I0650729

FOR SEVENTY-FIVE YEARS: THE UNIQUE MAGAZINE   ISSN 0898-5073
Summer 1998   Cover by Jason Van Hollander

That Is Not Dead Which Can Eternal Lie . . .

We're ba . . . a . . . ck!

Welcome, just in time for our 75th anniversary, to the pages of *Weird Tales*®, The Unique Magazine, the greatest of all American pulp magazines, once home to H.P. Lovecraft, Robert E. Howard, Clark Ashton Smith, Ray Bradbury, and even (believe it or not) Tennessee Williams.

To fill you in briefly: Terminus Publishing Company revived *Weird Tales*® in 1988 and published nineteen issues, numbers 290 through 308, up until 1994. Then we lost our license when Hollywood came calling and offered Weird Tales, Ltd., the owners of the title, scads of money for use of the title in a television project. Quite sensibly, WT, Ltd., took the aforesaid scads. The television project, ultimately, failed to pan out. Now *Weird Tales*® returns as a DNA publication, in association with Terminus Publishing Co., Inc. We have been able to rent the title again and resume publication.

Have we ever been away?

You will notice that this issue is numbered 313 and the last "official" issue was #308, so that implies that the four issues of *Worlds of Fantasy & Horror* count as *Weird Tales*®. For one thing, we find it enormously convenient to avoid renumbering everyone's subscriptions. But there's more to it than that.

When we lost our license back in 1994, we didn't want to quit. The obvious alternative was to think up *another* title which fit behind the big red **W** on the cover and keep on publishing, with continuity, so that the letter column in the first *Worlds of Fantasy & Horror* referred back to the previous *Weird Tales*®. But for the title on the cover and contents page, it *was* the same magazine. So, think of *Worlds of Fantasy & Horror* as *Weird Tales*®-in-exile, a means of keeping the magazine alive until we could get the title back.

What's in a name? If the name is *Spicy Oriental Zeppelin Stories,* maybe not very much, but *Weird Tales*® has, for most of this century, commanded respect. We can only promise you that we intend to continue with a magazine worthy of that name.

We have complete confidence in our a new publisher, Warren Lapine, of DNA Publications, who is one of the most successful and capable fiction magazine publish-

ers in the business. His science fiction magazine *Absolute Magnitude* and his vampire-fiction magazine *Dreams of Decadence* actually *make money* in a time when most magazine publishers are feeling a sense of doom and gloom, and, particularly, small-press horror magazines seem to be dying like may flies. We have joined Warren Lapine's stable and feel very comfortable there. Our future seems brighter than it has been in a long time. Quarterly publication of *Weird Tales*® will resume, as of this issue. You will continue to see stories by your favorites — and by bright new talents — in future issues. We have some on hand by S.P. Somtow, Tanith Lee, Nicholas DiChario, and quite a few others.

One other change: since George Scithers is no longer officially Publisher, he and Darrell Schweitzer share the position of Co-Editorship, and the "Editorial We" becomes, once again, a genuine plural.

Meanwhile, half of the aforesaid "We," Darrell, found ourselves, flattered, honored, and more than a little surprised by events at the 1997 World Horror Convention in Niagara Falls, New York. We attended in the capacity of Editor Guest of Honor and found the whole thing decidedly eye-opening —

Let's dispense with the formalities. This is Darrell here. The other guests of honor were writers Joe Lansdale, Poppy Z. Brite, and Ramsey Campbell, and artist Rick Berry. In such company the thought inevitably occurred to me that, after attending (by now) literally hundreds of other conventions in lesser rôles, Maybe I Had Arrived.

But arrived at what? Conditions in the horror field have been *so* dire in the past few years that I was left wondering if there would be anything left to have a World Convention *about.*

"I have a feeling this may be either a pep rally — or a wake," I said before the affair. It was neither. It was more like a visit to an intensive care ward. Reports of the patient's demise may be a trifle exaggerated, but Horror is, right now, on the critical list.

Let me say right away that it was a pleasant weekend, everyone was very nice, the Falls are as wet as ever (though the Americans turn them off at night) and the twin towns of Niagara Falls themselves (New York and Ontario) retain that subtle atmosphere of down-at-the-heels tackiness so reminiscent of a somewhat run-down section of the Atlantic City boardwalk plunked down in the middle of the continent.

It might best be summed up in the fun-house maze called Dracula's Haunted Castle on the Canadian side, which has an impressive exterior; loud, blaring speakers announcing the frightful delights within; and enormous, dripping fangs between which one walks to reach the entrance. But the inside is not quite as good — and scarcely more elaborate — than the "haunted house" you may have put together with your friends at Halloween when you were twelve.

In fact, the one the twelve-year-olds in my neighborhood put together, which scared the crap out of me when I was perhaps six, was considerably more imaginative. There was this girl dressed up as a witch in what might have been an old wedding gown. She *glowed* from the blue light behind her, and she offered me a jar of what I later realized were olives. "Reach in," she said in an alluring, spooky voice, *"and feel the eyes."* At that point I ran out screaming.

And she didn't have to rely on a guy popping a paper bag behind your back to deliver the frights, which, I kid you not, the Niagara Falls Dracula castle did.

Delivering the frights is what the game is all about, and the impression I got at World Horror was that no one is delivering much of anything right now. The convention was notably lacking in professional activity, in stark contrast to the bustling World Fantasy Conventions, where authors, agents, editors, and publishers gather by the hundreds to make the deals that determine what you'll be reading for the next year or so. Representatives of the major New York publishers were conspicuously absent.

I try to convince myself that the Niagara Falls Dracula castle isn't quite the appropriate metaphor for the state of the horror field right now. And yet . . .

At the time of the convention, there was *no* "horror editor" at any publishing house in the United States. There was a time, ten or so years ago, when great quantities of black-covered, gold-embossed paperbacks with demon children or show-through drops of blood poured into the bookstores, when becoming a horror writer was actually a valid strategy for a beginning novelist who wanted to make a living. There was, admittedly, a flood of crud; but lots of good books got published too. The Dell Abyss line promised (and sometimes delivered) great things. The horror field gleamed with prosperity. Writers left fantasy or science fiction, hoping for greener pastures (and bigger paychecks) in the horror field. Editors gathered at conventions to court the writers. The writers gathered to court the editors. The New York publishing world spent lots of money on parties and promotional events.

That's all gone. At the Niagara Falls convention there was talk that A Certain Publisher Who Shall Remain Nameless was starting a horror line with the worst possible contracts and might get away with it, as the only game in town.

STAFF:

Publisher: Warren Lapine
Editors: George H. Scithers
& Darrell Schweitzer
Managing Editor: Carol Adams
Art Editor: Diane Weinstein
Assistant Editors: Kyle Phillips, Jan B. Berends, Pat Buard, & Robert Waters
Computer Consultant: David J. Williams III
Typesetter: Owlswick Press
Printer: News Publishing Co., Inc.

MANUSCRIPT SUBMISSIONS:

Before sending us your material, please send us a business-sized envelope, with postage affixed, addressed to you, for our guidelines. The address for this and all other editorial matter: *Weird Tales*®, 123 Crooked Lane, King of Prussia PA 19406-2570.

The address for all subscription and back-order matters: DNA Publications, Inc., PO Box 13, Greenfield MA 01301-0013.

Yes; we read unsolicited submissions — but *only* if they are in standard manuscript format. To survive, all editors insist on a few Rules: each submission must be in proper format and must include a return envelope, addressed to you, with enough postage affixed to bring the manuscript back to you. If you want us to discard the manuscript if we don't buy it, tell us so, but include a business-letter-sized envelope, addressed to you, with proper postage affixed, so we can send you our comments. No loose stamps, please!

We recommend either of two books on writing (after all, we wrote one of them!): *On Writing Science Fiction: the Editors Strike Back!* by Scithers, Schweitzer, & John M. Ford; $19.50 in hardcover; and Barry B. Longyear's *Science-Fiction Writer's Workshop,* $9.50 in trade paperback, available from the Owlswick Press, 123 Crooked Lane, King of Prussia PA 19406-2570. These prices include shipping & handling; in Pennsylvania, please include 6% sales tax.

We are not responsible for manuscripts in our hands or in transit. You *must* keep a copy of every manuscript you send out. You *must* put your name and address on the first page of every manuscript. And please: *no* binders, folders, or padded envelopes; and especially: *no* registered or certified mail for which we would have to stand in line at the post office!

The great Empire has fallen; and the surviving writers, if lucky, will be serfs.

Take a look in the horror section at your local chain bookstore. It's a lot smaller. Once you take away the brand-name writers who don't *need* a category to make their books sell — King, Koontz, McCammon, Brite, Campbell — you'll discover that the whole section is filled by less than twenty writers, and some of those books are reprints, such as the recent Carroll & Graf edition of William Hope Hodgson's 1908 classic *The House on the Borderland*.

And what about magazines? There was a lot of talk about magazines at the World Horror Convention. What particularly threw me for a loop was that I found myself regarded as a hugely-successful, senior figure. What this turned out to mean was that *Worlds of Fantasy & Horror* (the Once and Future *Weird Tales®*) is one of *two* bookstore-distributed magazines in the field which has been around for more than a couple of years and has a circulation in four figures. (The other one is Richard Chizmar's *Cemetery Dance*.) The editors on the magazine panel with me spoke of 200-copy print-runs. Writers told how wonderful it was to get a whole cent a word for fiction, and how they'd take just copies if need be, to get published. (*Weird Tales®* and *Cemetery Dance* pay three cents a word and up.)

Now I had never seen ours as a large operation at all. But then I always saw us to be in the broader spectrum of fantastic-fiction magazines, along with *The Magazine of Fantasy & Science Fiction*, *Asimov's Science Fiction*, and *Interzone*. In that company, yes, we are one among many. In the context of what was being accounted as "the horror field" in Niagara Falls, I guess *WoF&H* must have seemed a titan. Or, to use an architectural metaphor, after all the skyscrapers and castles and gigantic temples have crumbled into dust, two modest little cabins in the back woods — ours and Richard Chizmar's — are the only things left standing, and therefore the most colossal edifices in the world. Perhaps the "field" is defined too narrowly.

I had another quite interesting conversation in Niagara Falls, with a fellow who ran a "horror" bookstore and boutique in California, one of those places where you can get, in addition to books and magazines, black t-shirts, skull jewelry, etc., etc.

The gentleman's store moved a lot of books and magazines, he said, particularly anything about vampires. Would he want to carry *Worlds of Fantasy & Horror*? Well, no. It isn't "horror." But our title says "Horror," and the current issue's cover has a naked demoness popping out of an eyeball, and we publish Thomas Ligotti, Ramsey Campbell, David Schow, and any number of top horror names.

No, he explained. That's not "horror."

Well, by way of a thought experiment, I asked (knowing perfectly well where this was heading): Would his "horror" bookstore carry a book by Clark Ashton Smith, surely one of the most nighmarish writers of all time?

No. Smith has some "dark" elements, I was told, but isn't horror.

Well how about Edgar Allan Poe? Not "The Masque of the Red Death"? Probably not. I don't want to tell the bookstore owner his business. He knows better than I what he can and cannot move, but I think this is the heart of the problem: If we define "horror" as scary fiction (with no other emotional tones allowed) which exists *only* in a modern setting, perhaps only in a Generation-X frame of reference, and if a "horror magazine" is one which publishes such material, to the exclusion of all else, then the field is very small indeed. There *is* a very intense, very narrow audience for punk/Goth/vampire fiction, but this is — dare we say it? — a passing fad, likely to last no longer than the "psychedelic" science fiction of 1967, or a story Henry Kuttner did in the late 1930s about space explorers who landed on the Planet of the Jitterbugs.

An editorial policy of all modern-scene horror — and nothing else — is limiting, especially for a magazine. Of the stories in our last issue, Ian Watson's "My Vampire Cake" wouldn't exactly do because it's funny. The Tanith Lee and Darrell Schweitzer stories are not "horror" because they have imaginary settings. (Which was why the bookstore owner disqualified Clark Ashton Smith. The paradox is this: If the story's about a Vile, Rotting Thing from beyond the grave, and it's set in New Jersey in 1997, that's "horror." If it's about a Vile Rotting et cetera and set on the Earth's last continent in the far future, or in ancient Hyperborea, that is "fantasy.") The Dunsany and Shipley stories in recent issues don't quite make it either, leaving, at best, Ligotti's "Teatro Grottesco" and R. Chetwynd-Hayes's "The Chair." So, in the eyes of that California store owner, our magazine isn't "horror" enough for his clientele, and he may be right.

While we'd like to get our magazine into that California store, at the same time we have to stop and realize that there's been a severe winnowing out, and we're just about all that's left standing. We must be doing something right. This isn't the time for us to start emulating the losers.

Our magazine continues to be what it's always been. *Weird Tales®*, throughout its 75-year history, has presented a *range* of imaginative fiction, from Conan the Barbarian to H.P. Lovecraft's Cthulhu Mythos to the psychic-detective stories of Seabury Quinn. It found room for stories of childhood terrors by Ray Bradbury (most of the ones that make up his classic collection, *The October Country*,) and H. Rider Haggard-esque (or Indiana Jonesish) Lost Race novels by Edmond Hamilton. We intend the same, with a common denominator, which may be best expressed by a wonderful phrase, used by a correspondent several issues back, to describe the ideal *Weird Tales®* story: "ominous and magical."

Roll that phrase around in your mind. Balance both halves of it carefully. That's what the whole field needs. Magic. Imagination. The ability to get *out of* a completely mundane frame of reference. *Fantastic* horror.

Too much horror has no imaginative content at all anymore. There's only room for so many serial-killer books. If writers, booksellers, editors, and even readers start seeing horror only in terms of gore and crazy people with knives, then everyone will tire of it very quickly. By all indications, that's already happened. The field is wasteland. Dare we suggest that the public is bored with more and more imitations of fewer and fewer books?

Good horror attracts as much as it frightens. It does not *repel*. It is a careful balance of *wonder* and *terror* — as Fritz Leiber so well articulated in various essays, and practiced superbly in his fiction. It does not, Stephen King's disastrous advice to the contrary, "go for the gross-out," something which King himself, fortunately, doesn't do very often.

At the Convention, a small-press publisher was gleefully reading from a new novella which went for the gross-out as much as possible — in fact to a degree seldom seen in legally circulated literature.

Well, fine. This is all very amusing, even as small boys amuse themselves at camp with disgusting stories told in the dark. But that direction seems to me a dead end. It's a great way to sell about four hundred copies in an expensive, limited edition and no more.

Meanwhile, H.P. Lovecraft sells in the hundreds of thousands of copies, all over the world. I've since suggested another topic for a convention discussion: "What Can the Horror Field Learn from Lovecraft?"

What indeed? Lovecraft was around before the rise of "Modern Horror" and he's still there after its demise. So maybe he knew something too:
Wonder and terror, carefully balanced.

Now we (lapsing imperious once again) admit we're speaking from the position of a winner (or at least a survivor), but none of the foregoing is intended to suggest we're happy with the state of affairs. We note with guarded optimism that horror books are still being published. As it was a couple decades ago, horror books now have to be slipped into other categories: mystery, science fiction, fantasy, and mainstream.

Bestsellers are bestsellers. King and Koontz still sell. They will continue to sell. Otherwise we suspect that horror fiction is going to have to hide out in the small presses for the next few years, until the buyers for the large bookstores forget just how badly all those horror paperbacks of the boom years sold. Then it will be time to start again, cautiously. We hope there will be more Wonder and less Gross-Out next time around.

More successful magazines will strengthen us all. One hopeful sign is *Wetbones*, a new magazine started by Paula Guran, who was at that World Fantasy Convention, with an attractive new issue, which, alas, hasn't had much distribution so far. (Our first impulse was to help. We carried copies back on the plane, to test-market in Philadelphia.) Send her a subscription. See her ad elsewhere in this issue.

We'd like to see other editors and publishers try. If newcomers would like a little advice from such an August and Senior Figures as Ourselves, it is this: Emphasize good writing. Keep the imaginative and fantastic content high. Use covers which suggest, not psychopathology, but fantasy. Design a magazine which would sell on the same shelf with *The Magazine of Fantasy & Science Fiction,* or even *Realms of Fantasy,* rather than one that looks like a small-press horror magazine of the kind that distributors won't touch. With a little camouflage, Horror can survive.

We Get Letters and not enough of them. However, we were pleased to hear from **Timothy Tucker,** who comments that the cover on #4 was "sort of a '90s update on Margaret Brundage," to which we suppose we'd agree, save that Douglas Beekman knows human anatomy far better than did the 1930s *Weird Tales* artist. Mr. Tucker continues:

S.T. Joshi's essay on child prodigies was very interesting, especially his harsh criticism of Poppy Z. Brite. It would be interesting to hear a response. This is my first exposure to Joshi's non-Lovecraftian criticism, but he shows himself to be just as astute here as he is in his massive Lovecraft biography.

It is hard to pick out one outstanding story this issue, because all of them were very fine indeed. Right now it appears to be a three-way tie for first among Tanith Lee's "The Sequence of Swords and Hearts," Thomas Ligotti's "Teatro Grottesco," and your own "The Sorcerer's Gift." Both your and Lee's stories successfully evoke a certain air of ancient myth and folklore. This air is one of the reasons I read fantastic fiction, because it is one of the few places left where such archetypes can be used. In addition, "The Sorcerer's Gift" is reminiscent of the works of one of my favorite authors, Clark Ashton Smith. I would gladly read more tales of Sekenre the Sorcerer, if you care to write them.

On the other hand, Ligotti's story is a fine example of updating the first-person-paranoid fiction style used by Poe and Lovecraft. The strange world of the Teatro definitely produces its share of mystery and chills. This issue seems to be a good one for tales in the style of Poe, because "The Chair" by R. Chetwynd-Hayes (is this a pseudonym?) is in the same vein, with a touch of the British ghost story thrown in. A fine effort.

To which we reply variously: No, the author's real name is R. Chetwynd-Hayes. The initial stands for Ronald. Mr. Chetwynd-Hayes is British, author of many published books, and recipient of a Bram Stoker Award for lifetime achievement.

You're quite right about the direct use of archetype in fantasy. That is one of its chief appeals, something which any successful writer in this field must understand, and be able to accomplish. As for Sekenre the Sorcerer, he began his career in *Weird Tales* #303 with "To Become a Sorcerer," which was expanded into a novel, *The Mask of the Sorcerer,* published by New English Library in 1995. (Alas, there is no American publisher yet.) The Sekenre story in the present issue is a "reprint" from the British magazine, *Interzone,* although it has never before been published in North America. Two more stories appeared in *Interzone,* which might be run in *Weird Tales*® if there is reader interest. One appears in the final (and 30th) issue of W. Paul Ganley's *Weirdbook,* another in the second issue of the new British magazine *Odyssey,* and yet another is forthcoming in *Adventures in Sword & Sorcery.* Yes, we would like to write more of them.

Jeffrey Goddin quotes the Irish writer Padraic Collum about Lord Dunsany: "His fantasy is of the highest order. There's not a social idea in it." Which could be the basis for a whole new editorial sometime. Ursula Le Guin remarked once that one reads Dunsany for his prose, "since he was a dreadful reactionary," so maybe it's just as well.

We might get another editorial out of a clipping from the *Philadelphia Inquirer,* which reads "Fla. Girl and 4 Other Teens Accused of Killing Her Parents," with a subtitle, "Police point to a 'Vampire Clan' A detective said: 'They apparently like to suck blood.' "

It all sounds much too much like the scenario of Christopher Lee Walters's "The Renfields" in this issue. However, as we've had the story in inventory for quite a while, it must be a case of art anticipating life.

Lelia Loban Lee writes:
In issue #4, your artist, Douglas Beekman, has outdone himself, with his fine painting of a winning moment in the annual Underworld Eyeball Rolling Competition, a sport too little appreciated on the surface, despite its large and loyal following of fans down below. It's unfortunate that the competitor's name does not appear in the credit, but I believe that Beekman depicts the 1988 champion from Eastern Stygia in the Middle-Distance Giant Eyeball Division. For those unfamiliar with Eyeball Rolling, this sport originated as an ancient feast-day ritual to tenderize the fruit of a week-long hunt. While the much smaller goat, human, and monkey eyeballs used in the Pixie Division do not require such treatment for culinary purposes (indeed, the modern style of competition frequently renders eyeballs unfit for consumption), a Cyclopean Giant Eyeball, such as the one shown in the Beekman painting, becomes quite a delicacy when rolled for six to ten miles, pressed, sliced thin, and served raw, with a generous slathering of bat-brain butter. The modern competitor must roll the eyeball (in a manner similar to log-rolling) with feet or equivalent appendages, depending on the athlete's species, up a steep, rocky incline to a precipice. The athlete must not only balance on the swiftly rolling, wet, slick surface of the orb, but must conserve sufficient energy to break into the interior at the finish, to demonstrate that the eyeball is now palatable. You can see from Beekman's painting what a rare degree of physical fitness Eyeball Rolling requires. I commend him for introducing this sport to the ignorant and frequently indolent dwellers on the surface.

Just how Ms. Lee came by her first-hand knowledge of this subject, she did not explain.

Franklyn Searight praises a new writer, Jonathan Shipley:
My selection for first place in the Winter 1996–7 issue goes to Jonathan Shipley's "From the Shores of Tripoli." I particularly enjoyed his effort because he comes across as an accomplished storyteller, and in my view the story is of the *utmost importance.* Shipley has not relied upon flowery prose to mask the absence of a decent yarn.

The Most Popular Story in issue #4 was Thomas Ligotti's ominous and magical "Teatro Grottesco," with Darrell Schweitzer's "The Sorcerer's Gift" a close second, and Jonathan Shipley's debut story, "From the Shores of Tripoli" a strong third. And the late Margo Skinner's poem "Prime" also attracted favorable notice.   Ω

SHADOWINGS
by Douglas E. Winter

sacrament \'sak-re-ment\ n {ME sacrement, sacrament, fr. OF & LL; OF, fr. LL sacramentum, fr. L, oath of allegiance, obligation, fr. sacrare, to consecrate}
1: a formal religious act that is sacred as a sign or symbol of a spiritual reality; esp : one believed to have been instituted or recognized by Jesus Christ. 2 cap: the eucharistic elements; specif: blessed sacrament.

Sacrament, by Clive Barker.
New York: HarperCollins, hardcover, $25.00.
Harper, paperback, 605 pp., $6.99.

Will Rabjohns, the protagonist of Clive Barker's latest and best novel, is a controversial photographer of endangered and dying species. "For most of his adult life he'd made photographs of the untamed world, reporting to the human tribe the tragedies that occurred in contested territories. They were seldom human tragedies. It was the populace of the other world that withered and perished daily. And as he witnessed the steady erosion of the wilderness, the hunger in him grew to leap the fences and be part of it, before it was gone."

That hunger is born of a hollow ambition that has driven Will since his youth: "He was not . . . designed for happiness. It was too much like contentment, and contentment was too much like sleep." In the novel's opening act, it brings him to Hudson Bay, where images of polar bears wallowing in garbage will provide a mournful conclusion to what may be his final book of photographs. In his forty-first year of life, he is lost to melancholy, the onset of middle age and a dire sense of things winding down. In a world that seems defined by death, his success seems meaningless, and the purpose of his photographs, and of his life, is unclear. "The less alive you were, the better chance you had at living. There was probably a lesson in that somewhere, though it was a bitter one."

When a bear is wounded, a misguided sense of responsibility leads Will into its violent embrace. This is death, he thinks: "This is what you've photographed so many times. The dolphin drowning in the net, pitifully quiescent; the monkey twitching among its dead fellows, looking at him with a gaze Will could not stand to meet, except through his camera. They were all the same in this moment, he and the monkey, he and the bear. All ephemeral things, running out of time."

It is not death, but epiphany. Ravaged and comatose, Will's body heals while his mind returns to the thirteenth year of his youth in England. The second son of Eleanor and Hugo Rabjohns — a philosopher and domestic tyrant whose later scholarship echoes Julia Kristeva — Will grew up in the shadow of his brother, Nathaniel (who, like Barker's own brother, Roy, seemed more truly his father's son); but when Nathaniel died in an accident, Eleanor withdrew into polite madness and Hugo moved the family from Manchester to the Yorkshire village of Burnt Yarley.

There, in a ruined maze known as the Courthouse — a madman's throne of judgment for those who would abuse animals — Will meets the man and woman whom he will learn to love and hate more strongly than his parents: "Jacob Steep, with his soot-and-gold eyes and black beard and pale poet's hands" and glorious Rosa McGee, "who had the gold of Steep's eyes in her hair and the black of his beard in her gaze, but who was as fleshy and passionate as he was sweatless and unmoved."

This curious, unearthly pair join with Will in the most crucial of the triadic structures through which his life has been defined: Will and his parents, Will and his childhood friends, Will and his photographic team, Will and his lovers — a series of incomplete men and women united and transformed by the enigma that is his life. Steep is the "Killer of Last Things," stalking the planet with knife in hand to put an end to each dying species. Once he had believed that, by recording each act of extinction in a journal, he could earn God's forgiveness; but now, like the elder Will, whose photographs no longer seem sufficient, Steep doubts the purpose of his life; soon he argues that, without purpose, there is no God — and no bounds to violence: "We're alone, with the power to do whatever we want." His consort, Mrs. McGee, mingles desires both carnal and fatal, played out through her "rosaries" — strange ropes that cavort like viperous extensions of her flesh. Their odd coupling has spanned three centuries, and Rosa's womb has carried eighty-seven children, all of whom died at birth.

Steep's ennui is leavened by the young and inquisitive Will, who offers the prospect of a new companion. Steep offers his apt pupil a simple but lasting lesson: "Living and dying we feed the fire." His secret knowledge of the darkness, and the need to hold it at bay, seems profound and seductive: "For an instant . . . Will saw himself at Jacob's side, walking in a city street, and Steep was shining out of every pore, and people were weeping with gratitude that he came to light their darkness."

Steep's tutelage is swift and certain: Will learns to feed the fire — to kill — by casting a moth into a flame. When, wielding Steep's thirsty blade, he butchers two birds, Steep asks him to imagine that they were the last of their species: "This will not come again . . . Nor this, nor this . . ." Such an act, Will realizes, could change the world.

When Will and Steep touch, the spilled blood summons something more, a vision of Steep's past. In 1730, elsewhere in the bucolic English countryside, Steep was sent to confront the visionary artist Thomas Simeon, whose talents had succumbed first to debauchery and then to the patronage of a mysterious mystic and satyric sermonizer named Gerard Rukenau. Simeon had been brought to Rukenau's retreat in the Hebrides to chronicle, in paintings, the construction of an arcane cathedral known as the *Domus Mundi* (literally, the House of the World). When Simeon left, Steep was dispatched to bring him home; but the painter committed suicide, poisoning himself with his pigments, rather than return to Rukenau. Before his death, he offered Steep the petal of a flower, and the meaning of the true sacrament:

I have the Holy of Holies here, the Ark of the Covenant, the Sangraal, the Great Mystery itself, right here on the tip of my little finger. . . . If I could paint this perfection . . . put it on a sheet of paper so that it showed its true glory, every painting in every chapel in Rome, every illumination of every *Book of Hours*, every picture I ever made for every one of Rukenau's damned invocations would be . . . superfluous.

Steep blamed Rukenau for the painter's death and rejected his teachings: "You gave him your genius; he paid you in lunacy. That makes him a thief, at very least. I won't serve him after this. And I will never forgive him." The rage of his apostasy translated into the zealous assault upon creation that became his life's work: "If the world were a simpler place, we would not be lost in it. . . . We wouldn't be greedy for novelty. We wouldn't always want something new, always something new! We'd live the way Thomas wanted to live, in awe of the mysteries of a petal." His passion for simplicity — and, in time, for absence — finds Steep, like the misguided forces of morality in *Weaveworld* and *Imajica*, seeking to cleanse the world: the building of a New Eden without error or imperfection — the ideal place to find God, to understand the purpose of his existence.

Steep's memories, like his lessons, taint Will, transforming a lost child into a lost man who desperately chronicles the last of things: "He shaped you, Will. He sowed the hopes and the disappointments, he sowed the guilt and the yearning." When, as an adult, Will looks upon one of Simeon's paintings, he recognizes the horrifying relationship to his own photographs: "They were the before and after scenes, bookends to the holocaust text that lay between. And the author of that text? Steep, of course. Simeon had painted the moment before Steep appeared: all life in terror at Steep's imminence. Will had caught the moment after: all life in extremis, the fertile acre become a field of desolation."

When Will awakens from the coma, very little has changed since his mauling by the bear — or since his youth. "They were in a world of endings, or early and unexpected goodbyes, not so unlike the time from which he'd wakened." He is living in the midst of death — of animals, to be sure, but also of friends, and especially his best friend and former lover Patrick, now dying of AIDS.

The past, once remembered, pursues Will with feral intensity. Lord Fox, an avatar of his guilt, haunts Will, forcing him to look upon the ravaged world with the unfettered eyes of his childhood: "God wants you to see," Lord Fox tells him. "Don't ask me why. That's between you and God. I'm just the go-between." The creature confronts Will with a conundrum, proposing that "the passing of things, of days and beasts and men he'd loved, was just a cruel illusion and memory, a clue to its unmasking." This revelation only amplifies Will's painful knowledge that he, like Steep, is a pretender: pretending to find purpose in life, pretending to be human.

Steep and McGee, awakened from their dire labors by Will's memories, return to Burnt Yarley and assault the now-aged Hugo Rabjohns. Without family or children, Will is a race of one, and Steep plots his extinction; but Will, who can no longer grieve, offers the perilous pair their only hope: knowledge and healing. When he touches his nemesis again, the vision he sees is both frightening and enlightening:

This is what Steep saw when he looked at living things. Not their beauty, not their particularity, just their smothering, deafening fecundity. Flesh begetting flesh, din begetting din. It wasn't hard to fathom, because he'd thought it himself, in his darkest times. Seen the human tide advancing on species he'd loved — beasts too wild or too wise to compromise with the invader — and wished for a plague to wither every human womb. Heard the din and longed for a gentle death to silence every throat. Sometime not even gentle. He understood. Oh Lord, he understood.

When Will tells Steep that God moves each of them, "the words, though he'd never thought he'd hear them from his own tongue, were true."

God was in him now. Always had been. Steep had the rage of some Judgmental Father in his eye, but the divinity Will had in him was no less a Lord, though He talked through the mouth of a fox and loved life more than Will had supposed life could be loved. A Lord who'd come before him in innumerable shapes over the years. Some pitiful, to be sure, some triumphant. A blind polar bear on a garbage heap; two children in painted masks; Patrick sleeping; Patrick smiling; Patrick speaking love. Camellias on a windowsill and the skies of Africa. His Lord was there, everywhere, inviting him to see the soul of things.

Will's journey home to Burnt Yarley and his childhood is but an arc of another and greater circle: he pursues Steep north to the most fertile of the Inner Hebrides, tiny Tiree — "the granary of the islands" — where Barker spent so many memorable days in his youth. There, hidden in an icy outcrop of rock, is the *Domus Mundi*, the legendary House of the World; but its interior is a grey darkness, lit with pale flames that disclose walls and floors made of filth and clogged with rotting trash, a sad mirror of the dying psyche of the world.

High atop an elaborate web of knotted rope and filthy woodwork waits the throne of Gerard Rukenau. Despite his serpentine looks, the mystic and messiah Rukenau is no satanic majesty, just a mundane man whose arrogance and pride have engineered his own prison and Hell. A step outside of the *Domus Mundi* would forfeit its gift of immortality; embittered and lonely, he has covered its glory with dirt and excrement, rigging the elaborate ropework to assure that he never has to set foot upon the House of the World again.

Rukenau was the bastard child of a church-builder. Rejected by his father, he determined to build a cathedral that God would so desire to visit that all of his father's churches would be left empty. He studied architecture and magic, learned the sacred geometries, and finally enlisted the aid of the Nilotic, an angel who could construct a temple so profound that "a priest might see the Creator's labors at a single glance." But a glance was not enough for Rukenau; he needed an artist's vision — the vision of a Thomas Simeon — to comprehend the glory of his labors.

When the outcast Steep, who had failed to return Simeon to the *Domus Mundi*, re-enters its halls, he greets his former master with the killing blade; but Rosa follows, scouring the filth from the walls and exposing the glories hidden beneath: a vast temple of life whose essence is "the throb and shimmer of living things," the "glorious . . . madness" that is the glory of creation.

As Rukenau dies, he offers a final revelation: Steep and Rosa are one. They are the angel known as the Nilotic, divided by his necromancy. Each half, male and female, has adapted to the world of humanity through their experience of gender, embracing the most superficial impulses of man and woman: to terminate and to procreate. "Living in the world with stolen names, learning the cruel assumptions of their gender from what they saw about them, unable to live apart, although it was a torment to be so close to the other, yet never close enough." Now, in the House of the World, a mere touch reunites them, Rosa's bleeding brightness merging with Steep, marrying him, becoming whole . . . becoming one.

The Nilotic moves into the heart of the House, intent on undoing it, and Will follows. "The deeper they ventured the more it seemed he was treading not among the echoes of the world, but in the world itself, his soul a thread of bliss passing into its mysteries. . . . He did not grieve, knowing his life was a day long, or an hour. He did not wonder who made him. He did not wish to be other. He did not pray. He did not hope. He only was, and was, and was, and that was the joy of it."

The journey takes him home again, to Burnt Yarley, where he walks the cold slopes of his youth, the forgotten places and faces that live inside him still, seeing them with sublime wisdom: "The creators of the world had not retreated to the heights. They were everywhere. They were stones, they were trees, they were shafts of light and burgeoning seeds. They were broken things, they were dying things, and they were all that sprang up from things dying and broken. And where they were, he was too. Fox and God and the creature between." Finally his footsteps lead to the place where the birds had fallen and, in time, to San Francisco and Patrick's house, where Will fulfills his promise to attend his friend's final moments. But when Patrick goes gently into the night, Will feels an unaccustomed discomfort. For the first time in his life, the man who watched and chronicled the dying of so many breeds feels like a voyeur. "Maybe it would be better just to go, he thought; leave the living to their grief, and the dead to their ease. He belonged in neither tribe, it seemed, and that unfixedness, which had been a pleasure to him as he went through the world, was now no pleasure at all. It only made him lonely."

At last, it seems, Will Rabjohns has awoken. He is

no longer content to stand idly by, watching, waiting, for death to come. "The season of visions was at an end, at least for now, and its inciter had departed, leaving Will to take his wisdom back to the tribe. To tell what he'd seen and felt in the heart of the *Domus Mundi*. To celebrate what he knew, and turn it to its healing purpose." There is only one place for him: "his only true and certain home, the world."

It is a lesson for both the artist and the man. The act of creation, like that of existence, must be defined on our own terms, not those of others — certainly not those of parents or teachers, critics or readers, and certainly not those of politics, whether social or sexual — and in terms of sacrament. Creating and living, Barker reminds us, are acts as sacred as those of communion, signifying or at least striving to signify a spiritual reality; if not, they are as purposeless and as vile as murder.

Sacrament is not simply the best of Clive Barker's novels, but also the most directly and profoundly autobiographical of his fictions. It is his first novel with an openly gay protagonist (which, even in these "enlightened" times, hindered its commercial prospects); and it is one of a handful of contemporary novels in which the sexuality of the protagonist, whether gay or straight, is absolutely essential to its plot. There is, however, no sense of polemic. Just as the novel cannot be read as a pæan to animal rights, its take on gay lifestyles is by no means a gentle, let alone an encouraging, one. In the very real world of *Sacrament,* gay and straight relationships are equally difficult, and troubled; Barker argues convincingly against gender stereotypes and roles, as well as warning of the dangers of defining oneself through them.

The plot is deceptive in its simplicity, a characteristic puzzle box of secret histories whose telling and retelling are the key to revelation. In these pages Barker revisits themes — notably, the urge for unity and transformation — that have been crucial to earlier works. It is no accident that *Sacrament* echoes another autobiographical novel, *Weaveworld,* at essential moments, but here Barker strips away the veneer of fantasy (which plays a minor role in the proceedings), finding the courage to create a metaphoric wonderland that cannot be ignored or dismissed as the stuff of escapism. *Sacrament* is remarkable, for Barker the fantasist, in its retreat from the elaborate mythologies of *Imajica* and the novels of "The Art" in favor of a

subdued unreality whose most chimerical qualities are biblical in character. It is equally remarkable in its refusal to concede that unreality, to suggest that its tropes have anything but direct and vital meaning for the reader — and the writer.

Will Rabjohn's profession as a photographer of dying species is an elegant and, indeed, inspired metaphor for the writer, the filmmaker, the artist of the dark fantastic — in other words, for Clive Barker himself. The truth is underscored in a telling aside about reviews: "The critical response to both the books and exhibitions had often been antagonistic. Few reviewers had questioned Will's skills — he had the temperament, the vision, and the technical grasp to be a great photographer. But why, they complained, did he have to be so relentlessly grim? Why did he have to seek out images that evoked despair and death when there was so much beauty in the natural world?"

Why, indeed? Darkness, Barker counsels, is very much in the eye of the beholder. The bloodthirsty scourge known as Jacob Steep is only the most recent of the light-bearing zealots who burn their way through the pages of Barker's fiction. Steep fears the dark, and desires more than anything to hold it at bay; but Will Rabjohns, like Clive Barker, wants to know the dark, to embrace its mysteries, to rid us of the fear of the unknown and all that is done in its name. *Sacrament* is a testament to the explorers of that darkness, and a challenge to those who would write in its name.

At one juncture, Will offers a brief riposte, discussing a New Age spiritualist who comforts Patrick: "Oh, there's light in my pictures . . . light aplenty. It just wasn't the kind of illumination [she] would want to meditate upon." [p. 306] Before the *Domus Mundi,* Will considered his photographs as a kind of bleak magic, one that, like his childhood killing of the birds, might work change in the world, but through negation and despair. But the light Will offers after entering the House of the World shines brightly: "Take pleasure not because it's fleeting, but because it exists at all." The light is one that his photographs, like Barker's own work in so many media, cannot capture, but which, with wisdom and conscience, can suggest and, indeed, exalt: "This presence of all things, seen and unseen, around and about, remember. There will be days in your life when you'll need to have this feeling again, to know that all that's gone from the world hasn't really gone at all; it's just not in sight." Ω

editorial addenda by Darrell Schweitzer

The Encyclopedia of Fantasy
edited by John Clute and John Grant
St. Martin's Press, 1997
1049 pp. $75.00

We can recommend this massive volume almost without reservations. It is a companion to the similarly

enormous tome, *The Encyclopedia of Science Fiction,* and it will — we predict — sweep all the awards next year. It will also prove to be a definitive reference work for decades to come, and turn out to be even more influential than the science fiction volume.

At first glance, the entries seem to cover the usual: authors, magazines, films, themes, motifs, etc. But the reader notices an great deal of jargon, most of it in small capital letters, which means that each such term has an entry of its own. Thus we are referenced and cross-referenced and cross-cross-referenced to such entries as TAPROOT TEXT, POLDER, WAINSCOTT, LANDSCAPES, MYTH OF ORIGIN, GODDESS, THINNING, THRESHOLD, ACCURSED WANDERER, FOREST, GNOSTIC FANTASY, SLEEPER UNDER THE HILL, and so on for some distance.

Ultimately it not only makes sense, but proves extremely illuminating. What's going on here is something very ambitious indeed: an attempt to create an entire critical vocabulary for discussing fantasy literature.

You might ask why this is necessary. Fantasy, after all, is older than everything else. It is older than the written word. (See, in this book, TAPROOT TEXTS, FOLKLORE, and several more.) But fantasy as a *genre* is a relatively recent development (see GENRE FANTASY) created by Del Rey Books in the mid-1970s under decidedly sub-literary circumstances. And while there are any number of author studies (of Tolkien, Dunsany, Cabell, etc.) around, these often occur within the context of mainstream literature and are written by mainstream critics whose realist or post-realist biases may not leave them quite compatible with the subject matter. It is surprising, but true, that fantasy does not have the same rich body of critical literature that science fiction does. There is very little which addresses topics within the context of a (now inescapable) fantasy genre, which has its own archetypes, tropes, and cross-references.

For example, a great many fantasies deal with the loss of magic. The dragons and wizards go away at the end. The adventure may be glorious, but by the time it's over we have a sense that this is the *last time*. Possibly a whole new age or cycle of history begins, as it does at the end of *The Lord of the Rings*. This can be a powerful metaphor for maturity, old age, the assumption of responsibilities, or other irrevocable change. It is not something found in just one book or one author, but recurrent throughout the genre. Clute and Grant call it THINNING. We need that term and a whole lot of others like it, which are unique to the discussion of fantasy. Such markers will trace the influence of *The Encyclopedia of Fantasy* for years to come.

The actual entries on individual writers, which range in time from Homer and Lucius Annaeus Seneca to Thomas Ligotti and Ellen Kushner (or, for that matter, Darrell Schweitzer), tend to be expertly done, with few exceptions. Only the Lovecraft entry (by David Langford and Colin Wilson) is seriously skewed, and even manages to cram several factual errors into a single sentence, as when we are told that "The Shadow Out of Time" was the Old Gent's "last finished work, written about the time he learned he had cancer." (Wrong on all counts: The story was written in 1934. Lovecraft did not become ill, see a doctor, or begin to express intimations of immediate mortality in

his private letters — our most intimate, and often only, source — until well into 1936; besides which, "The Haunter of the Dark" was written later than "The Shadow Out of Time.")

Any review of *The Encyclopedia of Fantasy* at this point has to be preliminary. The only way to honestly report on such a volume is use it for several years and *then* review it, which isn't very practical. It is too massive to be read from end to end. Those cross-references are like little wormholes which weave in and out of the text, depositing us, sometimes, in surprising places, like a whole long section on Tarzan movies, which is better than you'll find in most film books. We can browse endlessly. We can turn to our own areas of expertise (Lovecraft, Dunsany, the *Weird Tales* writers, Mervyn Wall) and find, on the whole, that the facts are sound, the analysis intelligent, and that the scope of the work as a whole is by several orders of magnitude more ambitious than anything previously attempted.

The Best of Weird Tales: 1923
edited by Marvin Kaye and John Gregory Betancourt. Bleak House (an imprint of Wildside Press, 522 Park Ave., Berkeley Heights NJ 07922), 1997
129 pp. $12.00

It would cost you thousands of dollars to obtain the contents of this book elsewhere. All other considerations aside, *The Best of Weird Tales: 1923,* is a real bargain. It is the first of a projected series, each volume selecting the best from a given year of "The Unique Magazine." Since 1923 issues of *Weird Tales* can easily cost you five hundred dollars apiece (more for the first few), *if you can find them at all,* here you have, for a modest price and with good production values, the truly unobtainable.

Think of it as a core sample, drilled from the lowest sedimentary stratum of pulp horror fantasy. As such, it is of enormous paleontological interest, even if we have to admit that a good deal of what came up was mud.

It's a deep, dark secret, hidden behind those astronomical prices for the fabulously scarce early issues, that *Weird Tales* did not make an auspicious start. Had the magazine only survived a year or two, it would have been no more than a curiosity, a failed first effort, for the most part poorly written, badly laid out, and wretchedly illustrated. Fortunately, the quality improved rapidly in just a few years, so that we may safely predict that the 1925 or 1926 volumes in this series will begin to show pure gold.

There's no doubt that editors Kaye and Betancourt have indeed picked the best of 1923. All of the stories are at least readable. They're fun, in a crude way, but only serve to remind us why the *Weird Tales* greats, Lovecraft, Clark Ashton Smith, Henry Whitehead, Robert E. Howard, and the rest *seemed* so electrifyingly wonderful at the time. Here's what the competition was like. (Not surprisingly, Lovecraft's "Dagon," reprinted here to represent the October 1923 issue, is conspicuously the best of the lot.)

The other stories are of varying interest. "An Adventure in the Fourth Dimension" by Farnsworth Wright (the very man who, as editor of *Weird Tales*, would bring about the magazine's amazing transformation a couple years later) is a pioneering, clumsy attempt at the sort of "funny alien" science fiction Stanley G. Weinbaum was to make popular in the mid-'30s. "The Two Men Who Murdered Each Other" stretches the long arm of coincidence outrageously, but has moments of effective description. "Beyond the Door" (one of the very few early *Weird Tales* stories Lovecraft liked) has a genuinely creepy atmosphere. "Lucifer," by John. D. Swain, manages a cruel, surprising twist. Most of the others are anecdotes of madness, revenge, and rudimentary hauntings, by writers who did not subsequently become famous.

But this was the beginning. Here you can see how a great tradition started.

Mosig At Last: A Psychologist Looks at H.P. Lovecraft
by Yōzan Dirk W. Mosig
Necronomicon Press, 1997
128 pp. $7.95

At the recent Cthulhu Mythos convention, Necronomicon, held in Providence, Rhode Island, at the very base of Lovecraft's old neighorhood of College Hill (along the steep streets of which your editor conducted a somewhat breathless walking tour), there were two guests of honor. One was Brian Lumley, which is obvious and fitting.

The other was Yōzan Dirk W. Mosig, who may not be a household name, but who is, in his own way, equally important. For the occasion, this volume essays was published.

It's astonishing to discover how little Mosig actually wrote. The bibliography lists a total fifteen articles about Lovecraft, all published between 1973 and 1980. The present volume contains nine of them, plus what appear to be four short original pieces.

Despite this, Donald Burleson, Peter Cannon, S.T. Joshi, and Robert M. Price all attest in their tributes at the back of the book that Mosig is a seminal figure ("the Northrup Frye of Lovecraft criticism," says Burleson), who raised Lovecraft criticism to the level of a serious discipline and paved the way for a whole new generation of Lovecraftian scholars, including Messrs Burleson, Cannon, Joshi, and Price. Dr. Mosig, a professional psychologist (who has added the Yōzan to his name after having become, among his other accomplishments, a Zen monk; he also describes himself as a follower of Bertrand Russell and B.F. Skinner), applied a variety of psychological approaches, not to Lovecraft's life, but to his writing. One dazzling piece, "The Four Faces of 'The Outsider,' " explores a single story as autobiography, as Jungian allegory, as a Freudian and mechanistic nightmare, and *makes them all work*, each facet providing new and striking insights.

More than anyone else, Mosig was the first to show us Lovecraft as a serious thinker and an artist of almost infinite depth. That he wrote only a small amount merely shows that if you say something important enough, you don't have to say it at great length.

(Available from Necronomicon Press, P.O. Box 1304, West Warwick RI 02893. Add $1.50 for postage.)   Ω

Flower Water
by Tanith Lee

illustrated by George Barr

Lady Emeraldine Morrow vanished, or died, yesterday; and the circumstances were reported in many of the papers. It was the bizarre nature of events and their number of witnesses, which led to the publicity.

In the midst of a private festival, as the sun began to set, Lady Emeraldine was rowed across her small private lake, to her small private island. Just visible from shore, she there commenced to regale her three hundred guests with vivid torrents of music on her harp.

Her many accomplishments, coupled to her great beauty, have been well known and much publicized for years. Also her enormous good humor, her happy, light-hearted disposition. And, in some circles, her apparent callousness.

The music rang out, chords, glissandi, and the sun sank into the woods, and the sky turned from crimson to the coolest mauve.

It was at this moment, in the last of the twilight, that Lady Emeraldine ceased playing, in the very middle of a spirited improvisation. As startled applause broke forth, a loud cry soared upwards from the island. Then came a burst of flame, a sort of explosion. Something quite small, dark and hard, shot into the air, then fell down into the lake, and with a sizzle, disappeared.

Guests swam or rowed in swarms to the island. They found a charred place beside the harp, which was itself unscathed. Of Lady Emeraldine there was no evidence at all.

There was of course talk of spontaneous combustion, or of abduction by fiery creatures from some other world.

Myself, I am strongly inclined to think that Lady Emeraldine was one of us.

Until I met him, under the coloured lamps of the Public Gardens, I had had an unpleasant life. My story is all too common. Father a drunkard. Mother a washerwoman. Put out at fifteen on the streets. Here

I unoriginally plied my trade in the oldest profession on earth, and with very limited success, being neither very attractive, nor very enthusiastic, and by no means a talented actress.

As the years passed, I had been also beaten and abused. I had thieved and been thieved from. I developed the expected passion for gin, and lost the last of my slight looks. Some of my teeth dropped out, my eyes were dim, my balance unpredictable. In this state, at twenty-four, here I was in the Gardens, not looking for custom, certainly, but tottering up and down, blearily eyeing the paper lanterns in mawkish solitude, before a police constable should behold and move me along.

When he spoke to me, indeed I took him for the police.

"Can't a poor girl come in and joy herself for five minutes for no cost, without she gets herded away?" I whined, in traditional, useless obstinacy.

"I don't suggest you go," he said, with a voice too educated for any of the police I had come across, which had been many. "No, stay with me."

"What, you want to walk with me, do you?" I croaked. I said, I was no actress, and though I had been trying, for at least five years, to act the pathetic sodden old harlot I had become, I was really no good at it.

"I'd like to hear your story," said he.

"Soon told. For the price of a gin."

"Champagne," said he.

At that I felt I should straighten up. "For the likes of me? What are you after? What's your game?"

He was young, rich, and handsome. He shone with health and wealth and grooming. He must therefore have some perverted whim. Fill me with expensive liquor and then slice me in scallops.

"We can remain at all times in the general gaze," he said. "I was only moved by your plight." But when he said that, he suddenly burst out laughing. I could see, in fact, he had the most carefree face I had ever looked at. I have seen one more such, since then. But I will come to that.

"Lead on then, Charlie," I said, thinking he was truly mad.

"My name is Raphael Pemberton. And yours?"

"Lizzie Lines."

We shook hands, and all about, very likely, the fashionable persons in the park glanced askance at us.

He took me to the open ballroom in the centre of the

Gardens, and straight off ordered two bottles of a famous champagne, on ice, also plates of oysters, bits of geese in aspic, jellies, cakes, and heaven knows what.

As I sat there I thought, *He must be going to poison me, slip something in my glass. Blame my demise on my weak condition.* I wracked my brains to remember strange deaths of blowsy, nasty whores in public thoroughfares, with a handsome gentleman nearby. Probably I had only missed hearing of them.

In any event, my life was not so grand I yearned that much to keep it, or so it seemed after a couple draughts of the champagne.

Raphael Pemberton, meanwhile, began to question me. He wanted to learn about this vile existence I had had. He could see, he told me, that I had suffered.

As I regaled him with my history, thickly laying on all the horrors, and inventing several new ones — my dying mother's bedside with the non-existent little ones snivelling in my skirts, my noble father renouncing the drink, and dying of want of it — actually he had been squashed by a runaway beer barrel — Raphael stared at me, his face working as if with grief until, every few moments, he burst out laughing again.

With the champagne I too began to see the funny side of me, and soon we were rolling in the aisles, a sideshow for the adjoining tables.

Additionally, I forgot to act my part. I became myself.

At last he said, between our gulps and hiccups, "You seem improved, Lizzie."

"Well," I said, "both my parents trod the boards — the stage, that is — before their luck changed. I had no talent, but I learned how to speak. Is that," I added, "why you're so amused?"

His pretty face fell. "No. Oh no, Lizzie." Then he bloomed, I have to say, like the rose in his buttonhole. "What a beautiful night!"

"Not bad," said I.

"Tell me, Lizzie," said Raphael Pemberton, as we began upon the third bottle, "would you like to be young and lovely again?"

"I'm not so old as I look. It's the gin wot's done for me, guv'nor. I was *never* lovely."

"For the first, then, Lizzie. How about it?"

"If you're buying."

"Selling, in a way. How old would you say *I* was?"

I squinted. Strong drink, by removing all pretense at focus, had oddly improved my vision. "Twenty-one," I said.

"Wrong, Lizzie. Seventy-one would be nearer the mark."

I smiled. Humour the fool. We were, as he had said, in the general gaze. And it seemed he had not poisoned me yet.

"You don't believe me, Lizzie Lines. Of course not. I look young. I'm handsome. And, evidently, well-off. The latter springs from the former. It can for you. I feel so happy, Lizzie. How do you feel?"

"I feel splendid. When the drink wears off, I'll be back where I was."

"Just imagine," said Raphael Pemberton, "there was a drink that never wore off."

"Oh yes?"

"A drink that, after one swallow, made you feel so well, so glad, as if — as if your heart was full of stars. Always just a little tipsy. Never a bad day. Never a sad night. No pain. No sorrow. Think of that, Lizzie."

"I am."

"Does it appeal?"

"What do you think? Besides, obviously it makes you young. Twenty-one, seventy-one. And good-looking. And it makes you rich, too?"

"Wealth comes from the rest. If you're utterly healthy, completely attractive, and your mind sharp, and your attitude merry at all times — you can't avoid riches, Lizzie, getting to be rich. Just think what you could have done, with all that."

"Well, Ralphie, I didn't have the chance, did I?"

"You have it now."

He gazed at me soberly for all of three seconds. Then he grinned. Well-being flashed and flamed from him. You could never think a blazing torch looked sick.

"This is a drink," I said.

"Yes, Lizzie. And I offer it to you."

"Why?"

"I have just one dose, and I must give it to someone."

"And why is that?"

"Because, outside the human frame, it's indestructible. I can't pour it away. Not down a drain. Not into the sea. I don't even want to lock it up because, in a thousand years, someone might find it. But you. I think you deserve it, Lizzie."

"Oh, yes. And why is *that?* For my terrible life?"

"Because you're such a bitch."

He told me then, as the dancers cavorted on the ballroom floor and the lamps burned lower in the trees, and the fourth bottle came; and I knew that, jolly as a jack-rabbit, in the morning I was going to wish I was dead — he told me about Aquaflora.

Someone had found a hidden spring, it transpired, beneath a temple in Italy dedicated, in pagan times, to the goddess of nature, Flora.

This someone, whose name Raphael Pemberton claimed not to know, had drawn from the spring — reputed, according to a Latin inscription about the fount, to restore, heal, and bless — one flask. An ancient legend declared that barren women had sought the fount and drunk there in order to bear children, also that cripples had washed in it and grown whole, elderly men got back their youth, and many other such tales. What had become of all these recipients of miracles had never been said, but in the end, the spring was shut away by the priestess for reasons of spite.

The modern explorer who found the spring did not think for a moment it possessed any unusual qualities.

He took the water as a curiosity. A day later, returning to the spot on other exploratory business, he found the spring had mysteriously dried up again. With the other excitements of his trip, he forgot the matter.

It was over a year later, once more at home, that the traveler again took notice of the flask from Flora's spring. By this time he desired to impress a young lady, and so he bore the flask into her house, told her that here was the wine of the goddess of flowers, and she, out of bravura, poured a few drops into her tea cup, and drank them.

Within a quarter of an hour, a change became apparent. Her undeniable prettiness had escalated into a potent glamour. A strain in her left foot, that had been annoying her for days, vanished. Her hair, which was not very thick, took such a turn towards the luxuriant that all the pins fell out in a downpour. Within the day she could see farther than the most far-sighted man in her father's regiment, could hear a bat squeak, and had mastered the piano forte, which so far had eluded her, to the point of rendering the "Minute Waltz" in forty seconds. Her skin was like cream, her grace that of a swan, and two missing teeth had grown back.

Her unnamed swain, the traveler, lost no time himself in sampling the juice from the holy spring.

Presently two of the most attractive people in the country walked to the altar.

"And lived happily ever after," said I. "I suppose, in *fact,* for ever?"

"No," said Raphael Pemberton.

It seemed that the fortunate couple somehow slipped from the annals of history, and after them only the flask remained, its contents next portioned out in several equal measures.

"How many?" I asked.

"That I can't say. The last will and testament which brought me mine, informed me of nothing but the basic tale, and that the fluid, which might be called the Elixir of Life, but which was only named as Aquaflora, would give me health, youth, physical glory, luck, and perpetual happiness." At which Raphael Pemberton lifted his marvelous face to the sky. "And it has! Oh God, it has!"

"But there are others?"

"Many. How many I have no idea. Sometimes — I believe I have unearthed one. People of great beauty

and talent. People who are never for a moment sad. I read once of a fellow screaming with mirth at a funeral. I sought him out. I'd been wrong; he was only subject to a rare laughing disease."

We drank a little more champagne. The sixth bottle now, I thought.

"You said," I said, "that you reckoned me a bitch."

"Well you are, aren't you?" said my host, smiling lovingly at me. "All around me I can see the poor and ill and needy and broken. But you're a clown, Lizzie. You mock us all and you mean no one any good, not even yourself."

"Fine words for a gentleman," squawked I.

But, "Look," said Raphael. And from his coat he drew out a tiny phial full of a muddy brown mess. "With my own mouthful of the water came this other one. It may be that these were the last two measures from the flask. One for me. One for someone of my choosing."

"So you want to waste it on me. On a bitch. What about your mother? Your wife? Your mistress? Your fancy boy?"

"All of those," said Raphael, careless, light of heart, "are long dead. You see, when I took my dram, I was aging and almost alone. I didn't hesitate. And when I looked into my mirror, what a roar I sent up. I've been roaring ever since. Oh, Lizzie. The worst news can't shake me. When I learned my only son had died, I had to hide my habitual, genuine smiles with a copy of the Times. If the world came to an end, there I'd be in space, charming as a comet, spinning with pleasure. *Nothing*, Lizzie, can bring me down. Think of it, Lizzie."

"But you want it for me as a *punishment?*"

"Not quite. It will suit you, Lizzie. You laugh at us all. It's in you already."

"There must be some catch."

"Can you think of one?" he asked.

I looked at him. After all the booze, I did believe the story, and the filthy-looking muck in the glass phial might well be a magic potion. My days had been devoid of any nice thing. Was I not due for some colossal change in fortune?

"It's poison," I said.

"It's water of flowers."

I had a strange notion then. I remembered some flowers in a vase in a public house where I had been

sitting on a sailor's lap, and the flowers were past their best. In the obligatory fight that followed, the vase was knocked down and the flowers spilled and the water ran out on the edge of my dress. What a stink it had, that flower water.

But the lights were growing dull; and I bethought me of the Last Chance, the Final Risk, which, in fairy stories and in the silly dramas my parents had acted on the stage, must be taken or lost for ever.

So I uncorked the phial, sniffed it — it had actually no odour — and sipped. I waited a little after that, to see if there were any burning or discomfort. Nothing happened. So I tipped the contents, the Aquaflora, down my throat. "Cheers."

"Cheers, Lizzie," said Raphael.

And then he got up, and we went onto the floor, and danced a polka.

I knew I was drunk enough to try, but soon enough I understood that now I had a mastery of this polka that is not given to many. And by the time they cleared the floor to watch us, and by the time the orchestra itself surrendered and stood applauding, and I felt my back was straight, and my corset loose at my waist, and my hair tumbling down the colour of polished coal, and my hand white on his sleeve, and I could see every tree to the termination of the mile-long avenue, and hear every individual hand clapping, I knew he had not lied.

The champagne was gone. I would never need a drink again. The world — was my oyster.

"I feel quite wonderful," I cried to Raphael.

"So do we all," he said, and his voice, for a moment, was black as iron from the pit, before he burst out laughing, and I with him, in ecstatic joy.

When I went home with Raphael Pemberton to his fine home in the square, I believed I was going there for the eternal reason, and for the first time in my life, I was looking forward to it. And, perhaps, even more than that, to the bathroom he promised with the enormous mirror, where I could see to the full what so far I could only feel.

The servants were in bed — or perhaps dismissed, I now sometimes conclude — and he led me up the stairs by low light, and opened the door of the bathing apartment, which led off his chamber.

I left that door ajar, and outside I heard him in his vast bachelor bedroom, talking to me as I stripped under the gas-lamps and showed myself the new Lizzie Lines.

I am accustomed to her now, this paragon of raven hair and hand-span waist and skin like lilies. But then I could not see enough, turning this way, that way. And licking all around my new growing teeth, and admiring my corn-less feet, washing myself the while in delicious pomades that now I could have for myself simply by smiling at a man — and to smile, when one is feeling so incredibly well and strong, and brave — and victorious — and safe and confident — is *easy*.

Meanwhile, Raphael went on with a sort of monologue.

To start, I scarcely listened.

But now, I piece to together somewhat, for in the end, I heard the end.

He spoke of all his shining days of happiness, not one with any flaw. And of his nights of blissful sleep unmarred even by any unappealing dream.

He spoke of his rise to wealth. Of all those idyllic spots he had visited and all those impossible conquests he had made. Of business ventures of pure success. Of the realization that, whatever he wished for, would soon be his.

And laughing, sometimes breaking into snatches of happy music and song, unable to restrain the sweeping delight of all and everything, which I too now had within me, Raphael now related how he had observed the miseries of the world, had looked upon its torments and its tears, even on its blood, and futile sacrifice, and never once had their shadows touched him.

"I've seen a woman hoarsely weeping at her husband's grave, I've seen the dead brought up in hundreds from a mine, I've seen a hopping child wasted by plague, and a city under a flood, and I've sung this very song, Lizzie.

"Lizzie, do you hear any strain in my voice? Do you, Lizzie. Regret, guilt, pain? No? I'm enwrapt in sweetness. For ever and a day."

I went out then, naked, in my exquisite flesh, and there he stood, Raphael Pemberton.

"Have you heard of the Last Straw, Lizzie? The one that breaks the back of the camel much overloaded? You, Lizzie, are it."

I laughed. I always laugh, now. Show me your wounds, I will lave them with laughter. If heaven falls, I shall fly above heaven. I cannot do otherwise.

"Perhaps you won't believe me, Lizzie Lines. I've offered this single phial of the elixir of life, this Aquaflora, seven hundred and eighty times, before I came to you. To the drunk I've offered it, and to the sober. To the rich and the destitute. To the sick, the dying, the agonized, and the mad. They all refused. This gave me some hope, Lizzie. But then, tonight, you crossed my path. I knew you at once. She'll take it, thought I. As so you did, Lizzie, you bitch."

And then Raphael Pemberton convulsed in a paean of hilarity, content, and pleasure, and as he did so, there broke from him one howl of anger louder than any thunder. Then he was on fire. He went up like a firework. Vanished in a few seconds. Lightnings, sparks, and gushes — I jumped back — laughing, of course laughing.

It took about a minute for him to be consumed in the golden detonation. And out of it there showered down only a veil of slightest ash, to touch the carpet scorched merely where he had stood. But one, tiny, wizened black thing there was, that shot up and fell back, and lay there, which might have been his heart. All that is, that a lifetime of fulfillment, happiness, and perfect peace had left of his heart.

There is no other phial of Aquaflora in existence; at least, I have none. Enviously, I deduce, you would read of the delirious wonders of my life, if I paused to repeat them. I have had all I want. More. A cornucopia. And, with good reason, I have never been sad. But, more to the point, even in the presence of the darkest and most awful, rent and desolate horror of this earth, never have I felt the faintest hint of hurt or sorrow. As for despair, I cannot even recall that angel with its sallow, leaden wings.

I look at you, without pity, for pity grows from fear. Your sufferings. Your endings.

With my heart brim-full of melody, I say, I the smiling, beautiful, and blessed, you cannot be more envious than I.

Your lovely pain, your tortures, and your anguish that I cannot even in a dream recapture. Your loss, your rage, expressed in the poetry of words and souls, tragedy, romance — cheated, I.

Melody and laughter have shrivelled, by now, my heart, little as a raisin, like the heart of Raphael Pemberton, who gave me this.

Far, far off, like a mist glimpsed fading on a hill, I think I see — nights when I sobbed or stormed, the glories of agony. The power of riven love. And my destitution, and my bad sight, and how my teeth left my mouth. My triumph over these paltry terrible things. My dignity. My inheritance, my rights, the sword's edge, honing me, telling me of my life. But perhaps it did not, and I was only what he said, and deserved only what I got from him.

One day I too will flare up and be gone. Like Emeraldine Morrow, whose withered heart dropped in a lake.

For now, all is lovely. All is well. It cannot be otherwise. Aquaflora. Stinking water from those stagnant flowers.

I have only had ten years of it. One was enough.

What will bring *me* the explosion of release, and let Lizzie from her prison of interminable, heavenly joy?

For me, as for all of them, perhaps, though quite unfelt, it is that last being freed from a Pandora's box of human truth. *Exasperation.* Ω

THE RENFIELDS
by Christopher Lee Walters

illustrated by George Barr

The ambulance streaks by below, sirens screaming, grey-black wheels pushing it down tonight's established route of panic. For a second the five of us glimmer in the red and blue and white; now we're fresh victims in the bruised light, then as pale and washed out as ghosts, now dripping crimson, like demons. Only Tia's cigarette remains constant, its tiny end flaring as she inhales. So we stand there on the closed overpass with garbage and rusting car bones at our feet, flickering between the dying, the dead, and the damned, until the poor vehicle is swallowed by the south end of Abbey Tunnel underneath us.

Tia blows jets of white smoke from her nose like a dragon, then pushes her cigarette through a diamond of chain-linked fence. Antonio leans out from the overpass railing where the fence is broken and whoops when the flowing butt strikes the windshield of a small car leaving the tunnel. Christian grabs him by the neck and pulls him back. Moon, the other girl in our group, moves closer to me and we watch silently. Christian's eyes are fiery tonight; he slowly works his lips in a half-pout, as if he's chewing something. He starts to scold Antonio but seems to lose interest and turns away to stare at the procession of tail- and head-lights below. Tia slides behind Christian and folds her arms on his narrow shoulders. Moon and I exchange glances like husband and wife.

"So what do you wanna do tonight, Christian?" Tia asks him seductively, her voice like oiled leather.

Moon steps forward so the light from below can crawl over her face. Even now she looks shadowed, her cartoon-sized eyes black and glitterless. "How about Seizure?" she offers. Christian shakes his head, despite Antonio's sudden excitement — there's a dancer there he's "sweet" for, to quote Christian.

"Nahhh . . ." A fly he's been twitching away lands on Tia's elbow and his hand snaps up like a trap to crush it. Tia flinches but says nothing, moves slowly to wipe off its remains.

He turns to face us and she melts from him into the grimed shadows. The night glows behind him, giving him an aura a yard wide on all sides. His face is a black hole in the center. "Tonight," he drawls slowly, so that his voice seems to rumble underneath us like the cars in the tunnel, "Tonight I think I want a man. . ."

"Ahhh, *shit,*" mutters Antonio. Moon grabs his hand and we follow Christian to the rotting pipes we use to climb up and down from here.

Christian's not like the rest of us. I don't know if he's a vampire or not, which is what he's told us all before, and why we follow him faithfully around the city committing and hiding our acts of love. He might be the Devil, though. He sees things, knows them before the rest of us. My last girlfriend, Dana, before I took her for him, said he was good at reading people, at figuring out their secrets. She said he'd have been a good mountebank about a hundred or so years ago. But by then I was already ignoring her. I asked Christian later what mountebanks were and he said the grandfathers of bunkshooters, which didn't clear things up much. But she was right; he *can* read people. And he knows when people don't trust him so I always do.

The bar is called Dorothy's, like in *The Wizard of Oz,* and the dance-floor used to be in a blue and white checkerboard design before all the feet scuffed the paint away. As gay bars go it's pretty sincere; it even has rooms in the back, despite all the danger nowadays. That's why Christian picked it to be sure — he likes things that remind him of the past, leftovers of previous decades. Tonight it's filled to capacity and we have to elbow our way single file to the bar. Someone feels my ass and I turn and kidney-punch him. At least I think it's the same man. But it does the trick, and no one else acts like they notice me.

By the time we reach the bar, Christian has left us; and before we finish our second round of drinks he has returned, face ruddy and a squiggle of blood lacing his chin. Moon signs this to him and he wipes it away.

"Can we go now?" Antonio asks a little too anxiously. Antonio's tall and muscular and wears tight, fringed clothing, like a disco cowboy. His shoulder-length blond hair frames high cheeks and green eyes. He gets noticed a lot in places like this and he's uncomfortable.

"Aren't you having fun yet?" yells Christian across the din.

Antonio shouldn't have spoken, I think to myself as I drink. I've learned to keep my eyes down and act bored when we go out, especially if Christian is in a mood, unless it's my turn to pick someone.

Antonio's not as swift. He looks enviously at Moon and Tia, who are sitting at the other end of the table with their arms curved loosely around each other, and decides to choose the direct approach. "No."

It's the wrong choice. Christian leers and his mouth is red like an open wound. "Tough shit, handsome!" he shouts. Then he leans closer and Antonio seems pulled by an unseen force to his face. Christian says something to Antonio that I can't make out, and Antonio blushes. Christian leans back and folds his hands behind his head.

"I think Tony here feels a great love for me, for all of us, don't you?" It's not clear if he's asking us or Antonio, who's keeping his eyes locked on his drink. Christian continues: "I think he feels like expressing his love. Like a faithful acolyte. Don't *you?*"

He empties Antonio's glass into mine and the beers froth like saliva, and then with a sudden brutality smashes it to the table. Wet diamonds sliver across the wood and I feel tiny pinpricks on my hands, like rain in a hard wind. I look around — as usual, no one seems to notice.

Christian idly fingers the glass, moving the shards away until only a large, mean-looking piece remains before Antonio. Christian spins it and it stops with the point glittering in Antonio's direction.

"Prove it to me, Tony. Cut yourself."

Antonio stays motionless for several minutes and I notice the smell of locker room. His face beads with sweat, mimics the play of light on the wet and messy table.

Christian watches him like a snake. Finally Antonio brings a trembling hand to the table and gingerly lifts the shard. The light bounces across the edges as it shakes. He places his other hand on the table and moves the glass towards it until the point indents his flesh. I look at Moon and Tia, whose faces betray the relaxed muscles of their bodies.

Christian growls, "Nooooo," and this time we all hear it despite the noise. Antonio freezes again. "Not good enough," Christian says. "Your throat. Cut your throat."

"That could kill him!" protests Tia. Again Antonio does not move. I realize I'm not breathing and force myself to look away.

"*Or,*" says Christian, the tone of his voice releasing us as if he had removed handcuffs, "or you can cut someone *else's* neck. I'll accept a sacrifice from one of these fine young men —" His hand sweeps the bar. "—if it's by your loving hand."

Immediately Antonio stands, the shard of glass falling away from sight beneath the table. He is angry, I can tell. Christian laughs as Antonio strides off. "You gotta quit thinking of yourself as one of *them!*" Christian yells after Antonio. "They're just *meat!*"

Antonio is swallowed, fringes last, by the crowd of men. Tia and Moon separate, and Moon gets up to get us more drinks.

I sneak a glance at Christian and his eyes catch mine. I look away, then look back.

"You have to be ready to help yourself if you want me to help you," he tells me. His eyes look almost sad. I try to match his expression and glance back in the direction of Antonio. Of course Christian's right; if we can't deal with murder now, how will we be able to accept it when it's a necessity?

The thing is, I say in my head, hoping he can hear, *I am. I would have cut my throat.*

I discover I'm not breathing again and look back at Christian. He smiles at me and I feel lightheaded, the way I always felt the first few weeks I knew him.

There is a scream, high and child-like, from the back of the building. The clubnoise shifts like a piece of music and takes on tense, panicked undertones. I look questioningly at Christian and he shakes his head. Of course not — he never leaves the bodies.

Antonio.

Before I realize it, I'm standing and Tia is already halfway to the door. We've been through this a hundred times in theory, like children drilling for imaginary fires, and we know the most important goal now is Escape. Moon pulls me with her and we jostle through the mass. I lose sight of Christian and finally see him as we go through the door — he's moving on the flaking dance floor with a very drunk, very short young man.

"Did you see him?" I ask Moon incredulously on the street. Tia is still ahead of us, and she slows to light a cigarette.

"In the mouth of the beast," Moon says softly. She moves ahead to Tia and I watch her walk. I try to imagine what she'll be like as an undead. So calm, so quiet, black hair long and straight; she's like an Indian princess or an Egyptian bride. She could easily be a model, I hear her mother saying. I see her more as an owl, or a hawk — nothing escapes her.

"Where's Christian?" Tia asks us.

"Still inside," I tell her.

She snorts. "He won't let Tony drown in there. He ought to, though. Stupid son of a bitch." She ashes viciously.

"He could tell on the rest of us," Moon reminds her.

We are silent then, sobered, shocked once again into realizing how unnatural our lives are. *This isn't normal,* I tell myself for the thousandth time. *None of this is. We're killing complete strangers —*

But the image of the first time he told me, his fangs dripping saliva and his hands clawing like a salesman's into my shoulders, wells up in my eyes.

You can join me, he whispers. *You can be one of us.* Tia's hoarse giggle behind him, starting and stopping like a car backfiring into crushed velvet. My mind, frozen by the sheer impossibility of him, forgets my body and I begin trembling.

Prove you love me and I'll make you one of us. Be my soldier. How long have you wanted this?

His smile is all needles, his eyes hold me like searchlights. "All my life," I whisper. *Oh God, it's the only thing that I ever wanted." I believe him completely, reject my doubts and fall down, my tears multiplying him in the corners of my vision . . .*

No, this isn't normal. But if Christian were crazy, he wouldn't be able to read minds like he does. If he were mortal he'd have surely been dead or arrested by now. He might not be a vampire, but I still have my hopes. Otherwise he'd be something worse.

He shows up from the opposite direction of the club, Antonio sheepishly following him like a beaten dog. There is blood all over Antonio's face, his shirt, his jacket.

"You botched the job, fucker." Tia spits on him when he is close enough. "You'll get us all caught —"

Christian slaps her. She quickly recovers and apologizes. He ignores her and jerks a thumb at Antonio. We need to get him cleaned up," Christian says.

"My apartment," offers Moon. I turn to look at Antonio as we start walking: his eyes are far away and dazed.

"He looks pretty shaken," I whisper to Tia, who is closest.

"I don't know why," she mutters. "He's done this before." Silence for several blocks. Then, even more quietly, "At least I always *thought* he had — have you ever actually seen him kill, or has he always just gone off like that?"

Christian glares at us and we are silent the rest of the way.

The next evening we meet on the rooftop of the condemned Clairent Hotel. The climb is hard and I'm breathing heavily when we reach the top; Tia's scraped herself on something rusty and is cursing, licking the wound between invectives. I think gratefully how much all this will change after the gift.

Christian, as usual, appears from seemingly nowhere. There is a noticeable absence, but no one asks about Antonio, and Christian doesn't offer.

"Tonight we'll go to Seizure," he tells us. He looks appraisingly at Moon and Tia, and nods his approval. "Both of you," he tells them, "tonight. Do this well for me and I'll know you're ready." He sees my face as we head for the fire escape and gives me a reassuring pat.

"Don't worry," he says so only I hear. "I won't forget you."

Seizure: flashing lights, heavy bass double-beating like the club's heart, smoky haze, smell of sweat, beer, fog-machine. The people here are leftovers; they dress like 1985-Underground, everything a shade of black, and steal glances at us when we enter. Rumors of our small group have started to spread, I'm certain; but our clothes are what draw the attention — by comparison we look like gypsies, like the Village People gone co-ed.

Tia walks like a cat in her dullest moments, and tonight she is supremely feline. The eyes of men in the bar follow her as she passes, and those who can break the spell are caught again by the brown velvet luxuriance of Moon in the doorway. Tia runs a finger over a stranger's shoulder and tastes it as if he were icing. Like Moon, she has a knack for it, and she's set out to prove herself to Christian once and for all. The man's eyes are glued to her the rest of the evening, and she ignores him the way an aristocrat would.

Two girls, both younger than I, smile nervously, unaware they are imitating one another. I stare back and let a sly grin wriggle across my lips like a centipede before I look away. Their faces are filed away in my head, in case I have a chance later tonight to go after one. Or both.

I go to get drinks and a tall woman with short hair and almost no clothes stops me — she's one of the cage dancers, Antonio's "girl." She quizzes me and I feign ignorance, and then push by her as she calls me names. I add her to my short list, telling myself I'm doing Antonio a favor. When I come back Moon is gone; she's dancing with a stocky, pink-scrubbed young man with no hair. *She's got one,* I think. Tia's nowhere to be seen.

"You sure you don't want me to do one tonight, Christian?" I've never asked like this before and the question spurts out before I can control myself. But Antonio's failure worries me, makes me understand how Christian might wonder if we've all been tainted by his inadequacy. Like Tia I'm burning to prove myself.

"Maybe," he says. He squints against the music. Christian doesn't like music at all. I drink and wait.

When Tia returns she doesn't come to our table; instead she walks past us towards the door. Her stride is even more animal-like, if such a thing is possible, and she languidly rolls her head one time around her neck as if to stretch it. At the bar a man drunkenly grabs for her hand, and she relents and leans in to him with half-closed eyes. They kiss. When she pulls away he licks his lips and furrows his brows quizzically as he tries to place the faint taste of copper on his tongue. She reaches the door — a rectangle of bluish light from outside widens and then narrows again, and she is gone.

"Wait for Moon," Christian orders me. He follows Tia to the door and it swallows him too.

Moon almost instantly appears by my side, making me jump. "You're getting really good at that sort of thing," I tell her. She smiles, and her teeth are outlined in red, as if she has been eating candy.

"Where's Christian?"

"Outside. With Tia."

Her expression is suddenly opaque. "Oh." She takes a gulp of my drink and shudders. "Well, let's go," she says finally.

Christian is draped over Tia in the alley across the street from Seizure's door. For a second I think, *Oh my God he's finally doing it* and then Moon calls out and the two of them convulse and jerk away from each others like sixth graders caught behind the school. We cross the asphalt to them; Tia stays in the shadows of the dumpsters, adjusting herself. Christian wipes his face and moves out into the light. There is red on his mouth but it's mostly lipstick. Moon and I stare — what is there to say?

"Did you do it?" he finally asks her, his temper bleeding through in the tone and rhythm. Moon nods and then, as if this were normal procedure, removes two Polaroids from her purse. She extends them to Christian, who snatches them away and concentrates for maybe twenty seconds on each one. Then he looks up at her.

"What the fuck did you do with his body?" he spits out at her.

"Oh, they'll find him, but not for a week or so. Maybe longer. He's wrapped in plastic in the ceiling of the old bathroom that doesn't work." Christian's face doesn't change. "The one where everyone goes to buy their drugs."

"I know where you mean." He looks down at the pictures again. I stare like a child at Moon's small black purse, trying to imagine how she must have planned, how she always must plan for these things. I wonder what else she has inside there — knives? Rubber gloves? Rope? Christian hands back the pictures and she returns them to the bag.

Tia at last moves from the shadows. Her pantyhose is torn on her left thigh, above and to the side of her kneecap. The white circle of flesh looks like a drop of paint on her leg in the streetlamp's two-dimensional light. Moon stares at her but her expression is again opaque. Tia mimics and returns it.

More silence. Disappointment and envy volt through my limbs. I weigh the pros and cons of simply asking if I can go back inside and am about to open my mouth when Christian clears his throat. "Follow me," he says, and he starts walking south towards the bay.

From behind us comes the crescendo of boots, and there is a sudden thud as Christian stumbles forward with a gasp. Antonio is hunched over, panting, eyes gleaming. His face is red and his hair stands out like a mane.

"You sorry fuck!" he bellows at Christian, who is stumbling around, face twisted with pain. "You LIAR!"

Christian makes a barking noise at Antonio and lunges for him. They fall backward and Tia screams.

"You *lied* to me! You shit! You can't do *anything*!" Antonio's voice comes in and out as they roll around, punching the street and each other. Finally Antonio scrambles back on hands and feet and Christian slowly stands, seeming to tower above us all. I blink and he's at his normal height, an inch or so below me.

There is blood on his lip. His own.

"You're not anything. Fuckin' coward." Antonio is almost crying, and he sits up, then stands, stomach heavy. The three of us watch silently, confused. I wonder why Christian is letting him go this far, why he hasn't simply killed him and ended it. Even Tia, strangely enough, hasn't moved since her scream.

Antonio rubs his jaw and looks at his bleeding knuckles. "Fraud," he says softly.

"You're not welcome with me any longer," Christian states in a grand manner. Antonio snorts. "You've proved unworthy of —"

"FUCK YOU!" Antonio shouts. His anger is building up again, I can see muscles knot in his bare arms. "You're crazy! You're like a little Napoleon! Man, I *killed* someone last night for you and — Jesus! You don't even know what you're talking about!"

"It *was* the first time," Tia says in amazement.

"Leave," says Christian.

Antonio is feeling more confident. "What are those, caps? Did you bond your teeth? Huh? How many times have you cut yourself in a bathroom stall just to smear a little blood on your lips to scare us? Huh? Fucking trick or treat!" He moves towards us, arms curved out from his torso, fists locking and unlocking.

Christian doesn't turn, but I know his next words are directed at me as surely as if he were leaning into my ear.

"What's the Golden Rule?" he asks.

"No witnesses," I say tonelessly. *My test. This is my test.*

"Break it," he says.

I hesitate only long enough for Antonio to understand, and when his expression changes to fear and he starts to move back I am on him like a wolf, biting his face because I have no weapons. He claws at me and kicks and there is a silent compression in my gut as his knee strikes. My vision dims, then sparkles. We both make wordless sounds. I go at him again, this time with fists, and after a moment he has thrown me into the wall. Pain swells shamefully around me like a body bag.

Christian attacks again. I look sideways at Moon and Tia and see them at a distance, wide-eyed and lost. Behind them a light comes on in a third or fourth-story window.

wrong failed wrong

When Antonio finally knocks Christian down I see the blood decorating Antonio like war medals. He isn't losing, but he's suffering. There is only fear in him now.

Christian is dragging himself away, not looking up. Antonio staggers after him. Silently, almost apologetically, Tia moves in and, with a precision I don't immediately grasp, slides her knife into Antonio's back. He screams, and that scream expands like a steam whistle against the metal and brick and glass, finally dissolving in the night air. He starts to turn and she punches him twice, pushing him to the ground and cutting his neck. His jugular sings vacantly, spilling black into the street. She locks her head and he heaves, vomiting.

I push myself up and look for the others. Moon has disappeared, but Christian is standing on the other side of Tia and Antonio and grinning madly. He nods to me and opens his arms. "THIS," he yells out, "is *FAITH! This is a SOLDIER!*"

Antonio's kicks grow weaker and weaker. The pavement around them glistens wetly. Tia, hands slick with blood and stomach juices, is gasping between mouthfuls; and my stomach begins to feel spongy, hollow. I've been here before, felt the ragged warm skin swell into my mouth as I sucked, fought the nausea of drinking someone to death with thoughts of romance and eternity, images of Christian. This scene isn't new but the point of view is, and no amount of imagination can dilute my uneasy perspective. There's a horror to it, a viciousness that wasn't there before.

"Tia?" I call out.

She looks up at me with rabid eyes and I freeze, suddenly cold. She's as close to a monster as I've seen any of us, even Christian. He walks up behind her and touches her head; and she screams and spins around, droplets flying from her face, her knife whirring through the air.

Christian flinches and holds his arm; inky blood wells up in the crevices between his elbow and the hand supporting it and runs in a thin stream to the street. Tia laughs, but not her usual laugh, and I begin to back up.

"You are a fucking fraud, aren't you?" She hisses her words through wet lips. Christian stands motionless, silently eying her. She cocks her head to one side. "Why didn't you stop him? Why didn't you stop me?" The knife winks as she moves it up between them.

Slowly, as if he's learning how, Christian's face begins to contort into a grin. Tia stops, confused. Christian begins to chuckle, his lips still pressed together; and then the laughter bursts out like a stampede and fills the air between them. Tia weathers it without flinching and finally presses the tip of her knife to his neck. He grows silent again.

"Why?" she asks him.

"You're still going to be Tia when you're a vampire, you know." His voice is soft and low now. "Nothing changes, really. You'll still have the same parents. The same childhood. You'll still be poor. You'll still be lonely."

"I don't care!" she screams. Her whole body shakes with the force of her voice.

"It's not like Bram Stoker, or Anne Rice, or Catherine Deneuve, or Carmilla. Or Bela Lugosi. Or Countess Bathory. Or even Vlad. It's just you. Only less."

"I don't care," she says again. Her voice is uneven.

"You'll still have been molested, you know." His voice is so warm now that he sounds like a father, all-forgiving. "You'll still have to deal with your hate. You'll still have had the abortion. The addictions don't go away, you know; they just change."

The knife is no longer dimpling his flesh. Tia is quietly sobbing, her tears blending seamlessly into the blood still wet on her face. "Please shut up," she cries. "This is all I want."

"Nothing changes," he repeats.

"I'll do anything. *Anything.* I've given up my whole life for this. Please."

There are police sirens about ten blocks away; I can barely hear them behind the buildings.

Christian surprises me then — he moves forward and holds her, his shoulder growing messy from the blood smeared across her face. She drops the knife to her feet, and her savagery falls away with it as she cries. The visual effect is ironic — they look as if he's just saved her from a deranged murderer.

The sirens grow louder. "We need to go," I call out, my voice sounding small and feeble.

Tia looks up, blinking stupidly. "What'll you do with the body?" she asks Christian.

He smiles. "There's nothing we can do," he says.

"Let's go," I say. "C'mon." The pain in my lower back is fading as my adrenaline starts coursing again.

Christian continues to hold Tia. She finally pushes him away but he refuses to release her. When she pries at his arms he tightens them, wincing at the pain in his elbow.

"Christian, what are you doing?" Tia's voice is high and panicked now.

He looks at me over her shoulder. "You'd better go," he warns. "They're gonna comb this whole place once she starts talking."

Tia is kicking and screaming now but Christian is immobile, granite-like. His flesh doesn't even seem to indent when her fingers claw at him. I back into an alley but don't turn away from them yet.

"They'll arrest me!" she screams. She struggles in his arms like a drowning swimmer. "My God, they'll kill me! They'll lock me up for the rest of my life!"

"The shorter, the better," he coos.

I should say something, do something . . .

"You've . . . Done . . . Enough!" he calls out to me over Tia's noise. The words are over-emphasized, dramatically spoken; I can't tell if he's being sarcastic or emotional. Either way, I feel ashamed.

Tia's screams fade as the sirens increase, and then both diminish behind me as I cross the city. When I get home, it's almost sunrise.

What little faith in Christian I still have, covering me like a residue from the night before, flakes off as I watch the television next evening: an image of Christian and Tia, bathed in sunlight, handcuffed, being led to and then from a building somewhere in the city. Flashes exploding all around them and the roar of reporters no different from the unending club noise, only tinnier-sounding on the speaker. I don't hear the words of the newscaster, but I can imagine what he's saying. I curse Tia again and wipe my eyes.

Moon doesn't knock on my door. It's locked, in fact; but she manages to get in anyway and is sitting across from me almost before I'm aware of it. I try to ignore her and she unplugs the television.

"We should've called him Judas when we chose names," she says to me.

I stare at her, not comprehending.

"Antonio," she explains. "If anyone betrayed us it was Antonio."

I start to argue with her but realize how foolish I'll sound, comparing Christian to old legends and fictional rules. I remember his words from the night before, what he said to Tia.

"They'll come to arrest us, you know," I tell her.

"Yeah, I know." She sighs. "He wasn't stupid. He knew who to pick, how to get a group together that would self-destruct without him." She cocks an eyebrow at me. "I suppose you're thinking about killing yourself, huh?"

I don't respond, my face reddening.

She smiles. "Thought so. You will too, I bet. I was going to ask you to come with me but I don't think so."

"I would've cut my throat for him," I say out loud, but not really to her. "I told him that."

"You *did* cut your throat, for all practical purposes. How many bodies have you left rotting around this city? Thinking in a month or so it wouldn't matter if they found your fingerprints?"

She drums her fingers on the dirty floor beside her. "Quit thinking about it. There was probably nothing any of us could have done. He worked us like mor-

phine, like a sedative — how do you resist a promise like that?"

My eyes are blurry and wet. "Then we were just idiots? Blind?"

Moon digs though her small purse and withdraws a makeup case. She begins to shade her eyelids; she plays with herself like this whenever she wants to think, I've noticed.

"Let's say he *was* the Devil, a devil," she says slowly, one eye softly closed. "He was still here to test our faith. He wasn't lying, not really." She blinks and does the other eye.

"What if he wasn't anything like that at all? What if he was just a crazed psycho playing around with us — manipulating us?"

"Whether he was anything or not, we were still tested, weren't we?" She drops the case back into her purse and begins to edge her full lips with a brush. When she finishes she stares at me. "Weren't we?"

I don't say anything, which is as good an agreement as any.

She closes her purse and stands, clears her throat as if she's about to give a speech. "I grew up believing in Church," she says, "In God and the Devil. In the American Dream. Nothing's changed, really — sin is sin, and if you try hard enough you can be anything you want." She stands. "Tia and Antonio failed. I haven't, not yet."

I watch her feet pass by. "I'm not giving up," she says from somewhere high above.

"I don't think it's your choice," I say sadly.

There isn't much else to say, and after a moment she leaves without a goodbye.

When I finally fall asleep, after throwing up a pint of bourbon, I dream of Hell over and over, shimmering through a haze of Moon's ashes in the distance like the promised land. Ω

by Christopher Lee Walters

THE GAME
by Melanie Tem

illustrated by Allen Koszowski

My father died last night. I know; I was there. I'm glad he's dead, but I'm going to miss him terribly.

We had what you might call a complex relationship. It was never abuse. No one could call it assault. What my father did to me all my life — and what, classically, my mother could not or would not protect me from — was never, by the letter of the law and probably not by its spirit, actionable. It was all in fun. No beating or burning, no lasting injury, no marks; my Daddy wouldn't do that to me.

And I wouldn't do that to him, either, once he got old and frail and dependent on me. I wouldn't hurt him in ways that anyone else would notice, or so that anyone, least of all him or me, would be forced to call it by its name. That would be too easy.

"Daughter! I'm thirsty!" His voice, once so playful and gentle and mean, had turned wimpy and clotted now, like stuffing leaking out of an old chair. He hadn't called me by my name since I was fourteen and had asked him to, had sulked and stormed and tried my ineffective best to insist. Dutifully, I went to get him a glass of water.

One of my earliest memories is of Daddy throwing me into the air and catching me, big hands hard under my arms. Over and over and over again.

At first it may have been fun. Then it wasn't. I was scared. I was dizzy. I wanted him to stop. I shrieked and kicked at him and twisted in midair until, I realize now, he probably almost dropped me and it would have been my fault.

My Daddy was big and strong and sure of himself, though, and I trusted him not to do that. He always caught me, and then he always tossed me into the air again. By the time he let the game be over, I was hysterical.

Then he'd hold me too tightly — to all appearances comforting me, maybe even intending to comfort me although I doubt it — while I sobbed and struggled to get free. Murmuring to me, "It's all right. It's okay, honey," he'd announce over my head to my mother, who had affected a perpetually and ineffectually worried stance. "We were just playing. She was enjoying herself. I don't know what happened."

Doing his bidding on what turned out to be his last day alive, I dropped two ice cubes into my father's glass and filled it with cold water from the pitcher I kept for him in the refrigerator.

I suppose I could get rid of that pitcher now; it's always in the way when I want something from the top shelf.

When I had just been learning to walk, he'd push me down. Never hard enough to hurt me; always, carefully, onto carpet or grass. Just a little shove to my shoulder and I'd tip over backwards, landing with my legs straight out in front of me, unable to get back up by myself. Sometimes I'd giggle. More often I'd cry. It didn't matter what I did. He would help me up when he was ready to, taking me gently around the waist and setting me on my own two feet again, or holding out his index fingers for me to clutch. Then later — never once did I see him coming — he'd nudge me again and grin as I collapsed at his feet.

I'd been a long time learning to walk. But once I had, I'd been agile, quick, and strong. I'd learned to stay out of my father's way and, at the same time, to position myself to make him stumble against a wall or trip over a threshold.

"Here's your water, Daddy."

"Thanks." Warily, he put out both hands to take the glass.

Quick as a rubber snake striking when you press a disguised button, I threw water on him. Not the whole glassful; that would be crass, and in his frail condition might make him sick. But enough to surprise him, to leave him damp and cold. An ice cube slid down inside the collar of his pajamas.

He grimaced and flapped his hands, like a bit out of a Marx Brothers routine, and gave a ragged yelp. It made me laugh. I stood over him and chortled for a moment or two before I hurried off to get him a towel, dry pajamas, and another glass of ice water. This one I planned to let him drink. It wouldn't do to pull the same trick too often; he'd taught me that half the fun was in keeping the victim guessing.

Growing up, I never had known what to expect; my father was accomplished. The older I got the more concertedly I'd tried to outwit him, but it hadn't often worked. I'd taunt him. Sometimes I could brush right past him and he wouldn't seem to notice me. Sometimes he'd smile in an affectionate, fatherly way and maybe tousle my hair.

Sometimes he'd grab me in what was supposed to pass for a hug, and then wouldn't let me go. He'd hold me just snugly enough that I couldn't get loose and he'd go on with whatever he'd been doing — reading the paper, cooking spaghetti, chatting with my mother who by this time would be looking even more distracted and helpless than usual.

I'd squirm and complain. "Dad-*dy!*"

"What?" He'd clown, pooching out his lips. "What? What's the matter with my little girl?"

"I want *down!*"

"You want what?"

"*I want down!*"

"*You want down!* Why?"

There'd never been a reason good enough. I'd had no control whatsoever over when he finally set me down. When he'd decided to, whatever his whim, he'd loosen his embrace and I'd run away, feeling beaten again and determined to get him next time. Next time had been a long time coming.

But soon I'd be strolling past him again, flirting, teasing, daring. Closer and closer, just to see what would happen. Sometimes nothing had. Sometimes he'd capture me and tickle me till I'd get sick to my stomach. "See?" he'd defend himself to my mother, who'd be watching us with her arms folded across her stomach as if to protect herself. "She likes it. It's a game."

We'd be lying on the living room floor companionably watching television, and without warning he'd lunge at me and flip me over onto my back so he could use my belly for a pillow. "Daddy! Quit!"

"Quit what?" he'd ask sweetly. His voice would be muffled, his beard prickly against my bared skin. "I like it here."

"I wanna see the end of the movie!"

"You do?" He'd pin me there until the credits rolled up the screen. Then he'd kiss me and effortlessly let me go.

When I'd worn shorts that rode a little too low on my hips, he'd sneak his hands around me from behind and poke his finger into my belly button. I'd loathed that. I'd told him so, sometimes patiently, often at the top of my lungs. But I'd frequently worn my shorts that way, and made sure he saw.

I'd pester him — untie his shoestrings, dribble grass into his coffee — until he'd come after me with a playful bellowing. Then I'd shout and cry in outrage while he held me down and licked me all over with such sloppy thoroughness that I'd thought I'd throw up. I'd wished I would; that'd show him. "Daddy! Stop it!"

"Stop what?"

"Stop it! It's gross!" And eventually, when he'd been good and ready, he had, but not because I'd wanted him to.

Once in a while when he had come in to kiss me good-night — often enough that I'd always been on guard until he'd been safely out of my room — he'd flop down beside me in my bed and I'd be powerless to get him up. For the first few seconds it would feel nice, and I'd snuggle against him. But then I'd want him out of

my bed, and it was *my* bed, and nothing I could do would budge him. By the time he'd left, in his own good time, I'd be furious and my nerves jangled, and I'd have dreams about being trapped or tied.

Sometimes, too, the perfect sweet revenge would come to me in a dream.

"Daughter," my father whined last night, unsteadily holding out his glass and watching me with his crafty old eyes. "More water."

"More *water?*" I pooched my lips at him. "You want more *water?* Why?"

"I'm *thirsty.*"

"You're *thirsty?*"

"Please bring me another glass of water."

"No," I said, with mock reasonableness, taking the glass from him. "It's almost time for dinner."

As my father and I had both aged, the balance of power between us had shifted. I'd started to win more often and suffer less retaliation. But he'd remained a worthy opponent. His mind, though fuzzy a lot of the time, had stayed clever, and he'd retained more physical strength and agility than he let on.

I'm positive, for instance, that sometimes he got up in the night and rearranged or outright hid things in the kitchen; many a morning I couldn't find the spatula or the cord to the coffeepot. I didn't give him the satisfaction of complaining. I just made do, and eventually the missing items showed up or were mysteriously replaced. I suppose now everything will stay where I put it.

He also used to collect the mail before I realized it had come, and he'd hide the phone bill or the disconnect notice from the power company. The challenge was whether I could keep track of the dates the bills were supposed to arrive. Of course, if they'd ever turned off our power or phone, he'd have suffered as much as me. The game had acquired a curious and exciting double edge.

I'd barely started fixing supper last night when he called me again. I took longer than necessary to go to him, first making sure the lid on the pot of potatoes was tipped so the water wouldn't boil over. I left the skins on to preserve some of the food value. Daddy could chew potato skins so it wasn't dangerous, but he didn't like them.

"Yes, Daddy." I stood respectfully before him with my hands folded, waiting for his instructions.

"It's time for the news."

I nodded and turned on his television. He had a remote control but wouldn't use it because he liked me to wait on him. I suspected he was also titillated by the risk: the more things I did for him, the more opportunity I had to play a trick.

My father and I understood each other. We were

very close. I wonder now how my life will be without him.

"Channel 9." He always said that.

I turned the channel selector to 7 and left it there. It took him only a split-second to realize what I'd done, and he was howling before I got out of the room. I chuckled all the way down the stairs. That was a good one. Even now, thinking about it makes me laugh, in a sad kind of way.

"Daddy, what makes a rainbow?"

Without missing a beat: "Birds go to the bathroom in different colors."

"Oh, Daddy."

"It's true. Robins make red, bluejays make blue, canaries make yellow, parrots make green."

I don't remember ever getting a straight answer from him to a question like that, and it had been particularly infuriating because I'd known he knew; he'd had information I'd wanted, and he wouldn't give it to me. I'd believed everything he'd said, and at the same time I hadn't believed a word. By the time he actually had deigned to tell me the truth, I'd never known whether to believe that, either. Sometimes my mother would intercede and try to give me accurate information, but I really hadn't wanted her to.

In high school, Daddy would help me with my algebra and geometry homework. He'd been a smart man and a good teacher. I'd learned from him better than from any of the teachers at school.

I hadn't been able to trust him, though. Sometimes he'd feed me the wrong answers, or tell me I'd worked a problem wrong when I hadn't. I'd learned to check the work myself, and to be able to defend what I'd done, and for that reason I'd got straight A's in algebra and geometry.

On the other hand, I still have nightmares. A whole semester's worth of equations or proofs with every one mysteriously wrong. Rules that fluctuate even as I write them down.

"Daughter!" There was something different about his voice that last time he called me yesterday; I knew instantly that this was serious. "My pill!" he croaked.

Out of old habit, my mind was spinning out ways to fool him even as I raced for his room. I could give him vitamins instead of the medicine. I could pretend to drop the last pill and make him think I couldn't find it.

Once again, my father beat me to it. When I stepped onto the landing outside his room, my feet went out from under me. I heard a cascade of taps and rattles as whatever he'd strewn on the steps — marbles, maybe; they make for terrific pratfalls — rolled, bounced, and scattered. I grabbed for the railing and missed. My leg twisted out from under me, and I heard the snap of my ankle before I felt the pain. "Daddy!" I cried.

From where I lay crumpled outside his door, I could clearly see into the room. My father was on the floor, blue-faced, fists to his chest. Unwillingly, I considered the possibility that this was not a joke. Which was worse: to take seriously a false alarm and be made a fool of by my father, again, or to assume he was pulling a fast one when he wasn't?

I tried to drag myself toward him, but I'd hurt my wrist in the fall, too, and it wouldn't support my weight. My elbow came down hard on a marble, right on the point of the funny bone, and my whole forearm blazed with pain before it went numb. My father called me. I hobbled on my knees as fast as I could, terrified and thinking how silly we must look. He was doubled over now, clutching his chest and wheezing, and I stifled a laugh as desperately I flung myself past him and yanked open the nightstand drawer where his medicine was always kept.

It wasn't there. I shoved my fingers into the back corners, slid the side of my hand along the edges. It was empty.

Then I remembered that the night before I'd palmed the pill bottle into the pocket of my bathrobe, happily anticipating the look of shock and horror on his face when he checked for it in his obsessive way and couldn't find it. My bathrobe was in the laundry room in the basement.

For a moment, delight won out over fear and pain. I may have laughed aloud. This was a *great* trick: I couldn't walk. The pills were down two long flights of stairs. And my father, whose heart had allegedly been on the brink of stopping for so many years that I had come to suspect the doctor of collaborating in a ruse, was now having a heart attack in front of me. Maybe.

Propped against the wall with my broken and now swelling ankle stretched out in front of me at an odd angle, I sat and watched him. The thought crossed my mind that he wouldn't know whether *I* was tricking *him* — maybe I had on an inflatable flesh-colored stocking; maybe I could walk if I wanted to.

He was moaning and gagging and gasping, "Daughter!" It annoyed me, as he surely knew it would, that he still wouldn't use my name. Then he died.

When his thrashing and then his breathing stopped, I tried to tell myself he was faking. But when I couldn't find a pulse in his wrist or a heartbeat in his chest, I knew one of us had gone too far. I stared at him, furious and contrite, and then I struggled to my hands and knees and crawled frantically out of the room.

It was a doomed and self-indulgent gesture. My father was already dead. But I had it in my head that if I could find his medicine and sneak a few pills down his throat, I could somehow trick him into coming back to life. Putting weight on my shin, even horizontally across the floor, caused excruciating pain, and my wrist kept collapsing. I went downstairs headfirst, bracing myself against the banister, or scooting and sliding in clumsy sideways positions. But I didn't allow myself to pass out, or to pause and rest, or to think about what I was doing except to repeat like a mantra that I was doing this for my father.

In order to reach the knob on the basement door, I had to brace one hand on the floor and stretch.

My hip must have been hurt in the fall, too, or in the arduous journey downstairs, because it was throbbing. The knob turned almost freely in its socket, and with grudging admiration I visualized my father sneaking down here and loosening the screws. Finally I outwitted him and got the knob mechanism to catch enough to open the door. It swung toward me, into the kitchen, requiring an awkward series of hunching movements that made my whole leg and now my flank ache.

I didn't even try to reach the light switch. I maneuvered until I was sitting painfully on the top step, then took a deep breath, deliberately thought of Dad dead and winning upstairs, braced my uninjured hand on the step beside me, and started down.

The stairs were rickety. The basement was dark. Once, when I was six or seven, Daddy had locked me down here for most of a rainy summer afternoon — accidentally, of course.

I'd been more furious than frightened, more challenged than anything else. When he'd come looking for me, about supper time, I'd hidden in the furnace room, not emerging until long after I'd started hearing the real panic in his voice.

Now I heaved myself into the laundry room and tugged the robe out of the basket of clean clothes. The bottle of pills was not in either pocket. It must have fallen out in the washer or dryer. Both machines were top-loaders and towered over me. Repeatedly I tried to hoist myself up, and fell back every time. My entire left side was numb.

I heard the door at the top of the stairs shut and lock. I heard my father laugh. Outraged, I yelled, "Dad*dy!* Stop it!" as I'd done so many other times in my life, knowing full well it wouldn't do any good. Even dead, he wasn't about to forfeit the game.

So I've been sprawled on the laundry room floor all night. Now and then I've heard his footsteps across the ceiling. I am virtually immobile by now, ankle and wrist swollen huge, head swimming, and I've drifted in and out of consciousness, but most of the time I've spent plotting revenge.

As of yet, I haven't come up with anything good. But I will, Daddy. I will.   Ω

by Melanie Tem

On the Last Night of the Festival of the Dead
by Darrell Schweitzer

illustrated by Stephen E. Fabian

". . . then all things which have been begun shall be finished."

— *The Litanies of Silence.*

On the first night of the Festival of the Dead, they were laughing.

All the capital rang with mirth; fantastic banners and kites festooned the towers and roofs of the City of the Delta. The streets swarmed with masked harlequins bearing copper lanterns shaped like grotesque faces which *sang* through some trick of flame and metal. That was a kind of laughter too.

On the first night, Death was denied. Children crouched by the canals and floated away paper mummies in toy funeral-boats. Black-costumed skeletons ran from house to house, pounding on doors, waving torches, shouting for the living to emerge and mingle with the dead. Revelers swirled in their shrouds, their death-masks revealing their ancestors, not as they had looked at the close of life, but with rotten features hideously, hilariously distorted.

That was the joke of it, that everyone was masked and no one knew who anyone else was. All gossip and insult and roguery might be done with impunity. Nothing mattered. Death itself was a jest. Surat-Hemad, the crocodile-headed Devourer, god of the Underworld, could be mocked.

But it was nervous laughter. Inevitably, even on the first night of the festival, some of the restless dead actually returned from their abode in *Tashe,* that shadowy country which lies beyond the reach of the deepest dreams. So the possibility was always there, however remote, that the person behind the mask, either speaking or spoken to, might actually *be* a corpse.

If not something far stranger.

"Is this the house of the great Lord Kuthomes?" the person who had knocked at the door said, holding out a small package wrapped in palm fronds.

That was all the two servants who answered could remember: the soft voice, the diminutive messenger with long, dark hair; probably a child, gender uncertain. The mask like a barking dog, or grinning jackal, or maybe a bat. Plain, scruffy clothing, maybe loose trousers or just a robe; probably barefoot.

They'd merely accepted the package and the messenger ran away.

Their exasperated master took it from them and ordered them beaten.

Lord Kuthomes tore the fronds away and held in his hands a small wooden box, cheaply made of scrap materials, without any attempt at ornamentation.

The box vibrated slightly, as if something inside it were alive, or perhaps clockwork.

Thoughtful, ever on guard against the trick of some enemy — for he *was* a great lord of the Delta and he had many enemies — he carried it to his chamber. As he entered, living golden hands on his nightstand lifted a two-paneled mirror, holding it open like a book.

Kuthomes sat on a stool, a candle in one hand, the parcel in the other, gazing at the reflections of both in the black glass. The hands shifted the mirror, showing the image in one panel, then the other.

As he had so many times before, Kuthomes searched for some hidden clue which might reveal treachery or useful secrets. He was a magician of sorts, though not a true sorcerer, wholly transformed, reeking of poisonous enchantment. His art sufficed to unravel such lethal puzzles as one Deltan lord might design for another. In this mirror, he had often learned the weakness of some rival. Once he had even reached *through* the glass and torn out a sleeping man's heart.

He hefted the box. It weighed perhaps two ounces. But he had an instinct about such things. He sensed strangeness, and in strangeness, danger.

But when he held the box up to the mirror, even with the candle positioned to shine through the delicate wood, he saw only his hands, the box, and the candle's flame. The depths remained inscrutable; they did not even reflect Lord Kuthomes's silver-bearded face.

The box stirred, humming like one of those metal lanterns the harlequins carried. For an instant, Kuthomes was furious. A festival night *joke?* He would have crushed the thing in his hand and hurled it away. But that same caution which had made him a great lord of the Delta again prevailed.

He placed the object down on the night stand, took a delicate calligrapher's knife, and, by candlelight, began to chip away at the thin wood. There were no envenomed needles, no springs, no magic seals waiting to be broken. The fragments fell away easily.

Inside was a sculpture about two inches high, of a laughing corpse-face, its head thrown back, its gap-toothed mouth stretched wide. Inside the mouth, a tiny silver bell rang of its own accord. Kuthomes touched

by Darrell Schweitzer

the bell with the tip of his knife and the ringing stopped.

Outside, the mob laughed and roared. Drums beat faintly, muffled, far away.

He laid the knife down on the table top, and the ringing resumed. It wasn't a matter of a breeze or a draught. He placed the whole object under a glass bowl and the bell still shivered.

He knew, then, that this was no thing of the living world, but a death-bell, manufactured in *Tashe* itself by dead hands, then borne up, like a bubble rising from a deep, muddy pool, through the dreamlands of *Leshe*, until it was present, very substantially, at the doorstep of Lord Kuthomes of the Delta. It was a token, a summons from the dead.

"Whoever has sent this," he said aloud, "know that I shall find you out and wrest your secrets from you, though you be already dead. You shall learn why Kuthomes is feared."

He rose and prepared himself, performing the four consecrations, forehead, eyelids, ears, and mouth touched with the Sorcerer's Balm, to shield him from illusion. His midnight-black sorcerer's robe came to life as it closed around him, its delicately glowing embroideries depicting a night sky never seen over the City of the Delta; the stars of Death, the sky of *Tashe*.

He regarded his reflection in the mirrors, only the robe visible in the darkness, like some headless specter.

The original owner of that robe, he recalled, had been headless toward the end, but well before he died, before others carried the remains away and finished the unpleasant, perilous business. He knew that to kill a sorcerer is to become one. The contagion flows from the slain to the slayer. Therefore a sorcerer must be disposed of carefully, by experts, not such dilettantes as he, who might occasionally require that the serpentine motif on a jade carving come to life on cue, or a sip of wine paralyze the will, or the face of a one man be temporarily transformed into that of the other. These were stock-in-trade for any lord of the Delta, to be applied as deftly as a surgeon's knife.

But no, he was not a sorcerer.

Therefore he also carried a curious sword in a scabbard underneath his robe, its strong steel blade inlaid with intricate, ultimately mystifying silver designs. It was the weapon of a Knight Inquisitor, one of those fanatic warriors from the barbarian lands across the sea, a sworn enemy of all gods but the Righteous Nine and especially of the Shadow Titans, who breathe sorcery like a miasma into the world. The sword was proof against all the magical darkness.

But Kuthomes, merely a man, had strangled the Knight Inquisitor with a cord, years ago, when he was younger and had the strength for such things.

He put on the jeweled, brimless cap of his rank and took up the death-bell in his hand, then passed silently through the halls of his own house in vigorous, graceful strides. He crossed the central courtyard. Up above, someone hastily closed a shutter. Even on such a merry

night, it was ill luck to look on Lord Kuthomes in his sorcerer's aspect.

A single lamp flickered in the atrium. There were still palm fronds on the floor, and a stain where the servants had been beaten. That would be cleaned up on his return, or made larger.

He slipped out into the street.

By now the night was almost over. Stars still shone overhead, but the sky was purpling in the East. He found himself in an utterly dark street, without a single lantern hanging from a doorway, a channel of featureless exterior walls. Higher up, the balconies were empty, the shutters invariably locked.

He stretched out his palm and held the death-bell up level with his face.

It laughed at him, but slowly now, the faint tinkling interspersed with silence.

Several streets away, someone shouted. A horn blew a long, trailing blast that began as music and ended in flatulence. Something fell and broke, probably crockery. Then silence again.

He walked confidently along that dark street until he stumbled, cursing, over what looked like an enormous, long-legged bird left broken and sprawling.

But Kuthomes did not fall. He regained his footing, crushing the death-bell in his hand. The thing felt like a live wasp, scraping to get free. Hastily, he opened his hand, then stood still, gasping.

Gradually he made out an inert reveler in some absurd costume: trailing cloth wings, tatters and streamers, a crushed and shapeless mask. There must have been stilts somewhere, or else a crowd had carried the fool aloft.

In his younger days, Kuthomes might have given the fellow a kick to the ribs, but now he merely spat, then continued on his way.

He tried to follow the delicate voice of the bell, turning where it seemed to ring louder or more frequently. But his ear could not actually tell. He wandered through the maze of streets, once or twice passing others, who hurried to get out of his way.

In a market square, he faced the East. Dawn's first light sufficed to reveal the solitary figure standing there: very short, clad in shapeless white, arms akimbo, bare feet spread apart, face hidden behind some cheap animal mask.

"You there!" Kuthomes dropped the insistent bell into his pocket and stepped forward, but the other turned and ran. For an instant he thought it was a dwarf, but the motion was too agile. A child then. He couldn't tell if it was a boy or a girl.

He pursued until his breath came in painful gasps and it seemed his chest would burst. Again and again he saw his quarry, near at hand but out of reach, vanishing around a corner at the end of an alley, on the other side of a courtyard, or gazing down on him from a balcony or from a bridge over a canal.

"Do not dare to trifle with me!"

On the Last Night of the Festival of the Dead

Bare feet padded on cobblestones. Hard boots clattered after.

But in the morning twilight Kuthomes could go no further. He had to sit down on a stone bench and lean back against a wall, gazing out over the central forum of the city. All around him the temples of the major gods faced one another. The rising sun made the rooftops and the many statues gleam. Divinities, kings, and heroes lining those rooftops and perched on pillars and ledges seemed momentarily alive, gazing down benevolently or wrathfully, each according to their nature. Yawning peddlers opened their stalls. A flock of pigeons stirred, murmuring on the steps of the temple of Bel-Hemad, the god of new life, of springtime, and forgiveness. But the house of Surat-Hemad, the lord of Death, was still a mass of shadows and black stone, the eyes of the carven crocodile head over the doorway aglow like faint coals with some mysterious light of their own.

Kuthomes half-dozed, exhausted, enraged that he had been the object of a *joke* on the first night of the Festival of the Dead. He set the death-bell in his lap, and still it rang, a far more serious matter than anybody's joke. He laid the sword of the Knight Inquisitor across his knees, and the ringing stopped. When he put the sword away, it resumed.

He couldn't think clearly just then, weary and angry as he was, but he was certain that he was proof against illusion, and that there was an answer here somewhere, in the haze and dust and fading shadows. If he concentrated hard enough, he would have it, and his revenge, later.

Was he not Lord Kuthomes, feared and respected by all?

Eventually he fell asleep on the bench and dreamed, strangely, that he, the feared and respected Lord Kuthomes, had ventured alone into the city at night, and that the city was empty. All the revelers, soldiers, courtiers, even the Great King himself had fled before him, and Lord Kuthomes's heavy footsteps echoed in the empty palace, even in the vast Presence Hall where he mounted the throne with the double crown of the Delta and Riverland on his head.

He sat still and silent in his dream, the crown on his head, crocodile-headed scepter in his hand, gazing into the empty darkness, until he heard the sound of the tiny death-bell approaching.

Someone shuffled and emerged from behind a column. Kuthomes stiffened and beheld a tall, cloaked figure approach the throne slowly, tottering like a very old man; no, swaying side-to-side like a crocodile reared up, imitating a human walk.

The thing opened clawed hands when it stood at the foot of the throne. The face beneath the hood was indeed that of a crocodile. In the open hands, nothing at all.

Here was one of the *evatim*, the messengers of Surat-Hemad, whose summons may never be resisted or denied. Kuthomes shrank back in his stolen throne,

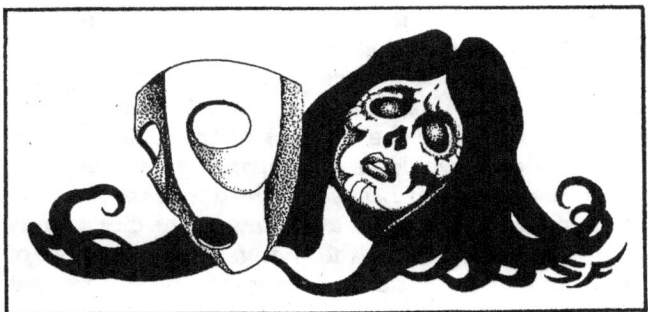

knowing that all his magic and even the silver sword were useless.

But the other tore off a crocodile mask, uncovering a laughing corpse face identical to that which held the death-bell, head back in a paroxysm of hilarity or terror, mouth agape. In the unimaginable depths of its throat, a tiny bell rang insistently.

Then the apparition breathed *laughter*, neither harsh nor exactly gentle, impatient, with a touch of petulance, and at last a voice spoke from those same black depths, soft, definitely feminine, a young woman's voice, maddeningly familiar.

In his dream, it was too much effort to recall. He almost recognized the voice, but not quite.

"Do you not know me?" the other said.

"No," he replied.

"Ah, but you did once, long ago."

"How long ago was that?"

She only laughed for a brief instant. Then the laughter was gone and the bell rang.

Lord Kuthomes shook himself out of his dream and found himself on the bench at the edge of the dusty forum, in the blazing mid-day sun. The bell, in his lap, still rang. No one had dared to disturb him, of course. Those who gaped in wonder suddenly turned their faces away, pretending not to have seen.

He took up the bell again and lurched to his feet, shouting for an old woman to fetch him a litter. When she had done so, she held out her hand for a coin. He patted his pockets, found nothing, then scowled and spat, tumbling into the litter, drawing the curtain behind him. The bearers set off, the litter lurching, swaying. Kuthomes felt sick by the time he reached his house.

Inside the atrium, the palm fronds and the stain on the floor were still there.

Later. There would be time for that later.

On the second night of the Festival of the Dead, they were dancing.

This was a more somber time. The streets and rooftops echoed with stately music. Paper masks from the first night floated in the canals or littered the streets. Now people wore beautifully carved and adorned wooden masks, ageless, ideal visages which did not so much hide the identity of the wearer as abstract it, like a name written in intricate, illuminated letters.

Musicians, clad in dark cerements and masked in imitation of the *evatim*, moved slowly from house to house, to palace and hovel alike, excepting no one, summoning the inhabitants to dance, to mingle in the wide forum before the temples of the gods. On this night the dead would truly return in great numbers, out of the dreams of *Leshe* and the darkness of *Tashe*, climbing up from the Great River and the city's many canals to walk among the living. It was a night of portents and revelations, of sorrows and bittersweet joys, reunions, secret dooms, and frequent miracles.

Lord Kuthomes had rested and bathed. He had pored over such books of sorcery as he owned and could read, unable to find any answer to the riddle before him, but still certain some enemy had laid a trap.

He would be ready. Once more he anointed himself four times and put on his sorcerer's robe. Once more the silver sword pressed against his thigh. This time even he wore a mask, beautifully wrought, set with gems and feathers until the features of Lord Kuthomes had been transformed into some fantastic, predatory bird.

When the revelers reached his door, he gave them such coin as custom required, then stepped out into the throng, moving along the dark and crowded streets, into the forum where moonlight shone on the roofs of the temples and the many bronze and golden statues. The gods seemed to be watching him alone, waiting for something to happen.

Even the Great King, Wenamon the Ninth, was there with all his lords and ladies, all of them masked, to do homage to Death. Kuthomes took his rightful place in the great circle of their dance. Once he held the warm hand of Queen Valshepsut, who nodded to him, and he to her, before he yielded to the King. Around and around dancers turned, as the musicians followed, pipes skirling, drums beating stately, muted time. Acolytes with lanterns or torches pursued their own paths at the periphery, the intricate revolutions imitating the cycles of the universe. In the center, priests of Death stood motionless in their crocodile masks.

Or were those perhaps the true faces of the *evatim*? The fancy came to Kuthomes that many of the faces around him, in the royal circle, in the crowd, were not masks at all.

In the midst of them was one who did not dance, who clearly did not belong: some scruffy urchin in a paper mask that was probably supposed to be a fox, in shapeless white trousers and shirt, bare feet spread apart, arms this time folded imperiously. He could see the figure clearly.

He broke through the dancers. "You there! Stop!"

But the boy was gone.

Then someone, whose touch was very cold and dry, whose grip was like a vise, took him by the hand and whirled him back into the dance.

He hissed, "Who *dares*?"

But the other merely bowed, with both arms spread

wide, then straightened and stepped back, in a half-formed dance step. He discerned a slender lady in rotting funeral clothes, but that meant nothing on this night. Her mask was plain and featureless white, with mere round holes for eyes and mouth.

Now the rhythm of the dance changed. The music slowed and the circles broke apart. Dancers clung to one another, drifting off in pairs into doorways and alleys, beneath canopies, there to unmask.

The stranger led Kuthomes into the darkness beneath a broken bridge, far from the crowd, into silence. They stood on a ledge above the black water of a canal. The other lifted Kuthomes' mask off and made to throw it away, but he snatched it back and held it tightly against his chest. She twirled her own white mask out over the water, where it splashed, then drifted like a sparkle of reflected moonlight.

"Do you not remember me?" she said, speaking not Deltan but that language universal among the dead, yet known only to sorcerers among the living and never uttered aloud. Kuthomes could make out enough: ". . . your promise . . . long ago. Our assignation. Complete what you began."

He cried out. He couldn't break free of her arms. Her breath was foul. Her filthy hand pressed over his mouth.

When she let go, he managed to gasp, "Name yourself . . ."

"Remember poor Kamachina . . ."

Then she was gone. He heard a splash. The black water rippled. He stepped out of the shadow of the bridge, into the moonlight and stood still, amazed and afraid.

The absurd thing was he didn't know any Kamachina. It was a common female name in the Delta. There must have been hundreds of servants, daughters of minor nobility, whores, whoever. He searched his memory for a specific Kamachina. No, no one. He tried to laugh, to tell himself this was another, tastelessly misconceived joke, that even the dead could blunder.

But then he got the death-bell out of his pocket and held it on his palm. The bell still rang.

On the third and final night of the Festival of the Dead, those who had received special signs assembled in silence on the steps of the black temple of Surat-Hemad, who created the crocodile in his own image.

The temple doors formed the Devouring God's jaws. Bronze teeth gleamed by torchlight. Within the great hall, two red lanterns burning above the altar were the all-seeing eyes of Death. In the vaults beneath the altar, in the belly of Surat-Hemad, dead and living commingled freely, and the waters of dream, of *Leshe*, lapped against the shores of the living world those of the land of the dead. On this night, of all nights, the borders were freely crossed.

The doors swung wide. Twenty or so pilgrims entered.

Dark-clad, bearing the death-bell and his sword, but unmasked, Lord Kuthomes filed in with the others, circling thrice around the altar and the image of the squat-bellied, crocodile-headed Surat-Hemad, then descended into the deeper darkness of the vaults. He walked among stone sarcophagi containing the mummies of great or wicked men, who might return at any time they chose to inhabit such earthly forms.

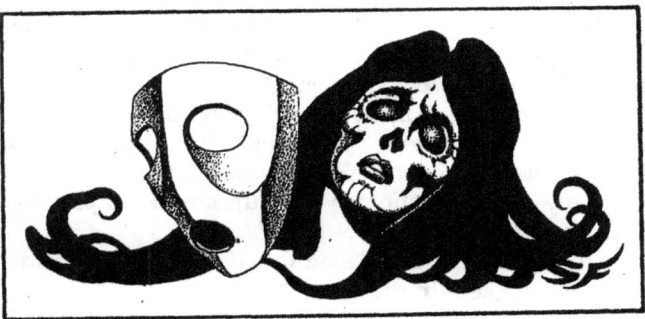

He placed his hand on the carven effigy of some lord of centuries past. The mummy within stirred and scratched.

His mind was clear, though he had not rested after the second night. He had searched his books and gazed into his mirror for long hours, coming up with no revelation at all. He knew, then, that he could only confront the dead and allow them to speak. His fate, perhaps, was no longer in his own hands.

All things return to Surat-Hemad, so the prayer went.

Yes.

Still he could not remember a specific Kamachina. He didn't know who the boy was either. The child's significance, in particular, eluded him. He did not fit.

All things —

He had even consulted a true sorcerer, an ancient creature deformed and transformed by the magic within him, who walked in swaying jerks like a scarecrow come alive in the wind, whose head flicked constantly from side to side like a bird's, whose noseless face was a mass of scars, whose metal eyes clicked, whose hands were living fire. The sorcerer laughed slyly in a multitude of voices, and turned away.

A priest of Bel-Hemad had merely shaken his head sadly and said, "By the end of the third night, you shall know who this lady is. I am certain of that."

Kuthomes had offered a fantastic sum of money, enough to startle even the priest.

"What is this for?"

"Help me escape. There must be a way."

The priest had merely shrugged, and Kuthomes stalked away from the priest's house, muttering to himself, striking people and objects in blind rage, pacing back and forth to fill the hours until the sun set and the third night of the Festival of the Dead began. The waiting was the worst part.

Dread Surat-Hemad, may all things be completed and finished and laid to rest, the prayers went.

Lord Kuthomes did not often pray.

Now he walked among the tombs of the ancient, sorcerous dead, the carven, laughing corpse-face in his hand, the tiny bell in its throat tinkling. Like all the others, he followed the sputtering tapers held aloft by the masked priests of Death, until all had gathered in an open space before a vast doorway.

A priest touched a lever. Counterweights shifted somewhere. Stone ground against stone, and the doors slid aside. Cold, damp air blew into the musty crypt, smelling of river mud and corruption.

Here was the actual threshold of the world of the dead. Beyond this door, he knew, down a little slope, black water lapped silently. Funeral barges waited to carry the dead — and the living — into *Leshe,* where madmen, visionaries, and sorcerers might glimpse Lord Kuthomes passing through their dreams.

Kuthomes hoped they would know and remember whom they had seen.

At the threshold, the tiny death-bell stopped ringing. Kuthomes threw it away, certain it was of no further use.

He reached under his robe and drew out the silver sword.

"You won't need that." A warm, living hand caught his wrist. The voice was soft, but not feminine, speaking Deltan, accented very slightly. The boy.

Kuthomes slid the sword back into the scabbard. "Who are you?"

"One who will guide you to your trysting place. Lord Kuthomes, the Lady Kamachina awaits."

"Explain yourself, or die."

"If you kill me, you will never know the answer, will you?"

"There are slow methods . . . which inspire eloquence . . ."

"But hardly worth the exertion, Lord. Come with me, and all will be made clear."

Kuthomes hesitated. Slowly, the other pilgrims crossed the threshold. What could he do but follow? The boy was waiting.

Hand-in-hand, the two of them passed through the door and into absolute darkness, where not even the priests with their tapers dared accompany them. The only sound was the sucking of boots in the mud. The boy seemed to know where he was going. Kuthomes allowed himself to be led. They groped their way into a barge and sat still, among many other wordless pilgrims.

Then they were adrift, and gradually stars appeared overhead, not those seen over the Delta on any summer night, but the stars of Deathlands, of *Tashe.*

He discerned crocodile-headed things in the river, thousands, floating along like a great mass of weed; but their bodies were pale and human, like naked, drowned men. These were the true messengers of Death, the *evatim.*

Someone in the company shrieked, stood up, and did a frantic, whirling dance, hands waving and slapping as if in an attempt to fend off invisible hornets. He fell into the river with a splash. The *evatim* hissed all as one, the sound like a rising wind.

Someone else began strumming a harp. A song arose from many voices, a gentle, desolate lyric in the language of the dead. From out of the air, from far beyond the barge, more voices joined in.

Many wept. Kuthomes was unmoved, impatient, tensely alert.

The boy took his hand again, as if seeking or offering comfort. He couldn't tell which.

They were deep into Dream now, and the visions began. Some of the others cried out from sudden things Kuthomes could not see; but *he* was able to behold vast shapes in the sky, half human, half-beast, like clouds moving *behind* the stars, pausing in some incomprehensible journey to glance down at those in the barge below. These might have been the gods, or the Shadow Titans, from whom all sorcery flowed. Kuthomes had no idea. He did not choose to ask the masked boy beside him, who, he was certain, *did* know.

From *Leshe*, Dream, as they passed over into the realm of Death, the rest of the adventure was like a dream, inexplicable, without continuity.

Once it seemed that he and the boy sat alone on the barge. The boy closed and opened his hands, and blue flames rose from his scarred palms. Kuthomes removed the boy's shabby mask, tossing it out among the *evatim*. By the blue light, he could see a very ordinary face, soft, beardless, with large, dark eyes; a man-child somewhere in the middle teens, with tangled, dark hair. Part of one of the boy's ears was missing. That struck Kuthomes as merely odd.

"Who *are* you?" he whispered in the language of the dead.

In that same tongue the boy replied, "A messenger."

"One of the *evatim* then?"

"What do you think?"

"You seem alive."

"Death, also, is a kind of life."

In another part of the dream they walked on water, barefoot because the river would not hold up Kuthomes as long as he wore boots. Ripples spread on the frigid surface. They walked through a dead marsh in wintertime. Among the reeds, skeletal, translucent birds waded on impossibly delicate legs.

Later still, the sky brightened into a dull, metallic gray, without a sunrise, but with enough suffused light that Kuthomes could see clearly. He and the boy walked for hours through sumptuous dust, until they both were covered with it. A wind rose. Swirling dust filled the air. By tricks of half-light and shadow, in the shifting dust, he seemed to make out buried rooftops, part of a city wall, a tower. But all these crumbled away when he touched them, then reformed again somewhere nearby.

Sometimes he saw faces on the ground before him, or in walls or doorways. He made his way through the narrow streets of a city of dust. The boy led him by the hand.

Here was the silently screaming dust-face of Lord Vormisehket, stung by a thousand scorpions; and here Adriuten Shomash with his throat still cut, sand pouring out of the nether mouth beneath his chin. Lady Neframe and her three children confronted him. She had hurled herself into a well with the children in her arms. So many more, faces and bodies sculpted out of transitory dust, forming and reforming as Kuthomes passed, dust-arms and hands reaching out for him, crumbling, reaching again.

He saw many who had been useful to him for a time, then inconvenient: Akhada the witch; Dakhumet the poisoner, who hurled tiny, darts fashioned like birds; even the former king himself, Baalshekthose, first and only ruler of that name, whose sudden ascent and decent both Kuthomes had brought about.

The boy dragged him on, pulling at his arm, completely plastered with the gray dust so that only his eyes seemed alive.

Kuthomes felt indignant anger more than anything else. Why should these phantoms accuse him? Such deeds were the stuff of politics. Those who wielded power must be, by the nature of that power, above the common morality.

It was only when they came to a halt by a broken bridge over a dust-choked canal that Kuthomes recognized where he was. Here, in dreams and dust and ash, was a replica, shifting and inexact but a replica nevertheless, of the City of the Delta, of a disreputable district where, many years before, he had promised to meet someone by that bridge.

In this place of dreams and death, amid the dust, the memory came back to him, clearly, like a book opening, its pages turning.

She was waiting for him, tall and slender in her dusty shroud. He knew her even before she spoke, before the caked dirt on her face cracked and fell away like a poorly-wrought mask to reveal empty eyesockets and bare bones.

Her voice was gentle and sad and exactly as he remembered it. She spoke in the language of the dead.

"Kuthomes, my only love, I am your beloved, Kamachina, whom you once promised to marry and make great."

He could not resist her embrace, or her kiss, though both revolted him.

"I never knew what happened to you," he managed to say at last.

He had been seventeen, an upstart from outside the city, youngest of many sons, driven out of his village with few prospects, ridiculed by the great ones of the Delta, desperate for recognition, for a position of any sort. He had dallied with a girl, the daughter of a minor official. Already he was precocious in the ways of the court, though he had yet to set foot inside a palace. His lies had the desired effect, with hints of plots and of suppressed factions soon to rise again; with the implication that Kuthomes was not who he seemed at all, but perhaps a prince in disguise, whose true name would make the mighty tremble. With this and more he secured introductions, a position. In exchange for the favor of the girl Kamachina, he promised to make her family great.

Later, when she pressed her claim and became inconvenient, he put her off, all the while whispering that she and her father were both mad, obsessed with absurd plots. At the very end, there had been the assignation at the bridge. The two of them would exchange marriage vows but keep them secret until the time was right for the revelation.

"But you never came," she said. On that final, sacred night of the Festival of the Dead, when uttered vows are binding forever, he had betrayed her, and, in her grief, she had flung herself into the canal and drowned.

"I truly loved you," she said. "You were my every, my only hope."

"I . . . did not know."

"I was great with your child. Did you know that?"

"I . . . had not seen you in several months."

"I could hardly confess such a thing in a letter."

"Someone might have intercepted it," he said.

She dragged him to his knees, then lay by his side in the cold dust.

At last he broke free, stood up, and brushed himself off.

"But all this was almost *forty years ago*. How can it matter now?"

She reached up and took him by the hand. "Among the dead, time moves much more slowly."

He looked around for the boy and saw him crouching nearby in the dust, hands folded over his knees, watching dispassionately.

"Is that your son?"

"I have no son," said Kamachina, reaching up for Kuthomes. "My child is still within me, waiting to be born." Once more she dragged him down into her irresistible embrace, pressing her corpse-mouth against his.

Kuthomes screamed. He fought her, drawing his silver sword, striking her again and again, slashing her head off, hacking her body to pieces.

But it was no use. She merely reconstituted herself, a thing of dust and dead bones, sculpted by some magical wind.

She caught his wrist in her crushing grip and made him throw the sword away.

"I'm sorry," he said. "I did what I had to do. I didn't know . . . If I could help you, I would, but it's too late . . ."

"What is begun on the last night of the Festival of the Dead," she said, embracing him once more, "is sacred, inviolate, and must always be consummated."

So it was that Lord Kuthomes came to dwell in the country of the dead with his Lady Kamachina. He was mad with the terror of it all for a long time. It seemed that he sat on a throne, and ruled as emperor among

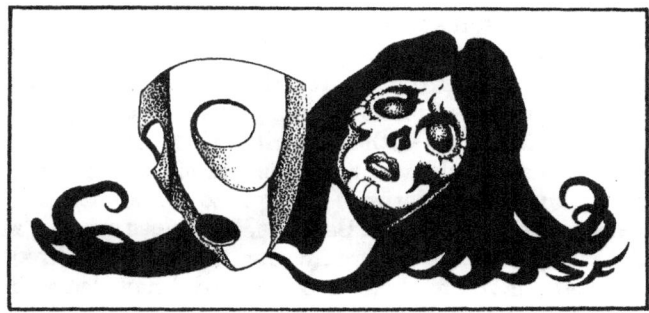

the corpses, but slowly, subtly, they turned from him, perverting his every command, until at last he was cast down, reviled, trampled into filth. He shouted that he was a great lord, that he was *alive* and they mere corpses, but they only laughed at him.

Dead hands tore his entrails out of his body, lifted his bleeding heart up before his face; dead lips drank his blood and devoured him. So it seemed, in his madness, though each time he awoke, he found himself whole.

He tried to bear all this in the manner of a great lord, silently plotting his revenge, but that was absurd, and before long he too was shrieking aloud at the hilarity of the idea.

"How shall I be revenged against myself?" he asked the ghosts. "How?"

They could not answer him.

All the while Kamachina was with him, touching him gently, whispering of her love. She alone did not mock him, nor injure him in any way, but her love was the worst torment of all.

In his madness his mind opened up. The speech of gods and of the Titans poured into him. There were many revelations, passed through Kuthomes into the dreams of men who awoke in the living world.

Gradually his pain and his madness lessened, and it seemed he had merely backtracked along a path he had once taken, then set out on another. His old life became the dream, the fading memory. Now he came to see himself dwelling, not in dust, but in an austere palace of massive pillars and black stone, there waited upon by ghosts, while his wife's belly swelled with his child.

"Is it not the duty of a lord," she said, "to provide for the comfort of those beneath him?"

He supposed it was. He didn't know anymore.

He sat with her in her garden of leafless trees and brittle stalks, listening as she spoke or sang softly in the language of the dead. He learned to play a strange harp made of bones as delicate as strands of silk. He came to behold the growing life in that dead garden, the nearly invisible leaves and blossoms like sculpted smoke, and he ate of the fruits of the trees, which tasted like empty air, and was sustained by them. After a while, he could recall no other taste.

She was delivered there, in the garden. The mysterious boy appeared once more, to assist the birthing.

"Who *are* you?" Kuthomes asked. "Can you not tell me at last?"

"I am the sorcerer Sekenre," the boy said.

"But, but, one so young —"

"For sorcerers too, as for the dead, time moves differently. I was fifteen when my father caused me to slay him, filling me with his spirit, and the spirits of all his victims, and the victims of his victims, all united in one, who must sometimes struggle to remember that he was once a boy called Sekenre. My voices are like a flock of birds. We are many. But for three hundred years and more, my body has not aged. I have learned and forgotten many things, as you, Kuthomes, have learned and forgotten."

"I too have a hard time remembering who I am sometimes," said Kuthomes. "We are alike."

"You are the loving father of this child." The boy Sekenre reached into Lady Kamachina's dead womb and lifted an infant girl out in his hands. Kuthomes thought his daughter looked more like a delicate carving than a child: skin translucently white, eyes open and unblinking, the expression severe.

Sekenre passed the baby to Kuthomes, who rested it in his lap.

"The world shall fear this one," Sekenre said, "but not for any evil in her. She is a mirror of the evil in others. In a hundred years' time I shall need her as my ally, against an enemy yet unborn."

"Therefore you have directed all these things, my entire life, to your own purposes."

"Yes, I have," said Sekenre.

Kuthomes shrugged. "I suppose one has to do such things." He felt, vaguely, that he should be angry, but there was no passion left in him.

Kamachina smiled and took the child from him.

Ghosts gathered around them, whispering like a faint wind.

On the last night of the Festival of the Dead, Lord Kuthomes emerged from the vaults beneath the temple of Surat-Hemad in the City of the Delta. He had grown very old. His once tall, vigorous figure was bent, his silver beard now purest white. No one knew him, or the bone-pale girl he led into the world.

His daughter clung to his arm, her eyes dazzled even by the gloom of the inside of the temple; amazed at everything she saw, whispering to him, for comfort, then out of excitement, chattering softly in the language of the dead. The grave-wrappings she wore had partially fallen away, revealing almost transparent skin. She seemed more to float on the air than to walk.

Outside, she had to cover her face from the starlight. Kuthomes found a discarded mask for her.

They walked through streets he remembered now only from his dreams. She had so many questions he could not answer. He took her tiny hand in his and led her to a place he had dreamed, where a certain magician was waiting. This man would nurture her for five years before an enemy killed him, bore her off, and came to regret the prize.

But these things were Sekenre's business.

Kuthomes departed without even bidding his daughter farewell, then hurried back to the temple of Surat-Hemad, and descended into the vaults, so that what had been begun on the last night of the Festival of the Dead could at last be finished. Ω

Three mad, hate-filled eyes blazed up with a living fire, bright as fresh-spilled blood from a face ringed with a writhing nest of worms. . . .

"Who Goes There?" by John W. Campbell, Jr.

BEDDY-BYE
F. Gwynplaine MacIntyre

illustrated by Allen Koszowski

Audrey had ripped off Betty's head again, and was knocking it around the room like a football. I was trying to carry on a civilized conversation with Sylvia, but Audrey drop-kicked Betty's head across the room; it landed in my lap, and Betty's blue eyes stared up at me while her mouth smiled patiently.

Sylvia frowned at Audrey. "I paid a lot of money for that doll, Audrey. You ought to take better care of it."

"It's a *cheap* doll! It's a CHEAP doll!" Audrey screeched. "I wanted one of those expensive dolls, the kind that talks when you pull the ring in her back. Betty is a CHEAP doll!"

"Well, you'd better put her back together, or you'll have no doll at all," said Sylvia impatiently.

"Oh, all right, Mom." Snuffling pathetically, Audrey harvested the various arms and legs of Betty from the places where she'd flung them, and started putting the doll back together. That's the problem I have when I date divorcées; they tend to have kids, and the wee kiddiewinks tend to be hideous brats. Audrey finished reassembling the doll — Betty's head was on backwards, reminding me of something I'd seen in a horror movie once — and held it up for her mother's inspection.

Sylvia nodded approvingly. "Very good, Audrey." She glanced at the clock, and then uttered the fateful words: "Time for bed."

"But, Mommmmmm . . ."

"Time for *bed,* Audrey. Go in and change, and I'll be there to tuck you in."

"Will you read me a story?"

Sylvia sighed audibly. "Aren't you getting to be a big girl now, Audrey? Big enough to go to bed without. . ."

"I want a story! I want a story!"

"*I'll* read her a story," I offered, picking up Audrey's storybook and glancing at the contents. The stories seemed innocuous enough: the three little pigs, the three little bears, the three little billy goats . . .

Sylvia eyed me gratefully, and then nodded to Audrey. "Go in and get ready for bed, dear, and then Uncle Fergus will read you a story and tuck you into bed. Take your doll with you."

I know what I'd *like* to tuck her into," I muttered, from behind the storybook. Audrey galloped off to the nursery, whomping Betty's head against the wall as she departed. For five minutes or so, Sylvia and I were actually able to carry on an adult conversation, over drinks, and then Audrey's hideous prepubescent lungs erupted from the nursery, "I'M READY FOR BEDDY!"

I got up, sighed heavily, and reached for the storybook. "Keep the gin cold," I said, kissing Sylvia and shambling off to meet my doom in the nursery. "This won't take long. . . ."

Audrey had flung her clothes all over the room and was now under the bed covers, presumably wearing her jammies. Her obnoxious face — a double-row of snaggle-teeth, surrounded on all sides by freckles — was grinning at me from the pillow. "Where's Betty?" I asked.

"Over there." Audrey pointed triumphantly. "Betty was bad, so I had to *punish* her."

I looked where Audrey was pointing. Betty the doll had been bound and gagged with handkerchiefs, spread-eagled across the saddle of a rocking-horse. I freed the doll, and looked at it; Betty's blue-glass eyes looked back at me impassively. I left the doll on the floor near Audrey's bed, then I pulled up a chair and started thumbing through the storybook. "Right. What story would you like tonight, then? The three little kittens? The three little ducklings?"

"I *hate* those stories! I HATE those stories!" Audrey's little fingers snatched the storybook out of my hands, and sent it whizzing across the room. The book struck the rocking-horse's face, and sent the wooden horse rocking back and forth crazily. "I want a *scary* story!" Audrey demanded.

A *scary* story? Well, now: *this* was a field in which I had some expertise; Audrey didn't seem to realize what she was letting herself in for.

"All right," I began, "Once upon a time there was a little girl, and her name was . . ."

"Audrey!" screeched Audrey. She was clearly determined to play an active role in the proceedings.

"That's right," I nodded. "There was a little girl named Audrey. One night she went to bed and went right to sleep, and . . ."

"I *hate* this story! I HATE this story!" Audrey screeched.

"I hadn't finished. Audrey went to sleep, and she started dreaming. In her dream, Audrey was *flying*. She was able to fly right up to the ceiling of her bedroom. She went up to the ceiling, and then went right *through* it, like a ghost."

"That's impossible," Audrey protested.

"No, it isn't," I said. "Audrey was asleep, remember? Her body stayed in the bed, and her dream-body — the part that was having the dream — was able to go through the ceiling. Like a ghost."

"Oh, that's different." Audrey seemed satisfied,

now that I was keeping the story firmly grounded on a scientific basis. "And *then* what happened?"

"Audrey's dream-self went right up through the roof, and flew around in the sky. She was able to fly anywhere she wanted, and go right through walls, and look into people's houses. But none of the people could see her or hear her, because Audrey's dream-self was invisible, like a ghost. She could look into their living rooms, and look into their dining rooms, and look into . . ."

". . . their *bathrooms!*" Audrey giggled, and clapped her hands with delight. "I *like* this story! *Then* what happened?"

"Well, Audrey kept flying around in the sky, and she saw other people flying around too. They were people whose bodies were asleep, like Audrey's body was, and their dream-bodies were floating around like Audrey was."

"I'll bet none of the people were Chinese," Audrey decided. "Because it's daytime in China when it's bedtime over *here.*"

"There were all kinds of people," I told her. "Men and women and children, and even dogs and cats. Animals have dreams too, so the dream-dogs and dream-cats had come out of their bodies, and were flying around with all the other dreamers."

Audrey pondered the consequences of this. "Were there any dream-*birds?*" she asked.

"No. Birds can fly anytime they want, so they never dream about flying. The birds were dreaming too, but in their dreams they were *swimming.* Dream-birds don't get to swim very often."

"Were there dream-*fish?*" Audrey wanted to know.

"Yes, and there was a dream-lion, because the lion over at the zoo was asleep that night too. All the animals were dreaming."

"Were there dream-*roaches?*" Audrey persisted.

"No. There weren't any dream-roaches, because roaches never sleep. Anyway, Audrey's dream-body was floating around in the clouds, and all of a sudden she met somebody she knew. Can you guess who it was?"

Audrey frowned. "This isn't going to be one of my friends from school, is it? I *hate* all my friends from school. Especially Ethel. She's so fat, when she bends over she wheezes, and . . ."

"No, it wasn't Ethel. And besides, Ethel's dream-self is thin; you probably wouldn't recognize her. Anyway, the dream-Audrey was flying around in the clouds, and who do you think she met?"

Audrey considered several possibilities, and then wrinkled her nose, "I give up. Who?"

"It was *Betty!*"

"Betty my *doll?*" Audrey glared distastefully at Betty; the doll was sitting quietly in her pinafore, staring at Audrey, and hadn't moved. "But that's *impossible!*"

"No, it isn't." I stealthily reached up and turned out the light, and now Audrey and Betty and I were alone in the dark. "Dolls sleep too, and dolls have dreams. So Betty's doll-body stayed here, and her dream-body was flying around in the clouds overhead. 'How did you get up here, Betty?' Audrey asked her doll.

"The doll looked at Audrey while they both flew through a cloud. 'You let me out, Audrey; remember?' the doll answered. 'You pulled my head off, and kicked it across the room. So I was able to get out of my doll-body through the neck-hole, and here I am!'

"Audrey thought about this while they flew through the cloud. 'I have to be getting home,' she said to her doll.

" 'So do I,' said Betty. 'Come on! I'll *race* you!'

"Well, Audrey turned around in a cloudbank, and flew back to her house as fast as she could go. But Betty the doll was right next to her, flying just as fast as *she* could go. They got back home, and Audrey flew through the roof of her bedroom, and then *what* do you suppose she saw?"

There was a silence in the dark, and Audrey fought back a yawn. Her seven-year-old body seemed to be getting tired at last after a long hard day of doll-bashing, but her seven-year-old mind seemed determined to stay awake "Wh–what did Audrey see?" she managed to ask.

"She saw her own body asleep in the bed, of course. And she also saw Betty's doll-body lying on the floor, with Betty's head lying nearby. Well, Audrey flew back to her own body, and was just about to climb into it, when suddenly . . .

" 'Beat you!' Suddenly Betty elbowed Audrey aside, and then *Betty* jumped into Audrey's sleeping body. Audrey tried to get in too, but there wasn't room in there for *two* people. Audrey was trapped outside her

own body, like a ghost, and all she could do was bang against it with her little ghost-fists, yelling 'Let me in! Let me in!' And then, all of a sudden . . . Audrey's sleeping body opened its eyes, and *woke up!*"

There was a faint gasp in the dark, from the direction of Audrey's pillow. The only nice thing about hyperactive brats like Audrey is that sooner or later the hyperactive cycle hits its down-phase, and then they *have* to go to sleep. I kept going:

"Audrey's body got out of bed and started walking across the room. Only it wasn't Audrey in there now; it was Betty! Audrey was starting to get frightened, because she didn't want to be a ghost forever. She needed a body! She looked around the bedroom, but the only body she could find was Betty's doll-body, with no head. Audrey's dream-self flew into it.

"Instantly, Audrey's body ran over, and snatched up the doll-head, and *snapped* it onto the doll-body! And now Audrey was trapped inside the body of Betty the doll, like a fly caught in a jar. So now Betty was Audrey, and Audrey was Betty."

I let that hang in the air for a moment. The real Audrey, tucked into bed, shifted nervously as if trying to stay awake. Finally she asked weakly, "Wh—what was it like?"

"To be a doll? It was terrible. The doll-body had arms and legs, but Audrey couldn't move them; dolls can't move by themselves. She could look out at the world through the doll's glass eyes, and hear with the doll's plastic ears, but she couldn't *speak*. Everybody knows that dolls can't talk, except for the expensive ones with the ring in their backs. This was a cheap doll."

"And . . . and *then* what happened?"

"Nothing much. Betty the doll, wearing Audrey's body, put on Audrey's clothes and pretended to be Audrey. She took her doll — who was really Audrey — and threw her in the bottom of the closet. Once in a while Audrey's mother would find the doll, and then Audrey would try to talk to her: 'It's me! It's me! Let me out! I'm Audrey!' But Audrey's mother couldn't hear her."

I let that concept hang in the dark for a while, and then Audrey asked: "Did . . . did Audrey *die?*"

"No, of course not. She couldn't eat or drink or go to the bathroom, but now that she was a plastic doll she didn't *have* to. Meanwhile, Betty was a real little girl now, wearing Audrey's body. All the schools burned down, so Betty didn't have to go to school. She had lots of fun being Audrey, wearing Audrey's clothes and doing all the things that Audrey would have liked to do instead of being a doll in the bottom of the closet.

"Years later Audrey's body grew up — with Betty inside it, of course — and became a teenager, and that was the year that Audrey's mother got killed in a horrible accident on the M4 motorway. Betty went to the funeral, pretending to be Audrey, and everybody thought she was crying but she was really laughing. She took all the money that Audrey's mother had left behind, and she went on a cruise around the world. And do you know what she took with her?"

There was silence in the dark, and then a sniff. "What?"

"She took a doll, of course. One special doll, from the bottom of her closet. Late one night in the middle of the Pacific Ocean, slightly to the left of Australia, Betty took the plastic doll with Audrey trapped inside it, and threw it into the ocean.

"But Audrey didn't drown, of course; doll-bodies don't breathe. She floated on top of the ocean for a long time, and then she sank to the bottom. And she stayed there at the bottom of the ocean forever. She couldn't *die,* not ever, because the doll-body was made of high-impact plastic."

There was another long silence in the dark. Audrey yawned again; her mind was trying to force her body to stay awake. "Is that . . . is that the end of the story?" she asked.

"Yes, it is," I assured her. "Of course, none of it would ever have happened if Audrey had managed to stay *awake* all night. It was only because Audrey went to *sleep* that Betty the doll was able to switch bodies with her."

Now I got up, and kissed Audrey in the dark. "Nighty-night. Try to get some sleep." I picked something up off the floor, and thrust it under the covers next to her. "Here's your *doll.*"   Ω

LIMERICK KNIGHTLY

Said the knight, "I once heeded your pleas,
"And I slew that old dragon with ease.
    "But now something seems queer.
    "Please explain to me, dear,
"Why our twins singe their clothes when they sneeze."

— **John Clayton**

OTHERWHYS

Why does Sun?
Why, Moon?
Ah, those are two different whys.

One why is of gaseous fire
— Trembling meniscus
On gravity's deep pool.
The other why, of that harem-captive
Marble odalisque
— Body of passive stone
So cold while Sun's gaze
Is turned away, yet
Agonizedly incandescent
If caressed.

Worlds are only moons of a Sun;
Yet the lover, the empress,
Visits her World daily,
Not fortnightly
In rotation.

Sun's touch warms World,
Does not scald.
Hence that jealousy
Of Moon towards World,
Envy that steals the breath
Away, crusting acne
On Moon's skin.

Moon would throw stones at World,
Flail World with the hair
Of comets . . .

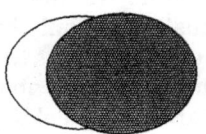

Why else does Moon conspire
To seed nightmares?
For Moon is vexed
If Sun is peering elsewhere
— Staring avidly out
At those others
Whom Sun truly adores:
Sun's flame-sisters
Stars lost so far away
Except to a gaze
Always centuries
Out of date.

Why, is the sigh
Of the sea-tide seduced
By bitter Moon . . .

One day Moon will plunge
Into warm World,
Shattering herself
In a rupturous and
Forced embrace.

What shall issue
From this genocidal union?
Eventually, some aeons afterwards?
Perhaps a new race
Of tortoise-roaches,
Of armoured ants
— Or of sapient spiders
That dream
And ask why.

Yet one why will be missing
From their understanding
— Being sunk in the bowl
Of a new ocean
Around which the breasts
Of lunar mountains rear.

— **Ian Watson**

... TO FAST IN FIRES ...
by Charles D. Eckert

illustrated by George Barr

Mallory was feeling old.

The close-cropped, graying veteran had been a civilian now, as well as Shift Leader, for many years. Yet everyone on the security detachment, including rookies lacing the periphery of the Team, still called him "Colonel." He had grown used to the familiar honorific, over time.

But time has a way of changing things.

"All clear, sir," Mallory said, looking at his boss with the seasoned objectivity of an experienced professional, thinking: *They keep getting younger. His predecessors seemed more my age. Now, even code names get recycled. I not only feel like their father, I'm beginning to look the part.* "Area secured."

"I'll go on by myself," Wanderer said.

"Unwise, Mr. President."

"Noted. Confine your people to the perimeter, as always."

"Consider it done."

Landscape gripped cold contours of fog.

Practically speaking, the best time to "close" any place open 24 hours is to do so in the so-called wee hours of the morning — 2:00 A.M. to 4:00 A.M. — or thereabouts. Few, if any, odd insomniac stragglers might find themselves "temporarily inconvenienced." A private visit could then be simply and properly managed. Colonel Mallory and the Team were pros at the process. Even the lights would, in fact *should,* be left on. Better visibility was a serendipitous result. Though, in this case, illumination shone only about half-way up the surface(s), and that but dimly, as seen from any distance in these obscured conditions.

Wanderer passed the slightly-larger-than-life-sized sculpture, cast to depict one understated yet remarkably poignant moment — bronze eyes, not merely *perceiving* but doing so with uncommon clarity, born of shared pain and experience — and made his slow way down the clean, narrow walkway, bound on the lawn side by a small chain barrier and on the other by spaced, wedge-shaped ground lamps shining up the polished black panels of engraved, gleaming granite, all etched with names.

So many names.

"... *inscribed in the order they were taken from us* ..."

A once controversial design gave distinct edificial impressions, rising out of slashed ground: smoothing gracefully, ascending to a vertex of two "wings" meeting at specific degrees of angle — according to his briefing — the center of an extended black chevron; descending thereafter, as the rougher stone path rose again to ground level, a total of almost 500 feet of long, reflective, darkened mirror.

Strange to recall there were no graves here.

Wanderer could hardly expect many to fully appreciate why he needed to repeatedly visit this place. It would never — *could* never — be easy to explain complex reasons to those who had not been of a certain age during troubled times, had not experienced an era from specific perspectives, had not burned with particular passions, had not endured what seemed unique pain.

A nation's wounds reflect those of its people.

Thus, Wanderer felt obligated to be here, at this — yes, holy — place, *sans* any distractions at all. Where, undisturbed among burnished Indian stones, his own healing might resume. What better way to start?

Yet something had happened during his first 'solitary' nocturnal visit. Shaken his very core. It recurred the second time, as well. Wanderer didn't think he was going crazy. In fact, he never seriously considered that possibility. No "agonizing self-appraisal" there. But with all the pressures of his job, *could* he ever be sure?

How?

Sometimes you just have to believe what you see.

Intense fog swirled and divided.

There he is!

Since the first time Wanderer had seen the soldier step out of the mist — not only had he been surprised, since he'd given explicit orders to be left alone, but also he had also been quite taken aback by the unfamiliar weapon (any weapon!) the soldier carried: where was security? — an indescribable calm surrounded Wanderer immediately. Then and Now. He somehow *knew* he was not in any danger. At least, not as he understood that term.

Spreading warmth proved oddly comforting: a presence, intimate, enfolding.

The soldier leaned his "Bloop Gun" — M79 40-mm Grenade Launcher — against the cool surface of the panel he always chose. He removed his helmet, with its bottle of "bug juice" in the band, put it down carefully in the damp alongside the big wooden butt-stock of the weapon so his hands could be free as he stood.

With an exquisite, touching reverence, the soldier —

an ever-so-painfully young *boy*, he always seemed to be at this point — reached out and up, fingertips quivering across a name traced in stone.

Same one, no doubt, as before.

The soldier froze there, rooted deeper than the roughened-rock pathway beneath wet/dried mud on worn, booted feet. Solid and singular, as the panel reflecting his jungle fatigues. Yet, for reasons unknown, Wanderer couldn't shake the visceral sensation that *others* — though no one to be seen — gathered around this lone, sweat-stained figure, sharing the otherwise unsharable.

Time ceased to matter.

Several distant pistol shots echoed faintly over the grounds — faintly to Wanderer's civilian senses; city sounds travel far in night's relative quiet — but sharp and clear to the soldier, who spun and crouched in a startling, cat-smooth movement, reaching for the re-assurance of his weapon.

The faint shots could have any number of origins, Wanderer thought: *a domestic disturbance; some cold, random drive-by with no articulable reason; a drug deal gone sour, or rival gangs disputing turf and market share. Could be anything.*

But what was it to this 'visitor'?

The soldier swept the area with what a previous generation called the thousand-yard stare. Taking care of business. A knowing smirk altered the now perceptibly aged(?) face.

"Get some —" the soldier whispered.

"Heard you comin', long way off."

"Sorry," said Wanderer.

"Typical F. N. G." The soldier shrugged. "You'll learn."

" 'F. N. G.'?"

"Fuckin' New Guy."

Been called worse.

"Everybody starts somewhere," Wanderer said.

"Got *that* right." The soldier shifted to a relaxed squat. "Make yourself at home."

"Wish I could." Wanderer tried to match positions without straining too much. "Sometimes, it's almost as if —"

"— You get the feelin' you're not welcome?"

"Something like that."

The soldier nodded. "Tough to forget the stares; weird accusations; the whispers. Like just touchin' folks, even breathin' the same air, might pass on a dose of 'Saigon Rose,' and they figure penicillin's no good. Not welcome. Yeah."

No graves, true; but much lies buried.

Wanderer's Kevlar overcoat weighed heavy in the chill.

"Keepin' busy?" the soldier said.

"They let me out occasionally," said Wanderer.

"Same here."

Wanderer had had lots of practice holding a smile.

"I've been meaning to ask —" said Wanderer.

The soldier's eyes retreated into his now cammo-smeared(?) face.

"— Who —?" Wanderer gestured to dark marble behind them.

"Nobody."

"I don't believe that," Wanderer said. "You wouldn't keep coming back for 'nobody'."

"Maybe not," the soldier said. "How about you?"

* * *

"Take it easy, man," a young Wanderer said to his friend, loud enough to be heard over blatting backfire. "County mounties have been know to rise out of the ooze."

The '52 Hudson's in-line eight engine roared with plass-pack authority — turning heads on all four corners of the street — slowing to a low, loping rumble, as it wound its throaty way down.

"Tough shitsky," Andy said with equal volume, caressing the chrome shaft of *The Green Hornet*'s floor shifter. "They can kiss my —"

Wide slicks screamed and spun out blue smoke, leaving long dual streaks on the pavement. Wanderer felt the gees pressing him back into the vintage comfort of the front passenger seat. Andy drove straight and rock-steady, with satin progression through the gears. A few fat June bugs splattered against thick windshield as the car consumed blacktop. City limits signs flew by — much too soon! — fading at frightening velocity from receding reflections in a cracked rear-view mirror.

Damn, that monster could move.

A famous local drive-in fast approached at the end of the curved short chute down State Road 11. Burgers & fries had been served at that location long before God, or at least since before anyone could remember, which amounted to the same thing. The decision was automatic.

Andy down-shifted with commendable aplomb.

There they were: two horny high school seniors, full of beer and bitching, cocksure young scoundrels and phony cocksmen suffering from testosterone overload, ready for bear and looking for love — or a reasonable facsimile.

It seemed as though they had known each other forever. Little League baseball, at first; all the way to summer jobs at the same factory. The odd keg, here and there. Nothing unusual, really, except double-dating a pair of salsa-hot twin sisters, which had its own set of pleasurable parameters. Other than that, their lives contained mostly stereotypical stuff.

But the times, they were a-changin'.

Grooving to the soothing dulcet tones of the Rolling Stones's classic "Honky-Tonk Woman" — which, or course, lyrically described situations with which they would have been only too happy to become accustomed — the topic of their soon-to-be graduation surfaced.

"What have you got on tap, man?" Andy said.

"You know I've always wanted college," Wanderer told him, leering at the nearest car-hop. "So, that's where it's at."

"Far out," Andy nodded. "School never was my favorite place. Gettin' my military obligation out of the way. I'll decide what to do after that."

They didn't speak.

Why do some dreams become nightmares?
If we select one crucial option instead of another, does someone else walk that alternate path in our place?
Time is a ruthless judge.

The Byrds' "Turn, Turn, Turn" wafted from the radio.

"You be careful, man," young Wanderer finally said, quietly.

"Aw, don't worry," Andy chuckled, soft-punching his friend's arm. "You know me. Look up *caution* in the dictionary; you'll see my picture. Besides, come right down to it, I've always done enough fightin' for both of us."

*   *   *

Wanderer shivered, like his thoughts, next to black granite.

"Hard to know the truth of that," Wanderer heard himself saying. "But he sure did the dying."

Pause.

"He's here," the soldier said.

Wanderer drew a shallow breath. "Yeah, I know."

Special needs require unique graves.

Reaching back for cold stones —

"Don't touch that!" the soldier said.

Both hands withdrew.

"Sorry," said Wanderer.

"My turn to apologize," the soldier said. "You grow possessive of things, before long. Even of pain. Can you dig it?"

"I think so."

Silence.

"Ridge was somethin' else," said the soldier.

Wanderer nodded in the foggy dark. "Ridge?"

"Short for Ridge-runner," the soldier went on. "Big ol' country bubba from near Fayetteville —"

"— I grew up close by —"

"— Anyway, it hurts to lose friends. Over and over, it gets worse."

"I can dig *that,*" Wanderer said.

"Bitchin'," said the soldier. "After a while, you close up. You figure if they're *not* friends, anymore, their loss hurts less. Besides, why get close to guys who might not be around that long? Most didn't even know enough, at first, to throw out their underwear in-country for causin' crotch rot. How could you expect 'em to understand anything important? But Ridge caught on fast. He was unusual in a lot of respects. Too smart by half, maybe. Ask how he'd come to be where he was, say, and he'd tell you one story, long and rambling. The next day he'd offer somethin' noticeably different about the same subject, or some other, and never bat an eye. Kinda funny, really. Set off bullshit detectors wherever he went. Yet Ridge was very smooth, and quick to see an angle. Managed to charm his way around **Mike Papas**, once or twice. Popular with the An Tan skivvy girls, too. Doin' his best to 'make the world safe for hypocrisy.' What the Hell? So were most politicians back home. But they were there; we were nowhere near; and it was Ridge's turn to walk point."

"Sounds simple," Wanderer said. "Good or bad?"

"I kindly fuckin' doubt he thought it'd be fun."

*   *   *

Ridge did fine, walking point, till he hit a tripwire.

"Tai Sao?"

Why?

The emaciated farmer kept bowing, gnarled hands clasped tightly in front of him, not only as though he were locked as well in indeterminate age, but also born, bobbing, in that position.

Who knows? Ridge thought through a haze of pain. *Maybe he was.*

"Tai Sao?"

Like everything else, proverbially, there was —

GOOD NEWS:

When artillery failed to suppress hostile mortar fire at the map coordinates called in, a

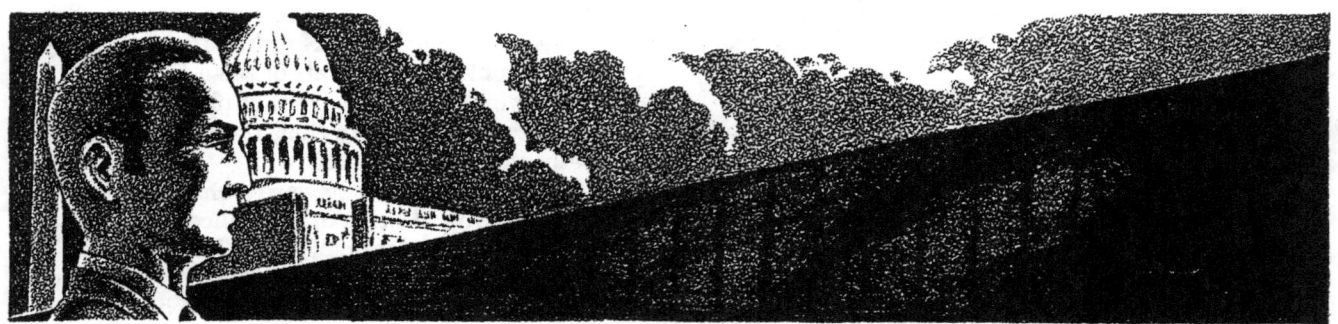

follow-up air-strike was urgently requested, same same. F-105 Thunderchiefs danced down. The Thuds laid napalm eggs where they'd crisp the right critters, then hauled ass. Three beautiful A-1E Skyraiders, with their old-time propeller sounds, hung around for shits & grins, basically, before heading back.

"Go Get 'Em — Done Got 'Em."

Local village untouched.

Number One!

And —

BAD NEWS:

Farmer's field(s) completely engulfed by rising, roiling clouds of flame-fed, fetid black smoke. No crops: no harvest. Family goes hungry. Village pinched even poorer than before.

"Shit happens."

Number Ten.

"Tai Sao?"

"I'm not sure 'why' either, Papasan," Ridge struggled to say.

No one could be certain what sort of mine it had been. Howitzer shells were highly prized for that purpose. Whatever it was, it had been big.

For an incredibly slow moment, Ridge had appeared to float both in and over a dense, expanding cloud of rapidly thinning pinkish mist, which dissipated with the shock wave that knocked down anyone close to its path. There must have been one hell of a noise. Curiously hard to tell. Hearing took time to return. Meanwhile, Ridge tumbled like a spent casing.

His legs were just gone.

* * *

Fog seemed to shift the soldier's features, as Wanderer listened.

"They rigged a poncho and carried him back to the Landing Zone, for Medevac. His groin was a first-rate mess, too, not just what was left of his legs. Tourniquets kept him from bleedin' to death. But he was goin' into shock. So, they moved as quick as they could. Still don't understand why he didn't scream more than he did."

Something about the definite change in the man's face —

"Lucky we didn't have to deal with a hot LZ. Yet anytime slicks swooped in for dust-off you could usually count on *somebody* takin' a shot at the Hueys."

— What was it?

"Anyway, Ridge mumbled about a lot of things: home, his mother, food, friends, girls — you name it."

And the voice, as well.

"You try to keep each other goin'. So, after the choppers were airborne, somebody held Ridge's head in his hands while the medics did their number on him. 'Hang in, buddy,' somebody said. 'You got the million dollar wound. That means stateside, son. Back to the world. No more of this happy horseshit for you. You're gonna be ballin' round-eye chicks. Real soon. You save some for me, now. Y' heah? You save some for me.' "

Wanderer's gut twisted and sank.

"Aw, he knew they was lyin'," the soldier hissed. "Ridge looked up and said: 'Man, if my willie ain't gonna work, I don't want to live.' "

Pause.

"And, by damn, he didn't."

Through his tears, Wanderer saw a heart-stopping countenance.

"Sir?"

I don't like interruptions! Wanderer thought, attention riveting on the annoying source. *This had better be important.*

"Urgent message on back-channels," Colonel Mallory said, "STAT."

"Now?"

"Yes, sir. A communication from *Crown.*"

Oh, well. Wanderer hadn't accomplished anything in his career without paying a price. Heavy ones, more often than not. Mary Todd Lincoln was a bitch on wheels, they say.

Past anchors present.

"I know I've asked you before —" Wanderer said.

It was hard to believe Mallory could blush.

"— And you'll get the same answer. You come here alone. You walk in solitude. You talk to yourself awhile, then we leave. That's all that ever happens. There's *never* anyone else here."

"But —"

"We're not in the habit of allowing strangers near you. sir. Not if given any choice. We like to think we're pretty good at what we do. No one is showing up to meet you. Not here."

Without graves, can anything truly be laid to rest?

"No," Wanderer said, "of course, not."

Mallory wondered, once again, whether he should include any of this in his report.

"Are you all right, sir?"

Wanderer very much admired this craggy-faced fellow. This frighteningly competent ex-military man, who now searched The Boss's features, knowingly, efficiently, yet with strangely sympathetic eyes. What had not *he* experienced in his long life and career? Deep down, *shouldn't* most combat veterans believe they're going to heaven because they've already served time elsewhere?

If so, where did that leave Wanderer?

> —*Doom'd for a certain term to walk the night,*
> *And for the day confined to fast in fires,*
> *Till the foul crimes done in my days of nature*
> *Are burnt and purged away* —

Pain kindled and flared, for all to see.

> —*But that I am forbid*
> *To tell the secrets of my prison-house,*

> *I could a tale unfold whose lightest word*
> *Would harrow up thy soul* —

"Sir?"

Wanderer turned to take in his surroundings once more.

> *Are even* **graves** *enough?*

Startled by his own reflection in the shining granite, Wanderer became convinced he could hear a whup-whup-whup of helicopters, a high-pitched doppler shrieking of jet engines overhead, astounding rate-of-fire out of "Spooky" (*How do I know about **that** gunship?*), in pseudo-symphonic conjunction with a crump and crunch of heavy weapons.

Stark silence — and a fragrance of monsoon rains.

"Later . . . Andy," Wanderer whispered — if not yet forgiven, at least doing **penance**, and *finally* approaching peace.

It didn't matter that only he could see his friend's smile.

"Let's get out of here."

"Yes, Mr. President."

At a snap of Mallory's fingers, the Team closed. Ω

IN THE NIGHT GARDEN

Strange orchids pale as consecrated bone
Flick serpent stamens over rippled glass
Preserving species centuries unknown
Outside this hothouse air where no winds pass
Save whispers. Cursed indeed the heedless hand
Which brought such seedlings from their lightless land!

Thick coiling vines entwine each trellis slat,
Yet bear no wholesome fruit to any mouth:
Such produce once — grown succulent & fat —
Drew forth assassins from Irem's fell south
To pay in witches' blood & wizards' gold
(For but a taste turned sternest tyrants cold).

No living presence tends these leafy rows
Which murmur endlessly in moonlit chill;
Their decadence of scent delights no nose
Still capable of such, nor ever will . . .
The last to tarry here & lend their toil
Now lend their flesh instead, in place of soil.

— Ann K. Schwader

RING RING!
by Seth Hill

illustrated by Allen Koszowski

Jeff is the guy your parents warn you about: "Too much trouble for this family." I guess we turned out to be too much trouble for a lot of families.

I don't really like Jeff — who does? — he's overweight and socially inept — but he's usually good for something outrageous. Like the time he got to school early, poured fake blood on the ground under the campanile tower, and sprawled face down in the blood with a suicide note pinned to his jacket. It was great. All the girls were screaming. The janitor covered him with a blanket and said a prayer. The principal had a team of psychological counselors there before Jeff jumped up and said he must have fallen asleep.

This time that we caused all the trouble, it was a long rainy two weeks. Stuck indoors. No driver's license until next year, M & D put the Nintendo in jail because I played it for seventeen hours straight, and I had to baby-sit little sister Suzie. How long can you sit in front of the VCR and watch a bunch of freaks yell, "It's morphin time"? I got desperate and called Jeff.

He brought a little gadget his uncle gave him. It was supposed to unscramble the Playboy channel. Suzie asked who wants to watch a bunch of boys play? We said shut up and crawled behind the TV to hook it up. I was sneezing from all the dust I never vacuumed. We turned on the TV. There was a blonde with big knockers in a tight dress. My palms got all sweaty. Then she started testifying for Jesus. It turned out we unscrambled the Family Bible Channel.

I clicked off the TV and said to Jeff, "When all else fails," and tossed him the phone.

First we ran all our standard phone jokes. We had been practicing these for so many years, we could string along anyone anytime.

The Raymond joke. Ring ring. Jeff asked, "Hello, is Raymond in, please?" "There's no Raymond here!" "Oh, sorry!" Then I called the same guy and asked the same thing, and Jeff with a different voice, and Suzie, and so on. Finally when the poor guy was getting really ticked off, Jeff called with his best British/snob accent and asked, "Hello there, this is Raymond! I say, have there been any calls for me?" Click!

The Donkey. "Hello, I really hate to complain, but your donkey is in my garden. Yes, I have the right number. . . yes, your donkey. What, you don't own a donkey? Well, don't worry, because I don't have a garden!" Click!

Bait the Attorney. I called 1-(800)-TOP LEGAL and used my most pitiful whine: "I work in a library. My boss made me climb that old, damaged ladder. The

books fell and broke both my legs. Now my boss says I have to come back to work. Yes, I'll wait until you call an attorney to the line. Hello, yes, now that you mention it, I do have headaches and chronic back pain. Yes, I'll wait until you call your general partner to the line. Hello, yes, now that you mention it, when I fell off the ladder it got recorded by a security system videotape. On the tape, you can see my boss walking over and kicking me in my broken legs." I strung them along until their salivating almost shorted out the phone, then Jeff came on and said, "This is the attendant at the State Mental hospital, has Arthur been telling one of his stories?! We're so sorry, he does this every time he breaks out of his room! Arthur, you have been a very bad patient! Whack, whack! Owwwww!" Click!

The phone jokes were good for grins for about an hour. But we ran out of ideas. Suzie wanted to try, but you can hear she's a little kid. Jeff told her to look up a number in the phone book, and he'd think of something new. She underlined a number. He dialled.

Ring ring. "Hello?" Jeff put on his deepest voice: "Hello, you don't know me, but I know you. I know what you do to your kids."

A long wait.

"Who are you?!"

"It doesn't matter who I am. What does matter is the fact that every newspaper, every radio and TV station, will know tomorrow morning what you do to your kids."

Click!

"Hey, man," I said, "That was pretty cold. That's going too far."

"Who gives a flying fig?" sneered Jeff. We both started yawning, so we called it a night.

The next day was dry, so I rode my bike to school. It's two miles. About halfway there, I was tooling along a nice street, lawns of real grass and fresh painted houses, birdies chirping in the trees and the sun making rainbows in lawn sprinklers. I was feeling pretty good. I passed this real ordinary house, and the light glinted off something on the sidewalk, and I had to swerve to keep from running over a line of thick red oil running from the closed garage down into the street. I stopped and looked at it, and this bald man next door opened his garage door to pick up his paper and pick his nose. He saw me looking, so he came over and looked too.

He asked, "What's that stuff, transmission fluid?" I

said I guess so. He said, "Boy, if McCartles blew a gasket in his car, he's gonna have a stroke. He keeps that thing clean enough to lick, isn't that right?" He was about to put his finger in the fluid, but he stopped. We both stood there, thinking the same thing. It didn't look like oil. It looked like blood.

"Hey, I gotta get to school," I said. He said he'd check and see if everything was OK, so I took off.

School was a drag as usual. I rode the same way back to check out that house. It was surrounded by yellow and black police tape and nosy neighbors. That same bald guy was picking his nose when he saw me and yelled, "Hey, that's the kid who was here this morning! Looks like he had to return to the scene of the crime!" He gave out a laugh like a jackass. A woman with her hair in curlers at three in the afternoon hit him in the ribs with her elbow and whispered loudly, "Keep your voice down, he's just a teenager."

I sat on my bike and asked what was going on. Mr. Picker looked all around at the neighbors and rubbed his head until it was shiny. He told this story so many times today, he must have got it perfect. "He was the nicest guy you ever knew, isn't that right? I rang the doorbell and woke up his wife and kids. They said he was sleeping. But they checked and said he wasn't in bed all night long, so. We tried to see in the garage but the windows were too dusty, and she couldn't get the door open, so. After an hour prying around we called the fire department, and they put a crowbar to it. What a sight, isn't that right?" The curler woman tried to grab his arm, but he was too warmed up to stop.

"What a sight. He hung himself by the ankles from the rafters, and he slashed both his wrists with a steak knife."

It's funny, but I don't remember riding the rest of the way home. I don't remember doing my homework. I don't remember what we had for dinner. All I remember is lying on my bed, thinking.

I called Suzie in and asked her who was the last person we called last night. She gave me her usual little kid dumb look that drives me crazy. "Hey, wake up, little Suzie!" I yelled at her. "Remember? Last night? You, me, Jeff? Phone jokes? Raymond? The Donkey? Bait the Attorney?"

Finally the light dawned. "Oh, those phone jokes. I don't remember. You never let me play anyway."

I chased her out and started looking through the phone book. And then it was my turn to feel dumb. I couldn't remember the name. It was Candles or Milktoast or something odd. You know how it is, the harder you try, the less you remember. Then it popped into my head that Suzie had underlined the name. So all I had to do was look through the entire phone book. It was seven hundred pages long, I could scan a page every five seconds, so that came out to about one hour.

I threw the phone book in a corner and got into bed. What the hell, who cares anyway?

At two in the morning, I knew I wasn't getting any sleep until I found out. I turned on my fluorescent lamp, opened the phone book and started on Aaaaardvark Bookstore.

By two thirty, I found it. There was the name McCartles, underlined.

I couldn't call Jeff then, it would wake up his parents. At six in the morning, his line was busy. I took off early for school to be sure and catch him.

He was late as usual. I said we had to go somewhere and talk. Jeff has to make a joke out of everything, so he lisped in a high-pitched voice, "Oh, we have to stop meeting like this!"

"Listen up, Jeff, before I beat the crap out of you!"

"Oh, you're so cute when you're mad!"

I considered busting his fat face, but I just turned away and started walking. He decided ditching school was a good idea, so he chased after me and started telling a joke about four nuns who decide to confess their sins.

I heard the joke three dozen times already, so I finally told him, "Jeff, shut up for a minute! We got to turn ourselves into the police station!"

That really got him going. "I heard of a sorcerer who turned himself into an eagle, but I never heard of anyone turning himself into a police station! Hey, that reminds me. This alcoholic, this miser, and this faggot go to hell, but the devil gives them one more chance. They get to come back to earth, as long as they don't even think about their favorite sins ever again. They're walking down the street, and the alcoholic turns into a liquor store. Poof! He vanishes. Then the miser sees a penny on the sidewalk. He bends over to pick it up, and both guys vanish! Get it?"

Jeff's like the Energizer Rabbit. I had to just wait until he ran down. It took an hour. By then we were walking along a train track, stepping on the old cracked stained ties, kicking up gravel. The rails were starting to rust. No trains, no people anywhere near, and that suited me just fine.

I told him the whole story.

He didn't say anything for a second. I thought he had a streak of decency, enough to feel guilty or something.

Fat chance. Not Jeff. He yelled, "Hey, I get it!" and started laughing. He thought it was a joke.

Finally I put it to him outright. "It's our fault this guy killed himself. We gotta turn ourselves in."

Jeff wouldn't buy it. He gave me a hundred reasons why we should keep our mouths shut. He said if I told anyone, he'd say I was lying.

I wish I hadn't done it, but I busted him a couple of times in the face. It broke his glasses, and he got a bloody nose. He wouldn't talk to me all the way back.

Jeff wanted to make his last class, but I didn't feel like going back to school. I wandered around downtown. Bought a big fat meatball sandwich and fries for lunch, but felt like barfing after the first bite. Walked down auto row and checked out the sports cars, but they sure cost a lot. I got a headache. Found ten dollars in my pocket and stopped at the porno theater, but it was closed for remodelling. Turned the corner and was standing in front of the police station.

Everything Jeff said kept playing over and over like my mind was a stuck CD. We don't know a hundred percent for sure we called that same guy; if we did, it's not our fault he aced himself; if it was, who'd ever find out; if they did, who could ever prove it; if they could, it's no crime to use the telephone; if it was, no one would believe us; if they did, they'd stick us in juvenile for a few months and we'd flunk all our classes and have to take the year over and the guy's still dead, and who gives a flying fart anyway?

On the other side, I couldn't come up with much. You're supposed to always tell the truth. Turn ourselves in to the authorities and take the consequences. Sounds like something your parents are always whining.

I asked the cop at the desk if I could talk to an officer, and he asked if I wanted to report a crime, and I said I guess so, and he said sure if I could wait a few minutes.

I was sitting there wondering where the bathroom was and looking at the smudgy photos on the wanted posters when five cops and a lady cop came in with two little kids. Everyone in the place came out, cops in uniforms and some I guess plainclothes, I heard them say the name McCartles once or twice, somebody else started saying "Will you look at this, will you look at this," and somebody else said, "He got off too easy hanging upside down bleeding like a side of beef."

Nobody noticed I was still there. I snuck a peek. One of the cops was holding the little kid's shirt open, and he had fresh burns and old burns all over his chest, but no burns on his arms or face or neck where they'd show.

Nobody noticed when I left.

It took me a while to talk Jeff into coming over. He had a new pair of glasses, and his nose looked OK again. I apologized up one side and down the other, and finally he gave me a grin and said, "Hey, you saved me a thousand bucks for a nose job, maybe I can talk my old man into letting me put it into car insurance."

I said it was still bothering me. "I rode my bike by the guy's house, now that's a coincidence, but it's not that big a town. It's the other part. We call this guy in the first place, you tell him we know what you do to your kids, and it turns out he really is a child abuser."

"What's a child amuser?" asked Suzie.

I didn't even know she was listening at the door. "Get out of here!" I yelled.

Jeff said, "Someone who spanks their kids too hard."

"I knew that!" sneered Suzie. She gave us a know-it-all look and walked away.

I got to thinking again. We didn't pick the name out of the book, Suzie did. "Suzie, get back in here!"

We showed her the name she underlined in the book and asked her how she picked it. She shrugged and said, "It just felt cold, that's all."

Jeff and I looked at each other for a few thousand years. I felt the book, but there was nothing cold or hot or lukewarm or anything. I asked Suzie if she could find another cold name. She said sure, felt a few pages, and pointed at another.

I nodded at Jeff. He dialled the number.

Ring ring. "Hello, you don't know me, but I know you. I know what you do to your kids."

We waited. There was a weird kind of gasp. Someone was on the line, but they weren't saying anything. Finally a woman asked, "Who is this?"

Jeff said, "It doesn't matter. What matters is, by this time tomorrow, every newspaper in town, every radio and TV station will know what you do to your kids."

The woman started crying. She said, "I can't help it . . . I swear I can't help it when they cry all day . . . I love em so much . . . I promised I'd get into treatment . . . this time I really mean it . . . I swear I'll get into treatment . . . I'll call the clinic, I been meanin' to do that for a long time. I hear they got a 24-hour hot line."

Jeff looked weird. All of a sudden, he looked a lot older. First time I ever saw Jeff when he didn't know what to say. I grabbed the phone, and I spoke very slowly. "I'll know if you're telling the truth. By this time tomorrow, if you're not taking care of the problem, everyone will hear about it."

Click!

Jeff asked Suzie, "Can you find any other cold numbers?"

She felt a few more pages.

"Sure," she said. "There's a whole bunch!"

Suzie sat down next to me, and I put my arm around her. I looked at Jeff, and he nodded.

I guess a lot of sixteen-year-olds never had this feeling. Finding something worthwhile to do in your spare time. Sounds like something your parents are always whining about. Funny. It feels kinda all right.

Well, gotta go. We got a lot of numbers to call.

Ring ring! Ω

by Seth Hill

STEPMOTHER
by Valerie J. Freireich

illustrated by George Barr

Danny dragged his feet as he came upstairs in answer to my call. I counted each step, thirteen of them, then listened as he traversed the narrow hallway to my room. He stood in the doorway, outlined in sunlight. "Come here," I said peremptorily, patting the place beside me on the bed. "Did Daddy give you cereal and your vitamins before he left for work?"

"Yeah. But I want to watch cartoons, Mom," he said.

"You can watch TV with me on the big bed."

He shuffled closer, then stopped out of my reach. Whatever it is I take from him, he'd sensed some loss.

"Don't you want to cuddle with me, Danny?" I asked.

He stared at the floor.

I stretched out my arms to him, ready to embrace. I could hear the pulsing rhythms of his young body, smell the aroma of his life on him. "I love you," I whispered, not in parody of emotions I don't possess, but rather a true statement of what I feel in the hollow places of my mind for those I need to fill that emptiness.

He looked up, saw me, the only mother he remembered. "Aw, Mom," he said. He came into my arms.

Beyond the sweetness of his essence, of his blood and flesh and bones, he smelled of fresh air and cleanliness, of spilled Cheerios and the random dirt that clings to small boys no matter how particular their mothers. There also was the tang of a fresh scrape across his knee, but I did my best to ignore that. His small head felt soft against my chest and the curve of it fit well beneath my chin. I let my arm slip down, to the tops of his thighs, and in one quick, smooth motion pulled him into the bed beside me. I squeezed him in a single fierce hug that took nothing at all, then relaxed my hold, but kept him trapped with my arm around his shoulders, beneath his head, circling back around, like a snake, to lightly press against his cheek.

"What do you want to watch?" I asked, reaching for the controller on the nightstand with my free arm. "Smurfs?"

"They're over." He wiggled just a bit, settling into position. He'd learned not to struggle.

I turned on The Chipmunks, those lucky beasts who'd found a convenient human home and fit in, oh, so well. Danny and I lay together. Gradually, like any six-year-old, he became absorbed in the cartoon drama. His body relaxed. I felt it, a melting beside me, and I waited, teasing myself, wondering how long before the next commercial.

My fingers stroked his face in exact time to my own complex rhythm, not so lightly that it would tickle, not

heavy enough to hurt. I moved closer, so that we were pressed together the full length of his body. His pulse and mine began to interact, then unite in one cadence. I pulled him so near there was no space between us; he was half atop me, his shorter legs intertwined with mine. Mesmerized by the television and my accustomed presence, he barely sighed as I began to lick his neck. I felt the glow of satisfaction, the uncanny weightlessness of the transfer, which brought my strength.

Only rarely do I take anything physical, but there was the spice of his little scrape; after all, I thought, a child's skin is very thin, and children heal so easily and well. Danny gave a sharp intake of breath at the tiny puncture, but didn't flinch. I sucked a bit of his precious blood into my mouth, letting it rest there as I lay next to him, nearly senseless with delight. Then as I swallowed, I rolled away, not wanting to risk damaging his health by drinking any more. He turned slowly to look at me. He smiled, a beautiful little boy with dark brown hair and long-lashed green eyes.

"I'm going to take a shower. You can stay here or go downstairs, again," I said.

He resumed watching his television show, raising a hand to scratch his neck, as if at a mosquito bite. I turned away.

"How's my night owl?" Mark asked, coming back downstairs that night after tucking Danny into bed. "How late did you stay up last night?"

I didn't love Mark — that is, I didn't need him — but I rather liked him. We'd had some fun together. "Only until one. That book is trash, whatever the reviews said. I didn't even read it all." Last night's novel, all six hundred plus pages, lay face down on the messy coffee table, beside last night's can of budget diet cola.

"I thought you couldn't put anything down, once you got past the first twenty pages."

"I can't. So I just skipped the middle four hundred."

He laughed, then sat beside me on the couch.

"Have you noticed how much TV Danny's been watching lately?" Mark asked. "He used to play outside all afternoon; now it's video games and cartoons. I've been wondering if we should limit it."

I frowned, considering. The boy was still healthy, though perhaps a bit pale. Not anemic — not from me, anyway; I was extremely careful. Still, it could be Danny was weakening. I'd been with Mark and Danny for two years, and hoped for several more, longer than anywhere I'd previously allowed myself to stay. "You know," I said, "TV isn't all bad. I think Danny's just tired. First grade is kind of rough — a full day away from home. He needs to relax and adjust."

"You're probably right," he said, but he drummed his fingers against the arm of the couch.

"I'll keep an eye on him." I patted his hand. "Anything on the tube for us?"

"Junk. New season starts next week, though." He looked up from a desultory perusal of the TV schedule. "Do you think there's anything unusual about Danny?"

I caught my breath. "How do you mean?"

"He's so quiet. Other boys his age run and yell. He doesn't even wriggle. He's so . . . polite and careful."

I glanced at him. "I've tried to be a good mother," I said.

"Oh, no, honey. It isn't you." He looked at me and smiled. "He couldn't ask for a better mother. You're so careful with what he eats, you take him all over to museums and special classes. I just wonder if . . . maybe something is happening in school. You know."

I knew, all right. Public discussion of sexual abuse of children had complicated my life for a decade. "You think . . . ?" I asked in horrified concern. "No. It couldn't be, Mark. There was a talk show the other day. They said there'd be some physical signs, some irritations. I haven't seen a thing."

Finally, he relaxed. He put his arm around me. "You're right. It couldn't be."

I might have left another family, slipped away after such a conversation, but truly, I enjoyed both of them. I convinced myself that to leave would be alarmist. "How was story hour?" I asked, picking Danny up at the library the next week.

"Mom," he said, with a rather superior and self-important air — as if he really knew the answer and was testing me — "why are stepmothers in fairy tales always bad?"

"Well, sometimes stepmothers are bad," I said. "You're just lucky." I laughed, leaning closer and ruffling his hair. He smelled sweetly of perspiration, a rare scent on my child lately. His lips were bright red from the fruit punch the librarians had passed out after the story, and cookie crumbs clung to his t-shirt. I wanted to hug him, but I'd already started the car and belted.

"Mo-om," he said. "I really want to know. Why are they *always* bad?"

"I don't know, Danny. Because that's what the fairies wrote in their tales."

He smiled perfunctorily. "But why?"

"There isn't a why. It just is as it is." I was sharper with him than usual, and he fell silent as we pulled out onto the road.

"You're not bad," he whispered. "You *have* to do your special hugging." There were tears in the corners of his eyes.

I gripped the steering wheel very hard. "Do you want me to stop?"

He slowly turned his head to stare at me. I could only glance at him, because of the traffic, but his eyes, I saw, were wise. "No, if you stop, then you'll leave, because you need it. So don't stop. I love you, Mom."

"I love you, too, Danny," I said. Such love isn't more coerced than any other kind.

"Then it's okay," he said.

I was afraid, but I didn't want to leave them. It would mean nothing to anyone that Danny understood and had asked me to stay; children are without the power to enforce their preferences. I watched Danny for signs that he intended to tell his father, but there were none. He seemed, in fact, happier than before, more jovial and readier to play. I gave him only quick, maternal hugs for weeks, though it made me achingly hungry to take so little. But I stayed.

"You were right," Mark said. "It was only the adjustment to school that made him so withdrawn."

"He was tired. He needed more rest than usual."

We sat side by side reading on the couch, the TV making its usual background noise. "He's crazy about you," Mark said. "He worries that you'll leave us, like his mother did."

"I won't." To reinforce the lie, I looked directly in his lovely eyes, so much like those of his son. At precisely the correct instant, I kissed Mark. He put his arms around me and I let him be the one to draw us together. His hands began to caress my breasts, a bit crudely, but with effect. I twisted so that I was seated in his lap, facing him. He began to unbutton my blouse.

The essence that I crave is a stronger, richer force in children than it is in adults, though sex is a temporary enhancer of that essence. Children are more resilient than adults, too; they can withstand my continual small takings better. Some of my kind may have other preferences, and I cannot say there is no element of sexual desire in my feedings, since I never take from girl children; still, I've kept sex and feedings separate. But I was hungry, and the lassitude that follows sex is an excellent disguise.

I moved against Mark, feeling the pounding of his pulse. His scent was grittier than Danny's and the rhythms of his body somewhat slower, even as the tempo continued to increase. He kissed my breasts, and it was an intrusion, an irregularity in my striving to combine the two of us in a very different way. I leaned closer, so he couldn't reach them easily, and began to lick his neck, feeling the pulse with my sensitive tongue. He moaned when for a moment our rhythms matched and meshed, then his pattern slipped away from me again. I bit gently into his neck.

He pushed me aside abruptly, so quickly that I ached at the loss of contact. He covered his wound with a hand, then took the hand away, seeing the blood. "Jesus Christ, honey," he said.

"Mom!" Danny screamed from behind us. "The

special hugging was only supposed to be with me!" He stood, just visible on the bottom stair, in his Superman pajamas. Like an explosion, he began to cry and scream incoherent words at us. At me.

I was half on the couch and half off, where Mark had pushed me, ready to eat but not yet fed. Mark turned, staring at his son. I jumped to my feet and ran to Danny. I tried to speak, to say, "What's the matter?" like a solicitous mother, but I couldn't form the words around the taste of blood roiling through my mouth.

I reached the boy and knelt in front of him, pulling him into my arms, pressing his small head against my chest, feeling his tears. His sobs began to slacken immediately as the drone of the television and the contact with me began to have their usual effect. We meshed so perfectly, so easily compared with the botched effort with his father, that I lost myself in that sensation for a moment of deep feeding, taking from his insubstantial essence. I bent my head over him, licking at his face and neck, sensing the blood that tender skin encased, feeling the warmth.

A strong arm ripped me away before I'd finished. I looked up from a child's height at Mark. "Special hugging?" he shouted. He raised his arm as though to strike me. He stopped himself, but I cringed, he looked so like a furious giant.

"No!" Danny shouted, interposing himself between me and his father. "Don't hurt her! She needs me."

Oh, he was right! The need to put my arms around the boy was crippling any other thought or sensation. "Please," I moaned, reaching outward with my arms.

Mark looked as though he'd swallowed bile. "Get up," he said, pulling me farther from Danny, then he yanked me to my feet. "What the Hell kind of bitch are you, licking my son . . . ?"

I wrapped my arms around Mark's neck. He stumbled and together we fell to the floor. I heard Danny crying and ached to comfort him, to hold him close against me and take something away. His pain? I placed my mouth against the puncture I'd made earlier on Mark's neck, and teased it open with my tongue.

Mark swatted at me, then succeeded in disengaging me from his body. He was panting, a heavy beat I matched easily enough. I reached out a hand. He stared at me, part horror and part disbelief.

Danny grabbed my extended hand, and threw himself onto me, pushing me to the floor. "I love you, Mom," he wailed.

Perhaps it looked innocent enough; perhaps Mark was tired. He didn't respond as quickly as before. Danny fed me, warmed me with his willing energy. I loved him, for every moment that I squeezed upon his essence, extracting kernels of his being, savoring the pleasures of his soul.

When Mark pulled Danny off of me, the boy was limp. "What did you do?" he demanded, puzzled, since he hadn't seen me do anything at all but accept the fragile weight of Danny's body on top of mine.

I rolled out of his reach and stood. "Nothing." My eyes dared him to contradict me. I had never felt so strong, never taken quite so much so rapidly, even during the quick, killing meals of the days when I fed on strangers.

He glanced down at the boy prone on the floor, then looked again, alarmed. "Is he all right?" Mark asked me, falling for the moment back into our well worn family rôles.

I came closer. I could hear the faint hiss of Danny's breath. His lips moved as he mumbled something, but his eyes were closed and his face was slack. "I don't know," I whispered.

"What the Hell just happened here?" Mark said. I saw the question, the 'special hugging,' in his eyes.

"Never," I said. "It was . . . something else. Not sex. I swear."

He shook his head. "Never mind. Help Danny. Please. Help Danny if you can."

I didn't need either of them. I could leave. What could Mark say I'd done, even if the boy died? Yet, I didn't want Danny to die. I'd planned to leave these two long before he was weakened to this point. Tentatively, I touched Danny's temple, felt the throbbing of the blood against the skin. Mark watched carefully, a hound ready to attack any false move.

My hand brushed against his cheek, then slipped down to his small neck.

There was so little there. Like empty cabinets, dreary and forlorn. I took my hand away.

"What are you?" Mark asked. "What did you do?"

I'd stolen something that I needed to keep myself alive. Something more fundamental to me than food and drink. Except, this time I hadn't stolen. Danny had given himself to me, and like a greedy guest I'd taken far too much.

I put my hand back against Danny's neck. I smelled the blood in him; it seemed thinner than before and the pounding more erratic. The soapy fragrance of his bath lingered on his skin. I bent closer, then stretched out alongside the still body, ignoring the sharp intake of breath from Mark. I matched Danny's new, slow rhythm easily enough, but nothing happened. There was nothing to draw from him, nothing left to take. I had it all.

Many have told me that they love me. *You're not bad*, Danny had said.

I was.

"I love him," I said. I felt tears, tasted the salt from them, remembered Danny's in the car. "I think I really do."

"Then do something! You're his mother!"

I pushed. I squeezed. I pressed. I forced something that was in me out, and that intangible force began to move. It was like reversing the flow of a water main; it seemed as perilous as driving against the traffic on a superhighway. It felt like giving birth.

I didn't stop until it was impossible for me to do more. I was exhausted. I lay on the floor with less in me than there had been at the beginning of the evening, yet I wasn't hungry. Beside me, Danny was awake and alert, but tranquil, preternaturally composed.

Mark was seated on the floor, facing me. "Thank you," he said, in the voice he used for strangers.

None of us moved for a while. I felt calm, unreasonably comfortable. Later, Mark took my hand. "What are you?"

"I don't know."

"When you did whatever it was you did just now, you seemed to glow. Your face, all of you seemed warmer, and you glowed."

"Danny needs to go to bed," I said. "He has school tomorrow."

Danny sat up. "No, I don't. It's Saturday."

"Time for bed anyway, tiger." Mark hugged his son, squeezing so tight I thought Danny would complain and break the serenity of my mood, but he didn't.

"Mom," Danny said, "will you be here in the morning?"

All the rhythms in the room stopped, waiting. I had no answer.

I stood up. I was lightheaded and felt myself sway. Mark caught me, steadying me. Our eyes met. "Of course she will," he said. "We'll tuck Mom in first; she needs it more. You go on ahead upstairs."

Danny ran off, full of vitality, so strong it was a pleasure to watch.

Mark stared at me. "Angel. The glow, the laying on of hands. You're an angel. You gave him back his life."

I laughed. I am, if anything, the opposite, a soulless wanderer who sucks bits of energy from the spirits of real people. Nevertheless, it was a good, a glorious feeling for once not to be lying or ashamed.

They put me to bed together, absurdly fussing over the covers, both of them touching me tenderly and without aversion. Danny kissed me good night. When Mark returned a few minutes later, he climbed into bed beside me and turned out the light. In the dark every gesture was defined by shifting springs and the sound of movement across sheets. Mark held me in his arms, not sex, not the other. "If you ever need to leave," he whispered, "you can always come back home again to us."   Ω

CANDELABRA

Candle's tallow scent,
with shivering flame,
old portals rent,
muttered forbidden name,
thus mannas vent,
and elder shadows tame.

— J. W. Donnelly

THINGS FADE

Things fade
like green numbers from a screen
leaking from the corners of life

First a curtain, then the sill
Within a month the closet walls
    are gone
And behind the hangers
There's nothing but a gray mist

Very soon it isn't even surprising
I cease to search for vanished things

So when the people start to go
It's just a minor, fleeting shock.

— Patricia Russo

by Valerie J. Freireich

THE BIBLE IN BLOOD
by Ian Watson

Illustrated by Jason Van Hollander

It was simplicity itself to let myself into Appledorn's hotel suite. The under-manager of the Strasbourg Hilton had provided me with a master card-key several days before Henry Appledorn checked in at the hotel. I'd replaced the security chain with one which would snap easily. The under-manager was a *sayan*, a friendly local who would readily assist Israeli intelligence. We can rely on thousands of such individuals in many countries.

Naturally, I hadn't told our French under-manager that I intended to confront Appledorn and his secretary and their visitor with a pistol in my hand. None of his business. He wasn't involved.

The Beretta fitted snuggly in my palm. Standard issue for Mossad field officers. .22 caliber. Loaded with dum-dum bullets.

In with the card-key. Turn the handle softly.

Ah yes, the occupants of the suite had chained the door.

Apply a shoulder. The links snapped.

"Don't anyone move," I said. "Don't make any noise." And I shut the door behind me.

On a chrome and glass table there rested a pile of parchment pages penned in Gothic script. The letters were all of a dark brown hue, the colour of dried blood. The open case and backbone formed a portfolio, for those sheets were looseleaf without any stitching or tailband as yet. Faded red silk ribbons would tie the portfolio shut. The case was bound in black leather with steel protectors at the corners. Though I couldn't see the front, its slight elevation from the glass of the table suggested that emblems embossed the surface. A steel cross, perhaps, and steel swastikas.

So there it was at last: the Bible Written in Blood.

To be strictly accurate, the *New Testament*. A good ninety-five per cent of the *New Testament*.

Not all of it. Herzwalde concentration camp had been evacuated, due to the approach of the Red Army, while the scribes were commencing their slow labour on the book of *Revelation*.

Our American bibliophile, Henry Appledorn, darted a protective glance at the huge, incomplete, unbound volume. Our book collector was tall and rangy, with a predilection to stoop. His curly hair had turned snowy, as befitted his seventy years. His was a Bassethound face, long and somewhat ruddy.

Despite my warning, Appledorn's hand strayed to touch the silk handkerchief in his breast pocket. Couldn't he conceive of his own death? Did my sudden intrusion merely offend him?

Ah, he was worrying whether I might cause blood to spurt on to the volume in question, staining it.

How quickly could he mop the parchment page clean with his handkerchief? What cleansing agents would distinguish between recently spilled blood and the older dried brown blood of the text?

Klaus Bauer, procurer of the volume from its hiding place in former East Germany, appeared to be calculating whether he might heave up the bulky tome to use as a shield — or to hurl at me, disarmingly.

Bauer was thick-set but whey-faced, as if he had shunned the sunlight for a long time. He looked so cleanly scrubbed with his large pink hands and shaven skull that he reminded me of a potato. His jacket and slacks were creamy and recently pressed.

The woman, Appledorn's secretary, avoided focusing on my gun.

"What are *you*?" she demanded. "An *occultist*?"

I'd been intending to order all three of them to lie prone on the carpet to allow me to inject each in turn, rendering them comatose, after which I would simply decamp with the book. . . .

Her question threw me. I had to know exactly what Gloria Cameron implied by it.

She was golden-haired, tweed-suited, her ruffled blouse trimmed with embroidered roses. Brown-leather brogues with brass buckles on her feet. Butch. Perceptive.

I imagined her equipped with a whip, and dressed in an impeccable SS uniform, striding through a camp of cowering women. I felt weak inside. My weakness became fury — and fascination.

Yet Gloria's accent was Scots, overlayed by a slight American veneer. She was a graduate of Edinburgh University, her speciality bibliography.

I ought to have carried out my plan by rote, ignoring distractions. However, within me — confronted at last by the Bible in Blood — my mother's dreams were stirring. And within those dreams lurked another person, namely my father. . . .

Facts are never simple. Facts splinter into a kaleidoscope of interpretations.

Early in 1943 SS Colonel Gottfried von Turm became deputy commandant of Herzwalde labour camp. He was lame in the left leg. He'd been invalided back from the Russian front, from the doomed attempt to relieve the Nazi forces penned in Stalingrad.

From the jaws of hell — into a cauldron of death. Death cooked up by his own kind.

Yet were the other SS quite his own kind?

For a Prussian aristocrat to join the ranks of the fighting Waffen-SS was quite unusual. The Waffen-SS were superhuman . . . *scum*. For the most part they were brutal peasants — trained to be Übermenschen. Their military officers lacked the most elementary sense of tactics, though they knew how to rampage, and SS fighting units always had better weapons than the regular army.

Gottfried had once implied to my mother (or at least she took him to be implying) that he'd been obliged to join this band of butchers so as to protect his own family from some ambiguous fate.

Soon after Gottfried arrived at Herzwalde, he conceived the project of the Bible in Blood.

That camp housed, among many other unfortunates, a fair salting of rabbis and other Jewish *Intelligenten* — unphysical men for whom the forced labour of quarrying stone and logging in the surrounding forests was especially lethal on top of the starvation rations, the beatings, shootings, the interminable freezing rollcalls.

Jews had committed *bloodcrime* by murdering the Saviour. Why, the mere existence of Jews constantly posed a genetic blood-threat to the purity of the Aryan race.

Especially in the eyes of the SS the pure blood that coursed through the veins of the German peasant was sacred.

Had not Alfred Rosenberg proclaimed a mystic philosophy of blood as the true Germanic faith? Had not Hitler endorsed this crazy sanguinarianism? Was not the SS a new priesthood of blood?

So therefore Colonel von Turm ordained that the most noteworthy rabbis and eggheads should be gathered together in a special blockhouse. There, they should redeem their bloodcrimes and purge their *verfluchte Judentum* by writing out the whole of the *New Testament* in their own lifeblood.

Was this a monstrous joke on his part? A malicious insult to the prisoners? Certainly, other SS personnel took it as such, applauding Gottfried's wit.

True, at first I believe there was *some* dispute with his superior or his fellow officers. Had not the Führer wished to erase Christianity in favour of a revived Odinic paganism? Ah, but not even Hitler could afford to offend the church too deeply. Besides, many of the SS peasantry had been deeply branded in boyhood with Catholicism.

Later on, those SS in Herzwalde would become quite fanatic in a darkly superstitious vein about the progress of the project. It seemed to them as though this scriptural work was obliterating the very essence of the Hebrew race in a magical fashion — just as they themselves were occupied in annihilating the physical existence of Jews.

Now, this was bound to be a long, slow project. For how much blood could easily be siphoned from the veins of the scribes by those scribes themselves? How

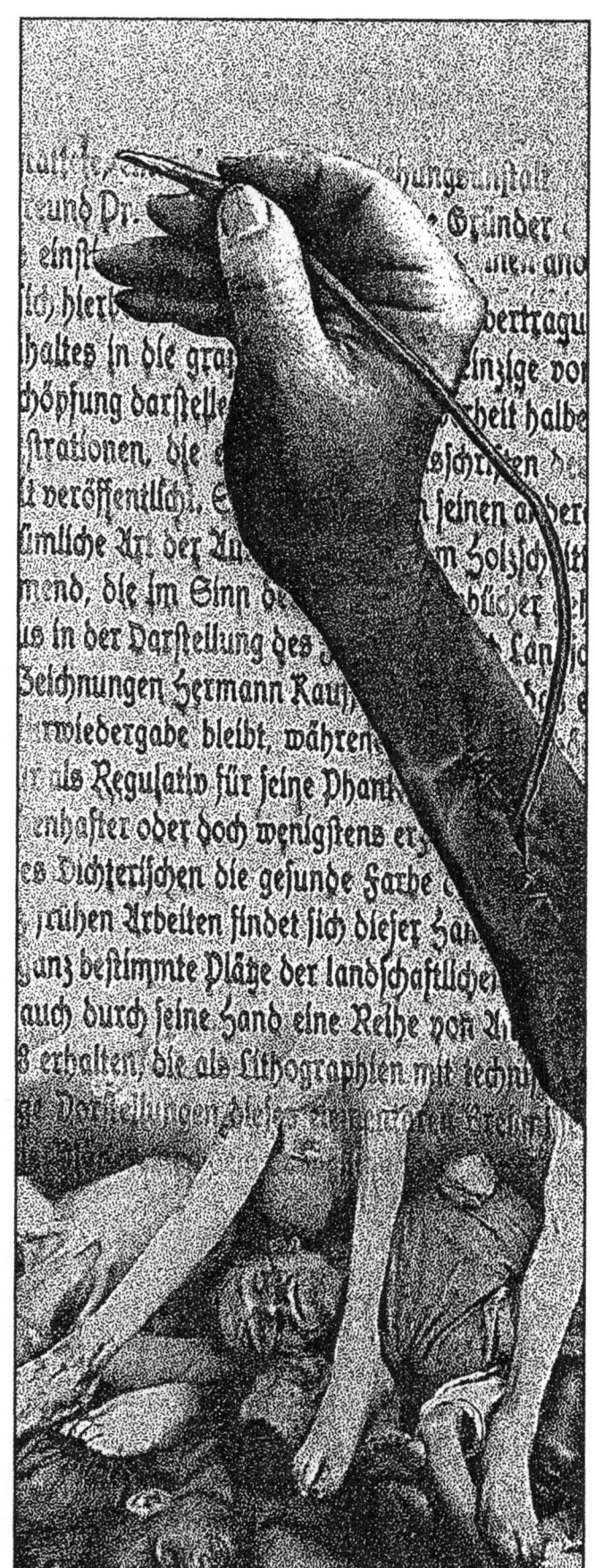

by Ian Watson

quickly would the bloodink congeal? What type of pennibs should best be used? How to ensure compatibility of calligraphy? How could the work best be divided so that costly parchment was not wasted by, for example, the *First Epistle to the Corinthians* ending at the top of one sheet, while the *Second Epistle* had already been started by a different scribe at the top of another sheet? And in the event of empty spaces, what decorative motifs should be employed to fill up the gaps? Swastikas? Death'sheads pierced with daggers? Crucifixions? Taunting pastoral scenes of Palestine?

These were exactly the kind of minutiae which obsessed the intellects of the SS who operated concentration camps. A hundred petty laws and prohibitions! With a savage whipping or hanging as punishment for infringement.

The Colonel played upon this savage pedantry.

What if the chosen Jews' blood was *anæmic* due to the scanty rations of watery garbage soup, black ersatz coffee, and stale bread?

Very soon the scribes' diet was being boosted with sausages and cheese from incoming parcels which the SS always stole (though they might occasionally let the wrapping paper be delivered), and with fresh fruit and eggs and rabbit stew.

What if the scribes' fingers were too numb to hold the pens skillfully enough to form the Gothic letters Gottfried insisted upon?

Why, *two* stoves must be kept well fuelled in the Scripture Block.

While the band of scribes regained some body weight and bloomed with renewed health, other less literate inmates of Herzwalde carried on labouring and dying of hunger and illness and beatings.

Aha! Was the Scripture Block — aside from being an insult to the faith of those within — also a cunning ploy to make its inmates resented and hated by other prisoners? The SS, permanently poised on the brink of capricious rage at Untermenschen, may have thought in this vein. *"See how those precious rabbis and eggheads grow fat while you become bones!"* In actuality, most residents of squalid, bestial Herzwalde had no surplus energy to spare for hatred. They hardly had enough energy to spare for conscious thought at all.

As I've said, the majority of the SS had no sense of *tactics*. . . . Might it be that Colonel Gottfried von Turm was in fact preserving, in his Scripture Block, the cream of Jewish people, the intellectual and spiritual leadership, for some postbellum salvation? Such an idea never crossed the minds of his boorish colleagues. Still, Gottfried must prevent any such notion from arising there — or taking root in the brains of his clever beneficiaries. Like some mystic high priest of the satanic Schutzstaffel he would rant about sacred and polluted blood.

Many of the assembled Rabbis, for their part, were knowledgeable about Kabalah. They knew the *Sepher Yesirah,* the Book of Creation, inside out, and the *Zohar* of Moses de Leon. They murmured while they dipped their pens in their own blood and copied the scripture of their oppressors. . . .

"What do you mean, Miz Cameron?"

The woman stared at me witheringly. So I jerked the Beretta towards her tweed-clad knees, threatening to cripple her unless words danced upon her lips.

Why hadn't Appledorn let her handle the acquisition of the book? Why did *he* need to be present personally at the handover in this hotel suite in Strasbourg, here on the FrancoGerman border? So that he could authenticate his purchase by smell and by feel and by sixth sense?

Suppose he had stayed behind in Florida . . . maybe the plane winging the book back to the States might have plunged into the Atlantic en route. It might have crashed on arrival at Orlando airport, incinerating the unique pages. . . .

Appledorn had to take control of the book right away.

What did he plan to do with it thereafter?

I'd *assumed* that he would lock it up along with other bibliographic treasures, reserved for his eyes only.

Now I wondered whether this was all he intended.

"Does your boss plan to complete the Bible?" I demanded. "Using whose blood? *Your own?*"

Gloria Cameron twitched.

"Do you intend to finish the book of *Revelation,* Mister Appledorn?" I harangued, sounding rather like a camp guard myself. "What *revelation* do you expect to achieve?"

Klaus Bauer stared from one to the other of us in bemusement. And with greedy regret. Had he somehow underestimated the value of the Bible in Blood to this collector?

Bauer asked me in German in a wheedling tone, "Are you one of the faithful?"

The faithful? The *faithful?* I hadn't heard this expression before. Did it refer to Judaism — or was it some neoNazi code? Did Bauer imagine that I wished to spirit the book away to some Hitlerian shrine? To some revived Wewelsburg Castle?

Bauer annoyed me. I shunned any conceivable association between himself and me. I wished him to sweat.

"I'm Israeli intelligence," I told him.

"Why," asked Gloria Cameron, "would Israeli intelligence wish to kidnap a *book?*"

Well, of course we wouldn't . . . unless the action served Israel's interests . . . which it hardly could, unless Kabalists were running our country.

"I ask the questions," I retorted.

Whether due to the strain of the occasion — this climax to a long search — or on account of sheer proximity to the book, my mother's dreams came welling up in me. . . .

SS Colonel von Turm limped, using a silverhandled

walking cane. With this he would lash out at the occasional tattered slave who didn't step smartly enough to one side and pull off his beret swiftly enough from his cropped cranium.

In fact, the Colonel never *damaged* any slave worker with his cane — unlike other SS who would beat an inmate to death. Perhaps he was concerned about snapping his walking cane. Perhaps not. A lick from the stick was equivalent to a shot of electric current in a moribund frog's leg. It galvanized the walking dead. They survived a little longer.

Von Turm's eyes were an icy blue. The ice of Russian winter; the ice of Prussian disdain.

He was wellfleshed.

He too needed to relieve the strain of the occasion . . . and maybe do something extra by way of lagniappe, as they say down Appledorn's way or thereabouts.

One afternoon, since it was freezing cold, the SS decided to order a new intake of women to stand naked on parade while they chose which to assign to the brothel block, which to the quarries, which to extinction. The women had been marched forty kilometres from their previous work camp, relocated to fulfil some whim or bureaucratic quota. Those who had survived the trek were desperately tired. Therefore, with the crops of their whips, the SS lifted the girls' tits to determine who was firm enough for brothel duty.

Aryans for the SS guards and for visiting soldiers. Jews for the common criminals who had become overseers of slaves.

Exercising the caprice of rank, and rather in breach of SS protocol, Von Turm ordered that my mother, Bella, should be sent to him for his use that evening. For she stood proudly. A tall, skinny waif, a starveling with large brown eyes and shaven head.

His quarters were beautifully furnished with loot, including a fine fourposter bed. On a table was set a carafe of milk, a bowl of sauerkraut, and a dish of meats and cold creamed potatoes. Bella, who was starving, only allowed herself one tormented glance at the Colonel's supper. And at his silk sheets.

"Undress," he said; and she shed a torn, soiled frock.

"You're too thin for me," he remarked, and terror seized her.

But then he tossed her a silk bathrobe. From a drawer he produced a lavish black wig for her to wear while she was in his room.

"You must eat first," he told her. "Do not eat quickly, or else you might vomit. Chew slowly. Drink slowly. Then you must sit and digest your meal."

Only an hour after she had finished feasting did he take Bella to bed, to relieve his tensions. Though he hardly spoke to her.

I could hear the percussion of a thousand wooden shoes on stone; and the squelch of a thousand feet tramping through slush and mud. I saw watchtowers and wire and roving searchlights. I listened to the chatter of bullets. I watched skeletal marionettes in striped pyjamasuits dangle upright for hours on end on parade from the invisible strings of their exhaustion. Strings snapped; marionettes collapsed in snow, in mud. I flinched from snarling dogs, whose teeth sheer hunger persuaded me were rows of almonds. I breathed the filth of the latrine abyss in the shithouse, surrounded by slippery, excremental steel bars on which to perch one's bum and vent the gruel of diarrhœa upon a million dissolving turds and the rotting corpses of those who had previously slipped backwards and drowned. The swollen tongues of hanged men on the gallows were blue, and looked delicious, like cured meat.

And I heard the rabbis mutter in their blockhouse as they copied the words of that loving Christian religion to which the world seemed to owe the massacre of the Albigensians, the Crusades, the Inquisition, the slaughter of witches and heretics, and the pogroms and the ghettos, because the blood of the Jew Jesus had been spilt; as they penned the holy words of their victimisers in their own heartblood . . .

Gottfried reserved Bella for himself alone. As the months passed by she grew sleek.

No doubt the Colonel concocted some spurious excuse to exonerate himself in the eyes of his fellow officers from the scandal of taking a Jewess as — effectively — his mistress. Those officers were by now much tickled with the Bible in Blood project, the Colonel's inspiration, so they regarded this other eccentricity of his with amusement, even addressing Bella as "Fraulein", although she continued to reside in the Brothel Block.

How did Bella respond to Gottfried's embraces?

At first woodenly, of course, exhaustedly, obediently — reserving within herself a kernel of her own dignity.

Yet presently . . . ah, the situation became fraught with ambiguity.

Von Turm remained taciturn towards her. How could he be otherwise? He could hardly involve her directly as a coconspirator against the ethics of the Schutzstaffel. Nevertheless, Gottfried's *body* seemed to speak to her in that fourposter bed.

True, when one's entire fate depended upon the whims of a powerful individual who belonged to an insane organisation, one might search excessively for

auguries. What did a frown portend? Or a grunt? What did the exact pressure of his hand upon the breast, compared with yesterday, imply? And the rhythm of his cock, or a gasp during orgasm?

Or a seeming *delay* of orgasm . . . ? Gottfried nursed Bella towards her own excitement by a bodily insistence that she should, she *must,* surrender herself to him sensually, now that her senses were back in working order due to better diet. This might merely be a further kind of oppression.

Yet she intuited that he would not reject her.

She was, to him, someone chosen especially to cherish — in his own bodily style. She was a person as well as an exemplar for the expiation of guilt — as well as someone symbolically saved from the slaughter in the way that he had saved some rabbis and eggheads.

She was the *personalization* of his act of charity or dictate of conscience. Thus it was entirely necessary that she should be, to him, an individual person. Always his body spoke more about his mood than his lips ever did . . . which led to that superstitious search for auguries.

Sometimes Bella felt furious that she was allowing him to unburden himself thus of bad conscience — that through sex she was shriving him to some degree. What did it really count that one Jewess was surviving through his *tactic* while thousands of others died? But she did not chose to reject her salvation.

She would never cry out to him, "I love you." In this mad place what sense would such a declaration make? Yet what did her body tell him? On the night when for the first time she climaxed, clutching him, digging fingernails into the firm flesh of this officer, he had flicked a cigarette lighter alight — no, he had *not* switched on a blinding lamp. And he had scrutinised her face briefly while she stared at him open-eyed; and he had nodded.

A true communication? Or only another evasive augury?

Nor did she imagine that any possible future could exist — for her, or for him.

With restored health, her halted periods had resumed. Late in 1943 she became pregnant by him an event which at first caused her a renewed pang of terror.

Would he blame her — as surely as if she had smuggled a knife into his bed, in the way that a truly *brave* victim might have done?

As for bravery, how many other prisoners in the camp had the energy even to contemplate such a suicidal, stupid act? In any case, she had those rabbis to think of . . . Von Turm's murder or mutilation would probably mean their elimination, not to mention her own flogging to death.

First and foremost, Bella's own body had already promised Gottfried something other than a knife in the night. . . .

Would he accuse her of having polluted him by allowing his seed to take root in her womb?

Indeed not. She would take extra vitamins. She would give birth in the Brothel Block — though he would not be present at such an event. She would rear her babe — though he would not see it — and she would continue to visit him.

Even this was within the gamut of SS caprice.

It could be done. For her. While others starved and died.

So I was born in the Midsummer of 1944. Herzwalde camp collapsed into chaos in March of the following year. The rabbis had barely begun work on the book of *Revelation,* yet it seemed that the prophecies of Armageddon were already coming true, prematurely.

A bomb, one of several stupidly dropped on the concentration camp, killed Colonel von Turm. The bombing killed prisoners too, but only one German, Gottfried. Yet obviously the end was nigh. Therefore the SS assembled the ablebodied to march them westward; and among the ablest bodied were those rabbis and eggheads of the Colonel's project, and of course Bella with me in her arms. In such circumstances I was a burden, yet one which the SS allowed out of some perverse sentiment towards their dead deputy commandant.

Chaos begat chaos as the sinews of lunacy stretched and snapped. Overnight, at a transit stockade previously used for cattle, the SS all decamped without troubling to machine-gun those they had escorted thus far.

Bella fled. Presently she found herself wandering with a band of other anonymous women, reduced to the status of tramps, starving herself to supply me with half-masticated, scavenged food which she spat into my mouth in the way that a mother bird feeds its hungry, squalling nestling.

Unluckily, those tramps fell in again with other ex-inmates of Herzwalde who knew exactly who Bella was. They beat Bella savagely as a mistress of a Nazi tormenter, for she had prospered while they suffered.

Though her injuries were patched up, Bella died of pneumonia.

Somehow, a nun took me to a camp for displaced persons. She only knew that I was Jewish, and was called David.

In that more benign camp, a miraculously reunited couple by the name of Abramowicz adopted me. Martha Abramowicz had been sterilised in a medical experiment, but had survived. As had Levi, her husband. I was their second miracle, a son.

Eventually the Abramowiczes reached Palestine, and Palestine became Israel. Ultimately I became a *katsa* of the Mossad, dedicated to foxing the enemies of Israel.

In lieu of other nourishment during the days of wandering, my mother may have told me tales. I would have needed to be preternaturally precocious to understand those tales — unless my memory was a perfect sponge, the incomprehensible contents of which could be stored for later retrieval, decoding, and interpretation.

Might this be partly the explanation? My memory is indeed remarkably retentive.

At puberty, I began to dream my mother's memories of Herzwalde. . . . These weren't exactly *horrifying* — not in the sense that I would wake up screaming. Rather, it seemed as though nightly I was engaged in a game, a game which dark gods played with people. The camp with its great rows of huts, its outer and inner wire fences, its watchtowers, latrines, kitchens, gallows, its special blocks, its SS residencies, its warehouses of loot, all, all this was an intricate and fascinating gameboard, a lifeboard and deathboard far more complex than any chessboard. Pyjama-clad pawns and grey-uniformed knights and bishop-rabbis and many other categories manœuvred there. Also, I glimpsed certain evasive pieces which seemed to bear no correspondence to ordinary reality. I called these the Sphinx, the Angel, the Harpy, and the Clown; though what they were I could not tell.

The more that I experienced the manœuvres, the more did it seem that some higher scheme presided over the camp. Some higher plan was emerging, ghost-like — in the manner of a vast message writ in invisible ink revealing itself line by line, under the stimulus not of warmth but of wretched death.

The final revelation of that message would be cataclysmic, yet potent, wrought of ultimate despair and prayer and conjuration.

Despair, yes despair. Despair that God might no longer be present in such a hell as the camp; that the camp represented an *absence* of God, a gap within Creation, a mad void where aberrant entities such as the Harpy and the Clown could caper, where the Sphinx and the Angel could construct themselves. Apocalyptic creatures! Yet not the banal Four Horsemen of Saint John, those projections of paranoia, jealously, and vengeance. Something much more *interesting*. . . .

Nevertheless, Godpower could still be summoned. Thus the Creator might be recalled into existence.

With the abandonment of Herzwalde, what became of the almost completed Bible in Blood?

The scribes didn't carry it away with them on their forced march. Nor was Gottfried von Turm alive to salvage it.

I spent many years — whilst engaged on other enterprises in Europe as a Mossad operative — in tracking down rumours of that legendary book which now lay spread open before me.

Surviving Rabbis (their faith reinforced, or else forsaken) and eggheads alike were distinctly reticent about their part in the affair, as though an oath of enduring secrecy bound them. . . .

For they had murmured over that book, uttering what were virtually incantations; and something strange and potent — yet abortive — had happened in that icy February of 1945, as Soviet forces fought their way progressively closer. It was something other than the seeming approach of Armageddon for the Third Reich. It was something connected with the prisoners' apprehension that they might all be summarily liquidated by a Germany in retreat. It was something which might magically *protect* the residents of the Scripture Block more effectively than Colonel von Turm. (If indeed they realized that he was their protector. The witness of survivors, on this point, ranged from incredulity to stubborn silence).

In my mother's fragmented memories, welling within me, was a hint of what this strange, potent, yet finally fruitless event had been. Only a hint.

Her *Gottfried* certainly knew more about it. Gottfried, of whom I was half. Yet that half remained veiled within *her* remembrance.

The rumour-web had finally attracted a spider, a spinner of cocoons in which to store prizes, a collector of bibliographic bizzarerie in the stooping shape of Henry Appledorn.

The German Democratic Republic had at last given up the ghost. In the process it yielded up all manner of monsters, including untold archives stored in secret cellars by the Stasi, those Marxist successors to the Gestapo. Out-of-work intellectuals were being hired to catalogue the morass of paper.

Whoever found the Blood Bible lurking in a Stasi crypt obviously realized its oddity, thus its potential value. Sufficient to buy a fine Mercedes, or several? He, or she, sequestered the volume for themselves, during this time of confusion, and put out feelers. . . .

Or perhaps our investigative entrepreneur Klaus Bauer himself discovered, from ageing ex-SS contacts, where the volume might have ended up under the Communist regime — as an unclassifiable curiosity which it might be prudent to keep hidden — and then he bribed the new custodians of the Stasi crypts.

The Stasi had often been chary about releasing Nazi documents or films from store to assist international quests for justice against Nazis. For thus they might be assisting that creature of America, the Zionist state. Colonel von Turm was dead, way beyond prosecution for war crimes. Better to keep such a weird anomaly as the Blood Bible stored in secrecy, if indeed the Stasi understood exactly what it was. Maybe they never really believed any scraps of testimony that they gathered. Maybe they viewed awareness of the book as potentially dangerous, a possible focus for neo-Hitlerian blood-dreams of unregenerate Nazis who had bored bolt-holes into the woodwork of the Bundesrepublik next door.

What Gloria Cameron had let slip made me realize that Henry Appledorn was no mere eccentric, ardent bibliophile. Unlike Bauer, he must be at least somewhat aware of the *event* which had occurred in Herzwalde during the final days.

Might he know *more* than I did? Had one of the surviving eggheads, after emigrating to America, then perhaps lapsing into poverty in his old age, told Appledorn an incredible story? Did Appledorn, himself confronting old age with disapproval, fancy himself as a Magus?

As a good *katsa* of Mossad, I was thoroughly accustomed to running scenarios of disinformation and duplicity through my mind, just as I was used to adopting false identities so that I could be one person one day, then another the next day.

Ha! I wouldn't be a good *katsa* much longer — not after acquiring the volume. I would be a disappeared, absconded *katsa*.

"I said, Miss Cameron, what do you expect from the book? What have you two heard about it? Come on, Mr Appledorn." I smiled at him. "I'm prepared to shoot one or both or you. The woman first, I think, to prove my intentions. Then you, Sir." With my free hand, I pulled out the hypodermic syringe. To allow them some hope, I explained, "I was merely intending to put you all to sleep with a jab. Now I may have to shoot you."

Miss Cameron licked her lips. "The noise will attract attention. You won't escape with the book."

"Oh, I think this is quite a soundproof suite. We are on what, the tenth floor? I happen to know that the rooms on either side and over the way are vacant. If any passing maid reports a problem, I'm sure that the under-manager of this hotel will cause all kinds of delay."

Thus I burned my *sayan,* but that didn't matter.

"Tell him what he wants, Herr Appledorn," begged Bauer in a cowardly tone.

A moment later Bauer launched himself at me, with a leap like a German Shepherd dog.

He knocked my gunhand down as I swung to fire. The first bullet must have passed through his jacket, but the second caught him, knocking him back from grappling with me; and I had stabbed him with the needle too. . . .

Appledorn uttered a bellow of affront — for the first bullet had passed aslant into the book, exploding outward through the rear board and the thick glass of the table beneath. The glass cracked into several jagged panes which nevertheless hung together. A hole bored down through the pages.

Gloria Cameron uttered a different, tremulous kind of cry.

For the top page — of *The Gospel According to Saint Matthew* — had begun to bleed. . . .

Red blood welled upward from the wound in the parchment just as though the heat of my bullet had reliquified the long-dried gore of the letters.

Bauer staggered aside, clutching at his hip. Part of his flesh had been blown away. He shook his head as the drug began to work on him.

That couldn't possibly be *his* blood on the book.

Bauer collapsed on a sofa. He was irrelevant now.

Through that tunnel torn in the book a wind began to whistle, the shriek of a wintry gale — which fast became lower in pitch, a vibrant powerful moan, as if the tunnel was fast widening.

And it was so. It was so.

The Cameron woman cried out again; and so, I think, did I.

A fissure opened through the book — a chasm.

A gulf that, howling, invaded the room, abolishing the furnishings and walls and the long, curtained window.

In their place was a cold dark river. A broad river. Little ice floes spun along it. Its banks themselves were gentle enough, but across the water indefinable walls and buildings mounted towards a steep ridge crowned by a long sombre fortress and a bulky cathedral. The Moon offered some illumination. Sparks of torchlight flickered here and there like stars fallen to Earth. . . .

I recognized those silhouettes on the ridge — even though they seemed strangely incomplete. Surely this was Prague. The river, the Vltava. The Cathedral must be that of St Vitus. The fortress could only be Hradcany Castle. . . . Yet it was a Prague of long ago. And in the winter, in the small hours of some morning.

Behind me, a jumble of buildings packed together in the obscurity. Jews' Town.

Three men laboured on the riverbank near the flood of wintry water. They were stooping, scooping, moulding handfuls of clay and mud. . . .

Had Appledorn and Gloria Cameron been sucked here too? I seemed to sense their presence. I myself was bodiless, a floating point of view, an invisible naked mind, a spirit.

Two of the men by the water were dressed in homespun doublets and leggings, soiled by the clay. The third, a white-bearded man with a curious cap on his head, wore a cloak.

With their bare hands they were moulding a body from the stuff of the riverbank. . . .

I knew who they must be. I could sense it.

They had to be none other than Rabbi Yehuda Löw ben Bezalel, and his son-in-law, and his trusted pupil. They were trying to make the golem, the artificial man of great strength who would police the ghetto which clustered close by.

Christian trouble-makers would smuggle a murdered Christian child into the ghetto, wrapped in a sack, as a pretext to utter the blood-accusation against Jewry and thus launch a vindictive, brutal pogrom.

The Golem was designed to haul such villains to justice.

Had this manufacture of a Golem ever really happened? Or had it only occurred in the realm of myth — a myth so powerful that many people nevertheless believed it? Jews turned to this myth for consolation in the dark hours of their despair. Even in the late twentieth century pious pilgrims visited Löw's lion-carved sarcophagus in the overcrowded Jewish cemetery to toss written appeals into his tomb, hoping for wonders.

Now this legendary event was happening before my gaze.

With his finger the Rabbi was drawing a face on the recumbent, lifeless clay-man.

"May the angel Metatron guide us," murmured the pupil. I could understand his words. Cautiously he asked his mentor, "Rabbi, will the Golem really borrow a soul from the domain of preexistence?"

Rabbi Löw paused. "Only a crude soul," he replied. "Our Golem will be speechless. Dumb. Without human words, always. Yet it will understand, and obey."

The Rabbi's son-in-law plainly felt qualms too, at this final moment. "Aren't we trespassing on God's prerogative?"

Löw mused. "The Divine Wisdom was obliged to become *creative*," he reminded them, "so as to justify His own existence to Himself. Man was formed in His image. Now Man must needs create too, all be it on a humbler scale."

Aye, desperate expedients for desperate times.

The three men whispered together.

Then Yehuda's son-in-law began to walk around the clay man, reciting as he did so a code of letters from the Hebrew alphabet.

"*Aleph . . . Vav . . . Aleph . . . Heth . . . Jod . . .*"

He circuited the clay body seven times — "*Heth . . . Samekh . . . He . . . Tav . . . Pe . . . He . . . Nun . . .*" — and as he walked, so the body of clay began to glow ruddily as an inner fire was stoked.

Next it was the turn of Yehuda Löw's pupil to pace around the body, uttering other permutations of Hebrew letters.

This was Kabalah.

True Kabalah. Pious Kabalah.

Sacred magic.

With a carved block of wood, Yehuda stamped a word upon the Golem's hot brow.

I could read the word. The word was *emeth*, meaning "true." Erase the first letter, and "true" would turn into "dead."

Into the Golem's mouth Yehuda pushed a piece of paper on which he had written the secret name of God. This piece of paper was the *Shem*, the program for the Golem. Remove the *Shem* from the Golem's mouth, and the artificial man would collapse back into clay.

Icy water swirled against the glowing body. Steam wreathed it. From the Golem's fingers nails sprouted. From its head hair grew.

In chorus, the three men recited: "And the Lord God formed man of the dust of the ground, and breathed

into his nostrils the breath of life; and man became a living soul."

With this last phrase, I felt myself being sucked towards the Golem — as if *I* was to be the soul that inhabited it!

As if my own soul was to animate that clay body and march obediently around the ghetto, unable to exert my own will, impotent to protest! Obeying orders numbly until some day when the *Shem* was removed from my mouth!

I fought.

I sought purchase with my nonexistent fingers and toes on the very air.

As I slid ever closer to entombment and a terrible oblivion, at the last moment the Golem opened its eyes. The pulling ceased; I was gently repelled.

The Golem arose.

"Your name," Yehuda said to it, "is Joseph."

And Joseph nodded.

"You are to guard us from harm, Joseph," the rabbi told it.

Snow began to tumble, slanting through the air.

Snow swirled, blanking out the scene. I could see nothing but tempestuous white flakes.

When these flakes cleared, instead of a river bank there were rows of wooden huts and roads of frozen mud. In place of a distant steeple, a watchtower. A searchlight stabbed out from its summit, cutting whitely through the night. In the distance, a whistle blew. From much further away — maybe sixty kilometres away — came a faint percussive thump of artillery. . . .

My mother's memories were alive. . . .

Within those memories stood Colonel von Turm.

I had leapt from her to him at last.

"Ich bin Gottfried," I told myself.

Yet what did I know of my identity? Though I probed, yet I could not penetrate. I was only a wraith, wrapped around this person. Of Gottfried's youth, his motives, his attitude to Bella: nothing. He might as well have been an animated man of clay, who could articulate nothing of his thoughts and feelings to me. I only knew what he did.

Resting his weight on his silver-handled cane, he stood surveying one nearby blockhouse. Within, a faint ruddy light glowed as if a dull brazier was lit in there. The Colonel had thrown a long leather coat over the shoulders of his grey uniform. Several helmeted SS guards were with him, toting their machine-pistols.

When they burst into the Scripture Block and illuminated it, almost all of the rabbis and eggheads proved to have quit their tiered wooden bunks. They thronged the floor space. Their Kapo was doing nothing about the situation.

Now, this particular hut wasn't as claustrophobic as most. It wasn't a sardine can. Space existed, for uniquely these slaves laboured in their own quarters. The far end of the hut housed a worktable surrounded by rickety chairs.

On that table lay the Bible in Blood. The letters on the open pages of parchment glowed ruddily, luridly luminous with inner light.

At the sudden intrusion, a murmuring of many voices ceased except one which continued to recite defiantly, insistently, "And man became a living soul. . . ."

From beside the table a naked corpse arose. Its skin was grey as wrapping paper. Its blue lips were bared in a rictus, exposing clenched stained teeth.

Obviously a corpse. Its sunken eyes were closed. On its brow was printed, in blood, a Hebrew word.

Emeth.

"And man became a living soul. . . ."

Its tongue, protruding through its teeth, had shrivelled to a white leaf.

No! That was no tongue.

That was . . . the *shem*.

The mud outside was frozen. Evidently the prisoners had smuggled in a corpse from another hut, or more likely from the charnel heap. Was not man's flesh made of clay? To clay, returning? Was this dead body not therefore equivalent to clay?

". . . a living soul, to be our protector, our guardian under God!"

The zombie-Golem opened its eyes, eyes that stared blankly. It began to cavort, windmilling its arms.

As the SS guards clove a pathway for the Colonel many prisoners scrambled into bunks or clung to the sides of those bunks like panicked monkeys.

By now the Bible had ceased glowing.

Gottfried stared at the scarecrow of a Golem, which turned now to face him.

"Kill it," he ordered his men.

Guns racketted.

The Golem's parchment skin tore, yet bullets seemed simply to pass through it. It rocked, but it did not fall. Its flesh burst, bloodlessly, but its bones could have been made of steel. Or of rock, of fossilised bones.

"Cease fire!"

The Golem still stood, swaying.

Gottfried stared at it . . . as though now he understood.

Some of the prisoners were moaning — not because they were afraid of a terrible punishment, but as if appalled at what they had achieved. Or halfachieved. A multitude of needle tracks in all of their arms kept tally of the blood they had yielded up repeatedly, day after day.

They had lost courage.

One of the eggheads cried out cravenly to the Colonel, "Take the *shem* from its mouth, Sir!"

Gottfried stood right before the Golem, although his men were hesitant.

It jerked. It froze again. Why should it attack this Colonel, who was a perverse — or honourable — protector of these prisoners?

Then it spoke — opening its vile teeth. At last it spoke. Or croaked.

"Ich bin *Joseph,*" it uttered. The *shem* lolled on its blue tongue like a long communion wafer.

Gottfried reached, and yanked the scrap of parchment from its mouth — so that the Golem lolled upright, motiveless, like any common or garden prisoner on parade who would soon die.

The Colonel spat on his glove, and smudged out the first letter of the word on the creature's brow. Oh he knew, he knew the tricks of the Jews!

The corpse collapsed. Its spirit had fled.

And so must I. For suction tore at me.

"Father!" I cried. "Tell me! Tell me!" Tell me so many things that you never told my mother. . . .

But that inhalation from elsewhere was overwhelming me, as if the very bellows of the world were breathing me in.

"Aitch-Jay!" cried Gloria Cameron. Our bibliophile hunched, lolling, spittle on his lips.

The book on the smashed glass table bled no more. There was no longer any wound from which it could bleed. The torn parchment had resealed itself like living flesh possessed of an amazing power of regeneration, a facility as considerable as that of the Golem itself.

Bauer was dozing, while blood continued to leak from his side through his clothes to stain the sofa.

"Aitch Jay!"

Henry *Joseph* Appledorn, of course.

It struck me then, fearfully, that only that coincidence of his name and the Golem's had saved my soul from being enveloped in the creation of clay. . . .

Either one of us might have been captured — him or me. Bauer? What about Bauer? No, he had already been rendered *hors de combat*. And Gloria Cameron was female.

Appledorn mumbled.

He staggered.

Aided by her, he sat down in an armchair.

He stared at me, out of grief-stricken, time-chasmed eyes.

His voice croaked.

"I had to patrol . . . for years, night after night. . . . And day after day I stood . . . motionless . . . in a back room of the Synagogue. I couldn't . . . utter a word. I was only . . . an animated *thing.*" He forced out all the words which had long been frozen. At first they emerged like nuggets of ice, then, as his voice thawed, in a gushing stream.

The cobbled alleys, the twisting streets so narrow that the eaves of houses almost touched. . . . Carved painted signs showing a swan, a lute, a crayfish, a giant key, as though each house was a member of some strange zodiac. Here was the building housing the first Hebrew printing press in Central Europe. There were the public baths. Here, a poorhouse; there, an infirmary. All crammed together. In a maze of alleyways. Which he must pace nightly, always keeping out of sight if he could, never speaking, for the *shem* was in his mouth.

And he was successful in his guardianship.

For presently a magnificent Jewish town hall was built. And the High Synagogue; and Klaus Synagogue; and Maisl Synagogue.

So successful was he that further services on his part seemed unnecessary. Frankly, his existence was an embarrassment. Consequently he was walled up, stored in darkness. Forgotten . . .

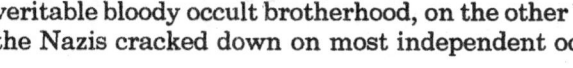

. . . till of a sudden he found himself standing in a crowded, noisome hut. Bullets tore his emaciated body — in vain, except that through the holes they made they let a breeze into him. He sucked that breeze together, and at last he gasped.

And the grey-clad officer pulled the *shem* from his mouth.

"The book could bring . . . power. So I heard," Appledorn confessed. He needed little prompting now. "Yes, I did hear it from an immigrant who had been in Herzwalde. But the book was still incomplete. . . .

"It's the only *actual* magic book I ever heard of. Books of spells and grimoires: they're just . . . weird words on paper. Nothing effective. This book was magic in itself! And that was because . . ." He frowned, trying to grasp the reason.

"Because God was absent from Herzwalde," I explained. "So therefore there was a chasm in creation. A gap. The rules did not exist any more — they broke down. The gap could be otherwise filled. I'm the son of Gottfried von Turm, the deputy commandant," I told him. "That is *my* book."

Though I had failed to commune fully with my father, I knew at last what his motive had been.

It had been different from what I had imagined from my mother's memories — ah, Bella's *deluded* recollections!

No wonder Gottfried had been taciturn.

Although on the one hand the SS constituted a veritable bloody occult brotherhood, on the other hand the Nazis cracked down on most independent occult-ists and occult groups who might in any way form a kernel of opposition to the Nazi regime. They suppressed these potential rivals. The Gestapo drew up lists of organizations little and large, even daffy ones, whose members must not be allowed any government employment, even as a postman. And this made perfect sense; for if the SS were occultly inclined, they must be the sole practitioners of dark and bloody rituals.

Gottfried von Turm had been an occultist of a different stripe, a solitary practitioner in a lonely tower, as it were. Yet he was also an aristocrat. Hence the Gestapo both punished him, and at the same time permitted him a National Socialistic redemption, by forcing his entry into the Waffen-SS.

Along with whom he fought, until he came to Herzwalde. In the camp he discovered a pressure cooker of horrors — a perfect crucible for an experiment. On the surface his project might seem more "benign" in its effects than the loathsome and lunatic medical mutilations which SS doctors performed upon prisoners. Yet it was a deep, dark investigation — by someone who bore Jews no particular animosity whatever, who might even arguably be aiding some of them. As intense heat and pressure might crush carbon into diamond, so might the spiritually humiliating toil of kabalistic rabbis in the Scripture Block, writing in their own blood — in an atmosphere of ultimate despair, devoid of God — create a magical device.

Ah, that *amalgamation* of Jewish blood and holy Christian words culminating in an Apocalypse!

What role did my mother fulfil in this? Oh yes, I *was* to be born — of a Jewess whose people were scribing the book, and of Gottfried's seed! This was the part of himself which Gottfried donated to the project. Most certainly I was to be born, a homunculus of him, a repository of his power — of that power which his project was distilling.

No wonder Gottfried was so silent in bed, so devoid of pillow talk. He was *concentrating*. No wonder he needed to remain detached from me, shunning my birth and my early infancy. For the project was not yet complete. The book wasn't finished.

And then that idiotic bomb killed him; and the book remained unfinished.

Now I understood why I could dream my mother's memories. And why I had felt so impelled to seek out the book.

"Do you think," I demanded of Appledorn, "that if anyone except me had fired a bullet into that book, the rift in reality would have opened up?"

Appledorn was trembling. Gloria Cameron regarded me . . . almost greedily, as if desirous.

by Ian Watson

"But," Appledorn managed to say. "But the Golem was a legend. . . ."

Yes, it was. In our own history it was a legend.

"There's another domain, Mr Appledorn," I said, with increasing confidence. "The domain of the Sphinx and the Angel, of the Harpy and the Clown." I had never uttered their names aloud before — names which indeed *I myself* had assigned to these entities. Nonetheless, those were the true names.

Appledorn wiped his lips.

"Take the book," he said. "I daren't own it."

"Aitch Jay!" protested the woman.

As though it was up to either of them to decide!

The American shook his head numbly. "I couldn't . . . The serving, the standing in darkness for years . . . I'd rather die than risk . . . something similar."

"Then you will die," the Cameron woman said to him bitterly. She wasn't threatening him, simply uttering a statement of plain fact. "In three or four years, ten years if you're lucky. You'll die, Henry *Joseph*."

"And therefore so will you one day, Gloria," he replied softly.

It was time for me to leave. High time.

I made both of them lie down upon the floor. Appledorn complied willingly; Gloria Cameron, less so.

I injected her, then him. Then I shut the Blood Bible, and tied the red ribbons.

The steel emblem embedded in the cover was a large mirror-image swastika, made of steel and inset with strips of mirror.

Lille is a fine enough city to hide in, though my stay will be relatively brief. I rent a little top floor apartment in the old town in the Rue de la Clef. David Abramowicz is no more. Now I'm Daniel Kahn, an author determined to finish a book. "About what, Monsieur?" "Why, about cathedrals." There's one substantial example just up the road. I make sure to visit the cathedral occasionally, to stretch my legs.

I take the blood from high up my arms so as not to produce obvious tracks which might attract the attention of antidrugs *flics*.

I arrived in this city with my book at the most opportune time in September — at the start of the vast rummage fair, the Braderie. By ancient charter the whole city centre is given over to thousands of stalls, street upon street of stalls selling old clothes, bric-à-brac, antiques, African carvings, tools, the rubbish from Granny's attic, carpets, curios, anything and everything. I even found a stall selling the extra parchment which I needed. In the evening, while music spewed forth and the whores patrolled, *tout le monde* feasted on mussels cooked in red wine and in cream at a multitude of tables which were further blocking pavements and streets outside of every café. Black mountains of empty shells arose. If a car intruded impatiently, tipsy diners tossed mussel shells at it in pique.

Half of the population of Flanders seemed to have descended upon Lille; and tourists galore. What more anonymous time to take up residence, and remain as if enchanted by the city?

My arms ache, and the fingers of my right hand are numb with forming the Gothic letters correctly. I must flex my fingers frequently. There's a whiff of blood in the room, and of sterilising alcohol too, since I wouldn't wish to become septic.

Presently I will reach those final words: *The grace of our Lord Jesus Christ be with you all. Amen.*

Amen. Amen. Amen.

So be it! Thus is it in truth!

Then I must bind the book; and having bound it, I shall fire my gun into that book once more, and the bloodstained parchment will split open to reveal the true territory of the Clown and the Harpy, the Angel and the Sphinx; and I shall discover what those beings are.

I myself, and my father within me. Ω

TENEMENT

Mama is out,
And Daddy's long gone.
The room is empty . . .
But the cradle rocks anyway.
Shadows strain
Against the walls,
Striving for a lullaby.
Baby smiles . . .
Reluctantly.
Already it has learned
To take what it can get.

—Kathleen Youmans

FOR SEVENTY-FIVE YEARS: THE UNIQUE MAGAZINE   ISSN 0898-5073
Fall 1998   Cover by Stephen E. Fabian

Weird Tales® is published 4 times a year by DNA Publications, Inc., in association with Terminus Publishing Co., Inc. Postmaster and others: send all changes of address and other subscription matters to DNA Publications, Inc., PO Box 2988, Radford VA 24143–2988. Editorial matters should be addressed to Terminus Publishing Co., Inc., 123 Crooked Lane, King of Prussia PA 19406-2570. Single copies, $4.95 in U.S.A. & possessions; $6.00 by mail elsewhere. Subscriptions: 4 issues (one year) $16.00 in U.S.A. & possessions; $22.00 elsewhere, in U.S. funds. Publisher is not responsible for loss of manuscripts in publisher's hands or in transit; please see page 5 for more details. Copyright © 1998 by Terminus Publishing Co., Inc.; all rights reserved; reproduction prohibited without prior permission. Typeset, printed, & bound in the United States of America.
Weird Tales® is a registered trademark owned by Weird Tales, Limited.

THE EYRIE

We get letters, but not nearly enough of them. There was a time when writing letters to the professional science-fiction and fantasy magazines was a major activity for fans. Before there was an internet, when fanzines were mimeographed and had circulations in the low hundreds, the way to make yourself known was to have a letter in every issue of *Startling Stories.* This excellent pulp magazine of the 1940s and '50s not only printed a novel in every issue (some of them, like Jack Vance's *Big Planet* and Arthur C. Clarke's *Against the Fall of Night*, now classics) and about the same wordage again in short fiction (making for a magazine about twice the size of a modern genre publication) but also had room for twenty pages or so of readers' letters in type of the size otherwise used for phone books.

It was, for some of the readers at least, great fun. The letter columns were the precursors of specialized newsgroups on the 'net and the on-line chat-rooms where fans and writers meet and exchange ideas. Personalities developed. "Letterhacks" became celebrities. Looking through old issues of *Startling Stories* (or its companion *Thrilling Wonder Stories*), a modern editor cannot help but feel envy and frustration. Most of those letters were good, and there were *so many* of them. It's been *our* experience that one gets about one publishable letter per thousand readers each issue; in the old days, how the mailbags must have bulged. (Then again, some readers found the letterhacking antics tiresome. When *Galaxy Science Fiction* started in 1950, the editor asked his readers if they wanted a letter column. He got *six thousand* negative replies.)

Times have simply changed. Maybe we're not as epistolary a society anymore. *Weird Tales®* in *its* grand old days never ran twenty pages of letters in tiny type, but it did run letters. Personalities emerged. Robert Bloch, then a teenaged fan, railed famously against Robert E. Howard's Conan the Barbarian, "May he be sent to Valhalla to cut out paper dolls!" and editor Farnsworth Wright then suggested that readers sharpen their axes because Bloch's own first story was about to appear; but Bloch's story ("The Feast in the Abbey") proved so popular that even Conan, in Valhalla, may have paused to commend him.

Letter columns give a magazine a sense of person-

ality and continuity. That's one reason why we, the present editors of *Weird Tales*, continue to encourage them.

But it's like pulling teeth sometimes.

We actually *have* extracted a letter which raises some interesting points; but, for reasons which should be obvious, we have chosen not to give the writer's name. This came back in reply to a rejection written by assistant editor Kyle Phillips. (Arguing back after you've been rejected, we hasten to add, is one thing a writer should *never* do. There is much to be lost and nothing to be gained from it.) Writes our rejectee of the wounded ego:

The problem with readers, and indeed with editors such as yourself these days, is that we are now in a society of "fast food" (analogy of course) service. That is to say that we have become so on the go that we no longer have the time, or even the desire to sit down and be entertained by a good piece of prose. This letter is in response to your rejection of my "yarn" [title given]. And before you believe this to be your average writer pissed about another rejection think you hard on the words that you read herein. [sic throughout] You will no doubt agree that your publication is not the magazine it once was in the hey day of pulp fiction. *Weird Tales* published fine stories by GREAT writers such as H.P. Lovecraft, Robert E. Howard, and so, you know this already.

The point I mean to make is that once your magazine was the standard by which other magazines were published. Today that is not the case, and do not take this personally. Of course readers want action, action, ACTION! Hell, that's all the crap box is feeding them — and it's all fast pace. Forget the setup and execution, just give us a few hours of senseless non-stop action and we'll be happy! So goes the outcry at the box office. [. . .]

All this brings me to this, sir; my works, even the shortest, will take time to appreciate, I speak in terms of actual reading. The reader sees it coming. There must be something lurking at the climax for this setup to pay off. And it always does where my prose are concerned. Furthermore, even more important with my yarns is the fact that they are poetic. Your remark, "if something sounds nice but doesn't further the action, cut it out and get on with things," may indeed be true, as you went on to say,

. . . otherwise readers will lose interest. However, I must justify my words as they are. "Art for art's sake," my friend. [. . .] Take a chance that at least a few of your readers would care to read poetic prose. If not my own, then someone else's. [. . .] I do so hope for the return of classic prose. Give me Robert E. Howard over Steven King any day!

Well, after invoking Schweitzer's Law of Poetic Prose ("If you have to tell us it's poetic, it isn't.") and quoting Ezra Pound's dictum that poetry must be at least as well written as prose, the above letter does give us quite a bit to chew on.

Start with Pound, then turn him around: poetic prose should be as well written as poetry. What is the most salient feature of good poetry? Compression. An extreme economy of words. A poetry editor might advise the writer that if a single word or even punctuation mark doesn't contribute to the overall effect of the poem, then throw it out and get on with the poem. Edgar Allen Poe voiced similar sentiments about the short story, and he was one of the great masters of poetic prose. There are no wasted words in "The Masque of the Red Death" or "Shadow: a Parable." Poe did not "take time out" to be poetic; he merely *was*. Schweitzer's Second Law of Poetic Prose is that as soon as you notice the writer stopping the story for poetic effects, that's just padding. Good poetic prose, such as Poe's, or Dunsany's, is as seamless as a sonnet. We thought that the rejected manuscript in question wasn't.

Otherwise the writer's complaints curiously echo those found in H.P. Lovecraft's letters. H.P.L. was enormously critical of *Weird Tales* in its heyday, for precisely the reason our correspondent is dissatisfied with our version of the magazine. Pulp fiction emphasized action, often to the exclusion of all else. Lovecraft wrote for *Weird Tales* reluctantly, regarding it as the least bad of a bad lot, where there was at least a little bit of breathing-room for literary artistry. In some of the other magazines of the day, there was none.

Actually we think Lovecraft's view of *Weird Tales* was a trifle unfair. *Weird Tales* (hardly "the standard by which all other magazines were published") was an extremely marginal enterprise in the '20s and '30s, barely able to survive from issue to issue, often years behind in its payment of authors. Editor Farnsworth Wright performed a delicate balancing act by mixing some genuinely literary fiction by Lovecraft, Clark Ashton Smith, or Henry S. Whitehead with, well, pulp trash of the pulpiest and trashiest sort, one of the trashiest of which was the serial "Skull-Face" by none

STAFF:

Publisher: Warren Lapine
Editors: George H. Scithers
& Darrell Schweitzer
Managing Editor: Carol Adams
Art Editor: Diane Weinstein
Assistant Editors: Kyle Phillips, Pat Buard, Robert Waters, Shawn M. Proctor, & Casey McCarthy
Computer Consultant: David J. Williams III
Typesetter: Owlswick Press
Printer: News Publishing Co., Inc.

MANUSCRIPT SUBMISSIONS:

Before sending us your material, please send us a business-sized envelope, with postage affixed, addressed to you, for our guidelines. The address for this and all other editorial matter: *Weird Tales*®, 123 Crooked Lane, King of Prussia PA 19406-2570.

The address for all subscription and back-order matters: DNA Publications, Inc., PO Box 2988, Radford VA 24143–2988.

Yes; we read unsolicited submissions — but *only* if they are in standard manuscript format. To survive, all editors insist on a few Rules: each submission must be in proper format and must include a return envelope, addressed to you, with enough postage affixed to bring the manuscript back to you. If you want us to discard the manuscript if we don't buy it, tell us so, but include a business-letter-sized envelope, addressed to you, with proper postage affixed, so we can send you our comments. No loose stamps, please!

We recommend either of two books on writing (after all, we wrote one of them!): *On Writing Science Fiction: the Editors Strike Back!* by Scithers, Schweitzer, & John M. Ford; $19.50 in hardcover; and Barry B. Longyear's *Science-Fiction Writer's Workshop*, $9.50 in trade paperback, available from the Owlswick Press, 123 Crooked Lane, King of Prussia PA 19406-2570. These prices include shipping & handling; in Pennsylvania, please include 6% sales tax.

We are not responsible for manuscripts in our hands or in transit. You *must* keep a copy of every manuscript you send out. You *must* put your name and address on the first page of every manuscript. And please: *no* binders, folders, or padded envelopes; and especially: *no* registered or certified mail for which we would have to stand in line at the post office!

other than Robert E. Howard, which actually does manage occasional flashes of color or atmosphere, but is mostly a second-rate Fu Manchu imitation paced as breathlessly and brainlessly as a silent-movie serial. *Weird Tales* used its serials in particular to reach for the low-brow, action audience. There were imitations of Edgar Rice Burroughs by Otis Adelbert Kline, featured prominently, often with several cover paintings, and stretched out over as many issues as possible, in a time when Burroughs books (or Burroughs serials, in much better-paying and better-circulated magazines like *Argosy*) sold the way Stephen King does today.

Not surprisingly, very few old-time *Weird Tales* serials are remembered as classics. But, dare we suggest that the old *Weird Tales* is sometimes viewed through rosy glasses? The magazine lasted a very long time (1923–54). It published a good deal of excellent material which has stood the test of time. But if you go back and examine the actual issues (at today's prices, a very expensive enterprise), you may be surprised to find that sometimes the classic (or even good) stories only occur at the rate of two or three per issue, and that the actual concentration of first-rate material was nowhere near as high as it was in *Unknown* or in the early years of *The Magazine of Fantasy & Science Fiction*.

If Farnsworth Wright (and his successor, Dorothy McIlwraith) managed to put out a magazine of, say, 50% worthwhile material, and they had to publish 50%

trash to keep that magazine alive decade after decade, then their efforts were certainly justified. That's a lot of good stuff, over time.

We are well aware that our *Weird Tales* is not the *Weird Tales* of the 1930s. It was our basic premise from the founding of Terminus Publishing Company, Inc., that our *Weird Tales* would not be an imitation of the past, but an approximation of what *Weird Tales* would have been if it had survived uninterruptedly until now.

We think it would have grown up. It might have evolved beyond the need to pander so obviously. We don't want to seem too full of ourselves, and we're well aware that it will take time to determine if what we've published will prove classic; but, frankly, we think that in some ways our *Weird Tales* is better than the old one, only in the sense that we don't have to publish Otis Adelbert Kline serials or the equivalent of "Skull-Face" or the Dr. Satan series when "weird criminal" stories became popular (think of it as cramming the magazine full of serial-killer stories to cash in on *The Silence of the Lambs*). We're glad we don't have to go to some of the ridiculous lengths the original *Weird Tales* did to get another issue out. Not that we have anything against action stories — or Robert E. Howard for that matter, most of whose work for *Weird Tales* was a lot better than "Skull-Face" — but we are beginning to suspect that our correspondent has not actually read the magazine very much, if he thinks that, after all the Tanith Lee and Thomas Ligotti stories that we've published, not to mention such delicately-textured works as Ian Watson's "The Coming of Vertumnus" (in *WT* #307), or even Darrell Schweitzer's Sekenre series, we are coming down on the side of non-stop action at the expense of atmosphere, character development, or, yes, even poetic prose.

We would really like to see more letters that we can quote and can put the correspondent's name on them. We got a nice one from **Christopher Dunn**, who comments:

> You picked the right name in your new publisher; a publication in its 7th [8th, but who's counting?] decade or so must have survival coded into its genes.

Mr. Dunn rates some stories, picking "The Bible in Blood" for its tightly controlled tour of real horror as well as fantastic in first place, and gives a favorable nod to "The Renfields" by Christopher Lee Walters. He also asks about the mysterious disappearance of the ad for Paula Guran's magazine *Wetbones,* mentioned in the editorial. Alas, that promising publication folded about the time our issue went to press. It is a real loss to the horror field, which could do with two or three strong and varied magazines right now, we think. So the ad got pulled and we missed the mention in the editorial. Sorry.

Nils Hedglin rates stories, then notes:

In the Eyrie, you discussed what horror is today and what it is not. If #313 is any indication of horror today, horror is child-abuse. Almost half of your stories had some aspect of child-abuse in them. From the parent/child relationship of "The Game," to the sadistic (albeit possibly deserved) bedtime story in "Beddy-Bye," to the revenge for the victims in "Ring! Ring!," to the supernatural abuse of "The Stepmother." Three of your other stories had significant abuse aspects to them too ("The Renfields," "The Bible in Blood," and the abandoned lover of the sorcerer in "On the Last Night of the Festival of the Dead"). Maybe horror in general is just the abuse of some power taken to an extreme.

We can certainly agree that lots of classic horror is about people doing bad things to other people. Maybe you're stretching it a bit to include "On the Last Night of the Festival of the Dead" on the child-abuse list, since it's about a grown man paying for the consequences of what he did in his callow post-adolescence; but we will admit that the preponderance of child-abuse stories in the last issue did leave us a little uneasy. It is *not* a message to writers that we want more stories about child-abuse. Rather, it's an almost unforeseen consequence of the magazine's prolonged ill-health before DNA Publications came riding to our rescue. We hadn't published an issue in a year. Issues before that were widely spaced. Our backlog was starting to get old. It is unfair to the writer when we buy a story and then sit on it for five years or so. *Worlds of Fantasy & Horror* #3 was a deliberate attempt to clear out the oldest stories in our inventory, and became, coincidentally, something of a Special Religion Issue. *Weird Tales* #313 was also put together largely out of stories we could not, in good conscience, keep unpublished any longer. It led to a somewhat unbalanced issue. We don't apologize for the *quality* one bit, but we do hope to have a little more variety in future issues.

Jack Williamson, who is one of the great grandmasters of imaginative fiction, and who wrote one of the few really good (and subsequently reprinted) serials in the old *Weird Tales*, sent his good wishes:

I'm happy to find *Weird Tales* still alive. The magazine was an important part of my own life back in the '30s. Farnsworth Wright was a great editor, admirable for his able dedication and the will to carry on so long in spite of the tremors and rigidity of Parkinson's disease. It was the only magazine market for fantasy — there was almost no book market. I recall it fondly. My favorite of all pulp covers is the wonderful painting of the golden tiger in the sky, done by J. Allan St. John for my serial "Golden Blood."

The writers, as we felt ourselves, were a tiny group of aliens lost in a world where nobody else understood or cared. I never met two of the

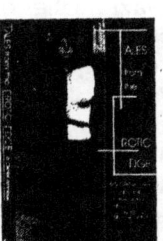
best-known stars, H.P. Lovecraft and Robert E. Howard, but Edmond Hamilton and E. Hoffman Price became life-long friends. I once drove with them to Auburn, California, to spend a memorable day with Clark Ashton Smith. I met a few others. All remarkable people, exciting to a farm boy from New Mexico. I was happy to be welcomed among them.

Never a huge success, the magazine was able to pay a penny a word, the equivalent of perhaps fifteen cents today, good money to me then. It survived in its first incarnation from 1923 to 1954, though times grew harder toward the end. Really "the unique magazine" in those early years, it was vital to its readers and deserves revival.

Kevin Filan writes (while in the course of submitting a story):

First, I should say "Good to see you again!" I was a voracious reader of *Weird Tales* back in the late '80s and early '90s. I still have *Weird Tales* #290 (the Gene Wolfe issue? Memory fades after all these years) packed away in my sister's garage. Now, almost a decade later, I picked up a copy of *WT* #313 and it was like I never went away! Back then you truly lived up to your name; I can remember horror, fantasy, science fiction, and more than one story that was simply "unclassifiable" but nonetheless wonderful. Maybe everything else has gone to

Hell in a handbasket, but *WT* is still a reliable good read. Congratulations and thank you.

WT #313 was uniformly excellent. I am not usually a "Swords & Sorcery" or "High Fantasy" fan, but Mr. Schweitzer's story was great fun and left me eager to read more of his work. (And I'm not just saying that because I sent a story along with this letter . . .) "The Bible in Blood" took a second read, but proved well worth it; Ian Watson is an excellent writer who obviously did his research. (As a onetime regular Nazi-basher on the newsgroup <alt.revisionism>, I've studied the Holocaust in some detail; his descriptions of "Herzwalde" are chillingly accurate.)

Most impressive, though, was Christopher Lee Walters's "The Renfields." He managed to pull off the damn-near-impossible feat of creating a new spin on the "Goth/punk-vampire-clan story" — a quintessential vampire tale without a single vampire. "The Renfields" is the best piece of psychological horror I've read since Dennis Etchison's "The Dark Country"; I look forward to seeing more from him in your magazine and elsewhere.

So do we. Believe it or not, "The Renfields" was a first sale. We were *enormously* impressed. So was Teresa Nielsen-Hayden of Tor Books. And, thank you for welcoming us back, but we hope that you were (or could become through purchase of back issues) an equally voracious reader of the four issues of *Worlds of Fantasy & Horror*, which we now think of as *Weird Tales* #309, #310, #311, and #312 in all but name.

The Most Popular Story is a feature we hope to continue in every issue of *Weird Tales*, but that depends on those of you who write in and tell us which stories you liked or didn't. For #314, we received a scad of congratulations, but received so few comments on the actual stories that the voting was completely inconclusive.

Ah to have *but a fraction* of one of those bulging *Startling Stories* mailbags!

Editorial Book Reviews
by Darrell Schweitzer

Pulp Culture: The Art of Fiction Magazines
by Frank M. Robinson & Lawrence Davidson
Collector's Press, Inc.
(P.O. Box 230986, Portland OR 97281)
1998, cloth, 204 pp. $39.95

Frank M. Robinson is the author of distinguished novels in various fields (*The Power*, *The Glass Inferno*, this latter with Thomas Scortia).

Lawrence Davidson has interviewed hundreds of fiction writers on his radio program, including many pulpsters.

Together, drawing largely from Robinson's legendary collection of pulp magazines, they have here provided us with a glorious, nostalgic journey through the lurid delights of yesteryear.

There have been other books of pulp-magazine artwork, but this one is special. Technically, it is the finest yet done, with computer-mediated repairs to some of the covers, which have cleaned up rips and wrinkles, and brought out the colors until they glow like new.

Sometimes, admittedly, the covers of pulp magazines were better than the contents. I don't know that anyone wants to read very much of the contents of, say, *Terror Tales* (a "sex-and-sadism" pulp which superficially resembled *Weird Tales* but had the ridiculous formula that all the supernatural menaces had to turn out to be fakes); but the covers are kind of fun, in the way that the posters to '50s exploitation films are fun. And what about *Zeppelin Stories*, purveyor of that immortal classic, "The Gorilla of the Gasbags" or, for that matter, *Harlem Stories*, which attempted to appeal to black readers without transcending stereotypes? Then there were *Saucy Movie Stories* and *Spicy Mystery Stories* and several others of, let us say, dubious reader appeal today. To be fair, one wishes one could read some of the issues of *Black Mask* and *Oriental Stories* and the first issue of *Weird Tales* or that legendary rarity, *The Thrill Book*, which was almost a weird/fantasy magazine until the publisher chickened out and diluted it with straight adventure.

This book is a pictorial history of the entire pulp era, from its beginnings at the turn of the century (when covers were pure as the driven snow and often of high aesthetic merit) down through the pulp magazines' heyday of the '20s, then into the '30s and '40s when a kind of decadence set in, as pulps over-specialized (and H.P. Lovecraft commented that the next thing he expected would be a pulp called *New England Newsboy Adventures*) and the covers became more cluttered. There was a strange sidestep into soft-core pornography in the '30s, with all those "Spicy," "Saucy," and such titles — though there was not, alas, ever a *Spicy Zeppelin Stories*, the authors quickly point out.

You will see many, very famous covers: Jack Williamson's favorite tiger-in-the-sky painting for the *Weird Tales* serialization is reproduced in all its glory on page 5. The *Tarzan of the Apes* issue of *All-Story* is present, of course, as are many, many rarities most of us are never going to see in the (so to speak) flesh.

The book also includes pricing information of these pulp magazines, and for this we have our only quibble: the prices strike us as a little high and must apply only to the very finest copies. The Williamson *Weird Tales* (April 1933) is listed as being worth in excess of a hundred dollars. In our experience, you can find one a lot cheaper if you hunt around at conventions a bit. Perhaps not as fine a copy as depicted here, but you can find it. As for *Zeppelin Stories*, maybe not.

Arthur Clarke & Lord Dunsany:
A Correspondence
edited by Keith Allen Daniels
Anamnesis Press
(P.O. Box 51115, Palo Alto CA 94303)
1998, 84pp., $19.95

This is a book for the specialist, a bit pricey for a trade paperback of its size; but there will be specialists (your editor among them) who will just have to have it.

Sir Arthur Clarke is, of course, one of the greatest living science-fiction writers, and a leading visionary of the space age.

Lord Dunsany was one of the century's great fantasy writers, who has also been (posthumously) a regular contributor to *Weird Tales*. It is because of this connection that we're reviewing the present book.

Clarke struck up a correspondence with Dunsany in 1944, when Clarke was 30 and Dunsany 66. Dunsany was still actively writing, though his greatest works, *The Book of Wonder, The King of Elfland's Daughter,* etc. were decades behind him. But Dunsany wasn't living in the past. What attracted Clarke to him was Dunsany's poetry about outer space. The early correspondence is largely about the dawning space age, which Clarke could see clearly. Dunsany's grasp of technical matters was less sure, but he too looked outward beyond the Earth. Both of them appreciated the aesthetics. Later letters move on to other topics, of considerable literary interest. Here we see Dunsany's first reaction to Lovecraft ("I see Lovecraft borrowed my style, and I don't grudge it to him.") and his responses to Clarke's own fiction.

The two discuss chess. They touch on numerous matters, literary and scientific. Clarke fishes for a Dunsanian blurb for his soon-to-be bestseller *The Exploration of Space* (and is a trifle embarrassed about his boldness in the afterword.)

An extremely worthwhile volume. Recommended.

The Boss in the Walls
by Avram Davidson and Grania Davis
Tachyon Publications
(1459 18th St. #139, San Francisco CA 94107)
1998, 122 pp., $50 (limited hardcover), $12.00 (trade paperback).

Both of your editors confess we are too much involved in Davidsonian affairs to review this volume, but we thought our readers would like to know that it has been published.

Avram Davidson was one of the all-time great fantasy writers. He was the subject of a special issue of *Weird Tales* in 1989 and graced our pages many times thereafter. He was the author of *The Phoenix and the Mirror, The Adventures of Dr. Eszterhazy,* and numerous other classics.

This posthumous novella, completed by his sometime collaborator and former wife from extensive scenes, fragments, and outlines, is as erudite as anything Avram wrote, scarier than most, and of interest to his many fans, or just to anybody who enjoys imagination and good writing. Ω

We moved again — sort of. Our publisher, Warren Lapine and his publishing company, DNA Publications, Inc., have just removed to PO Box 2988, Radford VA 24143–2988. This is where you should send *your* change of address. Always let us know your old address (with ZIP code) and of course your new address, also with ZIP code. Your copy of Weird Tales® is less likely to miss you if you let us know your new address a few weeks in advance. Our *editorial* address remains at:
123 Crooked Lane, King of Prussia PA 19406–2570.

THE DEN

by S.T. Joshi

The recent departure of James Turner as managing editor of Arkham House allows us to reflect upon his achievements during his more than twenty years as editorial director of the leading small press in the field of weird fiction, and also to consider whether any legitimate successors to Arkham House's position are in the offing.

To contemporary readers, all too many of whom are unaware that horror fiction did indeed flourish before the advent of Stephen King, the mystique that Arkham House continues to hold may perhaps be puzzling. Certainly, the fact that this publishing firm was founded by August Derleth and Donald Wandrei initially for the sole purpose of preserving H.P. Lovecraft's work in hardcover made Arkham House a monument to the devotion that friendship can inspire. The uniformity of design that Arkham House preserved under Derleth's editorship (with the celebrated "Holliston Black Novelex" covers and their gold spine stamping) lent an added distinctiveness to its publications. But Arkham House gained its devotees chiefly by being the principal hardcover publisher of such pulp legends as Lovecraft, Clark Ashton Smith, Robert E. Howard, and Seabury Quinn, along with such of their disciples as Robert Bloch, Ramsey Campbell, and Brian Lumley. Let it pass that much of what Arkham House published would probably never have been published by other hardcover firms on the basis of its actual quality: Arkham House's line nurtured a nostalgia for the pulp magazines even among those who had never lived during the pulp era.

Arkham House itself, of course, is by no means *passé*, although it was quiescent for much of 1996 and 1997. But over the last decade a number of other small presses have emerged to take up the slack in the wake of Arkham House's relative paucity of publications and its shift to "cutting edge" science fiction.

That shift — a significant point of criticism on the part of Arkham House loyalists and devotees of weird fiction in general — was in fact never as complete as many have believed. To be sure, books by Michael

Bishop, Greg Bear, Lucius Shepard, Bruce Sterling, and other young science-fiction writers represented an increasing number of the two or three books that Arkham House annually published; some of these volumes did indeed have a significant horror content, but by and large they belonged in the realm of science fiction. We tend to forget, however, that Turner also arranged for the republication of Clark Ashton Smith's best work (*A Rendezvous in Averoigne* [1988]), and issued landmark collections of the fantasy tales of Tanith Lee (*Dreams of Dark and Light* [1986]) and the horror fiction of Ramsey Campbell (*Alone with the Horrors* [1993]). And, of course, there were the textually corrected editions of H.P. Lovecraft's work produced under my editorship, along with such Lovecraftian anthologies as the revised *Tales of the Cthulhu Mythos* (1990) and *Cthulhu 2000* (1995). Even if some of Turner's other selections in the horror/fantasy field were suspect (David Case's *The Third Grave* [1981], David Kesterton's *The Darkling* [1982]), his continued nurturing of Russell Kirk and Basil Copper is noteworthy.

And yet, the gradual but inexorable shift from horror and fantasy to science fiction, under Turner's aegis, had some interesting and perhaps unexpected consequences. While each of the Arkham House publications remained impeccable both in design and in intrinsic literary quality, it is somewhat ironic that Arkham House had almost no impact upon the horror "boom" of the late 1970s and 1980s. Perhaps, indeed, it could not have; for with horror becoming a spectacularly commercial phenomenon with such best-selling writers as Stephen King, Peter Straub, Clive Barker, and Anne Rice, a small press could not possibly compete with the million-dollar advances offered by major publishers.

There is perhaps a still further irony: that "boom," now finally dying of inanition, has produced relatively little work of lasting literary merit; and now that the horror market is contracting in the commercial arena, perhaps it is once again time that small-press publishers in the field take their rightful position as both the preservers of the heritage of weird fiction and the vanguards of new and pioneering work.

Have any such publishers emerged? Several candidates are certainly putting themselves forward. Ash-Tree Press (P.O. Box 1360, Ashcroft, BC, Canada V0K 1A0) has in the last few years published a surprising number of reprints of classic ghost stories, and deserves the admiration of weird fiction devotees for its resurrection of the work of A.M. Burrage, H.R. Wakefield, E.G. Swain, and others. These reprints might be seen as analogous to Arkham House's reprints of the best work from the pulp magazines; but of course Arkham House was not content merely to revive older work, but actively fostered newer writing, something Ash-Tree has not done to any great extent. Moreover, the Ash-Tree Press books have extremely small print runs and are very expensive (something that does not seem to have changed even with the proprietors' move from England to Canada).

These same virtues and drawbacks also affect R.B. Russell's Tartarus Press (5 Birch Terrace, Hangingbirch Lane, Horam, East Sussex TN21 0PA, England), which — similar to August Derleth's founding of Arkham House initially for the purpose of publishing Lovecraft's work in hardcover — began life devoted to the salvaging of Arthur Machen's fugitive writings. Russell has done outstanding work in gathering Machen's uncollected or unreprinted fiction (*Ritual and Other Stories* [1992; rev. ed. 1997]; *Ornaments in Jade* [1997]), issuing some of his immense body of essays and journalism (*The Secret of the Sangraal and Other Writings* [1995]), and even promoting criticism of Machen's life and work (*Machenalia* [1990]). Lately Russell has ventured into other realms, issuing the work of the modern Welsh writer Rhys Hughes (*Worming the Harpy and Other Bitter Pills*) and editing a volume of previously unpublished stories, *Tales from Tartarus* [1995]). He has also published my edition of the selected writings of the obscure nineteenth-century Irish writer Henry Ferris (*A Night with Mephistopheles* [1997]). But, as with Ash-Tree, the extremely limited print runs of Tartarus Press books (sometimes as few as 200 copies) make Russell's enterprise virtually invisible.

Necronomicon Press (P.O. Box 1304, West Warwick, RI 02893) has recently engaged in reissuing Clark Ashton Smith's work in thematically arranged volumes (*Tales of Zothique* [1995]; *The Book of Hyperborea* [1996]), not to mention such curiosities as Ramsey Campbell's sword-&-sorcery tales (*Far Away & Never* [1996]) and the round-robin novel *Ghor, Kin-Slayer* (1997), based on a fragment by Robert E. Howard; but its series of chapbooks of original fiction has regrettably gone into abeyance. Instead, it continues to focus on Lovecraft's own work (*The Ancient Track* [1998], an edition of his complete poetry) or criticism of his life and work (my biography [1996], the first Necronomicon Press hardcover).

There are many other worthy small presses in our field, ranging from Kenneth Abner's Terminal Fright Publications (P.O. Box 100, Black River, NY 13612), which should be remembered if it issues nothing other than Brian McNaughton's scintillating collection of fantasy tales, *The Throne of Bones* [1997]) to Sam Gafford's Hobgoblin Press (P.O. Box 806, Bristol, RI 02809), which is about to embark on the ambitious enterprise of issuing the complete works of William Hope Hodgson in thirteen or so volumes, to Perry M. Grayson's Tsathoggua Press (6442 Pat Avenue, West Hills, CA 91307), devoted to works by or about Frank Belknap Long, Clark Ashton Smith, and others of the Lovecraft circle. But perhaps the most notable small press of recent years is Fedogan & Bremer (3721 Minnehaha Avenue South, Minneapolis, MN 55406).

This company began existence in the late 1980s on a somewhat curious premise: it was consciously determined to succeed Arkham House by publishing those works which August Derleth or Donald Wandrei had, as early as the 1960s, announced for publication but never in fact issued. And yet, F&B's first "publication" was not a book but a tape recording of Lovecraft's sonnet cycle *Fungi from Yuggoth* (1986), capably read by John Arthur, although the musical background by Michael Olson is a little too obtrusive and "New Age" for my taste. Another three years passed before F&B actually issued a volume: Donald Wandrei's *Colossus* (1989; out of print). This book had indeed been announced for publication in various Arkham House catalogues, but the finished book does not duplicate Wandrei's conception for it. He had envisioned it to contain nothing more than the long story "Colossus" (1934), its even longer sequel "Colossus Eternal" (1934), and a lengthy introduction. (Wandrei had told Richard L. Tierney that there was to be a third, unpublished story as well, but whether this story was ever written is in doubt; if it was, it was not found among Wandrei's effects after his death on October 15, 1987.) Evidently the editors of the F&B *Colossus*, Philip J. Rahman and Dennis E. Weiler, found this idea too constricting, so they chose to issue a large volume containing the entirety of Wandrei's science-fiction tales, gathered from his previous Arkham House volumes (*The Eye and the Finger* [1944] and *Strange Harvest* [1965]) and containing several uncollected tales as well. It was not until eight years later that F&B got around to issuing the tales of horror and fantasy for which Wandrei is best known, but that volume has now finally emerged: *Don't Dream* (1997).

These two volumes allow, for perhaps the first time, a comprehensive study of Wandrei's work as a writer of imaginative fiction. While I do not have the space here to conduct such a study, I can at least suggest some avenues for exploration. In the first place, the distinction between "horror" and "science fiction" is pretty tenuous in Wandrei's work; like his mentor Lovecraft, Wandrei was a pioneer in the fusion of these two realms. The editors of these two volumes acknowledge that in some cases the distinction is merely a matter of emphasis.

Wandrei's earliest fictional works were sketches or prose poems in the *Minnesota Quarterly*, the student magazine at the University of Minnesota. Several of these (mostly gathered in a separate section of "Prose Poems, Essays, and Marginalia" in *Don't Dream*) are uncommonly fine, revealing a verbal witchery that would endure throughout Wandrei's literary career. But as early as 1927, when he was nineteen, Wandrei had broken into *Weird Tales* with "The Red Brain," and for the next half-dozen years that magazine would be his chief market. But when *Astounding Stories* revived under Street & Smith's ownership in 1933, Wandrei quickly switched gears and wrote a substantial number of science-fiction tales that made him one of the luminaries of the pre-John W. Campbell era. These latter stories are, of course, chiefly gathered in *Colossus*, although a fair number appear in *Don't Dream*. Along the way Wandrei also broke into such rarefied markets as *Esquire* and *Argosy*.

Lovecraft believed that Wandrei possessed one of the most genuinely cosmic imaginations of any writer he knew, and certainly this is his chief distinguishing characteristic. "The Red Brain" (originally titled "The Twilight of Time") is perhaps a somewhat juvenile expression of the idea, but the tale still works for me. Even now I get a kick in reading the story's conclusion, when the only hope of halting the spread of the "Cosmic Dust" that is overwhelming all entity seems to reside in the brain of the title: "The hope of the universe had lain with the Red Brain. And the Red Brain was mad."

Then there is "Colossus," recognized as a landmark of science fiction even though it seems to raise more chuckles than thrills today. But I remain capable of suspending my disbelief at the thought of a spaceship that can "reach a maximum velocity of thousands of light-years, *per second!*" and thereby break through the known space-time continuum into another realm in which our own universe is itself but an atom. (At the same time, of course, the inhabitants of the spacecraft become as large as our universe, rendering it impossible for them ever to return to it.) "Colossus" is a story whose breadth of scope is such that it could not be encompassed within a single story, and its sequel — although no doubt inspired also by commercial considerations — thereby became a necessity.

In both his science-fiction and his horror tales, Wandrei is capable of achieving certain moments of utterly unnerving terror or awe that go far in redeeming his several deficiencies — occasionally slipshod writing, clumsiness in the handling of plot sequences, wooden or unconvincing characters, and poor dialogue. Perhaps his best weird tale is "The Eye and the Finger" (*Esquire*, December 1936), a madly irrational tale in which an ordinary man returns to his cheerless apartment to find a disembodied eye on the top of his bureau and, later, a hand hanging in midair with its finger pointed directly at him. No explanation is made to account for these bizarre events; they simply occur, and the diction is so matter-of-fact that we are compelled to believe it. "The Tree-Men of M'Bwa" (*Weird Tales*, February 1932) is not far behind in its depiction of individuals who have become living trees.

Wandrei's literary career was largely over by 1940. Why this is the case has never been satisfactorily explained. Richard L. Tierney's long and detailed introduction to *Colossus* offers some hints, but no more. Certainly, Wandrei's induction into the army in 1942 would not have allowed much time for creative work; but even upon his discharge in 1945 he made no effort to renew his literary career with the exception of preparing his novel *The Web of Easter Island* for publication in 1948. Of course, Wandrei was spending a great deal of time editing Lovecraft's letters (and it should be noted that the final two volumes of *Selected Letters*, appearing in 1976, seem largely to be based upon compilations by Wandrei even though they do not bear his name as coeditor), and Tierney asserts that it was Wandrei who did the bulk of the selection and editing of Derleth's fine anthology of macabre poetry, *Dark of the Moon* (1947). Over the next several years he engaged in brief stints at comic-book writing and songwriting, but only a few stories were produced.

By the 1950s, however, fortunes took a marked turn for the worse for Wandrei's family, and he was forced to spend more and more time taking care of his ailing mother and sister. The death of his brother Howard in 1956 did not help matters. In letters to Derleth, Wandrei frequently announced that he was at work on a variety of massive philosophical or aesthetic treatises, none of which were published and may not have been completed or even begun. His last work of fiction appears to have been the poignant end-of-the-world story, "Requiem for Mankind," published in Derleth's final anthology, *Dark Things* (1971).

I may note here that in 1932 and 1933 Wandrei wrote two novels in quick succession. One of them — whose original title was *Dead Titans, Waken!* — is what we know as *The Web of Easter Island*. The other — long thought to be lost — survives in manuscript as *Invisible Sun*. This latter is a mainstream novel, although with occasional fantastic elements, and contains some of Wandrei's finest and most daring writing. The manuscript for *Dead Titans, Waken!* also survives, and is markedly different from its later revision; a case could be made that it is somewhat more effective in its original form. These two novels will be published by F&B in one volume under my editorship.

F&B's most significant contribution to weird fiction to date is the publication of two volumes of Howard Wandrei's fiction, *Time Burial* (1995) and *The Last Pin* (1997); the first contains his horror and fantasy fiction, the second some of his detective tales. I had previously known next to nothing of Howard Wandrei aside from the fact that he was a superlatively brilliant artist and illustrator; as for his fiction, I could recall nothing save for Lovecraft's quip when he heard the title of Wandrei's "The Hand of the O'Mecca": "It sounds like an Irish Arab." Later, when Lovecraft actually read that story, he remarked in a letter to R.H. Barlow (April 20, 1935): "I'm hang'd if I don't think the kid is, all apart from his pictorial genius, getting to be a better *writer* than big bwuvver!" There is good reason to believe that Lovecraft was right.

I actually wish to consider Wandrei's detective stories first, even though they are obviously outside the purview of the weird tale. Although Wandrei initially attempted to duplicate his brother Donald's success in horror fiction, and had a few items published in *Weird Tales,* by the 1930s he seemed to sense that hard-boiled mystery was where his strengths lay.

He quickly gained a foothold in both the "spicy" pulps issued by Culture Publications and the various magazines of the Trojan Publishing Corporation chain. These latter, like the spicies, wanted a lacing of sex and nudity — which also seems to have come naturally to Howard, as it rarely did to his more strait-laced brother Donald — but, unlike the spicies, wanted no incursion of the supernatural. The result was a really admirable series of substantial novelettes written under a variety of pseudonyms. Perhaps they are not quite up to the Raymond Chandler standard — but then, whose are?

Two of the most piquant are "The Man with the Molten Face" and "League of Bald Men," which both feature a unique detective — Ferris Gerard, the mayor of the small town of Niles Park, who had suffered a horrible accident in which much of his face was mutilated. A remarkable surgical operation, using some sort of resin to take the place of his destroyed jaw, allows Gerard literally to remold his face at will and thereby conceal his identity. Implausible as this may be, Wandrei manages to pull it off. "League of Bald Men" is to my mind one of the most enthralling tales ever to come out of the detective pulps; with little alteration it could be adapted today into an exciting action film. Many of the other tales in *The Last Pin* are not far behind.

Wandrei was apparently forced by magazine requirements to throw in a certain amount of sex or sexual situations beyond the requirements of the narrative; but it is interesting to note that, according to a note by D.H. Olson, editor of the two Howard Wandrei books, "the versions of [some of the] stories reprinted here . . . are appreciably more risqué than those which were actually printed" in the magazines. Wandrei had a particular flair for describing women's costumes and overall appearance; he displays far more

knowledge than most male writers do in points of clothing, makeup, and the like.

The interesting thing is that many of the stories in *Time Burial* are also of the hard-boiled type, but of course they cross the line into the supernatural. Perhaps this would not have been a surprise to the original readers of the magazines (notably *Spicy Mystery Stories*), since this mingling of detection and the weird was the premise on which these magazines were based. But reading these stories now, we gain an added thrill when we find some crime scenario veering off insidiously into the supernatural.

I do not find any moments of that clutching fear that distinguishes a few of Donald Wandrei's tales; but on the whole there can be no question that Howard Wandrei was a notably more polished and skillful writer than his brother.

D.H. Olson's lengthy introductions to both *Time Burial* and *The Last Pin* should be singled out for praise. Although they in part cover the same ground (understandably so, since the books are designed for different audiences), they tell a compelling story of Howard Wandrei's strange life — a life that included an arrest for burglary at the age of seventeen and several years spent in a reformatory, a turbulent marriage, suspicion of wrongdoing in the later 1940s when some members of Trojan Publications were indicted for embezzlement, and an early death of cirrhosis of the liver.

Two more volumes of Howard Wandrei's mystery tales are promised, along with at least one volume of Donald's detective tales. If F&B had done nothing but issue these books by the Wandrei brothers, they would deserve the gratitude of lovers of the weird.

I have not left myself much space to discuss F&B's several other publications, even though these other titles are somewhat uneven. Robert M. Price has produced two volumes of "Cthulhu Mythos" barrel-scrapings in *Tales of the Lovecraft Mythos* and *The New Lovecraft Circle,* and F&B has made another error in publishing Richard L. Tierney's disappointing Mythos novel, *The House of the Toad.* But they are to be commended for issuing Karl Edward Wagner's last story collection, *Exorcisms and Ecstasies,* two collections of Hugh B. Cave's work, *The Door Below* and *Death Stalks the Night,* and books by Robert Bloch, Basil Copper, Carl Jacobi, and other standbys. On the whole, the F&B line shows careful judgment in the publication of old-time pulp material as well as newer work. It and other small presses may well be leaving commercial firms behind in perpetuating the best that our field has to offer.   Ω

THE MAD ARAB RETURNS

Higgeldy piggeldy, Abdul Alhazred came
Back from the Darkness to pen something new.
His agent had told him, "Your readers are raving.
Sequels are hot, Ab; write *Al Azif II*"

— Lawrence Barker

STARS ABOVE, STARS BELOW
by Tanith Lee

illustrated by Stephen E. Fabian

When the dust-storm had ended, Taira walked out into the desert. A court woman, she could not travel quite unattended. But she left her guard at the Temple of the Gate, pretending she was going in to pray. And her little slave, Aspa, she left in the last oasis by the road. By now, used to her whims, Aspa did not scold her; he was ten years old, at eight he had been impossible.

Taira walked along the road, then off the road into the rust-coloured desert, which was, in the sunfall, the soft shade of a fading, browning rose.

One final palm tree stood up from the dunes. A huge red palm, with beneath it a small altar to the desert God. Votary offerings left there had been covered with fine pink sand from the storm-breath of the God, who was savage, thankless, and unkind.

Taira's feet were bare, for court women went barefoot in the palace and city, whose floors and upper streets were kept as smooth as glass. Warmth remained in the sand like a caress. She found this comforting, yet the comfort was useless. Everything had been tinged by utter loss. It was so enormous that she scarcely felt it as anything separate. The loss had become like breathing, or even awareness. Loss was not a condition of life. Since the age of fourteen, Taira had served the priestess-queen Het-Ambaret. And this month, Het-Ambaret had died. Already the death ritual had been spoken. There was one line of it which said: *The lamp of my heart has been put out. Though it may again be lighted, never again will it burn with the same flame of love.*

Tonight, when the Lion Moon rose, the death barge would set sail upon the river. Taira would stand in the barge behind the sarcophagus of Het-Ambaret. It was a journey of three nights and two days, to reach the Tomb.

Taira, the chief maiden of a priestess-queen, was proud. She did not want anyone to see her weep. So she walked into the desert of Kumr Ar to do it. And here she was, a mile from the marble city, a mile from the cool river.

Dimly on the sky, the city lights glimmered, and Taira caught the strands of some music, teased out by the last wind-breath of the desert God. Above, the stars had unveiled themselves; and the little moon, the Kid, was coming up, tiny and almost opaque; but later the smallest of all, the Blue Moon, would rise, glowing, the Virgin.

Peace lay in the cup of the desert, as well as terror and violence. For this Taira had come here. But as she stood alone, and composed herself for grief, no tears rushed from her eyes. She felt their pain, their scald, but no release.

She thought that she, a being of red amber like the planet, must now be growing dry like the planet, barren of water. But the planet was old, and she was young.

Taira thought deeply of Het-Ambaret. Her grace and beauty, her playfulness, her serenity, her gentleness. She had never struck Taira, or any of her women. And once, when Taira had been sad, over some love-affair, Het-Ambaret had singled her out, and come to console here, staying with her a whole afternoon. A Skilled huntress, Het-Ambaret had even once brought Taira a portion of the kill, a sign of high favour, at which the surrounding court clapped, laughing, praising Taira and wishing her good fortune.

And now Het-Ambaret lay in her gilded coffin-box, which showed on its painted lid the image of the priestess-queen as she had been in life.

Thinking still, Taira could not weep.

So she thought of Het-Ambaret divining in the temple of her Goddess, moving among the sacred things, pausing, selecting, while the priests wrote her findings on their slates. She had seldom been wrong, even in great age. As, in age, she had never lost her beauty, becoming only thinner, and more inclined to meditate and to sleep. At last she slept and did not wake. It was Taira who found her, in her gilded chair on the terrace. The moons were high in the sky, all three, the Blue Virgin the smallest and lowest and brightest of them, giving her lucency to the night like water.

Long ago, Het-Ambaret would have gone up to the highest roof, and sat there, all her ladies about her, if the had the energy to climb so far up the palace steps; sometimes Taira followed alone. And then quite often Het-Ambaret would vanish away. The cool of night would grow chilly even in summer. The women often walked down again without their queen, knowing that she had sought solitude, and was communing with the heavens.

Thinking, thinking, still, still Taira could not weep. She gazed up into the sky. The little pale-grey moon had moved some way, and already she should turn back.

She had not shed her tears. They lay inside her like drops of hot iron. Dry like the planet, dry with sorrow, Taira returned across the desert.

At the oasis, Aspa came out without a word, and pattered after her, carrying her folded wooden parasol. At the Temple of the Gate, the guardsman, not know-

by Tanith Lee

ing where Taira had gone, complacently fell in behind the boy.

Along the glass-smooth marble streets they went, towards the palace of columns, the stair, the quay where the barge waited on the river.

Gongs sounded from the temples and all the high places of the city, to mark the rising of the Lion Moon, which was white, like lions of the desert.

The death barge of Het-Ambaret slid from the quay, itself a phantom.

The women sang: "She will go up . . ."

Ten rowers dipped and stirred with their oars, making hardly any sound start from the thick, shining waters of the river. Above, against the darkness, lit by all its red and rosy lights, the polished sandstone columns railed the façades of slender buildings, the great open windows, hung each one with a fretted golden or silver lamp. To the river's edge descended terraced gardens, planted with palms and traceried tinsel trees, where night birds called in wild moon-voices. But all these things swam by, and were soon gone. The lesser, more sombre fringes of the city soon appeared, and wharfs lit by fire-baskets, where soldiers stood, raising their spears to salute the barge. Then the wharfs gave way to vineyards and to fields, pierced by canals, until everything melted into the desert. Presently, on the farthest inland horizon, three tall, volcanic mountains were visible, and farthest of all a volcano called the Torch, on which a blush of flame faintly flickered always.

The river grew wider then, opening out, and the desert, and its intermittent garland of palms, moved to a distance. Now there were predominantly only night and water.

It became cold. The river flowed here from the Mountains of Ice. All rivers flowed from these mountains. All rivers flowed from these mountains, crossing by and through the cities built mathematically on their banks, and so on down to the abstract Sea of Smokes. But the Place of the Tombs was not so far away as that.

The Kid was low in the sky now, and the Blue Virgin smouldered between the volcanoes. Around the white Lion, stars burned in clusters. The river shone, but nothing reflected in its movement save in fragments, not even stars or moons.

In an arbor at the boat's centre, the painted case lay, with the queen in it. How small the coffin looked.

Two ladies sat on either side, and two at the front. But Taira must stand behind the coffin, a sentinel. It was her duty, and the honour shown her.

Over her head hung the veil of mourning.

The women sang, sobbing sometimes, the death hymn. Taira listened. But the hymn seemed remote, not even sorrowful. The barge was ghostly; and the passing of the city, the threads of land now unravelling on either side, here and there set with an oasis, or some monument or statue, interested her but vaguely, so her mind wandered.

She will go up among the stars.
Like a star she will live among the stars.
She will be winged as the stars
Are winged, with light.

The soft drum beat in the stern, making the stroke for the rowers.

If one looked carefully, on a clear night, a lion's face might be made out on the surface of the Lion Moon. But Taira could not see it. After an hour or so, another dust-storm, rising elsewhere on the land, obscured the lion's face with a tawny veil like Taira's own.

The colouring of Taira's people was inside one spectrum. The hair, if undyed, mahogany red, the eyes reddish bronze, jasper, amber, the skin all the tones of reddish tan, from shades like powder to the depth of a copper mirror. But Het-Ambaret had been of another kind. She was generally black, and her eyes gold, freckled with shadow.

This the painting on the cask-lid showed exactly.

As the barge continued downriver, sometimes people came by day to the banks, and threw flowers into the water. Or, at certain points, where temples of the Goddess had been built, a privileged few might row out, and be permitted, while the barge was at anchor, to step on board.

Children stared at the painting of Het-Ambaret in wonder.

There were others of the queen's kind, but in this region only seven, and now she was gone.

"Was she truly black?" the children asked Taira.

"As black as night," said Taira.

"But her eyes were golden stars," said a little boy, prophetically. Taira thought of Aspa, who was not prophetic at all.

The other women were moved. They cried openly. But Taira's tears stayed locked inside, hurting against her.

"She was the loveliest and best," said Taira, in a calm voice.

This was on the first day, and in the purple sky the sun blazed.

At noon, the barge again put down anchor. Under an awning, the women slept, as the rowers slept at their oars. Taira did not sleep. This was part of the ritual, and a herbal wine had been prepared, to help her stay wakeful. But Taira felt no need to sleep, had forgotten sleep.

The women had begun to tell her, from a few days after the queen's death, that they saw Het-Ambaret in their dreams. The priestess-queen was alive then, and spoke to them in her own magical language, which they had partially come over the years to understand. Her voice, as they recalled, was like a pale golden chime.

In the dreams, she was as she had been in her youth, plumper, and silken haired; but also she now, of course, had wings.

From Taira alone, pain apparently excluded such a

visitation. Not once had she dreamed of the priestess-queen, though during Het-Ambaret's life, Taira had often dreamed of her. And as the post-mortem dreams failed Taira, so she had gradually given up sleep. In a way, it was similar with her tears; she would not, then could not shed them.

Today as the rest slept, she sat by the coffin-cask, and leaned her cheek against the planed wood. She spoke to Het-Ambaret in her mind. There were no reproaches — Why did you leave me? — mortal things had little choice.

Instead Taira thought, *Do you remember all those years ago, when we were so young, and we played the ball game in court?* Or, *Remember how happy we were when you first predicted the end of the drought, and the rain came, the first in two years* . . . But then, *Oh, where are you?*

In the ancient time of myth there had been a Flood, which covered all things. But before that time, the stories said, people had been winged even in life, and had flown out to the moons, even to a place on the tiny Blue Moon, and built cities there. This country of the Blue Moon was like Kmur Ar, the Red Land, also a desert, with one vast river.

Myth told too how the Land of Life beyond life had its entrance in the skies between the planet and the Blue Moon. Here the planet's river flowed up mysteriously into the purple sky. At first there was sunset, and then night, black night sown thick with stars. But one would know it was not the night of the land of mortal life. Because all at once the river, though it still flowed onwards, turned also to utter black, and was set with stars. So you drifted in your boat of death, between the star-gilded banks, where silver palm trees grew, and stars shone bright above, and just as bright and fixed they shone below in the river, and there was the sound of mystical sweet pure singing, beyond all physical voices ever heard.

At last, a sunrise would commence at the end of the river of stars, and here the Afterlife began.

The Afterlife held no censure, no punishment for any, and even for the worst transgression there was merely teaching, grief, empathic penitence and expiation. Which would at last fade away into the delight and freedom of eternity. But no one had described, even in myth, the nature of the Afterlife, beyond its indescribable bliss. They told only of the river of stars above and stars below which led serenely into it.

Het-Ambaret was supposedly there.

I must recollect that she is, thought Taira. *I must hope that she is.*

And she was, if so, glad for Het-Ambaret. So glad. But she thought too that never again in ordinary life would she, Taira, be able to see or hear Het-Ambaret, or softly smooth and comb her hair, or feel the warmth of her touch, or smell the fragrance of her — not once. This was as if it had been said to Taira, *Summer will never return* — or worse — *Summer never was real.*

They passed three more cities. At the third a great ceremony was held, and hundreds of voices soared in the hymn to the dead. Gold and silver and jewels flashed, and flocks of birds clouded from the trees, while the sacred Ibu dippered their beaks in the river. The scaled river serpents which had legs, padded up to the bank. They were thrown bread soaked in wine and red honey. They snapped the loaves up, jaws clashing, and the Ibu drew back, offended.

Taira, many nights and days now without sleep, her blood full of unshed tears, felt pain like a spike driven through her. So much *life* — and this little death that filled the world. She seemed herself so light her feet did not meet the deck of the boat.

She drank some of the herbal wine. Not to keep from slumber — for surely she would never sleep again — but to stop her thirst — her dryness, her drought.

They poured honey before Het-Ambaret's cask, and put down dishes of baked meat and river fish, and beer and milk, for her Goddess liked all these things, and she had liked some of them.

A handsome man from a high family leant over the coffin and laid on it a pink lily, the kind that grew tall among the reeds. Het-Ambaret's women fluttered, even in their sadness. On his long dark hair the sun found streams of brilliant copper red; his eyes and skin were very dark.

That evening, just before the barge departed on the last stretch of the journey, this man came aboard again, and bowed to Taira.

"Lady, may I hope to see you again, in happier times?"

"You are kind," she said, "to wish me happier times."

"At the great city below the Torch, in a month, might I visit you? Meanwhile, may your sorrow leave you and joy return."

She saw in his dark eyes a promise of sexual desire, and perhaps more, perhaps the ember of love. Only these had made him precipitate. He was not unsympathetic. At any other hour she would have quickened. But not now.

She smiled sadly at him. She was too courteous to say, *Do not trouble.*

The rowers rowed them away.

The swift sunset poured out like red honey into moments of lilac twilight. The night rose, with all the stars above.

Taira thought of Het-Ambaret, her body held firm and pristine by the embalming of the priests.

Taira thought of kissing for the last time the soft brow of the priestess-queen, which had grown cold, and hollow and doll-like with death. And of her shut eyes, the suns of which would never be revealed again.

Taira's tears moved behind her whole face, a wall of water, a Flood, the inundation. But all her doors were locked against them. She had lost the key.

On the third night, they came to the City of the Dead, which lay far downriver, but still many miles from the Sea of Smokes, where all the planet's waters finally perished in boiling steam — so travelers declared.

The drum had stopped beating. The rowers raised their oars. The barge rocked mildly, and the current alone moved it.

They drifted in among rows of towering tombs, which ran for miles beside the river and out into the dunes, and even went down into the water itself, like marble and sandstone animals which had come there to drink.

Reeds grew here taller than a palace guard, whose head must always at least touch the lintel of each city's Soldiers House. The pink lilies had gathered in nets, and the purple irises which matched the sky. But now the lilies were simply pale, and the iris black.

There was a colonnade of pillars that led away from the river. The river ran off in a canal there, between them. The barge went into the canal without any guidance.

A current existed in the canal, perhaps natural, quite swift.

The rowers sat silent at their oars, and the women sat silent. But Taira raised her head and saw the stars above the columns, and under her hands she felt the wood of the painted box. She thought, *Now they will take even this from me.*

The death temple of Het-Ambaret's Goddess came from the night at the end of the canal. Before it had been made a great statue of the Goddess. Thought a giant, she was formed like any woman of Taira's people, but from the way her face had been carved, her nose and ears and mouth, one saw she was really of Het-Ambaret's kind.

She had a collar of skeins of colored precious stones, and earrings of gold. In her carven skirt was a door. Which, as the barge approached, moved slowly open without a sound.

The barge slipped in through the door, and dropped anchor.

Steps ascended from the water, to a terrace, where priests and priestesses were gathering now. They carried tapers, which burned like a thousand golden eyes of the dead.

The painted casket of the queen was taken up, and carried among the priesthood, and Taira walked after, her head held high. They were singing in the voices of life, the praises of Het-Ambaret. And Taira sang with them.

Suddenly, without shame or fear, without thought, the tears flooded easily from Taira's eyes, and dropped like heavy rain, striking her feet in hot, wet, unhurtful blows. It was so easy to weep, after all. It was so easy, so simple.

The light of the tapers glittered on her tears.

The hymn said now:

Her body is here, her body held in memory,
The memorial of our respect and honour,
The avowal of her beauty and virtue.
But she is in the land of life,
Where for ever she is living,
As in the heart, for ever she is loved.

All Het-Ambaret's women wept, loudly now, sobbing, and holding each other's hands. Taira with them.

The voices of the priesthood sang high up, sweet and pure, the prologue of supernatural songs to come.

For the beauty of the world was only an echo of a higher world.

All things must die, every man and woman, every beast, every tree and reed. Even the planet, Kmur Ar, the Red Land, one day would be a husk that lay empty upon the shore of a dusty sky. But the river of stars would remain.

Taira thought, I could not weep, it was impossible, and now I weep. It is so simple to weep. I could not love any other, but now I can, it is so simple to love. And I have thought it is impossible to live beyond death. But I shall live beyond death, and I shall see her again, and hold her in my arms, my queen, who lives beyond death now. And this too will be simple and easy. As easy as weeping.

For a moment, neither a vision nor a dream, only a thought, Taira saw Het-Ambaret flying, winged, with a star on her forehead. And Taira's tears in the taper light made the stone roof above sparkle, as if with stars, and where her tears had fallen on the stone floor, they sparkled too like the stars below. Ω

Author's note:

To speculate an ancient race might once have lived on the planet we call Mars, is fanciful, but not entirely ridiculous. More fanciful is, perhaps, the notion that at one time the 'Martians' reached the planet called by us Earth, and validated our own species. That a younger Mars generated water-courses seems to be a fact. But if so, fancy again conjures a recognizable resemblance between a waning desert Mars, her civilization clinging to the banks of yet-fertile rivers, and the Black Land of Egypt, a desert quenched only by the nurturing Nile.

In Egypt, certainly, the cat — whose kind may well have originated there — was loved and reverenced. Used in temples as diviners, and worshipped directly in the person of the cat goddess Bastet (Bast, Pasht), cats had servants and slaves allocated to them, and lived royally. If anyone killed a cat, the sentence was death — if the crowd had not already stoned the murderers or torn them in pieces. After their lives, sacred cats, like high-caste humans, were mummified, and buried, sometimes with regal and priestly rites, as the cat necropolis at Bubastis on the Nile bears witness.

As for the mysteries of true love and true loss, they have many forms, and are surely universal among any race, human or otherwise, which possesses imagination, compassion, and emotion. Ω

THE MONODON MONOCEROS

"The little whale with rare and giant horn,
The narwhal is one type of unicorn."

— **Anonymous Rime**

As grand as any fierce rhinoceros,
Archaic and majestic and uncouth,
Behold the *Monodon monoceros!*
His own straight horn is nothing more, in truth,
And nothing less than one long, huge, front tooth,
Evolved through time from need by nature's law:
Once prized for oil and ivory horn, forsooth,
As well as for those ivories in his jaw
The narwhal yet lives on! — a thing of miracle and awe:

Into what further stars, beyond all earthly care,
Might he, like other species past, himself withdraw,
With all his kind, to seek the seas of Otherwhere?

No fancy lingo can disguise that everything is linked:
His gain to Otherwhere means . . . here he would become
                                                extinct!

— **Donald Sidney-Fryer**

I MET A BEAST WITH CLOVEN THOUGHTS

I visited the wivern.
It began as a whim, on
summer nights when
Splinters of Stars passed
near enough to touch.

I've lost myself.
the muted wings of
the fiend spread across my mind;
into memories
echoing madly.

In the tabloids I had read
of people who disembark
and wander an astral
plane. Those nights I tried
to be like them. I floated,
or so I thought, above myself,
and tried to find my cat
who'd wandered off beneath
the moon.

wayward thoughts
themselves
burgeoning
mime-like
silent,
feeling utterly alien
with eyes like ice
this disjointed terror of
prey. let me think.

I found instead this wivern,
soaring above a land of
barren cliffs.
This creature thinks two
thoughts at once. It
makes me feel a bit unhinged.

a desperate worm
sodden,
stranger still
lost and cold
possesses me,
it truly does.

— **Steven Rogers**

UNTIL TIME CRACKS
by John B. Rosenman

illustrated by Fredrik King

Speers, the manager, didn't notice the figure until he was locking the theater doors. He watched it glide across the darkened stage, thinking that something in its manner was strangely familiar. After a moment he turned, waddled down the aisle, and stood directly before the stage.

"Here now, you'll have to leave!"

The figure froze, then turned toward him.

"The king my father! Dost thy spirit speak?"

Speers moved closer. "You're not supposed to be here, Mister. You have to go!"

An arm rose, thrust out at him. " 'Where wilt thou lead me? speak; I'll go no further.' "

Speers frowned, recognizing the line. Could this fool think he was Hamlet, meeting the ghost of his murdered father? Or maybe he was just drunk. Either way, Speers was not about to let an incident mar the play's successful run.

"If you don't leave, I'll call the police!"

"Say'st thou so, poor ghost? And dost thou *truly* see me?" The figure leapt forward and knelt at the front of the stage, window light bisecting its face.

Speers felt stunned. So quick, and spoken with such conviction! Now this nut knelt above him with half his face in darkness, half in moonlight. Speers rubbed his eyes as if to break a spell.

"Look," he faltered, "you can't —"

"Thy hand, my lord, and a leap of faith awaits!"

Speers blinked at the hand held down to him and reached up without thinking. Before he knew it, he was hoisted into the air, swung about, and deposited on stage. As he landed, a coin fell from his pocket and rolled across the boards.

"You must be mad!"

A dim smile. " 'I am but mad north-north-west: when the wind is southerly I know a hawk from a handsaw.' "

"Stop quoting from the play!"

"How shall I address thee, then? In the vulgar parlance of the times?"

"Yes!" Speers started to add something when he noticed how the man was dressed. Cloak, ruffs, doublet, hose, medallion . . . yep, the whole bit. As if it weren't enough to have a crazy who thought he was Hamlet, he had to *dress* like him as well!

Speers started to edge around the man, thinking that if he reached the control panel, he could shed enough sanity on the situation to dispel a hundred nut cases. Let him try reciting the bard in the glare of klieg lights!

But as he moved around him, the man majestically raised his hand. "Stay."

And Speers stayed. As if transfixed, he could go no farther.

"I'm not mistaken? You really *do* see me?" the man said, his language becoming more like that of the twentieth century.

Speers swallowed, wishing he had sent this lunatic flying through the door by now. But then, despite the poor light, he could tell that the man was far taller and more athletic than he. Not that it would be hard, for Speers, who had never married, was a squat man who had often heard himself called a 'fat little runt.' More than physical fear, though, there was something about this man that . . . held him.

"Yes," he said, "I really do see you."

"Praise the stars!" The man pressed his hand to his forehead in what should have been a ham actor's gesture but instead conveyed vast and compelling relief. Speers squinted, seeing the man's features more clearly. So sensitive and intelligent they were, so brooding and tormented.

The man dropped his hand and whirled, his elegant, patterned cloak swirling. Strange. Hadn't Hamlet worn a plain "inky cloak" to "denote" he was grieving for his father, the dead king? But then the play was so vast and Hamlet wore different costumes and displayed countless facets. Prince, philosopher, mourner, madman, lover and learned swordsman: these and others denoted but did not exhaust the rôle's limitless range.

The man swung gracefully back. "When you first spoke and I turned, methought I saw my father 'In my mind's eye.' So 'tis not strange that I addressed you as if you *were* my father's ghost. Indeed, for a moment I thought it so. But even if it were, the truth about myself is stranger. You see, I am . . ."

Speers waited, wondering if the man was an escaped mental patient.

"Well, what are you?" he finally said. "An intruder? A deranged spectator who's seen this play once too often and actually thinks he's Hamlet? Who *are* you, man? If you tell me, maybe I can get you some help."

The other slowly raised a long, tapered finger. It wove in the air like a succulently baited hook and caught Speers's attention despite himself. He watched the finger turn and end up pointing at its owner.

"I," the man intoned, "am Hamlet's ghost."

"Come again?"

A sigh, prolonged and heartfelt. "I am Hamlet's

spirit, doomed forever to walk these boards. Sometime after the first few performances, I found myself alive, speaking lines through an actor, then wandering alone afterward on the empty stage. It was as if I'd been suddenly just summoned into being."

" 'Summoned into being'?"

"Alas, yes. That first night I even beheld Shakespeare, my glorious creator! And for nearly four centuries now, wherever *Hamlet* has been performed, there too I must abide. Whether 'tis a professional troupe, or the rankest and most foul, I am conjured without my consent and must accompany the actor who assumes my name."

Slowly, he turned and gazed out at the dark and empty theater. "Ere you laugh, know'st that the play is now being performed on stages in nineteen different countries on this ancient globe, and that I exist in multiple guises upon them all. Such is my fate!"

Speers stared at the shadowy presence, forgetting his fears that the 'intruder' was a dangerous psychotic. The man spoke with such a compelling mixture of modern and outdated English that he seemed indeed to be the historical embodiment of the rôle. If Hamlet had trod the boards of a million stages in the past four hundred years, he might very well speak and act this way.

No, *he* was the one acting crazy now! This man was a fruitcake pure and simple, as cracked and demented as they came. He'd better get help fast.

But before he could do anything, the man skipped toward him and lightly touched his shoulder. "O'er the centuries, I've seen thousands of actors 'drown the stage with tears' and strive to capture my essence. From Booth to Burton, Burbage to Barrymore, all have failed. Sometimes, perchance, they have come nigh. But all have been found wanting. Garrick was too bombastic, Olivier too dreamy, Chamberlain too Hollywood. Oh, their names are legion! Suffice it to say that a thousand times I've hoped, nay, ten thousand times I've prayed, but always, *always,* I've seen my dearest wish dashed. 'Swounds, I've endured it, knowing always, though I know not how, that if just *once* an actor succeeded in becoming me, that at last, I would be set free!"

Rapt, ethereal, cursed — so did the face appear in the shadows. Speers tore his gaze away to the dim, barely seen reaches beyond the stage. In infinite distance, perhaps, the mezzanine and the upper balcony rose. Or perhaps it was the sixteenth century again, and it was an open-aired, three-galleried playhouse of Shakespeare's own time. . . .

His eyes returned, as if drawn by a magnet, to Hamlet. But that was insane. This . . . apparition wasn't Hamlet! Hamlet was a fiction, a character in a play who never even existed . . . and the play was a fiction too! As manager of this theater, he had dealt with actors and actresses before, seen them backstage with all their illusions and finery stripped bare. They were pot-bellied, droop-breasted, sallow-skinned,

by John B. Rosenman

painted-up and be-costumed lies. Sometimes they even had dentures and bad breath! For him to actually believe such a concoction was . . . well, it was crazy, that's all!

He opened his mouth, determined again to order the man to leave, but all he could say was one word. "Free."

"Aye, verily!" The man removed his hand from Speers's shoulder — had he held it there all this time? — and turned sideways, displaying a profile of profound and sensitive suffering. "To escape 'The slings and arrows' of this eternal bondage . . . 'Tis a consummation/ Devoutly to be wish'd'!"

Something stirred within Speers. Hamlet — he had just spoken phrases from his "To be, or not to be" soliloquy, the most famous words in all of drama! How could he not recognize them, having failed so miserably himself in auditioning for the rôle in college? "Stiff and inept," the director had called him, and everyone had laughed. No, he was not likely to forget either their scorn or the director's wounding words, not if he lived forever!

Speers wet his lips. "But if you're set free, what will become of you?"

For a second time, the man smiled. "Ah, if even once an actor speaks my very soul and pronounces it 'trippingly on the tongue' as its great creator ordained it, why then I'd be set free forever."

"But you'd die!"

" 'To sleep: perchance to dream.' "

" 'Ay, there's the rub,' " Speers countered. "But doesn't it bother you that there might be no 'undiscover'd country from whose bourn' you could return? That you might pass forever into darkness?"

A whisper from the shadows answered him. "May God grant me such a boon. Despite the play's grandeur, I have become so unspeakably weary of my eternal indecisiveness and inability to act. Look you, should I avenge my father and kill Claudius, or is his ghost a lying demon that seeks to deceive and damn me? I've been so 'sicklied o'er with the pale cast of thought,' that for four centuries I have been a mere 'John-a-dreams' who dawdles and does nothing until it is almost too late. Oh, I am tired beyond telling of assuming an 'antic disposition' and acting like a bedlam inmate with brilliant but blasted wits who tricks such 'arrant knaves' as Rosencrantz and Guildenstern. And Ophelia, whom I love! A million times she has drowned and closed her fair eyes for my sake!" He sighed. "To pass forever into oblivion and escape such tedium, would be a sweet consummation indeed."

Speers stiffened, trying to throw off the hypnotic net this visitor had cast about him, but it seemed woven of his own desires. Did he really want to believe such a lunatic? Whether the man was mad or not, Speers actually had to force himself to move away.

"You tell a good story, Ham— . . . uh, Mister. But you haven't explained how such a thing happened. What 'summoned you,' as you put it? Surely other rôles don't

create their own ghosts or alter egos. Did Claudius or Ophelia? Or Dr. Faustus? What about Hedda Gabler or Willie Loman? Or —"

"Methinks not," Hamlet said. "I alone have been chosen."

"And why is that?" Speers said, trying — but failing — to sound mocking.

Hamlet moved toward him and caught his hand before he could retreat. "Mayhap for the same reason *you* attempted the rôle in college, Mr. Speers. Because it is the greatest part ever written, 'mythic' and 'archetypal' as some critics call it. Mark you well: Is it not a rôle which can be endlessly and variously interpreted according to one's mood and whimsy? Is it not a tabernacle with countless rooms for the imagination? A peerless and endlessly faceted gem?" Taking Speers's other hand, he pulled him so close that their breaths mingled and Speers felt his heart surge into his throat. "And because it *is* the supreme and ultimate rôle, Hamlet has acquired its own life, its own undying spirit that must endlessly suffer in it."

Speers strained but could not break the other's grip. For a ghost, he seemed so solid and real! And Hamlet — no, this *man*, who was so young — claimed to have actually observed him, Speers, try to perform the rôle in college over thirty years ago! How could he know such a thing when he wouldn't even have been born yet? Though it was impossible, Speers felt a dagger's thrust of shame.

"If . . . If you *were* there, you must have seen how pathetic I was. They all *laughed* at me! I was a wretched Hamlet."

"Nay, you were not so wretched."

"I *wasn't?*"

Hamlet shook his regal head. "It was your director, that prattling villain of turgid bombast who was at fault. E'en then I was a close cousin to your thoughts and beheld your promise."

"My . . . promise?"

The face moved even closer, so close it was barely an inch away.

"I was e'en more a twin to your reflection than I am now," Hamlet whispered. "I dwelled within your deep but unripe heart, sensed the inspired construction you wished to give my story. E'en then I saw your vast promise and hoped that you might some day be the one to fully capture my spirit and give me rest."

"You must be mad," Speers said, though he did not mean it. His wavering and vacillation were gone, and he now believed everything. This man . . . this being . . . *was* Hamlet! "I . . . I'm only five feet four inches tall, weigh a hundred and ninety-seven pounds. Plus, I'm fifty-four years old and . . . and *bald!* Surely, I can't be Hamlet!"

"Ah, but these are but 'the trappings and the suits of woe'," the other said, "for you 'have that within which passeth show.' "

Speers recognized the lines, although they were turned around. In them, Hamlet had told his mother for four hundred years that he was more than what he appeared to be.

"I pray you listen," Hamlet said. "Why do you think that you alone in the past four hundred years have been permitted to see me? Is it because you are my successor, the only one who is worthy? Or because you share Hamlet's pain and confusion, his disillusionment with a corrupt and fallen world, his inability to act constructively and reform his life? Could it be because you alone share his soul?"

Speers trembled. "No."

"Listen," Hamlet continued. " 'God's bodykins,' man, you can *be* each and every Hamlet who strides across the stage and meets his father's ghost, or urges his mother to reclaim her virtue, or fights Laertes to the death in a tragic duel. As close as their thoughts and very souls you can be, and you can drink in the applause and acclaim of a thousand and more audiences! Come, have you not endlessly *longed* for such fulfillment, such a . . . consummation?"

Tears trickled down Speers's cheeks. "No."

"Oh fie! Even now your eyes, like portals of your soul, betray you. Why else have you lingered as a mere merchant in the profession that cast such scorn and calumny upon your head? Was it not to be as close as you could to what you loved by whatever means possible?"

Speers looked at his hands, clasped in Hamlet's. Could such a miracle be possible? *Could* it?

"You say I can be all these actors, the ones who play you?"

A nod. "The good, the bad, the indifferent. You can possess them all, on a million stages. I offer you the greatest rôle of all time."

"But . . . what will become of me? After a century or two, I mean. After I become as weary and tired of it as you? Who will save *me?*"

Hamlet smiled. "Mayhap a successor like yourself. One among all the others who is worthy."

"But what do I do if he *never* comes?"

Hamlet stepped back and adjusted his cloak, then touched his medallion. For the first time, Speers saw it was engraved with the seal of Denmark, the prince's realm. "Then you will be Hamlet forever," he whispered, "as well as an endless host of actors who play him." He smiled gently, then shook his head. "But I think not. Your appearance makes me feel that my creator was right when he had me finally learn that there's a purpose in providence and an ultimate peace for the soul, 'a divinity that shapes our ends,/ Rough-hew them how we will.' " He sighed. "Even if I'm wrong, and you toil until time itself cracks in the joints, you must decide."

Decide. Soundlessly, Speers repeated the word. He had no family, and no one who loved him. And the only thing he loved himself . . .

Did he really have any choice? Even if he risked playing Hamlet forever, wasn't it worth it?

As close as the actors' thoughts and souls . . . isn't that what he'd said? Yes! He could bathe in endless applause and adulation, embrace his dream by holding audiences spellbound on a multitude of stages.

Yes, Oh yes! Of *course* it was worth it. He would risk eternal damnation and hell itself for such a chance.

Ancient eyes read his decision. "To speak lines I wish the bard himself had written in my play: 'You know what you must do/ 'fore you can bid me adieu.' "

Speers found that he did know. Slain by Laertes' poisoned, traitorous sword, he sank to the stage and gazed up at the face that no longer looked so haunted and weary. As Speers spoke, Hamlet began to fade like a ghost.

> O I die, Horatio;
> The potent poison quite o'er-crows my spirit;
> I cannot live to hear the news from England;
> But I do prophesy th' election lights
> On Fortinbras: he has my dying voice;
> So tell him, with th' occurrents, more and less,'
> Which have solicited. The rest is silence.

Above, the visitor had become the merest shade, his face now that of Horatio, Hamlet's dearest friend. As Speers's senses faded and he slipped toward oblivion, he waited for Horatio's benediction. And when it came, his heart sang.

> Now cracks a noble heart. Good night, sweet prince;
> And flights of angels sing thee to thy rest!

A moment later, when Hamlet rose, he was alone. " 'Good night, sweet prince,' " he whispered.

And all the stages in the world awaited him. Ω

THE POCKET WITCH

Such a convenience,
Near at hand, until she grew
Too big for his britches.

— Catherine Mintz

by John B. Rosenman

GILLS
by David J. Schow

illustrated by Allen Koszowski

There had never been a lagoon, brown or black or otherwise; never *really*. Even without the help of civilized humans, the topography of the Amazon Basin both vanished and changed on an hourly basis. Soon only handfuls would remain — pressed leaves and desiccated insects on view in some museum.

Manphibian sat cross-legged in a mesh recliner, on a teak deck which surrounded a pool shaped like Brazil, working his way through a tumbler of iced coffee as the sky over the Valley slowly shaded to nicotine. He thought calmly about his place in this world. Out here, the lung part of his dual-purpose breathing system had to labor thirty percent harder just to sort oxygen from the particulates and feed it to his body's aeration network. He killed the coffee, slurping it through a straw since his fishy lips had never been able to close all the way.

"Burrraaacck," he said. He looked close at the webbing between his claws. Mites again. Dammit.

Manphibian had the coolest bathroom in all of Hollywood. Stainless steel fixtures; porcelain trim in aqua.

The pool outside had a specially constructed tributary that could feed right into the jacuzzi when the little steel security hatch was raised. The jacuzzi seated four, the shower, ditto, and the in-name-only tub was actually a large bronze dish set into mosaic tile. It looked like the world's biggest birdbath, but Manphibian could extend his arms and legs and do a horizontal cartwheel-revolve inside without ever bumping the rim.

Manphibian stripped away his sunglasses and worked himself over with bug spray and a toothbrush. He did not have teeth, but had found toothbrushes to be excellent tools for cleaning his eusuchian scalework. Then he showered off. The taps were for hot, cold, fresh, or salt. He usually did not bother to dry; lack of moisture was bad for his armored skin and his scale ridges could rip towels to ribbons by the truckload. Besides, his entire house was more or less waterproofed, the most obvious evidence being the layer of hardball rubber that covered the floor everywhere except in his "swamp room."

"Arroooggh," he said, with satisfaction.

A studio guy was coming up here for a meeting today. Some new newt from Production. Manphibian felt sure it was to discuss not *a* project, but *the* project — a remake/update of his debut feature film, buzzed and rumored for about a decade now, and counting. The movie that would reinvigorate the franchise and put Manphibian back in the Monster Top Ten of all time.

It excited him.

On the far side of the deck, Sofia was sunning her bush. The very concept of pubic hair was another potent turn-on for Manphibian, whose fluted penis had already telescoped from beneath its protective sheath-plate, self-lubricated with electrolytic secretions. The head and shaft featured Croataline tessellations which kept the penis anchored during underwater mating; Sofia called them "pleasure ridges." Women wanted Manphibian because his unique metabolism destroys pesky viruses and invasive micro-organisms — one of the reasons he can regenerate missing parts and live so long. They also wanted him because he was different, and almost never needed to come up for air.

Before wandering back to the deck, Manphibian put his shades back on. They were special goggles, custom-ground to keep the sun from hurting his delicate metallic eyes, and fashioned to overcome his lack of external ears. He checked himself in the bathroom mirror. Smooth.

Manphibian flipped Sofia to hands and knees and mounted her. The species concept of foreplay was unknown and irrelevant to him, although Bryce the agent had mentioned it. Once. The act was finished inside of forty-five minutes.

Manphibian had met Sofia at a film retrospective of his work. Her favorite novel was *Mrs. Caliban,* by Rachel Ingalls, and her curiosity was predictable but honest. The amazing thing was that she had stayed with Manphibian even after the gloss of the new or the spice of the different had dissipated. She could have had any weightlifter on Venice Beach. She was possessed of long, tawny legs, small feet, about ten pounds of rail-straight, burnished brown hair and perhaps the only pair of 38-Ds in Los Angeles that were real breasts. Most importantly to Manphibian, she read books. He would sit in his bronze tub and she would share books with him, reading aloud by the antique glow of oil-fed hurricane lamps, her eyes a color Manphibian had never seen before in any creature of the sea — an arid brown, almost tan, like fossilized sandstone beneath a sheen of oil.

One of Manphibian's favorite short stories was about a Japanese man catapulted back to 1745 by the Hiroshima mega-blast, to be mistaken for a sea monster by the Scots who net him. His skin color is "yellow like a slug's belly" and "covered from throat to ankle with brilliantly colored images of strange monsters."

Communication is attempted but there is no common ground . . . hence, obvious monster. Manphibian can relate. That beleaguered Japanese in the story had lacked the benefit of professional representation.

Sofia orgasmed like a broiling thunderhead, plateauing into a weird sort of Zen state. When Manphibian disengaged, she kissed him and jumped into the pool to paddle around. The way human beings swim amused Manphibian; like dogs trying to fly. The way Sofia swam just aroused him. Sometimes he stroked up from beneath, to penetrate her as she floated. He had to remember not to hold her under too long.

The pool was always clean. In the matter of the elimination of bodily waste, Manphibian did not suffer what Bryce unfortunately refers to as the "goldfish syndrome."

Manphibian's backstory was pretty much a rags-to-riches thing. En route from South America, he did bayou time, making friends with the water witches and the Peremalfait. His nostalgia was for python jerky, alligator wine, and mocha native girls by the village-full. In California, he could live like a king. Down in the Amazonas, he could be a god.

So why was he still here, outmoded by decades? The ongoing mutation that was his lifeforce had vacuformed him into an antique. Today, sitting by his anti-linear pool, Manphibian had himself become nostalgia. So . . . why?

Manphibian knew "why" the day he had met Sofia at the seminar. The day a crowded auditorium had stood and applauded his old black-and-white adventures in 3-D. Perhaps that was the day that he admitted he was hooked. It was the reason he was waiting around, today, right now, for some chinless VP of Production to toss him a table scrap.

Sometimes, when Manphibian got depressed, he drove his Dodge Marlin all the way out Mulholland to the sea. The last time he did this, he was mugged by bangers who stole his Platinum Card. Now Bryce, the agent, wanted him to have a bodyguard.

Dixie Kay Snow, Manphibian's very first cinematic leading lady, had called to ask if he could help her get a new agent. Not many parts were being cast for ingenues whose prime had slipped past the spoilage date decades ago. Then she asked if she could borrow ten grand. Manphibian sent her a check for three, knowing he'll never see *that* money again, even though his tax bracket still hovered at 48%, due mostly to his participation in merchandising.

Overall, Manphibian did not go out as much as he used to. While he enjoyed celebrity in cautious doses, he resented being asked to stand in the koi pond at the French Quarter Restaurant while snickering people snapped stupid photos with cheap, idiot-proof cameras. Every fucking time.

"I think my client was seeking more of an ecological feel," Bryce told the studio guy. "You know — a save-the-rainforests sort of vibe."

by David J. Schow

The enemy, whose name was Shelby something, nodded importantly. His college major must have been "nod." Manphibian already hated Shelby's suctorial mouth.

Bryce was sitting on the waterproof sofa, dramatically framed by a floor-to-ceiling aquarium stocked with outrageously-colored exotics. Manphibian's actual snack tank was back near the pantry because it was not built for ostentation. Bryce was backlit, the room light falling to place Shelby in the interrogation hot spot. All this negotiative strategy had been mapped for Manphibian earlier; now Bryce expounded, for Shelby's benefit:

"Tens of thousands of acres are getting cleared down there, day to day, for three reasons — timber, fuel, and agriculture. As a metaphor, it's irresistible in terms of plot: the bad guys, in messing with Manphibian, are jeopardizing a one-of-a-kind intelligent creature in the process."

Just a week ago, Manphibian had read the latest hopeless attempt at a screenplay. No meat to it. Just by-rote formulaic monster vomitus. If there had been any meat to the story, or characters, or plot, then the writing would have classed as butchery . . . but it lacked any emotion so strong.

But Shelby the Development Nod had a blank, puzzled expression marring his soft face.

Bryce pressed dutifully on: "Manphibian stands for everything that is ancient and enduring and on the verge of being lost. For this story to get up and walk, it's got to evolve some legs. It needs a subtext. Some depth."

Shelby the Nod moved his head around. "See, the major problem is, I think we need a *new* version of Manphibian. A kinda Nineties version."

Manphibian and Bryce stared at each other. It was as if the proposal had been to update the title of Poe's "City Beneath the Sea" to "Bite the Brown Bubbles."

The Nod expanded on his brilliant creative epiphany: "See, I showed the original Manphibian flick to my kid. He's thirteen. And he *wasn't scared.*"

They waited. Scary was easy. Put a claw-tip right on the wet surface of someone's eyeball and you got *scary.*

"See, we think the — uh — monster needs a redesign." He unveiled a Xerox of a sketch.

Scary? thought Manphibian. *Shelby's teen bratling should get a glimpse of his dad, naked with a hard-on.*

The critter on the paper had a humanoid torso with extra abs and the muscle cut of a comic-book superhero. The legs were backward-jointed, like those of a dog. The head was snaky, blunt as a lead bullet, and hanging off the end of a neck straight out of Loch Ness. Its hands were too Goddamned big. It had great big scary teeth and no pupils in its eyes.

"See, the artist is going to stab at another draft, 'cos this is basically what *we* like, except, of course, that women have got to want to — uh — fuck it."

Human women had to be sexually attracted by this ostrich-legged, peeny-headed slime worm. Kids would

yowl, *let's get* TWO *of the action figure with Real Kung-Fu Stupidity and Glow-in-the-Dark Agenda!*

"*Aarrraaaaccck!*" Manphibian frowned. Suddenly the room smelled like anchovies. Perhaps marinated in arrack.

"You're dead wrong, Shelby, and I'll tell you why," said Bryce. "If you say the name Manphibian, everybody knows what you're talking about — even people who've never seen the movies. You're messing with an icon."

"Every other monster we own, we've remade," said Shelby. "Updated them and redressed them and kept them parallel with the times. Didn't hurt a one."

"None of those remakes were hits."

Manphibian noticed that the drawing vanished as quickly as it had been produced. It was awkward and grotesque, not gracile, not logical; a bogey to be crudely Frankensteined from liquid rubber and toxic catalysts. Inside this soulless fake would be a wage-scale guy who hated his job.

"Doesn't matter. The originals were B-features. Bottom of the double bill."

"They're B-features with enough time behind them to resonate. You weren't even around when they premiered."

No, in fact, Shelby the Nod had not been even a concept back then, let alone a pitch. To Manphibian, Shelby looked about 35 human years old, max.

"And we're not talking about an aged actor, either," Bryce kept on, flinging both syllables of *ag-ed* at Shelby like daggers. "Manphibian doesn't age like humans. He'll be ready for action when we're dust. He could certainly kick your ass around the court, right now."

Manphibian crossed his legs and folded his claws over his knee, flexing the fins on his forearms so the stiletto spines fanned aggressively out. It would be wonderful to kick Shelby's ass. Or to maybe vise one butt cheek in each claw and split Shelby up the dotted line like a zip strip.

"Do you know who wrote the draft of the script you have?" Bryce was confident of Shelby's answer.

"You know I inherited this project when Allan Arnold Whitner left the studio," said Shelby, crunching the ice in his already-depleted coffee cooler.

"Not exactly factual," said Bryce. "You're here to fish, because Allan Arnold Whitner was fired by Samantha Coltrane, who paid half a million for a *Jaws* retread scooped up by her two favorite comedy writers. Samantha doesn't want the investment to sit on the shelf. You don't want Manphibian, so clearly you're here to lube up our rear ends before darling Sam rugs the franchise out from underneath us. You want us to sign off on the licensing rights. You want to own Manphibian the way Universal Studios owns Bela Lugosi's face."

Manphibian had heard two stories about old Bela's visage, and the images and tie-ins it represented. One was that Bela's heirs had sued and lost the right to a cut of the franchise. The other was that they had won, then lost their right to a cut on appeal. Of course, old Bela had not *really* been Dracula — maybe that had been the big boobytrap of his life.

Shelby was cornered, black eyes darting for escape routes. He employed the usual desperation move, which was to shift the spotlight of blame onto the writers. "Now, those guys Cangrejo and Lampreé are not just comedy writers. They're good writers. They wrote three in a row for Samantha that yanked a hundred-mil-plus each. Their stuff is tank-proof. You shouldn't judge —"

"I bear them absolutely no malice," said Bryce. "They took a pay gig offered by their producer. I probably would have done the same. But all you have to do, to tell their hearts weren't in it, is read the script."

Manphibian nodded in agreement. *"Orrrrrpp!"*

Sofia drifted through with most of her R rating covered and distracted Shelby the Nod by recharging his glass. Playing hostess interested her for about five minutes at a time in real life, but it permitted Bryce and Manphibian a vital huddle. Before Sofia poured, Manphibian made sure there were burst mites in the coffee. She winked at him like a child playing spy.

"It's a railroad, and we're on it, and the tracks go straight off the cliff into the nearest and most convenient abyss." Bryce had a knack for summation.

"Graaaaah," said Manphibian.

"But you have a power old Bela didn't have. We can't stop their moronic idea for a movie. We can't stop the movie. But we *can* stop them from calling it you-know-what. And if they can't say the magic name, they *have* no remake of anything. Because all the merchandising is shackled to it. They can't have any 'Manphibian'-trademarked toys and snacks and CD-ROMs on the racks in time for Exmas — because *you're* Manphibian, and they can't touch your name and cut you out without us swooping in piranha-style."

Manphibian liked that. *Piranha style.*

"I mean, I guess they *could* call it *Manphibian-*LIKE *Creature from a Darkish, Not Totally Dissimilar Lagoonal Pond . . .*"

Manphibian *urrrped* his approval. Bryce could be a funny guy. He could make monsters laugh.

"The trade-off is this. You can't let them know how badly you want to be in this movie, because they'll just use your desire to do things right to leverage you out. But if you tell me you can live without it, just for now, I'll fucking rip them wide on merchandising and in two years we'll have enough money to make our own version. James Bond did it and Frankenstein's Monster did it and we can do it for you. Because you've got the time on them. You can wait forever and they'll be gone tomorrow. This asshole Shelby will be a memory by the time we manage to get three people into the same room together for a new meeting. There'll be some other big butt warming his useless desk. Hell, at that point, maybe Samantha Coltrane will have moved

on and maybe we'll get a person who has some respect for what you do. So what do you say, Man?"

Manphibian ruminated Bryce's proposal, bobbing his knobby forehead at the key points. The time angle was particularly interesting. American moviemakers really needed to take a more Asian view of long-term cycles instead of using the next two weeks as their event horizon.

Shelby was slurping his third mite-laden iced coffee and trying to see Sofia's tits at every opportunity. Manphibian sucked several deep breaths, the delicate lamellae below his jaw flowering to grab air to oxygenate his attack systems. When he was pissed off he could literally swell to a size even more intimidating than his normal seven-foot-three. His spines extended and his eyes went that peculiar flat silver color which indicated he was not in the jolliest of moods. He glided up behind Shelby as silent as a mime. He opened his massive webbed claws; at full flex, fifteen inches from thumb to pinky talon. He thrust out his chest like a Ray Harryhausen dinosaur and cut loose with a window-rattling *"Hooorraaaar."*

Shelby the Nod blew a fan of coffee and crushed ice out of his nose, urinated in his pants, and was out the door inside of ten seconds, stumbling three times and losing a shoe as he fled.

He looked pretty damned scared.

Manphibian thought that later tonight he should pay Shelby's slacker brat a visit, too.

During the time absorbed by the meeting, seventeen square miles of Amazon rain-forest had been consumed. The paper used for the injunctions filed at Bryce's behest could easily have covered the Ponderosa — twice — while rare species of birds and insects skipped the "endangered" phase and did a smash cut

straight to extinction. Cattle now grazed on the clear-cut acreage not used for the manufacture of cocaine. Intrepid explorers seeking backwaters threaded with subterranean cavern networks which concealed ageless monsters would be disappointed by the wasteland awaiting them.

There was only one lasting way to make a proper lagoon, one that could engird and hold the slippery ghosts of myth: One third stock footage, one third backlot, and one third location shooting.

The notice in the *Hollywood Reporter* bespoke the commencement of principal photography on something called *Gills* — a hasty retitling of Shelby the Nod's beloved no-brainchild. It still depressed Manphibian, who tore out the page, crumpled it, and consigned the wad to his low-flush toilet. Advance heat on the underwater creature-feature had nonetheless caused Manphibian merchandising to come to a rapid boil.

Dark, sinister, foreboding, beautiful lagoons — the only place they could last is in the collective memory of the people whose imaginations have been enchanted by them. Manphibian knew that in the jungle, he could be a god, accepting forbidden sacrifices and watching tribal dancers shake virgin booty. And when the tribe had no further retreat, when their native land ran out,

it would all crash and burn. Past that life there would be nothing. The wilds are always conquered, and are thus impermanent . . .

. . . unlike Manphibian, who swam in powerful, meditative strokes through filtered, clear water, thinking that it is better to make a movie commemorating such loss than to actually suffer it.

He thought about forbidden ceremonies. Erotic rituals. Hollywood bullshit. Goldfish Syndrome, in terms of guys like Shelby the Nod.

Manphibian relaxed by his pool in the hills, pondering his place in this world. Perhaps he will have the pool repainted to a jungle theme — reeds and weeds.

His thoughts were about the fear people feel when their windshields are shattered on the freeway by imbeciles armed with marbles and Wrist Rockets. Fear of drive-bys and psychos and the random quake that could kill you with a piece of your own home. Fear that ran the gamut from getting your mail dipped to losing your sense of identity.

Manphibian thought about fear. About squandered natural resources. About lotus, and laurels.

That reservoir haven for joggers and make-out duos, the Lake Hollywood Reservoir, was so close, he could walk from here. And even though his mouth was not built to do so, Manphibian smiled. Ω

hell book

DEVOURER OF THE NEWLY DAMNED:

When the bronze-colored night settles over Hell, the mountainous *Vhyhinnom* flutter out of their hiding places to seek the souls of the newly damned.

©1997 Jason Van Hollander

by Jason Van Hollander

O TANNENBAUM
by James Van Pelt

Christmas *is* about friends. You have to believe this and not get discouraged. Look around you. Everyone here is poor — some poorer than you — some are crazy, but look at them, eating donated turkey, opening baskets full of clothes that are meant for them. All gifts of love. All symbols of human kindness. Today, of all days, you can't give up.

Here, pull up a chair. You look hungry. Grab a plate of turkey. Go ahead. Fill it up with dressing too. Everybody always shares. As long as I've lived, people have been kind. Maybe today I can give you a little in return for all that's been given me.

So there won't be any surprises, let me tell you something straight up front about me as an explanation. This Christmas day, I turned twenty-one — it's my birthday, I think, but not sure. It's different for me. Lots of people don't know for certain when they're born. They're abandoned at birth, so a birthday is assigned to them, probably one pretty close too. A baby, you can tell within a month or two how old they are, but that doesn't work for me. See, I have to count days, because for me, it's always Christmas.

Well, that's not exactly true. Lately it's been Christmas — the last five years ago or so, and for the five years before that, it was the last day of the Saturnalia. And before that, one kind of winter solstice celebration or another as far back as I can remember. My years, of course. Not your years. Really, for me, it's always Christmas.

Like this morning, I woke up in this shelter. The cot felt solid under my back, and the bed roll was worn but clean. Smelled old, you know, but not bad. Some folks were already stirring.

Guy next to me sat up coughing. Young looking fellow like yourself. Maybe my age, but a real dry cough that doesn't bring up anything, and he kept going for a couple of minutes.

"Got to quit these coffin nails," he finally said, lighting one up, tears still streaming down his cheeks. He took a deep drag. "Gonna be a good one today. I can tell." He offered me a smoke. See, first thing that happened to me today was an act of generosity.

I shook my head. People moving all around. Elderly ones, or the touched ones, talking to themselves. Bundled up, mostly. Like that guy over there — three trashed coats and two grimy scarves. Hat pulled over the ears. It's warm in here, but homeless folk hold their clothes tight.

Gina entered my head then. I hadn't thought of her at first, and that made me sad, you know, 'cause every time we talk now it's probably the last. Without a miss for two-and-a-half months I've called her in the morning to say hi, to see how she is.

My months, that is, not yours. Like I said, everyday is Christmas for me, and for me, two-and-one half months ago was 1914 when this soldier I met, Humphrey, asked me to call Gina. He sat next to me in the trench; I'd found out earlier in the day that we were twenty miles from Yrpes. German trenches weren't a hundred yards away, but you couldn't see them. Broken spirals of barbed wire, torn up dirt, a busted ambulance were all I could see. Night had fallen, and it had gotten very cold. A sentry walking by, head low, broke through a layer of fresh ice that had formed over the mud, so every step crackled, then squished. We had to pull our feet back to let him pass. The soldier's boots made a silly little squeaking sound when they pulled free.

Humphrey laughed. He was tired and scared, an eighteen year old Brit with a downy, blonde moustache and blood-shot eyes. He laughed at the ridiculous sound though, and then he started telling me about his family and his girl friend, Gina. He talked for an hour, low and passioned and non-stop. He made me swear to contact her if he didn't make it home.

"It's Christmas," he said, and he didn't say anything about where we were or what we were doing. He leaned his head against his gun and shut his eyes and by the light of the winter moon told me about Christmas in Lancashire, where he was born. I wish you could have heard his voice, kind of low and broken. He was a lot more down than you. "They're roasting chestnuts," he said. "And eating quince pudding, and telling each other stories. My Uncle Charles will bring out a cask of stout — he makes it himself — and they'll tap it open. He'll pour pints all around. Charles and Aunt Edna will be pie-eyed and toasting to the King's good health. Gina will be with them." Humphrey paused for a long time at that. No other sounds up and down the trenches, just cold, milky light pouring down on us, and the air like ice razors pressed against our cheeks. Finally, he breathed, "Oh, Gina, my good girl, my black eyed girl."

"Do they sing carols?" I asked. It had been a good day for me. Everyone clapped me on the shoulder. Ruddy faced fellows, mostly young, like myself, like you. "Merry Christmas, old sport," they'd say. "Separated from your company, are you? Good thing you Yanks are in it now," and they'd offer me stiff shots of warm brandy from hip flasks that suddenly appeared.

"Yes," said Humphrey. "They sing 'O Christmas

Tree.'" and he started to sing it, very softly, and I could tell he was crying. His voice, clean and clear, carried in that icy air, and it seemed like the only sound in the world, all tied up in the night sky and the moon and the barbed wire, and when he got to the part that goes, *They're green when summer days are bright; they're green when winter snow is white*, his voice cracked and he could go no further.

It was the saddest thing I have ever seen in my life: Humphrey slumped down in the bottom of the trench, lost and far from his home, from his Gina, the marvelous dark-eyed Gina who was hanging popcorn strings on a Christmas tree in a fire-lit room surrounded by Humphrey's parents and sisters and brothers and Uncle Charles and the homemade stout a million miles away.

And the echo of Humphrey's Christmas carol still rang in my ears, and I realized it wasn't an echo. It was the same tune, but the words had changed. Humphrey looked up too. He canted his head to one side and listened. Clear, so clear, as if the singer was in the trench with us, we heard a voice singing Humphrey's song in lovely baritone. It sang, "O Tannenbaum, O Tannenbaum . . ."

Humphrey hopped up then, and so did I, and looked across the no man's land. A face looked back. A German face under a pointy helmet, and he waved a tiny, white handkerchief at us. Humphrey dug into his back pocket and waved his own handkerchief. I don't know who climbed out of the trench first, the German or Humphrey, but I followed Humphrey across the cratered ground to the broken lines of barb wire in the middle.

Humphrey didn't even pause at the wire. He stepped over it, his hand out, "Merry Christmas, old chap," he said.

"Fröhliche Weihnachten mein Freund," the German said back, and they shook hands.

I stood behind them, arms wrapped around me against the cold. The moon, bright as any flare. All the way up and down the lines, as far as I could see, men were tentatively climbing out of trenches, walking toward the enemy, embracing, pulling out pictures to show each other.

Humphrey handed me a flask, his eyes shiny, his face alive with merriment. "It's Shnapps," he said. "It's Christmas Schnapps."

I fell asleep that night in the trenches, and I woke up the next day, a year later on Christmas in a hospital in London. Called Gina on the telephone. Told her I was a friend of Humphrey's. Found out he had died in January, but she was so glad to hear from me. Asked me if I was the "Yank" Humphrey had written to her about.

We talked a long time. It was another good day. In the hospital they brought in big baked hams. Cut them up in the wards. Even the sickest of the sick. Even the amputees and fellows who'd been gassed in the battle who couldn't hardly breathe, were happy. I made sure

they sang "O Christmas Tree," because I knew I'd made a friend. For the first time in my life I could talk to one person from day to day. Gina told me to keep in touch. With the telephone, I could. No matter where I was on Christmas day, I could call her.

So when I woke this morning, the man in the cot next to me offered me a smoke. A fellow from the kitchen told me that they'd be serving turkey and all the fixings in a couple of hours. Some kids from the high school are coming over later to carol with us. I asked him where the phone was. Yesterday — last year — Gina wasn't doing so good. Her heart, she said, was weak. "But you're sounding good," she had said.

"Yeah," I said. "The years have treated me well."

I made the call. She's in a nursing home in San Francisco. Moved to America in '57. I was afraid. The phone rang for a long time. Not many nurses on Christmas morning, and then someone answered.

I asked for Gina. Gina who, she said, and I told her. "I'm new here," she said. "I don't know that patient." Papers shuffled around on her end. She put the phone down, and someone mumbled to her in the background.

You've got to understand. I've never known anyone for more than a day. A day is all I get. I don't understand why. When the morning comes, I wake up, and it's Christmas. Sometimes I won't sleep for a couple of days, but everyone sleeps. It can't be avoided. Maybe I vanish in the night. Maybe a year later I appear when no one is looking. Who can tell? I always wake up in a place where a stranger could go unremarked, an army, a hospital, a festival, a flop house and soup kitchen like this one. I don't know if it's a curse — there's lots I don't know — but all I get is a day a year, and I'm a stranger that no one knows.

Then Gina came on the line. It was her voice. I've heard her grow old. "Hello, old friend," she said. "Merry Christmas."

"Merry Christmas," I said.

Each year she's been there. Each year. She's ninety-six now. I'm twenty-one today. It's my birthday. In three-hundred and sixty-five years for you, I'll be twenty-two, but I want to tell you something. It's important I think.

I hear rumors of bad things in the world. I hear about wars; I've even seen some, but in my experience, human beings are good. They're generous. They share with strangers, and they reach out to someone they've only talked to on the phone once a year for eighty years. If you could just see things from my perspective, you'd understand, even without friends, people are good. There are reasons to hope.

You shouldn't give up. People will help, like you've helped me by listening like a friend.

And you know what else? I wonder if you could do me a favor. You could? Great. I wonder — would you mind if I phoned you next year, here? Do you think you could find your way back here on Christmas to take my phone call? It would mean a lot to me. Ω

RENT
by Brian Stableford

illustrated by George Barr

At first, Jez thought that the vamp was just another freak, just another weirdo, just another shit with a screwed-up soul.

Jez knew lots of freaks. Some people — including the female whores who strutted their stuff on the King's Cross meatrack with the rent boys — would have said that *all* his johns were freaks, but that was just naked prejudice. Jez was a liberal, and he didn't give a damn where his johns wanted to squirt their semen, as long as they paid the going rate for the location in question; but even he had to concede that more than a few of the guys were seriously weird and definitely freaky.

At first, he thought the vamp was one of *those*.

The vamp drove a black BMW, polished so assiduously that it gleamed. Jez couldn't imagine the neatly-manicured vamp labouring over the machine with an old rag and an ozone-friendly can of Mr. Sheen, so he assumed that the job was contracted out. The first time he ever saw the BMW kerb-crawling the rack he noticed the girls edging out with a little more enthusiasm than usual, not just because they smelled the money but because they smelled the *pride* behind that polish. But the vamp wasn't interested in girls, and they soon learned to turn away in disgust when it came nosing up from the station.

That first night, Jez thought the vamp just *had* to be crazy. For one thing, he took Jez home to a brand-new glass-faced block in the Docklands, to the place where he actually lived. Not many johns did that, certainly not on a first date; even the ones who lived alone and only wanted hand relief, were nervous of the neighbours and scared half to death of becoming blackmail targets. The vamp ought to have been twice as scared, given the nature of his nasty little habits, but he wasn't. The vamp didn't seem to be scared of *anything*. He had nerves of steel.

Even that seemed like one more symptom of serious weirdness, in the beginning.

The vamp didn't have fangs, of course — not Christopher Lee-type extended canines, anyhow. Nor did he go straight for the jugular, the way vampires were supposed to do. He looked for veins in the same places the regular mainliners did, in the soft white flesh of the arms and the legs. He'd break into them very carefully, nibbling away with his pearly-white front teeth, then suck for twenty or thirty minutes at a stretch. It took the vamp far longer to take his drink than it did to shoot his wad, which he always did afterwards, into Jez's mouth, but he paid well enough

for the time he used. It hurt, of course, but so did lots of other things, and hurt was just one more thing that got added on to the rent.

The bites certainly didn't look like the little round holes that Christopher Lee left; they were more like ragged love-bites. They healed very quickly, though, and they never got infected, and Jez soon decided that the horror stories which passed up and down the rack about the things you could catch from human bites must be exaggerated. Most of the horror stories that passed up and down the rack were exaggerated, though some weren't; it was difficult to figure out which were which but Jez was fifteen years old and learning fast.

The first couple of times with the vamp, Jez found the business moderately sickening, but for that sort of rent he was always prepared to swallow his pride, along with everything else if necessary. After the first couple of times, it got much easier. He got used to it. He had plenty of opportunity, because the vamp was a man of regular habits, and the BMW always made straight for his spot; one of the other kids told him that if the car came cruising when Jez was otherwise occupied, it just went straight on through and out the other side.

Jez wasn't stupid enough to reckon that the vamp used him regularly out of affection; he figured that it was probably because his veins were easy to get at, because he was strictly a snorter and a dragon-chaser and never used a needle. Even so, he began to award the vamp a leading role in his fantasies of making a big enough score to skip the rack altogether and go independent. Like all the boys, he resented having to hand over so much of his take to the management — after all, he was the one renting out his tender young flesh to be poked and chewed; all *they* were renting to him was a square yard of pavement that they didn't even own. They supplied the junk too, of course, and an eight-by-twelve in a converted Victorian semi, but Jez knew how easily replaceable *those* services were, as long as you could come up with enough pictures of the queen.

It was only natural, in the circumstances, that Jez was able to think positively about the possibility of being taken on permanently by the vamp, in spite of the ragged lovebites. It was, after all, far less blood than the usual kind of donor was required to give, and the vamp never asked any awkward questions about HIV. Jez had never been tested and didn't intend to be; he couldn't afford to care, or even to try to figure out the odds as to whether the junk he smoked and sniffed would kill him before his immune system's season ticket finally expired.

Apparently the vamp didn't care either, maybe because he already had it, maybe because he had nerves of steel. Either way, he qualified for a starring role in Jez's dreamland — for a while. In fact, the vamp didn't stop being a prominent figure in Jez's dreams even when Jez started wondering whether he might, after all, be something other than one more freak, something more ominous than one more shit with a screwed-up soul, in a world where shits with screwed-up souls were by no means scarce.

Their conversation mostly consisted of mocking jokes. The vamp had a great line in deadpan answers to teasing questions.

"Will I become a vampire after I die?" Jez asked, once. "That's what's supposed to happen, right? — a vampire's victims generally become vampires themselves."

"You don't have to wait until you die, Jez," the vamp told him, serenely. "You could start right away, if you saved your money the way I do instead of blowing it all on synthetic endorphins and ersatz ecstasy. You could buy your own place and pick up some kid fresh off the train, and bleed him to your heart's content — or even her, if your fancy goes that way. If you really want to be a vampire, that's the only way to do it. There's no way to extend a lease on a body."

By degrees they built up quite a double act.

"Hey, Vamp," said Jez, when he felt entitled to be a little more familiar, "I bet I know what you do for a living — you're in the city, right? You're a bloodsuckin' capitalist who got filthy rich by exploitin' the toilin' masses, right?

"Got it in one," the vamp conceded. "I'm the sole proprietor of one of the oldest and most respected firms in the Golden Square Mile. My family have been managing investments since the beginning of the Industrial Revolution."

"Bullshit," said Jez. "You don't expect me to believe you got a *family*, do you? I bet you've been doin' it all yourself since day one — except you sometimes have to disappear for a while and then come back pretendin' to be your own son, so that nobody gets suspicious."

"Alas," the vamp replied, wistfully, "even vampires aren't immortal. I only wish we were."

Jez enjoyed the conversations, at first. It made a change — most johns were too paranoid to say much more than "How much?" and "This'll do." Most johns wouldn't look Jez in the eye, but the vamp did, without the least trace of embarrassment or shame or shiftiness. Nor was his stare at all mesmeric, as might have been expected if he'd been a *real* vampire — "real" meaning, in this paradoxical instance, the kind you could watch at work for a couple of quid on a rented video. The vamp had a gaze much softer and infinitely less haunted than Klaus Kinski's, though he was sexy

enough in a dignified kind of way. Jez figured that if the vamp had girls working at his offices in the city the air was probably heavy with unrequited lust.

"How come you got garlic in the kitchen, vamp?" Jez asked him once, after he'd done a bit of snooping. "Not to mention mirrors all over the place. Ain't you got no sense of *propriety*? Why don't y' hang a crucifix on the wall, f'Christ's sake?"

"Like every other species, vampires are subject to the rigours of natural selection," the vamp assured him, calmly. "All the ones who could only go out at night, or who couldn't be seen in mirrors, or got frightened half to death by the sight of a crucifix, ended up with sharpened stakes through their hearts. My kind are the only ones left. But I don't go in for crucifixes — one ought to show a *little* respect for the lost undead, don't you think?"

"Great," said Jez, laughing. "All the true blue Draculas got impaled, and only the harmless ones survive. With us normals, it's always been t'other way around."

"Oh, we're not *harmless,*" the vamp corrected him, in a voice as mild as milk. "We're civilized, discreet, modest, . . . but not *harmless*. Only the fittest survive, Jez — only the cleverest, and the strongest, and the best."

It was good fun, for a while. It might have been a fraction sicker than talking about what the greenhouse effect was doing to the weather or why England's batting had collapsed in the test match, but it certainly wasn't as sick as exchanging merry quips about the first signs of Karposi's sarcoma, or what you get when you cross a green monkey with a traffic warden, or any of the other contributions which the great gay plague had made to the oral cultural intercourse of the London Underworld. Jez was tempted once or twice to ask whether vampires were doomed to extinction now that AIDS was here to stay, but he never did; he figured that if anything were to qualify as overstepping the mark, that would probably be it.

There was no particular point in time when Jez's attitude to the vamp began to change. There was no sinister clue to catch his attention and make him shiver with unease, let alone a ghastly revelation. In fact, it didn't seem to be anything to do with the vamp's behaviour at all; Jez thought that the change was purely in himself, and didn't make much sense. It took the form of a creeping paranoia which stole up on him like a wasting disease. If there was a single starting point, it must have been some fugitive dream which he had forgotten completely by the time he woke up, or came down.

Logically, the relationship ought to have continued to become more comfortable; the two of them might even have learned to trust one another. As the weeks of their acquaintance turned into months, Jez found out more and more about the vamp. He knew not only the vamp's real name and his real address, but which

© G. Barr - 1998

bank and credit cards he used, where he got his groceries, where he had been to school, what kind of music he liked . . . all the little data which fleshed him out into the perfect image of a human being. But the more Jez found out — the more intimately he came to know the innocence of the image — the more the suspicion stole upon him that it really was all *image*, all sham, and all disguise, and that the only real and true thing about the vamp was the particular way he used his teeth and his prick, in that order, in the course of their expensive rituals.

At first, Jez was happy enough to construe his suspicions about the vamp's fundamental unhumanity as a natural extension of their joking relationship — was it not the case, after all, that such suspicions were a tacit assumption of all their humorous banter? But in time, although Jez and the vamp did not cease to joke with one another, the comedy wore thin. The idea that the vamp was just another freak seemed to shrivel up inside Jez's head, of its own accord, soon to be reborn as an anxiety that the vamp might in fact be thoroughly and utterly *normal* — by his own alien, unhuman, diabolical standards.

That anxiety was all the more pernicious, and all the more persistent, because Jez did not know exactly what it implied. He became gradually afraid, without quite knowing what it was that he was afraid *of*.

That was when his questions gradually became more pointed — and, inevitably, when the answers became gradually more evasive.

"Who'd you put the bite on before you took up with me?" Jez asked. "The old-timers on the rack say they never saw you before."

"Does it matter?" the vamp countered. "It was no one special — I paid him the way I pay you, and at much the same rate, allowing for inflation. Rents are cheaper up north, I hear, but that's because no one wants to live there."

Jez was from the north himself; the rack was full of northerners, put there by the state of the nation.

On another occasion, Jez asked whether everybody's blood tasted the same, and whether the fact that he was so often coked up to the eyeballs made his blood more addictive than the blood of a non-user.

"A connoisseur gets to notice subtle differences after a while," the vamp informed him, punctiliously. "But it's not as obvious as the difference between burgundy and claret. As to the hypothesis that my compulsion might have intensified by virtue of drinking the nectar of too many drug-addicts, I can only say that it sounds just a little far-fetched."

Later still, Jez asked what would happen to the vamp's considerable personal fortune, given that he had no son and heir to leave it to, adding the sarcastic suggestion that he might care to leave it to the Blood Transfusion Service.

"Oh, I intend to have an heir," the vamp assured him, blandly. "There's plenty of time for that, dear boy . . . plenty of time."

The vamp looked to be well on the downside of fifty; he kept Grecian-2000 in his bathroom as well as a mirror, and there was not one jot of evidence to suggest that he ever kept company with members of the opposite sex. Maybe that was the crucial incongruity which finally sowed the seed of something crazy in Jez's addled brain — though the crack through which it crept was, of course, already there.

Truth to tell, it wasn't just the vamp who had begun to seem a little less sick and freaky to Jez; the whole world was beginning to appear ordinary by its own implicit and thoroughly unhuman standards.

Jez wasn't particularly worried when he first began to feel the movement in his guts. It didn't seem to be painful, even when he hit dirt after a high; to begin with it was just *there*, disturbing simply by virtue of its presence. But it got steadily worse.

As time went by, he found it more and more difficult to sleep. Every time he lay down — whether he was drunk or sober, high or low — the quietness of his own limbs showed up by contrast the activity of whatever was inside him. Sometimes, he watched his own stomach, trying to see the skin bulge and stretch where the thing was shifting in its restless fashion. He began to run a tape measure around his waist every day, worried about the possibility that he was expanding from within; but he wasn't — in fact, he was getting thinner.

He thought that he was getting paler too, but it was difficult to tell. The rack was full of pallid faces which grew gradually whiter as careers progressed along their customary trajectories. No one else on the rack saw anything in his face or his gait or his manner that seemed worthy of comment, and if ever he mentioned to one of the other boys or one of the more maternal whores that his guts felt as if they were practising their boy-scout knots they would just laugh, and tell him he ought to have *their* problems.

Jez was no wimp, and he would have ignored the feeling if he could, waiting patiently for it to go away, but the nature of the feeling simply wouldn't permit that. It was too intrusive, too consistent, too close to the core of his being. He couldn't help but worry about it, and he couldn't help his anxiety transforming itself by inexorable degrees into an obsession.

Though he never actually *saw* the thing shifting under the skin of his belly he became absolutely certain that something was in there, that it was alive, and that it was feeding off him. He knew it wasn't a tapeworm or a tumour, but imagined it instead as something resembling a newborn rat or a blind mole, with massive jaws filled with tiny teeth, which it used to clamp on to his intestine in order to draw out the best of his blood — blood newly-enriched by the products of digestion.

It didn't take long to guess what the entity might be — to "formulate an hypothesis" about the thing, as the vamp would undoubtedly have phrased it. At first, the idea that came into his mind seemed too way-out, and Jez knew that even the vamp, despite his love of understatement, would have found a dismissive description far more colourful and contemptuous than "just a little far-fetched." But he couldn't shake the idea loose, and the longer it stayed with him, the more its incredibility was eaten away by familiarity. Every night, while he took his place on the rack, waiting and waiting while the creepy-crawlies inched past in their Astras and Cortinas and Volvos and Datsuns, the thing would gnaw away at his entrails — gently and painlessly enough, but no less horrid for that — and the idea would gnaw at his mind, gently and painlessly but no less horrid in its turn.

As the creature in his belly grew, so did the idea in his brain. They grew together, like shadowy twins, until the one was a mature homunculus, as sleek as strong as any fond parent could wish for, and the other was a full-grown fantasy, as vivid and venturesome as anything that morphine or magic mushrooms could ever hope to compose.

The fantasy which possessed Jez's mind took off from the supposition that the vamp *wasn't* just a shit with a screwed-up soul, like every other city gent who liked a bit of rough from the rack, but that his taste for blood was merely a matter of the routine nourishment of his species. Perhaps, Jez somehow could not help but think, this was one john who wasn't even queer, because he belonged to a kind which didn't have two sexes at all, but only one. Perhaps, Jez somehow could

not help but fear, this was one john who was only doing exactly what came naturally, for the proper purpose which nature intended. Perhaps, Jez somehow could not help but believe, the heir which the vamp fondly intended to have had already been conceived, after the fashion of his alien kind.

When Jez first wondered whether the strange stirring in his belly might have something to do with the vamp his immediate inclination was to share the joke, but he couldn't. He didn't see the vamp that week, and by the time the black BMW came cruising again he was well past the point where he could think the churning in his gut was anything trivial and temporary. He didn't want to mention it to the vamp, because he didn't want to see the vamp's reaction. It was like the blood test he'd never taken — one of those moments of possible confirmation which were best postponed forever. He was scared that if he told the vamp that something was eating away at his guts, the vamp would smile — not an amused smile, but a *proud* smile; the smile of an expectant father.

Jez thought — and *believed,* despite one or two brave attempts to doubt it — that the vamp had shot an alien spore into his fertile gut, where it had taken root and begun to grow after its alien fashion, and whence it would in the fullness of time emerge, the moment of its birth a baptism of blood.

In time, it became a little more painful, but never unbearable. Without hurting him unduly, the thing simply wore him down. By the time the creature in his abdomen had been gnawing at him for two months, Jez was so listless and so starved of sleep that simply taking his place on the rack became an ordeal. The intervals between enquiries began to get longer, and the management began to quiz him about the decline of his takings. If it hadn't been for the vamp, the management might have decided that he wasn't worth his spot, given that more fresh meat arrived just around the corner with every inter-city 125, but the vamp was still a regular, and one well-used to meeting sky-high city rents without a murmur.

The vamp never commented on the way Jez looked, or enquired after the state of his health. The blood, it seemed, was still good — and the vamp, in any case, had other reasons for keeping in touch. Those reasons didn't have to be spelled out; their relationship had reached that magical pitch at which they no longer seemed to need words to help them understand one another's motives and desires.

It still went on, day by day and week by week. Jez lost twenty kilos, and became as weak as a kitten. Eventually, after one more quiz administered more in sorrow than in anger, he lost his place on the rack, and knew that he couldn't complain. The management had had no choice, in the end; they were men of business, after all. The vamp hadn't been around for a while, and no one except Jez could be certain that he wasn't gone forever.

by Brian Stableford

The management even overrode his strenuous objections and sent him to the hospital, but the hospital couldn't make a bed available and the doctors sent him back to the eight-by-twelve after leeching a generous helping of his blood in order to carry out tests. Jez didn't tell them about the creature inside him, because he could tell that they didn't want to know, and would refuse to see it on an X-ray. He could tell that the doctors didn't want to take him in — that they'd rather he simply vanished, or at least had the elementary courtesy to die somewhere else instead of wasting time that they would far rather devote to the deserving sick.

By this time, Jez was in bad trouble. The worst of it wasn't that he was playing host to the vamp's offspring but that he was cut off from his connection.

If the hospital had admitted him, they'd have been obliged to feed his habit after some sort of fashion, rather than see him shrivel up to nothing at all, but the management worked on a strictly cash basis. They had done their bit, and owed him nothing; he'd never taken the trouble to pay into any kind of pension fund. He didn't have any friends among the other rent boys, and although some of the older whores sometimes seemed to experience a ghostly maternal affection for the prettier boys, there was no way that sort of pantomime affection was going to be convertible into any kind of supply.

Even so, Jez was home for two whole days, in bed but not sleeping, before he called the vamp and begged for help.

Any run-of-the-mill freak or weirdo would have put the phone down on him, but the vamp didn't. The vamp listened. Jez wasn't particularly glad about that, but he wouldn't have been glad if the vamp *had* cut him off either; he knew that there was no way out.

The vamp brought the black BMW to the semi, and came upstairs to Jez's room. He didn't waste any time; he just picked Jez up in his arms, all wrapped up in a blanket, and carried him down to the car. He laid Jez out on the back seat and he drove home to the brave new world of the half-reconstructed Docklands. He installed Jez in the spare room, and brought him a cup of hot, sweet tea.

"That's no good," Jez pointed out, politely. "I need some stuff — white and pure. I can't feed your lousy kid unless you can feed my head as well as my guts."

The vamp only held the cup to Jez's lips, patiently but insistently, and in spite of what he'd said, Jez drank it. He knew, somehow, that the vamp wasn't going to get him any hard stuff, or give him any money so that he could get it himself. Now Jez was in the spare bedroom, it was Jez who owed rent, in cash or in kind — and Jez knew that if it was to be paid in kind, it wouldn't be paid in the *usual* kind.

"Why me?" asked Jez, when he'd finished the tea. "Why'd you pick me?"

"Why anybody?" countered the vamp, with a shrug. "We can't even pick and choose our own selves with any degree of rationality or any semblance of good

aesthetic judgment, so why should we be any better at picking the others on whom we elect to inflict ourselves?"

He was a philosopher to the bitter end, was the vamp. Jez might have admired him for it, if he hadn't been so desperately in need of a hit.

When the vamp left him alone, Jez thought that it would soon be all over. In fact, he felt so close to the end that he was certain that the vamp had misjudged it, and would be too late returning to witness the birth of his son and heir — but he didn't know whether or not that would matter to the vamp, who was, after all, unhuman.

As things turned out, though, Jez had longer to wait than he thought, and the vamp *had* come back.

It was night-time when the moment finally came, but the light was on. The vamp was sitting by the bed, patiently waiting. When Jez began to retch and gasp, the vamp unhurriedly pulled the duvet back, and unbuttoned Jez's shirt to expose the pale white belly within. Then he stood back to watch while the thing inside chewed its way out, ripping and slashing and tearing with its tiny clawed fingers and its tinier teeth.

The vamp could have brought a razor or a carving-knife to help it on its way, but he didn't. His kind obviously didn't believe in cosseting their young; the ones who couldn't make it on their own must simply be deemed unfit to live. The vamp just stood and watched, his face devoid of any expression, while his son and heir fought his messy way out through the surprisingly resilient flesh of the host who had carried him to term.

Jez watched too, though he would rather have been shocked into insensibility. He watched the rip in his belly from the moment it first appeared until the much later moment when the thing which was so laboriously making it was ready to squeeze through, stained top to toe with blood and flushed with the triumph of its first success in the harsh and hazardous game of life.

The pain had always been muted before, but it was given free rein while the thing was extracting itself, and the agony increased steadily all the while. Jez would have given anything for a hit powerful enough to blast him into orbit, but he was down at ground level, flat in the gutter without a shooting-star in sight. There was nothing he could do to fight the pain except stuff his knuckles into his mouth and bite down hard, as if the self-inflicted pain might somehow exorcise the other. Strangely enough, it did help.

Eventually, though, the creature was free. It didn't look much like an ordinary baby, but there wasn't any particular reason to expect it to.

The vamp picked it up.

Jez looked down at the bloody wreck of his abdomen, and slowly unclamped his teeth from his bloody hand. He realised, pathetically, that he was not going to die. In spite of everything, he was not going to die.

He didn't immediately understand *why* he wasn't

going to die, but in the end he looked up from his rapidly-healing wound to stare at the vamp. Then he saw that father and son were looking down at him with earnest concern, sincerely glad to see that he was getting better.

Jez's mouth was full of the taste of his own blood, and as the pain gradually ebbed away, he realised for the first time how supremely sweet and nourishing that blood must be, in the mouths of those who were that way inclined. Ω

THE HAUNTING OF H.M.S. DRYAD
by Reginald Bretnor

illustrated by Denis Tiani

I had always felt there was something strange about my friend Captain Edmund Casebolt Crankshaw, who owns and manages the Dryad Hotel on San Francisco's Embarcadero, so I really wasn't too surprised when he told me the place was haunted. After all, it's been there for much more than a hundred years, built over the hulk of H.M.S. *Dryad*, which sank at her moorings like so many other ships when her crew deserted her for the promised riches of the Gold Rush in 1850. Her mizzen mast still stands in the middle of the lobby, and the saloon bar, The Bilge Pump, still occupies her after cabins, which her officers thoughtfully waterproofed before she went down. Still, the haunting puzzled me, for — though he's always a perfect gentleman — the Captain was no man to trifle with, which I felt sure even a ghost would realize. His card says *Master Mariner*, but it always seemed to me that he'd be more at home on the quarterdeck of a man-of-war.

I had joined him at his table at the end of the bar, just under the partly draped Dryad figurehead which had once graced the ship's prow, and Mickey, his huge Fijian bartender with the filed teeth, had brought me my first bourbon and water on the house. It was a Friday night, and there was the usual Friday crowd of other students and junior faculty members from U.C., arguing as always about whether science fiction should or should not be called speculative fiction — as though the word science might put a hex on it. The oil lamps in their brass gimbals — the only illumination allowed — cast a soft light on the mellow panelling. The Captain usually began by asking me how my work was progressing — I was hoping to become an undersea archaeologist, and naturally he was interested — but tonight he obviously had something else in mind.

"Captain," I said, "you look sort of worried."

He frowned thoughtfully, sipping his Pusser's Rum. "Andrew," he answered, "I am, and I might as well tell you as anyone. Truth is, this bloody old place has a ghost. Doesn't really bother me — just the guests, and especially young couples who have something else very much in mind. He — I'm sure it's a he — hangs around two or three weeks at a time, sighing and moaning and groaning distressfully, usually when they are just going to it, and of course he manages to ruin it for them. Sometimes they pack up and move out immediately, and naturally I refund their money if they've paid in advance. But then he'll go away for months — once it was actually a couple of years — but invariably he returns."

I looked over at a group just two tables off: Jean-Pierre Danziger from the French Department, who was into all sorts of New Age stuff, a tall, stringy stranger in late middle age, who looked annoyed about something, a couple of grad students I didn't know, and a weird woman called Ludmilla Gooch, a very large woman wearing heavy braids, a sort of cross between a monk's habit and a holoku made of corduroy, and all sorts of heavy charms and beads. I'd heard that she'd taken up channeling, was writing a book about it, and had attracted quite a circle of followers. I saw that their conversation had lapsed, and that they were doing their best to listen to ours.

I alerted the Captain. "From what I know of her, if she hears about this spook of yours she'll start pestering you and insisting she can get through to him, and she'll make enough noise to have the whole place wondering what cooks."

"Well, *that* we don't want, but I know her type. The species is indigenous to Berkeley, and seems to recur generation after generation. But — well, thunder! I've tried everything else. I even had Father Halloran, the police chaplain, down here trying to exorcise him. Who knows? Do you suppose . . . !"

"Uh-uh!" I shook my head. "Would you believe anyone who claims that a Phoenician sailor who died about seven hundred B.C. speaks through her with the Wisdom of the Ages, and does it in *English*? To say nothing of French and all sorts of unknown languages?"

The set of his jaw told me he had come to a decision. "Andrew," he said, "I think I'll give it a try. It's that Phoenician seaman who's convinced me. If she's faking him, I should know in a minute. Would you be kind enough to ask her for me? Don't tell her why. Just say I'm interested and that I'd appreciate it if she and her party joined us in that little cuddy behind the bar. Besides, that way we'll keep her from noising it all around."

"Well, if you say so," I replied dubiously, "but don't say I didn't warn you."

I rose and went over to their table. "Dr. Danziger," I said, all politeness. "You may remember me — Andrew Lochead? I took a course from you three or four years ago. Perhaps you'll introduce me to your company? Captain Crankshaw has heard a great deal about Mrs. Gooch, and he's extremely interested in her research. He asked me to invite all of you to join him in his private room behind the bar. He's already told Mickey to bring you another round and we'll be able to talk without being disturbed.

"Bah!" exclaimed the stranger, "Research indeed!"

Danziger cleared his throat. "Well, er — well, that'll be up to Ludmilla," he said, "as she seems to be the center of attention. Um — this gentleman, Mr. Homer McWhinney, is a friend of hers. But I myself regrettably can not attend. Actually, I am with some other people," and he pointed to an even odder group three tables away.

I could hear Ludmilla shuffling her feet back into her sandals under the table, and knew that the invitation was accepted.

"I can see by looking at him that the Captain's a very old soul," said she. "I'll be happy to channel for him."

She stood up, holding a poisonous-looking drink in one hand, swaying her braids and clanking her beads and things. The two grad students, male and female, agog at the prospect of free drinks, declared they were delighted to meet me, even though Danziger never did formalize the introduction, and Mr. McWhinney grunted disgustedly but did not abandon us. I saw the Captain rise, smile a gracious smile that immediately dissolved the severity of his countenance, and, bowing to the lot of them, led the way past Mickey and the figurehead to the cuddy behind the bar.

Mickey had already set their drinks out before their assigned chairs, and Ludmilla gratefully took both her glass and the recliner which unprotestingly accepted her more than ample weight. She kicked off her sandals, sighed, and wiggled her toes.

"Do make yourselves comfortable," said the Captain, a bit redundantly, and I made the introductions.

Rather to my astonishment, Ludmilla came right to the point. "Captain," she declared, "as I told our young friend here, you're an old soul, and these days I don't get to meet too many of 'em. So I won't beat around the bush. You've got problems on the Other Side? Right?"

"Rather," replied the Captain.

"I thought so. I can feel it all around us. Two-three more of these —" She looked thirstily at the greenish fluid in her glass. "— and I'll go into a trance and let Marduk come in. "He'll help you if anyone can."

She was, I'm afraid, an unattractive woman. Her nose had a porous look about it. Her eyes were muddy. But somehow I knew that over the years she almost certainly had had any number of lovers, of whom the obnoxious McWhinney was probably the latest; and oddly enough I began to wonder whether her channeling was as fraudulent as I had believed.

We had three rounds of drinks, Captain Crankshaw sipping his Pusser's Rum, I myself going easy with my usual, McWhinney hypocritically guzzling expensive Scotch, and the grad students eagerly ordering drinks they'd read about but couldn't afford.

The Captain sat there very patiently, making small talk about the Dryad Hotel, H.M.S. *Dryad,* the Gold Rush, and the California Historical Society.

Finally Ludmilla tossed off what remained in her

by Reginald Bretnor

glass, belched delicately, and announced that she was ready. The two students looked at their own glasses disappointedly; so did Mr. McWhinney, who started from his seat, muttering something about not putting up with a lot of drivel.

"Dammit, Homer, *shut up!*" snapped Ludmilla.

"Surely," murmured the Captain, "you will not abandon us after putting up with our company and my Scotch?"

McWhinney sat down again.

Now Ludmilla was lying back in the recliner. Her eyes were open, but they had lost something of their muddy look and whatever they were focused on did not seem to be in the room with us.

There was a long silence, Then, abruptly, a voice issued from her throat. It was not her voice. It was male, harsh and deep and powerful. "I am Marduk!" it proclaimed. "Marduk the Admiral, Marduk who conquered the sea, who explored the vast waters of the world. What do you want with Marduk?"

The voice was unbelievable. Its English, grammatically correct and clearly understandable, was spoken with an accent — or rather a melange of accents — so strange that I was at a loss to place it. It evoked images of Carthaginian soldiers prodding reluctant elephants over the Alps, of Honest Abdul's Used Camel Mart in Beirut, of shouted orders along a hundred far-flung waterfronts.

"I, Marduk, greet you — especially you, Captain Crankshaw, master of this unfortunate vessel, sunk in this Bay very much like my own so many years ago. . . ."

"Are you trying to tell me Phoenician spooks speak English?" snorted McWhinney. "I can't understand why Ludmilla allows herself to —"

"*Who in Baal's name is this old fart?*" shouted Marduk. "*Throw him out!*"

"I'm afraid I'll have to," said the Captain, just as Mickey stuck his head in the door, showing all his teeth. "Or Mickey will."

Ludmilla's lover subsided.

"Admiral Marduk," the Captain said. "Your knowledge of our language astounds me. Forgive me, but how the devil did you learn it?"

Marduk's laughter roared throughout the cellar. "Captain, I have had two thousand, six hundred, and some odd years to learn languages. Because of my mistakes — some might call them sins — I have been forbidden to reincarnate, and my destiny has been to follow the sea. I have been in battle on I know not how many men-of-war — *Revenge, Bonhomme Richard, Victory.* I have listened in their wardrooms in fair weather and foul. At Lepanto, the Armada, the Battle of the Saints, Trafalgar, Jutland. I have paced the quarterdecks of merchantmen, and listened to their sailors' yarns in ten thousand fo'castles. And almost never have I been able to manifest myself, to join them in their chatter.

"Only when there have been Finns aboard, because in the sailing ship days so many of them were wizards, carrying their bags of wind. And when I have, I've usually been taken for Davy Jones or the Flying Dutchman — do I *sound* like a Dutchman? — and once even for your own Ancient Mariner, but at least they didn't ask me to prophesy, or tell them about their past lives, or reveal the Secrets of the Universe like most landlubbers would. That is why I am so grateful to this lady for making it possible for me to converse with a fellow shipmaster.

"Captain Crankshaw, I shall do anything I can to help you. I know your vessel's history, and yours too. Often I have admired how you have done your duty despite all difficulties. Ah, how I wish I had had you with me when I discovered this glorious bay so long ago. Had you been, my stout ship never would have sunk when my wretched crew ran off, tempted by the native women."

At that, my ears pricked up. A Phoenician galley sunk in San Francisco Bay — what a subject for my dissertation! And with photographs of what remained of her, of the artifacts!

I looked at the Captain. "M-may I ask him?" I whispered. All my doubts had vanished.

"Presently, Andrew. I know what you're thinking of. After a bit, I'll ask him myself. But first I have my own problem to consider."

"Ha-ha-har!" roared Marduk. "You have indeed. The matter of your Chief Bo'sun's mate, the good, devoted William 'Opkins."

"You mean —" The Captain leaned forward eagerly. "You mean *he's* the ghost who's been bothering my guests?"

"That is right," replied Marduk. "Would like me to bring him in? I'm sure our good hostess wouldn't mind."

"Please do."

There was a long silence, during which the Captain whispered in my ear. "Hopkins," he said, "was one of those who let greed for gold tempt them from their duty. It astonished me — that is, years later, when I finally heard about it. He not only deserted. He took the ship's cat with him to the gold fields. Her name was Emma, so the crew always called her 'Lydy 'Amilton.' You know, after Nelson's mistress."

Abruptly, a new voice broke in, a masculine voice but neither as deep nor as authoritative as Marduk's.

"Ow, Capting, Capting!" it cried out. "All these bloody years I been lookin' fer yer, and now — now —" The voice broke into horrendous sobbing. "Now, at larst, I can tell yer 'ow sorry I am. You wouldn't believe 'ow I've suffered, me and Lydy 'Amilton. It was in a plyce called Second Garotte where they killed me, them Yankee brutes, and arf of 'em Irishmen, and Lydy 'Amilton too. I do believe they et 'er, poor creature!" He broke off once more, overcome by sobbing, and a new voice piped up.

"Meow," it said.

"There she goes, sir!" exclaimed Hopkins. "Remember 'er? She's rubbin' agynst yer 'ind leg, she is, purrin' up a storm. Carn't yer feel 'er, sir?"

"I can't, Hopkins," said the Captain. "But I'm touched by her devotion. It's a shame the whole crew couldn't have shared her dedication to duty."

There were more tragic sobs as Hopkins poured out the story of his almost century-and-a-half-long search for someone who could explain his contrition to the Lords of the Admiralty, and to 'Er Majesty the Queen. First, it 'ad tyken 'im years just to find 'is wye back to *Dryad*, only to find 'er sunk, and 'e styed around a bit but not even the Capting could 'ear 'im . . .

"Meow!" said Lydy 'Amilton.

"Well, now you've finally been able to make yourself heard, thanks to Admiral Marduk and this lady here, so what can I do for you?"

"Oh, sir, If yer please, Capting sir, you can discharge me from 'Er Majesty's service, so I'll be free to go on to where this 'ere Admiral Marduk says I ought to be."

"Very well, Hopkins," said Captain Crankshaw. "In my opinion, you've pretty much paid for your crime, disgraceful as it was, and there's certainly no way even the Admiralty could have you hanged from the yard-arm. So consider yourself, as of this moment, discharged from the Royal Navy, I suppose without prejudice."

"God love yer, Capting! Oh, thank yer, thank yer. Oh, sir, ayn't there nothin' I can do to repye yer? I could stye on a while and 'aunt anyone yer sye —"

"That," said the Captain hastily, "will not be necessary."

"Then, sir, I'll be on me wye — and, sir —" He hesitated. "— can I tyke Lydy 'Amilton with me? I know she's Crown property, but we've been together ever so long —"

"By all means take her, Hopkins. And the best of luck to both of you. *Good*bye."

"Goodbye, sir, and when yer time comes I'll be lookin' forward to seein' yer agyne."

I thought I felt a tiny wisp of cold air pass my face. Then Marduk was back again, laughing his head off. "My friend," he bellowed, "I'd not have let the man off so lightly. I'd have at least persuaded him I'd found a way to keelhaul ghosts! And now would you like to hear the story of my mighty voyage and its sad ending?"

"We should be delighted." The Captain signalled to Mickey for a refill all around, and McWhinney quelled some sort of derogatory comment he had been on the point of uttering. And it *was* a mighty voyage, so much so that I actually found myself listening eagerly, not even really impatient for the sad ending, when I hoped to learn where the remains of his vessel might be found.

After they cleared the Pillars of Hercules, a great storm had blown them north and west, so that they almost touched the tip of Greenland; they fought Indians in what were to become Quebec and New England; they traded for rich furs, which served them well along the coast of Mexico, traded in turn for gold

and slaves, some female for their delectation, some male to do hard labor and serve as sacrifices when the weather threatened.

Down the coast of South America they sailed, rounded the Horn at the cost of several slaves, beat out into the Pacific, and apparently reached what was to become Polynesia, then were blown to the continent's west coast, where they had dealings with the remote ancestors of the Incas, and on past Mexico to California.

Finally they reached the Bay. They had run out of female slaves, and the natives in the locality turned out to be very friendly and hospitable — so much so that Marduk's ship suffered the same fate as *Dryad*, with the one difference that she sank completely.

At this point Marduk heaved a great sigh. "I often suspected," he said, "that I was being punished because I did not sacrifice enough slaves to the gods, but in recent centuries I have started to wonder whether it was because I sacrificed too many. Ah, a man grows soft and sentimental in his old age . . ."

And then I could restrain my own eager curiosity no longer. "Admiral Marduk," I said respectfully, "exactly *where* in the Bay did your ship go down?"

"Ha-*ha!*" he exclaimed. "Boy, do you think to get her treasure? By the time she sank, there was precious little left that my scoundrelly crew had not absconded with."

"You misunderstand my friend Andrew," said the Captain, and he went on to explain my interest in undersea archaeology.

"Hah! That is different," said Marduk. "Bring me a chart and I will point out the exact spot."

"A chart?" The Captain frowned. "I'm afraid we don't have one, but I'm sure there's an auto club map of the area somewhere — that ought to do it."

"What absolute crap!" sneered McWhinney, who had just downed his drink. "Everyone knows Columbus discovered America, and he didn't get anywhere near the Bay. Anyhow, what's all this Marduk garbage? Marduk was a Babylonian god, and he'd have been long out of date by the time this character came along."

"*Indeenaq!*" Marduk yelled. "You — you turtle's anus! My *father* named me Marduk. You are named after a Greek poet who, if he ever lived, has been dead longer than I have, and it was not your unknown father who named you!"

"Well, you've got no business pestering my Ludmilla. Hell, she could be channeling somebody useful, like what's-her-name Shirley MacLaine's gang and just raking the dough in!"

Marduk started to say what he would do to him if only he was in the flesh, but as he finished in an unknown tongue we could only guess at the gory details.

In the meantime, the Captain had risen, called Mickey to the door, given him whispered instructions, and returned with a large-scale map of the upper bay and a fresh drink for McWhinney, who accepted it ungraciously. He winked at me. "An Embarcadero Special," he said, *sotto voce.*

He spread out the map, oriented it carefully, and pointed out salient points to the Phoenician. They commented on minor changes in the topography over the centuries, and he started moving his finger like a Ouija board pointer. Suddenly Marduk cried, *"There! There is where those eels' turds scuttled my ship, my beautiful ship."*

The Captain's finger stabbed down, and he used a felt pen to mark the spot with a large red **X**.

It was well up the delta of the Sacramento River, and I realized, dismally, that the wreck was, after all these centuries, undoubtedly under forty or fifty feet of silt.

Either my expression gave me away or the Captain read my mind. "Andy, Andy," he said, "do not despair. Remember modern technology — but just be very, very careful who you let in on it."

Having had some experience with what can happen to original discoveries too carelessly broadcast by eager graduate students, I knew that his point was well taken.

"The Captain is your friend," declared Marduk. "He will help you, and I too shall be there — I promise you! You will make sure that I, Admiral Marduk, will get full credit in today's world for first discovering this magnificent harbor?"

"We'll do our damndest," promised the Captain, and I echoed him.

"You can always get in touch with me through this lovely lady," Marduk asserted. "No matter where I am — Bremen, Capetown, Cap Finisterre — I will come immediately."

McWhinney, having swilled his drink almost in a gulp, started to say something offensive, but couldn't quite manage it. He dropped his glass, and his chin fell forward on his chest. He started to snore.

"A very reliable compound," said the Captain. "It was used in the sailing-ship days to shanghai sailors when a ship was short handed."

"Throw the turd overboard!" advised Marduk. "I wish I could stay and watch, but I've been here too long already. I have other duties to perform."

We bade him good night, and a moment later Ludmilla came awake, orienting herself and reaching for her glass, which Mickey had thoughtfully refilled.

"Hey, did he show?" she asked.

The Captain informed her that he had indeed, that they had had a most interesting and informative session, and that both he and I couldn't thank her enough.

She looked at McWhinney, now sprawled face-down over the table. "Oh balls!" she exclaimed. "Here's old lover boy drunk again. Somebody help me get him in the car and I'll roll him home to bed — the useless bastard. Would you believe he's a high school history teacher? Would you believe there's a high school in Oakland where they *teach* history?"

She stayed for three more of her green drinks, which I must admit she held admirably. Then Mickey and the Captain and I helped her load him into her car after we carried him to the parking lot, and we watched her drive away. The two grad students had disappeared.

"Well, Andrew," said the Captain, "now aren't you glad I took her seriously? Just think, poor 'Opkins and Lydy 'Amilton, free after all these years to go on to wherever. And up the Bay, there's that galley waiting for you. Now will you be going directly home to Berkeley, or would you rather come back in and chat for a bit? I've a feeling you've got a few questions you'd like to ask me."

Once more, I was amazed at his perceptiveness. The session with Marduk and la Gooch had intensified the feeling I'd had about there being something strange about him.

"Captain, I'd like very much to — and you're right about the questions — that is, if you don't mind?"

"Not at all, my boy, not at all," he said, "and my Juliana — she's Javanese but that's her Dutch name — will probably join us there. She speaks only Dutch and her native language, so she won't contribute much to the conversation, but most people are content just to look at her."

I followed him back into the cuddy, where Mickey had our drinks ready for us; and presently we were joined by an absolutely gorgeous Javanese girl. She looked like an idealized dream of Bali, and instantly I found myself undressing her in my imagination. I'm afraid I blushed.

"Don't worry, Andy," he said. "She won't be offended. She knows just about everyone does it."

He stood, seated her; and Mickey served her what looked like a glass of dry sherry.

The Captain smiled. "And now, Andy," he said, "what about those questions?"

"Well sir —" I hesitated, then went on as he nodded encouragingly. "Captain, there were several things this evening. That Phoenician admiral acted as though he'd known you a long time. So did Hopkins. And you yourself acted as if you'd known both Hopkins and that cat, Lady Hamilton. And I've met several people who say they've known you for years and you never seem to get any older. I hope you won't mind my saying so, but — well, it is kind of weird."

"You're quite right," he said. "You have no idea just how strange it is. I'll tell you about it — I know you won't repeat anything I say, and anyhow nobody's believe you if you did. The truth of the matter, Andrew, is that I did know poor 'Opkins. I knew him because I was in command of the *Dryad* when she put into San Francisco Bay, so I was held responsible for the crew's desertion and for the fact that some of them managed to get back into her and scuttle her when they heard that our Consul and I had sent to the Admiralty for a replacement crew by the fastest means then available. In the meantime, some of my officers, and the ship's carpenter, who'd remained loyal, had done their best to waterproof her aftercabins, just in case, which was fortunate, because the city was starting to fill in the waterfront as fast as possible, covering up the sunken and sinking hulks with thousands of wagonloads of earth.

"There was nothing we could do to stop them. By the time another Royal Naval vessel brought us the crew I'd asked for, the *Dryad* was as you see here now."

He sighed heavily. "Unhappily," he said, "the report had been brought directly to the attention of Her Majesty the Queen, who — as you may remember from your history books — was *not* amused. Her order came to me directly — by a Queen's Messenger and written in her own hand. *Dryad* was to remain on the active list, and I was ordered to remain in command "until such a time as the crew could be returned, properly punished, and the ship made ready for sea service," all of which was, of course, patently impossible. I imagine that, what with other matters, the Crimean War and whatever, she probably forgot about me; but my pay kept coming in, first through our Consulate, then less formally through one of the banks, and always in golden sovereigns — they must have a lot of them still stowed away. Well, I made the best of it. I had some family money. so I bought up the new bit of land they'd filled in and put up the hotel, which at least has been interesting."

"But Captain Crankshaw, I — I'm still puzzled. How — how on earth? — after all, *everybody* ages."

His face hardened. His gray eyes looked out to a horizon I couldn't see. "Andrew," he declared, "Her Majesty the Queen was no ordinary woman. Do you realize that, at the age of barely eighteen, she ascended an imperiled throne, totally unprepared either by training or experience, and during her more than sixty-year reign brought us to our pinnacle of power and prosperity? Consider her Ministers — Wellington, Disraeli who crowned her Empress of India, even Gladstone. Andrew, she had those mysterious *powers* royalty was always believed to possess. Even George III, in his madness, wandered the streets of London curing the King's Evil, as one of your historians — Davidson, I think his name was — discussed in detail. In short, her orders were to be *obeyed*. If I aged, I could not have obeyed them. If I had been a young man, more people would have noticed that I grew no older and made more of it, but I was already in my middle years, when no one really notices. In any case, most people's memories are short and muddled. Nowadays they'd probably say my subconscious had some thing to do with it."

He was silent for a moment. Then he smiled. "There are times, Andy, when I regret not having gone on to be an Admiral and finally retire to Norfolk and write my memoirs. But in may ways I've had a rewarding and interesting life." He and Juliana smiled at each other and I began to feel like an intruder. "I've had adventures I otherwise never would have had, and met people I never would have met. And there's more ahead. I can hardly wait till you dig up that galley of Marduk's — I'm sure you will. That'll really set those Columbus people on their ear, though I do feel a bit sorry for those who claimed the honor of the Bay's discovery for Sir Francis Drake."   Ω

THE EXPECTANT FATHER TO HIS UNBORN CHILD

My Jewish friends have told me that a child,
Before it slides its way to being born,
Possesses these: The secret names of God;
The hidden sources of Heaven; All the wild
Fulfilling wisdon that its parents mourn
Their foolish loss of. It is not the rod
Of education nor the chains of work
That rob us of the Marvellous, but the spite
Of Angels: For a stroking finger seals
The child's mouth into silence. Thus some clerk,
Some Bureaucrat of God, denies out right
To Wonder, as around us life congeals.
Sweet child, resist. Deny that curtain's fall:
Bite the Angel's finger. Tell me all.

— Peter Atkins

by Reginald Bretnor   **43**

AGAINST THE GRACE OF FIRE
by Batya Swift Yasgur

Three men and a boy, three boys and a man, and who the hell cares? There were four of them, man-boys, the youngest still with downy growth on his upper lip and slim grace in his thighs and hips, the oldest grimly bulging above and below, his bushy mustache stout and loud. Brothers, no question. Four.

And they held me down in that wooded patch, once a halcyon scrap of untramelled nature, between the library and Main Street. Ripped and ripped, till shreds and tatters and threads hung here and there over my shivering body, a quivering snail with shattered shell, a tiny white pupa whose cocoon has been rent. Rip, then stab, as they tore and stabbed and burned their way into my secret and holy passage. Thrust and stab, pouring the scum of shame into what was once innocent and inquiring, once a pristine and loving space of intimacy and trust. Tearing, thrashing, beating against its numb and pleading walls.

Until they left me, tears mingled with their sweat on my face, red and white fluids oozing, congealing, drying in sticky puddles between my legs

And inside, in my gut, in my ruptured and violated loins, a furnace, flames of blood and smoke sizzling and rising in sustaining fury. Rage, driving my knees to crawl, my hands to clear bramble and brush, my shaking form to rise, rise after collapse, rise through exhaustion, rise through my own screams which still roared in my ears. Rise and walk, stumble, grope through night calls of owl and cricket, rise and walk. Until Main Street and the Police Station at last.

Indignities.
Police procedures. Police doctors, scraping and peering into my lacerated and humiliated once private spot, now public property, display of the state, as specula and slides were inserted. DNA, semen samples, blood types. Yes, yes, I said wearily, do what you have to do. As I heard her — once my most intimate and privileged friend — crying in outrage, haven't they done enough?

Mug shots. Grim faces, baleful eyes, contemptuous glares in album after dreary album. Nothing.

Rumbles and mutters. Investigations, more interviews, more questions. Leads. Similar to crimes elsewhere — more leads. Then nothing.

Nothing.
Support groups and counselors, earnest and well-intentioned, throwing shiny pennies into my screaming abyss. Nights of sleepless darkness, the television puddling its feeble light, parading its tinsel comfort across the hollow spaces, as sleep treacherously smiled,

hiding under pillows, only to bounce downy lips and bushy mustaches, prying hands and searing thrusts against my drooping eyelids.

One month. Two, then three.

It was clear, it became as clear as the fire which had sustained me. I needed help: Rosita.

Rosita. Onyx-eyed, onyx-haired, ruby lipped, childhood neighbor and best friend. In whose kitchen I had passed hours of awe and delight with her mother, Señora Garcia. A family where curses and demonic influences were taken for granted, as germs are accepted in the modern hospital or classroom. Where las almas and los spiritos visited and dropped in like friendly or officious neighbors. To Rosita and Señora Garcia, then, and their brujera.

"Bah!" Señora Garcia spat. "Los policías. Ain't worth nada, believe me. I give you Señora Carmen's number. She will fix everything for you."

And so, nervously — because here I was, a modern, rational woman with a degree from Barnard College and an MBA from Wharton — clutching a scrap of paper with scrawled directions, seeking out a magician. A medicine woman. A shamaness. A brujera.

Ah, this must be the place. My knees announcing their skepticism with a series of trembles, I knocked on the door, expecting a stream of Spanish words. "Come in, it's open!" a voice called in utterly Barnardian English.

I pushed the door, expecting to see a gypsy fortune teller's booth — mysterious and eerie drapes, crystal balls, incense, perhaps crosses or pentagrams or whatever magicians use, and a raven-haired woman with darkened eyelashes, long red fingernails and scarlet robes, muttering incantations over a candle.

But the woman who came to the door was slight and sandy-haired, dimpled and denim-jeaned. "Expected some old witch, huh?"

"I —"

"Forget it. Sit, sit, and tell me what I can do."

"I want revenge. Four men, they raped me like animals. No —" I glanced down at a cat which had slunk out of the kitchen and was rubbing against my leg. "Not like animals. Animals mate. Maybe they copulate. They don't violate. These guys did, and I want to do it all back to them. And worse."

She regarded me with steady hazel eyes. "OK. I see that this is true. But you have to do everything I tell you."

There was something about this woman that inspired trust. Maybe it was the complete absence of magical trappings and pretensions, maybe the clarity and depth of those eyes, there was kindness and mystery and impenetrability there, levels of power I had never encountered. "OK. Anything."

"Good. Do you have any object of theirs?"

"Of course not."

"Well, then, how about the clothing you were wearing?"

"I threw it all out." I shuddered, remembering how I had carried what was left of my skirt and blouse to the incinerator.

She shook her head and sighed. "This isn't going to be easy. You'll have to take me to the spot where it happened."

I blanched. "But —"

"You said you'd be willing to do anything." Her eyes burrowed, drills of crystal, and I nodded slowly.

Back to the wooded patch, then, my cries still echoing, bouncing off trees and moss, witnesses to ravagement and violation, my blood screaming from the soil. Señora Carmen, her nose quivering, was sniffing the ground, gathering bits of grass and bark and dirt into a container. I gasped as she pulled a large pearl-handled knife. "I'm sorry —" her voice wavered for the first time — "You've already been through so much —" And with a flash of her wrist she had my skirt up, the knife had whisked under my panties, and she was holding a lock of pubic hair. Her arms were steady and cooling on my neck as I leaned over and vomited chunks of foulness pouring on land already defiled. "It was necessary," she said, handing me a handkerchief. "Now we can move ahead."

"You will find them," she told me a week later, "at Ed's Eatery in Hoboken." She handed me a piece of paper with the address, then she pulled out a box. "Here. Open it."

A mundane cardboard box, a box that could hold potatoes or photocopy papers or stored toys in someone's attic. I opened it and there were four small dolls inside. They were made out of some kind of clayey substance, clad in the moss and leaves Señora Carmen had collected, and their hair I recognized, too, with another heave of the belly. Four dolls, four plunderers.

"You will take these." Her voice was emerald, hypnotic, I was nodding. "You will go to the diner, you will look at them, you will watch them, you will walk over to them, you will stand before them, you will look at them, you will take this —" she handed me a long pin, it could have been one of my mother's hatpins, but it had an odd symbol on top, something that could have been a cross but had squiggly lines — "and you will stick it in any part of the body you want, and you will watch what happens."

And the heat inside surged and leaped and the fire smiled and sizzled and beckoned.

And there they were.

Three men and a boy, three boys and a man, and who the hell cared? There were my four man-boys, fingers sticky with ketchup and mustard (hands of blood and semen), shoveling cheese burgers into their mouths (those mouths, raven caves of yawning lust).

Clutching my box, the fire ready to leap, I looked at them, I watched them. Watched their faces — faces that had seen me in rawness and humiliation — heard their laughter, coarse and porcine.

Hugging my box, the fire coursing now through veins of rag and scar, I crossed the room and stood before them.

They gasped when they saw me. The biggest, his mustache still quivering with ketchup, dropped his burger, the youngest's eyes skittered to and fro. Then a leer spread over the mustached face, a slow sweep of the lip into a curl, a sneer of power, of knowledge, of ownership.

The sneer did it. The fire burst forth, I whipped the doll out of its box, the biggest doll, and drove the pin into its groin.

He stood up, then, clutched his groin, doubled over, writhing, strangled pain spewing from his mouth, together with his dinner.

The murmur of restaurant conversation ceased, faces turned to us, three horrified brothers, one stricken screamer, one blazing woman.

I pulled out the pin and shoved it in again, right into the center point between the legs.

His eyes bulged, the scream that tore from this throat sent the other diners shrieking to safety, he clutched at himself, screaming and screaming. Blood was pouring forth as I withdrew the pin and stabbed, again, this time at the heart.

And as he slumped to the floor, the next brother got it in the eyes. Eyes that had beheld my degradation, had violated my sacredness. And the next brother in the ears. Stone ears that had ignored my screams.

Then there was one left.

The youngest. He trembled before me, cowered and shook before my gaze.

And then I remembered. Twice she had said it, hadn't she? You will look at them, you will walk over to them, you will look at them. Look at them not just once, but twice.

I had done it all, but had not looked at them. Not really. Not that second time. There was one brother left, and I must look at him, must force myself to see whatever I would see. And watch what would happen.

I must look at the peachiness still clinging to his lip, bridge to years of innocence. Look at the slimness of hips and thighs, the shaking of hands. Look at his eyes. Look, look, look.

And see, suddenly, his eyes, powder blue like the carpet in my bedroom when I was a child, reflected off the dresser mirror, and through those eyes, into his childhood bedroom. Drawn into those eyes, through those eyes, I found myself in a sorry concatenation of four chests and four beds, walls resounding with blows and screams, four boys cowering under flimsy sheets as a monstrous lout lugged his massive form to their bedsides, their butts red and weeping, their maleness hiding, tiny and shy, from his searching, sausagelike fingers. In the caverns of his still boyish eyes, the black coils of molten memory, the childface of dew and light retreating, pushing into the foreground a mask of claw and darkness.

And remember — then — my classmate Minnie, scrawny, pimply Minnie whose name was a natural invitation to the razor of fifth grade derision, "Skinny Minnie." And remember Randy and Maureen, glowering over me. "You either say you hate her, or we're going to hate you." And my voice, wavering as I hurled the ultimate insult, the name that swam her through rivers of tears, until eight grade when her parents moved away: "Skinny Pinny Minnie." Basking in their approval, but hating them, hating Minnie for her sniveling victimhood, hating myself most of all.

This man-boy, younger than the others, eager for their approval, for the solidarity and protection of brotherly Unity in Hatred — he was no different from me. What he had done, I had done. I shivered in the inner prison of his terror, his past and his present, and I knew I had to give him his future because it was mine too.

She had told me to look at them again, Señora Carmen, and I hadn't. Now I looked, and I saw myself.

I held up the doll, water battling fire, my tears falling on the hatpin in searing drops. I advanced, step by step, as he shrank back into his chair. I held the doll in front of me, a torch of heat and light.

"Go." Then louder. "Go, I won't — I can't — harm you. Let there be one person in your life who hasn't violated you." His pupils were dilated, enormous black holes in the blue sky, his mouth opened slightly as if he were trying to say something. "I'm going to hold onto this." I thrust the doll in front of his face and he flinched. "You rape anyone else and I will set this doll on fire."

Back, then, to the wooded patch, the fire smoldering but quieter now, three dismembered dolls and a hatpin in my hand.

To bury the dolls, under that ground of desecration, allow green to grow from the ruins of memory, allow the sprigs and shoots of delicate Spring to grow from the staff of winter. Standing there, standing there in that strange and curious glade torn into the forest like a pit of memory; odd shafts of light, pincers of memory, coming in and out of that secret place. Placing the dolls in the ground and slowly, piece by piece, covering them with clumps of dirt, then backing away from that place in those odd shafts of light, staring, dreaming. And from that place over my heart where the fourth doll nestled warm as ice, a coldness as deep as fire lancing through me. Carrying, trundling that doll through all of the eaves and spaces of my life to come. Carrying thus, until that clear and questing moment, that redemptive moment, when it would be time to wrench that ice and fire from me and place it in that oldest and deepest of places, that final place, that place from which all creation must come.

And to which it must go.   Ω

NIGHT

What if the sounds outside my bedroon window were
          not the gently scraping of the bare tree limb on the cool glass,
          but the desperate scratch of one long dead,
          wanting in to warm his bare bones.

What if the sounds outside my bedroom window were
          not the night song of the insects and the reptiles
          harmonizing on the still country air,
          but the low humming cries of those disappeared.

What if the sounds outside my bedroom window were
          not the thunder rolling like boulders on hard ground,
          but my own dimension shifting slowly
          out from under me.

To leave me hanging
in the thin air.

— Donna Taylor Burgess

A TALK WITH S.P. SOMTOW
by Darrell Schweitzer

S.P. Somtow, whose real name is Somtow Papinian Sucharitkul, is a native of Thailand, who began writing science fiction while living in the Washington D.C. area in the middle 1970's. Some of his science fiction books are *Starship and Haiku, Mallworld,* and the "Inquestor" and "Aquiliad" sequences. He won the John W. Campbell Award for best new writer in 1981. But this was only one of his many careers. He has also been a leading composer of Thai avant-garde music, a musical ghost-writer, a seminal horror writer (*Vampire Junction* and sequels and *Moon Dance*), and he has directed two films, *The Laughing Dead* and *Ill Met By Moonlight.*

Worlds of Fantasy & Horror: So, you are not merely a well-established fantasy and horror writer, but, I understand, virtually an ancestral figure.

Somtow: Yes, it was Philip Nutman who first said in *The Twilight Zone* magazine that I was one of the four ancestral figures of the Splatterpunk genre. Frankly, although I didn't know it at the time, I've exploited it. I admit it. I've used "Grandfather of Splatterpunk" on numerous blurbs. It's amazing to me that such a label is necessary, because actually my work hasn't that much in common with Splatterpunk, except of course for large amounts of gore. And even that — I've mellowed a lot, as far as the large amounts of gore are concerned.

WoF&H: We're talking about *Vampire Junction,* which was a 1984 book. Twelve years ago and you're the *grandfather* of a literary movement that's already passed its peak?

Somtow: Yes, I would consider the entire movement to be dying in its infancy, probably because there is a limit to what one can achieve in such a narrow interpretation of the horror genre. But many of the things that I tried to do in *Vampire Junction,* like writing a novel that's structurally based on MTV videos — which is really how the novel is put together — those are things that were new to horror writing and were take up by many people, whether they used that label or not. I think that this is now a common feature of horror writing.

WoF&H: It seems to me that the inherent limitation in the Splatterpunk aesthetic, if we may call it that, is that once you've shown everything, you've *shown everything,* so there is nothing left to show. It's like bringing on the monster in the first reel, so there are no more shocks later on.

Somtow: Yes, that's why I've stopped showing things. I've shifted from the showing-everything bit to my mainstream novels, because it's a little more new there. In the book that I'm writing now, *Bluebeard's Castle,* which sounds like a horror novel but isn't, there are a couple of very intense serial-killing scenes that are just passed by in a couple of pages. The whole novel is not like that.

WoF&H: Here again you have encompassed an entire trend in a couple of pages.

Somtow: [Laughs]. Well, yeah . . . One of the reasons that I had to do that is this is a novel being published in weekly installments, and so one doesn't have more than a couple pages to encapsulate entire trends in.

WoF&H: Are you writing this like a 19th-century novel, in that you turn each installment in a week before it appears?

Somtow: No, I fax it in two days before it appears, which gives them no chance to change anything. So I've managed to be really out there, and they haven't been able to do anything about it. So it's very exciting. The first novel I wrote in that way was *Jasmine Nights,* and I found myself becoming more and more daring because of the knowledge that they would print it, no matter how daring I was. So it was a real watershed for me in terms of what I dared to write about.

WoF&H: Where is *Bluebeard's Castle* being serialized?

Somtow: It's being serialized in *The Nation,* an English-language newspaper in Bangkok. Now the English-speaking community in Bangkok is small, but it's frightfully cultural, so I can put in references to really obscure things and it doesn't faze them, which is one of the best things about it.

WoF&H: You could probably slip a horror novel in on them and they'd never know the difference.

Somtow: Well, there are scenes which appear to be horror. The odd thing is that the editor at Hamish Hamilton, who originally bought *Jasmine Nights* after it had been rejected by thirty publishers, had never heard of me, because she didn't read horror or any other genre. She said to me, "I was able to read your novel with an unprejudiced eye because, of course, I don't read genre."

Now that the editors at Hamish Hamilton know that I'm a genre writer, they've rejected *Bluebeard's Castle.* They're seeing all these tiny little genre clues in it, which were also present in *Jasmine Nights,* only they didn't know that I was a genre writer. So it's a double-edged sword.

WoF&H: Have you got a publisher yet?

Somtow: Not yet. I'm going to do what my agent did with *Jasmine Nights,* which is wait until it's finished. I seem to do a lot better that way, financially at least.

WoF&H: It sounds like a book someone could publish as horror anyway if they wanted to, like that last Tom Tryon novel, which wasn't really a horror novel at all, but was packaged as one.

Somtow: It was a Boy Scout Camp coming-of-age horror novel. It *is* horror, but not what you'd think of as horror.

Yes, they may decide that *Bluebeard's Castle* is horror, and if that's the way I have to go in order to pay the mortgage, then so be it. But it really isn't.

WoF&H: Apparently horror is absolutely dead as a commercial category right now. So they'll call it "dark suspense" or something like that.

Somtow: The only problem with calling it horror is that this book is hideously funny. All these awful things happen in it, like the heroine has RU-486 administered to her secretly, so her fetus can be aborted and made into a voodoo fetish without her knowledge, and so on and so forth. But she has this cynical sense of humor and is always saying things like, "Yes, it was terrifying, but I was starting to get turned on by it all." This tone is something that might make it a hard sell as a straight horror novel.

WoF&H: Maybe the horror readership is sufficiently jaded that they'll go for it, in the same way that, on one level, Ramsey Campbell's *The Count of Eleven* is a successfully funny serial-killer novel.

Somtow: Yes. That's what I am hoping will happen that people will approach it already jaded, or else it will reach a completely fresh audience that likes to be cynical and likes to satirize itself.

WoF&H: Do you think in terms of being a horror writer or of your work being horror fiction, or do you just let it fly where it may and then let someone else figure this out?

Somtow: I never have thought of myself as a horror writer, and it was only the fact when I did *Vampire Junction* they made me change my name that sort of split me off into a new genre.

WoF&H: Tell the story of why you changed your name.

Somtow: It's a very simple story. Berkley books said that if I changed my name, they'd make me a star. I did and they didn't. But I didn't want to change it too much. It's been a cumulative thing, because, although each edition of *Vampire Junction* has never sold that well, all together it has been quite a large best-seller. It's pretty steady.

WoF&H: I could see it and its sequels as a series of movies. An immortal twelve-year-old vampire rock star has a certain appeal. What a wonderful role for Macaulay Culkin at one point . . .

Somtow: [Makes sound of distaste.] Mary Lambert, who directed Madonna videos, and then went on to do Stephen King movies, *Pet Sematary* and so on, is

very interested in doing the book. We pitched it to Paramount at one point, and the producer there was an ex-starlet. In the middle of the pitching session, she actually asked us if it had vampires in it. So this is about intelligent Hollywood can be at times. She said, "Oh. This book has vampires?" She also asked Mary Lambert who she was. It was very odd. But it seemed to me that someone who had done MTV videos — she is very famous for doing the Madonna videos, which are very erotic and dark at the same time — and was able to infuse eroticism into it, would be perfect. She really wanted to do it. She wanted to have Leonardo DiCaprio play the role of Timmy Valentine — he's a little old, but it might work quite well.

WoF&H: There may be times when it's more important to get a good actor than to get the age precisely right. It would be very difficult to find a twelve-year-old who could play that part, and if you could get a sixteen-year-old instead, who's good, or somebody who just looks sixteen, then go for it.

Somtow: I agree completely. I've done three *Vampire Junction* books, and I am a little worried that it may be my fate to have to produce another, because sometimes I can go to a publisher and say "I have all these great ideas for books," and I start reeling them off, and they're kind of ho-humming, and then I say, "Then I'll just do you a sequel to *Vampire Junction.*" Then they just send a contract. This is frightening to me.

WoF&H: If you're successful enough, you could meet the fate of Edgar Rice Burroughs. You could end up writing twenty-five of them, and readers can predict whole chapters in advance. So I guess you need to reinvent yourself every once in a while.

Somtow: As you know, I really hate to repeat myself that much, and this has gotten me into really bad trouble as a writer. I could have written five hundred *Aquiliad*s or five hundred *Mallworld*s. Or maybe five hundred Inquestor novels. I could have been as big as Stephen R. Donaldson if I'd written five hundred Inquestor novels, for example. Or I could be like Douglas Adams if I had written five hundred Mallworld books. What can I say? I just can't bring myself to do it. There is always a strong temptation to do so, because it's the only way to make money.

WoF&H: Well, you've had your own flirtations with the movie industry.

Somtow: [Laughs.] You could call them flirtations if you like. *The Laughing Dead,* even though it has never been released in this country, has acquired quite a reputation as a cult item, because of the various well-known science-fiction writers who appear in it having their heads crushed, and so on. It seems to show up regularly at every science-fiction convention in the video room. In fact it got a rave review from Michael Weldon of *Psychotronic Film Guide,* which is the imprimatur of greatness among bad horror movies. Then I did the Shakespeare film, because I decided that at that budget I might as well do something relentlessly intellectual instead of just another slasher film, to see what would happen. They didn't go for that either, you know. I made the film and I am still looking for a distributor for it.

WoF&H: You refer to the genre you're working in as "bad horror films," not just horror films.

Somtow: Yes, I have not been working in horror films, *per se.* I have been working in bad horror films, which is a completely different genre from horror films, okay?

Bad horror films contain certain elements which are very important. For example, a mysterious villain who speaks in a British accent. There are certain tropes that are required. Therefore, even though my character in *The Laughing Dead* was a Mayan death god, I still had to speak in a British accent because it was a tradition in the bad horror film that this must occur.

WoF&H: Then we're defining the bad horror film as one which is self-aware and campy, with its own aesthetic, like underground art which may be deliberately ugly and crude. All this is different from the merely inept.

Somtow: Absolutely. I am not using "bad horror film" as a pejorative in any way. It is merely a genre with its own tropes, its own sensibilities. I've tried very hard to make my Roger Corman film a bad horror film. But unfortunately it wasn't quite bad enough when it came out, because they had tinkered with the screenplay too much.

Roger asked me to do an adaptation of Bram Stoker's "The Burial of the Rats" as a film, and he just gave me a list of sets that he had acquired the use of in Moscow. They had things like the Bastille, Versailles, these huge historical sets. He said, "Well you can write anything you want as long as it has this title, and I have to have the first draft next week." This was my job interview. "You must use every single one of the sets on this list."

I thought I would create the ultimate bad horror movie in my script, but it didn't work out that way. For one thing, Roger told me that he wanted it to be really wild. But I didn't know that that was a code Roger Corman word for having a lot of tits. I thought he *really* wanted to be really wild. The script is about the young Bram Stoker being abducted in France by lesbian highway women who are controlled by a mad queen who plays a magic flute and thinks she's Marie Antoinette, played by Andrienne Barbeau. The lesbian highway women induct him into the ways of feminism, while sitting around being scantily-clad at the same time. We have both left-wing liberal indoctrination and hideous male-chauvinism at the same time, which is kind of cool.

WoF&H: But in a self-aware, parodic way.

Somtow: However, most of the hilarious, pseudo-19th-century dialog that I created as been replaced by rather stodgy dialog. Only a few lines, like "I am the Pied Piper's twisted sister" remain.

WoF&H: Do you think you could move into the related genre of good horror films?

Somtow: I don't think I'd want to. I think I'd rather move from bad horror films to a completely different genre, like a mainstream film. Well, that's a silly word too. But the film that I just set up was an art film of the most owing caliber. It a cross between *Sleepless in Seattle* and *The Crying Game*, set in Bangkok. Unfortunately for me, Margaux Hemingway was one of the three stars attached to the film, so, because she committed suicide, I was kind of fucked. I'm still hoping to get it back together again somehow. But this was a film that didn't have a taint of horror to it at all, although it does have a shaman who gets possessed by the god Shiva.

WoF&H: There you go. That's enough. But how to you go about getting a film together. A lot of people would like to be movie moguls and make their own films, but you actually got to do it. So what's the difference?

Somtow: The first time, we were subsidized by Lex Nakashima, a well-known science-fiction fan. He simply had the money, so that was great. The second time we did it, I sold five-thousand-dollar shares to my relatives and to many other people, who are now breathing down my neck, so I'd better sell the film fast. I got a $100,000 grant from Mr. Sondhi who owns *Buzz* magazine in L.A.. He's a Thai guy. Because it was culture, Shakespeare and all that, we were able to get a lot of people who wouldn't otherwise do a hideous low-budget film to work for us. Timothy Bottoms, who is definitely an A-list actor, signed up to do it. Other actors, like Robert Z'dar, who is only known for being the Maniac Cop and other monsters in horror movies, wanted to do it so he can say he's done Shakespeare. So we had actors from both sides agreeing to do it.

WoF&H: To get back to horror fiction, we're talking about all these campy, self-aware horror films, but surely you have to control such tendencies in fiction. I don't think there's such a thing as the bad horror novel.

Somtow: Not at all. I think that my horror novels are about as different from my horror film projects as it is possible for two things with the word "horror" in them to be. But there is one thing that they have in common, in a way, is that both the bad horror film and my novels rely a great deal on the hipness of the viewer or reader to catch numerous references. But in my B-movies, those references are to other bad horror films, but in my novels, they're references to works of literature. So it's a different audience.

WoF&H: What do you think makes good horror fiction?

Somtow: I don't know. At first one ought to say that all fiction deals with love and death, and horror, of course, deals with love and death in a very more visceral way. But I haven't been scared by a horror novel in some time, so that's probably not it anymore. If it brings me even a slight flutter of how I felt as a child reading *Some of Your Blood* or something like that, then I feel that I am reading a really good horror novel.

WoF&H: Can you get this feeling while writing something?

Somtow: I aim for that. It's happened only a few times in my writing, when I've actually become absolutely terrified. It's happening less now, I confess. That's why I'm trying to reach out to something even darker, in some ways. I have been doing a series of extremely blasphemous stories lately. I thought maybe that would work.

WoF&H: It would to believers in whatever you're blaspheming.

Somtow: [Laughs] That's true. But even though I am sort of pan-religious these days, I was still brought up in a strict Buddhist/Anglican environment. Therefore I have two very powerful sets of traditional values working on me.

WoF&H: The readers would be interested, so why don't you say something about your background?

Somtow: When I was six months old, my parents and I left Thailand. My Dad was in the middle of doing his Ph.D. at Oxford, so I grew up in a very dissociative way, because I actually thought I was English. One of my famous statements from my childhood was, "I'm English and you're foreigners," which I said to my parents once. [Laughs.] Then, when I was seven years old, we moved back to Thailand. I spent five years there. I had a tremendous case of culture shock, and I got out of that by retreating into a study of the Greek myths and the classics, and so on. All that is narrated in my semi-autobiographical novel, *Jasmine Nights.* Everything in the book is sort of true, although not in that order or to that extent. Things like the fellating grandmother who removes her false teeth before the act, that, for example, is true.

WoF&H: I know you were educated in Britain, but you have lived in the United States off and on for many years.

Somtow: I grew up in four different countries, but after I started going to school in England, I pretty much stayed there until I was in my twenties. Then I went to Thailand to try to become the Harlan Ellison of avant-garde Thai music. But I got so burned out by that that I came to America and accidentally became a science-fiction writer. I actually stayed in America without going anywhere much for about five or six years, but now I have a double life and actually spend a lot of time in Bangkok.

WoF&H: What this must give you is a genuinely unique perspective, by virtue of being an outsider in several cultures at once.

Somtow: Yes, that's right. Wherever I've gone I've always been an alien, which is very frightening, perhaps the most frightening thing about my life. Even when I am with my most intimate family members, I am still culturally a little off from them. I'm the black sheep in both cultures. It's rather scary.

WoF&H: Doesn't this make you observe more, because you take less for granted.

Somtow: Absolutely. I've always said that this is the reason that I've ever acquired skills as a writer at all. I'm spending more time in Thailand, which is really a wild place right now, and which has caused me to see many more things. As you probably know, Thailand has gone from sort of 1920 to the 21st century in the last ten years. It's amazingly wrenching to see the transformation occur. When I was a child, my house was at the edge of a paddy field, and right now Bangkok is the city with the highest pollution and noise rate in the world, and skyscrapers go up everywhere you look. It's got the world's largest shopping mall, strangely enough. Not only does this mall have a roller-coaster in it, but there's a little water park where you can get into bumper boats — on the eighth floor of the shopping mall. It also has the biggest bookstore in the world, by the way. I believe it is like five hundred thousand square feet.

WoF&H: This has also given you a great sense of the absurd.

Somtow: Very much so. Let me give you an example. The last time I was in Thailand, a woman jumped off a building that my family owned in Bangkok. She jumped off and committed suicide, which is very tragic. So then my family had to have the building exorcized. So they sent a fax to the local shaman. That's how things work there. Of course they had to have a religious ceremony right away, to appease the spirit of the woman who had jumped off the building, so it wouldn't jinx the building. But these are people going around in their Armadi suits and acting very modern, and yet they do these things as a matter of course. It wasn't a special deal to them. Of course shamans have beepers and fax machines. There are astrologers in shopping malls.

WoF&H: Just like in the United States.

Somtow: Yes and no. These astrologers actually do your whole chart. They have all the figures in their heads. They're like idiot savants of astrology.

WoF&H: I see how you can get very powerful horror fiction this way, from the fear of never fitting in anywhere. Do you feel this?

Somtow: I do fear it and I live with it every day, so it provides an undercurrent of unease in my life wherever I am, certainly. Do we have enough material now?

WoF&H: Just about. We have a few minutes of tape left, so we might as well use it. I could ask you the meaning of life. Or is that passé now?

Somtow: Well, it's not forty-two. In my new *Riverrun* trilogy, I try to answer the question of what is truth, which is pretty deep. The hero is writing an essay about truth. Since it goes through lots of alternate universes, the same essay is shown again and again in terms of the latest universe the characters have fallen into. And the answer he comes up with is that everything is true simultaneously.

WoF&H: I suppose the ultimate question then for the writer is how do you write about truth and horror and your deepest fears without laughing? Is it a good idea not to laugh?

Somtow: I always laugh. As you know, Darrell, I've dealt with some of the most profound questions of life by means of comedy in my works, even in my darkest works. Ed Bryant pointed out that scene in *Vampire Junction* where the kid's entire family has been killed and turned into vampires, and they're sitting around feasting on the blood of a corpse in a video arcade, and they say "You must become one of us now." And the kid realizes that this is the first time he's seen his family have a meal together in years. [Laughs.]

WoF&H: Are there also things which are too uncomfortable to be dealt with in any other way except by laughing?

Somtow: Absolutely. Just because you laugh does not mean it's funny. Just because you're terrified doesn't mean it's not funny either. The interface between humor and horror is something that *Bluebeard's Castle* really deals with. So I'm afraid nobody is going to buy it because no one will be able to make up their minds as to whether it's a satire or a novel of suspenseful terror.

WoF&H: It could be both.

Somtow: That's what I'm saying. It is both. But they're going to have to decide what it is before they can sell it. Maybe they'll make a funny cover and a scary cover and have them both out at the same time. That would be good.

WoF&H: One cover could have a laughing face and the other could have embossed entrails.

Somtow: Yeah. I could see that. Or they could do it front and back, and it could be one of those display dumps where the books are facing both ways.

WoF&H: Ultimately everything dissolves down to marketing.

Somtow: I hate to think that, but I've become pretty cynical about marketing. I've decided that I'm just going to write whatever I want to and let them decide how to package it. My work seems to be better since I have stopped worrying about what it's going to have on the cover!

WoF&H: That's probably a good place to stop. Thank you, Somtow.   Ω

ARGUMENT:

No thing hates me.
Au clair de la lune
Faceless evil cuddling other sheets
Than mine, would have me
For its own.
A pricked balloon, clair audient,
Telling visions, can own naught.
My creed my touchstone:
Nothing is not sacred.

I may get something from nothing,
But I reserve the right
To choose what.

— **Virginia Kidd**

THE HERO'S CELLULOID JOURNEY
by S.P. SOMTOW

illustrated by George Barr

The first time I saw the Lady of the Lake was at the Steinfelds' party. A lavish do, they have it every year; the extravagance of the bash is directly proportional to the tax write-off their accountant has told them they need to bring them down one bracket. Hate their parties, I really do; they rarely have anyone useful at them, just your usual Z-grade starlets, predatory agents, out-of-work screenwriters, dealers, pimps, and parasites. Not my kind of people. The only thing the Steinfelds and I have in common is the support group. Matilda Steinfeld (maybe you saw her on *Oprah*) is recovering from persistent memories, perhaps falsely implanted by her previous therapist, of Satanic childhood abuse; I am recovering from something far more mundane — my wife was hacked to pieces by a serial killer while I, tied to a chair, did nothing.

The Steinfelds' gazebo was hidden behind a wall of oleander; unless you knew your way around the estate, there was tendency to miss it. I had every reason to believe I was alone — alone, that is, save for my double Black Label on the rocks — when I hung up my shorts and lowered my shopworn, ample body into the hot tub. I just wanted to get away from these loathsome people long enough to clear my head. The cocktail canapés had not agreed with me. At first, I mistook the tickling sensation in my abdomen for some incipient digestive problem. Then, looking down into the water, tastelessly illuminated as it was by a shaft of pink light and a shaft of blue, I saw a mass of some kelplike growth undulating somewhere in the depths. Perhaps the pool man hadn't been in that week? But that was so unlike the Steinfelds — each of their house's fourteen bathrooms had color-coordinated toilet paper, for God's sake! — and it occurred to me that perhaps I should be getting frightened.

Perhaps I should even scream.

S.P. SOMTOW

But I couldn't, you see. That's why I'm in the support group. I don't feel terror anymore. I freeze up. I just flash back to being tied up in that chair, the *Three Stooges* necktie cutting into my wrists, my wife's wadded-up bra rammed into my mouth, choking me . . . and that madman slicing her, slowly, methodically, like a deli chef . . . like a slow-motion ginsu infomercial . . . grinning from ear to ear.

In any case, it was just as well I didn't. The mass of reddish seaweed churned about in the bubbles for a while; then — as the timer buzzed and the water went suddenly clear — I saw that it was human hair — a lot of human hair. It was attached to one of those pale, pre-Raphaelite faces: a thin, delicate nose, lips red as a coral snake; her hair was so long it formed a kind of robe around her nude body, though now and then a plump, firm breast went peek-a-boo; but I have not yet mentioned the eyes. They were as wide and vacuous as a Japanese cartoon's; they lent her a dreamlike quality which, had I been capable of fear, should have exacerbated it. Instead, I got out of it by cracking jokes, as usual.

"Well, well," I said, "if it isn't the Lady of the Lake. Got a sword for me, babe?"

She sat up, looked me over, and said, "Indeed, you're not quite the way I imagined you."

"Like the accent . . . what is it, Irish?"

"No, it's more Welsh than Irish; something in between, indeed." Now that she was sitting up, I realized she was startlingly beautiful — wet-dream beautiful, in fact. I was glad that I was no longer prone to penile embarrassments.

"The Steinfelds sent you over, didn't they?" I said. "But you know, I'm not much in the business anymore. I seem to have a sort of negative Midas touch. You wouldn't believe that *Home Alone* meets *Jurassic Park* could bomb, would you? But mine did. Sure, they still let me keep an office on the lot . . . I'm down the hall from Harry Gittes . . . but nobody takes me seriously anymore. I go in one day a week. The rest of the time I'm down at USC, teaching *The Hero's Celluloid Journey: Carl Jung, Joseph Campbell, and the Contemporary Filmmaker* to first-year film students. It's a wildly popular course. I like to think it's because I'm a grand old man, I mean, middle-aged of course, who used to hang out with all those '60s legends, but really I know it's because I'm the Greg Hoffman who was falsely imprisoned for the axe-murder of his own wife in the big scandal that was on *Hard Copy* and *A Current Affair*; it's *that* that makes me an icon, not a few second-rate thrillers from the '70s."

Mostly, by the time I'm about halfway through this speech, my audience has begun to twiddle its thumbs. I've perfected the spiel as a way of keeping my distance from people. It usually takes about five minutes to alienate a total stranger; but this woman listened to me raptly, her gaze never leaving my face. Was it the hair weave? No, she was staring straight into my eyes, seeing past the barriers, past the bullshit, into places I

myself no longer dared look. And because she would not look away from me, I could not look away from her; and the more I looked, the more I knew she could not be real; beauty such as hers is a virtual beauty, spawned by persistence of vision in the dark gaps between the lit frames of a motion picture.

I said, "What's your name?"

"Bridget," she said, which is the name of a Celtic goddess.

"You don't look like a Bridget. You ought to have some poetic, foreign-sounding name like, I don't know, Anastasia, Arabella, Antigone."

"We'll never get to the Bs at this rate, Greg."

"Wait! You know my name! The Steinfelds *did* send you after all. Haven't I seen you before somewhere? Cover of *Vanity Fair*? Or dancing with Madonna, cheek to cheek, tongue to tongue, that raunchy new video, can't remember the title? Bridget *who*? Oh, but of course, that's not your stage name."

Steam hung in the air. She shook her head, clouding the water. "There's no need to talk," she said. "You're not really saying anything."

I took a deep slug of the Black Label, then reached behind me to hit the timer switch again; leaned back to receive the full pressure of the jets against my back.

"You know why I'm here," she said.

"No idea. Some kind of casting couch deal, maybe."

"No, you *do* know. You said it when you first laid eyes on me, indeed. I've come to give you that sword."

"Yeah, right. Excalibur."

She laughed. "You are the one! Thank the Old Ones; I've been searching right long enough, let me tell you. You've named the quest, you've named the sword."

"Well, of course I have. I have to teach this shit to freshmen who all think they're going to be the next Martin Scorsese."

"You are the hero who does not know the meaning of fear."

Well, that was true enough, in a way. If being so traumatized that you can't feel any emotion whatsoever qualifies as not knowing the meaning of fear, she had me there.

"And you've kept yourself pure for seven years."

"Pure? I'm impotent. I haven't been able to get it up since, you know, the . . ."

And I still couldn't bring myself to say it aloud.

"Others have wronged you grievously, yet you have not spoken ill of them."

"You're just like that fucking state prosecutor," I said. "You've already made up your mind. Now you're twisting everything about me into your crackpot theory that I'm the next King Arthur."

She smiled at me. In the water, I could see the glint of metal. The pink and blue lights lanced the clouds of steam. A pommel was rising from the froth. I looked away. "I think I should be getting back to the party," I said. "It's been good talking to you."

"But I have to give you this sword."

"Hey, give me a break. I do the Arthurian mythos three days a week, 4 to 6 P.M. The rest of the time, it's strictly reality. If you find your fantasy world bleeding into real life, I know a good support group you can join."

I got dressed and waddled through the crowd that thronged the lanai, staggered over to the valet parking without even bothering to say goodbye to the Steinfelds. The place was madness. They let *anyone* here. I even noticed one of my pupils, Angel Serafino, a pre-med who was just doing my class for kicks. "Hi, Mr. Hoffman," he said, and waved at me. He was one of the bronzed young Californians who belong on the covers of cheap romance novels; his date, bedraggled and bespectacled, seemed an improbable match. They were both bearing down on me, but I was in no mood to discuss movies, and I knew that that was all Angel ever thought about. Horror in particular. Ordinarily I would have exchanged a word or two, but there was something in the air — some fragrance — that just made me want to flee.

Not now, I gestured, and managed to sneak through some French doors, down a corridor, and out toward the valet parking.

I climbed into my Ferrari — I'd been thinking of having it altered to accommodate my girth — and whizzed back over the hill to Tarzana. I can't afford Bel Air anymore, but I don't give out my new address much.

At home, I poured myself another drink, and then another. But I still couldn't stop thinking about Bridget. It was hard to escape the notion that I had had some kind of archetypal encounter. It all made perfect sense. From a Jungian point of view, Bridget would have been the earth-mother in her positive, nurturing aspect; a Freudian could easily see that the proffering of the sword referred to the possibility of curing my impotence, though my refusal to accept it might point to some, ah, bone of contention between my Superego and my Id.

The psychiatric resonances were so perfect that by my third Scotch I knew that the whole thing had been a dream. In fact, I was looking forward to telling a suitably embroidered version of it at the next support group.

Presented for your consideration: Gregory Hoffman, producer without a past, neuroses in the *n*th degree. Aspects of my emotional dysfunction: no pictures of my children to be found anywhere in the condo. (I knew, of course, that I had two grown children, Roseanne and Mortimer; but I had no memory of them.) Moreover, I had forgotten what my brother Joshua looked like. (Surely not like me. We were adopted.) There were no pictures of family members at all. Especially not Jennifer.

Looked at from the mythopoeic viewpoint, I certainly fit the profile of the lonely hero who did not know his origins.

I curled up on the sofa, turned on the gavel-to-gavel coverage of the Menendez trial, and slugged down another double shot.

It occurred to me that my two-bedroom condo in Tarzana was not substantially different from my cell on death row — the one they'd kept me in until somebody bothered to analyze the sperm stains on Jennifer's shredded pantyhouse. Of course, by then, the serial killer had done away with a few more women, and *Hard Copy* had done that episode that showed me sobbing, protesting my innocence, and one of those true crime writers — not Ann Rule, some second-string clone — had already churned out a big fat fantasy novel characterizable as nonfiction only by dint of its 2,647 uses of the word *allegedly*.

I mean, I was in jail. I counted them. Nothing else to do.

The studio had to give me my old job back, of course. It was the right thing to do. Even when *Me and My Velociraptor* bombed, they were kind. I got to keep the secretary from Brooklyn with the *faux* North London accent.

I couldn't remember that much about Jennifer's death, or the trial, or the months on death row. I had had a lot of time to think about it all — seven years in all — five since they took me off Xanax and got me on Prozac. In the support group, I sometimes made up whole incidents — worked myself into a good cry — I was one of the group's star performers, second only to Matilda Steinfeld. But you know, that evening after my encounter with the naked woman who claimed to be a Celtic goddess, sitting in a near-fetal position on a Southwestern-style sofa in an unassuming condominium, with too much alcohol in my bloodstream and too much bewilderment in my brain, I realized that I only had three clear memories of that entire year, and this is what they were:

One. The serial killer had a certain smell. Sometimes, in my memories, he had a chainsaw, sometimes an axe, sometimes some sci-fi contraption; sometimes he had a hockey mask, like Jason, sometimes a red-and-green-striped shirt like Freddy, and sometimes, like Mrs. Bates, he appeared in my memory as the drag queen from hell. But he always had that smell — it was a particular cologne. The cologne was called Oscuridad. Darkness. It smelled of autumn leaves — bittersweet and with a hint of decay, mortality. All right. It was *my* cologne. I used to mail-order it from Honduras. The lab said it was all over the body. Coincidence? In court, I swore I had no memory of killing my wife.

Two. I remember my brother Joshua calling me up in jail. He said, "You're free. I'm coming down to pick you up. By the way, Dad's dead and you've been disinherited — he shot himself before we found out you didn't do it. And Mom's Alzheimer's is a lot worse. I've had her put away. Oh, and they gave me and Morgan custody of your kids. You're not allowed to see them. I know the governor's signed the pardon and all that, but it's gonna take a while for the paperwork to go through on those kids, and . . . well . . . you know. They went through a lot of teasing at school. They're both in therapy now. I think you'd better stay away from them at least for now. So as far as family's concerned, it's just you and me for the time being. But hey, I'm here for you."

That was when I realized for the first time that everyone, even my closest relatives, thought that I'd actually done it. Since the day my brother picked me up and dropped me off in front of the Beverly Hills Hotel, I had still not spoken to any of them. I could tell that they thought that this whole semen sample thing had been some brilliant legalistic sleight of hand by that Halperin guy, my attorney. And who could blame them? Because — and this was the third thing that was crystal-clear in my mind, drugs or no drugs — I hated Jennifer's guts. She was an insatiable, controlling, petty, gold-digging, vacuous, self-centered whore. I had married her for her beauty, which was legendary; I could not divorce her for fear of losing the house, which I lost anyway.

I had always wanted her dead.

When her throat was slit and that noise like a broken air conditioner came whistling through her severed windpipe and I knew for sure she was going to die, I came in my pants.

Seven years later, I had still not had another orgasm.

Four-thirty or so in the morning: I had the worst hangover imaginable, but I was used to that. I staggered to the bathroom to take a leak. I had barely unzipped my fly, though, when the mist began roiling up from the Stygean depths of the toilet bowl. Anxiously, I searched for my asthma medication.

The pommel thrust up through the tendriling fog. I recognized the hand that clasped it, but I was really too far gone to care, I began to piss, noisily and carelessly, not even bothering to lift up the seat. By now the entire hilt had come through, and I saw that it was cunningly sculpted in the shape of a many-coiled dragon whose eyes were cabochon star sapphires. It was all some kind of strange metal, too, not steel or bronze but something weirdly iridescent, like that titanium costume jewelry they sell down in Venice along the beach . . . it looked like the work of some second-rate optical

effects house. It's virtual reality! I told myself. The studio had been doing a top-secret VR project. Maybe I was the guinea-pig or the butt of some executive prank. Or — yes! a diabolical plot to drive me insane so that I would voluntarily void my contract and check into Cedars Sinai for observation! — but I was all too familiar with that plot. I had even produced it once. Even so, it did explain things in an almost rational way.

Then the toilet bowl shattered and *she* emerged. Carrying the sword, her hands raised above her head, clasping the hilt, the sword point hovering strategically over that zone which, if exposed, would have reduced the vision from art to pornography. As she moved to proffer the sword, she shook her head and her fiery hair fell across those unseen pubes; it was clear that the entrance to her a womb was a thing of unimaginable power, that it was not vouchsafed a man like me to gaze upon it and live.

"But this isn't very dignified," I said. "Somehow one doesn't expect Goddesses to come busting up out of toilets."

"This is the '90s, Greg," she said. "And you know as well as I do that Los Angeles is a desert, and all its water brought here from distant reservoirs; this city is an artificial flower."

"Well, I didn't mean to, uh . . ." I found myself more sober than I wanted to be. Why couldn't the hangover come back? But my head seemed clear, preternaturally clear.

"I don't mind being pissed on, really I don't," said Bridget. "You have to understand that I don't share your civilized repudiation of bodily functions. Once, men shat directly into the earth; now, there is a porcelain conduit that hides from you the fact that you are earth; what you eat is of the earth; what you void — even that final voiding into wormy oblivion — goes into the earth to be reborn. I am the mother, I am the earth; I swallow your shit and transform it into new life; I am woman, that greatest mystery of the universe; I am one, I am many, I am all creation, creatrix, the self-created."

Wow. She sure knew her Joseph Campbell.

"Care for a drink?"

"Indeed! Grasshopper. Frappé, if you've got a blender."

"Okay. But put that thing away; it makes me nervous."

"How can I? *You* must take it from me. It is your destiny."

"But first, I must agonize." I knew that from my own course material. "I have to come to terms with my hero's nature. You know how it is." I knew she couldn't argue with that.

"All right," she said, wandering out into the living room as I followed her (I had an irrational fear that she might try to steal something, like my stereo or my soul) and staring with undisguised curiosity at the trophies of my past lives — the David Hockney over the fake fireplace, my dead wife's Oscar, my leatherbound, unopened complete works of C.G. Jung — "I'll leave it someplace where only you can get it." She cast about the room for a suitable hiding spot.

"There's a broom closet right by the hallway," I said, "right next to the teakwood elephants."

But she made straight for the Southwestern three-seater — and then, with a Valkyriesque screech, plunged the whole thing, all the way up to the hilt, into the plump pink-and-gray sofa back.

"Jesus, take that thing out — you know how much that thing cost? Don't expect me to have industry parties with a great big sword stuck in my sofa."

"You haven't entertained in years, Greg. And anyway, I can't take it out; only you can."

"I see. *The Sword in the Sofa*. I love it. Classic Disney meets *The Big Chill*. It's a winner."

"Don't be flippant, Greg. You can joke all you want, but you know as well as I do that all men are fated to live out some low-budget remake of the hero's quest. You're not exempt from that. You think you're not a man; you think there's no emotion left inside you, no fear, no grief; you think you can get rid of all your inner longings by slugging down Scotch and barfing up your silly little witticisms. Well, you're not just a shell of a man. There's no such thing as that. Inside every paunchy, mediocre studio executive with a dark past there's always a real human being crying to be set free. Do you think I'd really come to you if you were really the nonentity you say you are? And I'm still waiting for that grasshopper."

She followed me to the bar. My hands were shaking as I poured the crème de menthe. I could see, past the étagère with the Hopi vases, that sword buried in my couch. I turned on the blender and stared at Excalibur. Well, anyone could see that pulling that thing out of there would be no challenge except maybe to an eight-year old. But it did look mighty hip, in a way; the jewel in the pommel gave a soft, pinkish glow that was quite color-coordinated with the rose, flesh and earthtones of the couch. That three-seater needed something anyway. Of course, I'd had it reupholstered after it became clear that it would be impossible to extract every molecule of Jennifer from the fabric; the killer had done a very thorough job.

We sat down with our drinks — I sorely missed my hangover and felt impelled to try to reinstate it — and watched Court TV for a while; they were replaying a bit of Lyle Menendez's testimony while two experts argued about childhood traumas. It was getting on to five-thirty now. I gazed at the hypnotic *verismo* on the little screen.

My trial had been televised too, but that was before Court TV; it had aired on CNN, midnight to five, interspersed with excerpts from the New Bedford rape trial. Watching Lyle, weeping and carrying on, I wished I had had my trial to do over. I wished I had been able to weep. I wished I had remembered those vivid details that could make television more real than the world. Then, perhaps, I would not have been on the cover of

People magazine with the caption, THE STONE-FACED KILLER.

"You should get some sleep," said Bridget. "You've a lot of work ahead of you."

"What about you? Is this going to be one of those 'just when you thought it was safe to go back into the water' situations? Am I going to be looking behind my shoulder every time I try to take a shower?"

"You movie people," she said, sighing, "you always think about how it's going to look on the trailer . . . but you are right. I'm going to have to stick around for a bit, until you grasp your destiny firmly in your hands and hold it up high and go charging off against the armies of darkness. But I'm a nurturing goddess."

"Which is another way of telling me you're the yenta from Hell."

"Go to bed."

"See what I mean?"

But I was tired . . . it was an almost supernatural kind of drowsiness, as though a sleeping spell had been spoken over me. I found myself lumbering in the direction of the bedroom. As I flopped down on the waterbed, however, I realized she had beat me to it. She was sprawled all over the left side, her thigh-length hair wrapped firmly about her hips. "Why are you in here?" I said.

"Any *other* large bodies of water in this dump?"

"You can't sleep here! Aren't you some kind of mother goddess? It's incest!"

"So what are you going to do about it?" she said, arching her back and clasping one of the bedposts between her fingers much as one might grip a sword handle, or an erect penis.

I knew the traditional answer to that one. Siegfried, sent by Gunther to capture Brünnhilde from the cave surrounded by impenetrable fire, had placed his magic sword Nothung between them as they slept so as not to violate the ex-Valkyrie's chastity. There was a sword stuck in a sofa right in the next room. All I had to do was —

"That's a trick question," I said. "I'm not pulling that thing out of the couch. Because if I do —"

"It means you accept everything I've been telling you; that you, indeed, are some kind of hero with some kind of destiny; that you're going to have to mate with your anima and wrestle with your shadow; that you're going to have to set out on a quest, slay dragons, salve the honor of beautiful princesses, perhaps even glimpse the holy grail; and you're going to have to accept that these things are possible, not in some Jungian never-never-land, but in a place as false and feelingless as Tarzana, in a milieu as hollow as Hollywood, in a time as tawdry as today."

Okay. The things she said were all commonplaces of the course I teach; in fact, my last lecture had used some of those very phrases. Perhaps it was their familiarity; perhaps it was the lilt and resonance of her voice; perhaps, after all these years, I still longed to be sung to sleep. But I began to drift; and in my slumber I floated through half-remembered images of childhood; I suckled at some mountainous breast that oozed forth blood and gall.

I got up mid-morning to take a piss, and the toilet was once more whole, and again I began to entertain the thought that I was having the acid flashback to end all flashbacks, thirty years too late. But the sword was still stuck in the couch, and Bridget was in the kitchen fixing eggs, lox, and bagels.

And the sword was still stuck in the sofa.

Stuck in the sofa.

I put my hand on the hilt. Gave it a little tug, enough to realize that there was nothing to it at all; it would glide out as smoothly as a well-lubricated penis. Then I saw her coming, so I hastily pushed it back in.

"Temptation?" she said. She had a demitasse of espresso and no clothes. In the daylight I saw that there was about her person a delicate mist, through which a school of tasseled rainbows darted; even in the concrete desert she could not be too far from water; she wrung what little moisture there was out of the air. Sipping the coffee, I watched her dancelike movements as she brought in the tray of bagels; the lox, like the ruby in the pommel, matched her hair. Uncanny. I bit into the fish. The sensation was indescribable. Yes, there was something of a woman's scent about that salmon. For a moment, I almost thought that my long-lost manhood was beginning to stiffen. Then I remembered. I was a self-made eunuch.

I also remembered something else. "You can't stay," I said. "Really, you can't, this time. It's the support group. They're meeting here this afternoon. Barbecue first, then therapy."

"Indeed, I'm sure I'll like your friends very much."

"But you haven't got any clothes!"

"I'm a size 8," she told me.

I went to the Galleria, told the sales clerk at the Benetton store to pick out something nice — managed to get away with under four figures for three items — and when I returned to the condo, Bridget was already hard at work cleaning trout. There was a basin of peeled, de-veined scampi in the sink, and a bucket of oysters waiting to be shucked. Clearly, she had not gone to the store — at least, I hoped she had not, in her current state of déshabillé — and it occurred to me that

I hadn't had any smoked salmon in the 'fridge the previous night, either.

I fetched myself a Bacardi and Diet Coke, and she pulled a plump, wriggling sea bass out of the disposal.

Oh yes. Though the weather report had put the humidity at less than one percent, the air in the condo was positively lubricious with feminine moisture.

"Are you becoming at least a *little* convinced," she asked me, "that I am nothing more or less than who I say I am?"

I didn't answer. I just took a couple of Valium and sacked out in an armchair in front of the Menendez trial, waiting for my fellow journeyers to arrive.

When I came to, they had all eaten, and the support group was in full swing. In fact, the Lady of the Lake appeared to be the life of the party, and she still hadn't put on any clothes.

Matilda Steinfeld was holding forth at the moment. "I was in sort of an iron cage," she said, "suspended from the roof. Well, it was more like a cave, not a room. There was an altar and there was a man with horns and a great big dildo with metal spikes. They made me kill my little brother, you know. I had to eat his heart. And he was screaming the whole time."

"Screaming?" It was a voice I didn't recognize. Still bleary-eyed, I thought it was Jennifer for a moment, but it was someone considerably younger. She wasn't extravagantly overdressed like the others. She had on a pair of stupefying spectacles. After a moment, I remembered where I'd last seen her — at the Steinfelds party, coming at me with that Serafino boy. "Your little brother was screaming *while you were eating his heart?* Oh, Matilda, surely you must realize that there's an element of fantasy here."

"Not at all," Bridget said. "I do it all the time."

She got a big laugh. I realized that the reason no one minded her nakedness was twofold; first, it fit in perfectly with the purpose of the support group; second, it became her.

But the plain-looking woman persisted. "But surely you've checked the hospital records . . . you've figured out by now that you never had a little brother."

"I know you're new here —" I began.

"Rachel," she said. "Rachel Goldberg."

"Rachel, but they must have told you the rules. When you're within the circle of this support group, you are allowed to state any fantasy you wish as fact. You are allowed to live your fantasy, without restrictions, without boundaries, and absolutely without any judgmental comments."

"Sorry," Rachel said.

"No need," said Mike Lazar, our therapist, who did not generally interrupt, "I should perhaps explain, Greg, since you've *finally* woken up, that the particular fantasy that Rachel is seeking help with is the delusion that everything in the universe has a rational explanation."

More applause. Was I being made the butt of some

joke? What had been going on while they slept? What was in that trout? Had my fellow travelers ingested the Christian *ichthys*, which every mythographer knows is actually the lost phallus of the dead-and-resurrected Osiris, for which the mother-goddess Isis nightly scours the depths of the Nile . . . and was not Isis but a somewhat more exotic manifestation of Bridget, who had come to me out of the waters of the Steinfelds' Jacuzzi? I turned to Mike Lazar, who was still basking in the others' applause. Only the mousy Rachel wasn't buying it. Suddenly I realized that I liked her.

And now they were raptly listening to Bridget's fantasy, which was, of course, that she was the Lady of the Lake who had planted Excalibur within the rocky confines of my sofa, who was now daring them all to draw out the sword and prove that they, not I, were the *kvisatz ha-derach* of the week. Lazar was the first. Laughing, he tugged, and tugged, and tugged, and then he shrugged, as if to say, Well, well, I've played along enough already, back to reality now! Then, of course, Matilda had to have a go, even though she found the whole thing ineffably Satanic; her husband, not strictly speaking a member of the group, tried it and actually budged it a notch or so, being the long-suffering saint that he was; Céléstine, the lesbian transsexual, refused to try at all, citing silly machismo rituals, the Brady Bill, and political correctness; and as for Rachel, she really did try; I could tell; she was straining every muscle in her body, and I caught, mingled with the sweat odor of her efforts, a whiff of Oscuridad . . . and then Bridget turned to me with a sort of *voilà* gesture and I said, "Oh no. You're not getting me this way. I'm not into peer pressure."

But that Oscuridad —

Oh, it opened the floodgates. Those fucking memories came welling up. Not the killing of Jennifer so much, but God, there were details, nauseating details . . . I distinctly remembered now that her trachea had taken three hacks of the razor blade to slit all the way through . . . remembered the spritzing blood . . . remembered a lot more of the killer, too, remembered him muttering, "Love, death, love, death, love, death" with each swing of the ginsu knife, remembered the way he laughed. It was a curiously high-pitched laugh, like a teenager playing at villainy.

Then I suddenly remembered the first time I had ever met Jennifer. I had come upon her and my brother Joshua *en flagrante* behind the oleander bushes . . . not at the Steinfelds' gazebo. I believe it was the Rabinoviches' cabana.

"Hey, Greg," Joshua had shouted to me. "Come and join us."

I always envied Josh his ability to copulate with women in odd locations, and in those days we always shared everything. I wasn't fat then, either. "Are you sure?" I said.

"Fuck yeah," he said. "She's just a shikseh anyway."

Jennifer giggled. She was a good giggler, one of

those "'cause I'm a blonde" kind of girls. We all had sex. It was uninhibited, '70s-style pre-AIDS sex. We never thought we'd see her again. But a year later, she was an Oscar nominee. That made being a shikseh acceptable.

It was, come to think of it, Thanksgiving, and it was the Rabinoviches' turn, and Jennifer was junior scream queen over at Stupendous Studios, having just debuted in *East of Amityville* — hardly Oscar material. Rabinovich is every three years, so that would have made it the year before we were married, which . . . suddenly I realized why Josh had wanted custody of my kids so badly, even before the family decided I was a serial killer. "That fucker," I said softly. "I'm a cuckold!"

"Not a word one hears much these days," Lazar said.

"So I read books," I said. "Not every producer is illiterate."

"That's good, that's very good, you venting your hostility like that; you're making great progress today, Greg. Maybe next week, at the Ben Davids, we can actually begin your descent into the private darkness that you fear so much."

Darkness! Oscuridad!

I caught another lungful of that cologne, and I started to go *really* wild. The scene of the crime . . . it was *true*, the hockey mask, the Freddy sweater, the Mrs. Bates wig . . . I hadn't made up any of those things . . . I could see the killer right in front of me, an amalgam of every slasher in the celluloid world . . . I heard that curious high-pitched laugh, could almost imitate it, knew it for a parody of my own laugh . . . knew that the killer was drenched in *my* Honduras cologne . . . had it been me after all? . . . no, no . . . "Who gave you Oscuridad?" I screamed. "Someone with a high-pitched laugh, who traipses around in a dress and wears a hockey mask and slices women in two?"

"Well," Rachel said, "my friend does sometimes borrow my pantyhose, but I hardly think —"

"God almighty, woman, your life is in danger! They never caught him, you know. The trail got cold after they put *me* away. Now I know what I'm supposed to use this sword for." I grabbed the hilt and it slid out easily. I brandished it as my guests dived under coffee tables and behind utility carts. "Finally I understand!

I'm the one who's got to go after the man who stalked and killed my wife. I'm the one who —" The sword felt good in my hands. Somehow the gnarled hilt seemed molded to the rills and indentations of my fists. "That's the quest that's going to restore my manhood . . . you're the princess I'm supposed to rescue . . . and the faceless killer is the dragon that's lusting to devour your — wait. I bet you're a virgin, aren't you?"

Hesitantly, Rachel nodded. I guess that maybe she thought the others would laugh at her, but no one did.

In fact, the whole group was in shock. It washed in as though they had sat through the entire *Ring* cycle. I put the sword down gingerly and they crawled back to their places. Then they started clapping. In our support group, it was traditional to applaud a good self-revelation.

Afterwards, they all clustered around Bridget like fireflies; perhaps it was the glamour of what Lazar called "the most sophisticated Autotheistic-Delusional Disorder I've ever encountered." This "ADD" was the good doctor's personal contribution to the jargon of the neurosis-of-the-month club, and he was proud to have prime specimen on hand.

I found myself alone with Rachel, in the kitchen, rinsing off the fish bones and stacking the dishwasher. My nostrils were full of that autumnal odor. It was the one scent capable of drowning out the fishy smell left by Bridget's conjurations. "Listen, Rachel," I said, "we can't fuck around. When I said you were in danger I meant it. Who gave you that Honduran *eau de toilette*? I'm obviously meant to track this guy down and kill him with Excalibur." It was just as I had feared. I had pulled the sword out of the sofa and now I had bought into the whole damn fantasy.

"A friend," she told me.

"What sort of friend?"

"Obviously not *that* intimate, since you were kind enough to broadcast my virginity in front of the whole gang."

"Can I meet him?"

"You see him every week. He's in that class of yours."

"He's in *The Hero's Celluloid Journey: Carl Jung, Joseph Campbell, and the Contemporary Filmmaker*?"

"That's the one."

"Which one is he?" Was it the pustulant-faced, beady-browed Elan Rosenberg, or the swarthy Levon Jihanian? Or was I succumbing too much to cinematic stereotyping? Perhaps it was someone who looked completely trustworthy . . . the leading man type . . . like the Matt Dillonesque Angel Serafino who always sat in the front row, taking copious notes and asking intelligent questions. The one who always reminded me of *me* as a young man. "It's not Serafino, is it?"

Rachel smiled. "Serendipity," she said, "*another* Jungian concept."

"But if Angel Serafino is the dragon, and you're the maiden to be rescued, shouldn't I be attracted to you?"

"You mean you're not?"

"Well . . . perhaps in a platonic sense . . . but . . . well, I'm incapable of, you know."

"Yeah. I read about that in *People*. I was little, then, though."

Alone with her in the kitchen, breathing in the fragrance that brought back not only the horror that held me captive but also the last outpouring of my last manhood, I realized that I did feel something. Not lust as such. It was the lust for lust. Lust in the second degree. "I don't know if it's you," I said. "Maybe it's just the scent of love and death that you exude."

"I'm told that impotence is all in the mind."

"That's all very well, but that's also true of reality."

"Screw this! Can't we just fuck?"

"In the kitchen? Surrounded by the carcasses of trout?"

She flung her arms around me. "I need you," she said. "I need to be filled up with something larger than myself. I need passion. I need enchantment." She thrust her tongue into my mouth and I attempted to respond in kind despite the limpness of my sword. She placed my hand upon her left breast and I gave it a tentative squeeze, at which she shuddered all over; she began shaking, and weeping, and she was forced to withdraw her tongue so that I could wipe her tears away with a paper towel. "Oh, I love you, I love you, I've always loved you," she said, which was hard for me to believe since I had just met her; then, as if worried that she had said too much, she retreated to the far corner of the kitchen, next to the electric pasta maker, and stared into the wall.

I felt an overwhelming need to love her, to protect her, a feeling so powerful it seemed to derive from some forgotten wellspring of my past.

"All right," I said. "I *do* love you. I *think* that's what this is."

"Thank you," she said, and kissed me on the cheek. But chastely, so chastely. Then, Helen Keller fashion, she wrote her phone number on my hand.

That night I lay down on a waterbed that held a slumbering goddess. Bridget's snores made tidal waves; the pillows pitched and yawed; the air conditioner squalled and howled; gradually it began to seem that I was thrashing on some intemperate sea, and that the goddess's form had become a piece of driftwood to which I clung in desperation — perhaps the sculpted prow of my wrecked ship.

I don't know how awake I was. I think this was one of those lucid dreams that I had often alluded to in the Jungian portion of my class, a sending from the collective unconscious. I was surprised that an ordinary person like me could be visited by such a dream. The sky was black and the water brackish. Excalibur, wedged between the timbers, served merely as a clothes horse for my rusted armor. From cloud to cloud, a dove flitted, and I wondered whether I had fallen overboard from Noah's ark. A voice cried, *"This is my beloved son, in whom I am well pleased,"* but was it referring to me? Was it proper to take up arms against a sea of troubles, or would that be mixing my metaphors?

Then, in the distance, I saw the maëlstrom. My raft was coming apart. We had gone from *Jason and the Argonauts* to *Journey to the Center of the Earth.* What movie was next? Would the Kraken wake? Would *Jaws 3-D* come hurtling through the waves?

Get a grip! I told myself. These celluloid allusions were just my fevered conscious mind desperately trying to trivialize the sending. I stood up, breasted the big wind, ignored the fact that we were swirling down the toilet bowl at the end of the universe. I took the armor from its stand. It fitted easily over my jockey shorts and yellowing undershirt. The tempest began to sand away the rust. I gleamed. In the ocean without sunlight, I myself became the sun-king that must die and be reborn to redeem the world. I seized the sword-hilt in both hands. The sword made a bright arc in the air. Lightning lanced the darkness.

But was that land I glimpsed on the far horizon, a black ribbon betwixt sea and sky? I plunged my sword into the waters like an oar. The swordpoint struck something hard. The waters parted. The naked-goddess/wooden-prow I clung to began plummeting into an abyss, a well whose walls were the ocean; we had gone from epic fantasy to the opening of *Alice in Wonderland.* As we fell, Bridget grew. At first it was only in the hips; they widened and widened until she resembled one of those Neolithic fertility-icons. Then her breasts began to bloat; rivulets of milk burst from the nipples; she sighed and she heaved and her skin began to buckle into mountain ranges, and her red hair was now the red of autumn, a billowing mass of dead leaves, and still she grew and grew and grew until I saw that she was the sea bed walled by towering water, that every pore of her was a volcano or a sulfurous geyser; that the earth was young and bursting with reproductive energy.

In the midst of the goddess, who now stretched from horizon to horizon, the goddess who had been the prow who had been the raft who had been the woman who had sprung from the spa at the Steinfelds' annual bash, there was me: Gregory Hoffman, decrepit studio executive and sometime college professor, my wrists bound to a kitchen chair by a *Three Stooges* necktie, and a bra crammed into my mouth.

On the sofa — the custom sofa which was the only link between my Beverly Hills past and my Tarzana present — there was my wife; above her, the ginsu-brandishing killer. The air was full of smells: the Oscuridad, the fresh blood, the fear — I was choking — straining against the necktie. The killer was raping and slicing. A shredded aureola whistled through the air. Yes, I watched it all with a certain detachment. He wore the hockey mask over the Freddy mask (they

advertise them in *Fangoria* magazine) and topped it all with the Mrs. Bates wig. Every inch of him was covered — he even wore white gloves, like a cartoon animal — except for the penis that, glistening, protruded from a pair of oversized Bugle Boys. Softly he murmured, "Bitch, bitch, bitch," and his voice, distorted by some kind of electronic thing strapped to his Adam's apple, sounded so oddly familiar — and there was a kind of love in the way he said it — and it put me in mind of the things I wished I'd done to Jennifer, the things I should have done, because of the things she did to the children and —

I fell into a dream within a dream now, strapped to the same chair, restrained not with a necktie but with my own terror, saw my wife, hair in disarray, storming through the kitchen, popping pills with one hand and gripping the lit cigarette with the other, stabbing first Mort's left palm then Mort's right, and the two-year-old screaming from the smoking stigmata and Jennifer's yelling, *"Christ killer Christ killer I want to be a Christ killer too,"* and little Roseanne is shrieking at the top of her lungs and —

Now a dream within a dream within a dream and it's my wife and Matilda Steinfeld laughing together at the kitchen table exchanging anecdotes about fake Satanic child abuse and comparing notes on the HBO special they'd had, debunking it all and —

And a dream within a dream within a dream within a dream and I'm making love to my wife on an inflatable raft, drifting along in the pool beneath the dry California sky, and she herself is the goddess, she herself is the dragon, she herself is the earth, and —

Snap! Matilda and Jennifer, coupling in the king-sized waterbed, with the children, hold hands at the bed's edge, watching *Bart Simpson* on the forty-inch monitor and —

Snap! Trying to get up out of the chair, shrieking at my wife to stop this witchery, and she smiles and me and sends me flying back into my seat and —

Snap! She's dead. Her windpipe whistles. Her killer's come dribbles across the sofa's custom fabric. He turns to look at me. My wife's blood isn't seeping in thanks to the Scotch Guard; it's in small puddles on the sofa and the carpet, and it's already starting to congeal.

My jockey shorts are stained with the piss of terror and the semen of arousal. I rip the *Three Stooges* tie,

by S.P. SOMTOW

bound up from the chair, hurl myself on my lady's murderer. My wife is the earth I'm standing on. The earth is spilling its blood into the sea. I have Excalibur. I slash at the air. My enemy, *the* enemy, the personification of darkness, runs at me with his ginsu-chainsaw-axe upraised. Weapon clangs against weapon. My enemy taunts me with his high-pitched laugh. He roars, he breathes flame; mother earth arches her back and fills the sky with fiery strands of hair.

He chases me. Trapped against the wall of water, I have to turn and fight. I thrust. He parries. From behind the hockey mask, his eyes glow. The chainsaw buzzes and I see woman after woman chained to the wall of ocean, every one dead or dying. I know I should be frightened, but am I not the hero who knows no fear? Suddenly I hear Rachel call out to me. "Daddy, Daddy," she says. I see her chained to the water-wall beside me.

"I'm not your father," I whisper.

We fight some more. Finally I stab him and he stabs me. He's weakened, maybe even dying. I stagger towards him. I strip away his mask. He is the person I knew it would be.

At last the fear, which I have kept frozen in place like the wall of water that surrounds me, visits me at last . . . just a few pinpricks of terror, then, all at once, deluging me with the explosive force of an orgasm, as the waters themselves crash down over the ocean floor, as the land contracts once more into the mortal form of Bridget, mutating back and forth from timber-prow to flesh . . . and now I'm adrift again . . . and the sea is calm . . . once more I'm clinging to the wood, swallowing great gulps of brine, gasping for air . . . and the sunlight is streaming down. I am bleeding from a deep cut in my side. I am mortally wounded.

I see my enemy bobbing up and down nearby. I paddle toward him with my sword. "Help me," he cries. "I think you've killed me."

"Help you?" I managed to croak. "You've killed me too."

"Yes," said the enemy, "but it's not my fault, it's neither of us's fault . . . we were just fulfilling our various destinies . . . c'mon, man, give me a break . . . hold my hand or something, man."

In the distance, now fettered to a phallic mast, I see Rachel; behind her, the white sail is unfurling; she seems to have transformed from a geek to something very like an angel.

"Gimme a hand, man," the killer says, "I don't want to die, not right away."

I hold out the sword; he grasps the honed edge, though it cuts his hands and the salt water makes him wince. He climbs on board the raft that is also the goddess, and we float on the sea that is also the goddess, catching the goddess's breath in our sails.

Our goddess-ship drifts toward Rachel. Behind Rachel is the sun, and above her head there hovers the dove of peace.

When I woke up from the seven-tiered dream, I realized I had become sober. It was an unfamiliar sensation. I had not experienced it for many years.

I lay on the waterbed with the sword between myself and the sleeping goddess. I got out of bed carefully, afraid that Excalibur would cause the bed to spring a leak.

I went to the bathroom to check for wounds. My side bore a faint, jagged bruise, hardly the death wound from the dream. I turned my palms over, searching for stigmata. There were none.

Then I went into the kitchen and poured myself coffee from the auto-timer espresso machine.

The first person I called that morning was my brother Joshua. The phone rang and rang; I barely recognized his voice when he finally picked up. "I'm taking back my life," I said.

"What life?" said Joshua.

"The life that's starting to come back to me, piece by piece."

"So! That support group of yours has finally gotten to you. What reeking dirty linen have you managed to dredge up out of your childhood? I saw Matilda on *Oprah* last year, hear she's doing a book; the buzz is Meryl Streep wants to play her."

"Don't change the subject."

"But I'm not. I've heard that satanic child abuse memories come in clusters; one person in the support group infects the others; pretty soon they've all come down with it. Saw the HBO special."

I said, "Joshua, you screwed my wife!"

He said, "Of course I did. You were there."

"But afterwards. You went on doing it, behind my back."

"Of course I did. You hated her. Remember?"

"Of course I hated her. She was cheating on me."

"No, no, she was cheating on you because you hated her. Who cares anyway? You killed her. Enjoyed it too, judging by the wad in your BVDs."

"You know as well as I do that I'm innocent."

"But in your heart, you killed her. That's the same thing."

"In my *heart*? What, you convert to Catholicism while I wasn't looking?"

"I had to. My latest shikseh is a stickler. Besides, one can always use more guilt."

"Yeah, Joshua, yeah. But there's one thing you have to tell me. It's true, you're right, I've been having these dreams, memories maybe. About Jennifer and the children. You know, violent stuff."

"Serves you right for falling asleep in front of the Menendez trial every night."

"I do *not* —" But he was right, of course. Even though I hadn't spoken to him in seven years, he still knew me inside out. "I don't know if the memories are real, Joshua," I said. "My past is in bits and pieces. I need an independent observer. What about *our* child-hood? Why don't I seem to remember any of it? I know we were adopted, but why? Were we babies? Were we like, abused kids from an orphanage? Was I a changeling, deposited on the Hoffmans' doorstep by a horde of gothic-punk fairies? I need a childhood desperately, any childhood."

"Maybe you didn't have one."

He hung up abruptly.

With searing clarity I saw that my life had been, not a steady progression of events, birth, self-awareness, childhood, puberty, youthful exuberance, middle-aged mediocrity . . . it had not had this algebraic arc I had always assumed it must have. It had been more like a series of unedited film clips. There were sequences that implied other sequences, scenes that promised dozens of possible outcomes. Sometimes there was more than one take; sometimes, where logic demanded that piece of exposition or a plot point, there was just blackness. That was why I did not feel like a whole person. That was why I could still receive visitations from mythic figures. It was part of the editing process. I had to take the jumbled fragments, pick out the shots, make a life out of the pieces.

It was the dream within the dream within the dream within the dream within the dream that made me realize that what I had thought of as my life might in fact be the final dream from which it was still necessary to wake before I could surface in the real world.

Of course, if I finally forced myself awake, there would be no more magic. No more goddesses. No more swords. I had to consider whether it was worth giving up those things.

I delivered my last lecture of the semester.

"Let's talk about good and evil today," I said. "Today, in the '90s, they are not fashionable concepts. We suffer from a collective delusion of rationality. We know that there is a *how* for everything and because of that we have come to believe that there must also be a *why*. If someone is depressed, they must have a chemical imbalance, or they must have been incorrectly potty-trained at the age of two; if someone is a brilliant artist, or a malevolent criminal, or even a second-rate, aging, balding studio executive such as myself, he must be that way because of a myriad variables that can be known and quantified: I mean his genes, his education, the traumas of his childhood, the chemistry of his blood. And even if we don't know why yet, we feel that if only we had an infinite amount of time, and an infinite number of books, CD-Roms, and therapist records, we could ultimately solve every equation, unravel every enigma.

"But is this true?"

"Just because the rational universe is *our* universe, does that make it the *real* universe?"

I get to this point every year in the course. Then I usually pause for a while, allow the students to try to grasp these cosmic notions. Some of the students are shrooming, stoned, or on acid. There used to be many

more like that; today there was just the stoner's corner, the upper left-hand segment of the lecture hall, which was perpetually shrouded in shadow. The acidheads were usually the only ones who could fully grasp the transcendent nature of what I was saying.

I noticed, though, that Angel Serafino, sitting in the front row, also seemed to understand. He watched me intently. It was as though no one else was present in the class; as though all the others were but props, computer-generated extras seamlessly matted into our private scene to lend it verisimilitude. And so, speaking directly to him, I said: "What if the question *why* were not only unanswerable — as we all know it must be — be also irrelevant? What if the archetypal situations we've explored in all the films we've covered this semester — *Chinatown, The Empire Strikes Back, Shane,* and *The Seventh Seal* — are simply the way things are, the irreducible building blocks of reality, the up, down, strange, charmed quarks of our existence? What if a madman is a madman simply because he is mad? What if a hero kills dragons and rescues virgins simply because a hero kills dragons and rescues virgins? What if the word 'because' is simply a crutch, a delusional clothes hanger for the hollow raiment of reality?

"That, my friends, is the final question we must ponder as we recall the celluloid journeys we have taken. What if the very fabric of reason were as fabricated as a schizophrenic's delusions? What if the truth is simply this: that knights are pure, that dragons breathe fire, that for each of us a sword lies buried in a stone . . . and that to the degree that each of us, inside his individual consciousnesses, deviates from these ancient truths, to that degree he is but a shadow, reflection, afterimage of that truth?

"For my next trick. . . ."

Huffing and puffing, two freshmen lugged in the sofa from my condominium. Excalibur, buried once more in the upholstery, glowed like a Hollywood neon sign.

"This," I said, "is Excalibur, brought to me by the Lady of the Lake a few nights ago while I was trying to enjoy a late-night soak in the Steinfelds' hot tub. Anyone who can pull the sword out of the couch will receive an automatic A+ even if they don't hand in their *Citizen Kane* and *Oedipus Rex* comparison sheet."

For the rest of the lecture hour, the undergraduates heaved, grunted, sweated, murmured mantras and yelled karate power words. I only took it for about ten minutes; I left them at it and went down the hall for a Clearly Canadian and a bagel. It came as not too much of a shock when, out of the frosted glass I removed from the refrigerator in the lounge, the image of a red-haired woman started to form. She was very small, no bigger than an ice-cube, but she was perfectly formed, and still draped in her hair. She looked up at me with those cartoony eyes, and she said, "Well done, my child, it's all coming to a climax; you're starting to find yourself again."

"Your child?" I said, incredulous at being so addressed by this R-rated Thumbelina.

Solemnly, she said to me, "The lake is the mother of all things."

I poured the Clearly Canadian (peach, I believe) over the shag carpeting as though it were a blood-libation to the earth; but before the liquid hit the floor it blurred, shuddered, grew into the familiar Bridget.

"That's better," I said, never having liked *I Dream of Jeannie*.

"I'm glad you've figured it all out," she said at last. "We will only meet once more, in the place where the waters meet the sky, in the place where the sun dissolves into the mist. You've been a good king, really; no complaints."

"What about Rachel?" I asked her. It was the piece of the puzzle whose solution I didn't want to accept. "Can't I — I mean, I'm not even going to get to —"

"Oh, indeed you'll screw, Greg," said Bridget. "You know the golden rule of cinematic art: if there's a loaded penis on the wall in Act One, it had damn well better go off in Act Three."

When I returned, the class was over; the room was empty save for Angel Serafino, who had not, apparently, stirred from his seat at the front of the class, had not even attempted to pull the sword from the sofa. Angel was wearing the Honduran Oscuridad. The reek of it was overpowering. More bitter and less sweet, less fragrant, more putrescent. It was the smell of love and death.

It was late afternoon now. In fifteen minutes, the traffic over the hill would become unbearable, and I would be stuck downtown until after dinner. How typically Angeleno of me to worry about the freeways when the entire universe was at stake! I sat down on the couch. Slugged down the dregs of the Clearly Canadian, put down the glass.

I knew who Angel Serafino was; I knew who Rachel Goldberg was; I no longer turned their pictures to the wall of memory.

"Hi, Dad," said Angel Serafino.

I waited.

"You do remember me now, don't you?"

I did. I had ripped the hockey mask from his face.

"You took the rap for me, didn't you?" he said. "You let them think you'd killed her. Why, Dad, why?"

"Because there had to be a reason for you to turn into a monster. I loved you, Mort . . . I can't bring myself to call you Angel . . . I never hurt you, never reproached you, never molested you, never warped your mind with cults or politics . . . there *had* to be something. You know. Bizarre rituals in the basement with your mother in black robes and a spiked dildo. Look at Matilda Steinfeld. All the things that happened to her. In the *Enquirer*, on *Oprah*."

"Dad, you know she made that stuff up. You think reality is like the Menendez trial, but it's not. There is absolutely nothing you could have done to prevent me from wanting to rape and kill women who happen to remind me of my mother. The fact is, I'm just another axe-murdering motherfucker."

I supposed that double-entendre to be deliberate, but I didn't find it funny.

"Why didn't you tell, Dad? You could have stopped me, man. Had me put away. I was only a boy. I had only killed one mother. I never quite got it right, and I could never quite find another mother to try it out on; oh, they looked a lot like her, even smelled like her sometimes, but the high just got less and less compelling. I murdered a woman in Houston a year later. I killed another one in Greece; no one ever found out, though; it was on one of those tourist islands. I got her good. Did you see on CNN, the one with the meathooks in the caves at Lascaux? That was me. And I'm going to keep doing it. I'm even going to kill Rachel — Roseanne — one of these days, when she starts to sag a little, like Mom was starting to; women are like balloons; if they start to sag you have to pop them, or the bang won't be as big."

"Does your sister know?" I said.

"Dunno. This meeting was her idea, really. She's the one who missed you desperately, tried to kill herself four times; she fucked some lawyer on your case so he'd give her access to the psych files, and that's how she knew you'd completely blocked us from your memory. Then she thought of the cologne I always used to steal from your bathroom . . . she wondered if the smell might be able to trigger, you know, all the repressed bullshit in your life."

"You're saying I couldn't face the fact that my son was a serial killer . . . so I repressed it . . . and that's how I ended up on fucking death row?"

"Hey, Dad, you *love* me. You couldn't reconcile your love with the idea that I'd sprung from your loins. Right? But you shouldn't have looked for a *because*. Enough *becauses*. You say so yourself. I don't belong here. I don't see things in the 16.7 million half-tones that the rest of the world sees. I see things in black and white. I am evil. You should have killed me. And now that you have the sword, you will."

Now I knew why he had listened so raptly in my classes. For years I had harangued these college kids about other universes, other perceptual systems, but I had only been playing games, juggling with words. My son understood. He had always belonged to the world of absolutes. And now I too belonged, and I could not go back.

I pulled the sword from the couch, knowing full well that in slaying my son I also slew myself.

He stood up from the desk. He knelt down in front of me, like Isaac before Abraham. We were about to step irrevocably into that world of absolutes.

But there was something pulling me back. It was seductive, this world where reason ruled and where nothing was eternal. I hesitated. "Before we go through with this," I said, "isn't there something we could have done together, father and son . . . you know, quality time?" I had searched through the raw footage of his childhood and found only a few fleeting scenes.

"You could have taken me places. Lunch at the Hard Rock Café, dinner at Dominicks, the roller coasters at Magic Mountain, even the Universal tour."

I knew that I would kill him by sunset. But I wanted to savor the last few hours of our relationship in some human way. I didn't want to just act out the timeless sitcom of our destinies like a robot, like a shadow puppet. So I said, "All right; we'll go cruising for a while, then I'll do it."

Around sunset, we did end up at Universal Studios. It was off-season, so the tours had ended for the day; luckily, one of the older guards still recognized me from the time I produced *Stranded in Eternity,* and we snuck into the back lot. I drove the Ferrari along the tramway in the gathering twilight; Mort and I shared the frisson of the *Psycho* house. We stood in silent awe in before the *Leave it to Beaver* residence; we couldn't get into the *Battlestar Galactica* and *Earthquake* and all the mechanical stuff, of course, but at length I parked on a side street, in front of a building (in which Jennifer had been murdered, not once but three times, in the film *Three Times a Zombie*) — and we walked along, past deserted brownstone shells, through ghost towns and Mediaeval villages, seemingly without aim . . . though I knew where we were headed. It was the Martha's Vineyard set, with the little lake that had often stood in for the Atlantic Ocean in *Jaws.*

We stood at the edge of the tramway, watching the sun set on the artificial sea. We pretended we were a loving father and son with genuine lives that stretched in non-disjunctive lines from birth to death. Because we'd grown up in show business, we knew all about the method; we convinced even ourselves. I held in my hand the hand that had dismembered the woman I both loved and hated. The simulated warmth between us was so poignant, so puissant, I almost wanted to turn back; yet I could not. There was still a final dream to awaken from.

We shared a strawberry ice cream cone, and then I plunged Excalibur deep into my son's chest. He did not groan. He slid forward along the sword as though to embrace me, drenching my Armani suit with gore. As he died, I felt a searing pain in my own side; blood gushed from wounds that tore spontaneously through

my two palms; and I knew that I too would be leaving this universe, that I would wake up for the final time.

I drew the sword from my son's heart, and flung it into the celluloid ocean. To the grinding music of double-basses, a shark fin rose from the water; it was Bruce, the tourist shark, somehow still circling even though the power had been turned off. When the shark had gone by, there was a woman walking on the waves; it was Rachel Goldberg. She was transformed. She was all woman, and still my little girl. She came to me across the water until she stood right next to me. The air was ripe with the autumnal scent of Darkness. Her feet floated an inch or two above the water, and she reached out and touched my wounded side. I winced.

"Daddy," she said.

"I can't," I said, and tried to push her away. Pictures flooded my mind: the naked little girl in the bathtub, giggling, the coy thirteen-year-old at her high society bat mitzvah, the adolescent who screamed "It wasn't my Dad" at Connie Chung before they dragged her away. Could these be buried memories? And yet they were still frames from a montage . . . there was no thread of a relationship running through those images.

She tossed her glasses onto the pavement and they shattered, and then she put her arms around me, across the body of her dead brother, and murmured, "Love you, love you, love you."

"But you're my daughter," I said.

"Oh, bullshit," she said, "you know as well as I do that I'm really Uncle Joshua's daughter, that you're both adopted, that I'm no real kin to you; but you can have all the titillation of breaking the incest taboo that you want . . ."

"You mean, like Woody and Soon Yi?"

"Oh, Daddy, forget all that nonsense. It isn't real. When the gods mate, it is always incest." And she pulled me over the edge. My feet slid over the pool of blood and the corpse that was already starting to melt into thin air. In fact, the corpse was slowly melding into the naked body of my daughter. Perhaps they had always been one, their binary quality another figment of a dishonest memory.

As my shoes hit the lake, both they and the blood began to swirl away from my feet, marbling the water with liquid red and black.

I looked back at the WELCOME TO AMITY sign with

its alluring, bikinied sunbather and the row of quaint New England shop façades. I knew at last that the world and all its denizens are façades, celluloid within celluloid. I was a shadow who loved another shadow. Those lips, breasts, hips, eyes, skin, hair, hands were all as substanceless as thought; but is not thought the source of all creation? We made love. In the darkling water, under the smog-streaked twilight. First she was Rachel-Roseanne, my daughter, a virgin, her mother's lipstick smudging her soft cheeks; slowly the woman in her awakened, and she was the Jennifer of my deepest dream, like the time we made love on the inflatable raft in the Olympic-sized pool in a Bangkok hotel at midnight; it seemed as though the water itself had become my wife, and I, a man-sized dildo, lanced the lubricious lake with the strength of a god; I hated her, I loved her, I killed her, I brought her back to life; and then, at last, she became Bridget, the source of all the waters, the great mother, the dragon, the world; and thus it was, at the heart of a kingdom of illusion that was itself the heart of a kingdom of illusion that was itself the heart of a kingdom of illusion, that the sword grown flaccid seven years before was given back to me at last; I found my lost manhood.

Would I have to awaken now? Must every human being be roused from shadowland? Were there only a few seconds of blissful madness left to me? Did it matter? I was loving the triple goddess, daughter, wife, mother; I was piercing the moon with my silver sword. The ocean was love itself. My seed burst forth not only from my penis but from my palms, my feet, and my wounded side. With the coming of manhood, fear returned to me at last. I trembled. I shuddered. I exulted in the feeling of this fear: the pounding heartbeat and the racing blood, the last, most vibrant colors of this transient world.

Any moment now would come the **snap** of final wakefulness.

Perhaps the last seven years of my life had been but a series of rêveries, that when the **snap** came I would still be in that living room in Beverly Hills, about to twist free from my bonds and lunge toward the murderer of my wife. Perhaps I would find that it was *I* who killed her, and that the brother, son, and daughter were merely different personalities trapped inside my head. Perhaps I would find that even Jennifer was one such personality, and that the person I was stabbing to death was, after all, myself.

Perhaps even that would prove to be a dream. If so, then all that a man can ever learn is that the one true journey ends in Oscuridad, and that darkness is another word for love.   Ω

FOR 75 YEARS: THE UNIQUE MAGAZINE   ISSN 0898-5073
Spring 1999   Cover by Jack Gaughan

Credibility vs. Credulity

We get books in the mail. That's one of the perks of being a magazine editor. Publishers send editors lots of new books for mention, review, or — sometimes — we're not entirely sure why, as when a copy of *The Tribble Handbook* showed up. We try to earn our freebies, with occasional editorial reviews, and with the convenient fact that one of your editors (Darrell) also happens to be book-reviewer for another DNA Publication, *Aboriginal Science Fiction*.

This puts us in a position to observe not just what is being published in the fantasy/horror field, but what publishers' publicists *think* belongs in the horror/-fantasy field. In the same way that science-fiction magazines get a lot of flying-saucer books, we've noticed a sudden influx of what might be called pseudo-fact books, such as two nicely illustrated volumes by W. Haden Blackman, *The Field Guide to North American Hauntings* and *The Field Guide to North American Monsters* (Three Rivers Press, trade paperback, $15.00 each). These are both filled with very dubious-looking photos, including a very famous still from alleged Sasquatch footage (or is that Bigfootage?) on the cover of the *Monsters* volume, which, we confess, looks to us remarkably like a man in a gorilla suit. Both books are arranged the same way a field guide to birds or butterflies would be, with little charts listing each critter's (or in the case of the *Hauntings* volume, specter's) range, habits, and frequency. This last is marked by cute little icons. Thus the Jersey Devil gets four little monsters and is thus rated quite common, as is the infamous Chupacabra (The Goatsucker), although fortunately gigantic anthropophagous owls are apparently much scarcer. Both books also give the searcher handy hints (and precautions) for amateur monster (or ghost) hunters.

The *Monsters* book is done with a certain detectable amount of facetiousness, as when the Jackalope (a rabbit with huge antlers) is accredited to "American folklore and creative taxidermy," but *Hauntings* is considerably more serious, presumably aimed at people who really believe that the Hull House in Chicago is haunted by at least four hooded phantoms and a "devil baby," and that the Amityville "Horror" is to be given some sort of credence. We are not told, "some people believe this" or "it is reported" but, quite unambigiously, that these things are so. Thus both volumes are what we classify as anti-educational material, since they perpetuate untrue information and make the public more ignorant, rather than less, about the way the world around them really works.

What, you may ask, has this sort of supermarket tabloid stuff to do with *Weird Tales*®? The answer is, we hasten to assure you, very little, no more than, say, Whitley Strieber's *Communion* has anything to do with the contents of *Isaac Asimov's Science Fiction Magazine*. The two Blackman *Field Guide* books are of only marginal interest to fantasy readers or writers. It's intriguing to read some of the older folklore, such as the story of the Bell Witch of Tennessee, which was the subject of a pretty good novel by Brent Monahan recently, but otherwise the general rule seems to apply here as with the more science-fictional stuff (saucers, abductions by alien xenoproctologists), namely that once a fantastic motif filters down to the lowest levels of popular consciousness and begins to appear in "true" books for the credulous, then the motif is probably too degraded for further literary use. We will qualify that by saying that if you want to write a haunted-house story and make it conform to traditional lore on the subject, then *A Field Guide to American Hauntings* might be worth skimming through. Such novels as Shirley Jackson's *The Haunting of Hill House* and Marvin Kaye's and Parke Godwin's *A Cold Blue Light* make excellent use of "true" haunted-house data. But you aren't going to produce a saleable weird tale by just dipping into *The Field Guide to American Monsters* and coming up with a beastie no one has written about yet. A *story* has to be a lot more than that. In fact, rather than going to the "true" material, wouldn't it be more fun to make up something which *sounds* like it belongs in a book like this but is entirely original? It's so easy to disarm the reader that way. Your editor (Darrell again) admits to deriving great amusement from the "authentic" Pennsylvanian German folklore inserted into his story "The Outside Man," which was originally published in Peter Crowther's 1994 anthology, *Narrow Houses*. It sounded very convincing, the Outside Man of the title being a kind of conscience-demon you meet in the woods when you have something really wicked in mind, whom you have to summon three times and tell your intent three times in order to make it true. This was even backed up with a spurious passage "quoted" from the otherwise quite genuine 19th century "hex" book, *The Long Lost Friend*. Maybe in time this particular Schweitzerian demon will find its way into "true" Field Guides and the like, even as did Arthur Machen's equally fictional "Angels of Mons." But the author made it up. Everything. What he'd learned from books like *The Field Guide to North American Monsters* was not the "facts" but the idiom of belief.

Okay, we'll admit it. We're skeptics, by which we mean the kind of folks who demand extraordinary proof for extraordinary claims, rather than just taking such reports on face value. We're rather doubtful about ghosts and psychic powers, regarding them as unproven, and certainly very doubtful indeed as to the existence of the Jackalope, the Jersey Devil, the Goatsucker, Mothman, or the Phantom Kangaroos of the American West. We're not very convinced by flying saucers and alien xenoproctologists either.

But *is* there a link between fakelore and fantasy? Aren't they both kinds of imaginative exercise?

It's always been our contention, although hardly our original idea, since H.P. Lovecraft said the same thing over fifty years ago, that the skeptical fantasy writer has a certain advantage, because he is in control of his material in ways a True Believer cannot be. If you honestly believe that magic works thus-and-so or that ghosts have certain characteristics, then such data are, for you, part of the realistic background of your story. If the needs of the story are otherwise, you're stuck, the same way Mark Twain got stuck about halfway through *Huckleberry Finn*. The story was going along gloriously until Twain suddenly realized that this was about a boy trying to smuggle a black man out of slavery, on a raft, on the Mississippi River, which flows *south*. American literature almost lost its greatest single book, as Twain put *Huckleberry Finn* aside for more than a year before he figured his way out of *that* one.

In fantasy, things you can't change are what we might call the eternal verities of the human heart: love hate, fear, loneliness, ambition etc. Get those right and you *can* do the equivalent of turning the Mississippi around. You can create a whole universe, up to the level of its gods. You get to *decide* whether there are ghosts or not. (One of the key questions to ask when making up original mythology is "Where do the dead go?" Perhaps they go into the belly of the great cosmic crocodile. See

STAFF:

Publisher: Warren Lapine
Editors: George H. Scithers
& Darrell Schweitzer
Managing Editor: Carol Adams
Art Editor: Diane Weinstein
Assistant Editors: Kyle Phillips, Pat Buard, Robert Waters, Shawn M. Proctor, & Casey McCarthy
Computer Consultant: David J. Williams III
Typesetter: Owlswick Press
Printer: Morgan Publishing Co., Inc.

MANUSCRIPT SUBMISSIONS:

Before sending us your material, please send us a business-sized envelope, with postage affixed, addressed to you, for our guidelines.

The address for this and all other editorial matters: **Weird Tales®, 123 Crooked Lane, King of Prussia PA 19406-2570.**

The address for all subscription, advertising, and other money matters: **DNA Publications, Inc., PO Box 2988, Radford VA 24143–2988.**

Yes; we read unsolicited submissions — but *only* if they are in standard manuscript format. To survive, all editors insist on a few Rules: each submission must be in proper format and must include a return envelope, addressed to you, with enough postage affixed to bring the manuscript back to you. If you want us to discard the manuscript if we don't buy it, tell us so, but include a business-letter-sized envelope, addressed to you, with proper postage affixed, so we can send you our comments. No loose stamps, please!

We recommend either or both of two books on writing (after all, we wrote one of them!): *On Writing Science Fiction: the Editors Strike Back!* by Scithers, Schweitzer, & John M. Ford; $19.50 in hardcover; and Barry B. Longyear's *Science-Fiction Writer's Workshop*, $9.50 in trade paperback, available from Owlswick Press, 123 Crooked Lane, King of Prussia PA 19406-2570. These prices include shipping & handling. If you live in Pennsylvania, please include 6% sales tax.

We are not responsible for manuscripts in our hands or in transit. You *must* keep a copy of every manuscript you send out. You *must* put your name and address on the first page of every manuscript. And please: *no* binders, folders, or padded envelopes; and especially: *no* registered or certified mail for which we would have to stand in line at the post office!

"To Become a Sorcerer" in *Weird Tales*® 313, in which your editor got quite a bit of mileage out of that one.)

Only a doctrinaire occultist "knows" how ghosts behave or what magical spells work and how. The occultist, writing fiction, is bound by that belief, even as the realist Twain was bound by the geography of the central United States. It certainly limits possibilities. Worse yet, as Lovecraft pointed out, the believer is less likely to give such elements much buildup, since to the believer a ghost is nearly as much a part of everyday reality as a streetcar. The non-believer is more likely to see the dramatic possibilities, and to move beyond the accepted, accumulated lore, which is precisely why we, as science-fiction and fantasy readers, don't find our imaginations all that much stimulated by the likes of *The Field Guide to American Hauntings*. We can do better. Lovecraft, who did not believe in ghosts, instead invented Cthulhu and the myth of the Great Old Ones.

And speaking of phantoms, before we get on with the letters, we must mention that we're looking for a disappearing author, one **Robert G. Evans,** formerly of Pennsville, NJ. We have a story of his on hand that we'd like to buy, but our acceptance letter to him bounced. We've tried to locate him through writers' organizations, to no avail. If anybody knows where he is, please ask him to get in touch.

And some phantom publishing credits. We buy *First North American Serial Rights* for stories published in *Weird Tales*®. That's a phrase every writer should take to heart. It means we are not buying the *story* but instead renting the privilege of being the first publisher to publish it in English, in North America, in a magazine. This does not preclude stories already published in England. But some readers ask us to point this out, and so we shall. There are actually four stories from Over There making North American debuts in this issue. Ramsey Campbell's "Kill Me Hideously" first appeared in a British small-press anthology, *Dead of Night*, edited by Stephen Jones. "His Shadow Shall Rise to a Higher House" by Thomas Ligotti originally appeared in a limited-edition, *In a Foreign Town, In a Foreign Land*, published by Durtro in 1997, and well on its way to being one of the great (and fabulously expensive) collector's items of our time: a small hardcover collection of four original Ligotti stories, published to accompany a CD of avant-garde music inspired by his work. The original sold for $65 a copy and is well out of print. We are proud to make such a story available to the general public, as we are to resurrect Lord Dunsany's "The Dance at Weirdmoor Castle," which originally appeared in *Homes and Gardens* for December 1950 and is copyright 1950 by Lord Dunsany and reprinted by arrangement with Curtis-Brown, Ltd. on behalf of the Trustees of the Dunsany Will Trust. Darrell Schweitzer's "The Giant Vorviades" originally appeared in *Interzone* #99 in 1995.

We got more letters this time than last, which is gratifying, and suggests that maybe somebody reads these editorials.

This one, from **Marilyn Mattie Brahen** didn't have to travel far, but we think it contains good advice:

I read, with an uncomfortable sense that I was seeing a doppelgänger of my former self, the disgruntled writer's letter in The Eyrie (Issue #314). "Fast food" indeed. A letter of my own was once published in Newsweek, *(responding to a mainstream author who inserted a fellatio scene at the editor's request to spice up her novel), decrying a reading public who had forgotten what sirloin steak tasted like, force-fed hamburger by publishers. Since then, and countless rejections of my own writing later, I've grown up, having met an editor about seven years ago who genuinely cares about good writing. Since meeting him, I chose never to submit to* Weird Tales, *so that charges of nepotism shouldn't fall upon our heads, as he, now my husband, is Darrell Schweitzer. My choice, honorable though it seems on my part, was probably one of great relief to him. He has extremely sharp standards, and my writing doesn't always measure up. But I must assure that rejected author: Mr. Schweitzer is a thorough reader. Like most knowledgeable editors, he can tell by the first manuscript page if a story is potentially publishable, and if so, will give it a fair chance. He also knows the difference between mindless action and a moving plot.*

At our writer's workshop, he's firmly blue-penciled my stories. Recently, he criticized a new one, pointing out flaws. I revised it and he reread it, only to tell me it still had little or no plot. "There's no conflict," he said. "Nothing happens to challenge your characters." While frustrated, I finally recognized that it lacked this basic element of fiction, and was as intriguing as "See Dick run. Run, Dick, run." And — drat — most readers long ago graduated first grade!

Now, under the circumstances (!), I do get to talk back, but wife or not, the story always comes first (Catherine de Camp once told him, the typewriter is "the other woman." I add sardonically: so are editorial criteria.) When my writing waxes poetic, and I attempt to justify it as artistic license, despite group consensus that I ought to cut the crap and get on with a story, my erudite spouse shrugs his eyebrows, and says, "Send it out and see what happens." A few rejection slips later, I come to my senses, and get back to work on that incomplete piece that revising and polishing (not wishful thinking) might make publishable. I've finally learned something from the criticism that he and our group dished out to me, as honestly as they could, trying for neat surgical cuts that wouldn't bleed too much. Invariably, I write a better story, and a few have been published.

So I suggest all disgruntled writers not quiver and fume more than a day or two when receiving a personal rejection letter. After all, it's only free advice, and we don't have to take it.

To which we can only add that the virtue of editorial advice as *free* advice is not inconsiderable. After all, there are any number of writing workshops, writing programs, and correspondence schools which expect you to *pay* for that advice. We will never do that at *Weird Tales®*.

That same letter in #314 also brought a comment from **Elaine Weaver,** who writes:

Choosing my favorite was not easy, but I finally settled on Tanith Lee's "Stars Above, Stars Below." The "Author's Note" at the end of this poignant tale made me smile. Contrary to the edict issued by our frustrated rejectee in The Eyrie, I did not *see it coming. This is also the case with Brian Stableford's "Rent," which ended on a note both touching and chilling. Catching the reader off-balance is one of the hallmarks of a* Weird Tales *storyteller, and one more reason to love the magazine.*

Nevertheless I was interested to learn that the spurned writer knows exactly *what the problem is with readers like me; all I want is action! No wonder I am always so tired!*

Famous SF and Fantasy grandmaster **Jack Williamson** responded to an offhand comment in last issue's editorial (about not *all* of the contents of the original *Weird Tales®* being deathless classics):

I had reason to be happy that Farnsworth Wright, to fill the magazine, sometimes bought stories that were not quite classics. My first contribution was inspired by a story (I think it had to do with the Spanish conquest of Mexico, though author and title are long forgotten) that struck me as so bad that I thought I might be able to do as well. Fortunately for me, Wright seemed to agree.

Incidentally, I think he would have been proud of #314.

We point out that Jack Williamson's first story appeared, not in *Weird Tales®*, but in *Amazing*, in the December 1928 issue, five months before our eldest editor was even born. His debut in *Weird Tales®* was with "The Wand of Doom" in our October 1932 issue. His most famous appearance here was the serial, *Golden Blood,* in six parts beginning in April 1933. His most recent novel is science fiction, *The Silicon Dagger,* soon to appear from Tor.

John Peyton Cooke writes from New York:

I did not know Weird Tales *was back among us until I saw the beloved logo peeking out from among the other magazines at Barnes and Noble. I bought it, of course. How could I not? Among the many unique things about the Unique Magazine is that its readers are true believers — not in the supernatural, but in* Weird Tales *for its own sake.*

More than ample justification for Weird Tales*'s*

continued existence is provided by Brian Stableford's superb, creepy "Rent." As a gay man, a fan of vampire fiction, a Weird Tales reader, and a Weird Tales writer (#295), I must say that I have a long-standing craving for this kind of tale, especially when done with such originality and grace.

Once again, George Barr came through with an exquisite illustration, the meaning of which I failed to grasp until I was well into the tale. Those hands across the stomach!

I do, however, have one quibble with "Rent" that applies equally to any work of vampire fiction that attempts to assert that HIV/AIDS will mean "death" of the undead. If vampires have managed thus far not to be destroyed by such infectious diseases as bubonic plague, smallpox, cholera, influenza, or syphilis (not to mention rabies, endemic in vampire bats), why should we believe that they will be laid waste by HIV/AIDS?

This untenable position was central to two tales by two usually reliable horror masters: "The Bedposts of Life" by Robert Bloch (Weird Tales, Summer 1991) and "Death in Bangkok" by Dan Simmons (Playboy, June '93). In both cases the HIV/AIDS "revelation" came at the very end and, instead of destroying the vampires in question, utterly ruined any credibility the tales might otherwise have had for me. I was glad to find that in "Rent," this anemic idea ran off in a peripheral vein and did nothing to abate the full aortic thrust of the story.

Actually it would seem more likely that vampires should *cause* AIDS rather than suffer from it, since throughout the ages the vampire myth has been a disease metaphor. This is developed explicitly in the film *Nosferatu* (both versions) in which the vampire leads a troop of rats into a city and brings the plague. Further, there was recently a fascinating special on PBS about a vampirism scare that happened (for real) in New England in the 19th century. Corpses have recently been discovered in their graves very obviously disturbed after death and mutilated, often staked down, or with the legs cut off and crossed over the chest, presumably to prevent the undead from walking anywhere. This was the work of terrified rustics trying to cope with a deadly tuberculosis epidemic they could not understand or control. In any case, it only seems logical that a supernatural creature which is already dead — really a form of predatory ghost — should be immune to physical diseases.

Christopher Dunn notes that *#314 was lighter weight, I thought. No bad stories, no great ones either. Well, with Lee and Stableford and Somtow you're not going to have any bad stories.*

Best is hard to say. I liked "The Haunting of the H.M.S. Dryad," but I'm never sure if light-hearted fantasy is the real stuff — though you'd think a long acquaintance with Discworld would have cured that, even if Zelazny (or Leiber!) hadn't. Liked "Until Time Cracks" and "O Tannenbaum" too.

Of course "Rent" is fine, even, yet again (so far as I know), an original approach to the vampire thing. But, after a while — well, it gets to be like another Ph.D. candidate looking for one more original bit of research on, say, "Shakespeare's Approach To . . ." The story's good, and I don't mean it isn't: tight, tense, grim, believable. But, still — more vampires? You know what I mean.

Well, yes. But you've also explained why we bought *that* story — "original, tight, tense, believable, etc." There's no denying that vampires are fashionable right now to the extent of a genuine cultural phenomenon. We won't deny, too, that we deliberately mention vampire stories on the cover in hope of selling more copies. But we also insist that vampire stories be good stories. We insist on that, far more than we insist on there being vampires present. If both happen to occur in the same story, great, it will sell copies, something no magazine editor is averse to.

Avery Hudson has difficulty choosing a favorite in #314, but ultimately settles on *Tanith Lee, whose two-paragraph vision of winged cat people gliding through the ether from the Martian to the Egyptian desert (in the middle of the story) is one of the best prose poems I've read this year.* He further adds: *It looks like you are continuing to provide fertile ground for writers and artists to experiment in traditional forms and express new concepts. After Poe's crystallization of the macabre tale in the 1840's and Lovecraft's "cosmic reality that predates human history and reason" a half-century later, weird fiction is overdue for a new idea. It would be great to see it land in* Weird Tales.

Keith B. Johnston suggests, as others have in the past, that we reprint earlier covers and illustrations, along with stories from earlier issues. We have to regretfully decline. Many *Weird Tales*® illustrations and covers have been reprinted, and certainly we couldn't do justice to them, reproducing what was a color cover in black and white on pulp paper. The book *Pulp Culture*, which we reviewed last issue, has numerous excellent reproductions of covers in it. There has been at least one book so far which consisted of nothing *but* reproductions of *Weird Tales*® covers. As for the stories, no, we don't expect you to spend thousands of dollars to acquire a complete *Weird Tales*® collection. But anthologies based on this magazine continue to appear at the rate of one every year or so. We already have a shelf of them. The original *Weird Tales*® is already one of the most reprinted-from magazines that ever existed. Also, not too expensively, the collector can acquire old copies of the magazines edited by the late Robert A.W. Lowndes, *The Magazine of Horror, Startling Mystery,* and *Bizarre Fantasy,* which consisted almost entirely of reprints from *Weird Tales*® and other rare pulps. They also managed to reprint virtually the entire contents to the 1931–32 rival magazine *Strange Tales,* copies of which would cost you a good $75.00 apiece. *The Magazine of Horror* can usually be found for about $5 a copy.

Chris Bevard apologizes for not having written before, talks about how much he enjoyed the letters pages in such independent horror comics as *Death Rattle* and Eclipse's *Tales of Terror,* and gives us his (welcome) story votes; but he also adds that he always thought handwritten letters to be "more personable." Maybe so, but we find them harder to read. We prefer typewritten letters, please.

The Most Popular story for *Weird Tales*® #314 was the result of (we are glad to say) more intense voting that previously. There were moments of suspense, and a few surprises, as one story edged the other out of the top slot, and then was in turn edged out, just barely. It was a close race, but the first place vote went to S.P. Somtow's "The Hero's Celluloid Journey," with Brian Stableford's remarkable "Rent" a very close second, and Tanith Lee's "Stars Above, Stars Below" coming in right behind that.

Editorial Book Reviews
by Darrell Schweitzer

The Cleft and Other Odd Tales
by Gahan Wilson
Tor Books, hardcover, 1998
333 pp. $23.95

Gahan Wilson's Even Weirder
Forge, 1996, trade paperback
239 pp. $16.95

Gahan Wilson has been a sometime contributor to *Weird Tales*® (illustrating the Robert Bloch issue, #300) with artwork and a book review column. We'd like to publish his fiction someday, as it too has the same admirable weirdness to it which has made him, since the death of Charles Addams, *the* macabre cartoonist (with only Edward Gorey as a possible rival). His prose fiction is far less known, because there hasn't been that much of it. *The Cleft* collects stories dating from the '60s to the '90s. The best of them are either very good jokes, like prose cartoons, or curiously profound fables (the title story), or quaintly old-fashioned little horrors, the sort you expect English adventurers to tell in the leisure of their clubs, circa 1920 — only nothing remains leisurely, safe, or predictable. Our favorite in this vein is the ink-blot story. It has no title, but the blot which keeps getting bigger and nastier as it moves through the text. Recommended, of course.

Gahan Wilson's Even Weirder is the most recent collection of Wilson cartoons, the title referring back to the previous one, *Still Weird.* Who can resist Mr. Wilson's grimly humorous explorations of life and death — ? We particularly liked the internet address on the gravestone, and the Grim Reaper who carries an electronic beeper when on call. Ω

SHADOWINGS
by Douglas E. Winter

> Some one said: "The dead writers are remote from us because we *know* so much more than they did." Precisely, and they are that which we know.
>
> — T.S. Eliot, *Selected Essays*

Three Gothic Novels.
by Charles Brockden Brown.
The Library of America, hc, 914 pp., $35.00

A man bursts spontaneously into flames. Disembodied voices speak from a closet. Religious mania incites the murder of innocents.

This is not a new novel by Stephen King, but a book that is two hundred years old: *Wieland, or The Transformation* (1798), the first novel by America's first professional writer, Charles Brockden Brown. Twenty years before Washington Irving's *Sketch Book* — and decades before Edgar Allan Poe's first short story — Brown abandoned a legal career to champion a new and uniquely American literature. *Three Gothic Novels*, which collects the best of his fiction, is a bicentennial tribute to this dimly remembered but highly influential wordsmith.

Born of Philadelphia Quakers on January 17, 1771, Brown transcended a sickly childhood and a wearying apprenticeship at law to pen a series of popular essays that convinced him, and his parents, that he could earn a living as a writer. Although his career was brief — Brown died of tuberculosis on February 22, 1810 — his ambition was intense and his output was prolific. He published six novels; founded, edited, and wrote for several literary journals; and, in the final decade of his life, crafted notable political critiques and Federalist tracts.

The weighty social commentary of William Godwin provoked Brown's first published book, *Alcuin, a Dialogue* (1798), a treatise on the rights of women and an early appeal for suffrage. The manuscript of his first novel, *Sky Walk, or The Man Unknown to Himself* (1797), was lost when his publisher died of yellow fever; but Brown labored on, creating, in less than three years, four of his novels, including the texts presented here.

A self-styled "storytelling moralist," Brown saw fiction as a moral force, but one that was populist — meant to entertain while provoking philosophical inquiry and debate. He embraced the structure and style of the Gothic romance, then twisted its impulses into a darker complexity that prefigured the insistent themes of American literature: murder, insanity, corruption, conspiracy, religious fervor, familial strife, distrust of institutions, distrust of self. Although flawed, with plots that move impulsively and illogically, and prose that ranges from the incisive to the overwrought, Brown's novels rank with, and occasionally transcend, those of his British contemporaries.

Wieland remains his best known work, and deserves its pride of place as the fountainhead of American Gothic. Although later novels demonstrate a more mature and controlled style, none surpasses the bravado of *Wieland* or its emotional intensity. Subtitled *An American Novel*, it is based upon a sensational crime of the era — a delusional father's murder of his wife and children — whose shocking circumstances were reinvented by Brown in order to explore their moral repercussions. Here, as in later novels, Brown brought more mundane Gothic concerns — romance, class, character, landscape — into collision with ultimate questions of faith, divinity, and eternity.

The narrative is an epistle from an archetypal Gothic heroine — Clara Wieland — whose placid life with her brother and his wife succumbs to a harrowing series of dire and seemingly inexplicable events: "What is man, that knowledge is so sparingly conferred upon him! that his heart should be wrung with distress, and his frame be exanimated with fear, though his safety be encompassed with impregnable walls!" Clara survives the persecution through a desperate kind of faith — a belief in revelation — but her brother's religious melancholy is sent hurtling into obsession. A mysterious voice commands him to kill his wife and children, and the deed sculpts him into a "monument of woe" whose only salvation is death.

Like another influence, Mrs. Radcliffe, Brown offers natural, if tenuous, explanations for the apparently supernatural events of *Wieland*, assuring the reader that the bright light of rationalism will resolve most, but not all, worldly fears. The crucial terrors, Brown urges, are those of the mind; and his fascination with the pathological would haunt each of his major novels.

Arthur Mervyn, or Memoirs of the Year 1793 (1799–1800) is the longest and most daunting of Brown's works. Originally published in two parts and inspired by Godwin's *Caleb Williams*, it is set, with accomplished realism, in one of America's plague years. As the yellow fever scourges Philadelphia, the narrator rescues and befriends young Mervyn, a wayward and misunderstood lad whose true nature — abused waif or devious scoundrel — remains ambiguous to the very end. The layered and occasionally perplexing story finds Brown manipulating Gothic conventions to present a stirring argument for civic responsibility toward the impoverished, the ill, the downtrodden.

Far more intriguing and entertaining is *Edgar Huntly, or Memoirs of a Sleep Walker* (1799), which is arguably the first American detective novel, as well as the first American novel to include Native Americans. Its introduction is a brief manifesto in which Brown proposes an American literature that is liberated, like the new nation, from its European past:

> America has opened new views to the naturalist and politician, but has seldom furnished themes to the moral painter. That new springs of action, and new motives to curiosity should operate; that the field of investigation, opened to us by our own country, should differ essentially from those which exist in Europe, may be readily conceived. The sources of amusement to the fancy and instruction to the heart, that are peculiar to ourselves, are equally numerous and inexhaustible. It is the purpose of this work to profit by some of these sources; to exhibit a series of adventures, growing out of the condition of our country, and connected with one of the most common and most wonderful diseases or affections of the human frame.

Edgar Huntly replaces the expected tropes of the Gothic ("Puerile superstitions and exploded manners; Gothic castles and chimeras") with elements of a peculiarly American darkness ("incidents of Indian hostility, and the perils of the western wilderness"). Its troubled narrator trails the sleepwalking enigma Huntly, who may have murdered his best friend, through a labyrinthine American fronteir. His dark passage through a maze of forests, caves, and cliffs soon comes to symbolize the moral dilemma at the core of the novel: whether criminology can understand and explain a mind in nightmarish conflict.

Indeed, it is the intensely psychological nature of Brown's novels, their unreliable narrators, their morbid curiosity, their willing descent into dementia and pathology, that sets them apart from their Gothic kin — and, of course, anticipates the tales of Edgar Allan Poe (who read and was no doubt influenced by Brown). Central to the human drama, Brown observes, is the tragedy of men and women wrestling with their inherent imperfection.

A character in *Arthur Mervyn* thus offers a despairing confession:

> What it was that made me thus, I know not. I am not destitute of understanding. My thirst of knowledge, though irregular, is ardent. I can talk and can feel as virtue and justice prescribe; yet the tenor of my actions has been uniform. One tissue of iniquity and folly has been my life; while my thoughts have been familiar with enlightened and disinterested principles. Scorn and detestation I have heaped upon myself. Yesterday is remembered with remorse. To-morrow is contemplated with anguish and fear; yet every day is productive of the same crimes and of the same follies.

Although his name may be forgotten, the novels of Charles Brockden Brown are a remarkable legacy, crucial not only to American fiction but also to the evolving literature of horror and the supernatural that would be perfected by Poe and other more famed successors, from the Shelleys to Hawthorne and Lovecraft — and, in time, to Faulkner, Shirley Jackson and, indeed, Stephen King. *Three Gothic Novels* is a welcome, if long overdue, celebration of an American original.

The Collector of Hearts: New Tales of the Grotesque
by Joyce Carol Oates.
Dutton/William Abrahams. 336 pp. $23.95.

Invisible Writer: A Biography of Joyce Carol Oates
by Greg Johnson
Dutton. 492 pp. $34.95.

An exquisite fable called "The Sky Blue Ball" introduces *The Collector of Hearts*, a gathering of recent stories by Joyce Carol Oates. Its narrator recounts the epiphany of her adolescent solitude: While walking in a strange neighborhood, a ball is thrown to her by someone on the far side of a high brick wall. The ball is blue, beautiful and new, "like a rubber ball I'd played with years before as a little girl; a ball I'd loved and had long ago misplaced; a ball I'd loved and had forgotten." She returns the ball to her unseen playmate, who throws the ball back to her, and the game of catch continues until interrupted by a desperate thought: "This is the surprise I've been waiting for. For somehow I had acquired the belief that a surprise, a nice surprise, was waiting for me. I had only to merit it, and it would happen." Now the ball is flung far from her, and recovering it nearly takes her into the path of a passing truck. Shaken, she returns the ball again, but the game, it seems, is over; when she climbs the wall, she finds no one on the other side — just the ball, worn and cracked and old, its sky blue color gone.

The bittersweet nostalgia that imbues *The Collector of Hearts* is a central motif of the Anglo-American ghost story; but for Joyce Carol Oates, the past is a spectre more haunting than anything the supernatural might have to offer. These fictions confront the loss of innocence — or the gaining of guilt — through experience or, more often, as reminiscence, repeatedly underscoring the collision of now and then. The revelation of "The Sky Blue Ball" is thus reprised in "Shadows of the Evening" and several other entries, including the delirious "Fever Blisters," in which two aged lovers reunite in the once-grand hotel that was home to their adulterous affair, only to learn a simple lesson: "It isn't romantic at all."

Now that commercial publishers have debauched "horror" as an acceptable literary descriptive, it is fashionable for writers of dark and fantastic fiction to apply more discreet labels to their work. Oates styles these stories, like those of an earlier collection, *Haunted* (1994), as "Tales of the Grotesque," which suggests, somewhat unfairly, a focus on the garish, the extreme, the absurd. If anything, *The Collector of Hearts* is subdued in its imagery and its physical violence — although there are moments of almost gleeful indulgence in the stuff of splatter films. Perhaps the most notorious is "Unprintable," which reads like a paean to the legendary E.C. Comics of the 1950s: a straightfaced adventure in ironic vengeance in which a prominent pro-choice activist is tormented by the revenants of aborted fetuses.

Other tales enact familiar scenarios of generational and gender oppression in which the old (and usually male) corrupt, if not obliterate, the young (and usually female). In the surprisingly literal title story, a fiftyish judge seduces a naive, gum-cracking defendant; it is not an act of romance, but of possession and, no doubt, murder. In a similar setpiece titled only with a black rectangle, Oates essays a woman's repressed, perhaps inexpressible, memories of the shiny Sunday on which her girlhood ended in sexual abuse. What Oates brings to these otherwise obvious plotlines is a remarkable voice, often that of the victim, which gives life and meaning — and truth — to events that lesser writers would merely play out for shock or sensation.

Unfortunately, these stories, although consistently skilled, tend to suffer in the collective. Unless read sparingly and with great patience, not as a book but for an occasional story, *The Collector of Hearts* proves a blur of obsessively similar themes and characters and plots; indeed, only "The Sky Blue Ball" and a handful of other tales remain unique and memorable. "The Affliction," in particular, offers a moving metaphor for the pain of creativity, considering the valedictory exhibition of a elderly artist whose artwork, in fact, is the extirpation of a mysterious disease. "[T]he affliction isn't fatal," he learns. "It's something you can learn to live with . . . . Until you scarcely think of it until it happens. And then, of course . . . you have no choice."

It is tempting to some to believe that writers — particularly those whose work is drawn to the dark side — are not born, but somehow bred. Clues are sought from their lives, preferably their childhoods, in the superficial belief that some dire event must have encouraged, if not engendered, their creative vision. *Invisible Writer*, the first biography of Joyce Carol Oates, offers far more reasoned and complex sensibilities. Written with Oates's cooperation by a worthy inquisitor, novelist and English professor Greg Johnson, it is a careful and detailed account of a life that is far from public. Despite a prolific literary career (and once gracing the cover of *Newsweek*), Oates is indeed invisible, known to her readers entirely through her writing. Certainly her past has its share of ghosts: an autistic sister whom Johnson portrays as an eerie doppelgänger; a university friend who suffered a homicidal breakdown; Oates's own near-breakdown and recurrent health problems. Just as certainly, those ghosts have been exercised, if not exorcized, in her fiction. But in reading Johnson's account of her life and her life's work, there is no doubt that, when it comes to writing, Joyce Carol Oates — like the artist of "The Affliction" — has no choice. She was born to write. Ω

KILL ME HIDEOUSLY
by Ramsey Campbell

illustrated by Allen Koszowski

"I don't read this kind of stuff myself, but could you sign it for my son?"

As Lisette clenched her fists on his behalf, Willy Bantam raised his heavy eyelids and gave the man ahead of her a full-lipped smile almost as wide as his plump face. "What's his name?" he said.

The man told him, and Bantam sent the son his best wishes on the title page of *The Smallest Trace of Fear*. Lisette swung her tapestry bag off her shoulder as the man retrieved the book, and the volumes in the bag nudged him none too gently at the base of his spine. She made sure he saw her place them in front of their author, who greeted her and them with exactly the smile he'd produced for her predecessor. "Sins of my youth," he remarked.

"They're not sins, and you aren't so old. I don't want them for anyone but me."

"Shall I sign them to . . ."

"Lisette."

"That's a pretty unusual name."

"Thank you," she breathed, and managed not to simper as she watched him begin to inscribe the title page of *Ravage!* She took a breath that tasted of saliva. "Would you put it in . . ."

"I am, look."

"I don't mean that. I mean, do sign them for me, I'll hold them even dearer then, but when you've finished, Willy, can I call you that . . ."

"That's who I was before I was William."

"You were when you wrote these, so will you be for me?"

"Anything for an old supporter."

He meant old in the sense of faithful, Lisette thought as he signed his original name. She was certain his pen was moving more fluently, happy to rediscover what it used to write. She waited for him to open *Writhe!* before she said "The thing I was going to ask you — when you write another book like these, will you put me in it?"

He didn't look up until he'd finished wishing her the best above his zippy signature, and then he gave her a straightened smile. "I'll see if I can find somebody called Lisette a role in one of the kind I write now."

"Don't be insulted, but that's no good. Shall I tell you why?"

"There are people behind you, but please."

"Because in this new one you never describe what happens to the girls who disappear."

"There's the scene where the policewoman has to try and say what she found."

"She doesn't even say three whole sentences. You used to write at least a chapter. The first girl in *Writhe!* got thirteen pages in the hardcover and sixteen in the paperback."

"My agent and my editor persuaded me you could imagine worse than I could ever describe."

Lisette saw the manager of Book Yourself frown at the queue behind her and direct more of the expression at her. "I'm not paying to imagine, I'm paying you to," she said.

"Then I hope these old excesses of mine give you your money's worth."

"I've read them. Thanks for them," Lisette said, and once they were nestling safely in her bag, hugged it to her as she marched out of the shop.

Beyond her Renault, which she'd had to park several hundred yards away, the lights of the department stores and fast-food eateries were padded with November fog. The street was deserted except for a man in a dark raincoat whose length and looseness put her in mind of a slaughterhouse. The lights lent his stiff expressionless face all the colours of a lurid paperback. As she stooped to unlock the car he arrived behind her, and she sensed a cold presence at the back of her neck: his breath as chill as his intentions, the imminent clutch of his hand? It was only the fog.

Five minutes' driving through the blurred streets of the city took her home. She lived in the middle of a row of youthful houses, each of them little wider than the garage that occupied most of the ground floor — no more than a slice of a house, she often thought, but all she needed. Having let herself into and closed the garage with the remote control, she unlocked the door that led from the garage into the house.

A narrow staircase lit by bulbs in cut-glass flowers ascended to the middle floor, half of it a kitchen and dining area, the rest solemnly described by the estate agent as a compact living space. In Lisette's case it was a library, its walls hidden by shelves stuffed with books. She crossed it to the farther staircase and climbed to the solitary bedroom.

She gave her secrets time to glimmer before she fingered the switch. The light seemed to draw the contents of the wall beyond the foot of the bed into a pattern she alone might sometime be able to interpret. The wall was covered with jackets of second-hand Willy Bantam novels and pages torn from them, framed by two female mouths stretched wide by screams, posters for *Ravage!* and *Writhe!* which Lisette had saved from a bookshop bin. She loved the mouth from *Writhe!* most — you could see the tongue starting to grow bigger and longer and harder.

She hung her coat on the back of the door and lay on the bed, her shoulders against the headboard. She placed one of the autographed books on either side of her on the fat quilt, then she opened *Ravage!* and read the inscription, running her fingers over the back of the page to feel how it was embossed by his signature. She was making herself wait, causing all her lips to tingle with anticipation, before she turned to her favourite scene.

". . . Sally had never known why he called them his ghoulies until she kicked him there. When he went into a crouch she thought she had put him out of action long enough for her to run, and then he jerked his head up, gleefully licking his lips. His hands came for her, except they were no longer just hands. His thumbs had stiffened and swelled huge. One moist throbbing thumb forced her mouth open, and the member slid over her tongue. The shock was so intense it was beyond shock, it was an experience she wouldn't have dared admit even to herself she'd dreamed of. She felt his other hand push her skirt above her waist and slide her panties down her helpless legs, and then the pulsing erection that was his other thumb slid deep into her. She would have gasped if she'd been able, and not only because of that — because a slick lengthening finger had found her nether orifice and wormed its way in. The rhythmic penetration was reaching for her deepest self from too many directions to withstand, and as wave after wave of forbidden ecstasy swept away the last of her control she fell back on the bed. When his face above hers began to change there was nothing she could do. . . ."

There was plenty Lisette could if she put her mind to it. She pushed one thumb in and out of her mouth, she bit down on it as the other stroked her clitoris and forged deeper while a finger poked between her buttocks. She moaned, she gasped, she writhed on the bed, raising her knees high and flinging her legs wide. She came within an inch of convincing herself.

When she was too exhausted to counterfeit any more pleasure she let all her muscles sag. For just a moment that state considered feeling like the release she'd laboured to achieve, and then the dead weight of frustration settled on her. It was waiting in the night whenever she lurched awake, and she was hardly aware of having slept when the bedside clock began to squeak at her to get ready for work.

Her car felt like a helmet not a great deal more metallic than her head. It gave her only just enough protection from the traffic, cars and lorries battling to be first past holes in the roads. All the workers crowding into the city were of a single mind that compelled them to rush along the pavements and bunch at crossings and flock across the roadways whenever lights summoned them. She parked as close to the glass doors of the Civic Coordination building as she could, then she buzzed to be let in.

A blank-walled lift carried her to the fifth floor. The switchboard room might as well have been windowless, since supervisor Bertha insisted on pulling down the blind as soon as the sun appeared in the window. Though the lines weren't due to open for five minutes, the girls were at their boards. "Here's Lisette," Vi said, blowing on her nails. "Bet she doesn't care if Tommo lives or dies."

"Double bet she's never seen him in her life," said Doris, appraising her face in a pocket mirror.

Bertha held up a hand as if to check it was as pale as the unsunned sky. "Hush now, ladies. She may not even know who our favourite gentleman is."

"Of course I do. He's one of your soapy people who's on every night. I wouldn't be watching him even if I had a television," Lisette said, and once the chorus of incredulity had passed its crescendo "I've a date with a man at a bookshop."

"I thought you saw him last night," protested Doris.

"That's why I am tonight."

"Is he one of your horrors?"

"He's the best there's ever been or will be," said Lisette, switching on her computer terminal as her board winked at her.

The caller was desperate for the times of a bus that had changed its route, the sort of call she and her colleagues dealt with every day. The world was full of people trying to catch up with it, and everybody had to find their own way of coping. Perhaps her workmates managed by doing away with their imaginations, she thought, and had to pity them for their need to care about someone who didn't exist. The point was to find out all you could about yourself, to store up that secret until you were alone with it, the prize you gave yourself at the end of the day — except that tonight she meant to win herself a bonus.

She dined swiftly at a Bunny Burger opposite the car park, then she drove to the next town. She was able to park almost outside another branch of Book Yourself that appeared to have brought many of its neighbours with it from her town for company. She let herself into the shop, and Willy Bantam saw her at once.

He didn't look at her again until the dozen people ahead of her had taken turns to linger. A fat man with a stammer moved aside at last, leaving her the aroma of his armpits, and the author met her eyes. "Back again," she said.

He was producing his smile when he saw the books she'd brought. "That's right, I signed these for you."

"Are you truly not going to write any more like them?"

"Nothing's changed since yesterday."

"Then I shouldn't make you. I've thought what you can do for me instead."

"What's that?"

She opened *Ravage!* at her chapter and turned it towards him. "Put me in this one."

"Put you . . . How . . ."

FOR Lisa

by Ramsey Campbell

"Cross Sally out and put my name instead. The way you describe her you could have been thinking of me. Here, use my pen."

When he didn't take it she planted it between his thumb and forefinger, and pressed her thighs together to contain an inadvertent stirring. "You only use her name five times. It won't take long," she said to enliven him. "She's Nell in *Writhe!* too, isn't she? Could she be your girlfriend?"

"It doesn't work like that."

"Here I am, then. Just this one," Lisette said, nudging the book towards him. "Don't worry, I won't sue."

He raised the pen, but only to level it at her. "For what?"

"Using me for the worst you could think of."

He laid the pen at the very edge of the table and pulled his hand back. "That's yours."

"Can't you use that kind of pen?"

"I can't use any for what you want."

"No, you don't understand. I said I wouldn't sue you, as if I could when it's me who asked for it. I won't be any trouble, I promise."

"Then please don't be," the author said, and looked past her.

"Are you embarrassed? Hasn't anyone ever told you why they read your books? All us girls want to be his victims," Lisette said, turning to the next in line, "don't we?"

The girl seemed in danger of blushing, even though that would upset her colour scheme — face white as bone and not much meatier, spiky hair the black of her gloves and boots and long tube of an overcoat — but managed to respond with no more than a series of alarmed blinks. "We do even if we won't say," Lisette told the author, and had to regain her voice, because he'd closed her book and was sliding it towards her with his fingertips. "Couldn't you just . . . ?"

"Your name's in it. You can't ask more than that."

"Oh, *thank* you." It seemed hardly possible that he could have substituted her name five times while she was busy with the other girl, but it would be worse than ungrateful of her to inspect the book in his presence. One acknowledgment of herself had to be all the magic Lisette needed. She bore her broad smile past the queue and smiled all the way home.

The garage closed itself behind her, the stairs lit the way to her bedroom. She took her time over removing her coat and unbuttoning the front of her dress, enjoying the delicious tension. She lay on the bed and took out *Ravage!*, which parted its pages at her chapter as though it was as eager to open as her body. Then her mouth widened, but no longer in a smile. Sally; Sally; Sally, Sally — Sally. Not a single use of the name had been changed to hers.

He'd lied to her, she thought shrilly as a scream, and then she saw he might only have told her he'd already signed the book. If he'd taken advantage of her willingness to trust him, that was worse than lying.

Everything of importance in her room — the Willy Bantam books, the fragments of them on the walls — seemed implicated in the betrayal; the mouths were jeering at her. She flung herself off the bed and was on her way to the stairs before she realised the bookshop would be shut by the time she drove back.

She'd been made to look enough of a fool. That wasn't her kind of victim. When she felt calm enough she reopened the book and read the description of herself — long slim legs, trim waist, full breasts, blonde hair halfway down her back. Only the name was false. "Not for long," she promised, and kept repeating it as she lay at the edge of sleep.

Next morning she was at the office twenty minutes ahead of Bertha and the girls. She might as well not have bothered: at that hour Bassinet Press was represented only by an answering machine. She left a message for someone who was privy to Willy Bantam's movements to call her at the enquiry office by name, then waited most of the morning while nobody did. No doubt whoever should have called would be going for an extended lunch as Lisette understood everyone in publishing did, and so she had to contact them before they turned into a machine. The moment Bertha wasn't there to see her phoning out Lisette dialled Bassinet Press and spoke low. "I left a message for Willy Bantam's person. Can I have them now?"

"I'll give you publicity," the receptionist said, which struck Lisette as a generous offer until another voice announced "Publicity."

"Are you Willy Bantam's girl?"

"Mr Bantam's publicist is on the road with him. Can she call you next week?"

"What road are they on? Where is he tonight?"

"Nowhere, I believe. May I ask who's calling?"

"I'm an old friend he used in one of his books. Where's he on next?"

"I think he's reading at a library tomorrow afternoon."

"Have you got the address? I want to surprise him."

There was a pause that might have denoted reluctance, so that Lisette was searching the depths of herself for some further persuasiveness when her informant returned with the address, followed by a question: "Can I just take your —"

"Don't spoil the surprise," Lisette said as she saw Bertha returning from her customary five-minute visit to the toilet. "Thank you for calling," she added, she hoped not too suspiciously loud.

She had apparently fooled the supervisor, but perhaps not Vi or Doris. She didn't say a word to any of her colleagues until she'd had lunch amid the tinny clattering of the basement canteen, followed by several strolls around the car park in pursuit of her clouds of breath to use up the rest of her lunch break. As soon as she was back at her desk, releasing Vi from hers, she said to Bertha "I know it's short notice, but could I have tomorrow afternoon off?"

Bertha turned from adjusting the blind, an irregularity of which had dared to admit a scrap of muffled sunlight. "Is it an emergency?"

Lisette grew aware that Doris was idle and listening. "It wouldn't seem like one to everybody, but —"

"Then we can't treat it as one, can we?" Bertha said with what might even have been a hint of genuine regret. "You know the rules as well as anyone. Forty-eight hours' notice of leave except in cases of absolute emergency."

This had never made sense to Lisette — it wasn't as though a substitute worker would be brought in. "I know you wouldn't want to be made an exception of and cause bad feeling," Bertha said, at which Doris gave a nod of agreement so meaningful it might well have contained a threat of telling tales.

Lisette pressed her headphones to her ears as an enquiry summoned her. Her professional voice sounded detached from her, entering her head from outside, but that wasn't new. A worse impression was, however — a sense that instead of being the role she played in order to afford her real life, this empty unfulfilled automaton serving a faceless public would soon be the whole of herself. It wouldn't be while she had any imagination left, she vowed, and remembered Willy Bantam's novels waiting on her bed. Her imagination wouldn't let her down so long as she refrained from wasting it on trying to concoct excuses she didn't need.

She'd hardly reached her bedroom and thrown off her coat when she opened *Ravage!* on her lap, its hard rounded spine digging into her crotch. From her bag she took the pen Willy Bantam had held. It felt cold, but grew warmer as she ran a finger up and down it while she used it to cross out the name that had supplanted hers in *Ravage!* Once she had written her own name everywhere it belonged she found the description of her in *Writhe!* and made it hers too, then she hugged the books to her and rocked back and forth on the edge of the bed.

That night her sleep was uninterrupted, even by dreams. The clock had to repeat its squeak to rouse her. She dressed at her leisure and strolled to the phone box at the end of the road, where she told Doris she was too ill to go to work. Back home she sat on her bed and stroked the Willy Bantam books until it was time to go to him.

She would have left earlier except for not wanting to be conspicuous when she arrived, but the two hours she gave herself proved not to be enough. Winds like tastes of a blizzard threw her car about the motorway and thwarted her even approaching the speed she would have risked. When at last she found the library, she was twenty minutes late.

It was one of several concrete segments surrounding a circular parking area, a plate that might have held a cake the segments had been part of. Besides the library there was a church, a police station, a fraud investigation office. Though the plate was several hundred yards around, it was almost covered with cars, so that Lisette was growing sweaty with desperation when she saw a space outside the library. It was reserved for the Disability Advisement Executive, but Lisette felt her need was greater. She parked as straight as she had time for and dashed into the library, where a notice-board tried to confuse her with a list of the day's events: a sale of videocassettes, a meeting of a writers' group, a demonstration of origami, a seminar for teenage parents, a course called "The Koran Can Be Fun" . . . The guest of the writers' group was William Bantam. Far better, the girl at Bassinet Press had misinformed Lisette. He wasn't due to start for five minutes.

Lisette hurried to the end of a corridor papered with posters for counselling services and found herself a seat in the midst of the large loud audience. She squeezed her bag of books between her thighs as a murmur of appreciation greeted the appearance of their author. He wasn't even bothering to look for her: he must believe she was either satisfied with his autograph or overcome by his trick. Then he rounded the table at the end of the room and saw her.

His jaw didn't quite drop, but his lips parted audibly before they snapped together. He poured himself a glass of water and downed half of it, then he set about reading from *The Smallest Trace of Fear.* He read the scene in which a willowy brunette became obsessed with the idea that she was being followed by the same car with different number-plates and was pitifully grateful to be picked up by her new boyfriend until she heard the rattle of several metal rectangles from behind her seat . . . "Dot dot dot is about the size of it," Lisette muttered, convinced he'd selected the chapter as a gibe at her. "Drip drip drip, more like." That everyone else present seemed impressed struck her as not merely a joke but a bad influence on him. She listened while people praised his subtlety and restraint and went on about his technique, all of them presumably writers so unsuccessful they had nothing better to do than sit at his new clay feet. Soon she was waving her hand, but Bantam and the librarian who was choosing questioners ignored her. As the author finished telling a woman that he didn't think publishers were biased against her or her class or her gender, Lisette sprang to her feet. "Can I speak now?"

Dozens of heads turned to find her wanting. "Are you a writer?" a long-faced shaky bald man demanded on behalf of all of them.

"Yes I am, and I wouldn't be except for Willy Bantam."

Bantam was searching for somebody else to recognise, but all the hands except hers had gone down. "What's your question?" the librarian said.

"I want to read you how it ought to be." Lisette pulled out the book: not her favourite — she was keeping that all for herself — but *Writhe!* "Lisette had been dreaming Frank was still alive," she read, raising her voice as people who could see the book began to murmur. "When she felt her calf being stroked she thought he had come back, and in a way he had. As the caress passed over her knee she parted her thighs. The long soft object squirmed between them, and that was when she knew something was wrong. But the worm that had crawled into her bed had stiffened, and as she gasped it thrust deep into her, spattering her with graveyard earth . . ."

The murmur of the audience had grown louder and more defined — tuts, throat-clearings, embarrassed coughs — and at this point it produced a voice. "You should save that kind of thing for reading when you're by yourself."

A girl brandished a copy of *Writhe!* "That's Mr Bantam's story, only she's not called that in it."

"She should be," Lisette said.

The girl gaped at her. "Is she supposed to be you?"

"Do you need to ask when you've read the book?"

The girl looked away, and so did everyone else. Lisette might have borne that much disbelief, but then she heard a muffled titter. "She's me all right. She always was," Lisette declared. "Willy put me in even if he didn't know he did. You heard him say he doesn't know where some of his ideas come from. You can't deny it's me when everyone can see me, Willy Bantam."

The bald man, shaking more than ever, broke the silence. *"Did* you have anyone in mind as your victim, Mr Bantam?"

"I'm glad you asked me that. There's only one person an author ever really writes about, and that's himself."

"That's stupid. How can he make out any of the girls are him?" Lisette protested, attempting to provoke a laugh with hers. "He's a Willy, not a Connie. Not a Cunty. Not a Pussy," she said, louder as the librarian gestured urgently at a uniformed guard. "Don't bother, I'm going," she said, grinning at the pairs of knees that flinched out of her way as she made for the aisle. "Just you remember everybody here knows I was in your books when you were Willy Bantam. I'll always be in them now."

She'd marched only a few yards out of the room when she heard hoots of incredulous laughter. What was he saying about her? She might have gone back to find out if the guard hadn't been following her, his face a doleful warning. She strode away, hugging her bagful of books so tightly they seemed to throb in time with her heart, to be transforming themselves into her flesh.

Long before she arrived home the fog was beckoning the night. The lights in her garage and upstairs were harsher than she was expecting. The one in her bedroom spotlighted her on the bed, naked except for *Ravage!* between her legs. "I'm there now, Willy Bantam," she murmured, and rubbed herself against the book as she crouched forward to read her scene. She didn't know how many times she read it before she had to acknowledge it was no use. He'd intervened between her and the book — his smug indifferent face

and his words in public had, and the jeering of his audience.

It wasn't until the binding gave an injured creak that she observed she was about to rip the book in half. Instead she closed it slowly as though it, or some thought it was capable of prompting, would tell her how to proceed. The notion kept her company in bed, and as the night settled into the depths of itself she saw what she must do.

The alarm had to make several efforts to waken her. Since the staff at Bassinet Press started work later than she did, her tardiness hardly mattered. She reached the office at least a minute before the switchboards were due to open, but Bertha frowned hard enough to darken her sunless face. "We'd given up on you. Are you better?"

"Getting there."

"We didn't think it was like you to have to stay off with a case of the girlies."

"Maybe I'm becoming a woman," Lisette said, and closed herself in with her headphones, ignoring the looks Vi and Doris exchanged. She dealt with enquiries until Bertha waddled off to relieve herself and remake her makeup, at which point Lisette suffered the next call to carry on twitching its light on her board while she rang Bassinet Press. "Will you put me through to William Bantam's editor, please."

"May I have a name?"

"Someone they'll want to speak to."

Quite soon a deeper female voice said "Mel Daunton."

"Are you the editor Mr Bantam has to talk to?"

"I'm the one he does. Sorry, can I ask who's calling?"

"You ought to be sorry. You should know who I am. He talked to you about me."

"You'll forgive me if I don't —"

"You and his agent and him got together to talk about what I could imagine before he wrote his new book."

"I don't know where you could have got that impression, Miss, Mrs —"

"He said it in front of witnesses at the bookshop here in town, so don't bother trying to tell me it isn't true. You can't take advantage of me any more than he can. Do you know what he wanted me to believe when I saw him yesterday? That the description of me in his books isn't me."

"I did hear something about that. If I can —"

"I'll bet he didn't tell you he said he was me. Even I haven't got the imagination to believe that."

"I'm glad to hear it. Can I ask what you actually —"

"I want compensation for the way he used me and then said he never did. I'm not talking about money. As long as you and his agent tell him what to write, I want us all to agree how he can put me in his next book."

"That might take some arranging. Give me your number and I'll call you back."

"It doesn't matter when we all have to meet, I'll

come," said Lisette, ignoring Vi and Doris, both of whom were staring at her. It wasn't until they turned to gaze past her that she realised what was wrong, not that she cared. A glance over her shoulder revealed Bertha in the doorway, hands on hips. "I'll call you tomorrow," Lisette said into the mouthpiece.

"I may not be here then, so if you could give me your —"

"I know what you're up to. Never mind trying to send someone to shut me up. I'll be there when you're discussing his next book," Lisette said, and cut her off.

She waited for Bertha to move into her view. The supervisor looked so unhappy and reluctant to speak that Lisette stood up at once. "You needn't say it. I'm fired," she cried, flinging the earphones at the switchboard. "Don't worry, I'm going to a better place," she said, snatching her coat off its hook, and stamped on whatever Bertha attempted to say to her back.

She was out of the only job she'd ever had, and already forgetting it. She knew who she really was, and before long everybody would. On her way home she parked in a side street she would previously have found too unpatrolled to brave and bought a tape recorder in a pawnbroker's. One of several men who were huddled under sacks in the doorway of a derelict pub erected his bottle at her for lack of anything more manageable. "I'll have worse in me than that," she told him.

It was almost noon, but it might as well have been dusk. Swollen lumps of light hovered above the pavements, thick glowing veils hung before the shops. The world had grown soft and remote from her, and the interior of her house seemed as distant: the closing of the garage, the climbing of the stairs, the crossing of the room full of redundant books. Only her bedroom was alive for her, and once she was naked she pressed herself against the wall that was papered with samples of Willy Bantam. She ran her fingertips around the screaming lips, she licked the pages of *Ravage!* The faint taste of ink seemed more nourishing than any meal. When she felt entirely ready she switched on the tape recorder and held in her hand the pen he'd touched, and widened her legs on the bed.

"Willy? Willy Bantam? I know you're going to hear this. I'm not angry with you any more. I can't be angry when we're going to collaborate. This is how I'll die in your next book. You won't be able to resist me. Are you listening?"

When she saw the flare of red that indicated the machine was, she closed her eyes. "Lisette pulled the cap off the famous horror writer's pen. No protection for her. She traced the contours of her full breasts with the tip, she ran it over her flat trim stomach and up

and down her long slim thighs, oh, and then she thrust it deep, ah . . ."

Before too long she was able to form words again, and meanwhile her other sounds kept the tape recorder working. "She felt it penetrate her virginity," she gasped, and steadied her voice. "She felt the ink that was his essence flow into her, tingling through her body. She felt herself starting to imagine like him, see into the depths of him, see things he would never have dared to see by himself. Now if she could just . . . just put them into words. . . ."

"That's as much as she managed to say," the policeman said, and switched off the tape. "By the sound of it she passed out shortly after."

"And then . . ." Bantam prompted.

"And then she lay there for weeks before anyone found her. She hadn't any friends or family, just books."

"I hope nobody's going to blame me for that."

"Most of them weren't yours," said the policeman, and paused long enough for his gaze to become heavily ambiguous. "We shouldn't need to trouble you further. Nobody can say you encouraged her."

"They better hadn't try." For an instant the author saw the woman as the sound of her taped voice had conjured her up — an unwelcome presence in the midst of his audience, at least middle-aged and already grey, flat-chested, thick-limbed, less than five feet tall and almost half as broad. "I wish someone else had," he said.

The policeman pushed himself out of the only chair and held up the tape recorder. "Will you want this when we've finished with it?"

"For what? No thanks."

"You won't be doing what she wanted."

"Writing about her? Too many of the papers already have."

"I can see you wouldn't want to get yourself a worse reputation," the policeman said.

Bantam saw him out of the apartment and out of his mind. He'd survived remarks more pointed than that in the course of his career. The woman on the tape was harder to forget, but a large glass of brandy helped, and put him in a working mood. Working cured anything. He sat on the bed with his lap-top word processor and reached out to turn towards him the photograph of his ex-wife, faded by years of sunlight and dust. He could almost feel her breasts filling his hands, feel her slim waist, long slim legs. "Bitch," he said almost affectionately, and began to write.   Ω

THE FAMILY FOOTBALL
by Ian R. MacLeod

illustrated by Allen Koszowski

Dad came home as a centaur that day. He rapped his hooves impatiently on the front door for someone to let him in. Me and my sister Anne were playing rats on the kitchen floor, running around the table legs and ticking Mum's legs with our whiskers as she fixed tea.

"Go see to your Dad," Mum snapped at me, "and you should be past these silly games. You know how much I hate those long pink tails."

I wandered grumpily down the hall, climbing back into human form as I did so. Dad's horse-and-man shape loomed through the frosted glass. He humphed at me when I opened the door as though I'd been a long time coming, then pushed past and trotted into the lounge. He tried to sit down on the sofa, gave up, and clumsily bent his four legs to lower himself down on the carpet.

"You should be doing your homework, Son," he said as I stood watching from the doorway.

"I'll do it all straight after tea."

"Well, just don't expect . . ." he winced. The long joints of his equine legs were hurting in the position he was sitting. As he changed into the shape of a large labrador, I stood waiting for the end of a sentence I knew by heart. ". . . don't expect to play football afterwards."

I nodded. If I hadn't already known what he was saying, his dog's vocal chords would have given me few clues. Dad was a physically clumsy man. He often changed shapes on the way home on the train when he'd had a bad day at work to try to get it out of his system. But no matter what shape he took, he was never able to make himself either well understood or comfortable.

At tea, we all came as ourselves. Only babies did otherwise, squirming from half-formed shape to shape as I could still (and with some disgust) remember Anne doing in her high chair.

Mum said, "I went to see Doctor Shaw today."

"Oh," Dad said, not looking, chasing a few stray peas around the plate with his fork.

"He says they'll need to do more tests to see what the problem is."

"You can get the time off at the shop?"

"They have to give it, don't they? It's the law."

"I told you when you started there, it's a mistake to work anywhere where there's no union."

"Well, I'm going to go anyway, day after tomorrow. I'm sick of . . . sick of this thing."

Mum was gazing down at her plate. She'd only given herself baked beans on a slice of toast instead of the gammon and egg the rest of us had. It had been the same now for two or three months, since her problem had started. She really couldn't face up to meat, and would have been happier — if she could have faced the indignity — climbing trees and nibbling at bits of green stuff out in the garden.

Anne and I had caught her doing just that on a couple of occasions when we were home all day at half term. Hanging upside down from the almond tree with her apron flapping over her face. She'd shooed us all the way out of the house, her face flushing between anger and embarrassment.

"You've got rights," Dad said. "Just you tell me if they cause you any trouble."

Mum said nothing. She dropped her fork onto the tablecloth with her good left hand, leaving a streak of tomato. I knew even then that she was going through a bad time, what with her right hand. At the moment, she had it hidden beneath the table, not so much because she didn't want us to see it — she'd given up after the first few weeks wearing gloves and bandages except when she went out of the house — but because she hated having to look at it herself. Her right hand was hairy, hairy with hairs that only petered out around her elbow. And it had the three long hooked claws of *Brandypus griesus*, the three-toed sloth or ai. It had been a mystery to us all how she'd even come up with that shape in the first place, as Mum wasn't a great changer, and was never very imaginative about it when she did. But it had happened in the night when she was asleep, which was always more difficult because you didn't have the normal control.

She put it down to the cheese she'd had before she'd gone to bed, and some wildlife programme she'd been watching — which was odd, because all the rest of us could remember seeing that night was a quiz programme, some football, and the news. "Well anyway," she said. "Tomorrow's another day."

"That's right," said Dad. "And I'm due some overtime from all the supplementary bills we've had to send out. How about we get a baby sitter for these two here and go out for a few drinks."

Anne piped in, "Please, not Mrs Bossom again."

But Mum shook her head anyway. "I'm sorry dear. I've promised to take the kids over for tea to see Gran. Of course, I'll leave something nice for you to microwave."

Dad nodded and chewed his food, glaring across at the microwave.

I finished homework at about eight, and ran out to play football on the balding patch of grass in front of our houses. Anne came too, and the rest of our gang were there, apart from Harry Blaines, whose parents were having marital difficulties and were always taking him off with them to see some counsellor as though the whole thing was his fault.

There was a problem: the last time we'd played, Charlie Miller had lobbed our plastic ball over the high fence into the Halls' back garden. The Halls were a mad and angry couple, and spent most of the time at home having rows and flying around the place as birds, pecking at each other and at anyone who dared to ring the doorbell.

We all stood around arguing in the twilight. But then I remembered something — there was an old leather football in our garage. Cracked and deflated, it had been there for as long as I could remember, tucked out of sight and reach behind the old paint tins. On the off-chance that it might be of use, I went in, found the steps and pulled it down in a shower of rust and cobwebs. The odd thing was this; when I managed to fit in the nozzle of my bicycle pump, it began to wheeze and expand even before I started to inflate it.

I played in the side attacking the goal towards the brick wall by the row of garages. We all sprouted tentacles on our heads to distinguish us from the other side. As usual, I was centre forward. So were the rest of the team — Charlie, Bob, Peter, the two Ford sisters — apart from Anne, who was the smallest and ended up in goal between the piles of trainer tops and pullovers. For some reason, she decided she could do the job better as a baby stegosaurus. I had to go over and have a quiet word with her after we had let in five quick and quite unnecessary goals.

"Saw your Mama in that shop today," John Williams came over and said to me as I stood rubbing a bruised feeler and catching my breath. "The shirt department. That's where she works, isn't it?"

"What if she does?" I said.

"You should have seen her. There was this man wanted his shirt taken out of the wrapper. You know, all the bits of card and the pins. Jesus H. Christ, your poor Mum was all over the bloody counter. Hasn't got two proper hands these days, has she?"

"At least she is my Mum," I said, which — as John Williams had a family who were all step-this-or-that — was a good below-the-belt swipe. I followed it off with a good below-the-belt kick.

When we'd finally finished fighting, we both felt better, and pleased with ourselves for being tough. I'd turned into a grizzly bear by then, and John was a tiger. But as always when you were fighting, you could never really manage the shape well enough to do any damage. That was probably a good thing, as I didn't really hate him anyway. He was just a loud-mouthed prat.

We got back to the game. The final score was Side With The Tentacles, 14: Side Without, 17. In my view, at least five of the latter goals would have been disallowed if there had been a referee. An argument started over whether we should settle the thing on penalties.

That was when Mum came out. She was in her old blue dressing gown and I could tell that something was the matter from the way she didn't try to hide her hand. Without saying a word to anyone, she walked out beneath the widening pools of streetlight and bent down to pick up the football. She said something to it, and held it close to her. Everyone just stood staring as she walked back inside.

Me and Anne followed her back into the house a few minutes after. It was getting dark by then, and penalties were out of the question anyway.

Next day at school was pretty ordinary. Steven Halier got into trouble in Maths for changing into a porcupine, and was hauled out to the front. We all laughed when Mister Craig pulled off Steven's shoe before he'd had time to properly change back into it and plonked it there on the desk, bits of shoe-leather, flesh and spines all mangled up together. As punishment, he made Steven leave class without the opportunity to get the thing back on, and he had to hobble around the playground all through the lunch break with only half a foot.

I always kept well away from Anne at school. She was four years below me, and beneath my heights of third form dignity. The girls in her year were all crazy about horses, and took turns changing into one so that the others could take rides. The whole thing looked incredibly stupid from where I was standing by the goalposts on the playing fields, talking about the mysteries of the universe and whether Jane Jolly in the year above us had really got glandular fever or had actually been missing all term so she could have an abortion. Still, I recognised my little sis as she lumbered past me along the touchline, hoofed and on all fours. It was generally easy enough to tell someone you knew well no matter what shape they were in. She was stumbling with a cheap-looking plastic bridle, having trouble with the weight of the fat girl classmate on her back.

After lunch, just as history was starting, Anne and I were both called to the headmaster's office. The headmaster was sitting behind his desk in the form of a big teddy bear. We both let out a sigh of relief to see him that way — Mister Anderson often assumed that shape, but only when he was in a good mood and wasn't after your blood. It wasn't a terribly attractive teddy bear — the eyes really did look like glass buttons — but he entertained the idea that it made him appear friendly and approachable.

"I've had a phone call from your Father at work," he said. "He's had to go off to the hospital now. It's your Mother, I'm afraid. She's been taken ill. Your Grandmother's coming round here to the school to pick you up."

Gran arrived a few minutes later in her little Austin and drove us back to the bungalow that she and Grandad had moved into after he retired from the fire service. Grandad didn't come, of course; Grandad didn't go anywhere now, except for walks. It had been a big family story about what had happened to him when he retired, one of those things that had gone past the stage of being sad — or even a joke — and was now simply accepted. After the first few job-free weeks of gardening and sitting around in the pub drinking more than he could afford, Grandad had started to get depressed. He said it was dog's life, doing nothing every day. Why, he'd ten men under him when he was working, with people's lives at stake. The Christmas when I was about six, Grandad had changed into a black and white mongrel with a jaunty eye patch, and he had never changed back since.

Gran now accepted Grandad that way, taking him for walks, buying tins of good-quality dog food at the supermarket, sending him to kennels and going off on holidays on her own. And so did the whole family. Not that Grandad was a particularly fun sort of dog to have around, the kind that you could throw sticks for and get into scrapes with. He was past sixty after all, crotchety half the time with rheumatism, his muzzle going grey. Still, he came up to me and Anne in the hall of their bungalow with his tail wagging. I patted his head let him lick my hand for a while before Gran took us into the lounge.

Gran made us both sit down. She still hadn't said anything about Mum. Grandad scratched his ear and curled up in front of the gas fire, which, as always — and even now in the middle of summer — was on, and muttering to itself.

"My dears, you both look worried," she said — which I suppose we probably did. It hadn't really occurred to us that Mum might be seriously ill, but once before when she had gone into hospital to have something done, we'd had to spend a whole week with Gran in the bungalow whilst Dad went to work and tried to cook himself spam fritters at home for tea. Grandad and Gran were fine in small doses, but not to stay with.

"Your Mum's really not that bad," Gran added. "But you know she's been having trouble with that hand of hers. Now," she leaned forward, as though she was sharing a secret, "it's started to spread. And she can't do a thing about it."

We went to see Mum in hospital that evening. The three-toed sloth business with her hand hadn't so much spread as taken over. She wasn't in any of the usual wards, but in a new place at the back of the maternity wing that had bare concrete floors and smelled like a zoo. Mum was behind bars, hanging upside down from an old branch, with big brown eyes staring out. The doctor warned us not to try to put our hands through the bars, because Mum had really lost all control, and, although sloths were herbivores, they could give you a nasty bite. Anne began to cry. She thought a herbivore was like cancer. I was older, and I guessed the truth — that Mum becoming a sloth wasn't that different to what had happened to Grandad, and that even though she hadn't done it deliberately, it was probably a kind of mental thing.

Mum just hung there, looking at us, her flattened muzzle gently twitching. She had a long shaggy coat that hung down around her, and the doctor explained that in the wild — and if Mum really had been a three-toed sloth — it would have been green with a special kind of algae. It was pretty boring really, and the chocolates and the stack of old women's magazines Gran had made us bring were obviously a waste of time. So as Gran twittered on uselessly through the bars about the WWI fête, me and Anne opened up the chocolates and started munching them and squabbling over the centres, wandering along the cages to see who else was here.

They were an odd-looking bunch. You can usually spot a shape-changed human from the real thing a mile off, but most of these were different. If it hadn't been for the medical charts with the names and graphs hanging by the padlocked doors, you'd never have guessed that most of them weren't what they pretended to be. Even Grandad, who'd been a mongrel for nearly five years now, wasn't anything like this convincing.

There was a lama, a coyote, a huge insect with mandibles like a lawnmower, and a creature-from-the-black-lagoon-thing that seemed to be rotting at the fins and smelled like an old canal. There were bubbling tanks filled with fishes. One of the was recognisably a catfish, but was scooting around the bottom of the tank on wheels. At the far end, there was a plastic chair behind a rope that we thought was just a chair until it moved when Anne climbed over and tried to sit on it.

"What's that supposed to be?" Anne asked, pointing to a patch of turf in a glass case. I looked at the medical charts clipped to the side. It said: *Lumbricus terrestris.* I'd just done that in science and was able to tell Anne that it meant an earthworm.

Dad arrived soon afterwards. He'd picked up a big

THE FAMILY FOOTBALL

bouquet of roses from the caravan that sold flowers in the hospital carpark, and pushed them towards Mum through a flap in the bars. Mum reached out a long, lugubrious hand and took them. One by one, she ate the lot, thorns and all. Between wincing, Anne and I could hardly stop ourselves from laughing.

We didn't have to stay with Gran and Grandad that night. Dad had taken time off from work. That was a relief — we didn't even mind the soggy spam fritters too much, although at the same time it was a little worrying. I mean, I thought as the three of us sat in the lounge watching TV afterwards, this in-the-head business must be a lot worse than the secret-down-below business that had got Mum into hospital before. By chance, the people in the soap opera we were watching were sitting around in someone's kitchen talking about another of the characters who had supposedly become ill a couple of episodes before but was probably leaving the series. They were all in the shape of armadillos — which Dad said was the only way these people could act — and there were subtitles in case you had any difficulty understanding what they were saying. It seemed that the ill character had had a nervous breakdown, and that, like Mum, he was in a special wing of the local hospital. A nervous breakdown, was, I decided, exactly what Mum was having.

Dad was grumpy. He shooed us off to bed like we didn't have any right to our usual books and baths. He didn't even ask if we'd done our homework, which any other time would have been reassuring.

Anne and I both climbed out of bed and squatted out of sight in the shadows at the top of the stairs as Dad rang up various relatives to explain what had happened. Mostly, it was an extended version of the stuff he'd told us, with the business about the hand and how Mum had been tired lately. But the last phone call he made to Mum's sister Joan was slightly different.

"Yeah," he said, sitting back on the creaky chair by the phone. "I guess it's all made it come back to her."

Dad nodded vigorously as Aunt Joan said something to him.

"Funny thing is," he said. "I thought she'd got over this thing years ago. I mean, you were there then, and I wasn't."

Eventually, he put down the phone and went back into the lounge, closing the door, turning up the TV loud as though he was trying to hide his thoughts. What thing, I wondered, lying awake in bed long after the house had gone silent. I was in one of those sweaty, tossy states when you're not sure whether you're awake or dreaming. I woke up fully with the figures of my alarm clock showing past two, and found that I had three long black claws on each hand, and that I was covered with hair. Although I changed back with no difficulty, the incident scared me. I knew now that what Mum had was a head-thing, but did that mean it couldn't be hereditary?

Next morning, me and Anne went to school as though it was any other day. The only difference was that Dad dropped us off in the car on his way to visit Mum at the hospital. Word had got around. All the teachers were nice to us that day, and even the other kids. Everyone seemed to know about Mum. I glared at John Williams when he came up to me during break, silently daring him to say the kind of thing that had got us into the fight when we were playing football. But one look at his face told me that it had gone beyond all that — that he actually felt sorry for me. More than anything, I think it was that that made me realise that Mum really was ill.

Gran and Grandad were there with Dad when we went to see Mum at the hospital that evening. And Grandad was human. Anne didn't even recognise him. He looked pretty neat, the way you want your Grandad to look when you're a kid, not old and stooped and smelly, but with silver hair brushed back and long, in a white colonial suit with a dark blue waistcoat and paisley cravat bulging out at the collar. The only thing he hadn't changed the jaunty black patch over one eye. It was probably a kind of birthmark.

Dad was very edgy. He'd come as a snake and kept climbing up over the bars as though he wanted to get into the cage with Mum, although at the same time he obviously didn't want to.

There was a doctor there too. A different doctor from the one we'd seen the night before. He was in a suit, and from the way he talked, I guessed he was a head-doctor, the type that you see in films. I thought, Oh no, we're going to end up like Harry Blaines, going to family therapy, but he turned out to be young and quite nice, and kept saying that he really thought Mum was doing well. She was eating plenty of leaves and fruit, and hanging there by her long arms the way sloths were apparently supposed to.

Back at home, Dad made us stay at the table in the kitchen after we'd eaten, which was the last thing we really wanted, what with the taste of his cooking and the room still filled with smoke from the blackened frying pan. But he said it was time we had a talk, and we knew from the look on his face (he'd turned back from a snake to drive the car home) that he really meant it.

"Your Mum," he said, "she didn't have a happy childhood. Well, she was a woman by then really, the time I'm talking about."

"But it was before she met you," I said, and Dad gave me a look as though he guessed that we'd been listening to him on the phone to Aunt Joan last evening. For some reason, the thought of being a sneak made me turn into an elephant. It was embarrassing — but for a while, I just couldn't help it.

Ignoring me — not even making his usual warning about the strength of the furniture — Dad went on; "Your Mum had a — a difficult time when she was in her late teens."

I nodded, my trunk swinging slightly and knocking

over the bottle of brown sauce before I had a chance to pull it back in. If Mum was late teens at the time, I guessed that it probably had to do with sex and babies. From my experience, there was not much else that kids of that age got up to, apart from maybe doing drugs and stealing cars, and I couldn't see Mum ever being like that.

"She wasn't very happy," I suggested, "and now she's not feeling happy again."

Dad nodded, and then he shook his head. "That's exactly it. . . ."

I thought he was going to say something more. And from the way Dad had his mouth half-open, he obviously thought so too. But, looking at us, he changed his mind.

Afterwards, me and Anne decided we might as well go out and play. Dad was shut in the lounge watching TV, one of those wrestling matches where they put Godzilla against King Kong and you can tell it's just people really and nothing like as good as the special effects you get in films. I looked around for the football, but it had gone from the garage. Dad had obviously hidden it, but I had a pretty good idea where to look — he and Mum were never very imaginative about hiding things. The football was tucked away with the dust under Mum and Dad's bed.

It was a good game that evening. And close. For once, Anne played out of goal — and she wasn't bad either, scoring twice, and with only one of them an own goal. We forgot about the time. Dad came out in his vest when it was almost dark and we were just having fun. He went mad when he saw the ball we were using. He put his hand up to hit me, and only just managed to stop himself.

Dad took the ball inside and dumped it in the sink in the kitchen, wrapped up in a towel as though he could hardly bear to touch it.

He found me staring at it when I came down after my bath to get a drink of orange.

"Son, I'm sorry about what happened on the green," he said, patting my shoulder with a shaky hand. "But under no circumstances are you ever to touch that football. Not you or even Annie. Not ever again."

I didn't say anything, and I didn't sleep much. In the morning, Dad took the football along with him when he dropped us off on the way to the hospital. He had it in on the front passenger seat, still wrapped up in the towel. To stop it rolling, he had put the seatbelt around it.

Grandad picked us up from school that evening. He was still a human, but I wasn't too keen on the idea of him driving Gran's Austin: normally, he travelled around in it with his head out of the back window, barking at pedestrians.

"Is Mum any better?" I asked, sitting on the front passenger seat beside him, thinking how odd it was to he talking to this smart grey-haired gent.

"I think she is," he said, smiling.

Grandad was keeping his eye firmly on the road. The skin around the dark patch on his left eye was crinkled. I could tell he was working up to saying something more.

"What has your Dad told you?" he asked.

From the back, picking the white dog hairs off her school blazer, Anne chirped, "He told us that Mum wasn't very happy once."

"Not very happy." Grandad shifted into gear as the lights changed. The car gave a jerk and nearly stalled. Grandad was okay at driving, but not that good. "I suppose that's right. You're, ah, both very young for the thing I'm going to have to tell you now. But we've spoken to the doctors at the hospital, and we reckon it's the best way. If you want your Mum to get better . . . you do want that, don't you?"

We both said yes. We were driving along the high street past the shops now. A couple of salamanders were lounging in the sun outside the new DIY superstore. I recognised them as tough older kids from school.

"Your Mum had a baby when she was . . . when she was far too young. Before she even met your Dad. You understand what that means?"

We both nodded. I decided it wasn't worth the bother of letting Grandad know that I'd worked that much out already.

"So we thought we could have the baby adopted. You know, given to some people who couldn't have a baby, but wanted one. It was a kind of . . . family secret."

"That the baby was adopted?" I asked.

"No." Grandad grated the gears. "That it wasn't. Even your Dad didn't know that when he and your Mum were courting. We hid it. I guess now we're all to blame, I suppose . . . apart from you kids of course. Your Mum couldn't part with the baby, and I don't think anyone else would have had him anyway. The poor little thing wasn't — isn't — right in the head. He can't change shapes like the rest of us. For a while, we didn't think he could change at all. He was always just asleep, not really growing or living. Then one day, I put him down in the corner of my study, by this old football. When I looked . . ."

We'd reached the hospital. Grandad parked the car at the far end, but we didn't get out.

I asked, "Did Dad know about this?"

Slowly, still gripping the wheel tight, Grandad nodded. "Just before they got married, yes. But he always found it hard to take. He couldn't stand to have Tom around, reminding him. That was why he ended up in the garage. There for years. As a football."

"And he's called Tom," I said eventually.

Grandad nodded. He reached and took both of our hands to help us out of the car.

"Come on," he said, "let's see how your Mum is. She's got Tom with her now."

We went and saw Mum. She was still a sloth, but

she'd changed her face enough to smile, and it was obvious that she was a little better. She had Tom, our old family football, cradled in her arms. Dad was Dad. I could tell he was fidgeting to change into a snake or something, but tonight he stayed himself.

We all stood around with the head-doctor, smiling and talking in big shaky voices. Eventually, Anne started to cry. I was glad when she blurted out the thing that had been worrying me too. I mean, we'd been kicking Tom around the night before. I could still hear that leathery slap he made when he hit the back wall of the garages. But the head-doctor was reassuring. Tom wasn't really like us. He was a football. He even probably liked being played. It was better, after all, than the years he'd spent hidden behind the paint tins in our garage.

Anne stopped crying, and I took hold of her hand. Now that everything was out in the open, I felt relieved. But Dad was just standing there, gazing down at the concrete. Apart from Mum herself, I suppose this whole thing was most difficult for him out of all of us. It took a week of visits to the hospital before he could bring himself to reach through the bars and take Tom from Mum's incredibly long arms. A few moments later, he had to give him back, but next day, he kept hold. Gran and Grandad were there too, and I suppose we were wondering what Dad was going to do next. But he surprised us all by lobbing Tom gently into the air, then kicking him on the volley towards me. He came over at head height, and I nodded him down towards Anne, and she caught him. It was perfect, one of those miraculous moments that hardly ever happen. And we all started to laugh and pat each other's back and in the excitement Grandad forgot he was human and started to bark.

That was the real beginning of Mum getting better. Next day, her head had changed back into the person we knew. And the day after that — after we'd borrowed Tom for a big game down at the park against the lot from the next estate — we came late with Gran back to the hospital to tell Mum about it, and found her sitting up on a log in her old house coat. She was complaining about the noise and the smell in her ward, but she was smiling.

They soon moved her to a proper ward. And not long after that, she came home for good. Even her right hand was back to normal. The head-doctor said it had all been a kind of hysterical paralysis. The hand had been a warning sign, but what probably tipped the balance was seeing me and Anne playing football with Tom out on the grass in front of our houses.

When Gran and Grandad came around for tea on the Sunday after Mum got out, Grandad had gone back to being a dog again. We all felt a little sad to loose him that way — he had been such a nice old man. But at least he'd changed from a mongrel into a red setter, and although he was still old — and he still had the black patch — he was more fun to be with from then on. We used to go around to Gran's to bring him along with us when we took Tom to play in the park.

Tom stayed a football. I supposed he always will, never changing, never getting old. Sometimes I talk to him, but I don't think he hears, or understands if he does. One evening that summer when we were playing with him on the green, the inevitable happened and he flew over the fence into the dreaded Hall's back garden. Knowing we couldn't just leave him there the way we had with all the other footballs, me and Anne went up and rang their front door. Mrs Hall answered. She was shaped as an octopus actually, not a bird at all. And she simply let us in to collect up all the balls and everything else that had landed in their garden over the years.

With all the other balls back, we still always played with Tom. Of course, the other kids knew about him, and were a little edgy at first, passing gently, using side-foots towards goal. But I realised that Tom was finally accepted when John Williams missed a penalty and ran over to the fence to yell down at him as though it was his fault. We all fell about laughing at that, and when I happened to look up at the top windows of our house, I saw that Mum was standing in the bedroom with the net curtains pulled back. She was smiling.

We were well into the summer holidays by then. Dad had had a couple of good pay cheques, and we agreed that all of us would go on holiday together, and abroad for a change. Dad, Mum, me, Anne, Gran, and Tom. Even Grandad agreed to change back into a human for the fortnight to save any problems with quarantine.

I can still remember packing my case for that holiday on the night before we took the plane. Filling up with books and shorts and tee shirts and cream for mosquito bites and clean pairs of pants. I could already picture that white beach, the white hotels, the cool old-fashioned streets at the back, the warm sea beckoning in the sunshine. First day, we'd all run out straight after breakfast and kick Tom across the smooth hot sand towards the breakers, changing into porpoises as we did so. Diving down into the stream of the ocean, bobbing Tom on our noses, dancing in the dappled light.

Which, as things turned out, is exactly what we did. Ω

SYMPATHY FOR ZOMBIES
by John Gregory Betancourt

Heat rose off the glistening white sand in shimmering waves. In the sparkling blue "Pirate's Lagoon," as the Cte D'Argent Hotel proclaimed it, swimmers frolicked; farther out, jetskis and sailboards cut white-frothed paths across the water.

"Take another drink, Miss."

Julie Novelle turned her head. A cabana boy, maybe eleven or twelve, dressed in the hotel uniform of khaki shorts and shirt, offered her a fresh strawberry daiquiri. She accepted the glass.

"Drink it, Miss," the boy said.

Julie sipped the cool, soothing daiquiri.

Heat shimmered across the beautiful white sand.

Far off, happy couples laughed and frolicked in the low surf.

She hadn't been wild about a vacation in the Caribbean at first. But she'd just come through a rather messy divorce — thank God there weren't any kids — and after the judge had awarded her custody of their house in the Hamptons, both Jaguars, and most of the money in their accounts, Tom had walked up with a pasty smile on his face and handed her a white envelope.

"Just to show there aren't any hard feelings," he said. "I need a vacation, and I want to make sure we don't bump into each other. Let's get on with our lives, okay?" Then he'd walked away.

Julie looked inside the envelope. It held a plane ticket to a Caribbean singles resort, plus other receipts. Everything had been paid for in advance, she realized.

He'd always been like that. Generous at the wrong times. She felt her heart soften, as it often had during their separation, but then she remembered his moodiness, his childlike tantrums, and everything else that had driven a wedge between them. Then she'd steeled herself. But she'd tucked the ticket into her purse. She could always cash it in, she told herself.

But somehow, she'd decided to go. They had always talked about a vacation in the Caribbean, after all. It had been a personal fantasy. And with the trip paid for . . . why not?

Julie sipped her drink and stared across the ocean. The water here was so blue, you could lose yourself in its depths. She'd gone swimming the first few days, and dancing, and partying. She'd joined other singles for the Recreational Director's planned jaunts. It had been fun. Everything here had been fun.

The best part had been the trip out to see Queen Jamorah, the Voodoo Priestess. They had gone late at night in a tour bus. Queen Jamorah lived in a shack in the middle of dense jungle.

One by one the other tourists pushed aside a bead curtain and ventured in. A few minutes later they emerged with knowing smirks or nervous grins.

Julie went last. When her eyes grew accustomed to the near darkness, she saw an old, wrinkled woman holding a rooster's claw and wearing a feathered headdress.

"You are called Julie," the old woman intoned.

"That's right," Julie said.

"I have a message," she said, "from one who is dead to you."

This was getting interesting, Julie thought. She leaned forward. "Yes?" she whispered, intrigued.

With a quick motion of her hand, the old woman threw something dry and dusty in Julie's face. It burned Julie's eyes and stung her throat; coughing and wheezing, she reeled back.

"Revenge," said the old woman, "has been paid for."

The floor turned beneath her. Julie felt herself falling and was unable to stop. Darkness came.

Julie awakened in her hotel room. For the longest time she lay in bed staring at the ceiling.

Finally the Recreation Director showed up. She took Julie's arm and helped her out to the beach. As the day went on, cabana boys brought her food and strawberry daiquiris, instructing her to "Eat this, Miss," or "Drink this, Miss."

The days passed, the crowds changed, and Julie drifted. Usually the cabana boys remembered to bring her inside for the night, and when they didn't she lost herself in the slowly changing constellations overhead.

"Look at me," a man's voice said.

Julie tilted her head back and saw her ex-husband. Tom wore blue Bermuda shorts, a white polo shirt, and designer sunglasses.

Queen Jamorah stood next to him, looking respectable in a bright floral muumuu. She peered at Julie and gave a nod.

"As you can see," she said in her thick accent, "she is a zombie, not a living person. She will obey your every command. She is your slave. Only remember one thing: she must finish every task she begins before she starts the next. She has no mind or will of her own."

"Check," Tom said, smiling. "Got it." He passed her a thick white envelope. "The final payment."

"I wish you luck," Queen Jamorah said. She hurried away.

Tom knelt. "I wanted to make up," he said, taking Julie's hand. "Say you've changed your mind about us."

"I've changed my mind about us," Julie felt herself saying. A tiny spark of rage flared inside her.

Tom grinned. "Good. Tell me you love me."

"I love you," she echoed.

"That's all I ever wanted," he said. "Follow me. I have a plane waiting. We'll get married tonight in Las Vegas."

Julie found herself rising to follow. The sea — the sand — the sky and the stars — she was going to lose them. For a second she hesitated.

"Follow me, Julie," Tom said again.

She walked after him. Inside, she felt something tighten around her heart. She tried to speak, to protest, but all that emerged was a soft, sad sigh.

"A whirlwind re-courtship," he murmured. "A break was all we needed, dear Julie. Our love is forever. Tell me that, Julie. Tell me you'll love me forever."

Julie's screams echoed in her mind. She opened her mouth.

"I'll love you," she said. "I'll love you . . . I'll love you . . . I'll love you . . ."

On and on she droned, like a broken record, repeating that phrase even when he told her to stop, because she hadn't finished carrying out his command. Forever, some distant part of herself noted, was a very long time indeed.

And she would go on telling him she would love him — forever.

"I'll love you," she said. "I'll love you. I'll love you."

After five minutes, when nothing he could say or do would shut her up, Tom's nervous twitchy smile turned frightened. And when he began to run, Julie followed.

"I'll love you," she called. "I'll love you — I'll love you — I'll love you —"

And she kept right on saying it, even when he began to scream. Ω

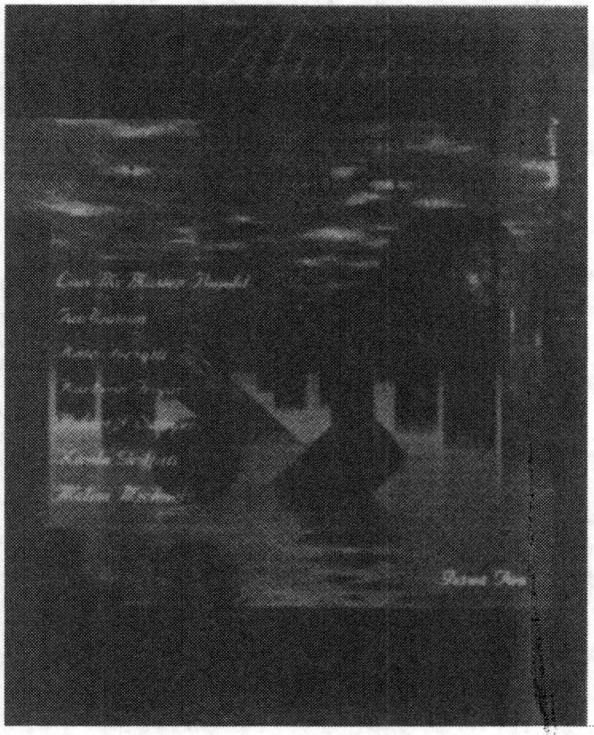

by John Gregory Betancourt

HIS SHADOW SHALL RISE TO A HIGHER HOUSE

by Thomas Ligotti

illustrated by Jason Van Hollander

In the middle of the night I lay wide awake in bed, listening to the dull black drone of the wind outside my window and the sound of bare branches scraping against the shingles of the roof just above me. Soon my thoughts became fixed upon a town, picturing its various angles and aspects, a remote town near the northern border. Then I remembered that there was a hilltop graveyard that hovered not far beyond the edge of town. I never mentioned to anyone this graveyard which for a time was a source of great anguish for those who had retreated to the barren landscape of the northern border.

It was within the hilltop graveyard, a place that was far more populated than the town over which it hovered, that the body of Ascrobius had been buried. Known throughout the town as a recluse who possessed an intensely contemplative nature, Ascrobius had suffered from a disease that left much of his body in a grossly deformed conditioned. Nevertheless, despite the distinguishing qualities of his severe deformity and his intensely contemplative nature, the death of Ascrobius was an event that passed almost entirely unnoticed. All of the notoriety gained by the recluse, all of the comment attached to his name, occurred sometime after his disease-mangled body had been housed among the others in the hilltop graveyard.

At first there was no specific mention of Ascrobius, but only a kind of twilight talk — dim and pervasive murmurs that persistently revolved around the graveyard outside of town, often touching upon more general topics of a morbid character, including some abstract discourse, as I interpreted it, on *the phenomenon of the grave*. More and more, whether one moved about the town or remained in some secluded quarter of it, this twilight talk became familiar and even invasive. It emerged from shadowed doorways along narrow streets, from half-opened windows of the highest rooms of the town's old houses, and from the distant corners of labyrinthine and resonant hallways. Everywhere, it seemed, there were voices that had become obsessed to the point of hysteria with a single subject: the "missing grave." No one mistook these words to mean a grave that somehow had been violated, its ground dug up and its contents removed, or even a grave whose headstone had been absconded, leaving the resident of some particular plot in a state of anonymity. Even I, who was less intimate than many others with the peculiar nuances of the northern border town, understood what was meant by the words "a missing grave" or "an absent grave." The hilltop graveyard was so dense with headstones and its ground so riddled with interments that such a thing would be astonishingly apparent: where there once had been a grave like any other, there was now, in the same precious space, only a patch of virgin earth.

For a certain period of time, speculation arose concerning the identity of the occupant of the missing grave. Because there existed no systematic record-keeping for any particular instance of burial in the hilltop graveyard — when or where or for whom an interment took place — the discussions over the occupant of the missing grave, or the *former* occupant, always degenerated into outbursts of the wildest nonsense or simply faded into a vaporous and sullen confusion. Such a scene was running its course in the cellar of an abandoned building where several of us had gathered one evening. It was on this occasion that a gentleman calling himself Dr. Klatt first suggested "Ascrobius" as the name upon the headstone of the missing grave. He was almost offensively positive in this assertion, as if there were not an abundance of headstones on the hilltop graveyard with erroneous or unreadable names, or none at all.

For some time Klatt had been advertising himself around town as an individual who possessed a distinguished background in some discipline of a vaguely scientific nature. This persona or imposture, if it was one, would not have been unique in the history of the northern border town. However, when Klatt began to speak of the recent anomaly not as a *missing* grave, or even an absent grave, but as an *uncreated* grave, the others began to listen. Soon enough it was the name of Ascrobius that was mentioned most frequently as the occupant of the missing — now *uncreated* — grave. At the same time the reputation of Dr. Klatt became closely linked to that of the deceased individual who was well known for both his grossly deformed body and for his intensely contemplative nature.

During this period it seemed that anywhere in town that one happened to find oneself, Klatt was there holding forth on the subject of his relationship to Ascrobius, whom he now called his "patient." In the cramped back rooms of shops long gone out of business or on some out-of-the-way street corner, Klatt spoke of the visits he had made to the high back-street house of Ascrobius and of the attempts he had made to treat the disease from which the recluse had long suffered. In addition, Klatt boasted of the insights he had gained into the deeply contemplative personality whom most of us had never met, let alone conversed with at any great length. While Klatt appeared to enjoy the attention he received from those who had previously dismissed him as just another impostor in the northern border town, and perhaps still considered him as such, I believe he was unaware of the profound suspicion, and even dread, that he inspired due to what certain persons called his "meddling" in the affairs of Ascrobius. "Thou shalt not meddle" was an unspoken, though seldom observed, commandment of the town, or so it seemed to me. And Klatt's exposure of the formerly obscure existence of Ascrobius, even if the doctor's anecdotes were largely misleading or totally fabricated, would be regarded as a highly perilous form of meddling by many longtime residents of the town.

Nonetheless, nobody turned away whenever Klatt began talking about the diseased, contemplative recluse; nobody tried to silence or even question whatever claims he made concerning Ascrobius. "He was a monster," said the doctor to some of us who were gathered one night in a ruined factory on the outskirts of town. Klatt frequently stigmatized Ascrobius as either a "monster" or a "freak," though these epithets were not intended simply as a reaction to the grotesque physical appearance of the notorious recluse. It was in a strictly metaphysical sense, according to Klatt, that Ascrobius should be viewed as most monstrous and freakish, qualities that emerged as a consequence of his intensely contemplative nature. "He had incredible powers available to him," said the doctor. "He might even have cured himself of his diseased physical condition, who can say? But all of his powers of contemplation, all of those incessant *meditations* that took place in his high back-street house, were directed toward another purpose altogether." Saying this much, Dr. Klatt fell silent in the flickering, makeshift illumination of the ruined factory. It was almost as if he were waiting for one of us to prompt his next words, so that we might serve as accomplices in this extraordinary gossip over his deceased patient Ascrobius.

Eventually someone did inquire about the contemplative powers and meditations of the recluse, and toward what end they might have been directed. "What Ascrobius sought," the doctor explained, "was not a remedy for his physical disease, not a cure in any usual sense of the word. What he sought was an absolute *annulment,* not only of his disease but of his entire existence. On rare occasions he even spoke to me," the doctor said, "about the *uncreation* of his whole life." After Dr. Klatt had spoken these words there seemed to occur a moment of the most profound stillness in the ruined factory where we were gathered. No doubt everyone had suddenly become possessed, as was I, by a single object of contemplation — the absent grave, which Dr. Klatt described as an uncreated grave, within the hilltop graveyard outside of town. "You see what has happened," Dr. Klatt said to us. "*He* has annulled his diseased and nightmarish existence, leaving *us* with an uncreated grave on our hands." Nobody who was at the ruined factory that night, nor anyone else in the northern border town, did not believe there would be a price to pay for what had been revealed to us by Dr. Klatt. Now all of us had become meddling accomplices in those events which came to be euphemistically depicted as the "Ascrobius escapade."

Admittedly the town had always been populated by hysterics of one sort or another. Following the Ascrobius escapade, however, there was a remarkable plague of twilight talk about "unnatural repercussions" that were either in the making or were already taking place throughout the town. *Someone would have to atone for that uncreated existence,* or such was the general feeling as it was expressed in various obscure settings and situations. In the dead of night one could hear the most reverberant screams arising at frequent intervals from every section of town, particularly the back-street areas, far more than the

usual nocturnal outbursts. And upon subsequent overcast days the streets were all but deserted. Any talk confronting the specifics of the town's night terrors was either precious or entirely absent; perhaps, I might even say, it was as uncreated as Ascrobius himself, at least for a time.

It was inevitably the figure of Dr. Klatt who, late one afternoon, stepped forward from the shadows of an old warehouse to address a small group of persons assembled there. His shape barely visible in the gauzy light that pushed its way through dusty windowpanes, Klatt announced that he might possess the formula for solving the new-found troubles of the northern border town. While the warehouse gathering was as wary as the rest of us of any further meddling in the matter of Ascrobius, they gave Klatt a hearing in spite their reservations. Included among this group was a woman known as Mrs. Glimm, who operated a lodging house — actually a kind of brothel — that was patronized for the most part by out-of-towners, especially business travellers stopping on their way to some destination across the border. Even though Klatt did not directly address Mrs. Glimm, he made it quite clear that he would require an assistant of a very particular type in order to carry out the measures he had in mind for delivering us all from those intangible traumas that had lately afflicted everyone in some manner. "Such an assistant," the doctor emphasized, "should not be anyone who is exceptionally sensitive or intelligent. At the same time," he continued, "this person must have a definite handsomeness of appearance, even a fragile beauty." Further instructions from Dr. Klatt indicated that the requisite assistant should be sent up to the hilltop graveyard that same night, for the doctor fully expected that the clouds which had choked the sky throughout the day would linger long into the evening, thus cutting off the moonlight that often shone so harshly on the closely huddled graves. This desire for optimum darkness seemed to be a conspicuous giveaway on the doctor's part. Everyone present at the old warehouse was of course aware that such "measures" as Klatt proposed were only another instance of meddling by someone who was almost certainly an impostor of the worst sort. But we were already so deeply implicated in the Ascrobius escapade, and so lacking in any solutions of our own, that no one attempted to discourage Mrs. Glimm from doing what she could to assist the doctor with his proposed scheme.

So the moonless night came and went, and the assistant sent by Mrs. Glimm never returned from the hilltop graveyard. Yet nothing in the northern border town seemed to have changed. The chorus of midnight outcries continued and the twilight talk now began to focus on both the "terrors of Ascrobius" and the "charlatan Dr. Klatt," who was nowhere to be found when a search was conducted throughout every street and structure of the town, excepting of course the high back-street house of the dreadful recluse. Finally a small party of the town's least hysterical persons made their way up the hill which led to the graveyard. When they approached the area of the absent grave, it was immediately apparent what "measures" Dr. Klatt had employed and the fashion in which the assistant sent by Mrs. Glimm had been used in order to bring an end to the Ascrobius escapade.

The message which those who had gone up to the graveyard carried back to town was that Klatt was nothing but a common butcher. "Well, perhaps not a *common* butcher," said Mrs. Glimm, who was among the small graveyard party. Then she explained in detail how the body of the doctor's assistant, its skin finely shredded by countless incisions and its parts numerously dismembered, had been arranged with some calculation on the spot of the absent grave: the raw head and torso were propped up in the ground as if to serve as the headstone for a grave, while the arms and legs were disposed in a way that might be seen to demarcate the rectangular space of a graveyard plot. Someone suggested giving the violated body a proper burial in its own grave site, but Mrs. Glimm, for some reason unknown even to herself, or so she said, persuaded the others that things should be left as they were. And perhaps her intuition in this matter was a fortuitous one, for not many days later there was a complete cessation of all terrors associated with the Ascrobius escapade, however indefinite or possibly nonexistent such occurrences might have been from the start. Only later, by means of the endless murmurs of twilight talk, did it become apparent why Dr. Klatt might have abandoned the town, even though his severe measures seemed to have worked the exact cure which he had promised.

Although I cannot say that I witnessed anything myself, others reported signs of a "new occupation," not at the site of the grave of Ascrobius, but at the high back-street house where the recluse once spent his intensely contemplative days and nights. There were sometimes lights behind the curtained windows, these observers said, and the passing figure outlined upon those curtains was more outlandishly grotesque than anything they had ever seen while the resident of that house had lived. But no one ever approached the house. Afterward all speculation about what had come to be known as the "resurrection of the uncreated" remained in the realm of twilight talk. Yet as I now lay in my bed, listening to the wind and the scraping of bare branches on the roof just above me, I cannot help remaining wide awake with visions of that deformed specter of Ascrobius and upon what unimaginable planes of contemplation it dreams of another act of uncreation, a new and far-reaching effort of great power and more certain permanence. Nor do I welcome the thought that one day someone may notice that a particular house appears to be missing, or absent, from the place it once occupied along the back streets of a town near the northern border.   Ω

FUTILITY

Echoes between
this sunlit & a stranger land . . .
echoes between
remind listening bones of green,
yet blight that green with gravelost hand
too far from flesh to understand
echoes between.

— Ann K. Schwader

THE GIANT VORVIADES
by Darrell Schweitzer

illustrated by Stephen E. Fabian

He found the giant crouching amid the frozen peaks of the highest mountains in the world. At that precise moment, he could remember little of his adventures coming here, of the hardships endured, and, perhaps, beloved comrades lost along the way. Even his own name seemed to shimmer just beyond his grasp.

But the voice out of his dreams told him clearly, as he led his emaciated horse onto the ledge, that what he saw across the adjacent chasm, huddled beneath the roof of the sky, was no mere pile of stones and ice. Here was Vorviades, cousin to the Shadow Titans and nemesis of the gods, devourer of light, enemy of mankind.

He made the sign of the dead for himself, crossing his arms briefly on his chest, tossing his head back to silently invoke the Righteous Nine Gods, performing, as best he could under the circumstances, his own funeral rites.

For his dreams told him that he had come to kill Vorviades, and he did not expect to survive the attempt.

Slowly the blizzard abated. The snowy curtain parted, and he beheld Vorviades, grown encrusted with centuries of waiting.

An avalanche roared into the gorge below. The monster turned its head toward him and opened its eyes. The giant's face looked like a thing of ice and stone, now torn free from the flesh of the mountains.

Calmly, the nameless man took his bags down from his pitiable horse, spread them out on the snow, and began to unpack, carefully unwrapping each piece of armor and strapping it on. Last came the ornately-inlaid, silver sword and gleaming sun-shield of the Knights Inquisitor, and his helmet, which was shaped like the face of an eagle.

Without hesitation, trembling only from weariness and the cold, he armed and bedecked himself as a champion of the Righteous Gods. He closed his visor, snapping the eagle's mouth shut. The clang echoed upward, toward Vorviades.

At the very last he removed his horse's saddle and bridle, and sent the beast down into the world wearing only a blanket.

Had the animal speech, he knew, it would be able to tell much, but the ending of the story would remain unknown, unless revealed by the Nine Gods in visions to the most holy.

For a confusing instant, he wasn't sure he even was a knight. He had some memory of another life, of a boatman who left his work by a river's bank when a dream summoned him; of crows picking at an armored corpse by a roadside, shrieking the words of dream; of the voice in his dream commanding him to take up another man's life, and another: the boatman, a slain knight, other wanderers. Souls processed into the darkness, but each time the hero rose again and continued his centuried quest.

Perhaps it really had been that way and he was an impostor, a madman, last of a series of madmen, who had stolen armor off a corpse. He didn't know. It hardly mattered now.

He drew his sword.

The snow in the air swirled away, revealing blue sky. The sun gleamed on silver blade, golden shield, and on the icy face of Vorviades.

"Do you not fear me, little man?" The giant spoke with the voice of wind howling among skybound crags.

The knight's waking dream told him not to fear, and he did not.

Vorviades slid down into the chasm in an even greater avalanche, the whole mountain seeming to split apart as his thundering limbs stretched themselves for the first time in countless years. Snow, ice, and powdered stone filled the air like spray, concealing the giant entirely.

When the knight saw Vorviades once more, the monster had donned a mask of battered, mottled silver. It rose out of the tumultuous snow-clouds like an ominous moon.

"Do you not fear me?"

For an instant the man was afraid, for he felt the voice within him quaver, as if the unseen and unknown sender of the dreams actually feared Vorviades.

Then the fear was gone, like sound cut off by a door suddenly shut.

The silver mask hovered before him, rising out of the abyss. He struck at it with his sword. Sparks flew. The mountains echoed the sound, and with the giant's laughter. Vorviades stood up to his full height, swelling like smoke, filling the entire sky, blotting out the sun.

"Do you not fear me?"

"No," the man gasped, unprompted by any dream. "I do not." Indeed, it was entirely too late for fear.

The giant crouched down again, but the sky remained dark. Somehow hours had fled away. Stars gleamed. The knight could barely make out the rough, hunched shape of Vorviades, diminished considerably but still huge, climbing up out of the chasm onto the ledge. Chivalry bade him wait until the giant was on the ledge before him.

by Darrell Schweitzer

Vorviades loomed perhaps forty feet above him.

"You have reason to fear me," he said. "Fear me when the cities are crushed beneath my tread. Fear me when the plains tremble, when the seas rise up and wash over the lands because I am wading."

"Not if you die here, on this ledge," said the knight.

"Not then, I freely admit."

The knight struck the giant again, but was brushed aside with the flourish of an enormous hand. He sprawled in the snow, perilously close to the rim of the ledge, rolling over on his back, his shield upraised to protect himself. He paused as he saw that the giant had diminished once more, and now was no more than fifteen feet tall.

"I have seen your death in my dreams, Vorviades. Many times. It must be true."

"Aye, true. But is it true *now.*?" The giant rushed at him. The knight leapt to his feet and struck again. He felt the blow connect, but found himself hurled through the air. Once more he rolled, at the edge of the abyss.

When he beheld Vorviades again, the giant was no more than ten feet tall, and seemed to be bleeding.

"I think it is true now."

"I myself have awakened *into* the dreams of many men," said Vorviades, "to bring them terror. I don't think it is over yet."

They fought on, the giant's fists crashing into the knight's shield, the silver sword flickering like a serpent's tongue, finding blood until the snow was splattered with it.

Now Vorviades was only a head taller than the knight, broad of girth and shoulder, but human-sized.

"I think it is over," said the knight.

"For you it is."

The giant had disappeared. The knight turned this way and that in the darkness, but could not find him. Then came the piercing, crushing pain from below and behind and he was hurled through the air once more, clear of the ledge this time, into the gorge below. His mind couldn't sort it out: the mountains and sky whirling, the clanging, crashing impact, pain spreading like the blood spurting inside his armor. In one dream he seemed to imagine the giant shrunken down to the size of a dwarf, calmly snatching a dagger from the knight's belt and ramming up into his groin before shoving him off a cliff.

He lay broken on the rocks far below the ledge. No, he could not accept such an ending. The dream had to be torn and rewoven.

He dreamed of Vorviades, grown huge once more, his mottled mask like the rising silver moon, reaching down tenderly, lifting up the dying knight, peeling away armor and flesh with surprisingly delicate fingers.

The knight wept, but for joy, for this was a hero's proper death.

Vorviades wept too, but only for an instant. Then he spoke as if he were addressing to someone else entirely, the dead man in his hand already forgotten.

"Dream of me, and fear me. I am coming for you, no matter how many such you send against me."

Vorviades sighed, and blew the knight's soul away as one might puff on a dandelion; and the man who still could not remember his own name sailed off into the darkness, to be judged and to dwell far to the south among the crocodiles, in the belly of Surat-Kemad, the Dreaming God, Lord of Death, whose mouth is the night sky, whose teeth are the numberless stars.

The Dream-Sender, dreaming, sat up with a shout, but did not wake. His voice echoed in the stillness of his tomb, and his dreams were filled with fear. He felt the earth tremble as Vorviades strode down from the mountains and began to cross the plains.

Therefore the Dream-Sender searched his dreams once more, frantically, to find another champion.

After King Angharad the Great had conquered all the lands between the northern forests and the Crescent Sea, fathered many sons, and brought peace to his wide domains, he was still a vigorous man, and it was assumed that he would reign for years to come.

But one night in his banqueting hall, before all his warriors and the ladies of his court, the king slowly poured out his winecup in libation to the gods and said, "I am summoned to conquer Vorviades, for I fear him."

At once, all were filled with consternation, that King Angharad could be afraid.

His queen, seated beside him, said, "Surely this was only some idle fancy of sleep, and you need not heed it."

But the king said, "I have dreamed truly."

That very evening, messengers came with the news that a city in a distant province had been overthrown.

"It was an earthquake," they said.

"It was Vorviades. The earth trembles when he walks."

Who knew of Vorviades? The historians searched the name out of books, but, but such books were old and filled with obscurities. The poets knew of him, but only stories. Hadrondius the philosopher, chief of the royal counselors and reputedly a wise man, merely said, "Lord King, you must defeat whatever it is you fear."

Therefore the king summoned his armies, and in the days that followed the earth indeed trembled, with the tread of King Angharad and ten thousand soldiers, off to battle Vorviades. They covered the hills like dark locusts. They looked down on the broken columns of the fallen city, and the king said, "Indeed, this is the work of Vorviades."

No one dared say otherwise.

The king summoned Vorviades with the blasts of a thousand trumpets. But the giant did not come.

The moon rose over the ruins, and the king declared the moon to be a silver mask, dented and tarnished, with burning eyes. He commanded his archers to shoot, and no one could say that they shot only at the moon.

In the midst of a forest, the king peered into the shadows between the great trees, and cried, "There! There is Vorviades!"

He sent his lancers charging for hours, until many were lost in the forest. Yet no one reported that they were chasing only shadows.

When a fire burned a whole district, Angharad said, "Vorviades has breathed."

When crops withered, he said, "Vorviades was hungry." Not even Hadrondius could make the king see otherwise.

Only when the army attacked a river with their swords and the soldiers began joking about baths and rust did anyone mutter anything, or look to the king and shake their heads sadly.

In time, though, everyone concluded that King Angharad the Great was mad. His courtiers slipped away, and his soldiers went over to his too-numerous sons, who fought over the pieces of his kingdom. Angharad watched the final battle from a hilltop, weeping, a ragged beggar now, alone and forgotten by the contending armies. In the end, two of his sons were beheaded. Two more died on one another's swords. The old queen perished before his eyes when her chariot overturned as she escaped one faction and was about to be captured by another.

The king raged on his hilltop, shaking his fists at the sky, while the smoke of battle rose. In the evening, in the bloody sunset amid the dust, he saw the giant Vorviades, clearly outlined against the sky.

"You!" he shouted with the last of his strength. "Why did you never fight me?"

The giant turned his masked face, which now gleamed like a second sun. He spread his hands.

"I have fought you all this time, and behold, I am victorious. Have I not destroyed everything you arrayed against me?"

"You never fought against *me!*" the king shouted. He reached for his sword, then fell to his knees sobbing when he found that he had no sword.

"Yes I did," said Vorviades, hurling his spear, which was the thunderbolt, to transfix the king.

The Dream-Sender cried out in agony as if he himself had been pierced, but still he did not wake. His tomb resounded like a great, echoing bell. Once more he whispered into the minds of men, commanding that Vorviades be opposed. But, in his own dream, he saw his champions like wooden statues, fierce enough, impressive enough in the darkness; but when the moon rose — and the moon was the mask of Vorviades — they were revealed to be only carven wood, useless as Vorviades knocked them down one by one and drew ever nearer.

Dreaming, the Dream-Sender cried out in his dream —

In a parched land, to the south and east, the boy Anzaxos lay down to sleep in an olive grove on a mountainside overlooking the crescent sea. On that bright, quiet day, when the air was still, the birds fell silent, and the sea gleamed like a warrior's shield, Anzaxos dreamed of Vorviades standing astride the mountains, reaching up to seize the sun in his hands.

Vorviades seemed to notice the boy as he lay there. He turned toward him, and his hands poured out blood and fire, until Anzaxos drifted in crimson depths, remembering lives which were not his own: a knight who died by the side of the road; another, pierced from below on an icy ledge; a king who went mad and saw his sons perish.

He feared the giant then, but some other voice spoke to him of glory, and of the path of the hero.

Anzaxos awoke and ran to his village to tell his parents, scattering sheep.

When he had told his story, his mother took him in her arms, rocking him side to side, saying only, "Small boys have big dreams sometimes, but they are only dreams."

He asked his father, "What *are* dreams?"

"Vapors in the head. You're better off ignoring them."

But Anzaxos could not ignore his dream, or forget it, and he spoke of it often, boasting that he would be a hero one day and kill Vorviades. At first people laughed or turned away, but when a traveller knelt before him and said, "You who dream true dreams, prophesy for me," he began to do so, repeating things the giant had told him in his dreams.

His mother cried out in fright. His father commanded him to be silent, but it was too late. The high priest's servants seized him and carried him off to the temple, and, while he sat trembling and afraid in a dark vault beneath the temple, his mother wept, his father pleaded, and a great deal of money changed hands.

Then the high priest announced that a little boy had been telling lies, no oracle had been discovered, and the gods had not spoken.

But before he was allowed to go home, Anzaxos fell asleep in the dark vault and dreamed that Vorviades leaned over him and whispered through his silver mask, "If not you, another shall come after you to fight me." Then the giant departed, laughing.

Anzaxos's father took him out to a shed behind their house and beat him with a rod until he swore that he was only telling stories and would tell no more. Then his family had to leave, because their farm had been sold. They begged by the roadside for a time, until a rich man hired them and to work his land as tenants.

The boy grew up alone and silent, toiling in the rich man's fields, never telling stories, nor pausing to hear when others repeated old legends of the battles of Vorviades or the madness of King Angharad. His father and mother both died, exhausted and sorrowful, but never angry, as if somehow they knew that it wasn't their son's fault, that he had dreamed truly of Vorviades and now all their misfortunes were the giant's revenge. The giant wanted to fight, so the stories went. Combat was his only pleasure, the object of his lust, and when he was denied it, he grew very angry indeed.

When Anzaxos finally married Dera, the third daughter of a poor family, and begat three sons of his own, he did not tell his boys any of those stories, nor did he mention his dream of Vorviades. He raised them to work the fields, hoping that between the efforts of the four of them, they might one day get out of debt and buy their own farm back from their master.

But Velatin, the eldest, preferred to run. He ran along the dusty roads and over the hills without ever tiring or suffering thirst. When his father demanded of him why he ran rather than worked, he called back, "I am chasing Vorviades."

Anzaxos fell to his knees and beat his fists in the dust, remembering what the giant had said, that it would be either he or one who came after who would go off to fight.

And in those days there was war in all the lands. Velatin, the Swift, ran in the service of his king, bearing spear and shield and wearing a crested helmet, as messenger, as soldier, sometimes finding time to write home to his father that he spied Vorviades beyond the horizon, in the sunset or the moon's rising, and ran to meet him.

Dera said sadly, "Vorviades has claimed our first-born."

Tired, gray, Anzaxos could only shake his head and remember his dreams.

Still the wars continued. Velatin, boldest of all the youths of his country, saw the giant Vorviades above the enemy hosts, or looming in the smoke above a burning city, and raced to battle him.

Then, one night the silver moon-mask of Vorviades appeared to Anzaxos, hovering beyond the bedroom window as he sat up in bed, and his wife slept beside him.

"Velatin is impaled on a post. Crows peck out his eyes," the giant said.

"This is just vapor in the head," Anzaxos said. "Go away."

The giant went, but Anzaxos wept until dawn.

His second son, Kalo, likewise left for the wars. He worked a huge device called a scorpion, which hurled a flaming spear.

"I'll use it to shoot Vorviades," he said. "I'll avenge my brother's death."

Anzaxos only wept more, and when word came that Kalo, too, had perished, he could not weep any longer, and accepted the news in silence.

His wife sickened. His third son, Naius, tended her lovingly, but one day he too came to his father and told how he had dreamed of Vorviades, and understood that he must be the champion of mankind against this monster. Naius was twelve years old. In those hard years, he had gone hungry a great deal, and was small and thin. From an accident in the fields, one of his legs

was crooked. In his piping voice, holding back tears, he said, "I have to go, Papa."

At last Anzaxos was truly angry. His shame and his hatred of Vorviades overcame any fear. Trembling, afraid he would strike out in his rage and injure his sole surviving son, he said merely, "No, I shall go in your place, as I should have gone long ago."

Then he put on the plumed helmet Velatin had once worn, and took up his spear and shield. Around his waist he strapped Kalo's sword. He bade farewell to Dera, who, in her delirium, did not know him and babbled of Vorviades.

"I dreamed truly," Anzaxos said to all he met as he took to the road. "The only lie was the deny that I had seen Vorviades. Look. The signs of his passage are all around us."

Old as he was, tired as he was, he ran, as Velatin had, not as far, not as fast, but he crossed old battlefields and saw the bones of the slain, noting the mark of Vorviades. He slept nights in ruined cities, listening to the giant's laughter on the wind. When he reached the shore of the sea, the sun was setting into the water, and there, amid the red and orange clouds, far over the sea, stood Vorviades, surveying all he had wrought.

Anzaxos caught the fading sunlight flashing on his shield. He shook his spear over his head. Vorviades gazed upon him.

"You!" Anzaxos shouted. "If you do not fight me, men will say you are afraid."

When the giant replied, storm clouds darkened the sky. The raging sea crashed upon the shore.

"At the Tarasian Gates, then, I shall meet with you in mortal combat, in one day's time."

Anzaxos was outraged. He was being mocked. "Coward! Your legs might be long enough, but you know I can't run that far in a single day. You're trying to escape me!"

"When the sun rises one more time," said the giant.

Anzaxos began to run, bearing his shield and spear, his helmet's plumed crest waving in the storm winds; ever eastward he ran, with the sea on his right. The greatest miracle was not his strength, his tirelessness, or how fast he ran. The storm ended, and the night continued. The stars turned in their courses, once, twice, five times and more, and the sun did not rise. Still Anzaxos ran, his endurance beyond anything human, beyond exhaustion or pain, in a kind of dream where he dreamt that he lay in a dark vault, far beneath the earth. At times he was not sure which he was, the dreamer or the runner, or the dreamer dreaming he was running.

The Dream-Sender said to him, many times, "You are my last, my best hope. You must prevail."

Anzaxos gasped, "Tell me of Vorviades. What are his strengths? What are his weaknesses?"

"His strengths are numberless and indescribable. He is the fury of mankind, which even the gods fear. His weaknesses, I have never been able to discover."

"That's not much help."

"I cannot help you. You must help *me*. My dread of Vorviades is unendurable, for I know that if you do not win he will find my hiding place and tear me out of it, and rend me to pieces in the light on the sun."

In darkness, what should have been ten days and nights passed, and by starlight Anzaxos came to that place where the Tarasian mountains part like gates swung wide, revealing the southern lands beyond. There he paused. He drank from a stream and waited.

In time he noticed that the stars were being blotted out, as if ink had been spilled over the sky, spreading relentlessly toward him. A dark shape rose up. Its silver mask gleamed so faintly he could barely make it out.

"Ah, Vorviades. I have waited all my life for you."

"Now let us finish this."

"Yes, now."

There was no combat. The giant reached down and snatched him up, as a child might a particularly curious and cumbersome beetle, then hurled him far out to sea.

The Dream-Sender screamed one last time, a wailing, despairing cry. The tomb resonated like a gong. Dust trickled down. Surely, he realized in sudden, hideous terror, Vorviades had heard and would be coming soon.

Yet he did not wake. He commanded the dream to continue, and reached out in it, cupping Anzaxos in his hands, forbidding him to die, summoning a great whale to bear him on its back.

Vorviades *did* find him, in the dream. The silver moon-mask rose out of the sea. The terrible, burning eyes opened. The storm wind spoke.

"Enough. Every time you try to repel me, you draw me ever closer. Surrender to me at last."

Now the Dream-Sender tried to end the dream. He dismissed the whale and summoned a storm to drown Anzaxos, lest Vorviades follow him and be led, inevitably, to the crypt of the Dream-Sender.

Now it was time to hide, to be silent, to become invisible, that not even the Shadow Titans, or Vorviades who was their cousin, could find him in the darkness.

But Vorviades breathed on the sea and calmed it, and blew again so that the wind carried Anzaxos all the way to the southern shore, where he was cast up in Riverland, near the City of the Delta.

Anzaxos awoke from a dream of his own death. He sat up, coughing, his throat fantastically parched, his limbs weary beyond imagining.

"There's some wine in the jug," someone said.

He blinked in the bright sunlight and groped for the wine. As he drank, he slowly took in his surroundings.

A tent-flap swayed gently in a sea breeze. Beyond it, he could make out swaying grasses and a sandy beach. The whole front of the tent was open to the sea, to let the cool breeze in.

The speaker, who had offered him the wine, was a child. A pang of remembrance came: his own sons, little Naius, who was paler, but not much smaller than this boy. His host could have been no more than fourteen or fifteen, with a soft, round face, large eyes, and unkempt hair. He wore what must have once been a plain white robe and sat cross-legged on the ground, writing in a book in his lap, every once in a while reaching for or replacing one of the pens and brushes he held between ink-splattered toes.

Before Anzaxos could question him, the boy turned his book around, displaying with obvious pride two pages of beautifully intricate calligraphy. It was an indecipherable script, all whirls and flourishes.

"Do you like my story? It is all about the giant, Vorviades."

Anzaxos tried to draw away from him, but was too weak.

"Don't be afraid of me," said the boy.

"I . . . I don't understand. All my life . . . Who *are* you?"

The boy placed a sheet of blotting paper over the page he had been working on, then closed the book. "To answer your last question first because it is the easiest, I am the sorcerer Sekenre. Whether I am the author of this story or merely one who records it, I am not at all certain. But I know that I shall profit from it, and find its meaning."

"But . . . it's not just a *story!* I have *lived* —"

"All that suffering, all that dying, did it happen because I wrote it down, or did I write it down because it happened; or is there a third explanation which only Vorviades can give us? This is a further mystery. I have pondered it for at least fifty years."

Cautiously, Anzaxos took another sip of the wine, then wiped his mouth with his hand.

"You're crazy, child. You can't be that old."

The boy began to pack his pens and brushes carefully in a case. As he worked, he spoke, and somehow seemed to change, not in physical appearance, but in manner, in voice, in presence, until Anzaxos had the impression that someone else, that a whole legion of others in turn, wore this boy's body like a garment, and now someone else entirely shared the tent with him. "Know that when one sorcerer murders another, the murderer *becomes* his victim, who lives on in the body of his murderer, but subject to him as a slave to his master — supposedly, though it doesn't always work out that way — and perhaps in the company of many more. Thus the power of the sorcerer grows. Sekenre, when he was truly young, started by murdering his own father."

The voice and manner changed again. "But his father wanted him to, and contrived it."

And another. "We are many."

Yet another. "The body does not age, but the culmination of our selves is very ancient indeed."

Anzaxos asked, "Do any of you . . . remember . . . or dream about Vorviades, or of some *other* who is his foe?"

Now the boy wrapped his book carefully in an oilcloth and put it in a shoulder bag. He seemed himself again, as if nothing had happened and he did not remember what he had just said. He got to his feet and stepped out of the tent, leaning over backward to stretch. He turned around to look at Anzaxos.

"Yes, I have dreamed of both of them, but only recently. I think I know how the story ends. Come."

Anzaxos tried to rise. "I'm so tired."

"You were always tireless before."

"Yes. And I think I can manage to be one last time."

Sekenre helped him to his feet.

The Dream-Sender came to them every time they slept, screaming in terror of the giant, warning that Vorviades was right behind them, pointing into every shadow, into the palm trees where moonlight flickered and exclaiming, "There! There is Vorviades! I beg you, go away and do not lead him to me!"

But Anzaxos and Sekenre journeyed ever southward, along the left bank of the Great River, to a place of pillars, where the tombs of ancient kings lay half buried in the sand. They camped there, seeking the final solution to the puzzle, the way into a maze which could be found only in dreams, despite the Dream-Sender's every effort to conceal it.

The Dream-Sender appeared to Anzaxos, walking across the moonlit river, ripples spreading from his path. He pointed a bony finger. His bird-faced mask gleamed. His iridescent blue robe wavered like water flowing over him.

"You! You *are* Vorviades! You've changed your form once again, but I know you!"

He raised his staff as if to strike, but at that moment Anzaxos awoke, and beheld only the river, the dawn sky, and herons wading by the shore.

Each night, as they slept, Anzaxos and Sekenre both dreamed of an ancient city of high, white, marble walls and golden rooftops, and of a time so near the beginning of the world that the gods themselves walked the streets of the place; for the world was new then, and the very gods had only just awakened from their birthing-places in the Great River's mud. The first of mankind lived there, and had the gods as their house guests. A certain sorcerer dwelt among them, but apart. When the gods stood up and saw their likenesses in shadow, and these shadows sprang to life to become the Shadow Titans, making the very gods afraid, it was with the shadows that the sorcerer conversed. He invited them into his secret chamber and conferred for long hours. From them he gained certain powers and many, many secrets. He was the first and greatest of his kind.

Each night Sekenre and Anzaxos dreamed too of corridors and doorways, of passages turning, of hidden stairs. Sometimes they found such things, and moved their camp accordingly. Sometimes they understood what they had seen to be only symbols.

This went on for twenty years, during which An-

zaxos grew older. Sekenre did not. Anzaxos, dreaming at night, began to prophesy by day, and travellers from the river stopped to hear him. Sekenre served as his attendant, gathering the offerings the travellers left. When the spirit left Anzaxos, and he no longer prophesied, flocks of birds swarmed over the ruins every day at sundown, leaving fish and fruits and grain scattered about. Thus the two of them were sustained. Perhaps Vorviades sent the birds.

The sun and wind darkened and gnarled Anzaxos, until, when he went to drink from the river, he beheld the reflection of what looked like animate driftwood with a wisp of white hair at one end. Sekenre merely darkened. The two of them were almost naked now, their clothing having fallen to tatters. Anzaxos saw that the boy's body, youthful as it was, was covered with intricate scars, like the elaborate calligraphy of a manuscript page, or the inlay on a warrior's sword. He understood that Sekenre was not young.

Sometimes, by day, he would dream — or remember; he wasn't sure which — another life, which was filled with glory and battles; and also of working fields and raising sons, who went away and died, first the eldest, then the second. He didn't know what happened to the third. He couldn't remember his wife's name. He was certain this was one more trick of Vorviades.

Sometimes he awoke cursing Vorviades.

Sometimes he seemed to be the Dream-Sender, peering fearfully into the world, certain that Vorviades was near.

Every day, Sekenre wrote in his book, and questioned Anzaxos about what he had dreamed.

Anzaxos felt that he was at sea again, drifting on the waves, carried along by the wind as if he were a feather, dissolving into nothingness. He forgot his anger. He felt only a fading regret and longed for release.

Then Sekenre found the way into the maze.

By torchlight, the two of them descended into the tombs. Sekenre touched a stone or spoke a word and some panel swung aside or a lion-headed god receded into the floor, and they climbed down further. Into the carven darkness they went, between huge pillars, through vast stone chambers, like insects crawling among the bones of a corpse.

In a low, narrow vault they found a sarcophagus; on its lid carven the image of a man with the face of a bird. Sekenre, for all his sorcery, wasn't very strong and needed Anzaxos to help him slide the lid off. The two of them grunted and heaved and the lid crashed to the floor.

The vault reverberated like a gong.

Within lay a man in an iridescent robe, wearing a bird mask, like the one depicted on the stone lid. Around his neck was a tarnished silver medallion of the moon.

"Behold the most ancient of sorcerers, Vorviades," said Sekenre.

"I don't understand."

"Nor do I, entirely. Come. Help me lift him up."

The two of them carried the stranger — sleeping or dead, cold to the touch, no heavier or lighter than a man should be — all the way back to the surface. All the while Anzaxos felt his mind overbrimming with terrors, with dreams hurled at him like the waves of a storm-tossed ocean. But the dreams were formless things and had no power over him. Instead he concentrated on memories of his past life, of his home, and tried to imagine what sort of man he might have become if he had never heard the name Vorviades. This left him angry, sad, and resigned all at once. He merely did what Sekenre told him to.

By the river's edge, in the bright moonlight, they laid the stranger out on the sand. Sekenre removed the mask, his hands trembling with excitement, his whole body tense with expectation.

But then the sorcerer merely sat quietly while the ancient face revealed crumbled away into bones and dust.

"I think I understand," Anzaxos said.

"Do you?"

"You wanted to murder this sorcerer, so all his secrets would be yours."

Sekenre paused, as if deep in thought, then handed the mask to Anzaxos. "The bird is called Hennet-Na. It seeks immortality by flying ever eastward, into the sunrise. But it never catches up with it. Eventually it flies all the way around the world and is burnt to death in the sunset. But that takes a long time. The mask of Hennet-Na may delay death for centuries, even as sorcery does, but neither is truly eternal. In the very end, Vorviades knew he was dying as even sorcerers must. He had mastered dreams, truly mastered them, so that what he dreamed became real. He was almost a god when he was young. He could create worlds. The giant which shared his name was merely his own implacable death, given shape by his dread of it. Now that his dreaming has ceased, the giant is no more."

"When you took the mask off —"

"I did not murder him. He merely *ended.*"

"And what of those who fought for him, against his own dream?"

"Merely implements, like brushes to write the story with."

"To be discarded when you're done with them?"

"Brought into existence for that sole purpose."

Anzaxos thought of his wife and his sons. So many wasted lives. He wept and laughed at the absurdity

that a discarded, worn-out implement should be able to do either.

"Come and assist me one more time," said Sekenre.

Together they cut reeds and to make a funeral boat. As they worked, it seemed to Anzaxos that a third person crouched with them, stirring impatiently in the shadows of the tombs. When they finished, and the bones of the dead sorcerer were placed in the boat, this additional presence was gone.

They waded out into the river, Sekenre shoulder-deep, until the boat caught the black current which flows upstream and they both felt the cold wind that blows out of the land of the dead. The boat drifted out of their grasp.

"I cannot accept this," Anzaxos said. "I am more than an old brush you throw away."

"What then?"

Anzaxos wept and raged. "I don't *know!* What life can I return to? I beg of you, please, help me."

Sekenre reached under the water and took the old man's hand. He squeezed hard. "I cannot help you. But you can help yourself."

"How?"

"You need Vorviades. Go after him. You'll beat him yet."

"But he is gone. You said so yourself —?"

"Believe in him again. Dream him back. Remember."

"I —"

"Find the dream. Look!" Sekenre pointed to the sky. "There! Do you see him?"

Anzaxos saw only the darkness, but he remembered knights and kings and a boy who had had a dream once, lied about it, and spent much of his life denying it until it would not be denied. Awake and yet dreaming, he was Velatin, who ran, and Kalos, who hurled spears with a device called a scorpion. He rose up and ran on the surface of the river as on smooth stone. He overtook the funeral boat, snatched the moon-medallion from among the piled bones, and put it on.

And he saw the giant Vorviades towering above the world, gazing down from behind the stars.

He shouted and he cursed and he ran, calling on the giant to come down and fight.

Later, Sekenre climbed up onto the shore, dried himself, and began writing in his book. He left several pages blank because he did not know how the story was going to end. Ω

The Classic Horrors

ALLEN K '98

At that instant the monster turned from Chivers, and the terrible cups, dripping with blood and fetor, descended on Maspic's own eyes.

Clark Ashton Smith
"The Dweller in the Gulf"

by Allen Koszowski

THE PIMP
by Lawrence Watt-Evans

Skin like white silk, pale as the sheets on which she lies, is marred by two deep-red scabs; beneath the skin blood is pulsing, hot and rich. For long minutes she stares down at that pulsing, caught between hunger and repulsion, between lust and fascination.

"She could die," she says, not looking up. She doesn't see whether the observer shrugs; she doesn't really care. At any rate, he says nothing in reply.

The white silk skin draws nearer, hunger overcoming repulsion, and she opens her jaws so far the dead muscles strain. She can feel her venom flowing, knows it's running down her fangs like water down stalactites, slow and thick.

Her vision is forced away from the girl's neck as her teeth set, sight lost in clouds of fine, tangled golden hair, and she closes her eyes.

Slowly, slowly, she presses her fangs against the white throat, the razor edges tearing through the scabs, cutting through the hard-clotted blood in a brief dry teasing before the new, fresh fluid wells up, blood and her own venom blending, hot and rich and bearing the flood of memories.

Eight years old, Momma's drunk again, and she's holding Amy by the blond braids they had plaited three days before, the morning before Momma's boyfriend had left; she's holding the braids so tight Amy can't move her head, can't turn to watch, but Amy can see from the corner of her eye as Momma pulls the steak knife from the drawer, the steak knife with the shining, serrated edge, and Momma holds it loosely in one hand for a moment while the other hand is clamped tight on the braids. Amy wishes she could pull free, maybe if her hair weren't braided she could, she could pull the hairs away, let them tear out of her scalp, and it would hurt but it would be over, she could run and hide.

But she can't pull out entire braids, and the knife is coming closer, Momma runs it across Amy's throat, very lightly, then a little harder, hard enough to snag and scratch ever so slightly.

"Amy," she says, "I don't know what I'm gonna do with you," and Amy knows that she doesn't mean that like the mothers on TV, she really means that she herself doesn't know what she's going to do, how far she'll go this time.

And the knife blade slides across again, stinging this time, and Amy feels something flowing down her neck and she knows it must be blood, she whimpers, she doesn't mean to but she whimpers, and Momma tells her, "Kneel down, Amy . . ."

And that's all; the blood has stopped flowing. The vampire opens her eyes, pulls her fangs free of the wounds, glances down at Amanda's chest.

It's not moving.

She peers closely at the silk-white throat, at the small smear of blood she's just left, looking for the old scars, but even her eyes can't find them, not for certain; a faint line, so faint she might be imagining it, so faint it might be just a crease in the skin from normal movement of the head, might be there.

But she remembers the feel of the blade across her throat, and shudders with inexplicable pleasure at the stolen memory.

"Sweet," she says, "But not enough."

"Take more, then," he says quietly, his voice a distant whisper.

"There is no more," she tells him.

He gets to his feet and crosses to the bed, stares down at Amanda's body. "She's dead?" he asks.

She nods.

"Damn," he says.

She smiles to herself. "I do," she whispers, but he doesn't hear.

"I don't know how many more I can explain away," he says.

"I said she might die," the vampire reminds him.

"I know," he says, "I know."

"I want more," she tells him. "There wasn't enough left."

He glances nervously at her. "I'll see," he says.

She waits calmly in the room, beside Amanda's cooling corpse, as he leaves; she hears the latch click, hears his footsteps retreating down the hallway.

To pass the time until his return, she remembers — not her own life, but the memories she's drunk from others.

She remembers the raw sexual passion that she felt when she drank the blood of a serial killer, the hideously erotic memories of his crimes, the power and glory of his hands on unwilling flesh, of his knife digging, of reaching into the wound . . .

And that blends into the memories of a boy trapped in a tornado-shattered home, the weight of a fallen ceiling joist driving his head onto the torn, bloody flesh of his mother, his hands flailing as he struggles to free himself, as he tries to fight free of his mother's body . . .

She recalls the sensation of giving birth to a monstrosity, the strain, the tearing, the gasp of relief and then horror as she sees what she's borne, as she sees, before the doctor can snatch it away, what's lived for nine months in her belly, sees it still twitching as it dies . . .

Reviewing them this way is not as good, not as involving, not as *rich* as drinking them in the blood, but it amuses her.

For the moment.

She remembers the jumbled unbearable love and hatred of a molested child, the feel of a father's flesh jammed down her throat, the hot sharp pain of torn and abraded tissue, blood spilling, trickling, spurting from a thousand wounds in a hundred different bodies, young and old.

All that wealth of experience, of sensation, lost to her own dead flesh forever, she can only taste through others; she hungers for the memories more than she hungers for the blood itself.

She places a hand gently on Amanda's still breast, sees cold white fingers on cold white flesh, and she reminds herself that though she still moves, she is as dead as the woman she has just slain, the woman whose life she has sucked away.

The thought sends a thrill through her.

She is dead, yet she endures.

As Amanda endured her mother's madness, as the boy endured his ordeal in the wreckage, as so many of her victims endured so much, she endures this sensationless imitation of life, taking what she can from those who yet live.

And perversely, she enjoys that, the thought that she's stealing what she cannot have for herself.

She finds a peculiar sort of hope in the awareness that she can still enjoy anything. She has been dead a very long time, yet she still finds this pleasure possible in her existence.

For a moment, her own memories stir, of a time when she still breathed — a vague blur of green fields and blue skies and a dark man who visited her at night.

And then there were the early days after her death, when drawing blood carried fear and shame and terror, when the taste of blood was a new and horrifying ecstasy.

She hadn't known, at first, that the blood would carry the victim's memories — but the blood is the life, and what is a human's life but memory?

At first, the blood itself was enough; she ignored the memories, tried to forget them. The blood brought warmth and a semblance of life; the memories brought only shame, and a sort of dull embarrassment that she so intruded on the lives of her victims.

But then, as the taste of blood began to pall, she came to appreciate the memories, the homely little moments — a father's story at bedtime, a lover's caress, a child's wild embrace.

With time, though, the novelty faded — one lover was much like another, the children's hands were all the same, she had heard every father's stories before. She began to seek the rawer, fiercer emotions for memories that could still stir her — the screaming hatred of a divorce, the wrenching grief of a friend's death, the slow agony of a parent's decline into senility.

Even that became dulled with repetition in time, for most of the lives she stole were so very similar, and her existence had become listless, boring, a weight to be borne — until the boy with the bandaged arm.

The dog's teeth closing on his arm, the desperate jabbing at the yellow-brown eyes, the incredible searing pain from wrist to elbow and the grim satisfaction as the animal's blood spurted up around his thumb . . .

She smiles, and runs her fingers lightly down Amanda's corpse.

The boy led her to Paul.

The boy's parents, worried about their son, took him to Paul for therapy, to get over the horror he had lived through. He was visiting regularly, though she didn't know that when she first tasted that young, sweet blood, blood that carried intense memory of just exactly how it felt to drive one's thumbnail through a dog's eye into the brain.

She heard the parents talking. She heard the mother explaining that the doctor thought the boy was suppressing memories that had been clear before, and the vampire worried that this doctor might suspect, might notice the scars on the boy's neck.

And to be safe, she found the doctor.

She found Paul.

She looks up at the door. Far away, she hears hesitant footsteps returning, echoing in the hospital corridor.

She found her pimp, found the man who brings her all the strange, the violent, the extreme memories for her to taste, to savor: The woman who had been held captive and gang-raped, the man who had been tortured in a South American prison, the couple whose little games had gotten so far out of hand that when the wife brought her mutilated husband to the emergency room he was given only a fifty-fifty chance of survival.

A slow smile spreads across her face.

The man might have made it, if not for the "inexplicable" blood loss.

That was the first death among Paul's patients. That was the point at which he could no longer turn back, could no longer pretend that his only motive was alleviating unbearable memories.

That was what he said at first — that it was an experiment, an attempt at treatment. The boy's nightmares were relieved when she drank away his memories of the attack, and Paul thought this could be a breakthrough for many of his patients. Even a temporary respite — and the effect *was* only temporary — could help.

She doesn't care about that. She is no psychologist. Paul's work, his theories, his degree, mean nothing to her except that he finds the most interesting treats for her.

And in a mental hospital, where no one believes if a victim tries to accuse her.

It's so beautifully simple — Paul asks an interesting patient to stay overnight for observation, all strictly voluntary, of course, nothing threatening, he says it all so well. The patient stays, and that night she drinks from a new well.

A symbiotic relationship, Paul calls it — blood and pain give her sustenance and pleasure, and in exchange her feasts lessen the mental suffering of her victims.

That was his excuse, until the first man died.

She doesn't need any excuses.

And then the door is opening, hard white light spills in, and Paul is there with his little cart, with the alarm device and the cold pitcher of orange juice.

"It's all right," he tells her, "No one will be coming by here for at least an hour."

She rises to her feet, eyes on Dr. Paul Burchard, on the trembling hands and the pale face, the white coat and the carefully-scrubbed neck.

He closes the door and steps closer.

"My turn," he says softly, as he lies down on the bed beside dead Amanda and tugs his collar out of the way.

Smiling, she stoops to drink of the nervous guilt, the perverse excitement, the nagging self-hatred of being a vampire's procurer; to drink also of the relief he feels in knowing that his torturing memories of dead patients will soon be as faded and dim as a photo left too long in the sun; to drink of the dread and anticipation that this time, this time, perhaps he'll die; to drink of the unreasoning lust he feels for her, for the vampire.

This is how she pays for what he brings her — and it costs her nothing.

Her mouth opens, her eyes close, and her fangs glisten in the lamplight as she descends.   Ω

TRIBAL SINGER

By firelight, our favorite tales
were woven in "... Once Upon A Time ..."
All seemed set in a place like Wales,
long after the church bells chime.

The woods loomed deep with claws & wings,
strange creatures found too soon;
Wolves & bears & flying things
would grace the hunter's moon.

Hanzel & Gretel, who managed to hide
behind the witch's well,
could see the oven open wide
and watch her cast a spell.

Music of trolls might kiss the dark
from bone flutes carved by hand,
cold as moonlight's dust-dry mark,
below the bridges' span.

One tower's window, bedecked with fronds,
sent out from its stoney lair
a trailing, braided rope of bronze:
The flax of Rapunzel's hair.

Across the moors, the swamps & sties,
beyond the river's flow,
our Knight beheld the Dragon's eyes
in red "reluctant" glow.

When "... Out Of The Long Ago ..." was done,
we said our evening prayers.
And — albeit slow — were sent along
to our bedrooms up the stairs.

Beneath warm blankets, thoughts roamed free,
our smiles & shivers earned;
Imagination stretched to see —
We listened, long ... and learned.

— **Charles D. Eckert**

MOVIN' ON
by Nicholas A. DiChario

illustrated by George Barr

Dad slow-dances across the living room, just the way those people dance in the black-and-white movies we sometimes watch on TV, except Dad only pretends to have a partner. He dances in front his favorite soap opera, making like he's romancing the new nurse on *Days of Our Lives*. He is very graceful, I think. That's how the women describe him.

"We have to go, my boy," Dad says.

"Today?" I say.

"Today," says Dad.

That's how it happens, mostly. One day Dad will decide it's time to up and leave, and off we'll go.

"Why, Dad?"

He stops dancing and looks at me. I don't like that look. It's the kind of look people get when somebody wakes them up out of a dream.

It was a stupid question. I go to my room. I don't have a lot of stuff to pack. Just enough to carry around in my duffel. We weren't here for very long. I empty out my dresser drawers. I hop on my bed and bounce on the mattress a few last times. The springs squeak. Dad comes in my room. He looks kind of dreamy again. I sit on the bed and look out the window. The sun is on its way down. The trees are going to hide the sun pretty soon, then the sun is going underground and it won't come up again till morning.

"What about Mom?" I ask Dad. "What are we gonna do? Just leave her again?"

Another stupid question. I think about telling Dad that this time I ain't going with him, that he can just go by himself, but I don't really want Dad to get lonely. Besides, this ain't all that great a place — kind of crowded, smells like cat poop from Mr. Bower's tabbies downstairs he can't get to use the litter box, and the mom doesn't like pizza, if you can believe that one.

Later, on the bus, Dad says, "You know, Junior, moms don't last forever. They come and they go."

I feel cold, even though it's pretty hot outside. The man on the Charleston radio station said ninety-four degrees. The bus has air conditioning, the kind that comes up the inside of the windows. You can stick your fingertips over the edge and make your fingers frozen numb. It's not a city bus; it's a Trailways.

I give Dad kind of a frown. "You and me come and go a lot, too, Dad."

"But you and me ain't real," he says like Groucho Marx, twitching his eyebrows, pretending he's holding a cigar. He knows Groucho always gets a smile out of me.

"*Horse Feathers!*" I say.

"*Duck Soup!*" says Dad. "Slap me five, my boy!"

I slap him five and we both of us laugh. I look out the window at the gray highway and the cars. "Where we going, Dad?" I ask him, even though I already know the answer.

"We'll know when we get there." He sits back in his seat and closes his eyes.

Dad's got short black hair and a squared chin, kind of like Clark Kent, and lots of muscles, too. Dad is beautiful. I know this because all the moms say so. "My God," they'll say, "your daddy is *so* beautiful." They say it because they can't help themselves. They say it almost like they can't believe it, as if I ain't even in the room. "So *unbelievably* beautiful."

Dad will just smile and blush, mostly. Depends what mom wants.

I stare at him for a while. He peeks at me through one eye. "Don't worry, boy," he says.

"Whataya mean?"

"You'll look the same way to women someday."

"Why?"

"Because you're my son," he says.

"But I don't look anything like you." The truth is, I got no idea what he looks like for real. Dad never looks the same for long.

Dad gives me a wink. "Someday soon you'll look exactly the way some little girl wants you to look. And then, when you're a teenager, you'll be every teen-age girl's fantasy. And then the women — the women who are lonely and hurting — they'll love you because they can't help themselves, because something will be missing from their lives and only you will be able to fill the void in their achy-breaky hearts."

"Why, Dad?"

He smiles and reaches over and pets my hair. "Because we ain't real."

I think Dad likes to confuse me. "But I'm here. You're here. That's pretty real, the way I see it."

"We will always be here, Junior, as long as there are women who dream, but being here ain't the same as being real."

"I don't get it. Are we here, or ain't we?"

Dad sits up straight. "It's not that simple. This is the way it is, and I want you to listen real good." Now he's doing Cagney — or Bogart — I get the two mixed up. "Sometimes a dream is so strong it makes something real. But no dream can last forever, and then what was made real becomes unreal unless it moves on, unless it keeps getting re-dreamed. Get me?"

Course I don't. I never do when Dad explains stuff.

I don't know why I bother asking. "I'm tired of movin' around, Dad." I give him my best pout. I remember this one place where we stayed for a while. There was a bunch of snow. I had a dog named Scooter. Actually he was the mom's dog. He wasn't much of a dog. A poodle. He didn't like getting petted a lot, but he'd flip over or play dead or do just about anything for a lousy dog biscuit. Sometimes I would sit at the window of my room with Scooter, and if the sunlight hit just right on the glass and the wind was blowing hard outside I could see snowflakes coming in through the edges of the window pane, right into my bedroom. I remember that place because we had a Christmas tree and a mom at the same time, and we all went to cut down the Christmas tree, and the pine needles stuck to my boots, and I remember how I tracked the pine needles across the rug in big green splotches and the mom — I can't think of her name right off — but I remember the mom laughing her head off about it, and me and Dad rolling around on the floor just having fun, and Scooter yapping like a maniac.

Anyway, I give Dad my best pout, but he pouts right back. I pull out my *X-Men* comic and pretend Dad's not sitting next to me at all, but it doesn't do much good. I know he's there, and he knows he's there, even if we ain't real.

When we get to the new place the first thing we do is turn on the TV. No cable. Dad hates that. He can watch his soaps all right but we can't get the good old movies at night on the American Movie Channel.

"Tomorrow I'll get a new job," he tells me. He will. He always does. He never works for very long, though, only until he finds a mom. "And we'll call the cable company."

"How long we gonna stay here?"

"You mean here in this place, or here in this town?"

I shrug. "Town, I guess."

"We might stay here a good long time, Junior." He always says that. "Rochester is a real nice place. They got a baseball team. Plus, the landlord says we're not too far from Hamlin Beach."

"A real major league team like in Atlanta?"

"Nope," says Dad. "Minor league club. The Red Wings, they call them. Nice new ball park, though, Frontier Field."

"Ain't the same," I tell him.

"New place never is the same, so quit the gee-whiz aw-shucks routine and unpack your bag."

"When we gonna get a mom?" I ask him.

"Pretty soon, my boy, pretty soon."

Her name is Lisa and we move into her place only a couple weeks after Dad meets her. She's got a big townhouse in this ritzy park called Garden Estates, with a guard at the gate. She's got air conditioning and cable TV and a microwave. She's got real pretty long brown hair that smells like strawberries.

She's older than Dad was last time we had a mom, but Dad has already adjusted. He's got some "stately wrinkles," Lisa calls them, at the corners of his eyes, and his hair has a touch of gray in it. She's a big shot lady egghead at some medical lab at the University of Rochester. Dad met her while he was emptying trash barrels in some restricted area. She came out of her lab to lambaste him, and that was the end of that.

Dad lets me stay up late our first night at Lisa's and we watch some old black-and-white movie on AMC starring Bob Hope and Bing Crosby. Lisa makes popcorn and we all of us laugh a lot. Lisa tells Dad it's OK for him to quit his job so he can find himself some more respectable profession. Sometimes Dad will really do that, if that's what the mom wants. But mostly she doesn't. Mostly she just wants Dad to herself. Lisa will be like that. I can tell by the way she can't stop touching him. "He's a perfect male specimen." That's her favorite thing to say about Dad. "Tall, dark, lean, with gorgeous greens." She calls his eyes greens, as if they're vegetables.

They talk about sending me to school in September, which I ain't too thrilled about, and Dad knows it. I hate going to school and having to deal with new teachers and new kids and everybody's dumb questions. Like, Where are you from? Who's your mom and dad? Do you want to come over and play after school?

I'll never forget how this dumb science teacher tried to tell me the sun doesn't really come up out of the ground in the morning, and then at night it doesn't go back underground again. He tried to tell me the sun is billions of miles away, and the Earth circles around it, or something crazy like that. "That's a lie," I told him. I told him I could see with my own two eyes where the sun goes down and where it comes up. I told Dad about it and Dad agreed with me. Dad said you believe what you want to believe, Junior. But the teacher said, no, "the eyes can deceive," and "we must learn to pierce through the dark veil of ignorance to what is scientific fact."

"What an egghead you are," I told him, just like that. He made me go to the principal's office, and I missed the bus, and Dad had to pick me up late. I've hated school ever since.

The next morning after the mom goes off to work and I'm eating Captain Crunch and watching the *X-Men* on TV, there's a loud knock at the door. Dad goes to answer it.

Some guy shoves his way in and pushes Dad over on the floor. Two guys rush in behind him. Dad tries to get up but the first guy kicks him smack in the face. I run for my bedroom.

"Get him!" one of them yells.

The two guys chase after me. I hop over the couch and beat them to the door but I can't slam it shut — this big guy sticks his foot in the way — so I run for the window but they grab me. I punch and kick and bite.

"Shit, the little bastard!" the guy says.

They stuff a rag in my mouth, get my arms tied tight

behind my back, and throw this sack over my head, over my whole body. Dad! I can't even shout. Dad! I hear a lot of footsteps and running around.

"Where's the professor?" somebody says.

"Out in the van," says somebody else.

"Does he know we got them both?" another guy says.

"Filthy bastard kid nearly bit off my finger."

"Is the professor coming in or what?"

"Should we drag them out?"

"He's coming, hold on a minute."

I hope Dad's OK. That guy kicked him pretty hard. I hope he ain't hurt or scared or nothing. I hear some other guy walk in the front door.

"We got them both, professor. Do we move them now or what?"

"All right, hold on a minute," says the new voice.

Everybody stops moving except for this one guy who walks over to me and grabs at my wrists through the sack. Then he walks over to Dad.

"Good, good," he says. "Back the van into the garage and throw them in."

"Professor," one of them says, "not that it's any of my business, but now that we've gone this far don't you think it would be best just to kill them? I'd hate to see them come back and start causing you trouble."

"Yeah," says somebody else. "If we're going to do a job, I like to do it right the first time."

"There's no reason to kill them," says the professor. "I'm not a killer. They won't be back. There's nothing left for them here."

"Are you sure about that? If we have to come back again, it's gonna cost you a lot more."

"I know what I'm doing. I've written two books on demonology that are standard text in most universities. Believe me, now that somebody knows what they are, they'll look for a safer place to operate."

"So you want your wife back, that we can understand. But you really don't expect us to believe this jerk and his kid are demons —"

"I didn't hire you to believe me. I hired you to perform a job."

"You're the boss," says the guy.

After that they toss me and Dad in the back of the van, and off we go.

It's real quiet for a long time except for the sound of the engine and the hum of the tires and every once in a while a horn or a siren. All I can smell is this crummy laundry sack, and this gas-and-oil kind of smell. The road is smooth forever but then it gets bumpy and me and Dad clunk around in the back. Finally I work the rag out of my mouth. "Dad? Dad? You OK?" He doesn't answer.

The van stops. The back doors screech open. The guys pull us out and toss us on the ground, but don't say anything. I hear the van pull away. And then there's just the sound of birds and flies. "Dad, we're in real big trouble. How we gonna get out of these sacks?"

"Don't you worry, Junior."

"Dad! You're OK! Jesus, Dad, why didn't you say nothing before?"

"Take it easy. Maybe I was testing you, to see what kind of stuff you're made of." I hear Dad squirm around on the ground. Then I hear this ripping sound.

"Dad, did you do it? Did you get out?"

"Maybe I did and maybe I didn't," says Dad in his Groucho voice.

"You did it! I know you did!"

Then I feel him tugging at my sack and all of a sudden the sack rips open and I can breathe, and I can move my legs again. It's a bright sunny day and we're out in the woods in the middle of nowhere. Dad unties my wrists and I hug him and he pats my back and I just start crying like a little kid. I hate when I do that but I can't help it. "I'm sorry, Dad, geez, I guess I'm not made of very good stuff. I'm sorry."

"It's OK, my boy, everything's all right now. Settle down."

My wrists are all bloody so Dad and me find this stream and we wash out our cuts, and clean 'em off with some leaves and stuff. I only got a few scratches, but Dad's face looks like hell. Anyway, we walk down this grassy hill, then we go through a field where the weeds come all the way up to my shoulders, and I can hear things I can't see rustling through the underbrush.

"Field mice, probably," says Dad.

"Where are we?"

"Don't know for sure."

We keep walking. At the edge of this field there's a dirt road. We follow that for a while, and finally come to a trailer house where there's a big black German Shepherd barking his head off. The dog is chained to a clothes pole. As we get closer to the house this old lady opens her front door and pokes her head out.

"I'm not looking to buy anything!" she hollers. She's wearing an apron, if you can believe that.

"I'm sorry to bother you, ma'am," says Dad, "but me and my boy been robbed and beat up out on the main road, and I was wondering if we might come in and get cleaned up a bit, and maybe use your telephone."

"Oh," she says, like she's heard all the stories about innocent old ladies getting robbed and killed by drifters pretending to be in trouble, but still can't believe people like that live in the real world. It's too late for her anyway. She got a good look at Dad and usually that's all it takes. She practically drags us in her house.

She's a plump old lady, with chubby arms and legs and everything. She's got a lot of hair, which I think is pretty weird for old folks. She's all apologies. "I'm so sorry I didn't realize you were hurt let me fetch a wash cloth and clean out that cut — it's a gash, a horrible gash — can I get you something to drink? Oh my God it must have been those Jefferson boys who live up on County Road 44 they're such trouble-makers — look at that swelling around your eye — did you get a good look at them?"

And Dad is playing her like a violin. "You're so kind, think nothing of it, we'll be all right, no sense in calling the police we didn't have anything of value — actually we didn't have anything at all. Me and my boy have fallen on hard times what with the missus passing away."

That professor should a had me killed for all the attention I'm getting. I wander into the old lady's living room. The place is filled with a lot of old-lady stuff, big surprise. On the wall there's a boring old painting of a wagon wheel leaning up against a red barn. There's a lot of knickknacks on shelves: wood salt-and-pepper shakers, little dogs and cats made out of glass, a shelf with just spools of thread and a bunch of sewing stuff on it, and another shelf with a big huge fat Bible. She's got all these old-lady afghans and fluffy pillows on the furniture, the kind that make you afraid to sit down. She's got a real ancient TV set, no cable. It's probably time for Dad's soap opera, but why should I give him the time of day?

I walk outside and the dog starts barking like a maniac again. I ain't scared of no dog. Never once met a dog that didn't take to me, except for that crummy poodle at what's-her-name's place, but that runt was nicer to me than to anybody else in his miserable little dog's life. I walk over to the dog and he stops barking and cocks his head at me and gives me this pitiful whine. Flies are buzzing all around his wet nose, and he smells dirty.

"I know how you feel, dog." I plop down next to him and hug the hell out of him and pet him for a while. Next to his dish he's got a bunch of big old rocks he must have dug out of the dirt. There's a chewed up rubber bone, and a deflated basketball with teeth marks in it. No dog house. Maybe the old lady lets him in at night.

I think about what it must be like when rocks and a bone and a chewed up basketball and an old hag are your whole life. Shoot, at least you can count on them day after day.

"Do you think I'm a demon, Shep?" I've always wanted a German Shepherd named Shep, ever since I seen *Hogan's Heroes*. "Maybe I should ask Dad, but I don't want him to get mad at me." Shep curls up with me and licks my hand, and the two of us stretch out together on the dirt. The sun is low in the sky. "Pretty soon the sun will go underground for the night," I tell Shep. "Don't let no stupid science teacher tell you no different."

"Junior!" I hear Dad call. I must have fallen asleep. It's almost dark outside. "C'mon in the house. Mrs. Lewis made us a nice big supper."

I haven't had a bite to eat since the Captain Crunch this morning. I get up and run for the house, and Shep barks after me. "I'll bring you some scraps later!" I run inside the house and sit down at the table. The kitchen smells like fresh bread, meat and potatoes, coffee, and something sweet like pie.

Dad and this nice old Mrs. Lewis are still talking up a storm.

"Children just don't have any respect these days," says Mrs. Lewis, wiping her hands on her apron.

Dad is already looking pretty old himself. A lot of his hair is gone. He's shorter, rounder, heavier. He's got a double chin. "That's because kids these days don't

by Nicholas A. DiChario

47

know where they came from," says Dad, "don't know how hard their grandparents and great-grandparents worked and struggled to make life better for them. Kids don't even care to know about that sort of thing these days."

"Ain't that the God's honest truth," says Mrs. L. She sits down at the table with me and Dad.

"Of course my grandson Junior here is different. Before my daughter up and died she taught him proper respect."

I listen to them chat for a while. Dad's story has changed some. Now I'm the poor, sorry grandson whose mama died of tuberculosis, whose drunken daddy abandoned him, and now here's Dad trying to care for another young 'n and hoping his heart won't fail him before the boy is old enough to care for himself. I catch Mrs. L staring at me with this sad look on her face.

All during dinner, Dad feeds her this line about how his ancestors helped blaze the Oregon trail, all the way west from Missouri, he says. He talks about how they had to fight the Pawnee and the Sioux Indians, trade off all their mules for ox because the Indians kept raiding their camp for the mules, and the ox held no value for them. He talks about all these dangerous river crossings and how they lost near a dozen wagons in the horrible rushing waters of Bear River, out past Fort Laramie, middle of God's country. I don't know where he gets this stuff. Sometimes I think maybe it's the truth, but I've heard so many different stories they can't all be true. Somehow Dad always comes up with just what a woman wants to hear.

Mrs. L says, "You are such a charming man, Mr. — oh, I can't believe I've forgotten to ask your name."

"None of this mister stuff," says Dad. "Just call me Jake."

"Jake? What a remarkable coincidence," says the old lady. "My late husband was named Jake."

"Is that a fact, Mrs. Lewis?"

"Call me Mavis," she says, taking hold of Dad's hand and squeezing. "You remind me so much of my late husband."

I can't take much more of this. I figure it's a good time for me to sneak some scraps out to Shep, even though we ain't had dessert yet. I grab a few bones, some potatoes, a hunk of bread, and out I go. Mrs. L must have got so wrapped up in Dad she forgot to feed the old boy. He wolfs down all I got in a few seconds. We play around for a while, me tossing the rubber bone into his rock pile, Shep fetching it and making me yank the bone out from between his teeth. I could stay out all night with Shep if it weren't for the lousy mosquitoes. After a while I can't stand slapping the bugs off me so I decide to go back in the house.

I walk inside, but nobody's around. I hear some sounds coming from a room back of the kitchen. I walk down the hall and find the bedroom door closed. I know it's the bedroom door. I sometimes hear women making lots of noise when Dad gets them in the bedroom.

I sometimes want to look, but I'm afraid Dad will get mad.

I don't know what makes me do it this time. Maybe I'm just sick and tired of being ignored. I turn the doorknob real slow and quiet. I listen to Mrs. L groan for a spell. My heart thumps crazy in my chest. There's a smell, an awful smell coming from the bedroom, not dirty like Shep, but more like there's something dead or dying in there. I wipe my palms on my jeans, and open the door a crack more. I can't see nothing except some candlelight flickering across the room. I can hear, though. Mrs. L is groaning like mad. The bed springs are screeching. I open the door a little more and sneak halfway through the crack.

There's Dad and Mrs. L buck naked on the bed. Dad is on top of the old lady. All I can see is their wrinkled white skin. Mrs. L groans. She's really hurting bad. Hurting like she's dying. I feel something hard knot up inside me. Dad, stop! I want to yell at him, but I don't want him to know I'm watching. And then she turns her head and I see her face — oh, God, she looks almost like a skeleton face — there's hardly nothing left of it. Old plump Mrs. L is almost all skin and bones all over her body. Dad is killing her! And then I hear her wail like somebody's twisting a knife inside her gut, and then she stops, stops cold and flops over like a rag doll. No more moaning or groaning. Her skeleton head rolls back on her slack neck, and she's got this sick, dead grin on her lips.

Then all of a sudden Dad glances over at me. "Hi, Junior," he says in his Groucho voice. "What's a nice guy like you doing in a place like this?"

Oh, God. I run out of the bedroom, out of the house. It's pitch black outside. Shep is howling like a maniac. I run up the dirt road, into the tall grass, trip and fall onto my knees, and I just start crying like a baby again. I don't know what it is with me. I don't know why I have to cry about everything. I'm just not made of good stuff.

I look up and see Dad standing over me. He's got his pants on, but no shirt. He's wearing that dreamy look again.

"Why, Dad? Why did you have to kill Mrs. Lewis?"

"Just wasn't much left in her for me to take, Junior. I didn't want to use her up, but that's what happens sometimes when somebody's old like that. The old are kind of defenseless. They've pretty much given away most of what they got."

I wipe the tears from my eyes. The crickets are carrying on, the owls hooting, the bull frogs croaking up a storm. "I hate mosquitoes," I say, swatting at my arms.

"We do what we have to do to survive," says Dad. "You have to learn that. We take what we need to live. We're not cruel about it. We give the women what they want. It's a give and take. It's a trade. You're old enough to understand that, aren't you, Junior?"

"Jesus, what the heck are we? Are we what that professor guy said we was? Demons?"

Dad kneels down beside me. "We're spirits, my boy," he says in his Groucho voice, pretending like he's flicking a cigar. *"Incubiiiiiiiiiiiiiiiiii . . ."*

"I wish for once you'd quit clownin' around, Dad." I slap my neck where a bug landed. "I don't want to be like you. I'm not gonna be anything at all like you. Not ever."

Dad stands up. He butts out his imaginary cigar in the palm of his hand. "Nothing you can do about it. That's just the way we are. It's our nature. When you get a little older, you'll understand what I'm talking about. You'll see."

No, I won't see. All I can see is Dad on top of poor old Mrs. L, all wrinkles the two of them, and there she is staring at me with her skeleton face. I don't ever want to see anything like that again. Of course I know what's coming next, so I figure I might as well bring it up. "I suppose we got to be movin' on now."

"Nothing left for us here," Dad says in his normal voice. I guess he figures I need time to stew. He's still got that queer dreamy look plastered on his face. He always looks happiest when I feel the rottenest, when we're about to hit the road. He holds his hand out to me and grins.

I get up on my own. "Ain't got no duffel to pack."

"We'll take some stuff from the widow's place. She's probably got a suitcase or two. Maybe she's got some old clothes packed away, coats or boots or shoes. Maybe a little bit of food. We'll see what we can use."

I turn around and start walking toward the trailer house. Dad sidles up next to me. Shep is still barking like a wild animal. "I better go calm him down, Dad."

"OK. I'll be in the house. You come on in when you're ready."

I walk over to Shep. He sees me coming but he just keeps barking. "Take it easy, Shep, calm down, boy."

He doesn't pay me no mind. He growls at me and shows me his fangs and his ears fall back, then all of a sudden he takes a leap at me. His chain snaps tight and yanks him off his feet, otherwise he would've bit me clean in half.

"What the heck's wrong with you? I didn't kill old Mrs. L. Dad did that. And he wasn't being cruel or anything. He gave her what she wanted. It was a trade."

Shep doesn't want to listen. Now he's snarling at me, and whipping his head back and forth, trying to bust his chain.

"Cut it out! Cut it out, Shep!"

Now he's drooling like an idiot, running around in circles, clawing at the dirt. He charges at me again. The chain snaps him back but he doesn't care about that, or maybe he thinks he can break it off or something. Stupid dog. Stupid idiot dog.

"Stop!" I pick up a rock from his pile and pitch it at him. It flies over his head. He keeps barking. "I said shut up!" I pick up another rock, a big one this time, and I step closer and he goes wild and rushes at me, and I take that big old rock in both hands and smash it down as hard as I can on top of Shep's skull, and he yelps and crashes to the ground.

His head is crushed in. I know it is. I felt it give. There's blood and fur all over the rock. I felt something else give, too. Something inside me. I drop the rock real quick. I'm all of a sudden scared of it. But I don't feel bad. I really don't. I did what I had to do.

A little while later Dad comes out of the house. He's carrying a couple of bags that look like the kind of bags sailors carry in those old movies about the Navy. By then I got Shep mostly buried under a stack of rocks and stones and some loose branches. "Had to do it, Dad. The dog didn't give me no choice. Had to shut him up before maybe somebody heard him and come to the house to check things out."

Dad says, "I understand." He takes out a cigarette and lights it up. Every now and then he'll have a smoke. Must be Mrs. L had some cigarettes in her trailer house. He's already looking younger and thinner. "Almost sunrise, Junior. Pretty soon the sun'll come up out of the ground like always, and it'll be another day, and we can put all this behind us. Whataya say?"

I take my bag from him and sling it over my shoulder. "Everybody knows the sun don't come up out of the ground," I tell him. "It's billions of miles away, and all the planets circle around it. I learned me that in school."

He puts his hand on my shoulder, and we both of us walk together down the dirt road, waiting for the light of day. Ω

TWILIGHT

By the ash-tree's root,
Faces of ice weep crystal tears
For forgotten gods.

— Catherine Mintz

ODE TO MY SCREEN SAVER

How you dance, how you dance.
You touch all the points
In your universe, you two,
Changing hue. Which of you
Was which mere moments ago?

You probe at your limits.
Boundaries rebuff you,
Reshape you, otherwise
You would fly away to infinity
Becoming too huge to see,

Leaving only a void of darkness.
Your cosmos consists of two beings
Waxing and waning. Does ours?
Maybe each of you is a universe
And our very own universe

Is accompanied forever by its twin
Unknown to us except when live fish
Fall from a cloudless sky
Upon city streets, flopping,
Gasping on dusty pavements

As if sea and land danced together
So quickly then flew apart
Before anyone could pay heed.
Unknown except when ghosts
Walk through walls into locked rooms,

Or when strange blips on radar screens
Dart away vertically from pursuit,
Disappearing into the unknowable.
Or when the fakir hoists the rope
Into mid-air, but that is a trick,

So we think — quick, quick,
Catch the blink when one world
Passes through the other
With barely a stirring of dust.
After staring at you for an hour

The book which lay shut now lies open,
And rain has become sunshine.
Mark the changes outside: that rosebud
Come into full bloom, the cat
Whose paw was surely white before,

Signs written in clouds and leaves.
I have the map of the world
Unfolded, and what do I find?
Somewhere between Spain and Poland
A new country has slipped

Into existence, opening new avenues
Along which its joyful citizens
Are cooking the fish which fell
From the sky. They're licking
Their fingers and laughing.

On my passport to that new land
You swirl together then apart,
Casting your spell in letters
Not of our own alphabet.
No wonder so many books appear

Nowadays, such floods of words
Created upon machines, each
Eager to decode your dance
In a thousand different ways:
Tales of Tahiti or Tokyo or Titan,

Ostensibly, yet I know otherwise.
Consequently I shall wash my books
To soak those proxy words away.
I shall paint their pages with milk
Then gently heat them to expose

The true text which you dance —
That single word far longer than
The human genome, word of creation
Of which we can only read such
A short sequence of syllables

Supposing we spend our whole life
Deciphering and writing them down.
You moving shapes, how you dance.
At least and at last, thanks to you,
The truth is within my grasp.

– **Ian Watson**

THE DANCE AT WEIRDMOOR CASTLE
by Lord Dunsany

illustrated by Fredrik King

It was at an inn by a big road through the flat land of East Anglia. Before a fireplace by which a dozen men could have warmed themselves in comfort seven or eight sat — men upon various businesses who had come in there from journeys in many directions, most to stop for the night, one or two to go on again in the cold after dinner, which all that were gathered before that fire had had. For some while all of them gazed at the orange light of the fire, and watched the slow change of the landscape that seemed to glow there, as though there were significance in it or things to be studied. And whatever calculations they made concerning the scenes in the fire they made in silence, but for the faint sounds that murmured from the pipes of those that were smoking. In the warmth of the room in which that fire was glowing the silence had lasted so long that any remark would have rung in it, and would have held anyone back who was, perhaps, about to slip through the quiet gateway of dreams.

"Why, I wonder," said one of those before the fire, "do we associate ghosts with Christmas?"

For a moment the silence fell back again after his words. And then from the depths of a chair there came a voice saying, "Everything has its season; butterflies, moths, swallows, cuckoos and lots of other things. I suppose ghosts have too."

"But why at Christmas?" the first man asked.

"I don't know," said the other and sank back again in his chair.

I was afraid that the conversation was going to be dull. For I was one of those seven or eight before the fire. And I could do nothing to brighten it. And then the man in the deep armchair began to speak again. "At any rate," he said, "I never saw one at any other time."

"Never at any other time?" echoed one of us weakly.

"Never," said the man in the armchair.

"Then you have seen a ghost?" said the one who had spoken first.

"Only once," said the other.

"Would you tell us about it?" I asked.

"Well, if the rest don't object, I don't mind," he said.

Everyone of us leaned forward, and a murmur of syllables arose, all encouraging him to tell his story of ghosts. One or two pipes were tapped out and refilled, and we settled down in our chairs before that warm fire to listen.

It was some years ago now [he said]. Some years. I was a foxhunter in those days. Still am in a way; always will be; though it isn't often I go out now. There was

less wire in those days. Well, about the ghosts. We had had a great hunt, and I was riding home alone. A great hunt, and I was out of country I knew. I had heard of the country through which I was riding, but had not been that way before. It was a part of the country called Weirdmoor.

It was one Christmas Eve, just as it is now, which is what reminded me of it. Not that I should forget it, in any case. It was bitterly cold, colder than what it is to-night. There had been some snow too, and there was a north wind blowing. I had heard of it because of an old castle that was there; a ruin called Weirdmoor Castle. And I had never been there, because none of us ever did go. There were stories about its being haunted. It wasn't that I was afraid of ghosts, but if there were none there, there was nothing to go for, and, if there were, they are chilly and clammy things and I saw no reason for not keeping away from them.

Well, there it was, a ruined castle standing by a bleak moor, with bats and owls in it and, there seemed, ghosts. No particular reason for going there, and nobody went.

But on this particular night, as I came over the moor, the north wind was going by me like a long knife, and I was wet from the snow that had melted on me, and my horse was tired and, ghosts or no ghosts, I wanted shelter, and there was no dwelling anywhere along that bleak road. I might have kept warm if my horse could have trotted, but I couldn't keep him at that without hitting him, and he had carried me well; always did; and I wasn't going to do that. And then an intenser blackness rose beside me out of the dark moor. It was Weirdmoor Castle.

My first impulse was to ride past it, as the members of our Hunt always did, if ever they saw it. It was merely the custom of our Hunt. And that is what I should have done, if there had not come at the same moment a blast from the north that was so especially biting that, cold as I was already and thoroughly wet, I felt that shelter of any sort was now a sheer necessity. My horse shook me with one great shiver, and suddenly I saw that the windows of the castle were all shining with what I took to be lamplight. Later I realised that the glimmer, whatever it was, had not arisen from lamps, and that, for that matter, there were no windows, but only black gaps in the masonry; but that was afterwards. At the time I thought that where there was light there must be warmth.

So I rode up to the doorway and hitched my horse to a rusted iron staple that must once have been a hinge

of the door. It was on the south side, so that my horse was sheltered from the appalling wind. And I walked in. The moment I had gone through the hanging curtains with which ivy half-covered the door, I saw that it was true what had always been said and that the place was haunted, and badly haunted.

One has read of bevies of ladies, and, for all I know, they should be so described; but here it rather seemed that there were gusts of them, that floated, slightly luminous, through the castle's dark interior, while the north wind sighed outside and stirred the air of the cavities in which there had once been windows, and set dancing the tendrils of ivy that hung loose from the walls. There was no roof on the catsle, and looking upwards I saw only racing clouds that rushed over strips of dim light; but whether such light as there was came from any remnant of day, or from the stars of the moon, I could not tell. The ladies that floated through the dark of the castle drifted together then, and seemed all to look at me, for all of them sharply turned their luminous faces towards me, then turned away and clustered closer together and were obviously talking of me. I could have no doubt of that. And what is more, I could feel that they found something wrong about me. For a while I wondered what it could be. Could it be my wet hunting-coat, or the mud on my stock, or the water from melted snow that squelched in my boots? And one by one I became sure it was none of these. And then the idea came to me what it was, a clear feeling, which I corroborated later, that I knew what it was they found wrong. It was simply that I was alive. And life was something that these ladies who floated in that dark castle found common and vulgar and coarse.

Then they seemed agreed about something. "One of us," they seemed to have said, "must receive him." And at once from the face of one of them, as far as I could see in the darkness, disappeared the amused criticism, to be replaced by a welcoming smile as she drifted towards me.

What she said as she smiled at me with her faintly luminous smile was said in so tiny a voice that you might have thought I could not have heard it above the howl of the wind through cracks in the walls, and the roar of it in the chasms that once had been windows, but it had a clearness like that of the shrill cries of the bats which were also piercing the darkness, and I heard every word.

"You are from Earth transitory, are you not?" she said.

And I said, "Yes," though I had no idea what she meant.

"Won't you join us?" she said.

So I said that I should be delighted. And she drifted back to the faintly luminous others, and I followed her, walking in my wet boots over the weeds of the floor. I bowed and said, "Good evening," to that dim cluster of figures, but saw from their vacant expression that evenings and mornings meant nothing to them, and I could not say anything apt about eternity and did

THE DANCE AT WEIRDMOOR CASTLE

not know what to say. But one of them, a graceful figure that swayed with her swirling silk skirts in the draughts that were waving the ivy, asked me if I did not come from the transitory ways; and, guessing what she meant, I said that I did. And she turned to the others and they all nodded and smiled, and I heard them muttering again, "the transitory ways," and their smiles put me at my ease.

I could not trace by their fashions the dates when they had been here, and the graceful lines of their dresses were too mixed up with the tendrils of ivy which hung and swung from the walls. I should have liked to have asked them something about their story, but coming suddenly thus among an assembly of ghosts, I was not so composed as they, who had before them only one stranger, and who were in their own home.

So it was they that questioned me. And in answer to their questions I told them that I had been hunting and that I had been taken far from home by a great run, and after a splendid fox. "Is it dead?" they asked eagerly then. And I guessed from the excited eagerness in their faces, and from all that they said later, that they cared only for what was dead; and again and again as they spoke I got the impression that, although they tried to hide it, all living things to them were vulgar.

They closed round me eagerly, asking for news. Had I seen any ghosts by the road? they asked.

"No," I replied.

Any spectres? Any phantoms?

And I saw from that that there were different kinds of ghosts and that all these were different things.

Then the north wind outside appeared to increase in violence, so that all the cracks in the castle and weeds in the windows were singing. And the lady that seemed to be the chief of the ghosts asked if I would dance with her. Well, of course, I could not refuse. And we danced, and the wind sang. A graceful figure and a lovely face, so far as I could see by the dim glow of it in the moonless and starless darkness. But no warmth came from her, and no warmth came to me from my dancing, but only an increasing cold that pressed in on me from the darkness and clamminess of the castle, and even from every one of those girls themselves whenever we danced near them.

Chillier and chillier I grew as I danced, and the waist and the hand of my beautiful partner were as cold as the leaves of the ivy covered with ice. And as I grew chillier still, I knew it was life that was ebbing. And as the music of the north wind in the crannies sank for a moment, I ceased to dance, and my chilly and lovely partner urged me to go on.

When I said that I feared that it was time for me to go, she clung to me still, like damp ivy. And something about her then drew the bare truth out of me, and I said, "The cold is beating me, and my life is ebbing."

And she said "Life!" full of amused scorn. But, if I was to live, I knew that I must get quickly out of the cold of that castle, even into the wind outside. For somehow I knew that even the north wind would be warmer, if I could only pull clear of the dead. But it wasn't so easy.

They were not able to move me. They couldn't drive me to dance. But there was an influence about them that, cold as I was now, was growing too strong for me, and they were all around me, and I no longer had the strength that I needed for pulling away. And my partner was fixing me with her glow-worm's eyes. I was growing colder and colder. How could I pull clear?

I grew colder and even colder, and my partner smiled at me, a welcoming smile as though I were coming over even then to the dead. And so I was. And at that moment my horse snorted, trying perhaps, poor brute, to drive some cold gust away from him. Life, I thought! Something alive!

"I must look after my horse," I said.

They all of them turned on me the faint gleams of their eyes. And then I heard them exclaiming with all their scorn, "A horse!" "A horse!" "A live horse." And more than that they had no need to say in order to show me the indignation with which they knew that I preferred something alive to them. And then the one that had danced with me said, "A live horse! Had you wanted a horse the Valkyries would have given you one, or sold it for fairy gold." Her indignation was rising, and the indignation of all of them, while my strength was ebbing away with my vitality.

I was moving towards the door and feared that I never would get there, for they were all round me now, like ivy, and their chill was gripping my heart. And now the door was only four or five yards away, but I felt I could no more reach it than one can run to safety in a nightmare. Their cold and their scorn were all round me, hemming me in. One moment I felt that their bitter cold had got me, and then there was warmth all round me and I suddenly felt I was saved.

It was the breath of my horse. In the warmth of that I was able once more to move, able once more to put my weight and my reason against imponderable and ghastly things. I patted my horse, unhitched him from the old staple and climbed up. As I got to the saddle the dance, or whatever it was, seemed all to die away. One faint wail of indignation or disappointment remained, hanging in the dark air. And the light, whatever it was, had gone from the windows.

That was Christmas Eve. I rode on with the north wind, which as I think I told you, was warmer than that dank castle.

When I got home it was Christmas. I don't suppose they haunt that place at any other time, or more people would have seen them than have; but I never went back to see.

That is the tale I heard one Christmas Eve at an inn, and I remember it yet. It was late when the man who told it ceased to speak and leaned back again in his chair, and it was warm and comfortable before that good fire, and I noticed that all but he were by then asleep.   Ω

BELLE
by Tina and Tony Rath

Once upon a time there was a girl called Belle. She was as pretty as a picture, a natural blonde and a perfect size ten, but she had trouble with computers. She was taking a secretarial course, and she would have been perfectly happy with it, if it had not been for the computer section. She was very good at photocopying, and she had a certificate for the safe use of the stapler, she made excellent coffee, and her typing was not all that bad, but show her a computer and her head seemed to fill with cotton-wool. One afternoon she was sitting at her keyboard in the classroom while the other girls were having a tea-break. She was desperately trying to make sense of the lesson she had just sat through, when the Principal walked in, followed by a very handsome young man.

"This young lady seems to be a very keen student," he said, smiling.

"Oh, my goodness, yes," said the Principal, who knew all about Belle, but who was not going to admit that any student of hers was a complete computer illiterate, after eighteen weeks of training. "We just can't keep Belle away from the keyboard. Run along now dear, and get yourself some tea," she added quickly, before Belle, who was a very truthful girl, could give the game away.

"Just a moment," said the young man. "She sounds just the sort of young lady we're looking for. When do you finish your course?"

"Next week," she said.

"Splendid," he replied and he gave her a card emblazoned with a golden crown and the words *King and Son* which was the name of his company. He told Belle to come for an interview as soon as she could because they could never get enough good, keen computer staff. And he smiled so nicely that Belle took the card and smiled back.

Belle decided to go for the interview because she thought she could explain that she was really best at things like photocopying and use of the stapler and perhaps there might be a vacancy for someone to do that kind of thing, and to make coffee for all the other people who were working on the computers. But when she got to the offices of King and Son she found they were in a huge building that seemed to be made of gold and white marble. There were crowns everywhere, even crowns woven into the carpets, and the entrance hall was so full of trees and fountains that it was more like a park than an office. She was so overcome and bewildered by it all that she found herself rushed through her interview and signing a contract of employment before she had caught her breath, far less explained about her problem with computers.

But then the handsome young man appeared and took her out to lunch. He turned out to be the Son part of King and Son and Belle discovered that he was not only handsome but clever and kind as well. They said very little at lunch, and ate less, but they sipped Perrier and gazed into each other's eyes and any chance that Belle might have had to explain slipped away. The rest of the week slid past in a delicious whirl. Belle met a lot of nice people, and had some very pleasant lunches, and she had really begun to enjoy herself — until Friday afternoon when Mr King's son led her into a little office on the top floor of the huge building, which had nothing in it but a desk, a chair, a computer and a huge pile of paperwork.

"There you are my dear," he said. "Just get this lot sorted out and I'll take you out to dinner." And he gave her a lovely smile and went out, shutting the door behind him.

Belle gazed hopelessly at the computer screen which glared greenly back at her. She pressed a few buttons but this made the screen flash so alarmingly that she burst into tears. And then, through her tears, she saw a button at the side of the keyboard which said, in tiny letters help and in desperation she pressed it. The screen went blank and for a heart-stopping moment she thought she had wiped all the data. But then it flashed into life again, and at the same moment the door opened and a strange little creature came in. She was no taller than a child of ten and her hunched shoulders made her look even smaller. Her eyes were tiny and quite red and her face looked as old as the century. But her hair was silvery blonde and hung down below her waist as fine and thick and beautiful as Belle's own.

"Have you finished in here, duck?" she said.

"No," said Belle, who thought she was the office cleaner. "I don't even know where to start." And she began to cry again.

The little creature peered up into her face and said: "What will you give me if I help you?"

"What!" Belle exclaimed

"You pressed the help button, so you must need help. But it's the same with computers as with most other things in life. You only get out what you put in. So, if I help you, will you promise to do something for me?"

Now, Belle had never read any fairy tales. She had been to a modern school where they only read socially relevant stories about children who lived in deprived inner-city areas, or pre-teens who worried about the size of their chests. So she said: "Oh, yes, anything, only please help me!"

The little old woman began to whirl round, so that her hair tossed and glittered in a mist all round her, and as she whirled she said: "Mr King's son has fallen in love with you. When he marries you, you must ask me to your wedding. You must tell him that I am your aunt, and welcome me as your most honoured guest. You must give me a seat between your bridegroom and your father in law, and give me the first glass of champagne that's poured and the first piece of the wedding-cake that's cut."

And she stopped whirling and stared at Belle with her tiny red eyes. Belle was not at all vain, although she was so pretty, and she did not really believe that Mr King's son would ask her to marry him. So she promised to do everything her strange visitor asked.

"Good girl," said the weird little creature. "Now go and fetch me a cup of coffee and I'll get started."

Belle ran to the little kitchen at the end of the corridor and made the best cup of coffee she had ever produced. It took her very little time, but when she carried the cup carefully back to the office the work had all been done.

"But — that's just like magic," said Belle.

"Isn't it just," said the little creature, grinning and showing some rather sharp little teeth. "Now my dear," she added, taking the coffee and drinking it down, boiling hot as it was, "don't forget my wedding invitation. Leave it on the computer here and I'll be sure to get it." And once more she began to spin round faster and faster until, before Belle's startled eyes, she vanished.

That evening Mr King's son flew Belle across to Paris in his private plane and during a most romantic dinner he asked her to marry him.

Now when Belle met Mr King's family and his rich friends she began to feel very uneasy about her promise to the weird little woman, and very unhappy about claiming her as her own auntie. But she had made a promise, after all, and perhaps the old woman was looking forward to her outing. And then again, she might not really turn up. So Belle propped one of her white and silver invitation cards on the computer keyboard in the little office, and hoped for the best.

The old woman did not appear at the wedding itself, and she was not in the long line of guests queuing to congratulate the happy couple, and Belle was beginning to feel safe. But when everyone was sitting down and the wedding breakfast was just about to begin there was a disturbance at the door and the little old woman came in. She was wearing a good black suit and her beautiful hair was piled up on her head and held in place with jeweled combs, but somehow this made her look weirder than ever. For a moment Belle was tempted to pretend that she did not know her, but she was good girl at heart, and pity for the wizened little creature made her stand up and walk down the room in all her bridal finery to greet her.

"I'm so glad you could make it after all, Auntie," she said loudly, though some of the guests, she thought, sniggered behind their hands, "you must come and sit with us."

So she sat down at the top table, between Belle's new husband and his father, and, true to her promise, Belle filled her a glass of champagne from the first bottle that was opened and gave it to her.

"Your niece seems very fond of you," said old Mr King, trying not to sound surprised.

"Oh, she is, sir, that she is," said the little creature. "And she's my favourite of all my nieces and looks just like I did when I was her age. I had lovely blue eyes, just like Belle's."

"But — what became of them?" cried Mr King, staring at her tiny red orbs.

"I was so fond of the computers sir, my eyes grew red and bleared with staring at the VDU," wailed the little old woman.

Belle stood up with her bridegroom to cut the wedding-cake.

"Ah, look at her pretty figure," said the little old woman. "I had a figure like Belle's, and not so long ago as all that, either."

"But — what happened to it?" said Mr King, staring at her hollow chest and her hunched shoulders.

"I was so fond of the computers sir, I couldn't be kept away from them, and I lost my fine shape stooping over the keyboard, night and morning, morning and night," keened the little creature.

Belle brought the first slice of her wedding-cake to the little old woman, as she had promised. Her skin had such a glow on it that it gleamed smoother and finer than the fine silk of her wedding-dress.

"I had a fine skin like that," said the old woman, "though you wouldn't think so now."

"But what became of it?" whispered old Mr King, staring at her yellow parchment neck and the dry folds under her chin.

"I was so fond of the computers sir, and the dust from the screens dried out my pretty complexion," she said. "And all they left of my beauty is my hair."

And she shook her head, until her long blonde hair fell down her back as rich and fine as Belle's antique lace wedding veil and for a moment they saw the pretty girl she might once have been.

And Mr King's son could keep quiet no longer and he said: "Never, never shall my lovely bride touch a keyboard again!"

And Belle winked at the little old woman and said, demurely: "Not if you don't want me to, dear."

And they all lived happily ever after.   Ω

by Tina and Tony Rath

UNLOCKING THE GOLDEN CAGE
by Tanith Lee

illustrated by George Barr

To be poor, not young, unlovely — and alone — is a composite fate inflicted on many by the Angel of Misery. And so it was upon Agnes Drale, who, thirty-three years of age, and in a faded gown and unfashionable bonnet, walked up the two miles of the drive, to her late Uncle's manor, carrying her bag, one evening in the early autumn of 18——.

Another might have had high hopes, but not Agnes. Although it seemed, by the terms of the curious will, she was now supposedly to want for nothing, she understood quite well that the house and grounds, the title, and the coffers of the fortune had passed to her eighteen-year-old cousin, Genevieve, who was already wealthy and notoriously fair. Agnes was to be this woman's supplicant. And although, as the will stated, Agnes was to live in the great house, and have everything she required, it was to come to her by means of asking.

Throughout her life Agnes had learned, utterly, that asking was ruinous, and mostly unwise. In church, at the age of ten, and on her knees by her narrow bed for three years more, she had asked God daily, nightly, to improve her looks. But God preferred to keep her as she was, thin and sallow; indeed He liked this so well, He added artistically to her appearance by bending her back and blearing her eyes, in the service of ungrateful and sometimes vicious children, so that now she had a sort of hump, and wore spectacles.

Other than God, the human race provided evidence of the inadvisability of asking: Those who did not wish to employ her or, having done so, pay her; those who did not care to take a cup of tea with her in her room, preferring other friends more galvanic; those, like her father who, when she was twelve, refused her desperate plea not to die and leave her.

Agnes had never met her Uncle; but he seemed to her, rather than a benefactor, a cruel and perverse man, wishing to play some game even from the grave — for things were said of him, of his journeys in the East, and his private pleasures, which included alcohol and perhaps other stimulants more foreign.

Genevieve, of course, he had once visited, when she was a glimmering, ormolu child of fourteen. Agnes he had never bothered with. The tone of his testament, conveyed to her by the lawyer, was of impatient remorse. As she did most others, Agnes had apparently annoyed him with her lack of means, and must be tidied up, like spilt milk, before he could depart the world.

Having just been ousted from her work as govern-ess in a drab, unclean, and misogynist household, Agnes had already packed her bag. She next came across the length of England, through the first flame of September, in a cheap, close, and bouncing public carriage. And so now walked up this drive, through this glorious park which, presently, was faintly tinged itself with the shades of butter, copper kettles, honey, rust, amber, and ruby wine.

When she reached the house portico, arranged with the Greek columns that showed one of the flighty turns of the building, Agnes activated the bell and stood in its clanging, to wait. Governess, servant, dependent, drooping under her hump at the great front door, she expected insults, and having to explain herself. But despite her droop, she was ready. For suffering and ill-treatment had done to Agnes Drale that which they usually do — soured and twisted her, made her bitter as the aloe, and hard, under the layers of her physical weakness, as a cold and ancient stone.

The cousins, Genevieve and Agnes, did not meet until the evening, the hour of dining, in the Old Hall of the manor.

The Old Hall was not, in actuality, very ancient, but had been arranged in the Gothic way, with a vast fireplace, black beams, and shields and swords to mingle with the portraits on the walls. An angled passage led from the Hall directly to the chapel, done in the same mode, that had, so the lawyer had informed Agnes, a royal crimson ceiling, with hammered silver stars. No one had worshipped in this chapel since its erection. The lawyer opined that Agnes might care to, holding, it seemed, to the common belief that the higher-class female destitute soon learned a rigid habit of prayer.

Now, amid the candlelight before the fire, Agnes observed, in her cousin, a pure example of the redundancy of praying.

Genevieve was a being of gold. She might have stepped from the heart of the sun. From her head poured loops and coils of golden hair, shining like the flames of the hearth. Her eyes, the colour of chestnuts, had each a golden sequin, that could have been caused by the candles, or by some inner, ever-present combustion. Her flawless skin was softly flushed as if gilded. She glowed, she gleamed. While her dress of gold-leaf satin had been fashioned to match all.

Agnes, sitting in her one shabby, dark, 'dinner gown,' her hair pulled tight, could only smile her twisted, little, invisible smile.

"This must be amusing for you, Agnes," said Genevieve. "Do you like Italian wine? I expect the French vintage was too dry for you. Or do you like dry things?"

Agnes, used to the quips and cuts of numerous employers, answered only when needful. Genevieve was patently furious that her cousin had dared to come. Genevieve had already made quite clear the fact that Agnes was normally to dine in her own sitting-room upstairs. Genevieve had explained that, while hairdressers and dressmakers and other slaves might arrive regularly at the house, and Agnes must feel at liberty to engage them as and when she wished, Genevieve did not predict Agnes to wish for very much. Agnes would have simple tastes. Agnes, unused to opulence, would intend, circumspectly, to avoid it. And so, to the frequent dinner parties, to the evenings of dancing, she must naturally consider herself, under the post-mortem avuncular law, invited — but Genevieve would not be offended by her absence.

"I made quite sure, Agnes," said Genevieve, as she ate the chocolate fruits, "a Bible was put beside your bed." Raising her dessert wine, golden as she, Genevieve declared, "I've no doubt you have several favorite passages in the Godly Book. Do tell me one. I'm sure it would admonish me to be virtuous, and I'm sure I need reminding."

"I seldom read the Bible," said Agnes.

"Oh, your weak eyes. How thoughtless of me. But then, doubtless you have large portions of the holy work by heart."

Agnes sipped the wine. It was sweet as the pain of toothache she had so often experienced. She said quietly, *"Curse God, and die."*

Genevieve started. She seemed shocked, or perhaps only behaved as if she were so. "What ever is that?"

"The Bible. You will find it in *Job.*"

Genevieve smiled. "What a serpent you are, in your dark dress. You must have something brighter. We must see your true colours."

Upstairs, in the large bedchamber which was now hers, Agnes looked from her window and beheld night upon the park, the huge, blazing autumnal oaks and beeches put out, and crowned solely with midnight. Stars shone, dull as hammered silver. Below, to her left, she made out the chapel, stretching away from the side of the house. It had seven long windows, each caught in a spiderweb of iron, and through these nothing was visible. The chapel seemed to Agnes more like an orangery than anything else, the skittish styles of the house here mixed to an extreme of unlikeliness.

On impulse, before blowing out her candle, Agnes opened the Bible at random. Running her finger down the page, she read this: *All wickedness is but little to the wickedness of a woman.*

A week passed. Agnes Drale became re-acquainted with familiar, anticipated things. Firstly, her despisement by the servants, and their carelessness with her,

manifested in their short replies, the cold and muddled food brought to her rooms, the way in which her furniture, of all the building, was left undusted. Secondly, her exclusion from the life of the mistress of the house, Lady Genevieve.

There were, however, new, and quite unknown, comforts — the softness of the bed, even undusted and not well-made, the tastiness and variety of breakfasts, luncheons, teas, and dinners, even tardily and untidily presented. To have her own private place at last, and somewhere to put her books, allied to the chance that she might purchase more. Soon enough she barred the sneering or glowering maids from her sanctum, and herself, not reluctantly, made up her own bed, her fire, and dusted the fine old chests and chairs. The park, too, with its massing of fiery dying colours, afforded her long and fascinating opportunities for exercise. Agnes did not know any more, it is true, how to be happy, but she had never had before a life such as this.

She met, during that week, only once with Genevieve. This was in a lower hall, near dusk. Genevieve was returning aflame, in a riding habit of Prussian Burgundy, with two or three gallant young men.

"Oh, Agnes, if you wish to join us for dinner . . . but I don't suppose you do. She is most retiring," Genevieve added to her court, and they laughed, a laugh that such women as Agnes have had from such women and men as these, since humankind was evicted from Eden.

Needless to relate, Agnes did not attend the dinner. Nor did she have plans to intrude upon the other, more lavish, dinner Genevieve proposed to give, to dignify her eighteenth birthday. This celebration had been carried from its correct date in August, due to the business of her having come just then into the inheritance of the manor. She was a child, unsurprisingly, of Leo. Agnes, whose Virgoean birthdate fell curiously on the very day of Genevieve's extravaganza, imagined only that the onset of her thirty-fourth year would pass without notice among Genevieve's birthday flambeaux and fireworks.

This was not, however, exactly the case. Five days before the event, one of the maids rapped harshly on Agnes' door.

"Lady Genevieve says you are to go down. Lawyer's come."

Agnes felt a clutch at her heart. From her past history, she knew at once a trepidation that some successful act had been made to exile her, after all, from her anchorage, despite all self-effacement.

Grey and rigid, she entered the drawing-room, and there posed Genevieve, herself like a ray of the sunshine which burst in at the casements, the lawyer fawning and sunning himself in her contemptuous light.

"It seems there's some box Uncle left for us, to mark our birthdays. Apparently he believed they lay closer together than they do." She expressed a glitter of distaste at such a notion. "This gentleman," the word spoke volumes of disdain, "has said that we must be present when the box is unlocked."

The lawyer uttered, trying — in vain — to impress by privy knowledge. "As I have said, my lady, the receptacle has never been opened, not since it was brought to his estate by your Uncle. But the documents assert that it contains a most valuable, indeed unique piece of jewelry, as I believe, of Eastern origin."

All this was rather lost upon Agnes, who, flooded by relief, had blushed a sudden, unbecoming red.

Nevertheless she went, as instructed by the lawyer, and stood nearby, while the container was produced and a key set in its lock.

The box was of some black wood, and intensely carved with coiled and embracing designs. The lock was horrible, although well-oiled, and gave out such a screech that Agnes' hair rose on her neck. Inside the box, alone on a nest of papers, shone out the roar of gold.

Agnes did not, immediately, determine what this golden article might be. But strangely it came to her, how different this was, this deep, hot, heavy, and mysterious alchemical metal, how unlike the golden gildedness of Genevieve, which even she, Agnes Drale, had confused with it.

"A bracelet," said Genevieve. She seemed amused, idle, neither impressed nor curious.

But as the lawyer lifted it out, and held it for her, ready, the rich lushness of its gold drained the sunlight, drained even, for a moment, Genevieve.

Genevieve said, maliciously sweetly, "Come and see, Agnes. Which of us can he have meant it for?"

"Evidently, for you," said Agnes, in a leaden voice.

It was only her now-ingrained servitude that spoke, her resignation. And yet, her voice sounded ominous, and cold as a bell.

Genevieve took the jewelry, an intricately-worked band, having in the midst of its circle a sunburst. With no scruple or hesitation, Genevieve undid the clasp and fitted and secured it to her wrist, the right one, brushing aside the lawyer's offers of assistance.

Slinking back, he said, "The papers relating to the ornament are here."

"Yes, no doubt. Reading of any sort bores me terribly. It harms the eyes, you know, and makes them dull, and blind."

She drifted to the window once more, holding her trophy — who could think of it as other than hers? — before her, outstretched the length of her creamy, rounded, lower arm.

The lawyer took from the box a paper, and put it on the table. Agnes leaned, almost involuntarily, to see. The writing was highly decorative, and did not look like the rather slovenly script of her late Uncle.

This wrist-ring, or bracelet, is known as the **Fraanghi** *or* **Frengeh**. *Although very beautiful, in the land from which it was taken, it was thought to convey a curse.*

The lawyer sucked his lower lip. "Dear me."

At the window, seethed in light, Genevieve, the lion's daughter, did not seem to hear.

Agnes read on, with her dull and blinded and bespectacled eyes.

A wise king, having this jewel, lived a full, long, and sanguine life. But, once the adornment passed to his son, this son, boastful and proud, made many enemies. It happened that he was found, then, the arrogant one, with the gem upon his wrist, but he was torn asunder. Then arose another king, a braggart, a cruel man, and he, wearing the jewel, was also found, **stripped to his bones** *in the forest. Beware then, for not randomly does the object keep its name.*

Agnes turned to the lawyer. "What language is it, what does it mean? *Frengeh — Fraanghi —*?"

The lawyer glanced at her. He said, "Your Uncle was a great traveller in India, Persia, and the East."

Agnes said, "There is another paper."

This time, he took it out and handed it to her.

She read aloud, *"The gemstone is purported to be that Fata Morgana, a* **yellow ruby**, *of which there are few or no examples. Those who have conversely suspected the jewel to be a topaz, of the red variety, amend that such stones are not often found in that region."*

There was nothing else in the box, but for a deep shadow. Agnes said, "There is no jewel. The gold is plain."

"It seems so," replied the lawyer.

Genevieve spoke in the incandescence of her window. "A jewel? Is there a jewel in it?"

"No, my lady. It must be that it has lost the jewel —"

Agnes looked, and the flash from the bracelet blinded her for sure. The light had sprung from its central part, the sunburst. Before the darkness cleared from her eyes, she heard herself speak distinctly. "Perhaps the boss opens."

"Let me *see*."

For an instant, Agnes beheld her glorious cousin clawing at her own wrist, the way a cat will at something it does not like, or likes too well.

There was a loud click. It was a noise a clock might make, in the moment before it stops.

"Oh! Agnes, come and see —"

No malice was apparent now. Genevieve cried out, as had the precocious, lovely, repellent, and greedy child she had been at fourteen years of age, the day her Uncle had visited her and brought her such wonderful presents, and she had danced for him the 'Dance of the Pretty Fairy,' and recited some sentimental ode, and everyone had sighed and clapped, but he had only gazed, with his thin, brown face and narrow, evil eyes — that she, the fool, had been too young and too self-enamoured to interpret.

Agnes moved to Genevieve across the room. She entered the flaming crystal of the light. And in the light, Genevieve became the palest ghost, but on her wrist, freed now from its cover, there scorched, amid the curve of gold, a gem, the red topaz or yellow ruby, just as the paper had specified.

Agnes, once more, heard from her throat the voice arise, as if another uttered within her. "It might have been made with you in mind, Genevieve."

On the evening of Genevieve's deferred birthday party, which was really her own, Agnes Drale descended the main stairway in good time.

Most of the upper house had been decked with gilt ribbons and swags of velvet roses. Tall, ivory candles burned at every turn, as if gas had never been invented.

A few heads were rotated as Agnes came into the reception room. Not at her beauty, nor in mockery, in mere perplexity. In the past slender number of days she had called upon the harassed dressmakers and coiffeurs, and had so changed her appearance that Genevieve, in the midst of admirers, did not for some time recognize her. Agnes had not aimed for the impossibility of charm or the veneer of sweetness. She wore an expensive gown of jet black silk, whose tailored shawling collar quite concealed the upper curve of her spine. On this was pinned a watch of finest silver, with seed pearls, tiny and of impeccable design. Her hair had been re-invented in a style more classic and less severely placatory, and had given her face, now mildly powdered, the stern and implacable look of the Roman dignitaries found on antique coins. Agnes, who had been, seemingly, bowed and apologetic, now looked more what she secretly was, formidable and unforgiving. As her eyes passed over the assembly, assisted by her improved and gold-rimmed spectacles, no one was moved to laugh at her. Best be wary, was the instinctive if hidden thought. They took her not for a governess, or poor relation, but some steely aunt, ready to despoil their pleasure if they were not careful, to cast them down. If one cannot ever be loved, it may be better, in the interests of self-preservation, to be feared.

In some way, Agnes perfectly understood this. Her glance, fortified also by a glass of malt-coloured sherry, was unwavering. Although she could not have said exactly how she had come by her abrupt assurance.

It was only Genevieve who, recognizing her cousin suddenly, burst into a peal of mirth. Genevieve, herself in a dress of saffron, her hair raised like golden fruits in a basket of combs, half spilling on her enamel shoulders, was even then extending her fair arm, for everyone wished to study her bracelet — the single ornament she had put on. Agnes, despite seeing the jewel on its emergence, was also drawn to do so once again.

"Why, Agnes, how magnificent you are!" But Genevieve's sparkling voice passed over Agnes' bending head.

There in its socket of gold, the huge, polished gem, substance of the wristlet called the *Frengeh:* Yellow ruby or not, one could not mistake what it was like. The clear reddish upper water that melted through the tinge of nasturtiums, to a base the shade, perhaps, of

a Harvest Moon. And over its face, a flaw, which must, being so remarkable, have made it even more valuable and curious, more esoteric, bizarre, and even sinister. This flaw showed itself as three soft bars of shadow, that were, unmistakably, like three stripes upon the pelt of a tiger.

"A tigerish stone," said the plump young lord who stood at Genevieve's elbow. "A tiger for a lioness, since her birthday, you know, falls more properly in Leo."

"The tiger abhors the lion," said someone.

"Does it not suit me, then?" asked Genevieve, playfully.

Her gallants laughed loudly. They laughed with countenances angled aside — they did not wish to dispute with the grim and elegant aunt who had spoken such ill-omened words.

As Genevieve glided away, they passed with her, like a cloud clinging to a sunrise. And Agnes remained alone, wondering what she had said. It was strange, was it not, that the golden bracelet, which had closely fitted the strong arms of kings, would be small enough to cling to the slim wrist of Genevieve. But men in the East were often small of bone.

Agnes turned her head, and saw, as if her reverie had conjured it, an apparition. Against one wall, was positioned a small and slender man, clad in garments that, to Agnes, suggested the East, his head bound in a scarlet cloth. His skin was smoky, his eyes as black as her dress. Seeing that she looked at him, he bowed, his hands beneath his chin.

But then the crowd of Genevieve's guests washed between them, he was gone, and all that was left, for a moment, was the impression of a woman's amber-coloured gown, moving away, as it almost appeared, with no one inside it.

The dinner was held in the Old Hall. As decreed, torches burned. Gilded candles pointed from garlands of autumn leaves and forced red flowers. An artifice, a palm tree with gilt fronds, dominated the table's centre.

Through the many courses, the soups and meats and side dishes, the desserts and savouries, the selections of wines, Genevieve was Queen. Her radiance beamed the table's length. As Agnes sat, eating her sparing, precise mouthfuls, she felt swell within her her own murderous hate, that which never before had she been able truly to acknowledge. As the gaiety and high spirits emblazoned the hot, fragrant, and overpowering air, Agnes mused inwardly on all the mean cruelties inflicted upon, and the careless wrongs done to her. A host of horrors marched across her mind, and in their wake swept Genevieve, a sun in splendour, putting all other light, all other slight, to shame.

After the feast, out they went, on to the terraces above the descending lawns, and watched as, garnet and diamond, fireworks were let off against the backdrop of black trees and night.

Agnes Drale noted the little slender man in his

turban, hurrying about the pitch, ordering the incendiary shows. While, as the fireworks soared, bursting with sharp bangs like artillery into their kalidescopes of flame, Agnes beheld how they reflected in the lines of the windows of her Uncle's unused chapel, unsanctified by prayer, throwing up crimson flares on its ceiling, where the still stars hung, as if it too were burning.

It was later yet, after midnight, when the cold champagne was served in the Old Hall, back into which they had mobbed to get warm, that the Eastern man approached Genevieve, and bowing low, hands joined, produced from thin air a yellow rose, unlike all the other madder roses, and put it at her feet.

"Oh, bravo!" exclaimed her lovers, who had arranged presumably for his participation. "Shall he read your future, Jenny?"

"Do say 'yes,' " cried the ladies, who wanted to have read their own.

Then Genevieve sat in a chair, the pivot of all things, a golden lamp; and Agnes waited in the distance, like a shadow. The Eastern man crouched by Genevieve's knee. He stared into her palm, He said, in a rhythm fluctuating like an autumn wind, "You are walking your true path, lady. Before you is your Fate."

A woman shrilled, tipsy and excited, "What is it to be?"

"It is shining," said the man, "like the morning. It turns towards you its golden eyes. Your Destiny is beautiful, lady, and you will not fail to meet with it. It purrs, like a cat."

Genevieve clapped her hands. The *Frengeh* flashed, another firework, its gold, the astonishing stone that ran from ruby to topaz, and was striped like a tiger.

"What about that, eh?" asked the lordling. "Cursed, ain't it?" He grinned.

The man from the East smiled, his eyes lowered to the floor where, applauded but untended, the yellow rose had been trampled.

"The jewel will have caused the death of mighty kings," he said. "But what need this lady fear? She is in England."

At that they howled with proud laughter. And Agnes Drale stood watching, smiling a little, just as he did. Yet through the smirch and haze of sinking lights, she saw now, deep inside the crowd, a woman in an amber dress. Her hair was dark, springing and trailing all around her face and throat. Her skin was tawny, and the lights ran on it like water. Her eyes seemed to come and go, now pale and flame-like, and now dark as the sky beyond the house, as if fireworks went on in them still. And as she turned a little, her gown might be seen to be striped, barred, an unusual pattern, just before she was gone.

Agnes shivered in the scalding room. And raising her sour and flat champagne, she drank it down. She was in the grip of that most primal and appalling and triumphant fright, which the ancients knew to call Terror. She was aware that all things were altered now, and that the drab world held more than she had thought, and that God, in some form, some fierce and unimaginable and awful form, existed.

"There is a wretch of a gypsy in my park," said Genevieve, peevishly, shedding her riding gloves. "She wore a dress of dull orange, and her dark hair all loose. I shall have men scour the grounds. She must be evicted."

Agnes did not argue with this statement. She ate her breakfast, there in the dining-room with its marble and velvet, where now she took her early meals. But as she bit into her kedgeree, Agnes recollected how, even prior to Genevieve's ride, she, Agnes Drale, had walked in the manor woods, and sensed that something was slinking behind her, hot in the frosty morning, something that smouldered on and off between the trees. And on the lake, the ducks kept to their island, while now and then, above, the song of the over-wintering finches fell mysteriously quiet.

Two grooms and three footmen were sent out from the house; they left jesting, and returned silent. Seeking for the gypsy, they had found nothing at all, save the burnt leaves down from the trees, the berries like blood, and feathers of some bird a fox had taken.

The servants were different now, in their attentions to Agnes Drale. In a matter of a month, they had come to respect her. As the last leaves scattered from the trees, so were discarded the prejudices and the glee of certain ill-used things for another ill-used creature supposed more vulnerable. Agnes was not as she had seemed.

When she brought back the surly young women to clean and tidy her suite of rooms, they took one fresh look at her, this Agnes seeming taller in her faultless black, straight and hard as the winter trees were coming to be, strong and impervious. And when their first efforts were not good enough, then she brought them back again by a couple of clipped words, to re-make her bed, to replace her higgledy-piggled ornaments in a reasonable order. They said, presently, she was obdurate, but just. After all, she knew what was right.

They did not say they had formerly sought to jibe at and prey on her weakness. They said they had mistaken her, been misled by a temporary loss of character on her part, and so not initially discerned that she was a lady, and so she expected — and deserved — their best.

It was Genevieve now they took to task, Genevieve who had always been capable of viciousness, throwing at them her hairbrushes, retracting their wages, her unsuitable whims and extravagances, her manner that had, they now affirmed, no dignity. She had hardly worn mourning black for her Uncle, and that was a disgrace, he had been dead only half a year. She slept most of the day, until eleven o'clock, like a pig, and then was out gadding in the town, or rode about the park until the poor horse was lathered, and carried marks on its side of her wicked little whip, so the head groom frowned and cursed under his breath. She said something had frightened her in the park, under the oak trees, something, some vagrant, a cry or call or sound — but she was profligate and drank too much for a lady, a bottle of wine now at her luncheon, and two or more at night. With these sudden unaristocratic humours and alarms, a look had come into the exquisite face of Genevieve, that puffed it out and dredged away its lovely colour. She appeared more human now, standing in her hallway, under the chandelier which tinkled and faintly glinted in the cold October afternoon dimness, twisting her whip in her hands, her eyes roving, screeching like a fish-wife for lights, like that guilty king in that clever play Miss Agnes had mentioned.

And now Genevieve, their *Lady*, had lashed them all with her tongue. She swore they had a criminal here — she had seen the woman, she, Genevieve, had *seen* the gypsy bitch — such a word! No lady would use it, Miss Agnes would not — seen her in an upper corridor. Not only some no doubt impecunious and thievish relation of the servants taken in secretly under her ladyship's roof, but permitted to steal about the rooms of their betters, pilfering. In vain they protested, scandalized themselves, for they laid claim, the servants, only to relatives of the purest sort, and with here and there merely the by-blow of some exalted person who had loved their grandmothers or their great aunts unwisely but extremely well.

As the girl nightly brushed Agnes' hair, found to be long and strong and wiry, with its strands of steel, and the sparks flew off it, she told Agnes of Genevieve's strange, new, and troublous ways.

"I think, Miss Agnes, if you'll excuse me —"

"And what is that, Beryl?"

"I think she may've taken her Uncle's own road."

"Which road would that be, Beryl?"

"It was — *Hump*, Miss Agnes."

"Hump . . . ? Oh, hemp. I see. Opium."

"He was haddicked, Miss. Terribly so. The drug makes you mad."

"So I've heard."

"She ups and screams at me, Miss, yesterday, as I was going through the lower hall — *'Look! Look there!'* She gives me a proper turn. I dropped all the napkins. And then she struck me. 'Can't you even smell it, you stupid —' Well, then she called me a nasty name. I said I couldn't smell nothing but for the fire burning in the little sitting-room, which was smoking. She says, 'Beryl, you —' that name again — and she hit me across the face. *'It's a dog,* she cries. *'One of the dogs is in — that filthy orange one — fetch someone to put it out!'*"

Beryl brushed, and Agnes Drale's hair crackled. The sparks flew past the lamp, and the little clock chimed eleven.

"But there *was* a smell. I *did* catch it. A whiff, like the zoölogical gardens in the city. It seemed — beg your pardon — to come from her ladyship. Perhaps something picked up on her skirt —"

Agnes thanked Beryl, and Beryl put down the brush, and drew open the neat and perfect bed. Inside the hour, lying on the laundered sheets, Agnes slept her now-usual sound and dreamless sleep, which as a rule continued until seven in the morning.

However, about four, something woke her. She did not know what it was, but yet she was impelled to rise at once, and seek the window.

How icy the panes of glass were behind the thickness of the curtains, and beyond this flimsy barrier, lay the great park, stripped bare now to its black bones, and holding up a canopy of stars. Her eyes, her neck, her head — turned, and Agnes looked towards the star-hung chapel that ran out from the house.

She was bemused by sleep, and yet awake. She saw calmly, clearly, the long black window-spaces in their iron webs, and next, faint and glowing, how some occult light passed up and down inside. It was the shade of a dying lamp, reddish or ochre. It reminded her of how she had seen the reflected fireworks display upon the crimson ceiling. Yet, conversely, *it* moved low down.

"What can this be? Who's there? Oh, what?" Agnes murmured. She trembled and her heart beat wildly, and yet she was removed from her own self, from the expressive emotion of her familiar body. She sat high up within the walled chamber of her skull, and watched the moving glow, now yellowish, now red, until it ceased to move and faded away like a dying, or a sleeping, fire.

Then, returning to the bed, she too regained her sleep and in the morning, perhaps, had quite forgotten.

That evening, Agnes Drale was summoned by her cousin Genevieve, to dine in the Old Hall. Here every night Genevieve had partaken of her dinner, alone or in noisy, festive company. While Agnes had kept to her modest if luxurious rooms, now her own meal was always served hot, and decorously arranged.

No one but Genevieve waited in the Hall. Of all things, a cold repast, on this frigid night that conceivably promised snow, was laid beneath the illumination of a mere ten candles. The gas was out. The fire burned sluggishly about a handful of logs.

"The heat — the smell of recently cooked food," said Genevieve, turning rapidly to Agnes, "excites — something." She added, feverishly, "Animals in the park — come to the windows."

"As the wolves do, in Russia," supplied Agnes, coolly.

"Just so. Indeed. What an isolate place this is. I may remove to town. Lord E——, you recall him, I expect, has offered me the use of his Small House, only fifty rooms, but I must manage. You, of course, won't mind remaining here."

"No, I should think it very cozy," said Agnes, amenably.

They went to the table, its waste of white cloth, and helped themselves from the dishes.

"The servants . . ." said Genevieve. "It's because I must speak to you very privately, Agnes. No prying ears or eyes. They gossip about me —" Genevieve was pallid, her face, on another, might have been described as engorged, swollen. Her grasp was unsteady upon the silver utensils, and three times they dropped from her fingers.

Agnes ate at a slow and even pace, and sipped from her crystal glass the apricot-coloured wine. Genevieve ate nothing, but drank eagerly. On her wrist was a dull mark; perhaps the bracelet, the *Frengeh*, had bruised her. Occasionally Genevieve would encircle this bruise with her other hand. At last she said, "Do you remember the jewel, Uncle's silly foreign bangle — it's so heavy . . . those times when I put it on. But the gemstone is spoiled. Three dark scorings across it — surely there's no such thing as a yellow ruby."

Agnes ate a tartlet. It was cold in the vast room, the fire soaking ever lower, casting a dark cinnabar glare, the candles flickering. The voluminous curtains were drawn fast at the long windows, to close out any wild beasts that might be gathering in the park.

"Agnes," said Genevieve, "I don't suppose you were ever — fanciful."

"In what way?"

"In — the way — oh, of ghosts, nightmares. Such things."

"Perhaps," said Agnes quietly.

"It is stupid of me," said Genevieve. "Never in my life — something is following me about, Agnes."

"Something is following —"

"Some *thing*."

"How exactly to you mean?"

Genevieve drained her glass, rose abruptly, and flung it from her. It smashed in stars at the edge of the hearth.

"It is preposterous and absurd. But — I know that it happens. I *hear* it. I — *smell* it. I see it pass, sometimes near and sometimes at a distance."

"But what do you see — or hear or smell?"

"I can never be sure what it *is* — the smell is hot and pungent. *Spicy.* Or — a dirty smell. Or there is a noise — soft, like — a cat, walking over the floors, but a big cat, Agnes, very big. And sometimes —" Genevieve stared at Agnes' face, not seeing her, "I hear it — *breathing.*"

"You're overwrought," said Agnes.

Genevieve gave a squeal of laughter. "I am *terrified!*"

"How could there be such a thing?"

"The bracelet," said Genevieve. She wilted suddenly; she drooped. Such a stance, over thirty-three years, had brought about Agnes' stoop. To Genevieve it was a posture novel as darkness to one who had never beheld the night.

"The bracelet Uncle left for you," clarified Agnes, diligently.

"Yes, yes — that horrible, gaudy gew-gaw. Oh God! I shut it up in its box again. I *hid* it in my dressing-room. And still — still — Oh, Agnes, I can't eat or sleep. I think I'll wake to find it crouching on my breast. I *dream* of it. It — *purrs*. Such a dreadful purr, rasping — like nails tearing velvet. I shall go mad!"

Agnes drank another mouthful of wine. She said, "You're unnerved, my dear cousin. Naturally, no such thing exists. But if you're in this state of mind, there is, after all, a certain recourse."

"Tell me! Quickly! Agnes — I beg you —"

"You must," said Agnes, raising her eyes, her spectacles gleaming bright, "turn to God. No other, my dear, can help you. Pray, Genevieve."

"Pray? *Pray?* Do you think —"

"I know it, Genevieve. God is attentive to every sincere plea. And only recollect, our Uncle built here a chapel, consecrated and ready for the most urgent use."

"The chapel," said Genevieve. And she spun about in the direction of that narrow door which led from the Old Hall, out into the angled passage, and so to the folly of the chapel with its orangery windows and ceiling of stars.

At this moment, the most curious sound stirred against the huge room. It might have come from outside the walls, or down the chimney, or out of the very air itself. It was indescribable, but as Genevieve heard it, she uttered a shriek, and Agnes rose to her feet, the skin crawling on her bones.

"Take a candle, Genevieve," said Agnes.

"Oh, Agnes — I'm too afraid — in the darkness —"

"Then I'll go before you. I'll go and see, and ignite the gas lamps that I've been told are fitted there, as here."

"But the light —" cried Genevieve "— may attract —"

"It is," said Agnes, in an iron voice, "the place of God."

"*Yes.* Yes, then. I will. If you — will go there first."

"Stay here, and I'll return for you," said Agnes.

And taking up one of the faltering candle-branches, she walked across the Hall, her spine erect as if fletched with the quills of lizards, her hands colder than the promised snow.

At the narrow door she paused. The sweat started icily on Agnes' brow. She said, "Take courage, Genevieve. All will be well." And passed into the corridor beyond.

Perhaps, because it had no windows, the corridor, that ran between other rooms unseen, was close and warm. It had a scent of fruits dried for cake — raisins, prunes, such items. At the turn, Agnes halted. The candles dipped and lifted up again their nervous flames. She went on.

The right-angle of the passage was only some four or five yards in length. At the end was a large door, secured only by a simple latch.

by Tanith Lee

As Agnes approached it, she seemed to hear a strange, muted noise, like tiny tinsel bells. She shivered again, touched the latch, and opened the door wide.

The chapel stretched before her, long and dim, its elongated windows dark, lit sidelong in a peculiar manner, by the vague, curtained lamps of the house. It was a slender oblong in shape, this chamber, and at its extremity a carved lectern stood, and before that, to either side, three carven pews with their backs to her. On the floor lay a red runner, velvet perhaps, and above soared the red arch of the ceiling where the silver stars winked back the candlelight.

Possibly it was the apprehension of Agnes Drale that made the atmosphere seem to tremble and ring. She had had so often to be brave in the face of many humiliations, attacks, and reversals, that courage was habitual with her.

Nevertheless, she moved stiffly, and put up her hand like a stick to the gas fitment she had perceived on the wall.

The gas fluttered and popped, and slowly the flame bloomed up, spreading down the aisle of the chapel and polishing the carvings on the backs of the pews. The second fitment was set adjacent to the lectern, and Agnes gathered herself to go there and attend to it. For she was not yet quite ready.

Beyond the long windows only the night finally showed, the glim of the manor put out. Around the lectern shadows clung, ascending into the crimson roof. It is now and then to be seen, this phenomenon, how a light, placed in an unexpected or unaccustomed position, may seem to throw a shadow that bears no relation to anything revealed by its rays.

Agnes stared, and then, intuitively, her glance descended and rested on the last of the right-hand pews, that which stood the nearest to the lectern. Its back was high, and nothing was to be seen, but the air was now so very hot, so intensely smothering, as if before some tropical storm. And in this choking, shimmering air, the quivering bells ran on, making dizzy Agnes Drale, so that she swayed, and her candles sank and died in her hand.

Something was rising after all, over the back of the last pew. Something was sitting up, a curve, a hump of darkness that rose into the light. Its colour slowly changed to amber, rich and royal, and over the amber scored the dark streaks and bars, and a stream of gold that ran from the lamps, on silk, or fur. It was the back — of an enormous beast, of a tiger, and yet, and yet, it was turning now, the golden sheen shifting, turning its head, to look at her.

Agnes Drale opened her mouth, but no sound came from her. She slumped against the wall, and was pinned there, unable to drop down.

It is a woman's face, but a woman's face that is the face of a beast, a face of amber, with human eyes that are the eyes of a demon, yellow as topaz, red as ruby, eyes that are not windows, for no soul is behind them,

yet *something* is behind them, and looks out. And the jaws are wide, and the long teeth, brown and stronger than steel, protrude from it. The dark hair falls that might be mistaken for a woman's hair, but not now. And a hand that is a paw rests on the edge of the holy seat, and the claws unsheathe, and they draw one thin line along the wood, delicate, soft, and never, never will be forgotten the noise they make, as this is done, nor the rasping ripple of a speechless voice, coaxing and impatient. *And the thud, the lash of the tail.*

It is hot now as the centre of a furnace, or a dying sun.

Come, Agnes Drale, leave your candles where they lie, go backwards slowly and with caution, feel for the door, slip out, and close it carefully once more, behind you.

Agnes re-entered the Hall, firm, not breathless, and Genevieve sprang up at once.

"Everything is ready," said Agnes.

"The gaslight —"

"There is light," said Agnes. "And God is there, awaiting you."

Genevieve draws herself up, haughtily. "Then I shall go alone." If it is between her and God, no other is needed.

Ten minutes after, Agnes is in her bedroom, while Beryl brushes her hair. Across the park, once, twice, three or four or five times, they have heard an odd note, a shrill, distorted, soulless scream.

"It must be an owl," says Beryl. "There it is again. It does go on so. I hope it won't disturb you, Miss."

"Not at all," says Agnes.

In the sombre month of November, when the white snow was down about the manor, the lawyer finished his work for Agnes Drale, the legal proceedings necessary now that the house, and its estate, were hers. As she sat like a queen in her black tussore, he offered her a last paper.

"You were curious, I remember, Lady Agnes," he said, making intent use, as he had throughout, of her inherited title, "about that bracelet your Uncle had brought from the East. I confess I was a little, too, myself."

"An unlucky gem, as prophecied," said Agnes. "It's locked away, and no longer in my keeping."

"I hope, my lady," said the lawyer, "that you also affixed the golden sun-shaped cap once more over the stone?" He chuckled frivolously. "You will see why, when you regard this document I have procured from the city museum."

"Oh, yes. I did do that. My servants were very uneasy. They had learned the jewel was cursed. Poor Genevieve."

The lawyer touched his heart in an affectation of feeling. "And the criminal is still at large —! A madman. Such a terrible, such an unthinkable end — eviscerated, rent, ripped, the blood splattered — the face torn off —" He displayed the purest ghoulishness of his time, or most times.

"There is a general belief," said Agnes, "that gypsies and their ferocious dogs —"

"Several had been seen, I gather," agreed the lawyer. "But to enter the chapel —"

"No one can explain," said Agnes. She nodded. The subject was closed; one did not argue with her.

She unfolded her palms and took the paper, and read it. As she did so, the lawyer, a true slave, and generously remunerated, stood respectfully smiling, to show how he was aware what nonsense he had just handed her. Ω

This piece of jewelry is mentioned in several ancient texts, and seems to date from the fourteenth century. The jewel is itself not mooted as a mineral but as a living energy, or animal. *When let loose in particular conditions, it may evoke, it is thought, violent and horrible death, the ingredients for this seeming to involve the emotions of hatred and jealousy, in opposition to callous greed. In the case of one ruler said to have died through it, the matter is proposed as the actual opposition of the two elements of the stone itself — vividity and hardness.*

The bracelet, which is formed of gold, also entails an enclosement over the stone, which, if the wrong or provoking elements are present, should in no circumstance be removed. Thus, it is the bracelet, the **setting** *of the jewel, which is named* **Frengeh**, *or* **Fraanghi**, *deriving of course from the Musselman word, meaning,* **A Cage**.

SENTRY

Licked bare and black
By dragon's breath, his old bones
Watch with living eyes.

— **Catherine Mintz**

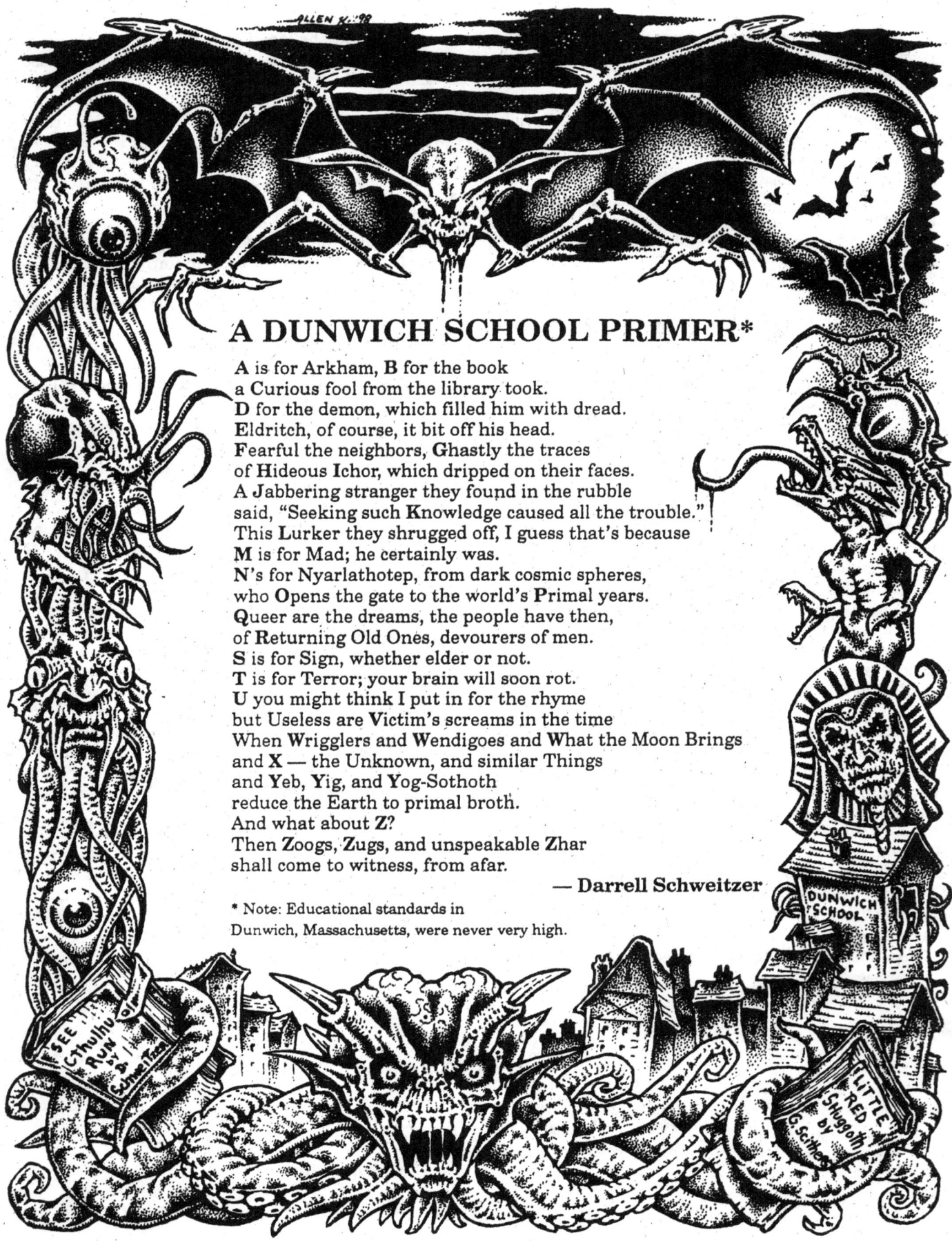

A DUNWICH SCHOOL PRIMER*

A is for Arkham, **B** for the book
a Curious fool from the library took.
D for the demon, which filled him with dread.
Eldritch, of course, it bit off his head.
Fearful the neighbors, **G**hastly the traces
of Hideous Ichor, which dripped on their faces.
A **J**abbering stranger they found in the rubble
said, "Seeking such **K**nowledge caused all the trouble."
This **L**urker they shrugged off, I guess that's because
M is for Mad; he certainly was.
N's for Nyarlathotep, from dark cosmic spheres,
who **O**pens the gate to the world's **P**rimal years.
Queer are the dreams, the people have then,
of **R**eturning Old Ones, devourers of men.
S is for Sign, whether elder or not.
T is for Terror; your brain will soon rot.
U you might think I put in for the rhyme
but Useless are Victim's screams in the time
When **W**rigglers and Wendigoes and What the Moon Brings
and **X** — the Unknown, and similar Things
and **Y**eb, Yig, and Yog-Sothoth
reduce the Earth to primal broth.
And what about **Z**?
Then **Z**oogs, Zugs, and unspeakable Zhar
shall come to witness, from afar.

— Darrell Schweitzer

* Note: Educational standards in
Dunwich, Massachusetts, were never very high.

FOR SEVENTY-FIVE YEARS: THE UNIQUE MAGAZINE   ISSN 0898-5073
Summer 1999   Cover by Jill Bauman

Weird Tales® is published 4 times a year by DNA Publications, Inc., in association with Terminus Publishing Co.,
Inc. Postmaster and others: send all changes of address and other subscription matters to DNA Publications, Inc.,
PO Box 2988, Radford VA 24143–2988. Editorial matters should be addressed to Terminus Publishing Co., Inc.,
123 Crooked Lane, King of Prussia PA 19406-2570. Single copies, $4.95 in U.S.A. & possessions; $6.00 by mail to
Canada, $9.00 by first class mail elsewhere. Subscriptions: 4 issues (one year) $16.00 in U.S.A. & possessions;
$22.00 in Canada, $35.00 elsewhere, in U.S. funds. Publisher is not responsible for loss of manuscripts in
publisher's hands or in transit; please see page 5 for more details. Copyright © 1999 by Terminus Publishing Co.,
Inc.; all rights reserved; reproduction prohibited without prior permission.
                              Typeset, printed, & bound in the United States of America.
Weird Tales® is a registered trademark owned by Weird Tales, Limited.

THE EYRIE

Portrait of the Editor as Patron of the Arts.

We don't have to agree with the opinion columns we run, but we confess we do by and large agree with S.T. Joshi's comments, later in this issue, on weird poetry. Poe, Clark Ashton Smith, Swinburne, Coleridge, Robert E. Howard, Walter de la Mare, and so many others once wrote magnificent ghostly, weird, imaginative verse, some of which (particularly in the 19th century) was as widely read as many novels are today. Now we ask: is poetry dead?

But at the same time we hear a certain Simon and Garfunkel song going through our collective editorial head, the one in which various pretentious types are asking one another questions about whether analysis is worthwhile or the theater is really dead. And once when we were a bit more pretentious than at present (and a whole lot younger) we parroted that very line to a theater person . . . and received the response that was deserved.

Our more mature conclusion is that while the metrical romance doesn't seem at all well these days, and cave painting is perhaps in decline, one gets into difficulty rather quickly when pronouncing any art form "dead," as long as even one single artist of ability is doing sincere work in the medium in question. The audience may be vanishingly small. But *dead* seems a little too final.

Let's say then that in 20th-century American culture, poetry has gone into hibernation. We think Joshi is right that it has declined to virtual irrelevance even among literary people, and we pretty much agree with his analysis of why. It's a standard challenge we offer: "Quote a famous American poem written in the past twenty years." You can't, because there aren't any. There aren't any famous poets either. Arguably Allen Ginsberg was the last, but more as a public figure than as an actual poet.

At the same time, as long as there are still poets out there and poems are still being written and (to whatever degree) published, then poetry isn't really dead.

But how many copies of the typical poetry collection are sold? How many just gather dust on university library shelves? Could it be that, in a country of 250 million people, poetry readers are, quite literally, one in a million? Is poetry read by anyone other than other poets?

Considering the circulation figures given for literary magazines in *Writer's Market,* then *Weird Tales®* is actually one of the most public outlets for poetry anywhere. Certainly for weird and fantastic poetry, we're just about the largest, and the highest paying. It gives us pause. What is to be done?

The answer is, we're going to go on publishing poetry. Since not everybody who reads *Weird Tales®* is a poet, here, at least, poetry is still read as it is supposed to be, by the public.

Maybe ours is a last redoubt; and poetry here is like some exquisite icon created at the Byzantine court just a few years before Constantinople fell to the Turks. The art of the Byzantine court about A.D. 1450 was still perfectly valid on its own terms, even if only a handful of people ever saw it. Maybe somebody preserved that icon and it was appreciated centuries later. Certainly it was better to have created it than *not* to have done so.

This, then, is our rationale for fantastic poetry, however diminished its audience or appeal may be. This is why we make an extra effort to sponsor poetry.

It may be a bit much for us to claim to be *the* center of the Poetic Universe; we feel a certain sense of stewardship, if you will, without taking ourselves *too* seriously.

Okay, if we're in charge, here's our agenda: While Ezra Pound may have been one of the principal villains who overthrew 20th century English poetry, he did come up with a ringingly good phrase when he said (in *The ABC's of Reading*) that "poetry must be at least as well written as prose." That is to say, it must be lucid. It must (to use Mark Twain's phrase) say what it proposes to say rather than merely come close.

We absolutely reject the idea that poetry must be "difficult," deciphered rather than read, and that if we don't understand it, it must be profound. If we don't understand it, more likely the author hasn't expressed himself well enough.

We refuse to believe that poetry just flows spontaneously onto the paper. We believe in craft, even as we believe in the craft of the short story. A certain editor, for whom we have a great deal of respect, once told us that he never sent poets anything but rejection slips back with poems, because he never once was able to ask for a revision and get back a poem he could publish. Very slowly, indeed with all due respect, we have come to appreciate that this is not so. We are perfectly willing to say, "the last two lines are unclear," or "don't you need an extra syllable in line 14?" Sometimes we *have* been able to get revised poems back in publishable form. This is not, we suspect, because we are so much more editorially perceptive, but because, in the fantasy field, we are perhaps dealing with a different breed of poet, who regards his work as somewhat less ineffable.

For poetry to regain even an audience as large as that enjoyed by the short story, then, first, it must be held to higher standards of intelligibility than are found in general poetry magazines; and second, it must have emotional content. A poem is not a cypher. It is, more often, a lyric, which appeals directly to the emotions. It also should be (here, at least) genuinely imaginative. It should make us see or feel things we have not previously seen or felt. We are not interested in tired rhymes with the same old ghosts and monsters in them. For that matter, we do not insist on rhyme at all, only that if the poet attempts rhyme or meter, it be achieved. We will take a limerick, a sestina, blank verse, or free. Form is anything that works.

STAFF:

Publisher: Warren Lapine
Editors: George H. Scithers
& Darrell Schweitzer
Managing Editor: Carol Adams
Art Editor: Diane Weinstein
Assistant Editors: Kyle Phillips, Pat Buard,
& Robert Waters,
Computer Consultant: David J. Williams III
Typesetter: Owlswick Press
Printer: Morgan Publishing Co., Inc.

MANUSCRIPT SUBMISSIONS:

Before sending us your material, please send us a business-sized envelope, with postage affixed, addressed to you, for our guidelines.

The address for this and all other editorial matters: **Weird Tales®, 123 Crooked Lane, King of Prussia PA 19406-2570.**

The address for all new subscriptions, subscribers' changes of address, advertising, and all other money matters is: **DNA Publications, Inc., PO Box 2988, Radford VA 24143–2988.**

Yes; we read unsolicited submissions — but *only* if they are in standard manuscript format. To survive, all editors insist on a few Rules: each submission must be in proper format and must include a return envelope, addressed to you, with enough postage affixed to bring the manuscript back to you. If you want us to discard the manuscript if we don't buy it, tell us so, but include a business-letter-sized envelope, addressed to you, with proper postage affixed, so we can send you our comments. No loose stamps, please!

We recommend either or both of two books on writing (after all, we wrote one of them!): *On Writing Science Fiction: the Editors Strike Back!* by Scithers, Schweitzer, & John M. Ford; $19.50 in hardcover; and Barry B. Longyear's *Science-Fiction Writer's Workshop,* $9.50 in trade paperback, available from Owlswick Press, 123 Crooked Lane, King of Prussia PA 19406-2570. These prices include shipping & handling. If you live in Pennsylvania, please include 6% sales tax.

We are not responsible for manuscripts in our hands or in transit. You *must* keep a copy of every manuscript you send out. You *must* put your name and address on the first page of every manuscript. And please: *no* binders, folders, or padded envelopes; and especially: *no* registered or certified mail for which we would have to stand in line at the post office!

What we basically want is to provide a forum where, should a new Clark Ashton Smith arise, he'd find an audience. As long as that's possible, weird poetry isn't dead.

And speaking of Clark Ashton Smith, we apologize to Perry M. Grayson of Tsathoggua Press (6442 Pat Ave., West Hills CA 91307) for not mentioning until now the copy he sent us of Donald Sidney-Fryer's *Clark Ashton Smith: The Sorcerer Departs* (1997, $7.00). This is a revised version of a 1963 essay, which remains one of the best pieces of writing about this important figure, who is still almost wholly absent from standard literary reference works. It is a combination of biography and literary analysis, by an author who is himself a poet of no mean ability. (We're happy to say we've recently acquired a long poem by Mr. Sidney-Fryer for a future issue.) The booklet concludes with the poem of the same title by Smith, which aptly sums up the state of the field after Smith's death:

The sorcerer departs . . . and his high tower is drowned
Slowly by low flat communal seas that level all . . .

Maybe what we can do here at *Weird Tales*® is at least lower the water level a bit . . . Between Joshi's column, this response, and the more than usual number of poems we have managed to fit into this issue, we hope you enjoy this, our Special Weird Poetry Issue.

Another book we recommend. *The Timeless Tales of Reginald Bretnor*, published by Story Books (4732 Hunting Trail, Lake Worth FL 33467) is a 1000-copy limited edition, a posthumous gathering of many of the best fantastic stories by the late Mr. Bretnor, the inventor of Ferdinand Feghoot and Papa Schimmelhorn. It is a worth tribute, containing fifteen stories and an introduction by Poul Anderson, and sells for $12.95 a copy. One of Bretnor's last stories, "The Haunting of the H.M.S. Dryad," appeared posthumously in *Weird Tales*® #315.

We get letters . . . :
The artist **George Barr** writes: *Just finished reading David Schow's "Gills." I laughed and loved it. . . . because there are parts of it that are so very nearly true.*

When I was living in Los Angeles (1968 to 1972) I got a call from a friend of mine, Bill Hedge, who was a prop maker, a sculptor, and an animator. He had just snagged an assignment to design and build a costume for a film called Octaman.

It was to be, of course, a creature-feature, and the creature was an octopus-like thing that menaced and killed people. Bill was a very skilled craftsman, but had no confidence in his ability to draw well enough to put across his ideas to a producer. He asked me to sketch out some concepts for him.

The thing that always bothered me about the gillman in The Creature from the Black Lagoon *was that, despite the beautiful detail of the costume, it was all too obviously a costume.*

I envisioned something that would crawl, all tentacled and squirmy, to — if possible — disguise the fact that it was a person beneath that writhing mass. I did drawings showing the overall look of the thing, where a man would fit into it, and how he would move in order to make his humanness less obvious.

. . . Bill asked me to go along to meet the producers. I don't remember both their names, but the one who did the majority of the talking was none other than Harry Essex, who, himself, had made the memorable The Creature from the Black Lagoon. *He considered it his greatest triumph. It*

was not that he didn't understand my concept; it was that what I had envisioned was exactly the opposite of what he wanted: a huge, imposing, very man-like thing that would stalk about on two legs "tentacle-ing" people.

It did not good to explain that an octopus, being a mollusk, had no skeletal structure, nothing to support its weight out of the water . . . that even Ray Harryhausen's monstrous creature in It Came from Beneath the Sea, huge as it was, probably could not have reached up out of the water to grasp the Golden Gate Bridge and flail about in the city. That would require bones. Mollusks don't have them.

Essex shrugged that off, saying this was a "crossbreed" between octopus and man, and that its walking about and "tentacle-ing" people was essential to his story.

"Tentacle-ing," it turned out, was his word for the uncoiling and lashing out that this creature's arms must be able to do, in addition to one tentacle being (bones or not) sufficiently rigid to stab a man through the midsection.

Reminding myself that I was being paid to cater to his ideas, I hurried sketched out a creature which incorporated a little of both our concepts. No, he said; it wasn't sufficiently manlike.

So I gave it a huge, octopus-like head (with the mouth he adamantly insisted it have: a modified sucker I invented on the spot), welded four tentacles into legs, and left the thing with four arms for tentacle-ing people. He suggested it have scale-like plates on its abdomen, "like the gill man."

It soon became obvious that what he intended was, basically, a remake of The Creature from the Black Lagoon, with a (slightly) different species and enough plot changes to make it seem (to him) like a new story.

I went home, did a slightly more finished version of the approved idea, and gave it to Bill for Mr. Essex's okay. He got it. Then — I'm not exactly sure what happened. . . . In any event, Bill turned the job over to a young friend, a teenager named Rick Baker. This talented kid, with his friend Doug Beswick, built the creature from foam rubber. . . . Then I heard no more about it . . . vague rumors that the film had been seen here or there . . .

Then, at a WesterCon in San Francisco, I met actor Kerwin Mathews, who had actually starred in the film. He had tactfully sidestepped the suggestion that we obtain a copy of Octaman to show at the convention. He said it wasn't really very good, and laughingly suggested that it had never actually been released, but had "escaped."

It wasn't until years later, when a nearby video store was going out of business and offering its stock for sale, that I found a tape of Octaman and learned why I'd heard so little about it. Words cannot express the awfulness of that movie.

If Harry Essex is still alive, I hope he has the good sense to be embarrassed by it. The creature in it does everything he wanted it to do, stalking up out of the swamp, tentacle-ing people right and left, and — yes — stabbing a man through the midsection with the rigid tip of a tentacle.

Octaman was made back in the days when only the head of each department actually got mentioned on-screen. So Rick Baker, who has become quite deservedly famous over the years (and has his name emblazoned on the video tape box because of that fame), gets sole screen credit for the monstrosity that Harry Essex envisioned as the star of his gillman remake. Enough time has passed that I'm amused rather than humiliated that I had anything at all to do with it. Bill Hedge is the lucky one; he got out before the sin was actually committed.

Then **R. Michael Burns** catches us in a little embarrassment of our own: . . . the football mentioned in "The Family Football" by Ian R.

MacLeod is clearly meant to be an English foot-ball, i.e. a soccer ball — not the American football shown in Allen Koszowski's illustrations. A small point, maybe, but it seriously distracted me from the tale. To this we can only repeat (without excusing ourselves) the old adage that editing magazines is like assembling jigsaw puzzles against the clock. A hole in the issue appeared. The decision to include the story was made at the last moment. We called up Koszowski and said, "We need a couple spots of a football with eyes." The issue went together . . . and nobody noticed, until now. Argh, to use a technical term . . .

Michael Mayhew points out the same failing, but still finds "The Family Football" *a wonderful piece of skewed, but perfectly thought-out world logic. I found myself caught up in, and totally accepting the plight of these middle-class lycanthropes.* It's hardly Allen Koszowski's fault that we forgot to tell him what kind of football it was, but does this suggest that a thousand words is worth a picture? Mr. Mayhew also has high praise for Schow's "Gills" as "very witty and reminiscent of Robert Deveraux's writing," and he also had good things to say about "Movin' On," "Kill Me Hideously," and "The Giant Vorviades." Regarding the latter, he asks about the pronunciations of some of the imaginary names, to which we can only reply that since the names *are* imaginary, there is no "right" way to pronounce them. We tend to apply English phonetics with just a faint trace of foreign exoticism, but nothing even as elaborate as silent letters or dicritical marks. Thus: "Vorviades" is pronounced Voor-VIE-a-dees, the last syllable being like the Greek, "Herakles," etc. Sekenre, our popular 300-year-old adolescent sorcerer, has a name misspelled from the ancient Egyptian, which he probably pronounces "Sekh-EN-ray."

Bob Waterman writes, *. . . the Tanith Lee story, "Unlocking the Golden Cage" was my favorite. Her story had a lot of "atmosphere," and her attention to detail had me reaching for a dictionary a couple of times. It took me into another world, a time I could escape to, and stories set before 1900 seem to make this possible for me. The fantastic seems more possible to me in settings before 1900. When I think of the category "Weird Tale," I think of Gothic images, candles, shadows, gloom, architecture, mist, dread, fear, high ceilings, and a deep personal loss, either physical or mental; from within or without.* This of course opens a very large aesthetic argument. Writers as diverse as Lovecraft, Fritz Leiber, and Stephen King have done very well with horrors appearing in the immediate, contemporary world. Bram Stoker got to have it both ways by setting the first four chapters of *Dracula* in remote Transylvania, then bringing his monster back home to London.

Elaine Weaver passed on an amusing comment from a family member who saw her reading Ramsey Campbell's "Kill Me Hideously," which was, *must be a love story.* Mr. Campbell would probably nod sagely, smile with just a hint of amused menace and say, "Well, yes."

The Most Popular story in issue 315, a little bit, but not all that much to our chagrin, as if we were the host who just upstaged all our own guests, turned out to be Darrell Schweitzer's "The Giant Vorviades," which narrowly edged out Ramsey Campbell's "Kill Me Hideously" and Tanith Lee's "Unlocking the Golden Cage," which tied for second place. These three were well ahead of the rest. Third place goes to John Gregory Betancourt for "Sympathy for Zombies." Ω

by S.T. Joshi

The subject of weird poetry appears today to be little discussed, and the poetry itself little read, for a variety of reasons having much to do with the overall status of poetry in our society. We need hardly be told that poetry has been, for long periods in Western history, not merely the dominant but in some cases the only mode of literary expression; so how has it come about that poetry is now so little a part of even the literate person's cultural baggage? Modern poetry seems utterly irrelevant to our present-day concerns, and most of us would be at a loss to name even a single contemporary poet who could authentically be called great. Is it that we have become insensitive to poetry, or that the poets themselves (as Lord Dunsany, unremittingly hostile to the tendencies of modern poetry, famously put it) have "failed in their duty" to express their age in a way that readers can understand? My own view is strongly on the side of Dunsany, as I will hope to explain as this column progresses.

But the domain of poetry offers much that can satisfy the devotee of the weird. Certainly, the pedigree of the fantastic in poetry is as old as poetry itself, if such instances in classical verse as Odysseus' descent into the underworld (*Odyssey*, Book 9), the various grisly or horrific scenes in ancient tragedy (Oedipus' self-blinding in Sophocles' *Oedipus Rex*, the deaths of Creon and his daughter in Euripides' *Medea*, and many scenes in the Roman playwright Seneca's tragedies), and Catullus' mad "Attis poem" (in which that hapless demigod castrates himself out of frustrated love for his own mother, Cybele) attest. Moving several centuries forward, we find the Romantic poets revelling in the weird —

Coleridge's imperishable *Rime of the Ancient Mariner,* Keats's *Lamia*, the spectral ballads of Thomas Moore and James Hogg, and so many others, culminating in the small but immensely influential body of Poe's verse, which was nearly as great a landmark in our field as his short fiction. Much of the best of this work can be found, of course, in August Derleth's compilation *Dark of the Moon* (Arkham House, 1947), although recent research has revealed that many of the selections were in fact made by Donald Wandrei, who was much more knowledgeable in the history of English poetry than Derleth was. I had once thought that, aside from the omission of *Lamia* and some other items I will mention presently, *Dark of the Moon* was well-nigh definitive; but my colleague Dan Clore is at work on an anthology of 17th-, 18th-, and 19th-century weird poetry whose selections will differ significantly from Derleth, and will unearth much meritorious work from such writers as Emily Dickinson, Thomas Hardy, and others not included in *Dark of the Moon.*

Two of the most noted omissions from the Derleth anthology were the weird poems of Ambrose Bierce (1842–1914?) and his pupil, George Sterling (1869–1926). Bierce, of course, was primarily a satirist, both in prose and verse; and the two large volumes of his *Collected Works* (1909–12) devoted to his poetry contain only a relatively small number of items that could be labelled weird. But among them are several distinctive dream-fantasies, several futuristic poems, and a number of cosmic verses that dimly anticipate the work of some of his successors. It was probably these last items that led Bierce to embrace the work of Sterling, whom he had known since the 1890s. Sterling's long "star poem," *The Testimony of the Suns,* is indeed a riot of cosmic imagery, and Bierce was so taken with Sterling that he deemed another long (and more purely horrific) poem, "A Wine of Wizardry," a greater work than *Hamlet!* This is of course a bit of an exaggeration, but Bierce was not far wrong in saying that Sterling had added something unique to literature. Sterling became a master of the sonnet, and some of his finest weird effects are embodied in that form, as in "The Black Vulture":

Aloof upon the day's unmeasured dome,
   He holds unshared the silence of the sky.
   Far down his bleak, relentless eyes descry
The eagle's empire and the falcon's home —
Far down, the galleons of sunset roam;
   His hazards on the sea of morning lie;
   Serene, he hears the broken tempest sigh
Where cold sierras gleam like scattered foam.

And least of all he holds the human swarm —
   Unwitting now that envious men prepare
      To make their dream and its fulfilment
one,
When, poised above the caldrons of the storm,
   Their hearts, contemptuous of death shall
dare
      His roads between the thunder and the
sun.

Is it any wonder that Sterling himself served as the mentor of the young Clark Ashton Smith (1893–1961) when the latter hesitantly showed his early poems to "the poet laureate of San Francisco" in 1911? It was Sterling who, as Bierce had done before him, tutored Smith in the niceties of meter, diction, imagery, and symbolism; Sterling who shepherded Smith's early volumes of poetry, from *The Star-Treader* (1912) to *Sandalwood* (1925), into print; Sterling whose suicide in 1926 was so traumatic to Smith that it was perhaps a significant factor in his shift away from poetry to prose fiction in the later 1920s. Clark Ashton Smith is not merely the finest weird poet of all time, but, if there is any justice in the world, one of the finest American poets of the century, and his *Selected Poems* (Arkham House, 1971) would be regarded as a landmark if literary history had not taken a very different direction at the very time that Sterling and Smith were producing their best work.

The 1920s is currently remembered as the era of Modernism; one would like to think that in the distant future it will be judged as the period when literature and perhaps other arts took a wrong turn that has condemned entire branches of aesthetics to irrelevance. Poetry is one of these. Whereas Sterling, Smith, and other conservative poets of their day still found strength and inspiration (as all artists up to their time had done) in the great work of the past — specifically, the poetry of Keats, Shelley, and Swinburne — the Modernists were so overwhelmed by the cultural heritage of prior ages that they felt that only a complete break from the past could cause their work to be "original" and vital. They failed to observe Ambrose Bierce's dictum: "The best innovation is superior excellence. The great men are those who excel in their art as they find it; the revolutionaries are commonly second and third rate men — and they do not revolutionize anything." We all know the result. Poetry fundamentally split into two types: one type, headed by William Carlos Williams (with posthumous support from Walt Whitman), regarded conventional metrical poetry as too restrictive, and so poetry became more like prose, and in many instances indistinguishable from it; another type was em-

bodied by T. S. Eliot, Ezra Pound, Hart Crane, and their followers, who, while also abandoning formal metre, felt that poetry must be "difficult" to express a complex and difficult age, and as a result their work became esoteric, obscure, and well-nigh incomprehensible even to the majority of literate readers.

To my mind, however, if poetry is not kept distinct from prose — not merely in terms of rhythm and metre, but also in terms of imagery, metaphor, and symbolism — then it is nothing. It is simply bad prose.

If the Modernists had paid some attention to their humble fellow-poets in the weird tradition, they might not have brought poetry to the dire state it is in. Many members of what has been called the "Lovecraft circle" produced outstanding verse, and did so very largely because they adhered to traditional metrical forms; but they also filled their poetry with the pungent metaphors and images that create an unbridgeable gap between verse and prose and render poetry the highest expression of the human aesthetic sense.

Lovecraft himself was by no means the leading poet of his own literary circle, and he knew it. Setting Clark Ashton Smith aside as an unapproachable pinnacle, Lovecraft's verse cannot even be judged comparable to that of some of his younger colleagues, whom he far outstripped in prose fiction. My edition of Lovecraft's *Fantastic Poetry* (Necronomicon Press, 1990, 1993) does contain a modicum of good work; but my forthcoming edition of Lovecraft's *The Ancient Track: Complete Poetical Works* (Necronomicon Press) — which will include even scraps of verse buried in published and unpublished letters — will be of interest only because we long ago reached the stage where every word of Lovecraft's, good or bad, is of some interest.

Donald Wandrei (1908–1987) perhaps ranks second only to Smith as a weird poet. He himself was thrilled by Smith's *Ebony and Crystal* when he read it in 1923, and he began corresponding with Smith the next year — two years before he ever came in touch with Lovecraft. Wandrei's two early volumes of poetry, *Ecstasy* (1928) and *Dark Odyssey* (1931), are choice items for the collector; scarcely less so is his *Poems for Midnight* (Arkham House, 1964), with its 750-copy print run. That volume, however, failed to include several poems from his earlier collections, as well as a number of uncollected poems, necessitating my edition of his *Collected Poems* (Necronomicon Press, 1988).

Frank Belknap Long (1901–1994) was also an able poet, although his output was slimmer and more uneven than Wandrei's. He too produced two early collections of poetry much sought after by the collector, *A Man from Genoa* (1926) and *The Goblin Tower* (1935; typeset by Lovecraft and R. H. Barlow), as well as a later gathering of his best work, *In Mayan Splendor* (Arkham House, 1977). But like Wandrei, Long omitted a number of his poems from this volume, and the remainder have now been gathered up in Perry M. Grayson's 1995 compilation, *The Darkling Tide* (Tsathoggua Press [6442 Pat Avenue, West Hills, CA 91307]).

The verse of Robert E. Howard (1906–1936) also deserves mention, and the slim Arkham House collection *Always Comes Evening* (1957) gathers only a small proportion of it. Howard's verse may be as voluminous as Lovecraft's, and it deserves to be assembled.

The members of the Lovecraft circle did their best poetic work in the 1920s and 1930s. Smith, of course (although in this context it is unfair to consider him in any sense a satellite of Lovecraft), went on to great work well into the 1950s. It is a shame that Derleth (himself a noted poet, although not primarily in the weird vein) delayed publication of Smith's *Selected Poems* for so long: Smith had completed assembling the volume by 1949, but Arkham House's financial difficulties of the 1950s, along with the general difficulty of selling large volumes of poetry, delayed publication until 1971, years after Smith's own death and just prior to Derleth's own. Hundreds of Smith's poems remain uncollected and unpublished, and it would probably require two or three large volumes to gather them all. David E. Schultz has long been at work on such a project, and we hope not merely that he can finish the job soon, but that some publisher will have the sense to issue it.

Since Smith's heyday, no one has attained to his eminence as a weird poet. Joseph Payne Brennan (1918–1990) did creditable work, and his *Sixty Selected Poems* (New Establishment Press, 1985) is an admirable volume. Arkham House has continued to issue limited editions of various poets, among them Stanley McNail and Donald Sidney-Fryer. McNail's *Something Breathing* (1965) was reissued in an expanded edition in 1987 by Embassy Hall Editions (Berkeley, CA), while Sidney-Fryer's *Songs and Sonnets Atlantean* (1972) is already two and a half decades old, and the author has done much good work in the interim; let us hope that his recent verse may appear soon. Of recent Arkham House volumes of poetry, perhaps only Richard L. Tierney's *Collected Poems* (1981) is noteworthy. G. Sutton Breiding, Bruce Boston, and many others in the small press have produced fine work, but their poetry is little read outside of a small band of devotees.

Now, however, two relatively young poets have stepped forward to claim the mantle of Sterling, Smith, and Wandrei. Their work in many ways reflects the dichotomy we find in modern poetry in general.

Keith Allen Daniels' *Satan Is a Mathematician: Poems of the Weird, Surreal and Fantastic* is issued by his Anamnesis Press (P.O. Box 51115, Palo Alto, CA 94303; their e-mail address is anamnesis@compuserve.com; $12.95), while Brett Rutherford has brought out *Whippoorwill Road* through Grim Reaper Books, a subdivision of his The Poet's Press (175 Fifth Avenue #2424, New York, NY 10010; $24.95). These are not either poet's first book by any means: Daniels made his debut with the exceptional volume *What Rough Book* (Anamnesis Press, 1992), while *Whippoorwill Road* gathers together the weird verse from Rutherford's many previous volumes. They are comparable in many ways, contrasting in others, and perhaps most interesting in exhibiting both the virtues and the failings of the modern poetic muse.

In his somewhat aggressive introduction Daniels resurrects the argument from C. P. Snow's lecture *The Two Cultures* — lamenting the intellectual cleavage between the humanities and the sciences — and hopes that his work can do its small part to bridge the gap. Daniels himself has a "daylight career in polymer science and engineering," and his back cover boasts a blurb from Roald Hoffmann, a Nobel laureate in chemistry. It is all very good to attempt to infuse the findings of science with poetic feeling, but I am not sure that Daniels has found the proper way of doing it. Consider the opening lines of "Bight of Sonic Blasters":

In benthic valleys where cetaceans wail,
half hidden by the veils of filtered sight,
with *gonyaulax* polluting every scale
and vesicle inherent in the bight
of sonic blasters . . .

I suppose Daniels would simply call me ignorant for not knowing the meanings of several of the scientific words used here, but I think there is a greater underlying problem that he fails to see: the plain fact that many scientific terms do not have sufficient poetic resonance to generate a poetic response. Much of Daniels' work in this volume is opaque (thereby embodying the second type of Modernism I outlined above), not merely because of the abundance of unexplained scientific terms, but because Daniels has resolved upon a tortured and contrived manner of utterance that defies comprehension by even the most alert reader.

I hope I am not revealing my prejudices when I say that almost all the memorable and notable poems in *Satan Is a Mathematician* (and there are many) are those that follow strict metrical schemes. In this book there are some uncommonly fine sonnets, as well as poems written in pentameter blank verse, regular quatrains, and the like. And Daniels has learned the all-important secret of verse: that the message must be conveyed by means of imagery, metaphor, and symbolism rather than by plain statement. Consider a few simple lines from one of the finest of the poems, a series called "Sciomancy Nights." One section, "An Evening with Aldous Huxley," has the following:

[he] knew . . . that dying's just a glitch,
a transitory bummer in the now
of being.

The range of tone in the book — from pensive reflection to tart satire to cosmic fantasy to outrageous humor and grotesquerie — is notable. If one could prevail upon Daniels to be a trifle less esoteric, then one might confidently predict that he is on the way to becoming a not unworthy successor to his idol, Clark Ashton Smith.

The first thing that strikes us about *Whipporwill Road* is that it is a superlative job of book production, in the finest tradition of Thomas Bird Mosher and Roy A. Squires. Rutherford himself notes: "The binding is done by hand, employing gluing, side sewing, and a cloth-reinforced spine. The outer wraparound covers are made from hand-made or artists' papers." And much of the contents fully equals the meticulous quality of the physical product.

Rutherford embodies the first type of Modernism I enunciated above, in which the rhythmical distinction between prose and verse is muted, and sometimes disappears altogether. Many of the poems are, I regret to say, nothing but prose. But there are enough genuine poems to redeem the volume. In the remarkable "Fête" (Rutherford's own favorite poem) we find not only the striking expression "I am Love's Antichrist" but the following flawless stanza:

I cough a cloud and let it blot the moon
so that no distant star may hear and mock
the oath that is sworn in the hidden copse.
Here! now even fireflies are dimming out,
now ravens avert their ebony orbs,
now sputter and die, ye will o' the wisp!
Not even a random thought can penetrate
this furry arbor of my wretchedness.

Or this from "He's Going to Kill Me Tonight":

Midnight. The Reaper's shift begins.
The minute hand tips past Reason,
careens into Murder's tithe of night.

The division of the poems into loosely thematic groupings is singularly felicitous, with the result that each poem strengthens or adds color to the others, and all gain a cumulative power by adroit juxtaposition. Perhaps the only drawback in the book is an unwarrantedly lengthy section at the back in which Rutherford, telling of the genesis of the poems, leaves himself open to charges of self-praise by the tenor of some of his remarks. Poets should resist the temptation to comment on their own work — at least in the manner that Rutherford does. But this is a small flaw in an otherwise highly creditable volume.

Why is it that poetry is no longer read? Why is it that there are, quite literally, more poets than readers of poetry? Some of it has to do with education: the schools do not teach the appreciation of poetry anymore. A large part of it has to do with the tendencies of modern poetry, which have alienated many potential readers with obscurity or prosiness. But weird verse has been inherently conservative, and appears to draw its greatest strengths from that circumstance. It is perhaps too early to state that poetry is a dying art; but we can at least maintain with confidence that, with poets like Keith Allen Daniels and Brett Rutherford, weird verse will continue to flourish for some time.

Two new books relating to Lovecraft call for some notice. *Lovecraft Remembered* (Arkham House, 1998; $29.95) is Peter Cannon's magisterial compilation of memoirs of the Providence writer, culled not only from previous Arkham House books but many other sources. Containing 65 items divided into seven broad categories, the book also features an incisive introduction and introductory notes to each of the sections by Cannon. No memoir of importance has been left out, and the volume can be regarded as well-nigh definitive. A striking dust jacket by Jason C. Eckhardt is the capstone to a book whose attractiveness in typeface, design, and binding is exemplary.

Still more physically sumptuous is *In Lovecraft's Shadow: The Cthulhu Mythos Stories of August Derleth* (Mycroft & Moran, 1998; $59.95), edited by Joseph Wrzos. Its chief feature is an array of superb illustrations by Stephen E. Fabian, along with a vivid color cover. Of the actual contents of the volume I am not much inclined to speak: Derleth seriously misconstrued the bases, and in some cases the details, of Lovecraft's pseudomythology, and in any event his stories are simply of poor quality as gauged by common standards of plotting, character description, and style.

The title of the book is therefore apt: Derleth is clearly in Lovecraft's shadow and likely to remain there. But Fabian's illustrations are in themselves worth the price of admission.   Ω

DAGGERS AND A SERPENT
by Keith Taylor

illustrated by Stephen E. Fabian

I.

The raiders came out of the desert like a sudden storm that whirled against Anubis's temple. Despite its high walls and pyloned gateways, it was no fortress. The Libyan savages swarmed over the walls of the outer court in moments, avid for plunder. In a moment more they had opened the bronze-hinged cedar gates. The guards who sought to stop them were speared or clubbed down, and their blood flowed in dark streams.

Other raiders rushed through the open gates to join the desert men. This second group sweated in ribbed horsehair corselets and padded caps with swinging tassels. Better disciplined than the naked tribesmen, they trotted forward under the weight of a long bronze-headed ram. From above, on the walls, their ram looked like a stiff-bodied centipede with sixty fateful legs.

Wheels rumbling, a war-chariot drove into the public courtyard. Its naked driver reined the horses back, while his passenger raised a hand and shouted orders. Lean, forceful, he wore a red pleated kilt and headcloth. The bearing of a prince marked him out — but a prince of bandits.

His soldiers swung back the ram, then heaved it forward to crash on the gates of the roofed inner court, which was not accessible to climbers. The whole building boomed like a drum. Within, priests, priestesses, servitors, and scribes milled in confused terror. Most hardly believed it was happening. Temples were not attacked in Egypt . . . it never occurred . . .

The second set of gates burst in. Libyans and men-at-arms charged together, yelling. The soldiers had been drugged with a potion that excited them to fury, as well as numbing their souls to fear of the gods; and they had been brutal men before drinking their lord's potion. Here was slaughter, the smell of new blood. Here before them lay victims and loot. The Libyans had their own gods, and in any case were outright bandits to whom anything in Egypt was fair plunder. They would slay and rob their present allies joyfully if a chance ever came. Surging through the smashed gates, they all behaved alike.

Wide-bladed spears sank into bellies, to be twisted and yanked back, spilling gore. Axes swung down on shaven heads. Eyes bleary with sleep and wide with consternation bulged in the horrified realization of death, then saw nothing. The priestesses and other temple women suffered worse. Their screams rose on the night wind and were silenced in the end by knives.

Bloody excitement stirred the man in the chariot as he watched, though he tried to conceal it beneath a haughty bearing. His father had impressed upon him firmly that this was business. He decided, reluctantly, that these creatures had enjoyed themselves for long enough. Driving among them, he swung a long-lashed whip and called harshly for discipline. Soldiers and Libyans alike shrank from the lash as though it was something immeasurably more dreadful, pressing against the courtyard walls to avoid it.

"Empty the store-rooms," the man commanded loudly. "Strip the place of gold and precious stones. I will see to the shrine."

The captain of soldiers saluted. "Yes, lord."

They scurried to obey. Stepping down from his chariot, the leader stalked through the temple's vestibule, a tall figure muscled like a hunter of lions — which he had been from boyhood. Of lions, and women, and power.

At the entrance to the inner shrine, he did not even hesitate before parting the rich hangings.

Murals of Anubis covered the walls. Here he embalmed a body with meticulous patience, there he performed the ceremony of restoring the senses — "opening the mouth" — on an upright mummy, elsewhere he guided the soul to the afterworld. These were his functions as god of the dead, the Lord of Tombs. The man in red smiled scornfully.

His glance moved to the diorite image of Anubis, with its golden kilt and jewelled trappings. The Announcer carried daggers. Around his forearm coiled a viper, the ancient instrument of death for a Pharoah. His head, traditionally, was that of a jackal, with snout and pointed ears.

Before the image stood a lean old priest. He peered like a mole in the yellow lamp-light. The

by Keith Taylor

intruder supposed there was little chance of this one recognising him, despite his noble rank, not that it mattered. Probably all he saw was a blurred figure.

"You are doomed beyond hope," the priest said in a surprisingly steady voice. "Do you not fear?"

"What? This?" The bandit leader waved an arm at the jackal-headed image of black diorite. "None of it has moved me since I was a boy, old priest. I should fear to strike against a temple of Amun-Ra, since he is revered by the Pharoah, and holds the great power of being in fashion. Likewise Osiris, who is both royal and beloved. But the jackals. No one remembers him while the blood runs hot, only when their time comes to die — and his Arch-Priest is not close to the circles of power. I have no fear."

"Then as well as a murderer, you are a fool. The Arch-Priest of Anubis is the greatest magician in all of Kheml. I do not pity your doom; you have earned it. But I pity your ignorance."

"Indeed." The man in red smiled mockingly — but his eyes flashed with stung conceit. He was young.

He shook out the lash of his whip and struck with it. Cubits of thin braided leather coiled around the old priest's body. The intruder uttered the words of a spell that made his throat vibrate, brief though it was. Then he loosened the whip with a motion of his arm and pulled it back.

The priest made a ghastly noise. Worse ones followed, though they did not issue from his mouth. His head began to twist inexorably on his neck. He tottered, then fell, as his legs turned around in the same way, with the hideous cracklings and tearings of complete dislocation at the hips. Muscles stood out in distortion through his skin.

After an excessively long while, he lay still on the floor of the inner shrine. His eyes stared at the dark ceiling, and his skinny toes pointed in the same direction, yet he did not lie on his back. His knobbed spine and shrunken buttocks faced upward, while his belly pressed against the floor, in a disconcerting and abhorrent reversal.

Traces of revulsion even touched the man in red, though morbid curiosity and the thrill of lethal power were far more strongly felt. He worked his shoulders back and forth as though to release tension. Then he briskly tore head-dress, armlets, collar, belt, and golden kilt from the statue of Anubis. Quenching the golden lamps, he tore them down, thrusting them into a sack with his other plunder. Leaving, he ordered a minion to take the precious hangings from the doorway.

A plain massive barge waited at the water-side to receive the loot. The brigand-noble supervised the loading to be sure that no one cheated. His whip trailed freely from his hand.

"Greatest magician in all of Khem," he repeated, smiling ironically. "Yes, I have heard that, Kamose, you whom sots and fools call Satni-Kamose. I have heard that and other rumours, too. But what charlatan does not make such claims?"

The barge sat low in the water as it moved out from the temple quay. People who might have come running from nearby villages chose to hide their heads and see nothing. The barge moved down a well-maintained canal towards the Nile. Looking back, the man in red saw the Libyans moving into the desert by the light of the temple's blazing gates. He dryly commended them to the care of their father Set.

A good night's work. My father plans the attack. I lead it. The Libyans, conveniently out of reach, take all the blame but a lesser share of the plunder. Let the upstart Kamose find the truth, if he is such a master of the sorcerous arts.

II.

"Shape of the black crocodile? May their bodies be accursed! May the destruction of Set fall upon them! They shall eat no food in the after-world, their names shall be expunged from life, they shall belong to the Devourer!"

The outburst of passion ended. Kamose, Arch-Priest of Anubis, returned to his ebony chair and sat brooding in anger. His linen robe hung in two parts from his upper body, he having torn it to the waist when he heard the news of the temple sack. The messenger who had brought those abominable tidings remained kneeling, discreetly quiet.

Kamose repressed his fury to a contained seething. *"Who?"*

"Savages from the west, holy one. Desert men. Libyans.

"So." Kamose looked again at the written report he had been given, his eyes and mind now intent; rage gained nothing. It made a man a fool. "Those children of darkness."

The missive was not in formal heiroglyphs. Kamose deigned to read it anyhow, a sign of his outrage. He twice studied the passage which described the condition of his subordinate priest's body, with the head and legs twisted backwards.

"You may leave," he told the messenger. "Say to my major-domo that I command food, drink, and raiment for you, after a bath."

Sitting alone, he considered the atrocity. Kamose was tall, with an air of sombre but great vitality, muscled more like a soldier than a priest. His hands and skin, however, were definitely those of a scribe. He carried Syrian blood from his grandmother; it showed in his blade of a nose and narrow, somewhat tilted eyes. Kamose shaved his head and observed all the other strictures of his priestly station, except for a little pointed chin-beard. He supposed it was his Syrian strain that led him to prefer it. Besides, it saved trouble. Ritual prescribed a false beard of like size and shape in any case, for certain occasions.

Frowning, he walked out on one of the terraces of his mansion. All around him lay fanes of gods and mortuary temples of former kings, with cemeteries of huge extent in between. Abdu was more a great necropolis than a town. At its western side, among the low desert hills, lay the dark granite temple of Anubis. It was far larger and older than the temple at Bahari which had been looted, but no more sacred to the jackal-headed god, Foremost of the Westerners. That was to say, Lord of the Dead.

Kamose administered all such temples. In addition he held charge over the graceful mortuary temple of Pharoah Seti, the Ramesseum itself, and many others. Their endowments were immense. Having them in his control had made him a number of jealous enemies, such as the entire priesthood of Thoth. Kamose wondered if some of them could be responsible for this horror. The first step in a scheme to discredit him?

Shrugging the torn robe back upon his shoulders, Kamose went thoughtfully to his own chamber. There he found Mertseger, and she was restless. Instead of discreetly keeping to the form of a tall, supple woman, she had let her legs merge into the mottled tail of a large serpent, while her forearms had grown scaly and taloned. Yet the sight was not horrible.

A lethal, ancient fascination invested her, springing, as Kamose well knew, from the most lurid fancies of man.

Half lifting from her couch in the rags of a purple gown, she looked at her master from ophidian eyes and greeted him with a kiss.

"Such transformations are ill in

this house," he said harshly. "You know that. I prefer that my servants imagine you to be a mortal woman."

"Then set me free!" Her tail lashed about, found a leg of the couch arid coiled in frustration around it. "To offend me by holding me captive so far from my home is a fatal thing, magician."

"To threaten me before you are able is foolish, too. Freedom? I think not, O Mertseger. Having delivered Buto from your haunting, and increased my fame in the Delta thereby, I would undo my credit if I allowed you to return. Besides," he added, "your needs are too malign, as wives and mothers bereaved can attest."

"What do you care for those mortals?"

"Little, perhaps, and yet I had a wife and children once."

The lamia hissed in mockery, running a forked tongue out between her delectable human lips. The contrast would have appalled a normal man; Kamose felt amused and aroused. Being a magician, he knew that Mertseger's perverse allure was her means of drawing victims to her embrace, and knew equally how they ended, but he stood in no such danger. Rather, peril to the lamia attended *him*. And she could assume a completely human shape when she willed, a socially advantageous power not shared by Kamose's other leman, the she-sphinx Nonmet.

"Once," she said. "As mortals reckon time, it was long ago, Satni-Kamose. You have changed much."

"While you have lived many times longer than I, and in all those millennia changed not, nor learned a thing." He ignored her use of the erroneous nickname bestowed on him by the vulgar.

"I am content," Mertseger answered, coiling. "And you? Did all that you learned from the Scrolls of Thoth increase your felicity?"

A smoking anger kindled in Kamose's eyes. He held his features impassive. "Daughter of serpents, don't seek, to provoke me. You might have the misfortune to succeed. Transform!"

She hissed again.

"Transform, Mertseger, or I deal with you harshly."

Scaly forearms softened. The talons became feminine hands. Mertseger's deadly tail shrank and bifurcated.

Kamose nodded. "You may be able to sate your appetites again. Men have sacked one of my temples with slaughter. When I learn who —"

"My good lord." Mertseger looked melting. She curled her human legs under her, posing in purple tatters. "I regret the gown. But your own robe is conveniently rent."

"So it is."

Kamose took her in his arms. Even Mertseger's serpent-tongue was now human, pink and flat, as the occasion proved perfect for him to discover and appreciate. With the increase of her pleasure her tongue reverted to the ophidian, not that Kamose minded greatly. Later still, her lower body changed back to the coils of a glittering snake, writhing and undulating. This presented her lover with a greater challenge. However, it was not his first experience of that, and he proved equal to the situation. But prudence dictated, even to him, that he should not sleep beside Mertseger. He stayed wakeful while she drowsed until the morning.

In the grey hours, memories hummed around him like gnats. After the tragedies of his youth he had travelled widely, learned to extend his life span, and on returning to Egypt, lived as an ascetic hermit for years — but he had wearied of that, finally. Again he entered human society, became a priest and arch-priest (with a great deal of hidden sardonic amusement) and turned to sensuous pleasures once more (though not quite of the ordinary sort).

Egypt had come to lamentable days. Kamose was not disposed to shudder and wail over this, since he knew how transient are both good and unfortunate times. Still, lawless plunder did not suit him; he had immense estates and wealth in his charge that might be ravaged by such action. He also had a dreadful patron in the shape of the mortuary god, to whom even he must render an account.

The stars grew pale. In his aspect as Khepri the Regenerate, the Sun appeared across the Nile. Mertseger awoke, stretching sensuously. She heard Kamose say firmly, "We travel to Badari, daughter of serpents. Prepare."

"Badari. Is that where — ?"

"Where the temple was despoiled, yes."

Mertseger hurried. Kamose had half-promised the villain responsible would be her prey, once he was exposed. Her heart beat like a young girl's.

III.

Kamose bowed low before the desecrated statue of Anubis. Although he knew well that gods were not perfect beings, and further that many of their attributes and legends were made by the men who worshipped them, he had long been bleakly aware that they existed and held fateful power. The jackal-headed lord of death at least was fair; he treated everyone alike.

Kamose had fasted and ceremonially washed. He wore a robe of seamless linen. In his hands he held a silver bowl filled with Nile water, which he placed on the bare altar.

"O Foremost of the Westerners, Announcer of Death, you who foresee destiny, reveal to your servant who hath done this impious crime! Let judgement and retribution befall them."

Kamose bent forward, staring into the transparent water. Incised at the bottom of the bowl was a picture of Anubis. Under Kamose's unwinking gaze the picture stirred, moved, and walked forward across the surface of polished silver, to vanish from sight and be replaced by other gods in procession. Horus the Living Falcon, son and avenger of Osiris; Sekhmet the Lioness, fierce, unpitying, armed with the scorching heat of the Sun; Isis and Nepthys, the mistresses of magic and mourners of Osiris; Osiris himself, wrapped as a royal mummy but with skin green as the verdure of renewed life; Thoth, vizier of the gods, ibis-headed divine scribe. Kamose's skin prickled coldly as he beheld that limning. Thoth was an even greater lord of magic and prophecy than Anubis, but Kamose had been out of favour with him for many, many years — ever since, as a youth hungry for knowledge, he had stolen from a tomb the master-scrolls of magic which Thoth had written.

Contempt changed the shape of Kamose's mouth as he remembered that young man — a dreamy, studious fool. He was gone now, perished as Crete, lost as Troy, and good riddance. Thoth had punished that theft in full measure. Kamose had to control a boiling of rebellious hatred even now, almost a hundred years later.

The water clouded. Shapes moved murkily through a mist of blood. Libyan tribesmen in tall head-dresses slew, raped, and then plundered. Soldiers of Egypt burst the temple doors. An arrogant figure killed the priest unpleasantly with one light lash of an enchanted whip. His face appeared clearly. Behind it loomed another face, considerably older, austere, cynical, and tired, yet resembling the younger man's to a marked degree.

The water grew transparent again, and for a moment, cut on the bottom of the bowl, Kamose saw a number instead of the formal depiction of Anubis — the number thirteen. The water rippled, the number was gone, and once more Kamose saw a jackal-headed figure bearing daggers and a viper.

"My thanks, great one," he murmured.

The revelation had been clear. Two nobles were the culprits, one senior, one young, very likely related if that strong resemblance was a guide; and the younger had led this blasphemous raid in collusion with Libyan bandits. Thirteen could only mean the Thirteenth Nome — the province of Sawty.

Treading slowly, a deep scowl on his forehead, Kamose went out through the roofed courtyard and the broken, leaning gates. Though the temple had been cleansed with water and sand, it still smelled of blood. The sacrilegious reek stung his nostrils.

Men shall die, and worse than die, for this act.

With an executioner's look in his eyes, he left the temple and went to the nearby house of embalming. Rows of cadavers which had been his priests and priestesses lay there, dessicating in beds of dry natron. Kamose examined them. He took particular notice of the chief priest's body. The embalmers had turned his wizened head the right way around on his shoulders once more. They had also seen fit to amend the reversal of his legs and fit the dislocated femurs back into his hip-joints, but the torn, distorted muscles told their story to Kamose even before he questioned the undertakers. He remembered what he had seen in the divinatory bowl.

"The whip of Selket," he said aloud. "Very few such lashes exist. When I find one — belike in Sawty — I have found my murderers. But first let me deal with that desert scum."

Kamose kept a vigil in the plundered temple that night, before the statue of Anubis, that would have seared another man's soul to ashes. Holding a viper and a dagger in his naked hands,

he invoked his jackal-headed lord. Also, he addressed himself to other gods of the dead: Neith, Wepwawet, and the slain and resurrected Osiris, "He Who Makes Silence." But Thoth's name he did not speak.

A black night wind blew through the outer courts and into the shrine. Bats and owls flew above the roof. Ghouls crept out of their lairs in ancient cemeteries to stare with purulent eyes at the temple, though they dared not come too near. Something they sensed or foresaw seemed to amuse them; now and then, one gave a shout of hideous laughter.

At midnight, a little golden jackal appeared. After circling the temple several times, it came padding through the burst gates, shrinking with each forward step. It showed no fear of the ghouls, which was strange. Nor did one of the vile grey shapes molest it. They allowed it to pass, and it almost crept on its belly through the inner court, whining as though summoned on a journey it would rather not make, by a power it could not resist.

"Welcome, little brother," Kamose said, turning.

Bending, he seized the jackal and raised it towards the plundered statue of Anubis. The beast gave a piteous yelp of terror and twisted convulsively in Kamose's hands. He held fast. The statue's red eyes seemed to glitter with awareness.

In an instant, the jackal became heavy as granite. Kamose quivered with the effort of holding it. With reverent dread he set the little beast back on the floor. It slunk out. Something dreadful, which it carried now like a burden, had possessed it.

It vanished like a shadow through the pylons of the outer gateway. No one reported seeing it again, but its tracks, unnaturally deep, led into the western desert before the wind brushed them away. It travelled deeper into the wastes, night after night, resting by day, neither eating nor drinking.

Long after it should have perished, the jackal reached a large Libyan camp. Music, singing, and festive laughter came to its sharply pricked ears. Looting the temple of Anubis had made these people prosperous. They celebrated freely. They feasted and danced. The jackal crept closer until the firelight gleamed in its eyes.

Then it rushed the camp. A horrible cry of release burst from its throat, enough to make the stars quiver. Asses and other cattle fled wildly into the desert as the jackal raced from hearth to hearth, but not one human creature fled, although there was much screaming. And all human voices in the end were silent.

The jackal was not seen by mortal eyes again.

IV.

"O my father, let us repeat this action!" The young man's eyes glittered with anticipation as he swigged beer, the rich dark beer made from barley and dates. "There are temples and to spare, the land abounds in them. Half belong to outworn gods, ill serviced and guarded; and the times are lawless. Who will suspect us? We can do as we please."

"Not yet, my son." Watab, Prince of the Thirteenth Nome, smiled like a crocodile. "There is a war to fight with our accursed neighbours. Have you forgotten that we needed the temple gold only to hire mercenaries? The plunder of the whole Twelfth Nome is more than the wealth of any temple, and we can pass off this private campaign as loyalty to Pharoah. Our old foes have been indiscreet at last. I have waited and planned for this longer than you have been alive."

"I yearn for the day we will make an end of them!" the younger noble said. He was not wearing red now. "Let's hire the mercenaries, then. Kushite bowmen. Shardana sworders. I'll drive my chariot through their gardens in the high blaze of noon!" He drew the lash of his long whip through his fingers.

"All that and more." His father pointed to the whip. "However, leave that toy behind, Paheri. Its effect is too distinctive. You performed your raid well, except for that one thing. Using the whip of Selket on the priest was an error."

"No doubt. I had a concern that I might encounter magic and need some swift magic of my own, but there was none." Paheri shrugged. "So much for the powers of Anubis."

Prince Watab's mouth drew downward in a bitter, weary expression. "I ceased to believe in the powers of any god long since, my son — or at least in their care for the actions of men and women. Clearly they have deserted us. Weak successors of the mighty Usermare contend for the Double Crown, and leave us princes and chiefs to battle likewise. Justice is no more than a feather in the wind. We cannot afford principle. We can only secure the future for our descendants in such ways as are left, and hope that for them there will be better times. This is ill, but it must be. Remember that. Always be cunning, ruthless, wary — but feign virtue well." He held out his hand for the whip. "And do not leave your signature upon any crime you commit."

"I'll remember that, father." Paheri showed a cheerfully cruel smile as he handed over the whip of Selket. "However, if I take alive any of those Twelfth Nome curs who slew my uncle and my brothers, I shall ask for that whip again."

"And shall have it."

"Falcon of the Sun!" Paheri exclaimed suddenly. "A ship is making for our quay! A prince's ship, by its appearance — or —"

Prince Watab shaded his pouched eyes and squinted. From the roof garden, he could see over the high walls of his mansion all the way to the river, though only poorly. Years, and the bright sun of Egypt, had impaired his sight. Not until the ship glided closer did he recognise it as a small galley with its sail spread to the wind. Except that its hull seemed dark, he could not perceive detail. However, his son owned sharp vision. Paheri discerned the emblem of a black jackal couchant upon a pedestal, displayed upon the galley's sail.

"Father," he said with seeming coolness, "a messenger from the temple of the dog presumes to visit us."

"So?" The prince's visage became like a formal mask. "Let us receive him."

Watab sat in haughty state to receive his guest, shaven head bare, body robed and jewelled. Paheri stood arrogantly behind him, bare to the waist except for collar and armlets. His military kilt of stiffened linen hung short on one side, long behind the right leg, in the royal fashion to which strictly speaking he had no right, despite his descent from a Pharoah. A sheathed sword lay nearby on a table. Two women with fans flanked the prince's chair, and a scribe with pen and papyrus sheets sat below the dais. Impassive soldiers guarded the door.

Watab's major-domo, a large and sonorous person, announced the visitor in a voice that cracked unprecedentedly.

"The Most Reverend Kamose, Arch-Priest of Anubis, lord."

Kamose entered, erect and saturnine. The soldiers at the door grew somewhat less impassive as he passed between them. Their eyes shifted uneasily to regard the priest-magician, as though guilt and foreboding had touched their spirits.

Kamose's own gaze remained fixed on the prince's dais. Robed in pleated linen, Kamose did not wear the full regalia of his office that day, neither the artificial leopard-skin nor the gemmed apron; only a broad collar, belt, and armlets of jet and gold. He carried a jackal-headed staff of black wood. Behind him walked lesser priests and scribes — and Mertseger, in spurious human form, robed as a priestess, the image of dedicated beauty. Paheri looked at her with lustful interest, and drew his own conclusions as to why she accompanied Kamose.

The lecherous foreign dog, he thought.

Kamose looked at the two nobles. Paheri's rashness and pride was easily read in his bearing. Watab covered his feelings better. His visage slack-skinned, gashed by lines of disillusion, still expressed authority and resolve. Father and son both had the symmetrical features of native Egyptians whose every remotest ancestor had been Egyptian too.

Their disdain for this upstart priest with a Syrian grandam was so complete they took it for granted. As the fact that they breathed air. Kamose had long been accustomed to that attitude. It amused him now. Even from criminals.

Watab said, "I make you welcome, holy one."

Kamose's tomb-black eyes held an implacable glitter as he regarded the prince. He answered grimly, "Thy welcome is rejected. I bring thee the judgement and condemnation of the lord of sepulchres, even Anubis. The reason is thy plunder and desecration of his temple, thy murder of his servants. I travel to the Delta now in order to place proofs before Pharoah. Therefore I bid thee and thy son Paheri to relinquish thy places in the world, and to accompany me in chains."

His words echoed from the stucco walls as though from the stone slabs of a deep grave-chamber — and the air seemed to darken. Paheri stared in amazement for a long time, then laughed contemptuously. His father's jaded, unscrupulous face showed a surge of furious blood.

"Madman! Will you slander us to the Living Horus? That shall mark the end of your priesthood."

"And perhaps of you," Paheri said, sneering.

"I have more proof than I require," Kamose said. "The least of it stands here. This woman is the priestess Mertseger, who survived the vile attack upon the temple wherein she served, and recognised thy son as the leading perpetrator, with his red garments and lethal whip. Also, divination bears out her testimony. The Libyan barbarians who were thy allies shall be brought manacled to witness against thee. Denial, therefore, cannot spare thee the consequences of thy blasphemous carnage."

"You are indeed mad," Watab repeated. "What is the testimony of savage brigands against a nomarch of Egypt? What are the divinations of a priest, one bribed no doubt by icy enemies? Your journey to the mouths of the Nile would be fruitless even if you were to arrive."

"Not that you shall," Paheri added. "Your journey ends here, *holy one*. Your witness, the woman, shall witness to nothing. Not you nor this retinue shall be seen again. Look around you. We keep many soldiers, O Kamose, and they answer to us, not to you or even to the Living Horus. These are evil times, wherein the power of the Double Crown is weak. The worse for you."

"But your enemies in the neighbour nome are strong," Kamose said calmly. "They will be glad of a pretext to attack you. If my galley comes to this port and goes no further, they will have their justification."

Paheri laughed aloud. "We have our own plans for those curs of the Hound Nome. Their treachery, not ours, is now established. Let them justify themselves if they can."

"Your galley will proceed downstream," Prince Watab said harshly. "Men dressed as you and your retinue will be seen on her decks. She *will* vanish before reaching the Delta, O fool, but not in my domain. You and your folk will sink with her. Meanwhile you may have accommodations in a strong storeroom. Take him away."

Two soldiers taller and stronger than Kamose converged upon him. He did not even glance at the hands that gripped his arms. His sombre gaze never left Prince Watab's face.

"Instead, depart with me and confess before Pharoah. You would be wise. I make this offer once.

"Twice, as I reckon, now," the prince answered ironically. "You wasted your breath to say it even once."

Kamose disdained a reply. He allowed the soldiers to remove him. As they departed, he heard Paheri say mirthfully, "I will attend to the woman."

V.

Kamose sat composed in subterranean darkness. He set his back against a great jar of oil. No light entered this cool storeroom below the foundations of Watab's mansion. Still, Kamose sensed the progress of the Sun with his sorcerer's perceptions. Twilight had passed, the stars had shone in the sky for a full hour, and Kamose sat in the dust of the storeroom as though at ease in one of his own temples.

His vessel, undoubtedly, had been overrun by the prince's men-at-arms shortly after Kamose had been cast into this dim prison. The priests and acolytes of his retinue would be lying bound in some similar place. Kamose smiled derisively as he thought of it. These rascals had something to learn.

The prince's son would surely be with Mertseger. He had boasted that he would attend to her. He! Attend — to Mertseger? Kamose's smile grew wicked.

The time was ripe.

"O great one, Anubis, Foremost of the Westerners, Lord of Tombs, Announcer, Restorer, God Who Opens the Way, send against this house the ones who have endured your retribution, even the Libyan robbers allied with Watab the Accursed. Send them now, out of the West that is thy realm. Kamose, Arch-Priest of thy temples, calls upon thee. Be it so."

The darkness in the shut storeroom could not have increased. Nevertheless, it seemed to thicken until it pressed on Kamose's skin. Baying from a vast distance, he heard the cry of a titanic jackal. Time flowed by like barely warm pitch. Kamose waited.

With his mind's vision he saw everything that transpired above. Loping, padding shapes moved through the night, standing more or less upright, anthropomorphic yet not human. They prowled through the grain-fields. Reaching Prince Watab's walled mansion, they began to clamber over the walls, just as other shapes had done at the doomed temple. A dozen skulking forms converged upon the gate-lodge facing the river. Kamose could imagine the choked cries, no doubt a wild shriek or two, and then the mortal silence.

I daresay I will soon enjoy release from this storeroom, he thought peacefully.

The door crashed wide before he had drawn another twenty breaths. Armed soldiers bearing lamps and weapons filed among the great sealed jars, the lined storage pits, and Watab himself followed. Rage and consternation warred in his face. Behind both, to Kamose's eyes, lay the beginnings of a ghastly fear. He struck Kamose twice in the face.

"Swine and progeny of swine! What have you done? What have you brought upon me?"

"You have brought it upon yourself. Let us go and see."

When Kamose walked from the storeroom, no one laid a hand upon him, but rather drew back from his presence. None mocked his appearance, either, though stubble had grown on his shaven scalp and dust thickly fouled his robe. One of Watab's soldiers whimpered, "Holy one — have mercy —"

Watab struck the soldier down, and thrust Kamose violently ahead of him. The priest laughed. They reached a portico that looked out upon Watab's cool gardens, with their fish-ponds, flower-beds, and costly foreign blooms. They brought no satisfaction to the prince now. He looked on them with bulging eyes and frothing lips, those walks of his that an hour ago had been secure pleasaunces.

Corpses floated in the nearest pond. Others sprawled across crushed iris and asphodel. Monsters with scarlet jowls, red of hand, moved towards the house. They walked bipedally, having the bodies, arms, and thighs of men, but their heads were the heads of golden jackals, with scavenger jaws able to crack heavy bone; and their legs below the knee, also, were as the hind legs of jackals, so that they leaned forward for balance as they came.

"It appears, Prince Watab, that just as did the functionaries of a certain temple, you are receiving guests you did not invite," Kamose observed.

"Send them away, or you die!" Watab brandished the whip of Selket for emphasis. "You control those devils, do not pretend otherwise."

"You should recognise them," Kamose said. "These are the Libyan warriors you paid to cover the deed of your soldiers. The Lord Anubis burdened a jackal with the power of his curse and sent it to deliver his judgement. Here it is. They, with their women and children, and all their descendants, shall wear the forms you see. Now they answer his summons, to wreak his will on their former comrades."

"Send them away!" Watab's voice sounded scarcely human.

Kamose shook his head.

"Refuse," the prince whispered, "and before they can advance another step, your whole retinue dies. Look behind you, demon."

Kamose turned around with an expression of polite but small interest. Soldiers along the portico held daggers to the throats of his priests and acolytes. Sighing like a man wearied with foolish behaviour, Kamose clapped his hands sharply.

The veiling illusion that had cloaked his retinue vanished. Watab's soldiers recoiled with yells and shudders from standing, ancient mummies. Buried in the desert sand beside clay pots of food and their weapons, long before the first pyramid was raised, they had been kept from decay by dryness only. White ribs showed through flesh like ancient leather. Their eyes had become void pits. Long teeth glinted dry in their jaws, and their hands were claws of bone.

Kamose said ironically, "It is my turn to advise you to look."

Howling, Watab swung his lash at the saturnine priest. One of the mummies stepped between them with dreadful quickness, its bony heel clicking on the tiles. The whip curled around it. Ancient tendons burst as its head and legs turned backwards. Two more liches seized the prince and wrested his whip away. He shuddered uncontrollably in their dead grasp, while his eyes acquired a disordered stare. Kamose took possession of the whip of Selket, coiling up the supple lash with distaste.

"If I required more proof against you, it is here," he said like a judge pronouncing doom. "Your son Paheri partook of your crimes, and he too must answer. Is he hiding?"

Watab said nothing. His mouth had become as numbed as his mind. He looked like a man floundering in a poisoned swamp where soon he must drown.

Kamose looked at him closely. "Ah, yes. He boasted that he would attend to the woman, as I remember. Belike he's oblivious. Let us go and find him."

He turned his back on the gardens, to lead the way through the prince's house. Watab followed, escorted by two lipless corpses, while a third walked behind with a splayed, grotesque gait due to its legs being dislocated and reversed. It seemed to grin with malevolence.

Watab lurched and stumbled as though his will no longer governed his own legs. To him it appeared that what had been his mansion was, in the space of an evening, annexed to hell and overrun by demons. Behind him, the transformed Libyans advanced through corridor and chamber, their jaws seeking the throats of his soldiers. Kamose walked before him, never looking back. Grey dust fell from his robes as he trod. To Watab's half-blind gaze it seemed like the long accumulations of the tomb.

VI.

Kamose knew what they were likely to find when they intruded upon the lamia and the prince's son. He felt untouched by pity for the latter. The harvest of Paheri's own deeds had ripened.

Yet Kamose felt haunted by a sadness which arose from the humanity he had never been able to eradicate, despite his direst efforts. He too had been a father, and lost wife and children to the vengefulness of a god. Each one of Prince Watab's dragging steps behind him was a heavy reminder of grief. He ground his teeth. Curse human feeling that could survive even decades of traffic with demons, and return to haunt him with misgivings!

He halted at the entrance to a chamber from which a sound of low moaning issued.

Kamose shackled every natural response. They would have included grey skin, sweat, and a twisting belly. Instead, he turned an implacably harsh face towards the prince.

"*See,*" he invited.

And Watab saw . . .

Head hanging limply over the edge, his son lay on a couch strewn with oryx skins. One arm lolled slackly towards the floor. Paheri had lifted the other to touch, to caress as though enthralled, the half-female monster that arched over him. Her long ophidian tail moved on the floor.

Worst of all was the hideous pliant softness of Peheri's ribs and thighs. They were broken as though in the pulverizing coils of a python. Despite those fearful injuries, Paheri continued to embrace the lamia even as he shuddered and died.

Kamose watched coldly. His natural horror at the sight faded, sinking into the past where it belonged, dead and buried with the scholarly youth of a century before. Let all temple-defilers meet such a fate. He stared with contempt at Watab, Prince of the Thirteenth Nome.

Who shook and babbled and clutched his head.

"Fool!" Kamose said. "I offered you a journey to Pharaoh's palace in chains. A kindly proposal. You should have accepted."

Watab turned shuddering away from the sight in the chamber. He began weeping, rough wild sobs that jolted his body in spasms. The withered mummies watched him impassively.

Jackal-headed creatures still bounded and loped through the chambers of his house, killing the last of his soldiers while red pools crept across his floors. Watab's sobs became gulping laughter that rose madly higher. Yes, he would threaten no one any longer.

Turning, Kamose strode from the house, through the garden and the gates, towards the stone quays by Prince Watab's private canal. He preferred not to bid Mertseger follow him. She might join him aboard the galley when she was . . . satisfied.

He could wait.   Ω

Author's footnote:
    Abdu is better known by its modern name, Abydos; Usermare is the pharoah we know as Ramses II.

THE DEAD OF WINTER
by Mike Lange

illustrated by Allen Koszowski

They held to old customs here. A guard did duty at the gate, as likely guards had done through years beyond counting; but the wall that circled the village, twelve feet high, and the sentry neither one could have stopped much that the world had to fling at them today. The man leaned, shivering, on his only weapon, a rusty halberd; Donal, with his pistols, wheel-lock rifle, and borrowed crossbow could have killed him long before being seen, let alone menaced by any polearm.

But he and the villager shared a common enemy — winter. The season had lifted its bitter siege and left the village alone but destitute, storehouses plundered, game driven into hiding where it survived at all, nothing to look forward to but long rain and waiting, somehow grimly surviving, until a crop came to fruit.

Donal was one of the wolves who had ravaged throughout the season, and he was a stranger here, in a land where any stranger was, simply for safety's sake, regarded and dealt with as an enemy. The guard stared bleakly at him a moment, then without immediate comprehension at the soldier's two heavily-loaded pack horses.

"I would say welcome, sir; but you might as well keep moving," the villager greeted him, gaunt with hunger but far more polite than many past who'd met Donal at gates or doors. "We've nothing to offer a guest here but misery, and you look to've had your share of *that*."

"I didn't think to be a guest," Donal replied with a nod of agreement — he was miserable, and grimaced as he slapped his left leg, his side off from the guard. I was hunting — I came this way by accident, but a lucky chance. . . . I think my foot's gotten poxy frostbitten." He jerked his head back at the other two, loaded horses. "If you folk are hungry, I've had a damned good hunt. I'd call it worth half the meat if you could let me in out of this cursed cold before my toes brittle up and break off."

That was a very real concern. Snow was on the ground, still, spring keeping lazily to bed while winter's darkness covered the land; even with a fire to step back to as soon as this rare visitor was

dealt with, the guard still felt the bite of cold. He understood how a man might trade food for mere warmth — and he could certainly agree to such a trade, when it was the other man offering the food at the gate of a famine-struck village.

"Go in," he allowed the soldier. "Welcome to you. They'll take care of you inside — and of the food," he could not help but add, hungrily eying the tarp-covered, bulky packs. Donal left him watching and went in.

By the time feeling had returned to his gray foot, Donal had drunk two brimming cups of brandy. The surest way of determining the degree of damage done his foot had involved pain, and he had absorbed enough alcohol to distance himself from the probing. Now the warmth spreading from his stomach felt far better than the hunger given a razor's edge by the smell of meat cooking.

He looked sharply up at the young lady who refilled his cup. That she'd come so close without his warily noticing it, who had spent half a lifetime on the lookout for the enemy — Donal reckoned maybe he'd had enough to drink, and she agreed, smiling at him but something like anger glinting in her eyes. She spoke to him through the big but cadaverous man who sat across the firepit from Donal: "You'd better go easy on the drinking, Wolfgar, empty as our bellies are. You'll end too drunk to eat, and our friend," she said with a lingering look at Donal that unsettled him in its sadness, "nearly lost too much for his good work to go wasted."

Then she walked away. Donal stared after her, aware and not caring that the man opposite watched him and grinned.

"That's Marie, the poor dear," the villager said, and met Donal's sharp glance with a level look and voice: "Pity her. Her husband died just before winter. She meant more than it might have seemed when she mentioned what *you* nearly lost — her man froze to death, afield after game for our larder. It was a cold year past," he mused in low melancholy.

Donal meant to speak of soldiers dying in

much the same manner, but reckoned Wolfgar would have ample reason not only not to care, but to rejoice; and he almost shrugged, but decided that that wouldn't be overly polite and might be taken for an insult by these very polite, grieving people. He shook his head. "Sad. But you lost more than just him, didn't you? " he asked, knowing more of winter's hardship than of manners. He realized that he had blundered only as the lord stared into his cup for a long moment, scowling slightly.

Then Wolfgar shook himself. "We lost a lot, but each one was of value — not just one more," he said at last, speaking as one not hardened to mass death; and Donal recognized his own callousness too late, in comparison with the other man's capacity for feeling.

"Well, sorry," he muttered. "I expect each one *was* more. I doubt you know — no loss of yours — but I see men killed about every day, it seems, and I don't *like* half of the few I *know*."

"No," Wolfgar admitted in a slow voice, shaking his head; "I can't understand you. It sounds to me to be a poor way of living, my friend."

Now Donal shrugged, and winced, and had a deep taste of brandy. "It is," he finally admitted, finding the bitter truth better than argument. He mused on that for a moment, but then, before he or his host had to speak further, he looked clumsily around at the sound of a woman's laugh. Yes, there was Marie. Auburn hair and slender — maybe *too* slender, and too pale, for they'd been hungry here — but pretty and pleasing to his tastes.

"Soldiering seems it'd be a lonely life," Wolfgar said, and, as Donal looked narrow-eyed at him, smiled knowingly. "I think also a one to teach a man to take what he can, when he can. . . . The other soldiers came this way, this winter, " he much less cheerfully added, "were plainly taught so."

"I plunder the enemy," Donal said warily, "not people I'm going to sit to a meal with. Or their women."

Wolfgar looked at him a moment, then smiled as if nothing of matter or nearly unpleasant had been spoken or thought. "We know about hunger in this village, Donal — and, for what it's worth, Marie is very much her own lady, not anyone else's. I mean only to give my blessing to anyone with the sense to take a gift freely given. More so, when he — or she," he specified for emphasis, "— is so plainly needing."

He did not leave it at that. Perhaps he could

not. "The custom here is that no one leaves hungry; that we feed them, see to their needs for the journey. . . . This winter," he said heavily, "made us poor hosts. We couldn't even do that for our own."

"I hope this doesn't burden you too badly," Wolfgar worried again, walking Donal to the hut he was to sleep in.

Old custom once more: a guest house, off aside from the homes of day-to-day. Donal wouldn't have been surprised to be told these people weren't even Christians, with their archaic sense of hospitality and distance in manner from the religious madness engulfing the land. Witch-hunters would have found such tolerance to be highly suspect, Donal reflected.

He was no witch-hunter and would not have been offended to learn they were pagan here. All that mattered was that he walked comfortably on the foot they'd doctored and had had his own food cooked for him, and had been allowed a moment or two of ease all-too-rare in his life. He hastened once more (perhaps lying, but he'd done far worse for far less cause) to reassure Wolfgar: "I could well spare it. Hell, I only gave you *half* what I had, where some would have wanted it all from me — and you've met the sorts who'd have given you not a damned thing in return for your welcome." He chuckled — his humor was good tonight. "I would be a poor sort of man to be sorry I gave what I did."

Wolfgar plodded on silently for a moment. Donal felt an unease about the town lord that ill-fitted a man who'd eaten his fill for perhaps the first time all season, tonight. "Will you do us a favor, then, Donal?" he asked at last.

"If it's within my power," Donal said slowly, haggling, "and not against my orders or good sense — certainly." He was hoping that Wolfgar would ask some sort of service he carried weapons for; he was a sort of whore and made that his business, not a form of gratitude.

"Stay inside tonight," was Wolfgar's whole request; and Donal, who was dead-tired, sluggish with drink, and hoping he was right about the nature of Marie's attention all through the feast, did not care to be told more. Wolfgar explained, though: "You, a Christian soldier, there's much you mightn't understand that's still got to be done tonight." The man was making no apology; simply telling Donal. "We don't want hard feelings of any kind after you've so plainly relaxed."

"You can preach the Black mass, for all you'll

bother *my* Christian soul," Donal darkly scoffed. "I won't stir. I've a stronger sense for minding my own business, than for God."

"God wasn't kind to us this winter," Wolfgar said in what seemed to be and yet somehow didn't sound like sympathy. "It was plain custom that carried us through — now you've fed us, tonight there's a thing to be done. Stay in. Please."

He left Donal alone at the hut. A fire had already been built inside, by someone whose pleasant scent lingered. Used to tents and sleeping bags, atop a cot if lucky, and usually too-cramped quarters to boot, Donal could hardly relax in the single spacious room of the house. At least, to that he attributed the knotting in his gut; anxiety — or longing, for all his assuring himself that he had nothing to be nervous of or to anticipate.

Which was why, as he gingerly tugged off his high boots and unlaced his shirt, his teeth caught, his heart leaped. A light tap at the door had startled him; there came a second soft knock.

Half a lifetime's hard-learned habits couldn't be even a bit set aside after just half a day of peace. He went to the door with one of his pistols in hand, his sword still belted on. He opened the door just enough to peer out, his thumb on the cock of the gun in case someone tried to burst in.

Marie only stood there, glancing over her shoulder. Donal opened the door further to stare into her wide eyes — eyes abrim with want and fear and ready defiance even if he hinted at scorn. It was as if he gazed a long moment into a reflection of his own feelings, and he hesitantly beckoned her in to find what else they might share.

"I'm no whore," Marie said quickly, entering gratefully. "Don't think that I am. Please."

"I *don't* think so," Donal said, and touched her thick, cold hair and delicate shoulder as she stood half-turned away from him. "I think no such thing at all."

She nodded, gave the ghost of a smile and turned to him. It was that same wistful smile she'd shown earlier. "Did they tell you — my husband —?"

"I know about it," Donal said with a slow nod. "He died; was hunting, like me. . . . I'm sorry."

Marie nodded and glanced away, but went on; it was maybe of more importance to her, than to him, but Donal listened: "You've come in — where he didn't come back — you brought us food," she said miserably, "but it's been worse

than a hungry winter, for me. I've needed more than just food. . . . Oh, you *must* think me —"

He cut her off gently, taking her face in his hands and kissing her moving mouth in mid-word. Then he said, "I think a woman can be just as lonely as I am, that's all. No whore," he pointed out wryly, "would have missed this."

There was really no more need for talk.

He was awake — not pleased to be, still tired, but awake.

With what he'd drunk and his exertions in Marie's arms, it was odd that Donal now roused to know that it was bitterly cold outside the heavy warmth of the bed, the room dimly lit by the red glow of dying coals where a fire had burned. And he was alone.

He rolled over, looking and feeling for certain, swearing softly. Did even a young widow, even here, have to leave and pretend to a decency that wasn't decency at all, in Donal's mind, but only damned narrow-minded stupidity? Why else would Marie have left while he slept?

Then it came to him, with the sudden realization that he was going to have to get up to piss, and quickly, that a woman — Marie — might well have gone out and in exactly that same need. Donal tried to smile, but found his face numbed with alcohol, exhaustion, and the awful cold of the darkness. He was still going to have to get up, though.

He was, after all, used to tents, to being crowded and heeding certain courtesies, and he had long since forgotten his promise to Wolfgar, not to go out. There was a bucket in the hut, but in the darkness he could not have found it and didn't look — the rule of not fouling his and his mates' nest was too much a habit for him to relieve himself within smell of the bed. He limped barefoot out of the hut, yawning and scratching his crotch, an idea in mind that, when he found Marie, she being also awake might enjoy —

Donal stopped dead a single step outside the hut. Before he saw anything, he heard from the nearest houses a weeping in the night, as if most of the village sat up in the darkness to mourn. Belatedly, he recalled that Wolfgar had wanted him to stay in; but he paused on the threshold. He heard the stamp of laboring hooves, the creak of wagon wheels and the crunch of snow beneath the great weight. Next the wagon hove into view, one of the great open-bedded sort of wains that were driven a circuit through towns where the plague had struck.

Wolfgar manned the reins. Donal saw corpses piled in the wagon bed. He stared, shivering, a trickle of urine freezing down his leg as fear shook loose his bladder and self-control. There hadn't been such a supply of corpses or expression of grief even hours earlier tonight — and now the master of the village turned the ponderous wagon toward him. . . .

Marie stepped slowly, seeming to be sleepwalking, from someplace where Donal had not seen her. She clambered stiffly into the rear of the dead wagon. Donal had seen far more than enough death to know now, as she slumped atop the bodies, that the woman he'd known tonight was dead and cold, curled in winter death.

Wolfgar saw him only then, too late for much to be done or said. He reined up the wagon much as would pause a step shy of startling a frightened animal into running — or into attacking by reflex, for Donal tensed dangerously.

"I asked you to stay inside," he reminded Donal, without anger, only grief and exhaustion in his rough voice. "Now go, Donal, go back in. You're not dressed to be out, and you don't belong with these others — do you want to join them tonight?" he asked with a sat nod back at the dead.

Donal would have killed the man who approached the house or him that night. He had seen the dead walk and had no way of knowing if who came could be trusted to be living, so he was primed to shoot, simply aching to be sure. He sat up with the fire raging, his head aching, all sense of easy well-being gone.

The gray light of a new morning finally sifted through the shutters. Only then did Wolfgar come knocking, his tap light, his words spoken softly to soothe rather than scare further: "I'd like to come in, Donal; I'm sure you'd like to be away from here. Will you open the door? Neither of us can —"

Donal flung the door open, pistols poised. There was no mistaking the menace he meant toward anyone who spooked him, even a little, after the icy shocks of the night before.

"No need for the guns," Wolfgar told him. "No one here means you any harm."

"No one —?" Donal said shrilly, his hands shaking so that Wolfgar feared one or the other of the snaphances might go off, as yet unintentionally. "Do you think I care to lay dead women before they're buried? There's no *harm* in that?"

"It's our custom, I told you that — the hungry are fed before they leave. Marie died starved for something more than food. *You* fed that same hunger, yourself, last night. Did you know any difference then?"

"You God-cursed —"

"You call us that, mercenary?" Wolfgar snapped, finally growing angry with his guest, too tired to be unnerved by the whiteness of the fingers curled about the triggers of Donal's guns. "You weren't among the men who came and plundered our winter stores, but I doubt *you* would think that to matter if our places were reversed. They laughed then — to the mighty goes the right. Well, God curse *you*, Donal, all we did here is hold to an old custom. I think," he said coldly, "that I like our way better, caring even for the wants of the dead, rather than not giving a damn who lives or dies. *Your* way!"

Donal felt the urge to kill rise like bile; but that was a violation of the ancient custom forbidding a guest to bring violence into a host's home. He found himself in vast respect and dread of custom's power, and lowered his guns. "You might have told a man," he muttered.

"To have you go back out in the snow and die?" Wolfgar countered wearily. "I was afraid that telling you might have driven you out. I'd no idea you'd have *chosen* that. If death means so little to you, then why do *our* dead bother you?"

Donal could think of nothing to say. It was true; death was so familiar — and small — a thing to him, that he had to wonder what about Wolfgar's reasoning he could not accept. He could not summon an argument, but he still shook his head in bewilderment.

"Is it just that you're unhappy that anyone but yourself — that *Marie* might have gotten anything out of last night?" Wolfgar persisted irritably.

"No," Donal said dully. "I'm glad it was — appreciated." She shrugged, started to speak; then, as best he could, put his first thought in somewhat more charitable words. "I'll leave, then. You people have certainly given — given me as much as I could ever want here." Ω

THE CLOWN WHO IS A WEREWOLF

My hands grow dark with hair.
Somewhere, my carefree self
dons a clown suit
for the parade,
cheeks yellow and blue,
nose red as blood.
The black around my eyes thickens.
The children test the happiness
like wet fingers in the wind,
dance along with my wobbly cycle,
my fluttering pantaloons.
The bones beneath my brows
push outward, deliver
more flesh to my ears
as they jerk moonward.
The nickelodeon cranks out
the song of candy floss,
of carousels,
of eternal boyhood.

Cracking, stretching, mutating,
my body breaks all its own rules:
shoulder muscles bunched together,
knees bent like gnarled tree roots,
arms reaching to dangerous lengths,
fingers frozen into talons.
The clown mimics, parodies, pokes fun,
cracks smiles from solemn faces.
My passions drive my sinews
like turbines,
blow me out the door
two steps behind
my night-numbing growl.
I hear the marching bands
around the next corner,
a parade headed this way.
Anger rises like bile
to the tip of my knotted throat.
The first thing I wish to kill
is a clown.

— **John Grey**

A SOFT VOICE WHISPERS NOTHING

by Thomas Ligotti

illustrated by Jason Van Hollander

Long before I suspected the existence of the town near the northern border, I believe that I was in some way already an inhabitant of that remote and desolate place. Any number of signs might be offered to support this claim, although some of them may have seemed somewhat removed from the issue. Not the least of them appeared during my childhood, those soft gray years when I was stricken with one sort or another of life-draining infirmity. It was at this early stage of development that I sealed my deep affinity with the winter season in all its phases and manifestations. Nothing seemed more natural to me than my impulse to follow the path of the snow-topped roof and the ice-crowned fencepost, considering that I, too, in my illness, exhibited the marks of an essentially hibernal state of being. Under the plump blankets of my bed I lay freezing and pale, my temples sweating with shiny sickles of fever. Through the frosted panes of my bedroom window I watched in awful devotion as dull winter days were succeeded by blinding winter nights. I remained ever awake to the possibility, as my young mind conceived it, of an "icy transcendence." I was therefore cautious, even in my frequent states of delirium, never to indulge in vulgar sleep, except perhaps to dream my way deeper into that landscape where vanishing winds snatched me up into the void of an ultimate hibernation.

No one expected I would live very long, not even my attending physician, Dr. Zirk. A widower far along into middle age, the doctor seemed intensely dedicated to the well-being of the living anatomies under his care. Yet from my earliest acquaintance with him I sensed that he too had a secret affinity with the most remote and desolate locus of the winter spirit, and therefore was also allied with the town near the northern border. Every time he examined me at my bedside he betrayed himself as a fellow fanatic of a disconsolate creed, embodying so many of its stigmata and gestures. His wiry, white-streaked hair and beard were thinning, patchy remnants of a former luxuriance, much like the bare, frost-covered branches of the trees outside my window. His face was of a coarse complexion, rugged as frozen earth, while his eyes were overcast with the cloudy ether of a December afternoon. And his fingers felt so frigid as they palpated my neck or gently pulled at the underlids of my eyes.

One day, when I believed that he thought I was asleep, Dr. Zirk revealed the extent of his initiation into the barren mysteries of the winter world, even if he spoke only in the cryptic fragments of an overworked soul in extremis. In a voice as pure and cold as an arctic wind the doctor made reference to "undergoing certain ordeals," as well as speaking of what he called "grotesque discontinuities in the order of things." His trembling words also invoked an epistemology of "hope and horror," of exposing once and for all the true nature of this "great gray ritual of existence" and plunging headlong into an "enlightenment of inanity." It seemed that he was addressing me directly when in a soft gasp of desperation he said, "To make an end of it, little puppet, *in your own way.* To close the door in one swift motion and not by slow, fretful degrees. If only this doctor could show you the way of such cold deliverance." I felt my eyelids flutter as the tone and import of these words, and Dr. Zirk immediately became silent. Just then my mother entered the room, allowing me a pretext to display an aroused consciousness. But I never betrayed the confidence or indiscretion the doctor had entrusted to me that day.

In any case, it was many years later that I first discovered the town near the northern border, and there came to understand the source and significance of Dr. Zirk's mumblings on that nearly silent winter day. I noticed, as I arrived in the town, how close a resemblance it bore to the winterland of my childhood, even if the precise time of year was still slightly out of season. On that day, everything — the streets of the town and the few people travelling upon them, the store windows and the meager merchandise they displayed, the weightless pieces of debris barely animated by a half-dead wind — everything looked as if it had been drained entirely of all color, as if an enormous photographic flash had just gone off in the startled face of the town. And somehow beneath this pallid facade I intuited what I described to myself as the "all pervasive aura of a place that has offered itself as a haven for an interminable series of delirious events."

It was definitely a mood of delirium that appeared to rule the scene, causing all that I saw to shimmer vaguely in my sight, as if viewed through the gauzy glow of a sick-room: a haziness that had no precise substance, distorting without in any way obscuring the objects behind or within it. There was an atmosphere of disorder and commotion that I sensed in the streets of the town, as if its delirious mood were only a soft prelude to great pandemonium. I heard the sound of something that I could not identify, an approaching racket that caused me to take refuge in a narrow passageway between a pair of high buildings. Nestled in this dark hiding place I watched the street and listened as that nameless chattering grew louder. It was a medley of clanging and creaking, groaning and croaking, a dull jangle of something unknown as it groped its way through the town, a chaotic parade in honor of some special occasion of delirium.

The street that I saw beyond the narrow opening between the two buildings was now entirely empty. The only thing I could glimpse was a blur of high and low structures which appeared to quiver slightly as the noise became louder and louder, the parade closing in, though from which direction I did not know. The formless clamor seemed to envelop everything around me, and then suddenly I could see a passing figure in the street. Dressed in loose white garments, it had an egg-shaped head that was completely hairless and as white as paste, a clown of some kind who moved in a way that was both casual and laborious, as if it were strolling underwater or against a strong wind, tracing strange patterns in the air with billowed arms and pale hands. It seemed to take forever for this apparition to pass from view, but just before doing so it turned to peer into the narrow passage where I had secreted myself, and its greasy white face was wearing an expression of bland malevolence.

Others followed the lead figure, including a team of ragged men who were harnessed like beasts and pulled long, bristling ropes. They also moved out of sight, leaving the ropes to waver slackly behind them. The vehicle to which those ropes were attached — by means of enormous hooks — rolled into the scene, its great wooden wheels audibly grinding the pavement of the street beneath them. It was a sort of platform with huge wooden stakes rising from its perimeter to form the bars of a cage. There was nothing to secure the wooden bars at the top, and so they wobbled with the movement of the parade. Hanging from the bars, and rattling against them, was an array of objects haphazardly tethered by cords and wires and straps of various kinds. I saw masks and shows, household utensils and naked dolls, large bleached bones and skeletons of small animals, bottles of colored glass, the head of a dog with a rusty chain wrapped several times around its neck, and sundry scraps of debris and other things I could not name, all knocking together in

a wild percussion. I watched and listened as that ludicrous vehicle passed by in the street. Nothing else followed it, and the enigmatic parade seemed to be at an end, now only a delirious noise fading into the distance. Then a voice called out behind me.

"What are you doing here?"

I turned around and saw a fat old woman moving toward me from the shadows of that narrow passageway between the two high buildings. She was wearing a highly decorated hat that was almost as wide as she was, and her already ample form was augmented by numerous layers of colorful scarves and shawls. Her body was further weighted down by several necklaces which hung like a noose around her neck and many bracelets about both of her chubby wrists. On the thick fingers of either hand were a variety of large, gaudy rings.

"I was watching the parade." I said to her. "But I couldn't see what was inside the cage, or whatever it was. It seemed to be empty."

The woman simply stared at me for some time, as if contemplating my face and perhaps surmising that I had only recently arrived in the northern border town. Then she introduced herself as Mrs. Glimm and said that she ran a lodging house. "Do you have a place to stay?" she asked in an aggressively demanding tone. "It should be dark soon," she said, glancing slightly upwards. "The days are getting shorter and shorter."

I agreed to follow her back to the lodging house. On the way I asked her about the parade. "It's just some nonsense," she said as we walked through the darkening streets of the town. "Have you seen one of these?" she asked, handing me a crumpled piece of paper that she had stuffed among her scarves and shawls.

Smoothing out the page that Mrs. Glimm had placed in my hands, I tried to read what was printed upon it in the dimming twilight. At the top of the page, in capital letters, was a title: **METAPHYSICAL LECTURE I.** Below these words was a brief text which I read to myself as I walked with Mrs. Glimm. "It has been said," the text began, "that after undergoing certain ordeals — whether ecstatic or abysmal — we should be obliged to change our names, as we are no longer who we once were. Instead the opposite rule is applied: our names linger long after anything resembling what we were, or thought we were, as disappeared entirely. Not that there was much to begin with — only a few questionable memories and impulses drifting about like snowflakes in a gray and endless winter. But each soon floats down and settles into a cold and nameless void."

After reading this "metaphysical lecture," I asked Mrs. Glimm where it came from. "They were all over town," she replied. "Just some nonsense, like the rest of it. Personally I think this sort of thing is bad for business. Why should I have to go around picking up customers in the street? But as long as someone's paying my price I will accommodate them in whatever style they wish. In addition to operating a lodging house or two, I am also licensed to act as an undertaker's assistant and cabaret stage manager. Well, here we are. You can go inside — someone will be there to take care of you. At the moment I have an appointment elsewhere." With these concluding words, Mrs. Glimm walked off down the street.

Mrs. Glimm's lodging house was one of several great structures along the street, each of them sharing similar features and all of them, I later discovered, in some way under the proprietorship or authority of the same person — that is, Mrs. Glimm. Nearly flush with the street stood a series of high and almost styleless monuments with facades of pale gray mortar and enormous dark roofs. Although the street was rather wide, the sidewalks in front of the houses were so narrow that their roofs slightly overhung the pavement below, creating a sense of tunnel-like enclosure. All of the houses might have been siblings of my childhood home, which I once heard someone describe as an "architectural moan." I thought of this phrase as I went through the process of renting a room, insisting that I be placed in one that faced the street. Once I settled into my apartment, which was actually a single, quite expansive, bedroom, I stood at the window gazing up and down the street of gray houses, which together seemed to form a procession of some kind, a frozen funeral parade. I repeated the words "architectural moan" over and over to myself until exhaustion forced me away from the window and under the musty blankets of the bed. Before I fell asleep I remembered that it was Dr. Zirk who used this phrase to describe my childhood home, a place he had visited often.

So it was of Dr. Zirk that I was thinking as I fell asleep in that expansive bedroom of Mrs. Glimm's lodging house. And I was thinking of him not only because he used the phrase "architectural moan" to describe the appearance of my childhood home, which so closely resembled those high-roofed structures along that street of gray houses in the northern border town, but

also, and even primarily, because the words of the brief metaphysical lecture I had read some hours earlier reminded me so much of the words, those fragments and mutterings, that the doctor spoke as he sat upon my bed and attended to the life-draining infirmities from which everyone expected I would die at a very young age. Lying under the musty blankets of my bed in that strange lodging house, with a little moonlight shining through the window illuminating the dreamlike vastness of the room around me, I once again felt the weight of someone sitting upon my bed and bending over my apparently sleeping body, ministering to it with unseen gestures and a soft voice. It was then, while pretending to be asleep as I used to do in my childhood, that I heard the words of a second "metaphysical lecture." They were whispered in a slow and resonant monotone. "We should give thanks," the voice said to me, "that a poverty of knowledge has so narrowed our vision of things as to allow the possibility of feeling something about them. How could we find a pretext to react to anything if we understood . . . everything? None but an *absent* mind was ever victimized by the adventure of intense emotional feeling. And without the suspense that is generated by our benighted state — our status as beings *possessed* by our bodies and the madness that goes along with them — who could take enough interest in the universal spectacle to bring forth even the feeblest yawn, let alone exhibit the more dramatic manifestations which lend such unwonted color to a world that is essentially composed of shades of gray upon a background of blackness. Hope and horror, to repeat merely two of the innumerable conditions dependent on a faulty insight, would be much the worse for an ultimate revelation that would expose their lack of necessity. At the other extreme, both our most dire and most exalted emotions are well served every time we take some ray of knowledge, isolate it from the spectrum of illumination, and then forget it completely. All our ecstasies, whether sacred or from the slime, depend on our refusal to be schooled in even the most superficial truths and our maddening will follow the path of forgetfulness. Amnesia may well be the highest sacrament in the great gray ritual of existence. To know, to understand in the fullest sense, is to plunge into an enlightenment of inanity, a wintry landscape of memory whose substance is all shadows and a profound awareness of the infinite spaces surrounding us on all sides. Within this space we remain suspended only with the aid of strings that quiver with our hopes and our horrors, and which keep us dangling over the gray void. How is it that we can defend such puppetry, condemning any efforts to strip us of these strings? The reason, one must suppose, is that nothing is more enticing, nothing more vitally idiotic, than our desire to have a name — even if it is the name of a stupid little puppet — and to hold on to this name throughout the long ordeal of our lives, as if we could hold on to it forever. If only we could keep these precious strings from growing frayed and tangles, if only we could keep from falling into an empty sky, we might continue to pass ourselves off under our assumed names and perpetuate our puppet's dance throughout all eternity. . . ."

The voice whispered more words than these, more than I can recall, as if it would deliver its lecture without end. But at some point I drifted off to sleep as I had never slept before, calm and gray and dreamless.

The next morning I was awakened by some noise down the street outside my window. It was the same delirious cacophony I had heard the day before when I first arrived in the northern border town and witnessed the passing of that unique parade. But when I got up from my bed and went to the window, I saw no sign of the uproarious procession. Then I noticed the house directly opposite the one in which I had spent the night. One of the highest windows of that house across the street was fully open, and slightly below the ledge of the window, lying against the gray façade of the house, was the body of a man hanging by his neck from a thick white rope. The cord was stretched taut and led back through the window and into the house. For some reason this sight did not seem in any way unexpected or out of place, even as the noisy thrumming of the unseen parade grew increasingly louder and even when I recognized the figure of the hanged man, who was extremely slight of build, almost like a child in physical stature. Many years older than when I had last seen him, his hair and beard now radiantly white, clearly this was the body of my old physician, Dr. Zirk.

Now I could see the parade approaching. From the far end of the gray, tunnel-like street the clown creature strolled in its loose white garments, its egg-shaped head scanning the high houses on either side. As the creature passed beneath my window it looked up at me with that same expression of bland malevolence, and then passed on. Following this figure was the formation of ragged men harnessed by ropes to a cage-like vehicle that rolled along on wooden wheels. Countless objects, many more than I saw the previous day, clattered against the bars of the cage. The grotesque inventory now included bottles of pills that rattled with the contents inside them, shining scalpels and instruments for cutting through bones, needles and syringes strung together and hung like ornaments on a Christmas tree, and a stethoscope that had been looped about the decapitated dog's head. The wooden stakes of the caged platform wobbled to the point of breaking with the additional weight of this cast-off clutter. Because there was no roof covering this cage, I could see down into it from my window. But there was nothing inside, at least for the moment. As the vehicle passed directly below, I looked across the street at the hanged man and the thick rope from which he dangled like a puppet. From the shadows inside the open window of the house, a hand appeared that was holding a polished steel straight razor. The fingers of that hand were thick and wore many gaudy rings. After the razor had worked at the cord for a few moments, the body of Dr. Zirk fell from the heights of the gray house and landed in the open vehicle just as it passed by. The procession was so lethargic in its every aspect now seemed to disappear quickly from view, its muffled riot of sounds fading into the distance.

To make an end of it, I thought to myself — *to make an end of it in whatever style you wish.*

I looked at the house across the street. The window that was once open was now closed, and the curtains behind it were drawn. The tunnel-like street of gray houses was absolutely quiet and absolutely still. Then, as if in answer to my own deepest wish, a sparse showering of snowflakes began to descend from the gray morning sky, each one of them a soft whispering voice. For the longest time I continued to stare out from my window, gazing upon the street and the town that I knew was my home. Ω

The Case of the Glass Slipper

by Ian Watson

illustrated by George Barr

Outside the heavy chintz curtains of those famous rooms in Baker Street the London fog, yellowed by gaslight, crept and probed for entry and hid the world from view.

To Sherlock Holmes, seated within, the fog always seemed to afford a paradoxical image of his own relationship with the world of crime. That world sought to conceal its malignant, insinuating activities from view; activities which he by subtle probing would reveal. It sought to conceal, yet its very smokescreen betrayed its position. This fog was an organism which carried the seeds of its own unmasking, as did any crime of less rank than the hypothetical "perfect crime" — which, Holmes reasoned, would be no crime at all, since crime must necessarily be imperfect. Did not crime represent a flaw in the logical structure of society?

His thought processes were interrupted — if not disarrayed — when the visitor whom he had been expecting was ushered in.

"Your Highness," Holmes said, rising.

The Prince was strikingly handsome despite the muffler he wore to guard his lungs from the fog, and to preserve his incognito. Nodding, he glanced around the room, taking in the roaring fire, the music stand, the leather-bound volumes on pharmacology.

"My colleague Watson has been called away to the bedside of an old friend," Holmes explained. He immediately detected the missing element which puzzled the Prince.

"Excellent! Then there will be no record of this visit, nor of my dilemma." When the Prince unwound his muffler, Holmes noted a very slight scar on the side of the Prince's chin compatible either with an old hunting accident or a boyhood fall from a tree. The poised dancer's — not duellist's — grace with which the Prince moved ruled out the second, maladroit alternative.

"I can assure you of Watson's entire discretion," said Holmes mildly.

The Prince waved his equivocation aside, politely so.

"Mr. Holmes, I come from a neighboring kingdom. Yet my kingdom does not neighbour

Her Britannic Majesty's realm in any ordinary sense . . ."

"In my experience the extraordinary usually yields to logical scrutiny."

"Which is why I have come to you. I believe myself to be the victim of a monstrous imposture, though I cannot put my finger upon the betraying detail."

"Pray proceed."

"At a Grand Ball in my palace I fell in love with the most beautiful girl in all the world. She danced with me till midnight; then, as the chimes of twelve sounded, she ran off without telling me her name."

"And what of her appearance, Sire?"

"Delightful, delicate, wonderful! She wore the most elegant gown. On her dainty feet were a pair of glass slippers, not quite size three and a half."

Holmes temporarily dismissed the question of shoe size and of how the dancing Prince determined this feature of his partner. Such a fellow might wall have drunk champagne from the girl's slipper. Indeed such a slipper, made of glass, was the only suitable receptacle for the legendary, chivalrous pouring of bubbly into a partner's footwear.

"She danced in *glass* slippers all night long?"

"Certainly. Ah, how we tripped the light fantastic! Then, so suddenly, she fled from my arms!"

"Of *glass,* Your Highness? Were they not fragile? If not fragile, how could her tender young feet . . .?"

The Prince dismissed these suspicions of the sage of Baker Street. "It is nothing unusual in my kingdom to dance in glass slippers. As she fled down the steps of the Royal Palace in apparent panic and disarray she left one of the slippers behind her on the steps. Thus I was able to trace my beloved runaway. It fitted the foot of only one person: Cinderella, a poor oppressed maiden who I believe must have been a changeling for some royal princess. She confessed. She told me how her fairy godmother changed a pumpkin into a fine coach, and white mice into footmen. We married joyously. And yet —"

"And yet?"

"We have only been married for a year and a day. Her temper grows sharp. She shows signs of becoming a shrew. She is constantly indisposed. I cannot think but that my own true Cinderella has been stolen away, abducted from my palace, and that a simulacrum, a golem of her, has been substituted. This imitation will gradually sour my whole life, thus too the life of the kingdom

whose well-being — as you know — is intimately connected with the well-being of its prince."

At this point Holmes took out his pipe and placed it in his mouth — though out of deference to his royal visitor he did not actually light the tobacco. Holmes paced to the window and back a few times. Presently he placed the pipe on a walnut table.

"Your Highness, I must know: prior to that last midnight dance, did you by any chance drink champagne from your partner's slipper?"

"Why do you ask?" marvelled the Prince. "I did not. But why do you ask?"

"Champagne may have made your partner's slipper *slippery.* Consequently it fell off when she fled down the steps."

"A slippery slipper? I did nothing to cause such a thing! I believe the consequence of spilt, drying champagne would be a stickiness rather than a slippery condition."

Holmes glanced momentarily at his volumes of pharmacology, his memory searching for a reference in those texts, then he nodded slowly.

"Without intruding too far upon the privacy of the royal bed —"

Gallantly the Prince shook his head. "I may add that Cinderella does not have . . . lubricious feet, delightful though they are to behold."

Holmes admired the discretion of the Prince, for he had told Holmes what he needed to know without invoking the vulgar word 'sweaty.' "In that case, Your Highness, there is only one possible answer. We arrive at it logically. Cinderella's slipper slipped off as she ran, yet when your heralds visited her home that slipper fitted her exactly and perfectly. Is that not singular? She did not deliberately kick the slipper off in order to run more swiftly, otherwise she would have kicked off *both* slippers. Therefore, on the night of the Ball the slipper did not in fact fit Cinderella exactly! It almost fitted her; it was slightly too large. Consequently, the Cinderella who lost her slipper at the Ball and the Cinderella whom your heralds visited are not one and the same."

The Prince held his brow, aghast. "How can that be? The one Cinderella and the other exactly resemble one another!"

"Except in the matter of temper," Holmes reminded the Prince. "And except as regard foot size. You yourself have already harboured the suspicion of a simulacrum, substituted recently, but the true state of affairs is more serious. the Cinderella whom you have married, You Highness, is either an identical twin of the Cinderella who attended the Ball — or much more likely she is a *clone*. Not a golem, no, a clone. There may be a number of Cinderellas. Your Cinderella fled from the Ball because of her lack of uniqueness. She fled to save you — and herself — from the revelation of shame."

"I do not care if she is what you call a clone. I love her. Where is she now? That is all I desire to know." The Prince slapped his brow. "Stop me, but I have married the other, and bedded her. A shrew in the making."

"If so," Holmes pursued sadly, though logically, "she must have a genetic predisposition to shrewishness." He carried on remorsely. "You have already said that her Godmother can transform mice into footmen. I can only conclude that, in addition to clandestine cloning of at least one of your subjects, experiments in recombinant DNA technology are proceeding secretly in your kingdom. Enticingly beautiful and gracious maidens are being created by the Godmother, with a whole range of specific *animal* characteristics. Shrewishness may be one of such!"

"This is a vile conspiracy!"

"Quite so, Your Highness. It is a conspiracy of monsters in beauteous human female form: identical, innocently seductive people with a coding for some bestial characteristic in their very make-up. She will pass this shrewishness on to your offspring, Your Highness."

"Oh, but my bride is expecting a child even now!"

"When she has given birth to a prince or princess of the blood — and of her blood too — a child who is partly a beast . . . I warrant that this Cinderella whom you innocently married will slip away back to the Godmother. She will not be missed, for another almost identical Cinderella will slip secretly into the palace to take her place, possessing other implanted characteristics which she will pass on to your next child. This new Cinderella may be foxy, a veritable queen. She will present you with a whore of a daughter. The Cinderella who follows her might present you with a *mouse* who will never win any neighboring prince's hand. Your household, Your Highness, will become a menagerie of subtle evil: a zoo very like our own Regents Park — of the Beast *inserted into* Man. The Godmother's plans are more cunning and poisonous than those of the evil Moriarty."

Holmes deeply pitied the stricken Prince.

"All this," the Prince said quietly, "proceeds from a slipper which fell off . . ."

"By elementary logic, Your Highness."

"What shall I do, Mr. Holmes?"

"I am only an investigator, Your Highness. My final recourse is always the justice of the law. In your land —"

"In my land I am the Law. The love of my subjects for me is the whole of the social contract."

"In your bed, through the agency of love, the state will be brought low through the machinations of the Godmother!"

"Must I kill Cinderella then? Must I stifle my own child, new born? Must I emasculate myself so that my subjects shall not know evil? How can I? The destruction of the capacity for love would destroy the social contract."

"How devious this plot is! How ingenious the Godmother!" Holmes paced the room in anger. "It is well that the good Watson is not present to hear this. As a medical man he would be stricken to the core by this foul misuse of recombinant DNA and embryology. You are involved in a struggle, Your Highness, against the direst evil in the person of this Godmother. She possesses technology far in advance of your own. Yet she must have some weakness, some flaw. It is my experience that crime always carries the seeds of its own destruction!"

"In the same way that Cinderella carries the ova of my destruction?"

"Indeed. Perhaps the key to the eradication of this beastly crime —" Holmes drew out a key from his fob pocket and opened a locked cabinet. Amidst phials of reagents, bottles of laudanum, hypodermic syringes, and antidotes to poison, there reposed a beautiful tortoise shell comb with a silver handle. This rested across a brandy goblet containing a red apple with bite marks on one side, pickled in clear alcohol. Next to this glass lay a spindle from a spinning wheel, with a spring-blade needle recessed into it. Carefully Holmes removed the comb.

"Your Highness, I have retained this comb as a memento from a previous case. The worthy Dr. Watson was able to ascertain in his small laboratory that it was treated with a certain nerve agent. When the comb is drawn through the hair so that it touches the scalp, it will induce paralysis. Not death, but a suspension of the faculties for at least a century. You must present this to Cinderella. Once she uses it, she will fall into a deep sleep akin to a cryogenic trance. Likewise the child in her womb. That child which she bears must not be born until you have searched out and found the secret laboratory of the Godmother; until you have compelled her — aye, upon pain of dancing on molten glass — to develop a viral DNA agent which will usurp the shrewish traits in your wife and unborn child! This viral DNA will eject the beastliness from all the cells of Cinderella's body, and from those cells gestating in her womb. *Then* you may revive her. *Then* the joyous birth of your heir may proceed."

From the same cabinet Holmes produced a tiny jar of red salve.

"Here is the antidote to the nerve agent. The good Watson was obliged to develop this to revive the victim in the case I mentioned. It may be applied by means of your own lips. It is a binary agent. In contact with human saliva, it becomes effective."

Carefully Holmes wrapped the comb and the jar before presenting them to the Prince. Modestly he acknowledged that nobleman's thanks.

"As to the other Cinderella clones whom you will discover, you must compel the Godmother to inject them also with the viral DNA anti-agent. There will probably be seven Cinderellas in all.

Bring the others back to your palace and lock them in the attics. If discreet, you can found a great dynasty — and who will be the wiser? As to your first love, let the glass slipper always be by your bed as a sure way of distinguishing her."

Half an hour after the Prince's departure, Dr. Watson returned. Coughing on account of the fog, he gratefully accepted a medicinal glass of whiskey.

"How is Hodgkinson, poor fellow?" Holmes enquired solicitously.

"Failing fast." Holmes' faithful scribe cleared his throat. "Did anything of note occur during my absence?"

"I received one visitor — whose identity I may not reveal, even to your good self. His was a problem which I could solve by simple deduction without leaving this room." Holmes reached in his fob pocket and displayed an emerald ring. "I may only say that he was suitably grateful."

"Can you say nothing else, Holmes?"

"My dear fellow, it concerned matters of state." The sage of Baker Street reached for his Stradivarius, and began to play.   Ω

PRETEND VAMPIRE

You don't want blood
You want poems about blood
Nosferatu dreams
    & a bloodless life
E.A. Poe short stories
    maybe a house in the suburbs

But what if you find it, blood,
    your own
Pooled, coagulating, messy
A wooden stake, I think,
    unnecessary

— **Kendall Evans**

GOT 'ET

My unfortunate cousin, named Steve,
complained that the ghouls would not leave
    him ever alone;
    they gnawed flesh and bone,
without giving hope of reprieve.

— **Darrell Schweitzer**

KISS OF THE HARPY

Volumptous vultures
preened and pecked,
brushed with sagging breasts,

teased with phallic tongues,
and in raptor's raptures
rode him to carrion death.

— **J.W. Donnelly**

A SINGLE SHADOW
by Stephen Dedman

illustrated by Jill Bauman

It was November, which made it nearly two months since I'd arrived in Tokyo, and the local shows had been much funnier when I hadn't really understood them — but the apartment was tiny and my bed was also the Tanii family's sofa, so I sat there and tried to read. Maybe by the time I went home, I'd have learnt the domestic deafness which is the Japanese substitute for privacy — not that I'd need it back in Perth, but what the Hell. When Mrs Tanii ducked back to the kitchen, I turned to Hiroshi and said, as sotto voce as possible, "Saw you with Shimako today. Does this mean you're back together?"

Anyone who thinks the Japanese are inscrutable hasn't seen one jump the way Hiroshi did. He stared at me for a moment, then whispered back, "No! Not me! Haven't seen her in a week!" and hurried out of the room. Miyume, his sister, glanced at him over the edge of her magazine, and then disappeared behind it again.

"Was it something I said?" I muttered, in English.

Miyume looked warily at me, then shook her head. "You must have mistaken someone else for him, Dai-Oni-San," she replied, also in English.

"Please don't call me that." Less than a week after I'd begun teaching, I'd become known as Tony Dai-Oni, Tony the Great Goblin-Demon. I mean, it's hardly my fault I'm red-headed, green-eyed, and nearly two metres tall, neh? "And don't try to tell me you all look the same, either. I know Hiroshi when I see him. He was even wearing my Cerebus T-shirt."

"There are nearly twelve million people in Tokyo, Tony-san," said Miyume, patiently. "There must be more than one Cerebus T-shirt. And if it was Hiroshi you saw, then it was not Shimako you saw him with." I could have corrected her grammar, but didn't. "You do not know her as well as you do Hiroshi."

That was true, but while I'm generally pretty good at remembering faces, I'm excellent at remembering pretty ones, and Shimako, while too young for me, was nearly as stunning as Miyume (whose name, aptly enough, meant 'Beautiful Dream'). Okay, so I've fallen in love with one of

my students everywhere I've taught — or so it always seemed at the time. Maybe one day, I'll find some way of knowing when I'm really in love, and settle down instead of hurrying to the next city. "Maybe," I conceded, just to see Miyume smile before she vanished behind her magazine again. I sighed silently, and returned to reading Kwaidan.

I've never been very good at researching the places I visit before I get there, and most of what I knew about Japan came from the Lonely Planet guidebook, a lot of Kurosawa movies, a crash course in the language, and the works of Lafcadio Hearn — a half-Irish half-Greek dishwasher, proof-reader and hack writer turned translator, teacher and folklorist (my sort of person, neh?). He'd written book after book of Japanese exotica ('Kwaidan' is Japanese for 'Weird Tales') a century ago, and written them so beautifully that no-one really cared whether the legends, poems and horror stories they contained were authentic. I lost myself for a few minutes in his story of the Rokuro-Kubi; when I looked up again, Miyume had gone, leaving the magazine on the floor open at the centrefold — a colour picture of a fairly pretty Japanese girl of about Miyume's age, naked except for a strategically placed octopus. Back home, it would have been considered pornographic, but this was a family magazine, with comics and a sports section.

One day, I thought, I might understand the Japanese language — but the Japanese themselves, never.

The next day, I saw Hiroshi and Shimako again — this time, at Shinjuku station. It looked as though he were following her, and she ignoring him, but that might have been some sort of courtship ritual. Suddenly, though, she ducked into the ladies' room, leaving him standing outside, looking foolish. He hesitated for a moment, then vanished into the crowd . . . or maybe into the toilets, or behind one of the vending machines; all I know is that he wasn't there when I looked again, a second later.

I didn't think of it again until I returned home,

and found him watching a video of *Terminator 2*. "Done your English homework?" I asked, teasingly, as I sat down behind him. He reached down and handed me a sheet of paper. I looked at it, and then up at the TV screen when I heard Hiroshi chuckle. The T2, shape-changed into the brat's foster-mother, had just impaled the foster-father . . . which meant that the movie had been running for at least half an hour. The homework, even if it'd been done with maximum haste and minimal enthusiasm, would have taken another half-hour. . . . "When did you get home?"

"About four-thirty. Why?"

I could've sworn I'd seen him on the other side of Tokyo at a quarter to five, at the earliest . . . and it was barely quarter past. "Any phone calls for me?"

"No," said Miyume, from the kitchen, before Hiroshi could answer.

"Thanks," I said, and started correcting Hiroshi's homework, wondering why he might bother lying to me. Maybe he thought it was none of my business — or none of anyone's business. He was only sixteen, after all, and Shimako already had quite a reputation as a heartbreaker: maybe the affair embarrassed him. But why was Miyume covering for him? Well, she was his sister, as well as a Psych major; she must have known him better than I did, and presumably had her reasons.

I finished correcting the homework, then reached into my day-pack for my battered copy of Hearn's *The Romance of the Milky Way* and turned to the chapter of 'Goblin Poetry'. It was weird, I thought, how many creatures in Japanese mythology were shapeshifters, routinely taking human form to deceive their victims — or maybe not weird, not in a country where gangsters openly wore the emblems of their syndicates on lapel pins, but certainly interesting. I didn't much mind that Hearn had decided not to translate the stories of the Three-Eyed Monk, the Acolyte with the Lantern, the Stone that cries in the night, the Goblin-Heron, or even the Faceless Babe, but I wished he'd been more impressed by the Long-Tongued Maiden and the Pillow-Mover. I also would have liked to have known more about how Goblin-Foxes turned old horse-bones into beautiful girls; it might come in useful —

"Still reading fairy-stories again, Tony-san?" I looked up, to see that Miyume was standing beside me, shaking her head. "Are you ever going to grow up?"

"Sit down and say that. Besides, this is anthropology."

"Anth— ?"

I tried to think of the Japanese word for 'anthropology', without success. "Ah . . . you've heard of Margaret Mead?"

"Yes, of course: didn't she do that book about Samoa, after all of the native girls had lied to her?"

"Touche."

"I suppose you think we turn into cats and foxes when your back is turned?"

I smiled. "Only some of you — you, for example. You're much too beautiful to be human, but you could be a cat, a flower, a tree — no, scratch that one, you're too short." I glanced at Hiroshi. "Maybe Shimako's the tree-spirit," I said, softly. Hiroshi ignored me, but Miyume covered her mouth and laughed.

"I assure you, I'm quite human," she said. "I don't doubt that Shimako is, too. And how many girls have you used that line on, before?"

"I think that one's an original."

"Thank you," she said, too politely. "What line did you use on your girlfriend in Taipei?"

"Mei? I tried writing her a poem, but my Chinese wasn't up to it, and her English . . ."

"And the one in Bangkok? Or Mexico City?"

"What are you trying to do, write my biography?"

"I'm trying to understand you, Tony-san. Isn't that what you're trying to do to us?" She leaned closer, and whispered, "Or do you just want to sleep with us?"

"Only you," I whispered back, without any hesitation; Mrs Tanii didn't understand English, and Hiroshi knew how and when to keep his mouth shut, "and only if it's what you want."

"Why only me?"

"Because it's only you I'm in love with. Don't Japanese ever fall in love without burning down Tokyo?"

In the tiny park near the apartment, there was a memorial to O-shichi, a seventeen-year-old girl who'd been burnt at the stake in 1683 for torching her father's house in an ill-advised attempt to re-unite herself with her samurai lover.

Miyume laughed, loudly enough that Hiroshi turned around to look at us. She glanced at him, and he hastily returned his attention to the television. "Of course we do," she said, in more normal tones. "We haven't always regarded it as the most important thing in the universe, or everyone's inalienable right, but then, neither

have Westerners . . . and we no longer think of it as the great dragon-demon, either. It's just something that happens."

I shrugged. I grew up on a farm, didn't even see a city until I went away to university, and I've long suspected that romantic love is like traffic jams and good bookshops, something you're much more likely to find in cities and the bigger the better. If you see a thousand women on the subway every morning, you can pick and choose, or at least dream: living in a small country town, you take what you can get. Me, I'd chosen to spend the five years since I graduated in some of the largest cities on Earth, cities so crowded you rarely saw your own shadow. "What about you, personally?"

"Me?"

"Have you ever been in love?"

She raised her eyebrows innocently, and smiled broadly. "Of course, Tony-san, but love is one thing, and sex another. Please remember, this is not Australia: rents are high here, privacy expensive, and most of us can not afford to leave home until we have been working for many years — often, not even then. Competition for places in the universities is much more intense — you must have heard of Examination Hell — so we have to spend more time studying." She pointedly didn't even glance at Hiroshi. "And our doctors will not prescribe the pills which your teenagers take for granted — perhaps because they believe them to be too dangerous, but possibly because they make too much money out of abortions. I know it's not romantic, but Japanese girls have learnt when and how to say 'no'; the meek little women who do everything men tell them are as mythical as your kitsune, rikombyo and gaki. In truth, we rule our men from birth; that's why they work so hard to keep what power they have, and why they never come home at night." Then she bent over, kissed me quickly on the tip of my nose, and ducked back into the kitchen.

I sat there, rubbing my nose absent-mindedly. Kitsune were goblin-foxes, and gaki were hungry ghosts, but what the Hell were rikombyo?

I found the answer in Hearn (where else?): a rikombyo, literally 'ghost-sickness', was a dopplegänger, an apparition created by unrequited love, or the love for someone now dead. In the poem Hearn quoted, the rikombyo stayed at home with the original, both yearning after the far-journeying husband, but Hearn also stated

by Stephen Dedman

that 'one of these bodies would go to join the absent beloved, while the other remained at home'.

I looked over at Hiroshi, and shook my head. Sure, I loved ghost stories and old legends, but this was one of the most modern cities on Earth, it was like believing that there were vampires in Washington . . . well, you know what I mean. Besides, Hearn had written that rikombyo were 'of the gentler sex', whatever that meant in Japan. . . .

I continued to stare, until the movie ended and Miyume began setting the table for dinner.

On Saturday night, Miyume took me to a party at Tokyo University, to meet her Psych class. I was suspicious of her motives — Hiroshi had told me that she had at least three boyfriends at the university at any one time and was careful not to show favouritism to any of them, so this may have been just another psych experiment — but what the Hell, I would have followed Miyume into a leper colony or karaoke bar.

Once at the party, Miyume disappeared into the throng, presumably giving equal time to her troika (triad?), and leaving me to dance and converse with a group of students who knew even less about Australia than I did about Japan. It was exhausting, but amusing, and at least no one asked me to sing; more importantly, it gave us a moment of real privacy on the way home, as we walked from the station to the apartment. Miyume had been teasing me about having drawn a crowd, and I was accusing her of the same. She denied it, and I asked, "So what were they? Rikombyo?"

She laughed unconvincingly, and said, "Of course not; there's no such thing. I told you that —"

I looked at her, and realised she was lying. She tried walking faster to get some distance between us, but it was a wasted effort; I could hop faster than she could run. "Then why do I keep seeing Hiroshi following Shimako when he's supposed to be somewhere else?"

"Then it couldn't have been him; you were mistaken . . ."

"No I wasn't. Was it a rikombyo?"

"I told you, there's no such thing; you saw someone who looked like Hiroshi . . ."

"Next time, I'll take a photograph."

"It won't work," she said, as we hurried through the park, and then stopped suddenly at the memorial to O-Shichi, her face white. We stared at each other for a moment, and then I asked, "You knew, didn't you?"

"Knew what?"

"About Hiroshi."

"No," she said, quietly. "I didn't know about Hiroshi until you told me."

"About rikombyo, then."

"Of course; I told you about them, if you remember . . ."

"They exist?"

"Yes, they exist," she said, heavily. "They're rare, and you can't duplicate them in a laboratory — it's been tried — but yes, they do exist."

We stood there in silence (apart from the passing traffic and the occasional plane from the nearby airport), and then I said, "Laboratory?"

"Psychologists have tried to create them, usually with hypnosis. It's worked sometimes, but not often enough for anyone to risk making a fool of himself by presenting a paper on it."

"Jesus."

"We still don't really know what causes them. What do psychologists know about love, anyway, right?" she said, with a twisted smile. "We know they're rare — but even if they were one in a million, there'd be twelve of them in Tokyo alone. They're real enough to fool anyone in most circumstances, but they don't cast shadows or show up on film. And we know they're sterile; we managed to get a sperm sample from one, and no, I'm not going to tell you how. There are old stories about men and women having sex with them; they're — said to be very good lovers, because they're eager to please and that's really all they exist for. Rather like butterflies."

"And do they die after a day, too?"

Miyume smiled. "You keep saying how often you've been in love, Tony-san; does that die after a day? However long the love lasts, unrequited and with that sort of intensity, they last. Usually, they just disappear. We've never found a body of one; I suspect a lot of suicide attempts are really rikombyo, but that's just a theory, I can't prove it."

I shuddered. "What'll happen to Hiroshi?"

"I don't know. Probably nothing; usually, they just get over it, find someone else who loves them back, fall sanely in love instead of madly."

The shock hadn't quite worn off by Monday, when the rikombyo followed Shimako into my English class — but Domeki-sensei was too polite to mention it, so what was a humble teaching assistant like myself supposed to do?

A few of the girls giggled behind their hands, but nothing more; Shimako herself remained as poised as ever. I was sufficiently startled that it took me (me!) most of the lesson to recognise the telltale signs of a teenage girl who's just gotten laid and is trying not to be too visibly smug about it.

I stared at the rikombyo while earnestly trying to explain Australian Rules football to the class. He was as inscrutable as the Japanese are supposed to be. I babbled on, wondering if this was a tremendous hoax; perhaps there was no apparition, only an obsessive teenager who'd skipped a class to —

No. I knew the Japanese well enough to know that this being tolerated, especially this near Examination Hell, was much less likely than a ghost in a classroom. The lesson continued harmoniously enough until the siren sounded for the next class — the second-last of the day, I remembered with relief. A moment later, I remembered that Hiroshi was in that class . . . and he always rushed there, hoping to see Shimako before she left.

Shimako seemed to be taking forever to pack her bag and leave the room; she was only halfway to the door, with the rikombyo puppy-like at her heels, when Hiroshi walked in.

Back home, it would have been the prelude to a screaming match, maybe even a brawl . . . but Hiroshi merely looked from one face to the other for a few seconds, his expression horrified, then stared straight into the rikombyo's eyes. It looked for all the world like one of those scenes from the Kurosawa films, the contest of wills between two samurai: for a moment, the apparition seemed to fade into the dingy painted wall — and then Shimako took a step forward, and then walked past Hiroshi without looking at him again. The rikombyo followed her out. Domeki-sensei turned to the blackboard, and began writing.

I was on my way to the station that evening, when I saw Shimako again. The rikombyo was still following her, but this time, he was wearing a Cerebus T-shirt again, with a new pair of Levi 501s and even newer Nikes — way beyond the Taniis' budget. He seemed taller, too, with clearer skin: in fact, I realised, though unmistakeably male, he looked more like Shimako than Hiroshi. . . .

I scanned the crowd for the real Hiroshi, but there was no sign of him.

I caught the next train to Shinagawa, and walked to the apartment. He wasn't in the living room, or his bedroom, but the place didn't feel empty. I tried listening, but the traffic noises from outside drowned out any recognisable sounds of movement. "Hiroshi?"

No answer . . .

I stood in the living room for a moment, and then noticed that Miyume's bedroom door was closed. I knocked on it softly, and there was a distinct gasp from within.

"Miyume?"

There was a sound inside that might have been scuffling, and then "What is it?"

"Can I come in?"

"No! Don't open the door!"

Despite myself, I smiled. "Okay . . . but I need to talk to you. Hiroshi . . . well, it's about your, uh, psych experiment. Look, I'll be waiting in the living room, okay?"

I collapsed onto the sofa, closed my eyes, and tried to think. Finally, I heard Miyume's door open, and then close again. I recounted the afternoon's events as concisely and dispassionately as I could, and concluded, "I guess the rikombyo's about equal parts Hiroshi's frustration and Shimako's narcissism, now. Is that common?"

"No."

"What'll happen now?"

"I don't know," she said, sitting beside me, smelling unmistakeably of dynamite sex. "It will probably disappear before very long."

"Or Hiroshi will . . . has he been home?"

"No."

I nodded, and opened my eyes. Despite her obvious worry, she was still glowing and looked even more beautiful than ever. "Your boyfriend — is he a psych student, too?"

"No."

"You might as well bring him out; he can't stay in there forever."

She smiled hesitantly, and something went click! in my brain. I rolled off the sofa, and hurtled down the corridor.

"Tony! NO!"

Opening her bedroom door would have been obscenely rude even in Australia; in Tokyo, it was probably a capital crime. But I had to know —

He was red-headed and nearly two metres tall;

I couldn't see what colour his eyes were in the dim light, but I didn't need to.

I don't know how long we stared at each other, but suddenly Miyume was standing behind me. "You said you loved me," she whispered. "Isn't it good to know you were telling the truth?"

I turned around, and then walked out of the apartment without another word.

The youth hostel had a nine o'clock curfew, which was ridiculous for Tokyo, but it gave me time for a few drinks and a decision. I was on contract until the end of the school year, so I couldn't leave Tokyo . . . but if I stayed in a hostel and stuck to a vegetarian diet, I could save enough for an airline ticket. It only remained to choose somewhere to go.

The more Kirin beer I drank, the better Taipei looked. I could spend some time with Mei, maybe get my old job there back . . . I changed a few notes for coins, and headed for the phone.

The phone rang five times before being answered by a man with a faint Australian accent. It took me a moment to recognise my own voice, and then I hung up immediately. Then I went to the bar, had another drink, and my shadow and I went back to the hostel and to bed.   Ω

CURSE OF THE SIREN'S HUSBAND

He watches from the wings
as she takes her final bows.
Hoarse screams fill the rafters.
Bodies roll through the aisles.
They surge against the stage
like lemmings in full flight.
Yet security stands ready
and security holds tight
to repulse her hapless thralls.
This steady wall of deaf men,
who cannot hear her songs,
has saved her more than once.

Her albums all go platinum.
Her concerts fill the halls
When the tickets go on sale
the lines queue for blocks.
The critics praise her artistry
and marvel at her range,
from a virginal soprano
to a rich and knowing bass
that includes a magic mezzo
and a pure contralto scale.

Yet once they are alone
in a sumptuous penthouse suite
— her make-up stripped away,
her gown a wrinkled heap
and the music far behind —
she collapses on the sofa,
a damp cloth across her eyes,
until her real self emerges
and her real voice opines:

"If you'd booked a second show,
we could have upped the gate.
That drum solo was lame,
the bass line somewhat thin,
and the stage was far too small.
Put the flowers over there.
Where *are* my fluffy slippers?
Don't forget to call Chicago.
Bring me more champagne!
Tomorrow I'll sleep in."

As they idolize her photos,
wearing headphones like a vice,
as they hatch erotic fantasies
far beyond their reach,
as they multiply their longing
to the sum of their lives,
her addict-fans could never,
in their dark and wildest dreams,
imagine how her siren's song
can become a harpy's screech.

— Bruce Boston

A GOAT IN TROUSERS
by Lord Dunsany

illustrated by Fredrik King

A fog that had been lying over the fields was going away at last along the horizon, with queer weird shapes rising up from it as it went; but for which I might never have troubled with the fancies that what I saw in a field gave rise to, though what I saw was odd in itself.

It was a goat wearing trousers. They were good grey trousers with dark stripes in them, and he had a smart black jacket too, and even a hat, jammed down on one of his horns, which came out through the brim. Boys play all kinds of tricks, with most of which one would have no reason to interfere; but, when I looked close and saw the quality of the trousers, it seemed to me that somebody might be put to loss and considerable expense, and that the unsuitable joke, or whatever it was, should be enquired into.

So with a view to reporting what I had seen I opened the gate of the field, which was the end of an iron bedstead, so that I need hardly say that this was in Ireland, for this convenient use of old broken-down bedsteads, so far as I know, is scarcely found elsewhere.

And, indeed, the far blue shapes of the Dublin mountains looked serenely over the field and that strangely-apparelled goat, and me going up to it to pursue my enquiries. And the first thing that I saw as I entered the field was a boot of patent leather which I supposed had been kicked off. I don't know where the other one was. And when I got near the goat it turned its head towards me. And I looked into its yellow eyes, and it looked right into mine, and seemed for a moment as if it had something to tell me; and then with a sudden shake it turned its head away, as though neither I nor my enquiries could ever be any use to it. And from all the enquiries I made, not only on the spot, but from many men, this is what seems to have happened.

Those pale-blue distant mountains must have looked down also on two statesmen walking along a street in Dublin on one of those days on which their calm grave faces looked clearly all the way down some streets of the city. And, as they went, one statesman said to the other, "It is a shocking thing that, with the great position that Ireland now has, there should be anyone in the country still believing in wise women and witchcraft and all that nonsense, when we should be showing an example to the nations."

"It is indeed," said the other.

"We must frame a bill," said the first statesman, "and get it passed into law as quickly as possible, making it an offence to take any fees for any pretended cures of man or beast, or anything of the sort. I'd like to make it a punishable offence even to talk of such things; but we can't do that. But if we stop those women receiving any fees, we will soon stop the whole nonsense."

And the other statesman was silent awhile, and then he said, "No. We can't do it by laws. The cure for it is education. It's all childish nonsense. But stamp it out in the minds of children, and by the time that they grow up the thing will be done with for ever."

"You're right," said the other. "And it's what we'll do. We'll send down a man, for a start, to give a lecture about it to every school in Leinster, and to explain to them clearly in simple words that wise women are all just nonsense, and witches and all the rest of them, and that they are only helpless old women trying to frighten children."

So a man was sent down from Dublin to go to every school in Leinster, and would lecture for a bit in a school, and go on to another as soon as he had convinced all there. And in the far gaze of the Dublin mountains men were saying, "Isn't it a good thing to have a man down from Dublin teaching the children sense?"

And the answer would come, "Sure it is. Isn't it time they learned?"

And another would say, "It was all very well in the old days, putting horns and tail on a man, or any other queer shape; but a belief in all them things doesn't suit modern ideas, and it is time it was put a stop to."

"It is indeed. Sure, you're right, and it is indeed. At the same time, wouldn't it be a pity to annoy the wise women overmuch? For who is there but they that has any cure for the falling of the palate? Aye, and for other ills and evils. Sure, who would there be to help us in our need, if that man were to incense them so that one night they all went away to wherever such people go? I only ask the question, meaning no harm."

"Isn't there the doctor?" said someone.

"Ah, doctors don't know everything," came the answer.

And heads were nodded at that. And the mood of the men changed, as the mood of the mountains changes, watching from beyond Dublin; and they began to doubt the wisdom of the man who had come to the school of their village to teach the children sense.

But the wise women were troubled. For the rumour ran all through Leinster that all their witchcraft was only to frighten children and that there was nothing in it at all.

The lecturer was a man named Mr. Finnegan; and after speaking to the children of the school of Donnisablane he was put up for the night by Michael Murphy, the young schoolmaster of that village. And the rumour of his coming had run for miles round and told everyone that he would be there. And there it was that Mrs. Garganey, who was a wise woman, had talked with Mrs. Gallagher, who was another, as soon as the rumour had reached her, and said to her, "What is to be done? What is to be done at all?"

And Mrs. Gallagher had brewed a pound of tea only the day before, and it was simmering in the great kettle on her hearth, which small though her thatched cottage was, had an ampler space than any hearth that you are likely to see in any big house in England.

And Mrs. Gallagher said as they drank their tea, darker than brownest chestnut, "I have answered many queer riddles and read strange destinies. And so have you, Mrs. Garganey. But for this we must send for the Wise Woman of Galway. For there is none but she that can deal with this man from Dublin, who is down here putting wrong ideas into the heads of the children, and telling them that we and all our most secret arts are nothing at all, and that what we learned from our great-grandmothers, and that they learned from the old time and from the great witches of those days, is nothing only mere nonsense. And he, what is he but only a small clerk puffed up with his self-importance, and knowing no more of where the big winds rise, or of what news they carry, than he knows of the growth of a buttercup. But he has the authority

46

of them that be in Dublin behind him, and there is no one able to deal with him but that great witch, the Wise Woman of Galway. So let us send for her, and see what shape she will put on him."

And send for her they did, however their message was carried, and she had harnessed her ass-cart at once and had driven by town and bog and meadow and wood all the way across Ireland, and was now come to Donnisablane. And Mrs. Gallagher said to her whatever such people say when they meet, and made whatever obeisance; and brought her to her house and put her ass in her bit of a stable and gave the great witch a cup of her dark tea. And Mrs. Garganey came to that house too, and the three conferred. And they spoke of strange transformations. And then the Wise Woman of Galway told them what they should do. And about that time a look came over the Dublin mountains, as though they all crept nearer to listen; so that their very hedgerows could be seen below, and their glens and valleys above, as they show when rain is coming.

But it was more than the rain that was coming. For the Wise Woman of Galway had bid summon the wise women from all the province of Leinster, and it was they that were drawing nearer. They harnessed their ass-carts at that summons, and came trotting. And those that had no ass for their journey ran.

And on the night of which I tell, whatever magic may be, there were more of them that make it in Donnisablane than in any other townland in all Ireland. And they came with a great cauldron, and drew all round the house of Michael Murphy, with Mr. Finnegan inside, and lit a fire under their cauldron among the trees of an orchard, and chanted their incantations and made their spells and did whatever witches do. And Michael Murphy looking out of a little window saw what was going on, and he ran to Mr. Finnegan and said, "Mr. Finnegan, sir, clear out of this and change your name and get to foreign parts. For the witches are after you."

And the man from Dublin said, "Now, you know that is all nonsense. Didn't I tell your children so this afternoon?"

"I know, sir. I know," said Michael Murphy. "And you put it very well. But look out of that window now towards the orchard. Look out; only don't let them see you."

And the man from Dublin looked out. "I see," he said. "I see there is something over there in the orchard."

"And it's all round us," said Michael Murphy. "Only there's a little path that runs along under the hedge of my garden, and you could get away by that. Only go quick, and go to foreign parts; for they're after you."

"I see," said the man from Dublin. "Mind you, it's just as I said: witches and cauldrons and spells and all that kind of thing are just nonsense. At the same time, to avoid any unpleasantness, I will perhaps do as you say."

Then he left the house, and that is the last that was ever seen of him.

I have made very thorough enquiries into the case; too thorough, perhaps, for they have established three separate theories. Some believe Mr. Finnegan fled to France, or one of those foreign countries, changing his name and his clothes, however his clothes got on to the goat. And then many believe that the wise women, whose whole profession he threatened, closed round him at the back of the garden and murdered him and put him into the cauldron in the orchard and boiled him, all but his clothes, and then dressed up the goat in the way that I saw. That is a theory that has been put to the police; and it is for them to investigate it, not I. But they seem to have investigated very half-heartedly and with no sympathy from anyone in the townland, where men were heard to say, "Why can't the gardai [police] get on with their work, and leave the wise women alone?" A sentiment with which the gardai almost seemed to agree. For, from all I hear, they questioned very few of the old women, and those politely and briefly.

The third theory, and the one perhaps the most widely held, though men say little about it, is that Mr. Finnegan is still alive and wearing his own clothes in fields around Donnisablane. But that is a theory of which I need say no more, for my readers would never believe it. Nor could I believe it myself anywhere away from the influence of the south-west wind, full of the scent of turf-smoke, blowing by old gnarled willows away over wastes of bog.   Ω

DRACULIMERICK

Said the Count, to Jonathan Harker,
as his prospects grew steadily darker,
    "You will have from my wives
    pleasures no one survives,
and then get a nice pretty marker."
— **Darrell Schweitzer**

WERELIZARD WARNING

The human-lizard metamorphosis
consists mainly of internal changes.
The only outward signs reveal
themselves as a failure to express
genuine emotion and the absence
of a certain spark that is visible
in the eyes of nearly all mammals,
even squirrels or bats or mice.

The disease is not transmitted
by means of bites or scratches,
but merely through repeated
or prolonged exposure to those
who have already crossed over
into the chill reptilian realm.

In its final stages the affliction
is not transitory or reversible,
nor is it in any way related to
the changing phases of the moon.
Werelizards remain werelizards
the rest of their unnatural lives.

Werelizards can be all around
wiithout you even knowing it.
At the bank. On the freeway.
Your auto mechanic or plumber
could easily be a werelizard.
Most lawyers are werelizards.
Politicians become werelizards
at some point in their careers.

If you think you are infected
there exist means to reverse
the process in it early stages.
Listen to music. Read poetry.
Surround yourself with those
you care about the most and
the ones who care about you.
Take a derelict to lunch.

The war between humanity
and werelizards is the oldest
of all conflicts and it must
be waged on the rugged and
shifting terrain of the heart
where every battle won or lost
can change the course of life.
— **Bruce Boston**

anybody home?

on the walls
all the mirrors
empty

in the bedrooms
every bed
empty

on the floors
heaps of clothes
empty

in the crawlspace
an eight-foot eggcase
empty
— **Steve McComas**

ONE SUMMER EVENING

by Catherine Mintz

illustrated by Janet Aulisio

Summer was the cruelest season. As the decades passed, the often-thwarted hope that he might heal faded into despair, almost indifference, but when the long golden days came they always reminded him of what he once was and renewed the pain.

He knit his long fingers together and sighed. The girl laughed at him whenever she caught him in this mood, and he had become skilled at concealing it from her, if not from the cats that lounged before the fire kept burning day and night regardless of the weather. They fled to the jungle safety of the garden whenever he unclasped the dark book bound in scaly leather.

So far, of course, the girl — chosen for her sunny personality: he had a horror of clever women — had been right not to take him seriously. The book was as useless as he himself and might as well have gone to start the kitchen fire on some winter morning, except of course that the stove used glass.

He got to his feet to pace. That he had been exhausted when he had placed himself here, at the conclusion of what he once saw as the fitting end of his labors, was no excuse. What had then seemed overwhelmingly desirable — an obscure life filled with simple routines and mundane pleasures — was not not even tolerable. Grief is a bad counselor, he reminded himself.

A siren wailed in the distance, and he frowned. It would take great skill to reverse the process. A delicate balance of influences had to be reached before he, with the — metaphorically speaking — small lever that was all he had allowed himself to retain, could once again move worlds.

He turned and looked out the open French doors.

The mist was forming over the river and the sounds of the works of modern men were dulled. Yet another perfect moment for the testing spell. He smiled bitterly. There had been many such moments and he had done his best every time.

So far nothing had happened. He had sat and waited, listening to the distant rumble of airplanes, until the cats had come home and the girl came in from the kitchen, smelling of herbs, spices, and her own warm self, leaned on the arm of his chair and charmed him into a better mood with wiles older than any man's.

Still, he thought, and took the book from the shelf. He sat down, unclasped the volume, and smoothed the page carefully. One more try before he turned the television on for the evening: he never had been one to simply quit.

Focusing his mind on the task to come, he reread the instructions he had penned so long ago. Magicking from memory without dire need was ostentatious. He preferred discretion when discretion would serve as well or better than showy workings.

Somewhere beyond the garden wall a car hooted urgently.

He winced, then spread his hands and spoke.

The spell having been muttered and sighed into the summer twilight, he leaned back and dozed until the scrabble of a cat's claws on the hearth bricks woke him. The gray tabby had caught a mouse — or — he leaned forward in his chair — perhaps it was a bat. His eyes narrowed suddenly. Holding out a hand, he compelled the animal to him with a skill long-disused, then prodded the small carcass with a long forefinger before giving it back to its rightful owner. Head high to keep the wings from dragging, the offended tabby carried the tiny dragon off to her private lair under the rose bushes.

His hands palm up, in his lap, he closed his eyes, felt power begin to fill his hollow self. In the garden, a small wind tentatively stirred the leaves, then a swirl of vapor formed above the beech trees.

Looking up from its fabulous feast, the gray tabby hissed as fat raindrops splattered the paving, wept down the window glass. She bolted into the house as the first stroke of lightning lashed the air.

Merlin laughed, and thunder walked the sky.

© G. Barr - 1999

SCARLET AND GOLD

Scarlet and Gold

by Tanith Lee

illustrated by George Barr

There were two brothers. But, as the day is not much like the night, so they were, or were not, to each other. The fact was, they had had the same father, the lord of the great Village of Seven-Willow, but their mothers were different. Chegahr had been got by the lord on a girl little better than a slave, one midwinter's night, in a barn, while the wolves were composing their songs to the moon. Chegahr was strong and square-built, swarthy and dark-eyed, and with the white-blond hair of the North. But Velonin, whom his father had got on his priest-law lady wife, respectably under a sheet in the High House, was slim and tall, with hair like a mountain panther's pelt and blue eyes like the best china plate.

My story does not begin there, however, (or perhaps it does, since without their being born, they would not be in it) but in the hour before sunrise some eighteen, nineteen, or twenty years later.

At this hour, be certain, Velonin was yet lying fast asleep, with his head on swansdown pillows.

Chegahr, though, was out on the plain beyond Seven-Willow, dragging along his sled, for which he could afford neither pony nor dog, and loading it where he could with fallen branches which the snow had brought down. Trees grew thick on the plain, and southwards became a forest; but being the son of a slave, he was not permitted to cut any tree, even a dead one. So his share of firewood depended on sloughings.

It was winter again, and the scene was worth a look, if Chegahr had had the space and the spirit to look at it. And he did. When you have not much, there is not much to interrupt you. So he stood and saw, in the narrow, silver light that comes before the dawn, the sweep of the white world, which was like a vellum page in some rich man's book, but a book not yet written on. Unless the woods and forest might be the words of some tale, the firs and the pines, all coated white but here and there with a little of themselves still visible. For miles the plain ran and at its end, which Chegahr had been told — he had never gone so far — was ten days' journey off, stood the wall of the Iron Heart Mountains. And they too were shouldered and crowned with white, against the ghostly sky.

Chegahr looked, and he saw it all, and he fed his hungry eyes. Even on the three white hares he saw playing not much distance off. And if he wondered, should he bring one down quickly with a stone for his dinner, he then thought better of it. He had bread and cheese and a jug of potato beer, which he had earned by his work for others. Let the hares keep their lives until he would lose his without them.

Meanwhile the night got on with its departure. It rinsed the bright stars off the sky, carelessly muddying and fading them as it always did, before stuffing them in its pockets, and slipping away over the western horizon behind Seven-Willow Village. And the sun began to stain the east over the mountains, spilling pails of itself up the stairs of the sky as usual, in its rush to get back and spy on what was going on.

Chegahr watched, and he enjoyed the rich red flush of the coming sun and the torn gold stitches of the clouds, just as he would have enjoyed his breakfast, if he had had any.

And then, ah, then. The sun did a new and very strange thing. Instead of rising blindingly up as always through the gap in the mountains, it shot right through the gap, fast as an arrow, and began to race towards Chegahr.

Chegahr stared, and then he prudently moved himself and his sled some yards to one side. At the same moment the three white hares went leaping away, and Chegahr pondered if he too should take to his heels. But instead he only planted his feet more firmly. For if the sun was running straight towards him, it was yet much smaller than he would have expected, and although, it flashed and sparkled, it seemed to burn nothing, not even, properly, his eyes.

After some minutes the actual sun rose in the normal way up from the Iron Heart Mountains. And then the bit of the sun, which seemed to have been fired out of it, began to cast a long blue shadow. And next Chegahr began to see what it really was.

"Well," said Chegahr, "is this less or more wonderful than the sun rolling towards me?"

Just then, the less-or-more-wonderful thing turned sharply sidelong, and Chegahr beheld properly what it was. And what it was, was this: It was a great gambolling sled, and it seemed to be made of hardened gold. Its sides were gold, and its runners, and its high seat, and all its curlicues and elegances; and it had a prow that was in the shape of a wild face, human, but with the beak of a bird. And this was all gold, as I say, ripe red-gold, that shone and glowed. The sled was drawn not by a horse or dogs, but by a team of snow-white wolves. And Chegahr had no doubt about that at all. They were hitched very oddly in two lines of six, with one enormous one, big as a lion, he thought, at the very front, who bounded forward, dragging the rest behind. These wolves were harnessed in deep red, and hung with golden bells; and by now Chegahr could hear the hiss and rush of the sled, and the pound of the four times thirteen pads that sprang up and pounced down on the snow. Was this not enough? Of course not, for the sled must have a traveller in it, and so it did.

Chegahr stared, blinked, and stared the harder. In the sled was a young woman, and he was sure she was young for she was only a hundred feet away — what was that? — and if the sun was beyond her, even so, she seemed lit up like a lamp, and he could tell she had skin like cream without one blemish or wrinkle in it, and eyes like hot chestnuts and lips like red currants. But she wore a blood-red gown, and oh but was it not embroidered in a border three hands high (and Chegahr's large hands at that) in golden patterns? And at her wrists were golden armlets and round her slender white neck a necklace of hammered gold, and on her head a cap of scarlet velvet trimmed with golden discs. And was not *this* enough? Yes, and too much, indeed. But there was more, for as with most such sights, marvels vulgarly outdo themselves. So, from her pure pale temples sprang out a mane of golden hair, not vivid gold, as the sled and bells and discs and other paraphernalia, but *icy* gold, like the sun gleaming through a milk-glass window. And this hair, believe me or not, (and I hold nothing against you if you refuse, for even Chegahr, who saw it, afterwards partly thought he had not) this hair poured over and down like a wind of light blown out through the top of her head, and swirled on and on behind her, over her gown, out of the sled, over the white snow, over the plain, back as far, it looked, as the mountains. And all the while, the scarlet cap bobbing on it, like a stopper coming loose in a bottle of bubbling wine.

But then the wolves pulled the sled away among the trees, down the aisles of the wood, where the snow-coated pines soon hid it. And after some ten or twenty minutes more, which Chegahr counted out as carefully as he was able, (imagining in his head, the tick of the clock in church) the last of the hair was drawn in too, and vanished after the maiden and her sled, into the wood.

Then Chegahr took up again the ropes of his own sled, and turning, he walked back to the Village, whistling.

Let me assure you, Chegahr had no intention of speaking a word of what he had seen. It is possible that, on Witch Eve or Christmas Eve next, when he might have gone to the church, and next the tavern, if some had begun telling fairy tales and legends of the Village, he might have added this anecdote: One morning I saw . . . But in no other form would he have risked it. He was the son of a slave who had been rash enough, before she died, to boast her baby was the child of the lord in the High House, and that was tale enough to hang about him, as thrown stones, spittle, and other kindnesses had swiftly shown.

However.

As Chegahr was walking across Church Square, to reach the alley behind the cemetery where he had his hut, five men were standing by the church door to smoke their pipes. And they were important men of Seven-Willow, the chair-maker and the horse-doctor, the rat-catcher and the roof-patcher, and the elder of the two priests, whose skin was thin as silk from spirits in a bottle.

As Chegahr came near, generally speaking, they would have paid him no heed. Except one might have muttered something, or one might jeeringly have laughed. Even if any of the nine hundred persons in the Village had work for Chegahr, they tended to send their servants or slaves to tell him so. And even the slaves were impertinent and sullen, for they were owned and had some value. By the by, too, Chegahr's mother's master had died in the year Chegahr was born. And this master had been the Village muck-carrier, who tended the midden and cleaned the privies. Even as a slave, Chegahr would have had no status. But if you are wanting to tell me that Chegahr would have done better to have left the Village of Seven-Willow the day after his mother's death, when he was just twelve years old, I may say he had often thought so himself. But then, the mountains were ten days away, and crossing them was another matter,

more like scaling the vertical air to reach the moon. While south and north were other obstacles, the haunted forest, a vast raging river; and anyway there were everywhere only other villages very like Seven-Willow, which to strangers were reported unfriendly, or treacherous. And though everyone spoke of a city to the north, and another to the west, who ever came from there and could prove it, or going there — returned?

Besides, which is more to the point, now and then Chegahr looked up and saw the rise above the Village where stood the High House, inside its walls. But I shall come to that, as will Chegahr, presently.

Now though the five important men stared at Chegahr. And the rat-catcher gave an oath, and the old priest marked himself with the cross. It was the chair-maker who roared, straight at Chegahr, "Hey, you dog, what do you mean by it?"

Chegahr stopped. He put on his mildest glance. Trouble had no interest for him, for its own sake. It wasted his time, which might be spent in more fruitful ways, such as gazing, thinking, and dreaming. He did suspect this bother might be about some Village girl, for sometimes it was. Although the Village men did not much like him, now and then a young woman might cast him half a look of a different sort. He was too wise to give the look back, but occasionally even modest indifference was not enough. (As with the scholar's wife, who had once stridden up to Chegahr, one summer as he was minding the Village goats on the plain, and slapped his face hard. "I dreamed last night you laid me on my back and straddled me!" had cried this amiable woman. "There's for that!" And then she had fetched him another slap. "And that's for making me like it." Her name was Majlena, but it was not the time for him to find out.)

"How did you get it?" now bellowed the roof-patcher angrily.

"What?" asked Chegahr.

"Behold him stand there and deny it," growled the horse-doctor. "See this, wretch? It's a pill to cleanse thoroughly a horse's bowels. Do *you* want to try it?"

"My thanks, I decline."

"Then tell your news."

"I have none."

"The scut!" cried the rat-catcher,. "I'll stuff a rat up him, I will!"

"Peace, peace," said the old priest, "we are before God's house. Chegahr, you must tell us the truth."

"It has snowed," said Chegahr. "The sun has risen. This is called the Village of Seven-Willow and I am Chegahr. What other truth is there? Enlighten me. I'll speak it."

Then the horse-doctor and the rat-catcher and the roof-patcher and *almost* the chair-maker — who began, and then decided against it — rushed at Chegahr and grabbed him hard and fast. And Chegahr, who might fairly easily have thrust them off and mashed their noses for them, did not. Because other than they, there were the rest of the eight hundred and ninety-five persons of Seven-Willow, not to mention the immediate chair-maker and priest, and even women, who made love with him in dreams, slapped him twice in daylight.

"What now? Fetch my tongs!" inventively shouted the horse-doctor. And, "I'll nail him on a roof," improvised the roof-patcher, but the priest said, "He must go up to the High House. His lordship must see and decide."

Chegahr was quite in the dark about all this. And stayed in the dark all the way up the path to the top of the rise, during which trek, various other people came to join the procession, including the boot-maker and the tavern-owner, and the scholar (he of the wife), many children, and sixteen young girls from Seven-Willow's five wells. And it was not until Chegahr got face to face with a glass mirror in his father's house, which was now the house of Velonin, his half-brother, that he knew. But I will explain at once. Chegahr had returned from the snowy winter plain with a most beautiful golden summer tan. It covered, uninterrupted, his face and throat, and had even bleached his blond hair at the front to white.

The High House had high walls; and within was an orchard of cherry and peach trees, now hidden in the snow. But before the house, which was partly of stone and partly timbered, lay an open snowy space, on which balanced one mournful statue. It was of a naked boy and two bare-looking dogs, from which the ice had mostly melted off. This statue, a wonder of Seven-Willow, had been brought to the house as a curious bit of the dowry of Velonin's deceased mother. Chegahr, who had heard of it but never seen — this being the first time he had entered his father's gates — thought only that the marble boy looked very cold, and was shut out of the house. But perhaps he had some cause for thinking in that way.

Then the great door was knocked upon and a house servant came, dressed better, of course, than any Villager, save perhaps for the horse-doctor and the boot-maker.

To begin with, everyone waited in a big cold hall, with tiles underfoot and a long window of coloured glass, showing a scene that looked religious, but not religious enough. In one corner lurked a clock, twice the size of that in the church, and variously about were set a barometer, a musical box (silent), and a ship in a bottle.

Then, from up the oak staircase, (imported), came a loud bang and a slither, which was Velonin throwing a large book at the announcing servant in vexation, and the servant falling over.

Then Velonin appeared in person on the carved gallery above the stair.

All but hatless Chegahr doffed their caps and bowed.

"What in the devil's name do you want?" shouted his lordship.

The villagers grovelled. Many began to blame Chegahr, while the priest made a sort of bleating noise, the rat-catcher swore, and the girls from the wells gazed blushing at their lord.

"Devil take you," said Velonin, "cluttering up the place." And he strode down the stair, into the hall, his breakfast napkin still in his hand. There he stood glaring from his best-blue eyes, and in his coat of pale blue satin. There were three gold rings on his fingers — and next down the stair, as if wishing only to stay with him, there wafted the scent of hot white bread and butter, roast chops, and a rare coffee, brought years ago, with cases of wine and champagne, it was said, from one of the mythic cities far away.

"You," said Velonin, pointing at the horse-doctor, whom he slightly knew, having met him now and then in the house stables, "what's up?"

But the horse-doctor gave Chegahr a push.

"Look; your lordship can see; it's written all over his face."

And it was then that Velonin, who was the half-brother of Chegahr, stared right into Chegahr's face, and into his eyes. And Chegahr did the same with Velonin.

"Then who the devil are *you?*" demanded Velonin, sensing insolence more than noticing the tan.

So Chegahr told him, "Your father's son."

"Stuff and nonsense. You look nothing like him," declared Velonin, going straight to the point.

"Neither do you," said Chegahr. "You're pale and dark and delicate like your mother. Just as I'm burly and blond like mine. But what's wrong with my face, then?"

And at that Velonin reached into his satin pocket and took out a silvered round of mirror held in a gilded frame.

Chegahr peered. He saw. He gave Velonin once more look for look. "Then I'll tell you," said he, "seeing as you're kin."

And on the gale of gasps at his effrontery, there before them all, and the barometer and the music box and the bottled ship, Chegahr told what he had seen. That was, the sled drawn by thirteen white wolves, the maiden in scarlet and gold, and her golden hair that poured behind her and passed into the wood after her, ten or twenty minutes after *she* was gone from sight.

Throughout Chegahr's recital there was not another sound. Even the clock seemed to give over its ticking to hear. While the young lord, Velonin, sat down on the stair, careless of his coat.

But as Chegahr finished it was the scholar (he of the wife) who cried out, "It is a Soracsh!"

And then the priest said, "Hush, good sir. Such goblins do not exist."

But, "What is a Soracsh?" inquired Velonin. At which Chegahr, not the scholar, thoughtfully answered, "My mother once told me of those. They are common enough in the North, it seems. A Soracsh is a sorceress. She has power over wild beasts, and her hair has abilities all its own."

But the scholar pushed through the other Villagers and stood frowning there, as if he had a quarrel with Chegahr yet did not know quite what the quarrel was.

"More than a sorceress," said the scholar, "for she is related to the wolves. She has their blood in her veins. But, my lord, do not believe this oaf, Chegahr. He is only trying to make dupes of us. He has rubbed grease on his skin and burnt it at the fire to make it brown."

At which Velonin stood up again. "Well," he said, slapped his napkin on his smooth, clean

palm for emphasis, "get off with you. But you and you, come upstairs."

At which the scholar and Chegahr exchanged an uneasy glance, and followed the lord up his stair, while two servants ushered the rest out, being only careful to tip the priest and the horse-doctor with enough to buy brandy.

In the dining room above, an elbow of a huge stove, enamelled black, white, and blue, gave heat and cheer. Chegahr and the scholar were seated on two gilded chairs, quite near the servant who had earlier been felled by the book, and still lay prone. Velonin sat back to the table, and picked up his bread, dipped it in the coffee, and ate it.

"Now," said Velonin presently, "what I need is a plan. Put on your thinking-caps."

Chegahr said nothing, but the scholar asked, "A plan, sir? For what? If you valiantly mean to try to be rid of the Soracsh, that would be most unwise because —"

"Be rid of her? What do you take me for? I'm eager to meet the lady. The trouble with this village," added Velonin, turning to Chegahr, "is its lack of cultural excitement. Take a city, now. There would be cafés and loose women and the opera. But here what have you? In summer there is drought and in winter there is snow. What else? A zero. Don't you think so?" Velonin added in a peculiarly familiar way to Chegahr. "What do you say?"

"To what?"

"To what *I* have said, of course."

"I say you'd be happier in a city."

"Oh come," said Velonin, taking a pinch of snuff elegantly, as if sniffing a wayside flower. "In any city I'd be thought a turnip. No, I must make do, lording it over you foul and hapless peasants. But a witch in the forest, now. That fires me up."

"For God's sake," said the scholar, "don't go near her whatever you do. She's not a witch, but a Soracsh, part wolf and part woman and part spirit, and all of her terrible."

"Oh stuff," said Velonin, "get out, you klutz."

So the scholar got up and got out, and outside, to reassure himself he was not a peasant, he took a pinch of his own inferior snuff, and horribly sneezed three times as he went down the stair.

"Well then," said Velonin to Chegahr, "what do you think?"

"I think you are one year older than I," said Chegahr, "but act like a child of six. I think you faultlessly arrogant and perfectly rude, and probably heartless and witless to boot. And I think that God, if God exists, is anxious to call you back to Him that He may beat you soundly and put you to bed in a grave with no supper, which is anyway more than you deserve. I think therefore also, that if you desire to court a Soracsh, which being I now recall my ma told me is quite likely to devour a man alive and raw, then go do it, with my blessing. It won't be the opera, but nor do you deserve the opera. You deserve the Soracsh. And *now* I think I shall go home."

At which Chegahr rose. But Velonin burst out laughing. He laughed so hard he knocked over his porcelain coffeecup and it broke. So hard, the stunned servant (who anyway had been shamming) came to and crawled hastily away across the room and left them entirely alone.

"You *are* my father's son," cried Velonin. "Where else did you get such a voice and a wardrobe of such words?"

"From my mother," Chegahr staunchly replied, "who on her death-bed, called out to the angels, 'Leave preening your wings, you vain creatures, and heft me to the stars.' "

At that Velonin stopped laughing. He said, quietly, "Mine only whimpered. She was afraid God would be like father. You seem to think so, too, with your beatings and supperless graves."

"You care a deal what I think."

"Maybe I do. Come, have some coffee, or there's Aqua Vita, there. What the old priest drinks, but better."

Chegahr only looked at him.

Velonin said, "How's this. You mind my house here. Keep it up to scratch. Kick the servants, sleep in the best bed, and so on. I'll take *your* fate and go after the Soracsh."

"*My* fate?"

"What else? Who saw the creature? You. And she tanned your hide for you. She left her bookmark in your pages."

Chegahr shrugged, but his heart was banging now like a drum.

Velonin jumped up. He took off his fine coat and dropped it on the floor. "And if I catch the Soracsh I'll make her my wife. That'll set things right."

"Oh, how?" asked Chegahr.

"I don't like unkindness to women," said Velonin. "I've seen plenty. Our dad. (Your mother was spared, not living with the brute.) That scholar who was here starves his wife 'for her own good' and speaks to her only at mealtimes, while she goes hungry and he eats. Even that servant who was lying by your chair gave his wife a black eye last night, which is why I took the opportunity to give him one this morning. Yes, viciousness to the sweeter sex seems natural in a man. Why suppose I'm different? So if I live, I'll have a Soracsh-wife who I won't dare anger."

That said, he strode from the room, and Chegahr was left standing in it, between the still-laden breakfast table with its white cloth and plate of roast chops, and the warm grumbling stove-pipe.

Now Chegahr was left inwardly debating the actions and speeches of his half-brother, as you or I might briefly do (or not), wondering if Lord Vetonin were superficial, thoughtful, careless, caring, rotten — or simply deranged. But we (you and I) must now leave Chegahr to his debate, and to his bizarre possession of that lavish house, and follow Velonin, done up in his fur coat and hat, and his boots, and with, despite all his words, a sharp knife to hand and a gun with an ivory stock, into the woods beyond Seven-Willow.

Naturally Velonin had known the plain and these woods since childhood. He had ridden about them on a horse, or even, sometimes, tramped about them with his father, various servants and hangers-on, or now and then with some party of other rural aristocrats from neighbouring villages. He thought of the woods, and the plain, as belonging rightfully to himself. But not being mad, or not mad in this way, he had the sense to know the southern forest, which the woods soon became, was no more his than the Iron Heart Mountains in the east.

The change from the woods to the forest was very strange, for it was not sudden, and yet it was suddenly felt. One moment the trees were scattered, and sunlight seemed to litter about from a cloudy or clear sky. And then the light was gone, to be replaced by a sort of dim luminescence. But in fact the trees had closed their ranks only gradually. With the loss of light, there came a monumental sense, as of terrific architecture. It was like being shut in some ancient church, among great crowds of tall, thick columns, whose crowns met vastly high up in a beamed and coffered roof without a single window or lamp. This overpowering awareness was the same, both summer and winter, save in summer it was a black-green church, and in winter a white-blue one. That was all the difference. Also the forest was very silent. Among the woods, even in winter, red grouse flickered, birds and hares, sables, ermines, and other animals were to be glimpsed and heard. In deepest winter wolves and ghostly deer foraged even among the thinnest trees. Once into the church of the forest, however, nothing stirred or made any sound. Whatever lived there kept itself hidden — or was invisible. So, with the crushing sense of enclosure and dimness came the idea of deafness and isolation.

Velonin had entered the forest before, surely, but never alone. And if he had noticed all these sensations, never before had he acknowledged them. Now he did so. And this made him stop quite still, staring about him, and up into the windowless roof of frozen boughs and shadow.

Just then some snow did fall somewhere among the trees. It was like a giant's dull gun being fired, and Velonin jumped in his skin.

Then he only smiled. "What better place for a sorceress who is half wolf?" asked Velonin of the trees.

All this time he had been guided by the spoor of his quarry, for all over the softer snow the runners of the sled and the paws of the thirteen wolves had left their impress, while from this point he noticed, twined like exquisite gilded thread among the roots and snowy scrub, occasional slender, long, long skeins of shed, pale golden hair.

Velonin now bent and picked up some of this hair. It was fine as silk, yet very strong. Only with difficulty did he snap a single hair, and that across the edge of his knife. It had a faint perfume too, like burning incense, and like peach-blossom, and like fresh cold milk. In fact, it had so many scents, these three and others, he began to think the magical hair had enchanted him and really had no smell at all.

Velonin had come out for adventure. He had come because he was impossibly bored. And because the Soracsh was now his fate, not Chegahr's.

So, quite quickly, he coiled up the strands of hair in his pocket, and went on.

The forest grew more and more grandiose and ponderous, until he felt himself almost bent

double under its weight. The trees were very old, hundreds of years, perhaps thousands; and here oily indigo hemlocks loomed among the snow-wrapped pines and spruce, and black firs which also had let the snow slip from them. At last Velonin leaned on a trunk and took out his pocket-watch. He saw from this he had been walking most of the day, and also that the watch had stopped, and then he seemed to realize night was coming or had arrived. Just at that moment, craning his neck, he beheld what seemed an extraordinary sight. In the roof of the forest was motionlessly gliding a huge pitted white lantern, which touched everything to silver fire. It was the moon, risen high up in a patch of coal-blue clouds; and below, before Velonin, there opened a wide clearing.

Even as he grasped this, and wondered if the clearing had been there a moment before, Velonin noticed another arresting thing. The further end of the clearing was not closed by trees but by a sort of stone-piled cliff. And even as Velonin gazed at it, in the cliff wall, one by one, a row of lovely tapering amber lights bloomed up. Then he saw that they were windows, and that the cliff was the side of some great house, which made the High House at Seven-Willow into a cow shed.

On the moon-whitened snow beneath, the amber windows dropped reflections. And then in one flame-lit window, and in its reflection too, came a slender shape, like the slim dark wick dividing a candle-flame.

Out into the night rippled a wordless calling cry that made Velonin's hair stand on end. And yet, it heated his blood at the very same instant.

"There, sure enough, is the Soracsh," said Velonin, "and she is calling to see if anyone is here at last." So he stepped forward boldly into the clearing, swept off his hat, and bowed low to all the windows.

She was only a silhouette, so he could not tell if she was as Chegahr had described her; but then there came a flash of light like three hundred tinders struck all at once, and over the window-sill poured a waterfall of shimmering gold. Only when it slid quivering and gleaming along the snow at his feet, did Velonin see she had thrown down into the forest the ends of some of her sorcerous hair. And then he heard her laugh.

There was no door in the wall. No trees grew near. Velonin looked at the fall of hair, which even a knife had trouble in breaking. Then he asked her, "Do you mean me to be so ungentlemanly as to climb up by your tresses?"

And the Soracsh called down at once in her wild voice, "Do you dare?"

"If it won't hurt you, lady."

"Oh, nor it will," said the Soracsh.

So Velonin put his boot to the wall and gripped the stream of her hair in both hands, and swung himself upward. And but for being so silken-slippery, the hair proved a serviceable rope, so Velonin climbed on and on, up the rough flints of the wall, up and up to her high lit window, and there she leaned, with her hands on the sill, laughing at him, her lips like red currants and her coffee-coloured eyes that had reminded Chegahr only of chestnuts, and her skin like alabaster. Velonin hung in her hair with his booted feet braced on the wall, and he thought she had only to cut loose this streamer of her crowning glory, she would hardly miss it, and he would tumble and break his neck. But he said cheerfully, "Good evening, fair lady. I hope my weight doesn't pull at your scalp?"

"Not at all," said the Soracsh, "but put your foot now on the sill, and I'll help you in."

So Velonin swung himself up on to the sill, and she gave him her white hand, and he sprang down into the chamber.

I do not know what places you have seen, or what buildings you have ever gone into, but I myself never entered a room like that in the Soracsh's house.

First of all the walls were encased in a glowing gold and bronzy green that seemed at first to be caused by the adherence of thousands of polished gems. But then you saw it was the static cara-paces of thousands of beetles, but whether alive or dead, or ensorcelled, or only sleeping, one could not say. The ceiling of the chamber, how-ever, the Soracsh herself presently explained. It was covered — or formed of — hundreds of flying birds, large and small, among which were even bluebirds and canaries, peacocks and swans. They all hung there, static as the beetles, their wings spread wide, and all the shades of emerald and beryl, agate, turquoise and nacre; and seeing Velonin admiring them, (with his mouth open) the Soracsh idly said, "When birds sleep, they dream of flying. These dreams I catch in a net, and there they are." So perhaps the beetles on the walls were likewise meant to be the *dreams* of beetles. Meanwhile lamps floated in the air to illumine all this, and they were distressingly like great burning eyes . . . so Velonin did not look at them for long.

The floor of the chamber, though, was more simple. It was solid glass, but in the glass, just below the surface, great fish swam about, tawny pike, and huge carp of brass and coral. Seeing him look, even more idly the Soracsh then remarked, "Oh, it is a lake."

"Indeed," said Velonin, but he sensed her slight displeasure, and realized that, as with many other women he had met, and several men too, she preferred her guest's attention upon herself.

So Velonin gazed at her, raised her hand and kissed it (and when he kissed her hand, it was in some particular way like drinking the best choc-olate, or taking a mouthful of roses and cream).

She wore a scarlet gown, but not the gown she had worn for the sled. This one left bare her milk-white shoulders. But her throat and waist were clasped by gold and on her head she wore a tall golden tiara set with scorching diamonds. (It must have been about this time that Velonin for ever mislaid his knife and gun.)

The Soracsh then clapped her hands, and a door, (which seemed to be made of two bears with smouldering eyes) flew open. In walked a pair of beings that Velonin took to be her servants. They were men clothed in black velvet, but for their heads and faces, which were those of wolves.

"Here is my good friend, Velonin," said the Soracsh to the wolf-men. (And how she knew his name is a mystery. But then, she was a Soracsh.) "Is dinner prepared?"

The wolf-men bowed, and stood aside, and the Soracsh took Velonin's arm, and they strolled through the bears into another chamber. And this chamber only had walls made of static water-falls but against them stood gigantic flowers on stalks like birch trees, and in their bells burned unseen lights. There was a table of glass (per-haps), laid with silver and gold cutlery and dishes, and goblets of crystal. For the dinner, it was meats and pastries and puddings and delica-cies. And there were hot-house fruits the like of which Velonin had only ever heard described, or seen in books.

The Soracsh sat at one end of the table and Velonin was seated at the other. And he noted that one of the wolf-men stood behind his chair. But then, the other stood behind the chair of the Soracsh, and their prime wolfish purpose seemed to be to help their mistress and her guest to food and drink.

Of course, Velonin was not quite ignorant of uncanny matters. He had had a nurse as a child, and knew from her that to eat or drink anything in the house of a mere sorceress, let alone a Soracsh, would render him her slave. So he toyed with the choice cuts and slices, and did not put them in his mouth, and he pretended to sip the choice wines, and did not swallow any. But every so often, one of the lit flowers would bend towards him, and he would see another of those shining eyes peering at him through the petals, obviously watching. "Well, madam," said Velonin, once they had been at table a while, "you must wonder what my purpose is, in calling on you."

"Not at all," said the Soracsh.

"Then you have read my mind, perhaps?"

"No need."

"I am beneath your interest? That grieves me." The Soracsh smiled, and Velonin became aware that she also did not eat or drink anything from the table, only played with it as he did. And he wondered if she had another dish in mind, which was raw dead man's flesh. And this notion made him smile as well, and he said, "My reason for visiting you, lady, was to ask if I might court you for my wife."

"I am," said the Soracsh, "a great deal older than you."

"Oh come. We are too sophisticated to be upset by such trifles. What are a few hundred years between friends?"

"Also," said the Soracsh, "I am unbelievably wealthy, and you only somewhat rich."

"That's true. But then, if you wed me, by law your wealth comes also to me, and I shall be as well set up as you."

"Besides," said the Soracsh, "we have nothing in common."

"Quite wrong. We have in common one most influencing thing."

"And what is that?"

"We both of us," said Velonin, "adore you."

The Soracsh only nodded. "That's not enough. In any case, you came to me because any who see

me must so come. That is my power, or one of my powers."

Velonin said, "I think you may be wrong. But we'll let that go."

"No, no," said the Soracsh, frowning, "are you saying that one has seen me and not come to me?"

"I heard some such tale. Doubtless a lie."

But he realized how close the flowers were leaning now and their eyes popping out at him, while behind his chair the wolf-headed man leaned so close, Velonin could smell his meaty breath.

"Why," said the Soracsh, "will you not eat and drink?"

"Madam, I'm in love. My appetite therefore is gone. Since your beauty is all the feast I desire."

But the Soracsh got to her feet, and when she did this, she seemed very tall, and suddenly the dining room was much darker, and Velonin began to think that he felt most uncomfortable, like a child put in an adult chair too big for it. And it was then he noticed the ceiling, and it was full of faces, but all these faces moved and made mouths at him, screwing up their eyes and wrinkling their noses and poking out their tongues. It was very disagreeable and unaesthetic.

"Velonin," said the Soracsh, "you fear that to eat with me will give me extra power over you."

"Not at all. I already adore you. What power can you gain greater than that?" But when Velonin spoke, his educated and pleasant voice sounded quite odd to him. And then he found himself slipping off the chair on to the floor. And the floor was made of snow. It was cold and silent and he saw how his feet and hands left prints in it, but the prints were of the wrong shape. "Ah now," said Velonin, "I've been a great fool," but he did not hear his voice at all now, only another noise which he had never made before.

And she, the Soracsh, had become tall as a pillar, tall as a tree, and she stood there and oh, how stupid he thought he had been not to ask himself where all her miles of hair had gone (for it should have been piled up on the floor); but now he saw that hair; and he and she and the two wolf servants were all tangled up in it; and out of it now there dissolved the illusions or maybe the realities she had conjured, the birds and beetles, the flowers and fish and burning eyes. *They had all been made*, thought Velonin, *out of her hair, even the dinner had been made of hair. And now only her hair remained.*

And it was like the web of a ruby and golden spider, and he hung in that web, and heard her say, "Do you think I need such nonsense to entrap you? No. When once you kissed my hand you were mine. And now you're mine for ever."

"I have earned no better," agreed Velonin. But the only thing that came out was a yowl. Then all the colour and eye-lamplight winked away, and there was simply a horrible ruinous white garden under the walls of a cold dark house. And the unkind moon stared pitilessly down, for she had seen everything long ago, nothing was new to her or worth a second look.

For nearly a month, Chegahr lived in the High House at Seven-Willow. One may say he lived like a lord, but also the rôle did not fit him, just as Velonin's fine coats, breeches and shirts did not — although, perhaps oddly, in boots and shoes they were of a size. A tailor had soon crept from the Village, and brought Chegahr some quite tasteful apparel, ready-made, and Chegahr had chosen a few items. But he would not pay for them from Velonin's money-chest, and had no money of his own beyond a few coins in a broken pot, left at home in his hut by the cemetery. So he was in debt to the tailor. But the tailor only beamed and fawned, sure now Chegahr had gone up in the world. Likewise the others who came to call: the younger priest, with his silver cross a-bump on his chest; the horse-doctor, now leering with would-be friendship; the vintner; the apothecary; and so on. Chegahr sent them all away. He had needed nothing but a few new clothes, so as not to dirty or untidy his brother's house.

And that was how Chegahr thought of it, the house. As his brother's.

Which was itself strange, because all his life until then, if he had been honest, which generally he was, Chegahr would have said, "That house is partly mine, by rights." But of course, he had never thought he would live in it. And now he did, he felt he rattled in it like a die in a box. He was not comfortable, in fact. The rooms were too big and he could not find things in

them. Their beauty he did not find beautiful — he preferred mountains, woods and sunsets. He got lost in the corridors and could not discover the indoor privy, which anyway he thought unhygienic. The bed was too soft. The servants seemed to spy on him — they were always underfoot. The luxurious food was over-spiced, too sweet, too complicated. The fine coffee, which is a stimulant to most people, made him bad-tempered and sleepy.

All that disappointed him, as well. Here was the life he had, vaguely, envied. But he had no use for it. The only hours that still pleased him were those when he could escape the servants and pace about, or sit near a window, doing what he always did when he could, dreaming, gazing, thinking.

So, in the end, he dreamed of Velonin, and in the dream Velonin was at the bottom of a long steep place, and howling. And when Chegahr had sat up and lit the candle, the light fell on a book, which had been Velonin's; and it was poetry; but Chegahr could not read it, so he somehow imagined the black print said: "Help! Help! O half-brother, help me or I'm done for!" And then when Chegahr thought about it, he recalled that Velonin had been gone a long while, far longer than he had needed to go into the forest and find the Soracsh, drop on one knee, offer a ring, give her a kiss and bring her back for a priest-law wedding, and the better truer wedding in the wide soft bed.

"But what is he to me or I to him that I should bother myself? When I was in the hut, with only the recollection of a dry crust to eat, did nice Velonin ever trouble himself? If I hadn't seen the Soracsh pass, he and I would never have met, even though we lived only half a hill's distance from each other."

But then the servants came bursting in, as they always did, and Velonin saw it was morning, the candle had burnt out, and wax had splashed the book. He saw it, as the servants threw wide the silk curtains and the light thundered in. The wax on the book had formed the shape of an animal with four legs and a tail, and its mouth was open howling, as if it cried, "Help! Help! Help!"

"Devil take the pest," shouted Chegahr, who to his dismay had, in the house, begun to speak sometimes rather as Velonin did, as if Velonin's speech had stayed like a haunt. "Devil take him," he added. "Or the devil *has* taken him. I should never have let him go. It was *my* fate. He knew it, and so did I. If I had the wit to resist my fate, the wit even not to know there was anything *to* resist — I had the wit to stop Velonin as well."

Then Chegahr had his breakfast, put on some of the plain new clothes, and going out, walked down through the Village of Seven-Willow, where everyone stared at him, and even dogs trotted at his heels, wagging their tails.

When he reached the scholar's house, in a secluded lane, Chegahr halted. He knocked loudly on the door. The maid opened it and she cried at once, apparently satisfied, "Master's away!"

Chegahr scowled. "When is he back?"

"Not for seven days. He is off to the funeral of another scholar, in the village of Tall-Wheat."

Just then the scholar's wife appeared. She looked thin and pinched, but when she saw Chegahr, her face flamed and her eyes grew very bright. And suddenly Chegahr saw that she was young enough to be the scholar's daughter, and also Chegahr remembered that Velonin had said the scholar starved her 'for her own good.'

"Let me in," said Chegahr.

"Never!" cried the scholar's wife in a shrill excited voice.

Then Chegahr stared at the maid, and as Velonin might have, "Be off, you goose," he said. And the maid ran away. Chegahr then said to the scholar's wife, "Madam, you slapped me twice. You owe me two words in exchange."

At this she stood dumbfounded.

Chegahr said, "The two words are, 'Forgive me.' "

Her mouth dropped open. He saw it was a pretty mouth. Her eyes were deep as pools and sad as the hearts of dark flowers.

Chegahr said, "What I did in your dream was very wrong. What can I say? None of us can control what we do in our dreams."

Then she blushed, and lowering her long black lashes, the scholar's wife said to Chegahr, "It was my fault. In the dream I made you go and pick poppies with me in a field. And then I flirted. I said, 'My husband is away from home.' And then — I kissed you on the lips. Naturally you felt able to take liberties afterwards."

"I'm sorry I don't remember it as you do," said Chegahr, thinking that perhaps he was, too. "But in that case I must give you the two slaps back."

"Why not," said she. "The scholar is always slapping me.

So then Chegahr stepped inside the house, shut the door, and kissed the scholar's wife gently, first on one cheek, then on the other. Then on her eyelids, and next on her lips.

"Oh, Chegahr," sighed the scholar's wife, "I have loved you wildly for three years." She no longer seemed thin and pinched but only slender, and aflame. "Come up the stairs, and let me show you the bedroom."

So they went upstairs, and Chegahr saw the bedroom, which had a good hard solid bed. And here the scholar's wife flung off her garments, and she was pretty all over, her body like a slim white dress set with two pink pearl buttons, and honey trimmings.

Near afternoon, by which time Chegahr had finally learned her name was Majlena, he put to her the questions he had meant to put to her husband. And as he had begun to suspect, Majlena knew all the scholar knew, and quite a lot more (as she had recently proved in the bed).

Chegahr left the house after supper, as dusk was coming down, and went up the street whistling. But when he came to the foot of the rise where stood the High House, Chegahr did not turn that way, but went on walking.

And those that saw him pass said, "There goes the lord's son, Chegahr," and the dogs dribbled and wagged their tails, but Chegahr spared them not a glance, for he had things on his mind.

It had taken all one day for Velonin to get deep into the forest. But then he had not been following his fate, but another's. Chegahr walked for a brace of hours, and then he only sensed that he was in deep enough.

All around the ancient church of trees stood still and silent, but here and there the cold heartless moon pierced through. And to Chegahr she was not heartless at all, only secretive.

He knew now all he had to do, for Majlena had told him, taking care he should memorize everything. This had not been so very hard either, it was as if some part of him had already been lessoned in it.

First Chegahr made a fire. Then he drew all round the fire with a stick a black circle in the snow, and sprinkled it with salt. Then he took off every stitch (just as he had earlier in the day).

Then Chegahr recited the rhyme that Majlena had taught him. He recited its four lines facing all four directions, starting with the west and ending with the south.

When he had done this, a great wind bowled through the forest, and the vast branches and boughs rustled overhead, and snow fell from them. But after the wind was gone, another snow began to fall, straight down from the sky. Chegahr nevertheless felt warm as a cooking potato, and when he glanced at the fire, it was a strange clear yellow. Chegahr felt his eyes drink this colour up, and they turned yellow too. And then he put back his head, and please believe me, he gave such a howl that every wolf in the land may have heard it. After which he crouched down on all fours, and he turned this way and that way, and then he heard it coming, heard it far better than that first time, the hissing of the runners of the Soracsh's sled.

Sure enough, she soon appeared, and she passed, as the wind had done, and through the white lace of the dropping snow he saw her, in her scarlet and gold, and the thirteen white wolves running six by six, with the huge one in front, and the gold bells ringing and the gold sled rushing over the ground with a white spray going up on either side, like two white wings. The Soracsh looked only straight ahead of her.

No sooner was she past, and off between the trees, than Chegahr leapt out of the circle, taking care not to touch it with his feet. And then he ran to where the flowing train of hair was still streaming on in her wake. There he waited, counting, and when he had reached nine or nineteen minutes, he jumped forward and caught hold of some of the hair in both his fists. The speed at which it was going pulled him over, but he landed soft on the hair, and after that he let it pull him on.

Presently the sled ran into a vast clearing, and directly ahead, in the moonlight, was a high wall of piled stones. The sled raced on, and Chegahr, borne so far behind, expected some magic door to open in the wall. But this was not what happened. Instead, the lead-wolf ran straight up the wall, and after it the other twelve, six by six, and next the sled ran up, with the Soracsh upright in it, and standing out now horizontally from the wall like a red and gold nail.

Chegahr may have uttered an oath, I am not sure at this point; but whatever else, he clung on

tight to the ropes of hair, and next minute he too was hauled right up the wall, after the sled, and only the silken thickness of the strands saved him from a grazing and, seeing how he was dressed, from rather worse. Over the wall's top had gone the wolves and the sled, and over the wall's top was dashed Chegahr. And there on the far side was a lighted ballroom, such as he had heard of now and then, in those cities far away. But not quite.

Rather than being dragged down into it, Chegahr now found himself all at once lying on a golden staircase, and so he got up and leisurely descended, looking about him all the way.

Chandeliers with flaming roses in them floated in mid air. Below were walls like marble, and a floor like polished silver, and everywhere grew slender blossoming trees, frothy with pink and purple and blue; and golden snakes were coiled in them, with eyes like topazes, and from the boughs hung golden apples and silver pears. Where the snow fell into the ballroom, it became sweets, the fashionable kind called *bonbons*.

In the middle of all this stood the golden sled, but it had altered to a golden chair, and in it sat the Soracsh (and Chegahr wondered where it was that all her hair had gone, for now it only reached her scarlet slippers). As for the thirteen wolves, they had changed, or were changing, into men in black velvet, and it looked very odd as they did this, as if they pulled their bodies up over their heads like a nightshirt. But even though they became men, and had men's faces, this time, they had the eyes of wolves still, intelligent, and far more human than human eyes. And as they laughed and called out to each other, they only barked and yipped and made similar wolf sounds, apparently disdaining speech. Even the lead-wolf, who was brawny, swaggering and tall, did no differently.

Chegahr reached the foot of the stair, and then he noticed that now he wore satin breeches and a shirt of silk and a coat of golden tissue.

"Well, Chegahr," said the Soracsh, "here you are."

Chegahr thought it no surprise she knew his name.

"I am here," said Chegahr, "to ask you about my half-brother, Velonin."

"No. You are here because you are in my power, and I made you be here."

Chegahr felt the fine clothes itch him, and when he looked at the marble walls, he thought he saw mountains and seas and skies inside them. And in the floor under his feet glittered stars; and all at once, there, under his gold-buckled shoes, the priestess moon appeared, veiled in light clouds, at whom now, he might look *down* in wonder.

Just then a great golden table sailed through the air and squatted before the Soracsh, and after that a second golden chair. On the table was a landscape of food the like of which Chegahr had never seen, even in the house of Velonin — no, not even in his hungriest dreams.

Chegahr regarded it, and two of the wolf-men ran up to him; but they ran up on their hands and knees, and panted, with great red tongues hanging out.

Chegahr stepped around them, went up to the table, and stared along it at the Soracsh.

"Eat and drink," said the Soracsh.

"Pardon me," said Chegahr, "I ate supper before I left home."

"Some wine then, Chegahr. See how good it is."

"Your pardon again. Wine makes me bad company," said Chegahr. "I shouldn't like to offend you."

"Well, but already you do," said the Soracsh, getting up now and coming around the table. "Oh, Chegahr, wouldn't you like to give me a kiss?"

"I have had kisses too, before I left home. Enough to last a little while."

Then the Soracsh stood very near to Chegahr, and she smiled at him. "Your eyes are yellow, Chegahr, and I had thought your eyes would be black. Why is that?"

"I have the wolf-blood, lady," said Chegahr, "just as you do. When I was made, the wolves sang loudly. But how this coat itches. I think it's tailored from your hair. Like the table there and the roasts and cakes, and like the magical walls and floor and all the lamps. What do you say?"

"I say I will have you, Chegahr," said the Soracsh, and she suddenly bared her teeth. They were white as the snow, but they were the teeth of a wolf, and her tongue was blue.

"Oh, that," said Chegahr. "Didn't you hear me say, I'm part wolf too? I can't live in a fine house. I can't wear fine clothes. I like to dream and play. I like the woods. Just tell me where you've put my brother, Velonin. He's only a man, and is unhappy here."

The Soracsh snarled. Her chestnut eyes turned red as live coals. She clapped her hands and everything flew up in the air: the table, the blossom-trees, the entire ballroom (even the moon in

the floor); and Chegahr and the wolf-men were floundering and staggering in the midst of it, and it was all a writhing mass of golden hair.

"Now," said the Soracsh, "I'll show you your Velonin."

And she gave Chegahr a shove in his (again) naked chest that sent him hurtling: He landed on a cold cushion of snow in an old garden that lay at the foot of a high dank dark towering wall. The Soracsh stood on the wall top, snarling down at him, gnashing her fangs. She looked small as a doll. And in the snow beside him was another tiny toy. It was a little wolf, made perhaps of dark wood. But as Chegahr stared at it, it spoke to him in a little wolf squeak, as if a mouse were trying to howl. Through this noise, Chegahr plainly heard the words, "Help me, brother!" Here was Velonin.

Generally, in Velonin's life, it had been thought gracious and cultivated to talk. In his childhood, too, he had been given lessons in oratory and debating. So now he began to tell Chegahr, in dramatic detail, all that had occurred to him. But he could only squeak in his little wolf squeak. And all the time, the Soracsh stood on the wall top, gnashing her fangs.

So then Chegahr said, "Be quiet, Velonin. You need only know this. *She* is dangerous as life and death together, but blood is thicker than scarlet and I find I have a heart of gold. Besides, I am mysteriously unhurt after being flung off the wall, which is encouraging. This is what I'll do. I'll put you into my mouth, and you must wrap your front paws round one of my lower canine teeth. And then, with the help of the cunning spells of the scholar's wife, which have already saved me a broken neck, I shall run very fast away."

Velonin may have wished to argue but he had no chance. Into the wide open mouth of Chegahr he was popped — and Chegahr's mouth seemed, even to little Velonin, very much larger than it had been. And the strong teeth stood very tall in it, especially the canines. Velonin therefore had no difficulty in gripping a left one with his wolf paws.

No sooner was this done, than Chegahr gave a huge spring, and up the wall he ran, straight up over the flints and stones, on his bare feet, which were hard and tough as pads on a beast. Only once or twice did he need the use of his hands in this frantic endeavour. And he moved as quickly as a lizard.

The Soracsh to be sure darted back, but at the top he went right by her, and she spat at him, and her spit was fiery stuff, but it missed him and instead burned a hole out of the wall. Meanwhile he was leaping from the wall's other side. Down he sailed, and hit the ground of the clearing as if he had springs in his heels (from all of which we might conclude, you and I, the scholar's wife truly knew a thing or two). And then Chegahr ran in good earnest.

Never in all his days had Chegahr sprinted so fast, nor would he ever have had to sprint so far. But he knew he was no longer quite himself, or perhaps he was more himself, for his yellow eyes showed him all the forest clear as day, and his limbs had muscles of steel.

"Do you hold tight, brother?" he grunted, as the towers of trees roared by.

And Velonin squeaked that he did; but he cowered in fear, clinging to that tooth, now blasted by the icy cold air rushing. in and now by the scalding hot breath (tinted by a hot supper and Majlena's kisses) gushing out, nearly champed as Chegahr spoke, afraid of being swallowed whole, soaked by saliva and bounced up and down.

But Chegahr pounded on, and as he did, he did not know if he were any longer a man, with a wolf in his mouth, or a wolf that bore along a man. Nor did he know if he ran upright on two legs, or parallel to the earth on four. And then he heard the thick **plush-slush-ssrrrh** of the sled behind him, and the bounding footfalls of the thirteen wolves.

So Chegahr, who had only been running: well, you see, now he *RAN.*

At this new speed the trees disappeared. They became a pouring wave of white-black, that here and there dazzled with the light of the stars which still fell, or maybe it was the softly falling snow. And now and then he leaped high over some narrow streamlet or slight chasm, or some arched root wide as a crocodile shown in one of Velonin's books — but saw none of them.

But he heard *her* behind him, the push and hiss and the thudding of the four times thirteen feet. And he heard her crack a whip, too, and sensed its golden flare across the flying dark, like the striking tongue of a serpent.

Then, what should happen, but Chegahr heard also the lead-wolf calling to him, and now it either spoke in the human language, or he had come to understand its growls.

"Halt, stay, give in! There's nothing to fear. My mistress is charming. Have *I* not served her all this while?" Chegahr knew better than to shout over his shoulder what he thought of that. Besides he did not want to deafen Velonin in his mouth.

But then the lead-wolf began to call in a sort of singing way that matched the rhythm of their running, both the white wolves' and Chegahr's.

"Won't you run with us? Wouldn't you like to? You could even take my place and lead, a fine one like you. Oh, I lived as a man, once. I took a man's pride and pleasures. I smacked my wife soundly and laid her on the bed. I drank my beer and ate my meat and once a year I bathed and read a book. Oh it was a comfortable life, that. But would I now exchange what I have? Ah, what it is to feel the kiss of the golden whip. What it is to fawn on her scarlet slippers. She is the fate of all men, Chegahr. But it takes wisdom to know it. Yes, she may belittle you, or throw you down. But in the end you are necessary to pull her through the world."

Chegahr thought, and the thought was like the single wink of a spangle in the whirl of his running, *If you want that, that you may have.*

But he knew by then where it was he ran to, although perhaps he had already known.

I cannot say how long Chegahr cannoned through the forest and the night, with the Soracsh after him, her whip cracking, her tongue blue, and her spit all fire. Possibly it was scores of hours, the night constantly renewing itself, as one might over and over sew up a tear in a sock. Or perhaps he ran for many nights together, all the nights it needed to prove to the Soracsh she had not caught him, or to him that he had not been caught. Then again, he ran so fast, and so speedily did she follow, maybe they reached the brink of the forest in half an hour.

For reach its brink they did.

And then Chegahr sped through the thin woods, and over the plain, while the snow tinkled down like white china broken and dropped in heaven.

And at last Chegahr saw, (although Velonin did not, for if a wolf can faint, he had done so, though still with his paws locked fast about that great wolf's tooth) Chegahr saw the dull sparse lights of Seven-Willow, some of which always sophisticatedly burned on through the dark.

Even so, in the east, though Chegahr did not notice it yet, a hollowness had come to indicate night's end.

Accordingly, as he burst across the last distances of the plain, a cock crowed in the Village. It was early, to perhaps be sure, but not by much.

At the cock's alarm, Chegahr sprang again, he sprang among the streets and lanes, under the shadow of the houses. And so stopped running. To any other who had made such speed, and curtailed it so suddenly, it might have seemed the sky fell on his back — but not so, and God bless the scholar's wife.

When Chegahr looked round, his sides merely heaving, and streaming sweat in the white cold of ending night, he beheld the sled too had come to a standstill, there, at the Village's edge, and all the thirteen wolves stamped up and down while their tongues lolled, and in the air, coiling and boiling, was the golden whip, and also billows of the Soracsh's hair, embroidering the dark, weaving between the falling snow, her hair which was running yet to catch up with her. But strangest of all to him in that moment was the beaked prow on the sled, which all at once seemed to have the face of Chegahr's father, the lord of Seven-Willow — but doubtless he imagined it.

And then he forgot, for he heard the Soracsh cry out.

She *screamed,* no less, and in no language he had ever heard, though he had translated the words of her wolf-pack.

But some heard her. Some knew. Oh, indeed.

All through the night-ending Village there was banging and shouting, a bumping and scurrying. And then an unlocking and opening, a slamming and damning and hurry.

Out they came, as Chegahr later said, like rats from a drain.

Some had their lighted candles and some a lit lamp. Some were in their night-attire and some in no attire at all, and some had put on their Sunday best.

There was the horse-doctor, a quarter in his coat, and three quarters not, and there the blacksmith in only his apron. And there came the shepherd too, all unshaven-woolly like a sheep. And there was — but I hope will pardon my not

listing everyone. For there were many others — with, however, among them, two servants from the High House, in two of Velonin's own nightshirt; *and,* and here I lay an emphasis, there was the scholar, who very luckily had returned extremely and suspiciously early, by means of a horse and cart.

Chegahr stood aside, and as he did he prized his little wolf-brother out of his teeth, and held him wrapped up for warmth in one hand.

"See, Velonin. Not your fate, nor mine. The fate of Seven-Willow. She gets what she deserves, and so do they. But she was too stupid to know it; it's we that have shown her. She'll hardly miss us now."

Just then the sled spun round and all the thirteen white wolves spun round with it, it pulling them. And with a blood-curdling merry shriek, the Soracsh was flying off again while her golden hair flapped and flew behind her. And so the crowds of men in the streets, and in all there were one hundred and fifty-six of them, pelted after her as fast as they could. As they went, they yelled, they dropped their lights, and hats and shoes put on now fell off, and now and then they pushed each other out of the way, or, at other moments yanked each other forward. Until finally every one of them (again, very luckily including the scholar) had tumbled down among the rolling, retreating wave of the Soracsh's hair. And wound round in it, clutching and clawing at it, like kittens in yarn, they were carried away across the snow. And it seemed to Chegahr that now the direction of the fatal sled was not that of the forest, but straight on, back into the east, towards the paling sky and the stone and flint wall of the Iron Heart Mountains. So he wished them much joy of each other and of it, one and all.

As Majlena threw open the door, which the scholar, bumbling out, had yet possessively closed, she cried, "But Chegahr, how big and yellow your eyes are, how large and sharp your teeth — and I never recall you were so hairy!"

by Tanith Lee

But Chegahr seemed to gaze right through her to her sweet bones, and he said, "What you see is only another side of me."

So then she kissed him. And after that she led him, and his brother Velonin, a curled up wolf that could have sat in a little box, to the bath she had prepared. In the bath were thyme and olibanum, myrrh and saffron, pepper and aniseed and califrass. Best of all, it was warm.

As she sponged them, Majlena, who was a real scholar, even in her dreams, sang over them old words. And as she sang, she washed off the hair and the yellow stares, she washed off the wolf teeth and the wolf form, and in the very end she washed off Velonin's reduction, so he would no longer fit in a box — unless it was man-size. And so at last in the firelight and the copper bath, there sat crowded the two brothers, two young men white with fatigue, which one could barely see, since the proximity of the Soracsh had tanned them both golden all over.

Then Velonin wept. Chegahr thought, *Now he will start thanking me in flowery phrases, on and on.*

But Velonin only said, "Oh, but I loved her, that Soracsh."

Chegahr answered, "She had a blue tongue."

"It would," said Velonin, "have matched my eyes."

For some while after, in the way of a hero in a play, or an opera, Velonin wrote poems to his lost love, the Soracsh. He wandered forlornly the snowy woods, declaiming, until one day, near evening, he noticed that every tree was strung like a harp with notes of green. And then he went back to the High House and ate a large supper. After which he threw out the skeins of gold hair he had kept — they had faded anyway, and smelled of frogs. Then he wrote to another village lord, at Tall-Wheat, as it happened. This lord had a daughter, and inside the year, she and Velonin were wed. She was a lovely girl, with flawless skin, and sensibilities. He was very kind to her, and became immensely witty. And her word was Law. Yet also she loved him.

But Chegahr and Majlena, they bought a wagon and two strong horses, and wandered away across the world. At night by their wayside fires, they would tell each other stories, and teach each other all they knew. In the end, they were, each one, as clever as the other, equal as two stars that give the same blue light, but they had only one heart between them. As for the Soracsh, I cannot say I have ever seen her, but I have met those who reckon to have glimpsed her sled. They relate how it is made of hard gold, and her hair of filmy, milky gold, and that her red dresses are dyed in the blood of men she has devoured raw.

Once, I did see where the sled had gone by. I was shown, in the mud of spring, the tracks of the runners. And of course the prints of huge wolf paws, which in number were then thirteen times thirteen. She had harnessed them in sixteen rows of ten, and two rows of four, with one huge beast at the front, all alone. Those that have seen it in person, say it runs like a scholar. Ω

CONDO SKELETONS

I walk among the unhaunted skeletons
Of the half-constructed condos,
The timbers opaque white in the macabre light.
The three-quarter moon
Hengs, belly down, in the western sky,
Glowing, unabashed, among the 2 X 4 ribs.

In some other light the workers will come to
Board up the ribs and plaster them over . . .
Memories of glowing bone moon light forgotten.

People will move in bringing their own lives,
Mismatched furniture
They will live and die
And the bare bone skeletons
Will be given spirits at last.

—Blythe Ayne